I0831748

Secrets in the Heartland Books 1-4

Secrets in the Heartland Books 1-4

Andrea C. Heckner

Copyright © 2024 by Andrea C. Heckner
All rights reserved. No part of this book may be reproduced in any manner whatsoever without written permission except in the case of brief quotations embodied in critical articles and reviews.
First Printing, 2024

This book which is a compilation of the first four books that I wrote. Each of the book has a dedication that is important to me and this book is dedicated to all of those people as well as all who have read my books, gave me feedback and encouraged me to keep going.

Contents

Dedication v

The Farm 1

1 ***1*** 3

2 ***2*** 7

3 ***3*** 13

4 ***4*** 21

5 ***5*** 27

6 ***6*** 33

7 ***7*** 39

8 ***8*** 43

9 ***9*** 49

10 ***10*** 57

11 ***11*** 63

12 ***12*** 69

13 ***13*** 73

14 ***14*** 77

15 ***15*** 83

16 ***16*** 89

17	***17***	95
18	***18***	99
19	***19***	103
20	***20***	109
21	***21***	113
22	***22***	119
23	***23***	125
24	***24***	131
25	***25***	137
26	***26***	143
27	***27***	149
28	***28***	153
29	***29***	157
30	***30***	161
31	***31***	167
32	***32***	171
33	***33***	177
34	***34***	181
35	***35***	185
36	***36***	187
37	***37***	191
38	***38***	195
39	***39***	199
40	***40***	203

41 41 207

42 42 211

43 43 213

Dismantling the Farm 215

1 1 217

2 2 221

3 3 225

4 4 231

5 5 237

6 6 241

7 7 245

8 8 251

9 9 255

10 10 261

11 11 265

12 12 271

13 13 275

14 14 281

15 15 287

16 16 291

17 17 297

18 18 301

19 19 309

20 20 315

21 *21* 319

22 *22* 325

23 *23* 331

24 *24* 339

25 *25* 345

26 *26* 351

27 *27* 357

28 *28* 363

29 *29* 369

30 *30* 375

31 *31* 381

32 *32* 385

33 *33* 391

34 *34* 395

Remembering the Farm 397

1 *1* 399

2 *2* 405

3 *3* 413

4 *4* 419

5 *5* 425

6 *6* 433

7 *7* 439

8 *8* 447

9 *9* 455

10	10	461
11	11	467
12	12	475
13	13	481
14	14	487
15	15	493
16	16	497
17	17	501
18	18	507
19	19	513
20	20	521
21	21	527
22	22	531
23	23	535
24	24	539
25	25	543
26	26	549
27	27	553
28	28	561
School Days		567
1	1	569
2	2	577
3	3	583
4	4	591

5	**5**	597
6	**6**	607
7	**7**	615
8	**8**	621
9	**9**	629
10	**10**	635
11	**11**	641
12	**12**	649
13	**13**	657
14	**14**	665
15	**15**	673
16	**16**	679
17	**17**	691
18	**18**	701
19	**19**	705
20	**20**	711
21	**21**	717
22	**22**	727
23	**23**	733
24	**24**	739
25	**25**	743

The Farm

Book 1- Secrets in the Heart
The Farm
Andrea Crist Heckner

Dedication:

This book is dedicated to the three people who inspired, pushed, and challenged me to write it.

David Heckner- Thank you for cheering me on and pushing me to take a chance and not always play it safe.

Michael Heckner- Thank you for your crazy ideas, outlining, and suggestions along the way.

Thomas Heckner- Thank you for your honesty, especially early on when the book had little to no formatting or flow.

The Farm-Book One of the Secrets in the Heartland Series was originally published in 2023. The version contained within this compilation is an edited version with no major changes to the story line or characters.

1

Prologue

Have you ever wondered how an ordinary person could know and interact with a serial killer and not know it until it was too late?

Chapter 1

Monday April 1, 2013

They say the first time you kill another human being is the hardest. He hoped that was true, because he had been puking his guts out for an hour after cleaning up. She told him multiple times not to think of it as murder and to remember the greater good, but she was not the one cutting into a live human being or cutting up the body for disposal. No, she left that to him. Sure, she played her parts and was never far away while he did his part of this plan, but he had noticed that she never got human blood on her hands. He wondered, not for the first time, if this was a step up. He had observed that she never spoke when the recorder was on, but had demanded that he talk his way through each step of what he was doing. She took notes but typed them on a laptop without internet capability. He was sure she thought he wasn't aware of these things, but he was. She treated him like an idiot, but he saw her scheming ways.

Wednesday April 11, 2018

Kelsey woke up feeling like she was underwater. Her limbs felt heavy, and it was dark and cold. Where was she? She thought for a moment;

she remembered walking out of the conference her boss, Cardiologist Dr. Hann, had sent her to. She had declined to stay at the hotel at the conference center because she wanted to spend as much time as possible with her daughter. Claire was four weeks away from graduating high school, and then she would move a hundred miles away for college.

Kelsey was sure she had gotten into her car and started driving. She must have been in an accident. Was she trapped in her car? Was she in a coma? She took a deep breath and realized she could hear a faint beeping noise. *Okay,* she thought; *I was hurt, and now I am in the hospital, but what was that awful smell?* Why would a hospital smell so bad? Just as she realized what it was, she slipped back into the darkness.

Friday April 13, 2018

Joe had just gotten home when the doorbell rang. It had been a long week at work, and he wasn't expecting anyone, so he thought about ignoring the door. But curiosity got the better of him. He lived twenty minutes out of town, so people did not just randomly ring his doorbell. It was one of the things that he appreciated about living in the country. As he approached the door, he could see through the glass that it was two people.

Joe opened the door and quickly realized these two had to be cops. He had nothing against cops per se, but two showing up on your doorstep unexpectedly was never a good sign.

"How can I help you?" Joe asked.

The older detective replied, "I am Detective Mitch Leet, and this is my partner, Detective Kass Minor. Are you Joe Learner?"

"That is me; why?" Joe replied. He was quickly growing anxious.

Detective Leet asked, "May we come in and talk to you?"

Joe was unsure it was a question, but replied, "Sure."

As the three of them entered Joe's house, he saw how the two detectives looked at him and his home. He wondered if he should call a lawyer, not that he knew a lawyer to call. The only lawyer he knew was his divorce attorney, and Joe had paid him enough already.

Detective Minor spoke for the first time, “Is your ex-wife Kelsey Learner?”

The question surprised Joe. Kelsey was wound as tight as can be and would never do anything that could involve the police.

Joe nodded and replied, “Yes, why?”.

To his question, Detective Minor asked, “And you are the father of Claire Learner?”

Now Joe was getting upset and again replied, “Yes, why?”.

Detective Leet was the one to answer. “This morning, Kelsey’s employer’s secretary called the non-emergency number to report that Kelsey had not shown up for work for the second day in a row, and they could not get ahold of her via phone. Almost simultaneously, Claire called nine-one-one this morning. It seems your ex-wife never came home on Wednesday. Claire thought, at first, that she may have misunderstood and that her mom was staying at the conference she attended. However, Claire panicked when she got home today after track practice, and her mom was still not there.” Detective Leet took a breath, and Detective Minor asked, “Where were you Wednesday?”

That was the moment that Joe knew two things: something terrible had happened to Kelsey, and he might need a lawyer. Joe asked the detectives, “Do I need a lawyer?”

Detective Leet replied, “I don’t know, do you?”.

Joe thought about the original question. *“Where was he Wednesday?”* He had nothing to hide about Kelsey’s disappearance, so he answered, “I went on a couple of audits near Columbia. I left at about eight in the morning and got home at about six that evening. I have receipts for lunch and gas. I have to keep good records for work. Would you like me to get them?”

Detective Minor answered, “Not at this point, but we will want to see them. What was your relationship like with your ex-wife?”.

Joe chuckled, “Well, she was my ex-wife for a reason. Since our divorce, we don’t speak unless it is about Claire. I am supposed to have Claire every other weekend, but she doesn’t like to come over, and I don't force her. I pay my child support and live my own life. We were young when Kelsey got pregnant, and we got married. That rarely ends well."

Detective Leet replied, "Do you know if your ex-wife was seeing anyone?"

Joe looked at him. "No. As I told you, we don't talk."

Leet asked, "When did you last see your ex-wife, Kelsey?"

Joe seemed to be thinking and then said, "It was like two years ago at one of Claire's track meets."

At that point, the two detectives stood up. Detective Minor handed Joe a business card and asked him to email those receipts to her. Detective Leet told Joe, "I think you should call your daughter. We will be in touch as soon as we know more or if we have more questions." As Joe closed the door, he wondered where Kelsey was.

2

Friday December 27, 2013

Mitch Leet waved one more time before closing the house door. He loved his kids, but was also glad when they headed back home. It had been hard since his wife had died six months ago. This was their first Christmas without her, and he thought they had done okay. His daughter, her husband, and their two kids had driven in from Kansas City for the weekend. His son and girlfriend, with her two kids, lived in Springfield, so they had just come for the day. He looked around the house and sighed. For the hundredth time today, he wished his wife Gloria was here.

He would never forget the day she died. He had been at his desk doing the paperwork to wrap up a case. He had been working a ton of overtime on it and was looking forward to spending the weekend making his absence up to Gloria. His phone rang, and he answered it. The caller had been Mr. Benjamin, the bank manager where Gloria worked. He told Mitch that Gloria had collapsed while helping a customer and was rushed to Memorial Hospital.

Mitch ran out of the station and flipped his emergency light on as he sped towards the hospital. He knew it was against protocol, but he would deal with that later if he had to. He went through the ER doors and saw a nurse he knew from having been here with victims and suspects over the years. She greeted him, and he told her about his wife being brought there. She checked where Gloria was and then walked him back towards a room. The curtain was drawn, and it seemed no one was there with his wife. Mitch thought *she must be okay if they were not still working on her.*

He never imagined how wrong that thought was. When he walked into the room, he saw the sheet pulled up over Gloria's face. He felt a hand on his shoulder and turned to find the nurse who had walked him back. He heard her say a massive heart attack and never had a chance, but it made no sense. Gloria was healthy. She gave him grief for his high blood pressure and often bragged to their friends that she was on no prescription medication.

He had called their kids while he sat in the room with Gloria. He held her hand as he told their children their mom was gone. He decided he would call his captain when he got home. He needed some time to say goodbye to the love of his life before he told one more person she was gone. The staff at the hospital had told him to take all the time he needed. He wanted to say that no amount of time would be enough to say goodbye to her.

Gloria's doctor called him days later to explain that she had died from a widow-maker heart attack and that only twelve percent of people survived that type of cardiac arrest. He also told Mitch that African American women were fifty percent more likely to die of a heart attack than other women. Mitch was glad she had not suffered, but it did not lessen his grief. He had never thought he would outlive Gloria.

They had met during their senior year of high school. He was playing basketball, and she was on the cheerleading team. He told her that the first night he saw her; he was dazzled by her beauty. She would bring up that cheesy line for many years, and he would often tell her that she still dazzled him. They dated on and off while he went to the police academy, and she worked on her degree in banking and finance.

Mitch asked her to come to his graduation from the academy. After the ceremony, one of the fellow graduates pointed her out and said he was going to talk to her. Mitch told him that was his future wife. He proposed to her that night at the chain restaurant they had gone to celebrate his graduation in front of his family and their friends. He did not have a ring to give her, so his mom handed him hers to put on Gloria's finger when she said yes.

They had gotten married the weekend after Gloria's college graduation. Their two kids had come quickly after, and most of those early years were a blur of work, sick kids, and juggling their lives. As their kids grew up, there were periods when Mitch felt that he and Gloria hardly spent any time together. Their respective careers had taken off at the same time. She had been made bank manager just a month after he was promoted to the Criminal Investigations Division as a detective. Having made it through their kids' teen years with some rocky moments and the joy of watching them graduate from high school and head out into the world, they had just begun to enjoy their empty nest.

Mitch sat on the couch and looked at the remnants of Christmas. He wondered when missing Gloria would stop feeling like a gaping hole in his heart. It certainly would not be tonight.

Friday April 13, 2018

Detective Leet's cell phone rang as they left the ex-husband Joe Learner's house. A local patrol officer who had heard about Kelsey's disappearance at roll call before his shift was taking his lunch break by Lake Springfield when he looked at the edge of the lake and saw the keys. He called it in, and Detectives Mitch Leet and Kass Minor headed over. When they arrived, the officer also pointed out the flip-flop. Not being sure they were the right keys, Detective Leet used a pen to pick them up. Any doubts vanished when the detectives saw that the key chain was a wood cut out that said *KELSEY. At that point, they bagged the keys and collected the flip-flop. They took pictures and put down markers as they went.*

Detectives Leet and Minor stood looking at the shore of Lake Springfield. Kelsey Learner's car keys and an unidentified green flip-flop had been found there. They disagreed about the flip-flop. Leet thought it had nothing to do with the missing woman and was just trash. In comparison, Minor believed it was not a coincidence that the two items were found on the same lake shore almost fifteen miles from where Kelsey Learner was last seen.

They had found her vehicle in the downtown Springfield conference center parking garage thirty minutes after talking with her daughter, Claire. The SUV's doors were unlocked, and her purse and a bag from the conference sat on the passenger seat. Kelsey's cell phone was inside her purse. The only thing that was missing other than Kelsey was her car keys. The parking garage appeared to have surveillance cameras but much to the detectives' disappointment, the cameras had not worked in weeks. It seems there had been a blackout during a thunderstorm, and the system had fried. The conference center's head of security had quipped that his employer never moved fast to fix things that cost a lot but were not noticeable to guests.

****

Kass Minor had wanted to be a detective all of her life. She grew up reading Nancy Drew books her grandma had on an old bookshelf. Every afternoon after school, while her grandma napped and Kass waited for one of her parents to pick her up, she would cuddle up with her grandma's cat and read the books. Kass imagined herself growing up to be a super sleuth. When she was a teen, she started watching Law and Order and quickly decided that she wanted to be a real-life version of Olivia Benson. Without the personal baggage, of course.

Kass went to Missouri State University, got a criminology degree, and then enrolled in the police academy. Her dad thought she had wasted her time getting a bachelor's degree if, in his words, "all she wanted to do was be a cop," but Kass had done her research and knew she had a much better chance of becoming a detective with the degree. She had started right out of the academy at a small-town police department. Being a beat cop was not her dream job, but she knew she had to put in her time. After five years on the job, she heard that a neighboring department had an opening for a detective in Criminal Investigations. She applied and has been with the Springfield police department ever since.

Working with Detective Leet was not always easy. He was old enough to be her dad and had a love-hate relationship with technology. However, he also was willing to listen to her ideas and had treated her fairly since day one. Kass remembered him telling her during the first case that they had worked together and that he treated every case like it was the crime of the century because, to the victim's loved ones, it was.

They disagreed on the best way to solve cases, with Leet liking to take a logical, sequential approach and Kass being likelier to let the evidence take her wherever it did. Between that and their disagreement about music, Leet loved old eighties hip-hop music, and Kass was a jazz fan; they often seemed at odds. But Kass knew they made a good team, and one thing they did agree on currently was that neither knew where Kelsey Learner was.

3

Wednesday March 19, 2014

Kelsey sat at the table and cried. It had gone smoother than she thought with Joe, and she knew she was making the right decision. Even so, it was hard to know her marriage was over. She and Joe should probably never have gotten married. They had so little in common besides Claire, but Joe was gone so much with his job that she had just floated along. That was until a week ago when she noticed Joe had returned to his habit of never getting naked around her. She snuck into the bathroom this morning while he was in the shower, and sure enough, the telltale marks were there. He had made her a promise when she caught him the first time a couple of years ago. He would never partake in the activity again. He told her she would never understand his needs, but that he understood it was cheating.

Standing in that steamy bathroom, she decided to wait until she was calm to confront Joe. She prided herself on approaching challenges with a quiet demeanor. She hired an attorney, learned what to do and what not to do, arranged for Claire to be at Lindsey's house for a sleepover that evening, and then waited at the kitchen table for him to come home. She did not want to fight and wanted Claire to experience as little trauma from her parent's divorce as possible.

Kelsey thought about Joe's reaction. He did not even seem to care that she wanted a divorce. He didn't even ask why. He agreed and went to pack a bag. He would stay at his brother Eddie's place until he found somewhere of his own. Now, she had to tell Claire, but that could be put off until she returned from her sleepover. Kelsey headed to bed that night, feeling like a weight had been lifted off her.

She thought about how Claire had reacted more than Joe had to the news. There was no way she could or would explain to her thirteen-year-old daughter her reasons for divorcing her dad. She had said they had grown apart and wanted different things in life. Kelsey's attorney had told her not to say negative things about Joe to Claire. She had not needed that reminder. She remembered how it had felt to be torn between parents who hated each other and made sure she knew all about it from a young age. She had always thought she wouldn't get divorced if only for her daughter's sake, but here they were. So, she made a new vow to herself never to talk about Joe negatively. Well, at least not in front of Claire. Who was she kidding? It wasn't like she had any girlfriends to talk to; her mom passed away when Claire was a baby. No, Kelsey kept her nasty comments about Joe to herself.

Saturday April 14, 2018

Claire stared at the wall of her best friend Lindsey's bedroom. Her mom had been missing almost four days. It was six in the morning on Saturday, and she could not sleep. Where was her mom? She was so glad her dad had agreed she could stay with Lindsey and her parents until her mom came home. When he called last night, he offered to come to stay with her, but she told him she did not want to stay in the house without her mom. He had talked to Lindsey's dad and then to her again, and it seemed settled that she would remain here until her mom came home ... Well, she didn't know what would happen if her mom didn't come home. NO! She would not think that way.

She remembered the detectives were coming back over this morning. Lindsey's dad, who was a police officer, explained to her that since she was a minor, they would be bringing someone else with them. She asked if she was in trouble and why her dad couldn't be there. He told her she wasn't in trouble, and then he just shook his head and looked away. She would be sure to ask the detectives about that when they arrived. Did they think her dad had done something to her mom? Why would they believe that? Her parents hardly spoke, and even when they were married, they never had big fights, just a lot of petty arguments, followed by the silent treatment.

Plus, she thought her dad had moved on with his life. Claire thought he had a girlfriend, although he had never told her that. But a couple of months ago, she called him one time and accidentally hit his home number on her cell and not his cell number. A woman answered and was rude to Claire, telling her that "Joe is busy." Claire wondered if the woman knew he had a daughter; if not, maybe she thought it was another woman calling for her dad. A few days later, her dad texted her that he had canceled his home phone service.

Claire decided she would get up and get ready for the day. She went down to the kitchen and wondered if anyone would mind if she started coffee. *Do I even like regular coffee?* She loved Starbucks drinks, but her mom often told her they were as far from regular coffee as a milkshake from a glass of milk. Okay, she had no idea how to make coffee, so she would have a glass of milk and wait for other people to wake up. She heard the shower upstairs and knew Lindsey's dad had to work this morning. She figured he would know how to make coffee.

****

Detective Leet sighed as he got in the car to go speak to the Learner girl. She had been a wreck when they talked to her yesterday. He hoped she was calmer today. Maybe Minor or the guardian ad litem would be able to build a rapport with the girl. They needed her to walk through the house with them and tell them if anything was missing. He also wanted to know about her parent's relationship.

He and Detective Minor had just finished talking with Officer Dan Peterson. The Learner girl was staying at his house. Peterson told him that his daughter Lindsey and Claire had been friends since they were five. He knew Kelsey also, and assured Leet that she was not the type to disappear. She would call or text his wife, Jana, when she would be just a few minutes late picking up Claire, which rarely happened. His wife had told him that Kelsey had left a voicemail for Jana the day that she disappeared. Kelsey had said she wanted to stop by and talk to Dan about something, and asked Jana to call her back if he was available. Dan Peterson figured it was something that needed to be fixed around her house. Kelsey was very cautious and only liked to hire someone to do a job once she knew that it actually needed to be done and what she should expect to be charged. Dan had helped her out since Joe Learner had moved out.

As they drove across town, Minor and Leet talked. They had agreed that Minor would take the lead in questioning the girl. They also decided to speak to her first and then take her back to her house to look around. He had checked with their commander, and they agreed they did not need a warrant to enter the house as long as neither the Learner girl nor the guardian ad litem objected.

Detective Leet began to think about his retirement again. *Am I ready?* He wasn't sure what he would do in retirement. His wife had been dead for several years, and his kids had moved all over the country in the last few years. He enjoyed fishing, but could he do that every day? On the other hand, could he keep doing this job? There were rarely happy endings, and whenever he thought he had seen the worst of humanity, another criminal reared their ugly head.

Detective Minor cleared her throat next to him. He shot a glance her way. He knew she wanted him to ask her what she was thinking, but he was unsure he wanted to. She often seemed to leap to the most illogical conclusions, and he thought she was overly reliant on technology, but she was his partner, so what the hell?

"Yes, Minor, what are you thinking?"

She snickered and replied, "I think we need to look into the husband more carefully. There is just something I don't like about him."

Leet thought for a moment, *another leap*. Her gut was supposed to make someone with a solid alibi, receipts from another city, a viable suspect. He shook his head and replied, "I think that would be a waste of time at this point."

There was no time to disagree because they had arrived at the Peterson house. It was three doors down from the home of Kelsey and Claire Learner. The guardian ad litem, Mrs. Brittany Carr, was already waiting in her car by the curb. The three walked to the door together. When Mrs. Peterson answered the door, she showed them to the kitchen, where Claire was waiting. They sat at the table and introduced or reintroduced themselves to the girl. Mrs. Carr explained her role as guardian ad litem and asked if Claire had any questions.

The girl quickly asked, "No offense, Mrs. Carr, but why do I need you here? Why can't my dad just be here?"

Mrs. Carr turned and looked at Detectives Leet and Minor, waiting for one of them to answer. When Detective Minor did not speak, he did, "I understand that you want your dad here, but we still have some questions for him, and so we would prefer he was not here when we talk to you. Mrs. Carr is an attorney, and she will be sure we don't ask you anything we shouldn't."

Claire stared at him, saying, "So, my dad is a suspect. But what crime do you think he committed?"

Leet was somewhat taken aback; he had met hardened criminals who would not look him in the eye and question him.

Leet took a deep breath, but before he could reply, Detective Minor spoke, "Claire, we don't know where your mom is, and we need to do everything we can to find her. I understand you are upset, but please let us do our jobs."

Claire looked at Detective Leet and then Detective Minor. She nodded her head and then said, "Okay. How can I help you find my mom?"

Detective Minor asked Claire to tell them about her mom. Claire took a deep breath and then started talking. "My mom is thirty-seven years old. She had me when she was nineteen, but that never slowed her down. She finished nursing school and worked at a hospital for a long time. She and my dad divorced about four years ago, and she returned to school right after that. She became a nurse practitioner and started working for a cardiologist almost a year ago. She doesn't date and never really goes anywhere."

Detective Minor nodded and said, "Okay. What does she like to do for fun? "

Claire blinked and then said, "Gardening."

Detective Minor replied, "Nothing else?"

Claire replied, "No, not really. I am unsure my mom knows how to have fun or relax."

Detective Minor continued, her questioning, "Tell us about your parents' divorce."

Claire sighed and said, "There is not much to tell. They were married. My dad traveled a lot. When he was home, they argued about petty stuff. Then, one day, my mom told me my dad was moving out, and they were getting a divorce."

Detective Leet could practically see the wheels turning in Detective Minor's head. It was not what either of them had expected. A messy divorce, lots of arguing, and maybe even a physical fight or two would fit the picture Minor had likely begun to form about Joe Learner. Detective Minor took a deep breath and asked Claire, "What can you tell us about your dad? Do you spend much time with him?"

Claire seemed almost confused at first, but then she stated, "I don't think I know my dad. As I said, he travels a lot for work, so even when he lived with us, it wasn't like he was here that much. When they first divorced, I went to my dad's every other weekend and for six weeks that first summer. But then he bought that ramshackle of a house out in the country, and when I went there, I could never see my friends. So, I told him and my mom I didn't want to go there on weekends, and no one seemed to mind. Then the summer came after that, and I had to go to summer school, so I didn't go to his house then either. He stopped calling to talk, and so did I. So no, I don't spend much time with him, and no, I can't tell you about him."

Detective Minor looked at Leet, and he nodded. They were done with their questions for now. Minor addressed Claire and Mrs. Carr,

"We would like to go to your house, Claire, and would like you to come with us. While we are there, it would help if you pointed out anything missing or out of place. Is that okay?"

Claire took a deep breath and answered, "Yes, that is okay."

4

May 2016

George Jeffers was fishing alone, which he did almost every morning. She walked along the edge of Perche Creek and pretended to slip and fall right in his line of sight. When he got there to help her and offered her a hand up, she plunged the tranquilizer into his thigh. George looked startled, but before he could react, he was out cold. That was when the man pulled up in the parking lot of the fishing spot and quickly helped her load George into the vehicle. They strapped him down in the back and even threw a blanket over him just to be safe. The ride back that day was nerve-wracking, but not nearly as much as when they got George inside, and he started cutting on him.

****

George's long-time live-in girlfriend, Irene, pulled up to the house they shared in Katy township outside Columbia. She was glad to be home, but a little pissed at George because he had not answered her phone calls for her entire drive home from Texas to Missouri. They went to Texas every winter and stayed in a condo she had inherited from her parents. George hated it because there was no decent fishing, so he had left two months ago to head home. Since they had driven to Texas together, he had flown to St. Louis and got a ride home from a friend. They had talked on the phone and were happy with how things stood. George had told her that he was fishing every morning and that it was just the retirement he had dreamed of all his working life. She could not understand him not wanting to do more, but as long as he was happy and was okay with her going off on her adventures, she figured to each their own.

The house had no lights on, which seemed strange since it was nine pm. Irene pulled into the garage and immediately noticed that George's car was not there. *Where could he be?* Okay, maybe he wasn't enjoying a quiet retirement consisting only of fishing after all. She wasn't due home for two weeks but had left early so she could be at a friend's birthday party. She would have told George all this if he had answered the phone.

She shook her head again, thinking about his refusal to have a cell phone. He called them electronic leashes and discussed how the police and government tracked people using the data. Okay, but tracked George doing what, going fishing or to McDonald's? She was tired and decided to unload her car and head to bed. Surely, George would be home soon, and then she would talk to him about getting a cell phone.

Irene woke up the following day to a quiet and empty house. Now she was worried. After drinking her coffee and getting ready for the day, she got in her car to look for him. She pulled up to the gravel parking lot of his favorite fishing spot. Sure enough, there sat his Buick Century. It looked like it had been there for a couple of days. She walked around the car and then down to the creek bank. George's tackle box sat next to a rock, but he was nowhere to be found. Irene decided it was time to call the cops. As she waited in her car for the county sheriff to arrive, she prayed George would be found and that this was a simple misunderstanding.

The deputy from the sheriff's office was kind to Irene, but he was younger than her kids, and she worried that he did not have enough experience to help George. As she saw the sheriff arrive, her mind was put at ease.

The sheriff asked her all the same questions. "How old was George? When was the last time she had spoken to him? Who else might have seen or spoken to George? Has he done this before?"

The last question surprised her, and she asked the sheriff, "Done, what before?"

He replied, "Disappeared for a few days here or there."

The answer to that was definitely no. The sheriff sent Irene home.

About a week later, the sheriff and another man arrived at Irene and George's house. The sheriff introduced the county medical examiner, and Irene thought she would faint. The sheriff told her they had concluded that George had slipped and fallen into the creek. He might have hit his head, which was why he could not get out. But regardless, he was carried away by the Perche Creek, where he had been fishing into the Missouri River. The sheriff informed her that it was unlikely they would ever find George's body. The medical examiner explained that, due to the preponderance of the evidence, George was being considered deceased. If there was no evidence that George was alive in six weeks, she could have him declared dead. He set down some papers that explained what he had told her and contained the case number. As Irene closed the door behind the sheriff and medical examiner, she slid down it and began to cry.

Saturday April 14, 2018

Claire walked with the two detectives and the attorney lady to her house. She thought if anyone was watching them, they probably thought they were a strange grouping. An older man, two middle-aged women, and a teen girl. Add that two were white, one was Hispanic, and one was Black. Yeah, she was sure they looked strange walking together. She was the one who suggested they walk over. She needed to get some air before they went in the house. She had stayed there without her mom for two days and was fine. It wasn't until she realized something might be wrong that she freaked out.

She kept thinking back to the argument they had on Wednesday morning. Claire was questioning whether she had made the right choice to start college in the summer early enrollment program. She would only have one week off between graduating high school and moving to campus. Her mom thought it was a great opportunity and could not see why Claire wanted to stay and hang out all summer. Claire responded by telling her mom that she didn't understand because she never had fun, which is why she had driven her dad away. Her mom had seemed too stunned to speak, and Claire got out as soon as they pulled up to the high school. She hoped those were not the last words she ever said to her mom.

Claire snapped out of her thoughts when she heard the lady detective say her name a couple of times. What was her name again? Claire turned and looked at her.

The detective said, "Didn't we just walk by your house?"

Claire looked up and saw they had indeed walked past her house. She just nodded and turned around. Claire wondered what the detectives were looking for as they approached the front door.

Detective Minor seemed to notice the home security camera mounted by the front door. She discreetly pointed it out to Detective Leet, who said he had seen it. As they walked into the house, Detective Minor told Claire, "Walk around and see if any of your mom's stuff seems missing. Also, do you know where the footage from the security camera goes?"

Claire took the detectives to the desk where her mom's laptop sat and logged in. Detective Minor asked, "Does your mom know you know her password?"

Claire shrugged and said, "All her passwords are my initials and date of birth." She then turned and began to walk around the house, with Detective Leet, while Minor watched the camera feed. Minor noted it kept the footage for ten days and decided to ask Claire's permission to take the laptop with them. Even though the system only recorded when it picked up motion, watching the footage would take a while. Minor got up and went to look around.

Detective Minor was not sure what she was looking for. Detective Leet had walked with Claire because they needed to be sure that Kelsey had not gathered her stuff before she left Wednesday morning and took off. She stopped at a wall of pictures. They were mainly of Claire at all different ages. In a few, Kelsey Learner was with her daughter. One shot caught Detective Minor's eye. She wasn't sure what it was about this picture of Kelsey and Claire at the beach, but it seemed off-center, and what was that bright green spot in the bottom corner?

Claire and Detective Leet came back just then, and Claire said, "All my mom's stuff is here except the clothes she was wearing, her purse, keys, and cell phone."

Minor turned to her and replied, "Thanks for checking. By the way, where was this picture taken?"

Claire replied, "That was at a beach in Florida. I am like thirteen in that picture. My hair is awful, but my mom loves that picture of us."

Minor asked, "Do you know what that bright green shape in the corner is?"

Claire looked at the picture, "Oh, that is probably my dad's foot. My mom folded him out of a bunch of pictures. I remember when we got to the beach. My mom was upset because my dad hadn't packed any flip-flops. He bought this bright green pair in one of those t-shirt shops."

Detective Minor was stunned by what she was hearing. Joe Learner had a pair of bright green flip-flops. She turned to Claire and said, "Do you mind if I take the picture out of the frame and unbend it so I can see your dad?" Claire just shrugged.

Minor took a photo of the picture hanging on the wall, then she carefully took the framed picture down and put it on the hall table. She took another shot of the image in its frame on the table. She then opened the frame and removed the picture. As she folded it open, Detective Leet walked up behind her. He asked, "What are you doing?".

She replied by pointing down at the picture of Joe Learner in bright green flip-flops. Leet said, "Well, I will be damned. I guess we do need to look into Mr. Learner a little more closely."

Detective Minor took another photo of the picture and then flipped the image over to see if there was any writing on the back. Someone, presumably Kelsey Learner, had written Clearwater *Beach, Florida, Christmas 2013: Joe, Kelsey, and Claire.* After taking one more picture with her cell phone, Detective Minor put the picture back in the frame and hung it back on the wall.

Detectives Leet and Minor thanked Claire for her help and walked out with her. As Detective Minor watched Claire, she wondered how this young lady would handle it if her mother never came home and, even worse, if it turned out that her dad was the one who made that happen. Minor could hear Mrs. Carr talking with Claire as they returned to the Peterson home. Out of the corner of her eye, she watched Mrs. Carr write something and then hand it to Claire. She thought it was likely her business card. She was sure Claire was utterly unaware of the possibility that Mrs. Carr would be a growing part of her life. If Kelsey was not found alive and soon and Joe continued to be a person of interest, there would likely be a court hearing with Mrs. Carr officially being declared Claire's guardian ad litem. Detective Minor thought, Let's *hope it doesn't come to that.*

5

June 2016

John arrived at Joe's house in mid-morning. When Joe had called and asked if he could come over and help him with a project on his truck, John had agreed, even though he hated working on vehicles. Hopefully, it would be quick, and they could go fishing and drink the beer John had brought in his cooler. He didn't understand why Joe didn't just have a mechanic fix the truck, but he guessed to each their own. He pulled up behind the old pickup they would be working on. That was another thing. Why did Joe drive around a nineteen nineties pickup truck? John knew he had a practically brand-new car provided by his work, but he never saw him driving that. Nope, only the pickup. How could he live without a backup camera, Bluetooth, or built-in navigation?

John walked over to where Joe was with his head under the truck's hood. "So, what are we working on today?" he asked.

Joe turned and said, "The alternator needs to be replaced, and I need an extra set of hands."

John replied, "Okay, but two things first. One, why not just have a mechanic fix it? I know you're not broke; I do your taxes. And two, we are going fishing when we finish this, right?"

Joe sighed as he looked at his friend. He explained to him before about his truck. Kelsey used to say that he loved the GMC more than her, which he had, of course, denied. But now it seemed that was probably true, since he still had the truck and not her.

The truck was a 1993 GMC Sierra that was in mint condition. Joe's dad had bought it brand new, and Joe had loved the truck even as a boy. He fondly remembered getting the truck as his high school graduation present. He had thought then and still believed it was the best present his parents had ever given him. He had taken meticulous care of the truck, including having the seats reupholstered in the last few years and the headlights replaced so they were not cloudy-looking. He did regular maintenance on the truck himself and, besides the seats and headlights, had fixed everything that had gone wrong since the day it became his. He was not letting some mechanic overcharge him for something he could do with a friend's help.

Joe finally replied to John, "We have talked about my not seeing a reason to pay some mechanic to fix things that I can, and yes, we can go fishing when we get the new alternator in."

The alternator was replaced two hours later, and the truck ran in tip-top shape again. John was ready to go fishing. Joe went into his house to wash up and change his clothes before leaving. He remembered when they went fishing last time, and John started messing around and tipped them both out of the boat. Joe was pissed about it that day but could now laugh with John about it.

As soon as Joe got into John's VW Passat, he started in on Joe's truck again. John asked, "Why don't you drive your company car? I never see you driving it. They give you a brand-new car every two years, yet you drive the truck unless you are working. How can you live without a backup camera, Bluetooth, or built-in navigation?".

Joe knew his friend would never get it, so he chose to ignore his comments mostly and replied, "I don't need navigation. I grew up here. I delivered newspapers and pizzas, so I know these roads. Plus, if I need it, my phone has navigation."

John chuckled and said, "Okay, man, but you never take your phone."

Fishing that day had been without incident or fish, and Joe was glad to be home. He had somewhere to be in an hour and a half and needed to get ready. As he took a shower, he thought about what a great day this was shaping up to be.

Saturday April 14, 2018

Joe sat in his house thinking about the last three years. He loved weekends. The sleeping in, the lack of structure to his days, the time to putter with his truck, and usually hooking up with her on Saturdays. He would never have thought meeting a woman on a hookup app could change his life so much. She was as different from Kelsey as one could imagine. Kelsey was pale and soft-spoken, and in contrast, she had olive skin and spoke to him in a way no one else ever had. Joe had been captivated from the start. He knew he needed to call her so they could finalize their plans, but a part of him was enjoying doing nothing. He wondered if he should tell her about the cops coming to see him, about Kelsey and her disappearance. No, it was best to leave that out of the conversation. Joe went to get the burner cell phone that they used to communicate.

He walked back down the stairs with the burner phone in his hand. He heard the doorbell ring. He instantly sensed that it was likely the two detectives who had come by yesterday. Because, after all, who drove out here to see someone without calling first other than the cops? Joe slipped the burner phone into his pocket, opened the door, and sure enough, there stood Detectives Leet and Minor.

Joe asked, “How can I help you two today? Did you find my ex-wife? Is she okay?”

Both detectives just stared at him. After what seemed like too long of a pause but was likely only ten seconds, Detective Leet said, “Mr. Learner, we would like you to come down to the station with us to talk more in-depth about Kelsey and your relationship with her.”

This took Joe aback. He thought *about my relationship with Kelsey. What relationship?* But he said instead, “Am I under arrest?”.

Detective Lett looked at him and, in what seemed to Joe to be a condescending manner, replied, “If you were under arrest, that is what I would have said, and you would be in handcuffs right now.”

Joe nodded and said, "Okay, I will get my shoes on and meet you down there."

This time, Detective Minor replied, "We would prefer if you rode with us, and we will be happy to bring you home when we are done."

Joe thought that was a horrible idea, so he said, "No, unless I am under arrest, which your partner said I am not, I will drive myself and call my lawyer to meet us there."

Now it was the detectives' turn to be a little startled, with Detective Leet asking, "So you need a lawyer to talk to us now?".

Joe said, "I have a right to a lawyer, and I will have one with me the next time we talk. Please leave, and I will meet you at the station. The address is on your card, right?"

Detectives Leet and Minor nodded, and Detective Minor said, "See you there." Then they both turned and walked to their car.

Joe closed the door and leaned against it as he thought, *Shit, Shit, Shit, I don't even have a lawyer, but I better find one.* Joe grabbed his work cell phone out of his bag and called John, thinking, *surely that guy knows a few criminal lawyers.*

John answered on the first ring, "Hey, what's up, buddy? Free to go fishing?"

Joe took a deep breath and explained about his missing ex-wife, the cops coming by twice now, and their request to talk to him at the station. He said, "So, John, do you know any criminal defense lawyers?"

John roared, "You should have never talked to them the first time without a lawyer. You know, they always think that the husband or ex-husband did it."

Joe asked, "Did what?"

To which John replied, "Made your former old lady disappear. But yeah, I know an excellent lawyer, and so do you. Mike Davidson. He is a member of The Club. Be sure you remind him you are in The Club, so maybe he might give you a discount. I have heard he is expensive."

Joe asked for Mike's contact info and then hung up with John, thinking; *Great, another lawyer to drain me of my money, and Kelsey is to blame for this, too.*

Joe called Mike Davidson, and the man was unhappy to be called on a Saturday. However, he did agree to meet Joe at his office in an hour, and then they would go to the police station together. Joe did what Mike suggested, gathered his records for the last week, and took a deep breath. There was no way the police had any evidence to show he had done something to Kelsey, and why would he? He didn't pay her alimony and was about to be done with child support. Wouldn't he have done it years ago if he had killed her or whatever happened to her?

Joe arrived fifteen minutes early at Davidson's office. As he walked in, he noticed how nice the office was, so John was right: Davidson was charging some high rates. He patted his back pocket to be sure he had his checkbook. Davidson had been sure to tell him to bring a check to pay his retainer. Joe had not even asked how much because he was sure it would be horrendous, and he couldn't deal with that until he had to.

Mike walked out of his inner office and brought Joe back. He asked Joe to tell him again about his last two encounters with the police. Joe reiterated that the two detectives had shown up at his house yesterday, telling him about Claire calling nine-one-one because Kelsey never came home. He then said that the detectives had returned this morning and asked him to accompany them. He had clarified that he was not under arrest. Mike asked him to tell him about Kelsey.

Joe asked, "What do you want to know about her?"

Mike looked at him and said, "You know what? First, write me that check."

Joe was surprised, "Okay, but why?"

Mike shrugged and replied, "Attorney/client privilege starts when you hire me as an attorney, and I need to know if you killed your ex-wife."

Joe gasped and said, "Wow, you don't pull punches."

Mike replied, "I cannot prepare a proper defense for you if I don't know all the details of what will come up."

Joe took a deep breath and said, "Okay, but some of what I need to tell you has to stay between us. I don't think the police know much about me or my past, and I don't want to open up things they don't need to know."

Mike stared at him and then said in a slow, steady voice, "I need to KNOW EVERYTHING."

Joe sat and thought about what he was willing to tell Mike, and decided; *Mike did not need to know everything.*

6

July 2016

Stress from work drove Pete Taylor to go for a hike, even though the weather wasn't the best. He thought about skipping his regular Saturday early morning hike, but he knew he would regret it later. He always felt much better when he went for a long hike. His brother Todd often met him for these hikes, but he had called to say he was skipping today because of the drizzle. Pete left all his electronics in the car and tucked his car keys in his hiking backpack. Even though the backpack was water resistant, he had ruined his cell phone this summer when he left it in the bag and hiked in the rain. That was an expensive lesson.

Pete stepped out of the car and took a deep breath. The fresh air and lack of other people at the trail head already had him feeling less stressed. Pete had planned to talk with his brother about quitting his job and returning to school, but that could wait. Enough thinking about work. As he started his hike, he daydreamed about the gorgeous woman he had seen around town lately. He wondered what would happen the next time he saw her if he walked up to her and asked her name. What would she say? Could he even do it? Even though she was significantly older than him, she was clearly out of his league, but hey, you never know.

As Pete ascended the first hill, he glimpsed someone lying on the ground ahead of him. He thought it was a woman, or maybe a teenage girl, and she did not seem to be moving. He decided to pick up his pace, check on her, and, if need be, run back to his car to get his phone to call for help. Pete was startled when he saw that it was the woman that he had just been thinking about. *Was she hurt?* He bent down to check on her just as she sat up.

He was so cold, and what was that annoying beeping? Pete was so disoriented. He realized he must be sleeping and that his alarm clock was going off. Why had he picked that alarm tone? It was so annoying. He must have been having a vivid dream about hiking in the rain. He felt like he was wet, but something wasn't right. He could not seem to move anything and couldn't open his eyes. He felt something cold on his chest, then there was searing pain. He sat upright, screamed, and then fell backward. It was like he was falling down a long, black tunnel.

Floating above him, he heard shouts. He could not make out who it was or their whole argument, but distinctly heard, "Stupid, and you fucked this up again" more than once. He wondered if it was his ex-wife yelling at him, but why was Cheryl near him? He dodged a bullet when he divorced her crazy ass after he found out she was sleeping with her boss. His last thoughts were of his crazy ex-wife. That would have rankled him if he was alive to know it.

****

The man sat alone in the cold, dark room. He was on his third whiskey because she was right. He had messed up. He thought; *In my defense, I am not an anesthesiologist, and you can't Google directions on how to put someone out for surgery.* Each time was different, and they had some success, but then something like this would happen. He knew he had done his best. But she was right; that did no one any good. They had to get rid of this specimen and start over with the selection process. He hated that part, although he knew she relished it. The picking someone, the stalking, the learning of their routines, the careful delving into their personal lives. They had agreed before they started that there would be no one married, no one with kids at home, and no one someone else depended on for their life. They had been careful over the past few experiments and developed a good system for identifying potential candidates. She was oh-so-good at the ruse near the end. She loved when she fooled these men and then got the better of them.

****

Todd Taylor let himself into his brother Pete's house through the attached garage. He had not heard from his brother since he had texted him back when Todd canceled joining Pete for a hike on Saturday. Pete was a dedicated hiker, and Todd was much more of a casual walker. He knew that Pete would have gone hiking without him. He and Pete talked or texted daily, so not hearing from him in four days was unusual. Todd had grabbed a pizza and a six-pack after work on his way to his brother's house. There was no sign of Pete in his house. Pete's cat, Boomer, started rubbing up on him as he walked through the house and then ran off, meowing loudly. Todd followed the cat into the kitchen and saw no food or water. He took care of that, not because he liked the cat, but because he knew his brother loved it.

After calling the Branson police department, Todd called their parents. His mom answered, and he had her put their dad on the other extension so he could tell them that Pete was missing. His mom was beside herself and had hung up her end of the phone. Todd told their dad he would call back when he spoke with the police. He opened the door for the responding officer. The young officer took down his report and told him a detective would contact him.

Todd waited another day before anyone called him back. The detective and Todd met at Pete's house. The detective, Jay Smith, seemed to think Pete was just off having a good time. Pete worked at a local tourist attraction, which had a lull time between Christmas and Spring Break. Todd had told the detective that his brother often had more days off than on during these times of the year. This convinced Detective Smith that Pete would go on a trip without letting anyone know his plans. Todd had tried to explain that his brother would never have left town without telling him and without leaving enough food and water for his cat.

****

Detective Jay Smith drove away from Pete Taylor's house. He did not feel that the young man was an endangered missing person. He was a young guy and did not have to tell his brother what he was up to. However, Detective Smith would cover his basis. He called in to find out if there was any information on Pete's car. The dispatcher told him that the Rav-4 belonging to Pete Taylor had been towed from the Lake Wilderness Hiking trail parking lot on Sunday. The SUV had been called in as abandoned by a park ranger. There was no sign of Mr. Taylor when they towed the SUV; it has been sitting at the impound lot since.

Smith knew he had more of a case than he first thought. He called Todd to inform him that his brother's vehicle had been towed. He set a time to talk to Todd the next day. He then drove to the impound lot and looked at the SUV. He saw no damage to the vehicle and could see through the windows that a cell phone was sitting in the cup holder. He would apply for a warrant in the morning to search the SUV.

In the days that followed, Detective Smith talked with Todd, Pete's parents, and a list of Pete's friends, the park rangers his ex-girlfriends, and even his ex-wife; three days of talking with people had resulted in no leads. It was like Pete Taylor had disappeared off the face of the earth from a hiking trail.

Saturday April 14, 2018

Joe and Mike walked over to the police station. It was only a few blocks, and Mike had thought the walk might clear Joe's head. Mike had explained that after talking with Joe on the phone, he had called Detective Leet and set up an appointment for them to speak at one pm. He reminded Joe for the millionth time not to answer anything without looking at him first and getting the okay. Joe felt like he was being treated like a criminal, but he trusted that Mike had much more experience with the police than he did, so he would do what Mike told him.

Mike walked up to the front desk and informed the desk sergeant that they were there to see Detectives Leet and Minor. The desk sergeant made a phone call, and a few minutes later, Detective Minor walked them back to a room. When they all sat down, Detective Leet said, "I am going to read you your rights and have you sign a paper saying that you have been informed and understood your rights."

Joe looked at Mike, who replied, "It is just procedure. It is fine."

Leet went on to read Joe his rights, and he signed the paper. Detective Leet slid the paper into a folder and turned to Detective Minor. She pulled what appeared to be a photograph out of another folder, laid the photo face-side up on the table, and stated, "Tell us about this picture."

Joe looked at Mike, who nodded. After taking a deep breath, Joe said, "That is a picture in Clearwater, Florida, from the last vacation the three of us took as a family."

Detective Minor stated, "Please tell us what you are wearing in this picture."

Joe thought that was an odd question, but turned to Mike to get the okay before answering. Mike nodded again. Joe said, "Shorts, possibly swim trunks and a t-shirt."

She said, "Okay, and what are you wearing on your feet?".

Joe looked down at the picture. "Some bright green flip-flops," he replied.

Detective Minor asked, "Is there anything significant about those flip-flops?"

Joe wondered why she was so interested in this, and without even glancing at Mike, he launched into the story about the flip-flops. "So, we get to Clearwater, and the girls want to go to the beach. We get ready, and Kelsey sees I am wearing my tennis shoes. She was super bitchy about how I needed flip-flops, so I went to some cheesy t-shirt shop and bought the ugliest pair I could find. By the end of the trip, it was a family joke."

"Do you still have the flip-flops?" the detective asked him.

He shrugged and then remembered that he was supposed to get Mike's okay to answer anything. Joe looked over at Mike and could tell he was steaming. Joe could not understand why. What could an old family picture and some ugly flip-flops have to do with Kelsey being missing? He heard something being set on the table. As he looked over, he saw a green flip-flop with mud on it sitting in a clear plastic bag with a sticker sealing it.

Mike immediately said, "What is this?"

To which Detective Leet replied, "A flip-flop. Looks pretty familiar, huh, Joe?"

Mike stated, "I think we are done with this interview. Remember, my client came here voluntarily."

Detective Leet looked smug and said, "Oh sure, no problem. We need to be getting back out to Joe's house, anyway. We obtained a warrant to search his house just before you got here. The Christian County Sheriff and the CSI team are there, and we want to discover what they have found so far."

Joe was genuinely shocked. "A warrant to search my house. What are you looking for?"

Mike said, "Joe, enough. Let's go. We need to go to your house and see that warrant."

Detective Leet smiled at them and said, "See you there."

As Detectives Leet and Minor watched Joe and his slick attorney leave, Leet hoped the forensic team had found what they were looking for at Joe Learner's house. He wanted to apply the screws to Joe and find Kelsey. Leet had come to accept that the woman was likely dead and knew that finding her body would help her daughter to accept this as well.

Detective Minor thought it would be a long weekend, but hopefully, they would have wrapped this case up by the end of it. Everything pointed to the ex-husband, Joe, but there were many unanswered questions. The most important of which was, where is Kelsey Learner?

7

October 2016

Cory Pratt loved running. He loved to find isolated places to run, and unlike many other runners, he liked to be alone and not listen to anything but his breathing and nature. He parked his car in the gravel lot by the trail he had found last week. He would run here again today. No one was on the trail last week, and he hoped he would be lucky again today. He thought about the fancy fitness tracker his parents had bought him last Christmas. They did not understand his running; he knew they felt it was a great gift, but he hated having anything on him when he ran. He even had one of those magnet key boxes under his wheel well, so he didn't have to bring his car key.

When Cory woke up, he was cold, and his whole body felt achy. What had happened? Had he slipped and fallen, or had someone in a car hit him? No, that máde no sense. He was on a trail. Cory could not clear his mind enough to sort out what was happening. Oh no, he smelled something rancid. Had he crapped himself when he was injured, that would be so embarrassing, but no, it smelled more like pig manure. Then he realized he could hear two people talking. They seemed to be in another room, and their voices were almost echoed.

A man said, "I am ready when you are." A woman replied, "The animal is prepared, so you may get started."

Cory wondered what that meant. Then he slipped into a state of unconsciousness.

Saturday April 14, 2018

When the detectives arrived at Joe's house, they saw that Joe and his attorney, Mike, were involved in what appeared to be a heated discussion while sitting on camp chairs on the lawn. Detectives Leet and Minor did not approach them and walked to the house instead. They signed in with the sheriff's deputy at the door and put on the protective gear the CSI team had waiting for them. The head CSI technician walked up to them as soon as they entered.

He stated, "I have something to show you now that you are here."

The technician approached the kitchen table and pointed to a clear plastic bag. The two detectives stared at the bag. Neither of them spoke at first.

Detective Leet looked at Detective Minor, "I have never said this before, and I doubt I will ever repeat it. That green flip-flop is our smoking gun."

Detective Minor nodded and asked the CSI tech, "There was only one flip-flop, right? Where did you find it? And what else did you find?"

He replied, "Yes, there was only one flip-flop, and it was in the back of his front hall closet, behind a box and several other things. Unfortunately, the warrant is particular, and we were just allowed to search for the flip-flop. Since there are no signs that Kelsey Learner has ever been here, there was no probable cause for us to expand our search. I suspect you will ask for a new warrant, and we will be back here."

Detectives Leet and Minor thanked the tech and decided that as long as they touched nothing, they should be able to do a quick walk-through to be sure they saw no signs of Kelsey. They walked through the place from top to bottom because you never know what one person might spot that others had missed. The house was minimally furnished, and there were no knick-knacks or pictures. Leet thought it looked tidy; in contrast, Detective Minor thought it looked sad. There was no personality in the home. The walls were all white, and the furniture was beige. Hardwood floors were throughout, but not one area rug for a splash of warmth and color. As they finished their walk-through, they both conceded that they had seen nothing that the CSI team had missed, and there was not much more they could do until they talked to their commander.

The detectives were walking towards their car when Joe yelled, “What the hell is going on?”

Detective Leet walked towards him and, when he got close enough not to shout, replied, “Why we are looking for Kelsey? You know the mother of your child. A woman that you once vowed to honor and protect.”

Joe looked like he had been sucker punched, and Mike Davidson addressed the detectives next. “I think my client was trying to ask when he can return to his home.”

Detective Leet replied, “Before they leave, the lead CSI tech will have you sign an evidence log stating what they have taken. Then you are free to return to your house, Mr. Learner.”

As the detectives drove off, Joe turned to Mike and said, “What now?”

Mike replied, “Now we wait to see what they do next. Are you sure there will be no surprises for me?”.

Joe assured him that there was nothing he had not told him.

8

December 2016

Dennis Clausen enjoyed being an apartment manager. He got free rent as part of his pay, and he got to do various things every day. What he did not like was collecting late rent. He would not have predicted he would be at Cory Pratt's door for late rent. He was a great tenant because he paid his rent on time and was quiet. Cory was a car salesman and had gotten Dennis a decent deal on his last car. He had called Cory multiple times and left several voicemails, but had not heard back. As he entered the building, he walked by the mailboxes and noticed a yellow tag on a mailbox. He looked at the label and saw that it read; *Please remove mail so delivery can be reinstated.* Dennis looked at the mailbox number; it was Cory's mailbox.

He had come prepared for Cory not to answer the door. After knocking and waiting, he put the notice of entry on the door. By law, he could only enter by posting the statement or with the tenant's consent. Dennis would return in twenty-four hours if Cory did not contact him. He wondered if he should call the police, but he did not have any reason to do so yet. The next day, as he opened the apartment door, Dennis breathed a sigh of relief that he did not smell anything terrible, like a dead body. He had never had that experience, but had heard horror stories from others in the property management business. He looked around and saw that no one seemed to be there. He left the eviction notice on the kitchen counter and posted one on the door. He hoped that Cory would contact him soon and clear this up because he hated doing eviction clean-outs.

At the end of the thirty days, Dennis contacted the Miller County Sheriff's office to file the eviction paperwork. With the papers in order, Dennis cleaned out Cory's apartment. He wondered where the young man had gone because he had left a lot of nice stuff behind.

****

The deputy at the Miller County Sheriff's office took the report of a missing person's report from a woman from Wisconsin. The woman reported not hearing from her son in six weeks. She called his work and found out her son no longer worked there. She had called him many times with no answer. The phone was going right to voicemail. She told the deputy that her son's name was Cory Pratt. The name rang a bell in the deputy's head. He ran the man's name through the database when he hung up. The man had been evicted a few days earlier. The deputy wrote up his report and talked with the Sheriff. The Sheriff determined that there was no reason to investigate. His opinion was that the guy had lost his job and moved on. It wasn't a crime to not call your mom. The Sheriff said he would call Mrs. Pratt back and tell her they would not be opening an investigation.

Saturday April 14, 2018

Detectives Leet and Minor stood in the forensics lab looking down at the two flip-flops; one had been found at the lake and the other in Joe Learner's house.

The forensics tech said to them, "Here is what we know for sure. These are both the same brand and size. They have similar wear patterns and appear to be the same color. It will take a few days for the chemical analysis of the materials to be completed, but we can agree at least preliminarily that these are indeed a pair of flip-flops."

Leet and Minor nodded and thanked the tech for his speedy work. It was time to brief Commander Davis on what they had found.

Commander Davis had agreed to meet the detectives at five pm. Working Saturdays was not his favorite thing, but time was of the essence when you have a missing person. When he arrived, they reviewed what they knew so far. Kelsey had last been seen at approximately six in the evening on Wednesday. No one had seen or heard from her since. They found her car, purse, and cell phone at the convention center. Her keys and what they now knew was her ex-husband's flip-flop were located on the shores of Lake Springfield. They had dive teams search the lake and found nothing besides garbage unrelated to their case. The forensics team had seized the second flip-flop in Joe Learner's house and had since made a presumptive positive match between the two flip-flops.

After presenting everything to Commander Davis, he called the assistant district attorney and requested a warrant to return to Joe Learner's house. This time, it would be a much more open-ended warrant so they could thoroughly search his truck, computers, home, and the surrounding land. The Assistant District Attorney, Liza Reinhart, had worked quickly to get the judge on-call to sign off.

They had to wait to seize and search his work vehicle and laptop because Joe was not the legal owner. Their commander had told them that ADA Reinhart said it would be Monday afternoon at the earliest before they heard back from Greatlands Insurance, Joe's employer. She had not expected an issue with searching the company car and computer or getting the company's records on Joe's whereabouts, but she had said it would be a few days. The company would be served with the subpoena first thing Monday morning. Leet knew that timeline also applied to getting Joe's cell phone records, which were also tied to his work. It seemed Joe did not have a personal cell phone, nor did he have a home phone.

As Detectives Leet and Minor drove back to Joe Learner's house, they talked about their case. Leet had to admit that it was shaping up to look like Detective Minor's hunch about Joe may be right. The forensics team would take Joe's truck back to the police garage as soon as they arrived. They would also take his personal computer to be analyzed. The detectives talked with the sheriff's deputy, who met them at Joe's house. Detective Leet knocked on Joe's door while Detective Minor spoke to the head of the CSI team. He presented the warrant to Joe and asked him to wait outside. Joe had seemed startled that they were back this evening with another warrant, but did what was asked of him.

****

Joe sat on his lawn once more, watching the police enter his house and, this time, tow away his beloved truck. He wondered if now was the time to come clean with Mike and then the cops. But no, they would not find evidence in his house or truck that he had something to do with Kelsey disappearing. He had a right to keep some things private which is why he had gotten rid of his burner phone.

Mike arrived just as the detectives walked out of Joe's house to their car. Joe yelled out, "How can you just take my stuff?"

Detective Leet strolled over and said, "Warrant."

Mike calmly said, "I think my client was trying to ask when his computer and truck will be returned?".

Leet addressed both men and said, "The items will be returned when the ADA releases them, so you will have to take that up with her office. Mr. Learner, I also suggest you contact your supervisor before they are served with the subpoena on Monday morning." Leet turned and walked towards Detective Minor, who stood at the car.

Joe turned to Mike and said, "What the hell is going on?"

Mike said, "Well, I guess that the flip-flop they found in your house earlier today matched the one they showed us at the police station. Somehow, those flip-flops are related to your ex-wife's disappearance. Any ideas about that?"

Joe had been thinking about the stupid green flip-flops since the detectives showed him the one this morning. He told Mike, "I went fishing with John a while back, and he capsized the boat. I lost one of my flip-flops that day. That must have been the one that they found."

Mike nodded and said, "Okay, so where was that and will John back up that story?"

Joe said, "It was on the James River. That is John's favorite place to fish. I am sure he will remember tipping us over and how pissed I was about it."

Mike seemed satisfied with this answer.

He started to walk away and added, "Detective Leet was right about one thing. You do want to get ahead of this with your supervisor. Just remember what I told you about talking to anyone about this. Keep the information that you tell them to a minimum. Your ex-wife is missing. The police are crossing their t's and dotting their i's by eliminating you as a suspect. Anything else that is asked of you says you don't know. Got it?"

Joe nodded, as this was the third time Mike had given him this lecture.

9

May 2017

As Joe walked into the banquet room at the back of the restaurant, he thought about how much his life had changed. He had been single for four years, and no one nagged him about his whereabouts when he traveled for work. Then again, no one worried about him or picked up his dry cleaning either. His boss had encouraged him to join a civic organization and build a local network. Joe couldn't think of a good reason not to be here, so he was.

Joe sat at a table beside the man sponsoring him, to join The Club. Joe had met him through his divorce attorney. John was a tax accountant, and the attorney had thought Joe might benefit from his expertise. While Joe was thankful for the tax help, he appreciated the camaraderie of another man who had been through a divorce. John was sometimes irreverent and crass, but Joe enjoyed having a few beers with him. When Joe mentioned his boss's advice about joining a civic organization, John quickly invited him to The Club.

Joe listened to the conversations going on around him. This was an eclectic group of people. He was still determining what The Club was all about, but meeting new people and having a good dinner several times a month seemed like something he could get used to. He could add it to his next self-review, earning him a few brownie points with his boss.

John handed him a laminated sheet and said, "We will be doing The Club pledge soon. I grabbed one so you can read along until you memorize it."

A large man walked to the front of the room and tapped on the microphone. As the microphone squealed, Joe wondered why seemingly intelligent people always do that. The man introduced himself as Alex Pointer, the current president of The Club. He led the group in the Pledge of Allegiance. Then Alex said, "Now we will recite The Club Pledge." When it was over, everyone sat back down. Joe thought that the pledge to The Club was a little corny, but it wasn't something that bothered him enough not to join. Alex asked any new members to stand and be introduced by their sponsoring members. After John had introduced Joe, the two men sat down, and John thumped him on his back. As the night went on, different people took the microphone and talked about the various projects they were leading. John leaned over to Joe and explained that he needed to volunteer to help with something. John did the books for The Club, which met his volunteering requirement.

Joe had heard a man, named Dr. Raul Moore, talk about building a new playground. He thought that sounded as good as any other project. When the meeting had broken up, Joe approached the small group where Dr. Moore stood talking. Joe introduced himself and asked about helping with the playground. Joe and Dr. Moore discussed the playground project, and Joe agreed to be at the site the following Saturday at seven am.

As Joe left The Club that evening, he noticed Dr. Moore standing in the parking lot by a cargo van. He seemed to be talking to someone in the back of the van. That seemed odd to Joe. Joe noticed the emblem on the side of the van: *All Creatures Veterinary Service- Doctors Paulina and Raul Moore.* Joe chuckled and figured that Raul was likely talking to an animal in the back of the van. That was something that he had never understood, talking to animals like they were people, but he had seen it many times before.

Joe drove towards the house he had bought after his divorce. He loved living outside the city. No light pollution, no nosey neighbors to wonder about his comings and goings or his occasional guest. The smells of the country, pigs and cows primarily, might deter others, but

Joe had grown accustomed to them. The news was playing on the radio. The commentator was reporting on a missing man from a neighboring county. The man had seemingly vanished about a month ago. Joe wondered if the police thought the man had taken off and started a new life somewhere. Before his divorce, Joe had fantasized about doing that many times. He remembered the day he had come home to find Kelsey sitting at the dining room table, waiting to talk to him. She wanted a divorce and asked him to move out of their house. Joe shook his head to clear his thoughts. *Why am I thinking about this?* He had a new life that Kelsey was not a part of.

The following Saturday, Joe arrived at the park just before seven am. It was going to be a beautiful summer day. He was glad he had a reason to spend the entire day outside. He spotted Raul's van, so he knew the veterinarian was there already. Joe grabbed his coffee and got out of his truck. He was halfway between his truck and the new playground site when he felt he was being watched. He turned in a circle, slowly looking around, but saw no one. He continued towards his destination but could not shake the feeling.

As he approached the new playground area, he saw a bunch of men he had met at The Club the other night. Raul had a clipboard and seemed to be the one assigning jobs. As Joe approached the group, several men greeted him and introduced him to other people they had brought. Raul asked Joe to be in charge of constructing the swings. All the main support poles were already in place, and the concrete had dried, so now it was just a matter of putting the swing set together.

Joe and several others worked for a few hours and completed the swing set. Throughout the process, Joe kept looking around to see if someone was watching them. He never saw anyone, but the feeling of being observed never disappeared. As Joe and another man cleaned up from the swing set project, Raul approached. Raul thanked both men for the group's hard work. He then asked if they wanted to stay for lunch. The other man declined, but Joe agreed and followed Raul to the picnic shelter.

When they reached the shelter, Raul introduced Joe to a stunning, dark-haired woman. She was Dr. Paulina Moore, Raul's wife. Joe wondered about the couple. Raul was a short, slightly pudgy guy with a receding hairline, and his wife was a petite, shapely woman who could have been a model for fitness gear. As they ate lunch, Joe learned they had met in veterinary school and had married when they completed their training. They were both in their mid-forties and had no children. The female Dr. Moore stated that the animals and their research were their kids. They were both big animal vets but were not opposed to working with other animals, such as farm dogs and barn cats.

Joe told them about Claire, although he had to fill in some gaps with guesses, as he rarely saw or spoke to her lately. Sixteen is a hard age for kids, especially when their parents are divorced. He wondered if Claire was still running track and reminded himself that he should call her this weekend to catch up.

The Moores turned the conversation to Joe's wife, whom he quickly informed them was his ex-wife. They seemed sympathetic to the fact that it was hard to be divorced in your thirties. Paulina asked Joe if he or his ex-wife had been the one to file for divorce and what their custody arrangement was. Joe found the questions invasive, but figured the woman was trying to make conversation. He explained that Kelsey had sprung the divorce on him and that she had full custody. He told them that Claire was supposed to come with him every other weekend and for most of the summer. However, since she had started high school, she didn't want to go with him. He had decided not to fight with a moody teenager. Paulina asked him if he thought his ex-wife had poisoned Claire against him. Joe thought about this for a minute. It did not seem like Kelsey's style to talk badly about him to their daughter.

He replied, "No, I think she is too busy with school, track, and her friends to spend time with dear old dad."

Joe steered the conversation to his job as an insurance auditor and his weekly travel for work. The Moores expressed interest in the places he went and laughed at some of his stories.

As Joe was getting ready to head home, Raul asked if he wanted to join him for lunch on Thursday at The Club. The Club also met every Thursday for lunch. Joe wondered why John had never mentioned this to him. He then explained to Raul that he would be gone for a few days to Wichita for work, which he did once a month, but he would try to plan to come to the lunchtime meeting in the future.

Joe got in his car and checked his phone. No missed calls or messages. Typical. He thought about calling Claire but figured his daughter was busy on such a beautiful early summer day. Her birthday was next week, and she would finish her junior year of high school the week after. He wondered if she would want to spend time with him this summer. Joe got the feeling of being watched again, but this time, when he looked around, he saw Dr. Paulina Moore looking at him. He waved, and she smiled and waved back. As Joe drove off, he wondered if it had been her the other times today. He had felt eyes on him, but why would she be watching him?

Sunday April 15, 2018

Joe pushed the end button on his cell phone. The call with his boss had gone horribly. Joe could hardly stand the man on a good day, and today was not good. His boss was upset that he would have to call the higher-ups and inform them about the pending subpoena. He told Joe to consider himself on vacation until this was sorted out. Joe had questioned him as he only had a few vacation days left, and his boss said that HR would contact him to work out the particulars. Joe thought, *Great, now he was dealing with the police, an expensive lawyer, and his company's less-than-stellar HR department.*

He had missed his meet-up last night with his friend. He wondered if she was upset with him, too. He thought about calling her to see if she was available today, but he knew they usually only saw each other on Wednesdays or Saturdays, and she liked it that way. Plus, he had tossed his burner in the river and there was no way he was going to use his work cell to call her. Normally, he would wash and wax his truck when he was feeling stressed, but the cops had taken it. He had no idea when he would get the truck back, but it better not be any worse for the wear.

****

Claire sat at the Petersons' house. The family had gone to church this morning, but Claire did not feel up to it. She could not stop thinking about her mom. She wondered if she should call her dad and see if he knew if there were any new developments. But wouldn't he have called her if he knew something? She knew she needed to return to her house and get more things. She was going to school tomorrow and required clean clothes before then. She walked home and stopped to look at the house. Her mom loved this house. It had been her grandma's house, and she had left it to Claire's mom when she died. Claire did not remember ever living anywhere else. She had overheard her mom talking on the phone a long time ago. She explained to someone that she owned the house and had no mortgage.

She wondered where her mom's SUV was. Claire could drive it until her mom came home. She decided to call Detective Minor and ask her. Detective Minor answered on the second ring. She told Claire that her mom's SUV was being processed for evidence, but as soon as it was done, she would help Claire get it back. Claire thanked her and hung up. She wondered if she should move back into her house. She was sure the Petersons would think that was a bad idea. She was only a few weeks from her eighteenth birthday, but was still a minor. Hopefully, the detectives would find her mom soon, and she would be okay.

****

Detectives Minor and Leet had started their day by talking with the lead forensics tech about what had been found at Joe Learner's house. Nothing. They had taken many fingerprints and collected some hairs and fibers, but until those were analyzed, they had not found anything. They had used ground penetrating radar and detected no disturbances to the ground on Joe's land. His personal computer and truck were being analyzed as they spoke. It was a waiting game for forensics, and they had no time to waste. They disagreed on what to do next. Detective Minor thought they should watch all the surveillance footage they had obtained from around the convention center and Kelsey's house. While Detective Leet thought it was best to look into Joe Learner's past. They agreed to tackle the task that they each had prioritized.

Kass Minor sat in the media room of the police department. She had been watching hours of images from every camera they had found around the convention center at three times the speed. As she drank her lukewarm coffee, Kass thought she saw something on the footage from the DOT traffic camera at the intersection closest to the parking garage. She backed the footage, slowed it down, and watched as a truck turned the corner and drove out of the frame. That truck looked like Joe Learner's truck to her. She noted the time at the bottom of the footage as five-forty pm. That was just twenty minutes before, the last time Kelsey was seen. She marked the portion of the footage she wanted to save and went to find Leet.

Together, they watched the footage several times. Mitch Leet turned to Detective Minor and said, "I wish this videotape were better, but yeah, that could be his truck."

Detective Minor suppressed a groan; how often had she told Leet that no videotapes were involved? Minor commented, "I am going to send it to the tech guys and see if they can enhance the image. Have you found anything interesting so far?".

Detective Leet told her about Joe being from Springfield his whole life. Joe had graduated from the University of Missouri; those four years were the only time he had not lived here. A news article had a picture of Joe and a group of other people who had helped build a new playground about a year ago. Joe had never been arrested and had no court records besides his divorce. Leet concluded by saying, "So, nothing of interest in this guy's background, but you know how people are often shocked when they find out someone is a killer? They say stuff like, 'he was a great neighbor' or 'he was such a nice guy,' so it doesn't surprise me that there was nothing to find". Kass was surprised that Leet had called Joe a killer. Detective Leet usually did not believe someone was dead until he saw the body himself. They did not have a body, and frankly, they had no idea where to look for Kelsey Learner.

10

Saturday September 2, 2017

Joe drove towards the Moore's farm. Everyone at The Club had been invited to a Labor Day weekend party. John had told him that the Moores threw epic parties. He had to park down the road from the driveway because so many cars were parked at the farm already. There had to be at least one hundred cars here. Walking up the Moore's long driveway, he noticed the large Trump 2016 flag flying above their barn. He saw large white tents all over the yard, smelled food grilling, and heard music playing. Joe looked for John or the Moores. He had talked with several of the other members of The Club but wasn't comfortable just walking up and joining them.

He spotted John standing in a small group by what looked like a bar. Of course, that is where he would be. He approached the group and talked with them for a while about the Cardinals. His dad was originally from St. Louis and was a die-hard Cardinals fan. Thus, Joe had been a Cardinals fan his whole life. The discussion quickly heated up as they argued about whether the Cardinals could catch the Brewers for first place. Raul Moore walked up to the group while the men shouted at each other about various players' performances and the chances. "Break it up, guys. This is a party, not a sports bar", Raul said jokingly. He added, "Come and get some food."

Joe had wondered what kind of food would be served, as he knew many veterinarians were vegetarians. As he approached the food tent, he saw something for everyone. He loaded his plate with pulled pork and sides. He sat down, and Paulina Moore joined him. She had a plate of salad and fruit. She smiled at him and asked, "Are you enjoying the party, Joe?" Joe was a little surprised she remembered him. Although he often saw her husband twice a week at The Club, he and Paulina had only met one time a few months ago.

He told Paulina he was having a good time and thanked her for the hospitality.

She smiled at him and asked, "Didn't Raul tell you could have brought your daughter or another guest?"

He nodded, as he had just taken a big bite of potato salad. After swallowing, he replied, "Yes, he did."

Joe had thought about asking Claire, but when he called to talk to her, she had excitedly told him about leaving for track camp. He turned the conversation to the Moore's farm by asking, "How many acres do you have out here?"

Paulina said, "It is a hobby farm. We have a little over thirteen acres. We mostly raise pigs and grow food for our use. Feel free to walk around the barn and visit the pigs." Paulina then got up, walked to other guests, and started a conversation.

Joe started walking towards the barn. He also lived in a farmhouse, but the barn had been converted into a garage and storage area. When he looked at the house, it included ten acres. The realtor told him the farmer behind him wanted to buy the land. In the end, Joe kept an acre for himself, and the farmer purchased the rest. It had made the house a great deal for him. He entered the barn and thought about how immaculate it looked. He wondered what they used their barn for. A small tractor and a riding mower were sitting to one side, what appeared to be file cabinets to another, and then, right by a door, three large refrigerators. The refrigerators had locks on them. Joe did not understand why the refrigerators were locked. He decided to see if the door led to a bathroom because he needed one. The door was closed with a deadbolt. This also struck Joe as strange. Joe was about to turn around and leave the barn when he felt a hand on his shoulder. Raul Moore stood there, staring at him. Raul inquired, "Are you looking for something?"

Joe shrugged and replied, "Paulina said I could come to look at your barn and pigs. I was hoping this was a bathroom."

Raul nodded and then said, "No such luck. We will have to return to the house to help you with that."

Joe and Raul started to walk back to the house. As they approached the pig pen, Joe marveled at how many pigs they had and how large they were. He said to Raul, "You must feed your pigs well."

Raul chuckled and said, "Pigs will eat anything, so it is not difficult to keep them well-fed."

Monday April 16, 2018

Claire swore everyone stared at her as she walked to her first-hour class. She was busy taking notes on statistical analysis when she heard herself called to the office over the PA system. She walked to the office, and the secretary told her the school counselor wanted to see her. She sat in the counselor's office and listened to the woman tell her that Jana Peterson had called to explain about Claire's mom. The counselor wanted to check how Claire was doing. Claire assured the woman she was ready to be at school and that she would let her know if there was any way she could help. She returned to class and tried to catch up.

At lunchtime, she met up with Lindsey. They sat outside and ate their salads. Lindsey asked how she was doing. Claire said she was fine and added, "I don't know about you, but I usually don't think about my parents while I am at school." Lindsey agreed she didn't think about her parents either.

Claire asked her, "Are people talking about my mom?"

Lindsey shook her head and assured Claire that she had not heard anyone discussing what was happening. They finished up their lunches and walked to their classes. Claire decided no one was staring at her.

Mrs. Peterson picked the girls up after school and drove them back home. Claire used to daydream about living with her best friend. She thought it would be nonstop fun, but now she just wished her mom would come home and things would return to normal. As they entered the house, Claire's cell phone rang. She answered the call even though she didn't know the number. It was Mrs. Carr, the guardian ad litem. She asked Claire how she was doing and set up an appointment for them to meet the next day. Claire was unsure why they needed to meet, and Mrs. Carr had said it was best to discuss it in person.

****

Detective Leet was poring over the records that the Greatlands Insurance company had sent so far. The company had transmitted the audit and expense reports that Joe Learner had submitted for the week that Kelsey disappeared. They had assured the ADA's office that they would send the cellphone and GPS records as soon as they had them. There was no discrepancy between the documents sent by the company and the ones they had gotten from Joe or his attorney. Mike Davidson had sent copies of Joe's work calendar and copies of the duplicate receipts Joe had first provided to them. It seemed Joe had appointments in Columbia until four pm. That would mean he could not have been back in Springfield until six thirty. Detective Minor had been wrong. It wasn't Joe's truck in the grainy video she showed him.

****

Sitting back in the media room, watching the footage from Kelsey Learner's house, Minor had begun to make notes. Detective Minor started with the newest footage first and worked her way backward. She would need to find out what kind of vehicles the neighbors drove so she could eliminate their comings and goings. She knew Kelsey had a dark blue Buick Encore, and she had seen her come and go from the house many times. Another blue Buick Encore likely belonged to someone in the neighborhood because it drove by often. The driver of the second Encore was very cautious as they were always going very slow as the SUV passed Kelsey's house.

Minor had watched almost all of the saved footage when suddenly, she saw something interesting. A person came from across the street and walked up to the front door of Kelsey and Claire's house. Detective Minor was sure it was a woman despite her nondescript clothing, hat, and sunglasses. The woman seemed aware of the cameras, keeping her head down and angling her face away. She rang the doorbell and then tried to open the front door. After being unable to open the door, she looked in the windows and all around the porch. She then walked down the stairs and around the side of the house. Detective Minor switched to another camera view and cued the date and time. Sure enough, the woman walked up to the garage, attempted to enter the side door, and then around to the back. She checked all around the deck and tried to open the back door. Once again unsuccessful, she continued around the house and walked back across the street.

Detective Minor printed pictures of the woman from several angles and noted the time and date of the woman's appearance. Minor returned to watching the last four days before Kelsey Learner's disappearance.

****

Detective Leet stood up to find Detective Minor and tell her what he had found just as his phone rang. The CSI technicians in the forensics garage had found something. Leet found Minor, and they headed down to the garage together. He decided not to mention Joe's appointment calendar just yet.

The lead forensic tech approached them and said, "I think you will like this. We were almost done processing Joe Learner's truck when one of the technicians decided to sweep between the truck's bed and the cab. That is where we found these."

He held up a picture of several long red hairs.

He continued, "From the picture of Kelsey Learner, we believe these are her hairs. We will send these for DNA analysis once we have a known sample of Kelsey's DNA. In addition, we found mud on the gas pedal that appears to match the mud on the flip-flops that were located earlier. That has also been sent to the lab so they can confirm if it is the same mud."

Detectives Leet and Minor thanked them and headed back to their office. Leet kept thinking that something was just not adding up. They sat together in the conference room, and Minor showed her partner the pictures she had printed. She explained what she had seen, and Leet agreed they needed to identify the owners of the vehicles that drove by and this woman. Leet told her about the records review and that there seemed no way Joe Learner could have been in Springfield when his ex-wife disappeared. He told Minor, "I am now wondering if this woman had something to do with Kelsey's disappearance."

Minor objected to Leet dismissing Joe Learner as a suspect. "What about the hairs we were just shown from the back of Joe's truck?" she asked her partner.

Leet replied, "I think we need to find more evidence."

11

September 2017

Kelsey dreaded parties but had only been working at Dr. Hann's office for about five months, so she thought she better show up. It was a small office, and there was no way her absence wouldn't be noticed. She did not know what to expect other than she knew it was a sit-down dinner. She had taken Claire with her when she went shopping the weekend before to find something to wear. Her daughter had vetoed most of Kelsey's choices, saying they were boring or frumpy. In turn, she had rejected most of Claire's choices, reminding her that bright colors did not go well with their red hair. When Kelsey had been pregnant with Claire, she had hoped she would not be a pale redhead like her, but her daughter was her spitting image. Claire had stopped growing at five foot three inches, just one inch above her mom's height. They both often joked about buying their clothes in the children's section. In the end, they found Kelsey an asymmetrical black dress.

Kelsey opened the door to the restaurant and walked up to the hostess. After explaining that she was there with Dr. Hann's party, she was shown to the private dining room in the back. She had heard of this restaurant but had never been to it. She was pretty sure it was the most expensive restaurant in town. She looked around the room and realized she was the last to arrive. She looked at her watch. No, she was not late. Dr. Hann welcomed her and showed her a seat next to a woman who had to be his wife. She had heard about Mrs. Hann from the receptionist and nurse in the office and had seen several pictures of her in the doctor's office. The woman had been a biology researcher at Mizzou before marrying Dr. Hann when he was in medical school. According to the woman in the office, she brought up her credentials whenever she could work them into the conversation.

Mrs. Hann introduced herself to Kelsey. "Hello, I am Helen Hann. You must be Kelsey." The women talked about their kids. The Hanns had two grown children who had scattered across the country. Helen told Kelsey, "I stopped working as a biology researcher when Chris graduated from medical school, and we moved here for his residency. I was doing cutting-edge research at the University of Missouri on organ transplants. Are you aware of how many people die yearly in this country waiting for a transplant?" Kelsey acknowledged that she knew about this alarming statistic from her time at the hospital on the transplant team.

Dinner was served, and the conversations tapered off as everyone enjoyed their delicious meals. As the main course was being cleared away, Dr. Hann asked Kelsey how she had enjoyed her meal. She told him it was one of the best meals she had ever had. He smiled at her, then she noticed he immediately looked away and resumed his conversation with the man to his right. She thought the man was the husband of the office receptionist, Becca. Kelsey had noticed before that Dr. Hann seemed uncomfortable socializing with the women in the office.

Kelsey turned down the after-dinner coffee or cocktail. The first was because the caffeine would keep her up at night, and the second was because she never drank if she was driving. Just as she had been the last to arrive, she was the first to leave. She decided to go to the ladies' room before she drove home. As she was washing her hands, Helen came in. The woman stared at her and said, "You are a pretty young thing." Kelsey was unsure how to respond, so she quickly said thank you and left.

Monday April 16, 2018

Detectives Leet and Minor sat down with Mrs. Carr and Officer Peterson. They had asked the two to meet to discuss how to handle Claire. Commander Davis had decided that they would hold a press conference first thing tomorrow. Davis felt that they were at the point where they needed the public's help to find Kelsey. He also felt that Claire needed to participate in the press conference. Detective Minor balked at this because she thought asking the teen to do it was unfair. They had agreed to allow Mrs. Carr, the guardian ad litem, to decide. In addition, they had obtained a warrant to collect personal items from the house, so they had a known DNA sample for her mom. It would be easiest if Claire let them in and pointed out which brush and toothbrush were her mom's.

As Leet explained what they needed and saw Mrs. Carr growing uneasy.

She let him finish explaining and then stated, "I made an appointment with Claire for tomorrow after school. I need to find out if she wants to be emancipated or have the Petersons be granted temporary guardianship until her 18th birthday. In addition, I was going to explain to her that I will be asking for a power of attorney for finance to be sure all the bills get paid in her mom's absence. I suppose we should go over there this evening and I will explain all of my parts and then you can explain yours. Will you be telling her that her dad is a suspect?"

Detective Minor looked at Leet and wondered how he was going to respond. Joe Learner had not been officially declared a suspect, but it wasn't untrue that he was their only suspect.

He took a deep breath, "I think we will tell her that he is a person of interest at this point. She needs to know why her dad can't be the one to make decisions for her right now."

Mrs. Carr nodded, "Either way, I must go before a family court judge for an emergency hearing soon."

They all headed over to the Peterson house in their respective vehicles. Officer Peterson called his wife on the way over and let her know they were coming, but asked her not to tell Claire. Fifteen minutes later, as they sat in the living room, Claire appeared confused by the meeting. She asked Mrs. Carr, "Don't we have a meeting tomorrow at three thirty?"

Mrs. Carr assured Claire she was right about the appointment the next day and added, "Some things have come up, and we need to speak to you this evening. Since we are here, I will talk to you about what we were going to discuss tomorrow, but I will let one of the detectives explain something to you first."

Detectives Leet and Minor looked at each other. Both had understood that Mrs. Carr had wanted to talk first. As they looked at each other, Mrs. Carr cleared her throat and said, "About her dad."

Detective Leet thought, *Oh, great start with the most challenging part. There was no cushioning this.*

Claire shrieked, "What about my dad?"

He knew Detective Minor would want him to tell the girl, so he said, "Claire, we need to let you know that, at this point, your father is a person of interest in the disappearance of your mother."

Claire was stunned. *What are they talking about?* She could not believe her dad had done something to her mom. Mrs. Carr was talking again, but Claire could not concentrate on her words. All she could hear was a rushing sound in her head. She ran from the room before she got sick to her stomach. Jana Peterson checked on her, and Detective Leet turned to Mrs. Carr. "That did not go well. Why the change of plans? We thought you would talk to her first.", he said.

Mrs. Carr shook her head. "I am sorry. I should have talked to you outside. As we drove over here, I could not think of how I would explain to Claire about the need to go to family court without her knowing why her dad couldn't just step in."

Leet thought her explanation made sense because he agreed they could only talk about what needed to happen, with Claire being as fully informed as possible.

Ten minutes later, Jana Peterson led Claire back into the room. Claire was even paler than usual, and clearly, she had been crying. Claire looked at the adults in the room, "I do not believe my dad did anything wrong, but I will do what you need me to bring my mom home," she whispered. Mrs. Carr explained the emergency family court hearing the next day, what she would be asking the judge for, and what the judge's options were. She ensured that Claire fully understood what would happen and turned to the detectives.

This time, the detectives picked up on Mrs. Carr's nonverbal clues and knew she wanted them to continue the conversation. Detective Minor addressed Claire, "We have two things to discuss. We need your mom's tooth and hair brushes so the lab can develop a DNA profile on her, so it is ready to go in case we ever need it. We have a warrant for them to ensure we are following all the rules, and a forensic tech is waiting at your house. We would appreciate your help to know which items are your mom's."

Claire nodded, with tears brimming in her eyes. She wondered if the detectives knew more than they were telling her.

Detective Minor continued, "We will hold a press conference tomorrow morning. We need you to be there. If you want to say something briefly, the public relations liaison for the police department can help you prepare, but you do not have to speak. We need you to stand there with us."

Claire was not sure she could speak at a news conference. She looked at Detective Minor and asked, "What are you all going to say tomorrow morning?".

"We will make a statement regarding your mom being missing since Wednesday evening and ask the public to please come forward with any information that they feel may help us to locate her."

Claire nodded again. She had seen these things on the news. It mainly seemed about missing kids, but she wanted to be there if it helped bring her mom home. Claire said to no one in particular, "I will be there, but I don't think I can speak."

Detective Minor assured her that was fine.

This time, when they walked from the Peterson's house to Claire's, they were an even bigger group. Not only were the two detectives, Mrs. Carr and Claire, but the entire Peterson family had decided to walk with them to support Claire. Claire went inside with just the detectives and the forensic tech. She showed them which toothbrush and hairbrush were her moms in the bathroom. She also gave them a recent picture of her and her mom. The photo was taken two weeks ago, at a neighbor's barbecue. Her mom printed it and put it in a frame by her bedside.

12

October 2017

Dr. Raul Moore pulled up to the barn he and his wife used for their veterinary practice. As large animal vets, people rarely brought animals to them. He and Paulina generally traveled to farms and ranches to treat animals. He parked and headed towards the barn. He needed to restock the veterinary van before heading to his next appointment. Deworming cattle was not glorious, but essential for keeping the herd healthy. He walked into the barn and remembered that the keys to the medication refrigerators were in the house. He thought again that they should make another set to keep with the van keys.

Paulina did not want extra keys. She had told him that having extra keys posed a safety risk. A few years ago, someone had stolen large amounts of Xylazine before they locked the fridges. The large animal tranquilizer was necessary for their work, so they immediately noticed. They had filed a police report and an insurance claim. The police told them that Xylazine had begun to be used to make methamphetamines. They had advised the Moores that they needed to increase their security. After the theft, they had locks on the medication refrigerators and the barn doors, although they often left the barn open. Neither Raul nor Paulina was willing to have security cameras as they felt cameras weren't secure from others being able to view them.

Raul went to the house to grab the keys and a hot drink. He looked on the hook in the kitchen and did not spot the keys. That was odd, because he knew he had put them there. Paulina was the kind of person who wanted everything in its place. He had adjusted to her ways over their twenty years of marriage. The only other place they could be was on Paulina's desk. She had done an inventory of the medications last night, and maybe she had forgotten to hang them back up. He knew she hated him looking through her desk, but he needed those keys.

Raul walked into the study and looked around. He rarely came in here, as it was Paulina's space. He had most of the basement for a man cave, which seemed only fair to them. Walking over to her desk, he looked for the keys. He was not snooping and did not want to disturb anything else in the room. Sure enough, he spotted the keys on top of the clipboard Paulina had used last night to do the inventory. He noticed another key peeking out from under a stack of papers as he grabbed the keys. Curiosity got the better of him, and he tugged it out. It looked like a safe deposit box key, but they didn't have a safe deposit box. He put the key back where he found it. He was not sure it was worth bringing it up to Paulina. He would have to tell her about being in her office to do so. He decided; *No, I will forget that key.*

Monday April 16, 2018

Joe spent the day sitting around watching sports on TV. It wouldn't have been a bad way to spend the day if he wasn't constantly wondering what the police were doing. He decided to take a shower before heading to The Club. He hated to drive his work car because he knew they tracked his every move, but he had no choice since the cops had his truck. As he drove towards The Club, he wondered how Claire was. He knew he should call her, but did not know what to say. Did she know the police seemed to think he had something to do with Kelsey's disappearance? If she did know, did she believe that, too? He remembered when she was little and would shout "*Daddy*" when he came home from his trips. She had always been so happy to see him and would sit on his lap for hours. When had that changed before or after the divorce? Not the sitting on his lap part; he knew that changed when she was in elementary school and began to think of herself as not a baby anymore.

He didn't know the answer, but knew he had no real relationship with her.

Joe parked the car and walked into the restaurant. As he walked into the banquet hall, it seemed everyone stopped talking at once and stared at him. Mike Davidson marched towards him and steered them out into a hallway. "Who the hell have you been talking to?" Mike bellowed at him.

Joe was taken aback and responded, "About what?"

"You idiot. Kelsey! The police. The search of your house," Mike said in a quieter tone.

Joe thought for a moment and then responded, "No one. Well, my boss, but I just told him what you said I should."

Mike looked at him like he was lying and, in a measured tone, replied, "Nope. That is not the only person because everyone in there is discussing you and your missing ex-wife. So, I will ask you again, who have you been talking to?"

Before Joe could respond, John came out to the hallway. He raised his arms as if surrendering and said, "I am sorry. I did not know the whole thing was a secret. I was telling people at my table, and pretty soon, everyone was talking about it." John said in a quiet voice.

Joe looked at him. "What? What were you telling people?"

John responded, "Well, you know that you called me to get Mike's number because the cops were looking into what you had to do with your ex-wife's disappearance."

Joe thought; *this guy is supposed to be my friend. Wow, just wow!*

Mike looked at the two of them and said, "Well, now that we know who the leak is, let's talk about some damage control." He told Joe and John how to respond to people and what they should not be saying.

The three men returned to the banquet hall just as the group finished saying The Club pledge. They took their seats, listened to various club businesses, and tried ignoring the stares people gave Joe.

Just as the dinner was being served, the manager said, "Hey, does one of you have a dark blue 2018 Toyota Camry? Because it is being towed."

Joe jumped up from his seat and dashed to the parking lot. That was his company car. What the hell! As Joe and other members of The Club watched Joe's company car being loaded onto a flatbed truck, Mike said, "It seems the cops got the warrant for your company car, too."

Joe turned to John and said, "Will you give me a ride home?"

"Before we eat dinner? That is the best part of these meetings?" John replied.

An hour later, after they had eaten dinner, Joe got into John's car. He was grumpy and decided to turn the tables on John about his choice of vehicles. "So, why do you drive this four-door foreign car? You are a single guy with no kids. You should drive a sports car. I know you can afford it. I have seen what you charge to do my taxes."

John never took his eyes off the road but without missing a beat replied, "I am glad you asked. There are three reasons I bought this car. Which, by the way, is my second Volkswagen Passat. I drove the first one until it had almost two hundred thousand miles and traded it for this one. So, reason number one is that this car gets incredible gas mileage, which is connected to reason two. It has an eighteen-gallon gas tank, so I only have to fill it up every six hundred miles. The third reason is that the trunk is massive. I can fit a body in there."

13

December 2017

Kelsey logged on to the research site from the computer in her office. Dr. Hann was at the hospital all day attending the medical review committee. Once a month, he took part in these meetings to review patient deaths and suggest changes or actions the hospital needed to take. Kelsey had seen a few patients for follow-up care this morning, but her afternoon was open. Everyone else was off this afternoon. Kelsey's primary responsibility was to answer patient calls. She had come to love her job at Dr. Hann's office especially these afternoons. There was only one issue, Helen Hann. The women seemed to hate her. While Mrs. Hann chatted with other staff members, she only glared at Kelsey.

This brought Kelsey to the research site. Kelsey wanted to find the papers that Helen Hann had written when she was at the University of Missouri. She would read them, and the next time Helen came to the office, she would ask her questions about the research. Since the dinner party, she learned that Helen had a Ph.D. in Human Biology. She was a doctor in her own right, but seemed to never use the title.

Kelsey got three hits after typing in Helen Hann and the University of Missouri into the search engine. They seemed odd to her as all had titles dealing with animals. Kelsey was sure Sue, the nurse in the office, had told her Helen's Ph.D. was in Human Biology. Looking at the titles, Kelsey understood why Helen had called her work cutting edge. The oldest article was entitled The Use of Animal White Blood Cells in Patients with Sickle Cell Anemia. Followed by an article titled Biological Similarities and Differences between Human Organs and Large Animals and then, finally, an article on The Future of Human Organ Transplants using Animal Donors. Kelsey sent all three pieces to the printer and continued to search the site.

She found several articles that Helen was listed as a co-author before earning her Ph.D. She also considered reading those, but decided the three she had already printed were an excellent place to start. Just as she was headed to the printer, her cell phone rang. It was the ringtone she had assigned to Claire. After talking with her daughter, she left the office to pick Claire up from school. It seemed that the indoor track was unavailable for use because of an issue with vandalism, so Claire's track practice was canceled. Kelsey wondered if she should give in and buy Claire a car, but no, she and Joe had decided to get her one for high school graduation. Even though driving her teen daughter all over was a pain, she knew she would miss it when Claire left home.

****

Moments after Kelsey left the office, Helen Hann let herself in using the key her husband had given her. She knew Kelsey was supposed to be the only one here, but she did not find her. She would make sure to tell Chris about this. He paid that woman an outrageous salary, and she was playing hooky. Helen walked into the staff area to make herself a cup of coffee. She heard the printer chugging away. It was strange that something would be printing when no one was here. She walked over and picked up the papers. Helen was startled to see her three published articles from many years ago. *Why would someone be printing those?* She waited for the printer to finish and shoved all the papers in her bag. She completely forgot why she had come to the office in the first place.

Tuesday April 17, 2018

Claire flopped down on the couch in the Peterson's living room. Today's events had been exhausting. First, the press conference and then the family court hearing. It seemed she was now an emancipated minor. The judge told her that, in essence, it was like she had her eighteenth birthday today. She was free to stay at her house alone, but the Petersons had also told her she was welcome to continue to stay with them. She turned on the TV and immediately saw her mom's face. Claire turned up the volume and listened to the newscasters talking about her mom and the fact that she had been missing for six days. There she was standing next to Detective Minor at the press conference. She looked ready to cry the entire time. She still couldn't believe she had the nerve to speak. She had read what the public relations person from the police department had written for her: "Mom, if you can hear this, I love you. We are looking for you." Claire wondered if her mom could hear the messages. She had begun to think she might never see her mother again.

Claire's cell phone began buzzing. She looked down and saw another unknown caller. Detective Minor had told her not to answer, but Claire could not stop herself. *What if the call is from my mom?* she thought but no, it was just another reporter. Claire hung up without even acknowledging the person. She needed to head home and at least get some more of her things until she decided where to stay. She opened the Peterson's front door and saw the street was full of television vans. Reporters and camera people were all over her front lawn. There was no way Claire was going home.

****

Joe did not remember the last time he slept until noon. It had to have been in college, but he had no reason to set the alarm since he was on leave from work and had no transportation. He had woken to the distant sound of his cell phone ringing. He knew it was downstairs in the kitchen, but was not worried about going to see who had called. He slowly got up and made his way to the kitchen. He started the coffeepot and then grabbed his phone. He saw ten missed calls. There were three calls from Mike, two from John, and five from numbers he did not recognize. He also had ten voicemail messages.

What the hell was going on? he thought as he poured his coffee and put it the phone on speaker. The first message was from Mike, "Call me as soon as you get this message" was all he said. Two were from John; who also asked Joe to call him back. Then there were two more messages from Mike, each sounding more urgent that he needed to speak to Joe. Joe hung up on the voicemail before it played the messages from the unknown callers. *Better call Mike back, he thought* and dialed his lawyer's number.

Mike's secretary put him right through, and when Mike picked up his end, he boomed at Joe, "Where the hell have you been?"

Joe replied, "Sleeping."

"Well, while you were sleeping, the police held a press conference about your missing ex-wife. They are asking for the public's help to find her. I am guessing it will not take reporters long to figure out who you are and start calling. We need to talk about what to say."

Joe thought about the missed calls from the unknown numbers and the voicemails. Those were probably reporters.

Joe listened as Mike told him not to answer the phone for unknown numbers. He also warned him to look outside before leaving the house because Mike predicted the reporters would soon be sitting outside his home. Joe reminded him that he had no vehicle and wouldn't be going anywhere. Joe thought about calling John back, but he wanted to see if he could watch the press conference. He sat in the living room and flipped the channels. Without a computer, he would need to find a station replaying the news program.

14

Wednesday January 3, 2018

Claire arrived home before her mom again. Winter sucked for her because there was no track. Sometimes their coach arranged for time to run on the indoor track but not today. She loved running and competing. She walked to the mailbox on her way into the house. There was a large envelope stuffed in the mailbox. She grabbed it and looked at the return address. It was from the Missouri University of Science and Technology in Rolla, Missouri. It was her first choice of college. She knew she qualified for the A+ student program to attend college in Missouri free of charge. She ripped open the envelope right at the mailbox.

She got in. She ran into the house and put the acceptance packet on the kitchen table. She could not wait for her mom to come home and find out. She read the letter more carefully. Not only had she gotten into Missouri University of Science and Technology, but she had also been accepted to the early start program. She was so excited and thought about calling Lindsey, but she wanted her mom to be the first person she told. She hoped her mom would agree to drive to Rolla this weekend so they could walk around campus again.

****

Kelsey walked out of the grocery store, pushing her cart full of groceries. She hated grocery shopping after work, but they had not been to the store in two weeks, so she needed to go. As she walked to her car, she looked around. She felt like someone was watching her, but she saw no one. It was not the first time she had felt watched in the past few weeks. She had mentioned it to Sue at the office, and the other woman had laughed. Sue thought it was probably random men looking at her because she was beautiful. Kelsey didn't see herself as beautiful and didn't think Sue's reasoning made sense, but she let it go. She thought, *sometimes, as a single woman, I start to feel a little paranoid.*

She put the groceries in the trunk and walked around to her driver's side door. That was when she noticed something on her windshield. She went to the front of her car. The word Home Wrecker was written in what appeared to be lipstick on her windshield. She took out her cell phone, took a picture, and returned to the store. She wondered if she should have filed a police report, but once the manager told her they had no cameras in the parking lot, she decided it was a waste of time. A few minutes later, the manager followed her out. He brought a rag and window cleaner with him. Together, they cleaned her windshield; Kelsey thanked the manager and drove home.

Kelsey entered the kitchen through the back door and saw Claire sitting at the table. Her daughter looked like she was about to burst with excitement. As soon as Claire saw her, she jumped up and hugged her and practically shouted. "Mom, I got in! I got into Missouri University of Science and Technology, including the early entry summer program."

Kelsey responded, "I am so proud of you. I knew you could do it. Let's put away these groceries and go out to dinner." Claire squealed and hugged Kelsey again.

As Claire got ready to go out, Kelsey thought she needed to encourage her daughter to call her dad and share the exciting news. She also needed to talk to Dr. Hann about a raise. He said they would talk about increasing her pay after six months when he hired her. That point had come and gone without any mention of a pay increase. She took the job knowing she was not going to be paid more by switching to Dr. Hann from her position as a registered nurse at the hospital but the set schedule had made it seem worth it. With a better schedule and Dr. Hann's assurance of pay increases, she had made the move. Even with Claire not having to pay tuition, there would be an increase in expenses.

Tuesday April 17, 2018

Detectives Leet and Minor met with the Criminal Investigations team after the press conference to go over where their case was at. Leet knew they needed all the help they could get, with the Mayor and the Chief of Police putting pressure on them to find Kelsey. It had been decided that other detectives from the department would lead volunteer searchers in looking for Kelsey around the convention center and Lake Springfield. Meanwhile, Leet and Minor would begin talking to people who know Joe, Kelsey, or both. They sat and made lists of people they needed to interview and agreed that Leet would interview the people connected to Joe. While and Minor would take the list of people associated with Kelsey.

They agreed to meet back at the station when they finished unless something significant came up. Leet figured he would start with Joe's brother Eddie, who he thought would be the hardest to talk to. He decided to head out and get this one done. The man lived in an older, run-down trailer park well-known to the police department. He pulled up to Eddie's trailer, which was mainly rust. He observed an old pickup truck parked in front of the trailer, and he could hear several dogs inside.

He walked up to the trailer and knocked loudly on the door. He heard someone holler, "What?" from inside.

Leet identified himself by saying, "Eddie Learner, this is Detective Mitch Leet with the Springfield Police Department. I want to talk to you about your brother Joe and his ex-wife Kelsey."

The door swung open, and a less-kept, overweight version of Joe Learner stood in front of him in nothing but a t-shirt and boxer shorts. The man had long, stringy hair, which he was either using it in a feeble attempt to hide his baldness or was too lazy to get cut. Eddie said, "Well, I guess you better come in then."

Eddie held open the door, and Leet entered the trailer. All the while, he kept his eyes open for the dogs he could hear barking.

Eddie must have sensed his apprehension because as he cleaned off a seat on the couch for Leet, he said, "Don't worry, the dogs are in their kennels in the back bedroom. They won't bother you. I suppose you are here to talk about that stuff I saw on the news about Kels being missing."

Detective Leet had never heard anyone else refer to Kelsey Learner as Kels, but he would leave that tidbit for now. He asked Eddie, "How about we start with you telling me about your brother?"

Leet looked around the trailer's living room while he waited for Eddie to answer. He had learned a long time ago that a good detective waits for someone to answer the question they have asked. Despite the messy appearance, he noticed the trailer seemed well cared for. The carpet appeared to be only a few years old, and although every piece of furniture was piled with items, it was in good repair.

Eddie cleared his throat and started talking. "My brother Joe always seemed to think he was better than me. He was good at school and went to college. My mom was proud because he was the only person in our family ever to attend college. Before my folks died, Joe seemed to have a perfect life, and they both made sure I knew about how great he was. But little by little, the mighty have fallen. What kind of guy cheats on someone like Kels?"

Detective Leet was taken aback. There had never been any indication that Joe had cheated on Kelsey. He wondered if Eddie was telling the truth? Leet asked Eddie, "Tell me more about Joe cheating on Kelsey?"

Eddie smiled, "I guess you didn't know about that. Yeah, that is why Kels divorced him. I only know because he stayed with me for two months when they split up. He never told me why until one night when we got drunk on a bottle of my dad's old whiskey that I had been saving. He told me he would never have cheated if Kels had been more adventurous. I tried to get him to tell me details, like if he was into kinky stuff or men or something but he clammed up."

"Eddie, what can you tell me about Joe and Kelsey's relationship before the divorce?" Detective Leet inquired.

Eddie shook his head, “Nothing. I didn’t spend much time with them. When my mom was around, I saw them and Claire on the holidays at her house, but once our mom died, that stopped. At the holidays, everything seemed fine with them, but anyone can put on a show for a few hours.”

Leet nodded, as he had seen these same patterns in his own family. “Do you believe that Joe could have done something to hurt Kelsey?”.

Eddie started laughing, “Joe is a major wuss. He cried when my dad hit a deer when we were teenagers. I cannot imagine Joe having anything to do with her being gone.”

Leet then asked, “Just as a matter of procedure, where were you last Wednesday around six pm?”

Eddie responded, “Where I am six days a week from three to eleven pm, the pork processing plant. If you need my time card or something, I can have them send it to you.”

Leet assured him that it was not necessary at this time. “Just one more question: why do you call her Kels?” Leet asked.

Eddie laughed, saying, “That was like a running thing with Joe and me. When he brought her around the first time, I called her Kels, and Joe hated it. So, I have kept doing it all these years to get under his skin.”

Detective Leet thanked Eddie for his time and pulled out one of his cards. “Please call me if you think of anything else I should know.”

Eddie nodded and stood up. He walked Leet to the door and said, “I hope you find Kels. I always thought my brother had won the lottery when he married her.”

Detective Leet sat in his car and looked at the list he had made of whom to talk to about Joe. Two more men were on the list; both were named in the picture from the playground building project in the newspaper article.

15

Monday January 15, 2018

Dr. Chris Hann stood in his garage staring at the new vehicle his wife had bought. He did not understand what she was thinking. If she wanted a larger vehicle, he would have been happy to go to the import dealer to look at the options. Instead, she had bought an American-made pedestrian-vehicle that he could not fathom. He wondered what account she had used to pay for it and why he learned of the purchase only when he pulled into the garage and saw it. Also, where was her Mercedes S-class? Surely, she had not traded that in for the SUV he was staring at. He thought to himself; *she does not have a practical bone in her body, but she is not that dumb, is she?* Instead of leaving for the office, he walked back inside to have what he knew would be an epic screaming match.

****

Kelsey walked to the sandwich shop across the street from work. She needed a break from the office. She had met with Dr. Hann to ask him about her performance and whether she would get a raise. He was kind and told her she was doing great but he couldn't give her a raise at this time. He explained that expenses were up, and he could not afford to pay her more. While she understood what he was saying, she wondered what expenses were up. Before he had hired her, he had had another nurse practitioner for many years, so it was not her. She wondered if he was considering retirement and becoming more cautious with his money. Whatever his reasons, Kelsey knew she would need to make a budget to help Claire.

Claire had called her dad the weekend after she got accepted to Missouri College of Science and Technology, and she had told Kelsey he was excited for her. What he had yet to do was offer to help financially. Kelsey knew that he knew that Claire would attend without paying tuition as long as she maintained her high GPA. Since they had both benefited from the program many years ago when they went to Mizzou. But he should also realize that tuition was not the only expense. The entire time they had been divorced, Kelsey had never asked Joe for more money, and she had not argued when his lawyer suggested he be done with child support when Claire turned eighteen.

This was different, though; they both had agreed when Claire was little that when the time came for her to go to college, they wanted her to graduate without student loans or having to work full time while she was a student. Kelsey needed to call Joe and set up a time to get together. Conversations like this were best done in person and, in this case, in a public place.

Wednesday April 18, 2018

Detective Kass Minor called Dr. Hann's office this morning to set up a time to come by and talk with the people who worked with Kelsey Learner. Dr. Hann's receptionist, Becca, had encouraged her to come at noon. She had told Kass that she would let the others know that the detective was coming by and would order some lunch for everyone. Kass walked into the doctor's office just before noon and introduced herself to Becca. The young woman showed her back to the staff room. She told Kass that Sue White, who was the nurse, and Dr. Hann were finishing up with their last patient before lunch.

While waiting for the others, Detective Minor reviewed her notes regarding what they knew about Kelsey Learner and her disappearance. Kass did not feel they had a real handle on who Kelsey was and what could have led to her being a victim of this crime. After about ten minutes, three people walked into the room together. Becca was carrying a bag from the sandwich shop across the street. Sue White and Dr. Chris Hann introduced themselves, and Detective Minor did so in return. She then asked them all to sit down with her. Becca took out an array of food and indicated they should all pick something to eat.

She told Detective Minor, "I did not know what you liked, so I ordered a salad with no meat and a turkey sandwich. I figured one or the other usually works for most people."

Detective Minor thanked her and picked up the sandwich. She had never understood vegetarians, but to each their own. She asked no one in particular, "Tell me about Kelsey."

Dr. Hann was the first to reply. He started by giving basic information about Kelsey's credentials, how long she had worked at the office, and the kind of work she did. He stated, "She is hardworking and very devoted to her daughter. How is Claire, by the way? I cannot imagine how hard this must be for her."

Detective Minor let them know that Claire was holding up okay.

Sue White was the next to answer: "Kelsey is so sweet, and she cares about everyone. Do you know where she is or what could have happened to her?"

Detective Minor had been anticipating this question and replied, "We are not sure what is going on at this point. That is the main reason I am here today. Do you recall Kelsey complaining about anyone harassing her or any problems she had with a particular person?"

All three other people shook their heads no. Dr. Hann added, "I do not think Kelsey is the kind of person anyone could have ill will towards. Do you ladies?"

The two women who worked for him again shook their heads no. Although Minor thought she noted Sue hesitate for a split second.

This conversation did not give Detective Minor any new information to help her solve this case. She decided to try to ask a few more questions. "Do you know if Kelsey was dating anyone?" she asked.

Sue White replied, "No, Kelsey told me once she felt burned by her ex-husband and was not interested in dating. I remember telling her it was a shame because she was young and beautiful, but she laughed that off."

Detective Minor asked Dr. Hann, "Please tell me about the conference she was at."

He seemed happy to discuss this topic and talked about the speakers and information sessions for several minutes. The information, at times, was a little over her head.

Detective Minor interjected when the doctor paused his dialogue and asked, "Did you also attend this conference?"

To which he replied that he had. She asked, "When was the last time you saw Kelsey?"

He said, "Kelsey and I spoke briefly about ten minutes to six Wednesday evening as I was heading into the Cardiologist dinner, and she was getting ready to leave. My wife, Helen, mentioned bumping into her when Kelsey was leaving and Helen was arriving."

Detective Minor noted this and asked, "Is there anything else you can think of that might help this investigation?"

Dr. Hann and Becca said no, but Sue hesitated again. She seemed to be holding something back. Detective Minor decided it was best to talk to her alone. She told the group, "As a matter of procedure, I would like to talk to each of you alone. Would it be possible to start with Sue?".

Everyone agreed, and Dr. Hann and Becca picked up their lunches and went to their desks to eat.

When they left, Minor got up and closed the door. "Sue, you seem to have something you are unsure you want to tell me. Please let me judge whether or not it is important.", Kass implored the woman.

Sue looked at her, sighed, and said, "Okay, so a few months ago, Kelsey told me she felt like someone was watching her. I blew it off at first, but then the incident happened at the grocery store."

Detective Minor was intrigued and asked, "What incident at the grocery store?".

"Well, I wasn't there, and Kelsey was shaken up about it when she told me, so I am not sure of all the details. She was leaving the grocery store after work and had that eerie feeling of being watched. As she got into her car, she saw some writing on her windshield. Someone had written 'Home Wrecker' on her windshield in what seemed like lipstick." Sue explained.

Minor was surprised that this was the first time she or Detective Leet had heard about this. She asked Sue, "Did she file a police report?"

Sue shook her head no and said, "No, she went back in and talked to the store manager. He told her there were no cameras were in the parking lot, so she figured it was a waste of time. I agreed with her when she told me about it the next day. Since she has been missing, I have second-guessed that decision. She might have actually been being stalked."

Detective Minor could not help but agree, but she kept the thought to herself. She asked Sue, "Do you know why the words Home Wrecker was used?"

Sue said neither she nor Kelsey understood why someone would write that.

"Sue, is there anything else you haven't told me?" Detective Minor asked.

Sue shook her head and looked like she was on the verge of tears. She said in a choked voice, "I will never be able to forgive myself if something terrible happened to Kelsey, and reporting the incident would have stopped it from happening. I like her."

Detective Minor wondered if Sue knew what was really behind Kelsey and Joe's divorce, so she asked. Sue told her that Kelsey never talked about it, and she did not want to push because they had not been friends that long. Minor thanked Sue for the information and then individually spoke with Becca and Dr. Hann. However, neither of them had anything else of substance to add.

16

Friday February 2, 2018

Joe sat at the coffee shop, waiting for Kelsey. He had arrived early to ensure he had chosen where to sit. He knew it was petty, but he hated how Kelsey tried to control every interaction. He watched her walk in the door and towards the counter. He noticed that his ex-wife looked like she had lost weight since the last time he saw her, and she had no weight to lose. He wondered if something was wrong with her. He wondered, *is that why she wanted to meet in person?* She looked around the cafe after ordering, spotted him, and gave a half wave. After getting her green tea, she walked over and sat down.

Kelsey took the lid off the top of the tea and blew on it. She seemed to be stalling, so Joe asked, "Why are we here?".

She chuckled and said, "I see you still hate small talk. I wanted to talk to you about Claire and college expenses."

Joe shrugged, "Okay, what about them? She won't pay tuition as long as she keeps her grades up. I figure she is set for a while. She can tell me if she runs into money trouble, and we can discuss it."

Kelsey swallowed a drink of her tea and said, "Come on, Joe, you know that it is not a scholarship. It is a reimbursement program. Claire may not understand the difference, but you do. I cannot put half the money towards the car we talked about buying for her high school graduation and pay the first semester's tuition."

Joe was becoming upset with Kelsey. It seemed to him that whatever he did it was never good enough for her. "Okay then, we won't get her a car. She doesn't need one at school, anyway."

Before Kelsey could respond, Joe got up and walked out of the cafe. She blew out a breath and was glad she had never told Claire about the car. Kelsey wondered how she could pay the tuition and get Claire a vehicle. She could always work weekends at the hospital once Claire moved away.

****

Joe needed to burn off steam. He drove home and grabbed his burner phone. He called her and confirmed the time for their meet up later. Since he had a few hours to burn, he called John and agreed to meet him to go fishing. John never had any kids, but he did have two ex-wives, so he must understand how unreasonable women could be. He could not believe Kelsey was trying to squeeze him for more money. Why would he step up and give Claire more? She didn't even make an effort to be in his life. Since Paulina Moore had suggested it, he had wondered if Kelsey had poisoned Claire against him.

Wednesday April 18, 2018

Detective Mitch Leet left a message for Dr. Raul Moore this morning, asking him to call back. He checked his phone when he got back in the car, and so far, he had no missed calls or messages. Leet had talked with Jerry Applegate, the third man in the picture, and was headed to his employer next. When they spoke on the phone, Jerry had told him that he didn't know Joe that well but hadn't hesitated to tell Leet he was happy to help. Jerry was the manager of a large truck stop gas station on the edge of Interstate Forty-Four. He had told Detective Leet to stop by whenever, and he would take a break so they could talk.

As Detective Leet pulled into a parking spot in front of the store, his mind flashed to the recent training the police department had sent him and other members of the Criminal Investigations division to on human trafficking. *Could Kelsey Learner be a victim of this growing crime? Were they wasting valuable time looking at her ex-husband? Was there any chance of ever finding her if she was kidnapped for this nefarious reason?* He did realize that she was older than the key demographic described, but her pictures showed a woman who could easily be mistaken for her late twenties. When he and Detective Minor both got back to the station, he would need to bring up this possibility to her.

Jerry Applegate was behind the counter helping a truck driver, who was upset about something regarding his points and free showers. Leet flashed his badge and indicated a table sitting off to the side. Jerry nodded at him and went back to his customer. A few minutes later, Jerry slid into the booth opposite Mitch Leet and asked if he would like something to drink on the house. Leet gladly accepted a Diet Coke and watched as Jerry walked off to get it. When he returned with the soda and a cup of coffee for himself, Jerry started talking. "I saw the story about Joe Learner's ex-wife on the news. Of course, everyone down at The Club was already talking about it. How can I help you with finding her?".

"What can you tell me about Joe Learner? You said on the phone that you do not know him that well. However, the way I got your name was a picture in the paper that featured Joe, Dr. Raul Moore, and yourself, so I know you have some knowledge of him," Detective Leet questioned.

Jerry nodded and said, "Yeah, I know the guy. He joined The Club maybe a year or so ago. I have talked to him several times at meetings, and we both worked on the playground project. Fuel Time was the project's corporate sponsor, so I ensured I was in the picture. That is the kind of thing that the corporate types like us to do. Honestly, I don't know Joe that well. You would be better off talking to his friend, John Andrews."

Detective Leet noted the name and asked a few more questions. It was clear that Jerry Applegate only had a passing knowledge of Joe Learner and could not help Leet to understand him better. He asked Jerry if he could provide more information on John Andrews. Jerry was happy to help and fished a business card from his wallet.

He told Detective Leet, "I got this from John a while back because I have some tax issues. My wife, Terri, is selling stuff online and we didn't include the income on our taxes. He helped me get that straightened out."

Leet thanked him for his time, the Diet Coke, and the business card; then, he returned to his car. He wondered if Detective Minor was learning anything helpful.

****

Detective Kass Minor walked into Memorial Hospital and then to the Labor and Delivery floor. Claire had said her mom's only friend was a nurse named Andi Waters. When Minor spoke to her on the phone, the woman was clearly affected by her friend's disappearance. She had told Minor that she was working a double shift at the hospital but to come by whenever. Detective Minor found Andi sitting behind a nurses' station, working on a computer. She introduced herself, and Andi Waters told her she was finishing some chart notes. She asked Minor to have a seat in the family waiting room and said she would come there to talk in a few minutes.

Andi walked into the room and looked around. It had been a quiet day on the floor, so there was no one other than the detective in the room. She told the head nurse she was taking her break to talk to Detective Minor. Worry for her friend had been occupying her mind all day. She had called Claire after seeing the press conference this morning. They had cried together on the phone, and Andi had told Claire she would come by tomorrow afternoon. She could not imagine what her friend's daughter was going through.

Andi asked Detective Minor, "Is there any news on Kelsey? I wish I were out with the searchers, but we are short-staffed here. I cannot believe she has been gone for almost a week, and I just found out today. What kind of friend am I?"

Detective Minor had no easy answers for the woman. She wondered if she disappeared how long her friends would go without noticing it. Probably a long time because, with her unpredictable schedule, they often went weeks and sometimes months with little more than an occasional text.

"We do not have any new information we can share now. I was hoping you might be able to help fill in some gaps about Kelsey."

Andi said, "Sure. What do you want to know?"

"How long have you and Kelsey been friends? Do you know if she was seeing anyone romantically?" Minor asked. She had decided to start with more straightforward questions and ease into the more difficult ones.

Andi told Minor that the two women had been friends for over ten years. They had met when Andi started as a nurse at the hospital on the transplant floor. She said that Kelsey had started as a mentor to her, and they became friends as they realized they both shared a quiet, sarcastic sense of humor. Kelsey had been married to Joe then, and Andi was newly married to her husband, Doug. The couples sometimes had dinner together before Kelsey and Joe's divorce.

"Kelsey never really talked about the divorce. Joe's cheating hurt her, but she never told me the details. She only told me that she had found evidence of his cheating, which he did not deny, and it was not the first time. My heart broke for her. No one ever wants to see someone hurt their friend. I think that is why she has never dated to my knowledge since her divorce.", Andi told Detective Minor.

Detective Minor was taken aback by this revelation about Joe cheating. She would have to text Leet when she left and tell him she was ready to meet to compare notes.

"Did Kelsey ever tell you or allude to being afraid of Joe or any violence in the relationship?" Minor asked.

Andi shook her head no and said, "Absolutely not, and Kelsey would have told me that. We had a mutual friend who had been in a domestic violence situation, and Kelsey helped her to get out. She was adamant that no one should be in a relationship where they were abused."

Minor understood this stance and wholeheartedly agreed. "Was Kelsey upset or worried about anything or anyone lately?"

Andi looked at Minor, took a deep breath, and said, "It has been a while since Kelsey and I have talked. I returned to work about three months ago after having our second baby. I have been so worn out between working and the kids. I always figured there would be time to reconnect." Andi broke down, crying.

Minor knew that the interview was over. She took a business card out, handed it to her, and asked her to call if she thought of anything that would help.

17

Wednesday February 28, 2018

Detective Kass Minor finished her report on the latest homicide case she and Detective Leet had conducted. They had the brother of the victim in custody. The victim seemed to have been fooling around with his brother's wife. The wife had the sense to run from the apartment when he caught them, but the victim stood his ground. When they arrested their suspect, he had given a full confession. He kept telling them it was justifiable. She wondered how seemingly sane people got to the point of killing someone they supposedly loved.

Kass stood from her desk and walked over to Detective Leet. They both were headed out now that the reports were done and their commander had given them the next few days off. Kass was going to go to her parents. It would be nice to take a break from murder, rape, and kidnapping. When she took the job as a criminal investigations' detective, she had known theoretically what her job would entail, but that was different from doing it daily. Kass often wondered if she could have a normal life while working this job.

She had been on only first dates for almost the last three years. The men she had dated were either too fascinated by her job or were put off by it. She did not want to date a fellow cop. While she knew he would understand the job, she could not imagine being in a relationship with someone whose life was in danger so often. When Kass told her mom this, she laughed and said, "I guess you can imagine how your dad and I feel about you."

"What are your plans for the next few days?" Kass asked Detective Leet. She knew that Mitch had lived solitary since his wife's death.

Leet looked up and replied, "Resting. This is a young person's game. For an old guy like me, these cases wear me out."

Minor nodded and replied, "I am not sure I will make it as long as you have. This job has already begun to take its toll on me."

Leet looked at her and thought about his daughter, who was only a little younger than his partner. He could not imagine her doing this job. He often wondered about Kass's personal life. She did not talk about dating or anyone special in her life. He could not imagine having done this job without Gloria and his kids to keep him grounded. Leet stood up and asked Minor, "Are you ready to go?" She nodded yes, and they walked out together.

****

Helen Hann sat in her car on the edge of the fast-food restaurant's parking lot. She met the man here whenever he had an update for her. She had another envelope of cash for him and hoped he had some good information for her. When she saw him pull in and park beside her, she unlocked the doors to her SUV. He got in and sat in the passenger seat. They did not exchange small talk, which was the way Helen preferred it. The man handed her an envelope. Inside was a typed report and pictures.

Helen handed him the money and said, "Keep following both of them."

He nodded his head and got out of her vehicle. Helen locked the doors and pulled out the papers and the pictures. She was starting to be able to visualize where each of them was regularly. She looked at the images that the man had taken. He had continued to not provide her with what she was looking for. Ever since she had found the ATM receipt in Chris's pocket for a cash withdrawal from an account she did not recognize, she knew. Now she was getting the proof she needed and formulating her plan for revenge. They would both get what they had coming to them.

Wednesday April 18, 2018

Detective Mitch Leet drove across town to John Andrew's office. He had called, and the receptionist told him that John should be there until five pm. He calculated the drive time and figured he would arrive by four-thirty, so there should be no chance that John had left by the time he arrived. When Leet arrived at the office, the receptionist told him that John was expecting him and walked him back to the accountant's office. John Andrews was the stereotype of an accountant in Leet's mind. He was slightly overweight, had short, thinning hair and glasses perched on the edge of his nose. Leet noted that the only personal items in the office were related to fishing or The Club.

John motioned for Detective Leet to take a seat and asked how he could help him.

"I am sure you know that your friend Joe Learner's ex-wife Kelsey is missing," Leet stated. John nodded, and Leet continued, "I am trying to build a picture of who Joe Learner is and his relationship with his ex-wife. What can you tell me about Joe?"

John looked at the detective momentarily and asked, "Is Joe a suspect?"

Leet noted that John had not answered his question, but had asked one of his own. People used this common diversion tactic when they did not want to share information.

Detective Leet chose his words carefully, "At this point in the investigation, we are focused on finding Kelsey Learner. We have not named a suspect in her disappearance. So, what can you tell me about Joe and his relationship with Kelsey?"

John responded, "I met Joe through our mutual divorce attorney about four years ago. I helped Joe to figure out the best way to file his taxes and account for his business expenses. Joe and I became friends because we are both divorced and like to fish. He is a good guy. He volunteers through The Club. The only thing I know about his relationship with his ex-wife is that she tried to squeeze him for more money a few months ago, and he was pissed."

This information was another surprise for Detective Leet. He asked John, "How did she try to squeeze him for more money? Do you know if they met in person or discussed this over the phone?"

John replied, "I am pretty sure they met in person at some coffee shop, and she thought Joe should help their kid with college. But the kid was going on a full scholarship, so it seemed more like a money grab because he was almost done paying child support."

Detective Leet asked John if there was anything else he could share or anyone else he thought the detective should talk to.

John responded, "No, no one else I know you should talk to. I can only say that you should be out trying to find out what happened to Kelsey and not harassing Joe."

John stood up to indicate he was done talking to Detective Leet and began walking to the door. He opened the door to his office, and Leet took the hint and left.

When Detective Leet returned to his car, he saw he had a text from Detective Minor. She was ready to meet back at the station. He started driving that way and called Dr. Raul Moore once again. Dr. Moore did not answer, and Leet left him another voicemail. He wondered if the man was avoiding him or was just really busy. Leet knew very little about what a large animal veterinarian would do daily.

18

Saturday March 3, 2018

Kelsey thanked the installer as he finished putting the security cameras up at her house. She knew that her friend Sue thought she was being paranoid, but she couldn't shake the eerie feeling of being watched for the past few months. She was unsure who it could be and wondered if she should contact the police, but what did she have to report? Feeling watched? The writing on her windshield? The hangup phone calls from unknown numbers? She was sure the police would agree with Sue that she was being paranoid.

As she walked back inside her house and locked the front door, Kelsey wondered what it would take to make her feel secure again. She couldn't go anywhere without looking around and worrying. She had read on the internet that anywhere between sixteen and thirty-two percent of people stalked by a stranger are the victims of violence from their stalker. Kelsey had been thinking about those statistics and wondered if they had made her more or less afraid. She had the cameras installed and had decided to take self-defense classes. She had even signed Claire up to go to the classes with her. She was planning to tell Claire about the class this evening. Her daughter was all about being an independent woman, so she would likely be excited to go.

****

Claire knew something was up with her mom. Why did she suddenly want to attend self-defense classes and have security cameras installed? She wondered if she should ask her mom. Although they were close, it was not like her mom was her confidant. Claire had Lindsey to tell her secrets to, and she had always figured her mom was so dull that she had no secrets to tell. She would go to the classes with her mom for two reasons. First, it would be good to know how to defend herself before she went to college, and second, she wanted to support her mom even if she did not know what had freaked her out.

Wednesday April 18, 2018

Detective Mitch Leet walked out of the diner carrying two dinner specials. He figured if he and Minor were going to work late, they may as well have a decent dinner. Detective Minor was walking through the door just in front of him. He told her he had gotten them some food and indicated they should go to the conference room. He followed her in and set down the food. She went to grab them both a cup of what passed as coffee at the police department.

"I found out a few things that seem to be important. How about you?" Minor asked him.

Leet replied, "I also found out a few new things. It will be interesting to see if they are the same new pieces of information."

The two detectives decided first to share what they had learned and then start a crime board. They often used a crime board when investigating a problematic case, and with Kelsey Learner now missing six days, this case had become just that. Leet indicated to Minor to start.

"Sue White, the nurse at Dr. Hann's office with her, told me Kelsey felt she was being watched and followed. She vaguely described an incident from a few months ago in which someone wrote 'Home Wrecker' on Kelsey's windshield."

He interrupted her and asked, "Why Home Wrecker?".

Minor shook her head and said, "Sue said neither she nor Kelsey had any idea why someone would write that on her car. In addition, when I asked Dr. Hann when he last saw Kelsey, he told me he saw her just before six at the conference center. Interestingly, he added that his wife, Helen, told him that she saw Kelsey in the parking garage as Helen arrived and Kelsey was leaving. She is my next person to talk to. I left her a voicemail, but she has not called me back."

Detective Leet chuckled, "I have the same problem with Dr. Raul Moore. I have left him three messages so far. We may need to go to his known address early tomorrow morning to catch him at home. Then we can go visit Helen Hann."

Minor agreed that sounded like a good idea.

She then continued telling Leet what she had found out. "After I left Dr. Hann's office, I went to Memorial Hospital and met with Andi Waters. She is a long-time friend of Kelsey's and was very upset. She told me that Kelsey and Joe got divorced because Joe cheated on Kelsey on more than one occasion." Minor looked at Leet to gauge his reaction to what she had just said. He did not look surprised.

Leet could tell that Minor had thought she would shock him. He said, "Joe's brother Eddie told me about the cheating, although he seemed to think it was just the one-time Kelsey caught him. It seemed that Eddie and Joe do not have a close relationship, but Eddie doesn't feel that Joe would hurt anyone. I ended up talking with Joe's friend, John Andrews as well. He told me something very interesting."

Leet continued, "According to John, Joe saw Kelsey a few months ago and was angry at her for asking him to help Claire financially when she went to college. I thought that I remembered that Joe told us it had been years since he had seen Kelsey. I checked the report I wrote on that first interview, and that was what he said. So, it would seem that Joe lied to us. It makes me wonder what else Joe is lying about."

19

Friday March 16, 2018

Joe sat at his desk at home. He had turned in all his weekly reports and was now paying his bills. He was looking forward to being done paying child support. In the last few years, he had run up sizable credit card debt not to have to cut back on his sessions with her. He knew paying back everything he had charged would take him a long time, but it had been worth every penny. He realized the looming debt was why he reacted badly when Kelsey asked him to chip in more toward Claire's expenses.

He did not feel like he owed either of them any more money. He wondered if he and Claire had stayed close and if she had continued to visit, if he would feel differently. He thought back to the relationship he had with his dad. They had been very close. So much so that his mother often commented that they were more like brothers than father and son. Their relationship had always been an issue between Joe and his brother Eddie. His dad was so proud of him when he was accepted to the University of Missouri. Joe was the first member of his family to go to college, and Claire would be the second.

He knew his dad would expect him to help Claire. Joe had only worked part time in college, and that was for spending money. His parents helped make sure that he graduated with no student loans. He was beginning to feel guilty for his reaction. He needed to reach out to Claire and offer to help her out.

****

Claire's phone rang just as she was leaving the locker room. The track meet was superb. She had won first in the 800-meter race, and the team she was running with had won the 4 x 200 relay race. She looked at her phone and was surprised to see it was her dad calling. She answered the phone, "Hi, Dad. Guess what? I won both my events today."

Joe responded, "That is great, Claire. What did you run today?"

Claire was excited to tell him about her performance in the 800-meter race. She also told him about the relay and how hard her team had worked to run it as a cohesive unit.

When Claire took a breath, Joe said, "It sounds like you had a great day. I was thinking about you this morning and about when you head to college."

Claire said, "Um, okay."

Joe went on to tell Claire that he wanted to help her with expenses while she was in college. Claire expressed her gratitude, and they agreed to discuss the details once she settled at school. After hanging up with her dad, Claire walked to the parking lot to find her mom. She was surprised to see her mom working on changing the tire on her SUV. Claire approached her mom and asked, "Mom, what happened?"

Kelsey looked up at her and said, "I am not sure. When I got to the Buick, I noticed it looked like it was leaning. I walked around and saw that this tire was completely flat. I am trying to change it, but will have to call for help."

Claire knew she was not any stronger than her mom, so she could not physically help her. "Do you want me to ask Coach Dunn if he can help?"

Kelsey said, "Yes, please."

****

Once Claire walked away, Kelsey sat down at the back of the SUV. She wanted to cry. Kelsey wondered if the flat tire was related to the other strange things that had been happening. She hoped she had driven over a nail on the way to the track meet and that the tire had gone flat as the Encore sat there.

A few minutes later, Claire, Coach Dunn, and a couple of young men walked up. They looked at the tire and told Kelsey they would have the spare on in minutes. Five minutes later, the spare tire was on the SUV, and the flat was sitting in the back cargo area. Claire was chatting with her friends, and Coach Dunn approached Kelsey.

"It looks like your tire was slashed. You may want to file a police report because it seems targeted to me since there are no other vehicles with flat tires.", Coach Dunn told her.

Kelsey thanked him for his concern and told him she would follow up. Now she knew that the flat tire was not just bad luck. Kelsey could not figure out who would do this to her.

Thursday April 19, 2018

Detective Mitch Leet pulled up in front of Detective Minor's condo building at six-thirty in the morning. He had stopped and picked up breakfast burritos and coffee on his way. They had decided last night to arrive at the Moore's farm just before seven am. He and Minor had agreed that people who managed a hobby farm and worked full-time as veterinarians would get up early in the day to care for their animals. Minor got in the car and spied the food and coffee.

She exclaimed, "You are a lifesaver. I ran out of coffee yesterday morning and did not remember that until this morning. Thank you so much."

Leet smiled and replied, "You are welcome."

He programmed the address of the Moores' farm into the car's GPS. He headed out of town to get this interview underway. As far as he had learned, Dr. Raul Moore had only a casual relationship with Joe Learner. He turned down the driveway of the Moores and noted the no trespassing sign at the start of the driveway. The gate was open, so he drove through and slowed down to not hit the ruts in the driveway at a rate of high speed. He looked at Minor and saw she had put her coffee down as he navigated the driveway. He noted that the Moores had several flags flying: a large American flag, a Trump 2016 flag, and the Gadsden Flag.

Detective Leet stopped his car in front of the house. He and Detective Minor walked up to the front door. Before either of them could knock, the door opened. A petite, attractive woman said, “Good Morning. How can I help you?”.

Detective Leet introduced himself and Detective Minor and asked, “Is Dr. Raul Moore here?”

The woman nodded, “He is here. I am his wife, Paulina. Please come in, and I will get him for you.”

As the detectives walked in, they noticed the house was fastidiously clean and tidy. They sat in the living room and waited.

Ten minutes later, a short, slightly pudgy guy with a receding hairline entered the room. “Hello, I am Doctor Raul Moore. Paulina said you are here to speak to me. What is it you need to see me about?”

“I left you several messages yesterday, and you did not get back to me. Since time is of the essence, we came out to talk to you this morning.” Detective Leet replied.

Raul’s response was to apologize and state that he had been very busy birthing animals.

Detective Minor said, “Okay, well, we are here now. We would like to know about your relationship with Joe Learner.”

“Um, okay. I know him from The Club. He has been out here once for a party, and I think he helped on the playground project that I headed up for The Club. I can’t say that I know him well. Is there something specific that you would like to know?”

Detective Leet said, “Did you ever talk to him about his ex-wife, Kelsey?”

“Well, I know he is divorced, and of course, I heard that his ex-wife was missing. He never talked to me about her, so I do not think I can help.”

“What is your general impression of Joe?” Detective Minor asked.

Raul shrugged and said, "He seems like an ordinary guy. Nothing that stands out in my mind."

Detectives Leet and Minor stood up. They thanked Raul for his time, and Detective Leet handed him a business card and said, "Please contact me if you think of anything else that may help us find Kelsey Learner."

When they returned to the car, Minor told Leet, "Both of them gave me a creepy feeling. Did you sense that?"

Detective Leet thought about what she was saying. He knew he was less intuitive than his partner. His late wife, Gloria, had often told him that he had no sense of people. This was not entirely true; he was great at knowing when people were lying to him. He did not feel that Raul Moore had lied to them about his relationship with Joe Learner, but Detective Minor was right that something was off about both of the Moores.

20

Wednesday March 21, 2018

Claire walked out of school and looked for her mom's SUV. Her mom picked her up on the days she had track practice. She had tried since middle school to get Lindsey to join track with her, but her best friend could not stand to be sweaty. So, Claire ran track, and Lindsey was on the debate team. Claire spotted her mom's blue Buick Encore at the far back of the parking lot. She wondered why her mom would park back there, but whatever. She started walking in that direction. As soon as she started walking, she heard a horn. She turned in the direction of the noise and saw her mom to the left of the entrance. That wasn't her mom parked in the back of the lot, just another SUV like hers.

Kelsey smiled at Claire and handed her the bubble tea she had bought her on the way over. She had been thinking about how much she would miss Claire when she left for college. Kelsey wanted to spend as much time as she could with Claire before she moved out. However, she did not want her daughter to feel smothered or for Claire to worry about how Kelsey would manage without her. She remembered when her daughter was a two-year-old, and people told her that parenting was at its hardest during that stage. Then later, when Claire was a pre-teen and teenager, she and other moms lamented that no, that was the most challenging stage of parenting. Kelsey now understood that the hardest stage of parenting is the one you are in the midst of struggling with. She had never looked forward to having an empty nest. She supposed that if she was still married and had a close relationship with her husband, she might be happier to have Claire move out. However, Kelsey did not have a husband with whom to enjoy a quiet, empty nest. She was sure that she would have many long, lonely evenings in her future.

Thursday April 19, 2018

Driving from the Moore's farm to Doctors Chris and Helen Hann's home was a journey through Springfield. They started in the countryside and went through a middle-class neighborhood. Then, into a working-class part of town, past downtown and all the apartments and condos that had sprung up in the last few years. Back into another middle-class neighborhood and finally out to the gated community where the Hanns resided. Detective Leet showed their badges to the man in the guard shack. He opened the gate for them and gave them directions.

Pulling up to the Hanns, Leet heard Detective Minor give a soft whistle. Indeed, the house before them was impressive. It was a Greek revival-style mansion with floor-to-ceiling windows and large front columns. Leet figured the house was probably seven to eight thousand square feet. The semi-circular driveway had a turnoff that led to the four-car garage. The two detectives exited their car and headed to the front door. A young woman in a black uniform answered the door. Detective Leet introduced them and asked to speak with Helen Hann.

The young woman inquired, "Is she expecting you?"

Detective Minor replied, "No, she is not, but we must speak with her."

The woman nodded and said, "Please wait here. I will go and let her know that you are here." She then shut the front door.

Detective Leet turned to Minor and chuckled, then said, "I guess we should have made an appointment."

Moments later, the young woman returned and opened the door. She told the detectives, "Dr. Hann said she would see you. Please follow me to the sitting room."

The detectives walked into the house and saw the young woman motioned for them to turn to the right. The sitting room was directly off the front door. Detectives Leet and Minor took seats as the young woman said, “Would you like something to drink? I just put on a fresh pot of coffee.”

They both declined the offer. This was not a social call. The detectives had agreed on the drive over that Minor would take the lead and that Leet would ask any follow-up questions he had when she finished. A short time later, the door to the sitting room opened, and an older woman walked in. She introduced herself to the detectives. “I am Dr. Helen Hann. How can I help you this morning?”

“I left you a voicemail yesterday, and since you had not returned my call, my partner and I decided to visit you. I am sure you know that one of your husband’s employees, Kelsey Learner, is missing.”, Detective Minor stated.

Helen Hann looked directly at Minor and nodded, “Yes, Chris shared that with me, and I saw the news conference as well.”

Minor continued, “We are wondering if you would tell us about the last time, you saw Kelsey.”

Helen appeared to think about the question before answering it. “I caught a glimpse of her when she left the conference that Chris paid for her to attend, and I was arriving to attend the dinner for the doctors and the spouses. We just exchanged pleasantries.”

The information Helen had shared matched what Chris Hann had told Detective Minor, but they seemed to have left out something. “How would you describe your relationship with Kelsey Learner?” Detective Minor asked.

Helen Hann shook her head and replied, “I do not have a relationship with her. She works for my husband. I saw her when I went to his office, and she attended one dinner he had for his employees.”

Detective Minor had no other questions. She looked at Detective Leet, and he asked, “What kind of vehicle do you drive?”

Helen seemed surprised by this and said, “A BMW M4 Coupe. Why?”

Leet replied, “Just following up on some leads.”

The two detectives stood and prepared to leave. Detective Minor took out a business card and handed it to Helen. “Please call us if you think of any information that might help us find Kelsey Learner.”

Helen walked the two detectives to the door.

As they walked to the car, Leet said to Minor, “Let’s head back to the station. We need to look at the pictures you printed and watch that footage from Kelsey’s house. I need to see if my hunch is right.”

Minor was sure that she knew what his hunch was because Helen Hann shared striking similarities to the woman she had seen at Kelsey’s house. Detective Minor was not one hundred percent sure what a BMW M4 Coupe looked like, but she did not remember seeing a BMW of any kind driving near Kelsey Learner’s house. She also firmly believed that Doctors Chris and Helen Hann owned several cars.

21

Saturday March 31, 2018

Helen Hann had carefully prepared her package for Kelsey. She wanted the other woman to know that she was on to her. Chris and Kelsey had been very secretive, but their time was almost up. Helen parked a few blocks away and put the package in a large purse. She looked like she was walking somewhere.

One thing that Helen had used to her advantage for a long time was her ability to blend. She was average in every way. She had gone to Sam's Club and bought the sweatsuit and shoes she was wearing. She looked positively middle class. She walked slowly up Kelsey Learner's steps, keeping her head down. She knew Kelsey had security cameras installed a few weeks ago.

She set the box down on the porch swing. Helen thought about ringing the doorbell but did not want to take the chance that Kelsey would see her. She would have loved to see Kelsey's reaction when she opened the package, but she would have to do with just imagining it. Would Kelsey call Chris to tell him? Somehow, she doubted it.

****

Kelsey sat on the edge of her bed, trying to get herself mentally prepared for the day. Today would have been her mom's sixty-fifth birthday. Her mom had talked about what she would do when she retired all of Kelsey's life. She had never gotten that chance. Her mom was just fifty years old when she was diagnosed with late-stage leukemia. There was little that anyone could do for her. Kelsey remembered how hard it had been to balance caring for a small child while having her mom in hospice care. She had been diligent in having regular checkups so that Claire never had to deal with burying her when she was young.

They cleaned out most of her mom's things when she inherited this house. She and Joe had painted every room and stained the hardwood floors. Kelsey loved this house. She had beautiful memories of living with her mom and raising Claire here. She was so grateful to her mom for leaving her the house and having insurance that paid off the mortgage. When they divorced, Joe had not fought her about the house. In all actuality, their divorce had been amicable. She wished that Joe had not reacted so badly when they met a couple of weeks ago, but there was little she could do about it.

Kelsey headed downstairs to get a cup of coffee and plan her day. She usually loved Saturdays, but she could not shake her melancholy. She sat at the table, made a grocery list, and then watched the footage from her security camera for the last few days. She had been watching it at double speed. The cameras only reacted to motion, but there was still a lot of footage to review because the cameras were set off by bugs and birds flying by, as well as every car that drove past the house. She had never seen anything of interest on the footage and had taken to only watching it on Saturday mornings. She stopped watching the footage before she got through it all and went to get dressed. She decided not to wake Claire up. It was a rare Saturday in the springtime that her daughter did not have a track meet.

Kelsey was walking down the stairs when something on the front porch caught her eye. She opened the door and saw a small package sitting on the swing. She knew it had not been there last evening because she had sat in the swing after dinner and read her new gardening book. She looked at the package and saw it was addressed to her but had no return address. It also had no labeling from a delivery service. Someone had dropped this off personally, but why not ring the bell and hand it to her?

She picked up the package and noticed it felt empty. After setting it on the kitchen table, she carefully opened it. Inside was a copy of a book cover entitled The Other Woman: Two Wrongs. On the back of the paper were taped cut-out letters that spelled out: ***You will be made to pay!***

Kelsey dropped the paper and began to shake. Who was harassing her and why? She never had an affair. She heard the floor creaking above her head as her daughter walked to the upstairs bathroom. There was no way she wanted her to see this. She grabbed the paper, shoved it back in the box, and threw it in the recycling bin by the back door.

Monday April 2, 2018

Claire woke up Monday morning feeling horrible. Her mom agreed she could stay home and rest. Around noon, Claire went to the kitchen to make hot tea. She saw that her mom had yet to take out the recycling. It was trash day; they only picked up recycling every other week. Claire grabbed the bin and walked it out to the curb. She went back up to bed and slept the rest of the day.

Thursday April 19, 2018

By the time they arrived back at the police station, Detectives Leet and Minor had learned that the Hanns did indeed own several cars besides the BMW M-4 coupe. They owned a Porsche 911 Cabriolet convertible, a 1966 Pontiac Catalina, and a Buick Encore. The Buick Encore, which was dark blue, was most interesting to the detectives. It seemed to Minor to be an odd coincidence that Helen and Chris Hann owned the exact same SUV in the same color as Kelsey Learner.

The first stop for Detective Minor was the computer forensics department. She talked to them about trying to enhance the parts of the footage from Kelsey's house that showed the blue Encore driving by. They needed to try to capture the license plate or at least a distinguishing feature. The team assured Minor that they would get started on that. In addition to attempting to digitally enhance the pictures of the woman who had walked around Kelsey Learner's house.

While Minor was with the computer forensics team, Detective Leet updated the commander. Leet had moved Helen Hann up on his list of potential suspects. Commander Davis agreed with Leet that they needed to look more deeply into Helen Hann. He also let Leet know that Greatlands Insurance had contacted the Assistant District Attorney's office to let them know that all the records for Joe Learners' work cell phone, the company car's GPS, and the tracking software would be sent electronically first thing tomorrow.

Detectives Minor and Leet sat and looked at the still pictures that Minor had printed, and both agreed that they could see physical similarities between the woman who had walked around Kelsey Learner's house and Helen Hann. The detectives would need to wait to see what digital enhancements the computer forensic technicians could do. Detective Minor suggested they go back to the conference center and see what the interior cameras showed about Helen Hann's time there.

Arriving at the conference center, the detectives spoke to the head of security. He told them he had backed up the entire three days of the conference after the first time the detectives visited. He pulled up the footage starting when Kelsey Learner walked from the coat check into the stairwell for the parking garage. The detective watched the footage for the next half an hour. They had yet to see Helen Hann enter the conference center. They asked the head of security to make them a copy of the footage he had saved. They would head back to the station and watch the footage to see if Helen Hann ever arrived.

Back at the station, after they had watched the footage several times, it was agreed that they never saw Helen enter the conference center. They did see Dr. Chris Hann enter the banquet hall just before six in the evening. He left the dinner with several other men his age at about seven thirty that evening. He then headed towards the hotel side of the convention center. Detective Leet and Minor agreed that the next step would be to get the hotel security camera footage and the key card information for the doctors' room. Detective Leet knew they might need a subpoena to get the records, so he went to see their commander.

22

Monday April 2, 2018

Doctor Chris Hann walked into the office building down the block from his medical practice. He never thought he would be divorcing Helen, but he could not take it anymore. He could not imagine dealing with Helen in retirement. He had made it all these years because he worked all the time. The thought of having to spend long periods of time with her had him reconsidering his options. He had met with the attorney for the first time over a year ago. He had begun moving assets overseas shortly after that. He knew Helen would try to bleed him dry, so he was trying to protect himself and their kids' inheritance.

Today's meeting was to finalize the details of his divorce petition and the timing of having Helen served. Chris would take a week off at the end of the month. He would have Kelsey cover all the follow-up appointments; besides those, his staff could also take time off that week. Helen was unaware of his vacation plan, and he had no intent on telling her. He would leave that Monday morning just like he did every work day and drive to the airport. She would be served with the divorce papers that afternoon. By the time he returned, she should have her own attorney, and the lawyers could hash it out.

After meeting with the attorney, Chris walked to the condo building he was buying in. He had put a down payment using his business account. When he applied for the mortgage, he used his work address. He talked to the doorman, who gave him the key to the unit he was buying. Chris would move in the day after he came back. His closing was scheduled for that day, and he would buy furniture and household items after he had his keys. He was happy for the first time in years. He would call his kids when his plane landed and explain, so they heard his side before their mothers.

****

Helen sat in her SUV and looked at the report the man had just given her. Chris had bought a plane ticket and a condo. She was sure he was going on a trip with his mistress and putting her in a nice condo. How did he think he would get away with this? She knew she had been drinking more lately, and Chris was upset about it. She had tried to explain to him that she was lonely with the kids all grown and moved away and that she had never recovered from losing their third child. He had yet to slow down his work schedule, and she could not restart her career. She had slowly lost herself over the years and did not know how to begin to rebuild. He had been unsympathetic and suggested that she figure it out. Chris had demanded many times that she stop drinking and go to rehab. She had never taken his ultimatums seriously before today. She needed to step up her plan to deal with Kelsey Learner.

Friday April, 20, 2018

Detectives Leet and Minor arrived at the station within minutes of each other. They were both hoping they were on the edge of a breakthrough in the Kelsey Learner case. They had been playing catch up ever since they got this case. It was a well-known belief amongst the police that the first forty-eight hours after a crime is when you are most likely to solve it. When it came to missing people, if you did not find them in that forty-eight-hour window, it was unlikely there would be a positive outcome. They had not even learned of Kelsey Learner's disappearance until forty-six of those hours were already up.

Detective Minor reviewed an email from the computer forensics team while Leet went to see if the subpoena had come through for the hotel. As Leet left the commander's office with the subpoena, Minor practically ran towards him. She stopped just before and held out a printout. The tech guys had isolated the license plates on seven of the images of the blue Buick Encore. Five of the images of the license plates were Kelsey Learner's license plate, but the other two were that of Helen Hann. Detective Leet thought, *well, now we are getting somewhere.*

He suggested to Minor, "Let's go to the hotel and see what their security footage shows us, and then we can bring in Doctor Helen Hann for a chat."

Minor agreed, and the two headed to the conference center hotel. After presenting the subpoena to and speaking with the manager of the hotel and the head of security, they were sitting in a room watching several screens that had been cued up to just before six pm for the day in question. They verified that the time on the footage was correct and then set it to play at triple speed. They watched it that way until Helen Hann appeared. It was six fifty-one pm, according to the timestamp on the bottom of the footage. She came in from the elevator that leads to the parking garage. She looked disheveled and was stumbling a little. She went directly to the hotel elevators. The detectives switched to that camera view when she got on the elevator. They watched Helen lean against the back of the elevator with her eyes closed until she reached the tenth floor. She shuffled out of the elevator, and the detectives switched to the tenth-floor hall camera footage. Helen Hann struggled to open the door to her hotel room, but she entered the room and closed the door at six fifty-nine pm.

The detectives continued to watch the tenth-floor hall footage at triple speed. Almost an hour later, they saw Dr. Chris Hann exit the elevator and walk to the room. He let himself in. They went back and watched the other cameras' footage to chart Chris Hann coming from the conference center into the lobby, onto the elevator, and then directly to his room. They watched for another half an hour and saw no activity. They put the footage back on triple speed and watched the night transpire without either Hann leaving their hotel room. They slowed the footage as Chris Hann left the room just before eight am the next morning. He headed directly back to the conference center. The detectives watched the footage, and it was not until ten thirty in the morning that the Hann's hotel room door opened again. Helen Hann walked out wearing the same clothes as she had on when she entered the room last night.

Detective Leet turned to Minor and said, "Now it is time to bring Dr. Helen Hann in for questioning."

Minor agreed with him but asked him to wait while she had the hotel make them a copy of the footage. Minor spoke to the head of security, and he agreed to email her the footage right away. As the detectives drove back to the station, they discussed what they knew about Helen Hann. Neither could figure out why she would have any motive to kidnap Kelsey Learner. Leet reminded Minor that figuring out a motive was not their job. He thought about all the senseless crimes he had investigated over the years. It was sometimes impossible to figure out what drove people to do what they did.

Detective Minor called Helen Hann and asked her to come to the police station to answer several follow-up questions. The woman told her she was nearby, running a few errands, and would be there shortly. When she arrived about a half hour later, Leet and Minor sat her down in an interrogation room.

Minor told her, "Before we get started, I need to read you your rights and then have you sign the form acknowledging that you understand them."

After completing that process, Minor opened a folder and took out a picture that showed Helen entering the hotel from the parking garage almost an hour later than she had told them. Minor said, "We are wondering about the discrepancy between the hotel security footage and what you told us transpired on the day Kelsey Learner disappeared. Care to explain."

Helen Hann stared at the detectives and said, "I want a lawyer."

The two detectives got up and walked out of the room. Helen was brought a phone, and she called her husband, Chris. The detectives listened from the other side of the one-way mirror.

Helen said, "Chris, I am at the police station and need a lawyer."

The detectives could not hear the reply, but it must have been short because Helen hung up the phone without saying anything else.

An hour later, Detective Leet got a call from the desk sergeant. Dr. Chris Hann and his lawyer were there to speak to him. He had the officer send them back to an interview room. Leet and Minor greeted the doctor and his lawyer. The lawyer told the detectives that his client wanted to know what was happening with his wife.

Detective Leet said, "We asked Helen to come in to ask some follow-up questions regarding the disappearance of Kelsey Learner. She refused to answer those questions and requested a lawyer. Are you her lawyer as well?"

The lawyer said, "No, I am not, but my colleague is on her way to represent Mrs. Hann. Would it be possible for Dr. Hann and me to observe the interview?"

Detective Leet responded, "I will ask my commander."

As they exited the interview room, Minor asked Leet, "Are they allowed to watch the interview?"

Leet responded, "I am not sure. I have never been asked to have one spouse watch the interrogation of another spouse. Let's ask Commander Davis and make sure ADA Reinhart will be present once Helen's lawyer arrives."

The commander turned down the request to have Dr. Chris Hann and his lawyer view the questioning. He told Leet and Minor to speak to them after they interrogated Helen. ADA Reinhart would observe the interview then let them know whether to charge her. They returned to the interrogation room Helen was now sharing with her lawyer.

The lawyer introduced herself as Angie Miller and asked, "Is my client being charged with a crime?"

Detective Leet replied, "We are trying to clear up some inconsistencies, so she is not charged with a crime she did not commit. We can charge her and let it all come out in court if you prefer."

"No, that is not what we want. Please ask your questions, and I will confer with my client regarding her ability to answer them at this time.", Ms. Miller replied.

Detective Minor pulled out the time-stamped picture of Helen Hann entering the hotel at six fifty-one pm. "When we met with you yesterday, you told us that you saw Kelsey Learner in the parking garage just before six pm the day she disappeared. You then said that you went to dinner with your husband. However, this is the first time you are seen at either the hotel or the conference center. Care to explain."

Helen looked at Angie Miller, who nodded her head. "I lied to you yesterday. I did not want to admit the truth because I have a drinking problem. I was drunk that evening. I do not even remember going to the hotel. I don't know if I ever saw Kelsey. Chris told me to say I did, but I have no memories from the afternoon of that day until the next morning.", Helen explained.

Detective Leet asked, "Why do you think your husband told you to lie?"

Helen looked up and said, "I am not sure, but I know he was worried I would be charged with drunk driving."

"All right, on a different note. Let's talk about the time you spent at Kelsey Learner's house.", Detective Leet stated.

"What?" exclaimed Angie Miller, "I need to confer with my client."

The detectives stepped out of the room and watched Helen and her attorney huddle together through the one-way mirror. ADA Liza Reinhart was standing in the room along with Commander Davis.

Reinhart told the detectives, "Commander Davis has reviewed all the evidence with me prior to your partial interrogation. So, I called the judge and secured an arrest warrant for Helen. When you go back in there, no matter what her answers are to any further questions, go ahead and arrest her. We are charging her with stalking and suspicion of kidnapping."

23

Friday April 6, 2018

Helen Hann sat across from Kelsey's house thinking, *how dare this woman destroy my family? After all these years and all that Chris and I have been through, I cannot believe he is having an affair with someone as young as our daughter. The time has almost arrived to make Kelsey pay for her scheming ways and then to be sure that Chris regrets his choices for the rest of his life.*

****

Kelsey drove home in the middle of the day to change clothes. A patient had gotten sick to their stomach, and Kelsey's pants and shoes had been dealt the brunt of it. She noticed an SUV just like hers drive away from the stop sign at the end of her block just as she arrived at the sign. She had seen many SUVs that were just like hers lately. She knew about the frequency of illusion theory. It wasn't like she was looking for blue Buick Encores, but her bias made sure she noticed one when it was near her.

Kelsey walked in the back door and took off her shoes. She carried them to the laundry room and finished undressing. She wrapped a towel around herself and went to take a shower. When she returned downstairs, she saw multiple missed calls from an unknown number. There were no voicemails, but she tried to call the number back. There was no answer, and the phone did not have voicemail set up. Kelsey texted Claire just to be sure she was all right. Claire had sent her an emoji thumbs up in response. She got in her SUV and opened the garage door. As she backed out, she would have sworn she saw a blue Buick Encore pull away from the curb and speed away. Her mind was playing tricks on her.

****

Helen was fuming. She had come so close to catching them in the act. She had just decided to head home when Kelsey arrived at the stop sign. Helen knew that Kelsey should be at work at that time of day. She turned her SUV around and called Chris's office. The receptionist, Becca, told her that Chris was at a meeting all afternoon. Helen thanked her and hung up the phone as she pulled up to the curb across from Kelsey's house. She arrived in time to see the garage door finish closing. She wondered; *what should I do.* She reached under the passenger seat and took out the bottle of vodka. She was sure Chris had either been in Kelsey's vehicle or would be arriving soon. She needed to decide whether to confront them now or stick to her plan.

She had just finished the bottle of vodka when she heard Kelsey's garage door open. Helen decided to beat Kelsey back to the office and watch as she and Chris arrived together. She would take pictures using her cell phone camera. She knew she would need that proof for when she confronted Chris. He was wrong if he thought that Helen would take this lying down. Helen thought, *Hell hath no fury as a woman scorned.* She truly understood this saying now.

****

Kelsey pulled into the parking lot of the medical complex where Dr. Hann's office was. She knew she would need to hustle to make up time, so she was not behind with patients all afternoon. Kelsey waved at Becca as she passed through the reception area. She found Sue, and the two were quickly immersed in their work. Kelsey was unaware that Helen Hann had arrived at the clinic until she walked into her office, and Helen was sitting behind her desk. She was about to ask Helen what she was doing when she realized the woman was fast asleep in the chair and reeked of vodka. Kelsey grabbed her laptop, walked out, and gently closed the door.

Friday April 20, 2018

When Detectives Leet and Minor reentered the interrogation room, Angie Miller informed them that her client wanted to make a statement.

"I admit I have been following Kelsey Learner. I suspected she and my husband, Chris, were having an affair. I needed to gather evidence so that I could confront Chris. I never did anything to harm her physically." Helen rapidly replied.

She and her attorney had clearly rehearsed exactly what Helen was to say. Detective Minor pulled out the pictures of the person who was seen snooping around Kelsey's home.

"These are pictures of you. You were trying to find a way into Kelsey Learner's house. Are you willing to explain what you were looking for?" Detective Minor questioned.

Without consulting her attorney, Helen replied, "I just wanted to understand her better and why Chris would choose her over me. I did not break in, but I figured that if she had left her door unlocked, it would not have been that big a deal for me to look around. All her doors and windows were locked, so I left."

Detectives Minor and Leet were pleased with Helen's answer, as it was impossible to be one hundred percent sure that it was Helen in the pictures. Now that she had confirmed it was her and what she was doing, it would be difficult for her attorney to argue that the photographs were unclear.

Detective Minor continued the questioning, "We have reports that Kelsey was being harassed. Was that something you were doing as well?"

Angie Miller answered before her client could, "Define harassment and what exact activities you think my client was involved in."

Although she had not heard of incidents other than the writing on the windshield, Detective Minor had a hunch that Helen Hann had not stopped with the one time.

"Specifically, did you write Home Wrecker on Kelsey's windshield?" Minor asked Helen.

Helen responded quickly, “Well, she was one, wasn’t she?”

Detective Leet jumped in at this point. “Was? Why did you refer to Kelsey Learner in the past tense?”

Helen looked at Angie, who shook her head no. Angie stood up and said, “Unless you arrest my client, this interview is over.”

Detective Leet also stood and said, “Helen Hann, you are under arrest for the stalking and the possible kidnapping of Kelsey Learner.”

Minor placed Helen in handcuffs, and an officer from the jail who had been waiting outside the door escorted her away.

****

Detectives Minor and Leet walked into the observation room to talk with Commander Davis and ADA Reinhart. The four agreed that the next step was to interview Chris Hann. The ADA asked the detectives also to find video footage of Helen Hann driving to and arriving at the convention center. Detective Minor went to get Dr. Chris Hann and his attorney.

When Chris and his attorney were seated, Detective Leet informed Chris that his wife was under arrest.

“She is currently charged with stalking Kelsey Learner; however, the ADA is also prepared to include kidnapping charges. We have some questions for you that arose from questioning your wife. I am going to read you your rights.”

After taking care of the procedure, Detective Leet asked Chris, “Why did you lie to Detective Minor about your wife's whereabouts on the evening Kelsey Learner disappeared?”

It was clear to both detectives that Dr. Chris Hann had already told his attorney what he was about to tell them. His attorney nodded at Chris, and the man began to talk.

“I want to apologize for lying to you, Detective Minor. I freaked out when I realized Kelsey had disappeared the evening that Helen failed to attend the Cardiology dinner. I am not even sure why I said what I did. I admit that my first thought was that I needed to protect Helen. She has been struggling since our kids moved away. I tried to get her help, but she refused.", Chris explained.

Detective Leet followed up by asking, "Why don't you tell us about what happened that evening?"

"What I told Detective Minor about my talking to Kelsey right before she left the conference center and then heading into the banquet hall was true. I had dinner and texted Helen a couple of times, asking her where she was. She never responded. When the dinner broke up, I think it was just before eight, I went to our hotel room. I was surprised to find Helen sprawled across the bed, asleep in her clothes. She had clearly had too much to drink."

Detective Minor asked the follow-up question, "Helen told us that she was stalking Kelsey Learner because you and Kelsey were having an affair. Were you and Kelsey Learner indeed having an affair?"

Chris Hann immediately shook his head and answered, "Absolutely not! I was not having an affair with Kelsey or anyone else. I was planning to divorce Helen and was making plans to do just that. It had nothing to do with Kelsey and everything to do with Helen. Did Helen actually stalk Kelsey?"

Detective Leet opened the folder and showed Dr. Chris Hann and his attorney the pictures they had of Helen driving by and walking around Kelsey's house. "Helen has admitted to driving by and walking around Kelsey's house and writing a harassing message on her vehicle. Do you have any information that may help us find Kelsey?"

"I have no idea where Kelsey is, but I want to ensure you know that Helen inherited her aunt's farm. It is out in the country. I can get the address when I get home and call you with it.", Chris Hann told them.

Detective Leet thanked him for the information, and the interview concluded.

24

Saturday April 7, 2018

Chris Hann had not been this mad at Helen in a very long time. He thought; *How dare she pass out in my Nurse Practitioner's office*? He had no idea what she had been thinking. He had apologized to Kelsey when she called him yesterday afternoon to explain the situation. Helen was out cold, and it was time to lock up the clinic for the day. He had told Kelsey to go ahead and lock up, and he would head over from the hospital to deal with Helen. She had woken just enough for Chris to walk her to his car. He had driven her home and put her to bed.

This morning, he sat drinking his coffee and waiting to see when she would come downstairs. This was not how he had planned to spend his Saturday, but this could not go on any longer. Helen would either agree to treatment, or he would tell her he was leaving. It was not how he had planned to have her find out, but he could no longer wait. At ten am, he heard the shower in the primary bathroom running. He wondered if he should have called his kids and told them how bad their mom had gotten. He knew that they would support him in saying she needed in-patient treatment.

Chris's pager went off. He checked the number and saw it was the hospital. He called the nurses' station of the Cardiac Care Unit and found out that one of his patients was not doing well. He would have no chance to talk to Helen this morning because he needed to leave for the hospital immediately. He scrawled a note to her, so she knew where he was. It was a courtesy he had shown her their entire marriage, and he thought about the irony of doing it when he was on the verge of divorcing her.

****

Helen was walking downstairs when she heard the garage door open. She was relieved that Chris had left. She had waited upstairs as long as she could stand not to have coffee. He usually played tennis at the club on Saturday mornings, so she was unhappy when she realized he was home when she woke up. She had a raging headache and did not have the energy to confront him this morning. Helen had decided that she needed to call her friend Margie. Margie had divorced her husband a few years ago when she found out he was cheating. Helen had been shocked by how big a settlement Margie's attorney had gotten for her.

Margie agreed to meet Helen at a local coffee shop. Helen got in her BMW, since her Buick was not in the garage. Plus, there was no reason to drive that crappy Buick today. She rarely went by Kelsey's on Saturdays, and if she did decide she needed to go there, she could always go to Chris's office and switch cars. Helen arrived at the coffee shop and found Margie seated in the back booth. It was as if Margie had sensed Helen needed to talk to her about something sensitive. Helen ordered a double espresso, as she needed the caffeine jolt.

An hour later, Helen left the coffee shop with the name and number of Margie's divorce attorney and a renewed sense of hope. Margie had helped her see that Helen could get her revenge, at least on Chris, through the court system. Helen knew that revenge on Kelsey was still something she would need to take care of herself. She drove out to her farm. When she had first inherited it, she was unsure what to do with the property, but now she was so glad she had not sold it as Chris had suggested. She needed to check if the work she had hired the man to accomplish was done and to her specifications. The time was drawing near, and she would leave nothing to chance.

Friday April 20, 2018

Detectives Leet and Minor reconvened in the conference room to review what they knew and what they would do next. As they waited for Commander Davis to join them, Detective Minor checked her emails on her phone. "Leet, we have an email from Greatlands Insurance with a file containing all of Joe Learner's work-related data from the day Kelsey went missing."

Detective Leet was not sure it was pertinent, "I think we should spend our time on Helen Hann. We already know she stalked Kelsey, and she has almost an hour of unaccounted-for time the day that Kelsey went missing."

Davis walked in and asked, "Where are we at in finding Kelsey?"

Leet explained that they needed to get a warrant for the farm Helen owned and find footage showing where Helen was before arriving at the hotel. Minor added that they needed to review the information from Greatlands Insurance regarding Joe. As well as trying to figure out what coffee shop Joe and Kelsey had met at two months ago. Minor believed there was a reason Joe Learner lied about that meeting.

"Great. Leet, you start figuring out where Helen was that night. I will work on the warrant, and Minor, you look through the information on Joe Learner. We will meet back here as soon as the warrant comes through." Commander Davis informed the detectives.

Minor and Leet looked at each other, and each nodded. They walked to their respective desks and got to work.

Minor started by looking through the GPS tracking data that Greatlands Insurance had provided for Joe's work vehicle. She quickly found a significant discrepancy. Joe Learner had not been in Colombia until four pm; he clearly began driving back to Springfield using back roads by twelve thirty-five pm. He arrived at his farmhouse by three pm. Minor wondered: *Why had he lied? Where was he actually when Kelsey disappeared?* It now seemed that she wasn't wrong; it was Joe's truck that she had seen in the grainy video footage.

Next, Detective Minor tackled Joe's work cell phone information. The cell phone data confirmed the GPS data. Joe Learner was at his home by three pm. Neither the cell phone nor Joe's work vehicle left again until the following day at eight am. Kass added to her list that she needed to determine what Department of Transportation cameras might have picked up Joe's journey from his farmhouse to the convention center.

Minor was becoming more convinced that she had been right all along and that Joe Learner had kidnapped his ex-wife. She grabbed the folder of information that Kelsey's bank had provided. She flipped through until she saw the transactions from two months ago. There was a charge from Supreme Bean Coffee Roasters, which stood out because it was the only time Kelsey had charged anything there in the six months of records. Minor made a note of the coffee shop's name and location. She would need to go and find out if anyone remembered Joe and Kelsey being there. It would be even better if they had video footage that far back. She got up and went to see Commander Davis.

****

Detective Leet had learned the gated community would require a subpoena to send the footage from the gatehouse. He also requested the Department of Transportation cameras' footage on Helen's most likely route from her home to downtown. He was not getting anywhere fast. Once again, he and Detective Minor would need to wait for their requests to be completed. He thought about Kelsey Learner. He had no idea where she was, but he believed she was dead. He wondered if Helen Hann had been helped in the kidnapping of Kelsey and who that could be. The woman seemed unhinged to him.

He looked up and saw Detective Minor and their commander walking toward him. Commander Davis indicated for him to join them in the conference room. Detective Leet walked into the room and observed Minor writing on their crime board. It seemed she had more luck than him and found out new information.

Commander Davis informed him, "We got the warrant for the farm that Helen Hann owns. I am sending the forensic team out there now, and the Greene County Sheriff's Department is meeting them. The farm is not within the city limits, but we will have jurisdiction because of the warrant being part of an ongoing investigation."

Detective Leet nodded and asked, "Minor, what are you writing?"

Detective Minor turned to Leet and said, "I am adding to our timeline. Joe Learner lied to us. He was back in Springfield by three pm."

"WHAT?" Leet exclaimed.

"Yep, his company has GPS tracking on their company-issued cell phones and cars. I tracked Joe leaving Columbia at about twelve thirty last Wednesday afternoon and driving home. He arrived there around three pm. The company-owned cell phone and the car stayed at Joe's house until the next morning. I requested the DOT send me footage of the route from Joe's farm to downtown. I am waiting for that now. What did you find out about Helen?"

Leet responded, "Not much. We need a subpoena to get the video from Helen and Chris's neighborhood gate. I also requested the DOT, but mine is for the route from the Hanns's home to downtown and from downtown to Helen's farm. It is now time for the hurry up and wait game."

Commander Davis stated, "It is almost time to bring Joe Learner and his attorney back. He has some explaining, but first, you two need to run down all these leads."

25

Saturday April 7, 2018

Claire had talked Kelsey into driving to Rolla again today to go to the Missouri University of Science and Technology campus. Claire had reached out to Residence Life, and they told her they could give her a tour of a dorm room. She wanted to start figuring out what she needed to buy and what she already had. Although she did not like to admit it, Claire was a lot like her mom. She did not like loose ends and was a careful planner.

Her mom had even let her drive. She looked over and saw that her mom had fallen asleep. That was another thing they had in common: car rides put them to sleep. Claire had plugged the address into the built-in GPS before leaving their house in Springfield. She wondered how often she would need to make this drive before she no longer needed the directions. It was reassuring to have the GPS to give her turn-by-turn navigation. She had shuddered to remember her mom describing printing pages of directions from the computer. Her mom had said that had seemed so much better than the paper maps that Claire's grandma used. Claire could not imagine using either one to get to a new place.

As she drove, Claire was so lost in her thoughts that she had not noticed the rising temperature in the Buick. Now it was getting uncomfortably warm. Claire fiddled with the air conditioner again, but it was not helping. She wondered what could be wrong with the vehicle. It was only a few years old and had just twenty thousand miles on it.

"Mom, I think something is wrong with the air conditioning," Claire said loud enough to wake Kelsey.

Kelsey sat up and asked, "What?"

Claire repeated, "The air conditioner does not seem to be working."

"It is warm in here," Kelsey replied as she tried to adjust the air conditioner controls. Nothing she did resulted in cold air starting to blow. "I guess it is good that we are almost to the campus. I will call the dealership Monday and make a service appointment."

Claire and Kelsey spent almost an hour touring the residence halls. Claire had made her lists and added the residence life app to her phone. She also learned how to look for on-campus jobs, which coffee shop was the best, and the age-old advice of not registering for classes before nine in the morning.

As they left the dorms, Kelsey joked with her daughter, "I think the Buick was trying to get you ready to be without air conditioning."

Claire rolled her eyes and said, "Come on, Mom. We both know you will rent me a window air conditioning unit."

Kelsey laughed along with her daughter and agreed that it was likely true she would rent Claire a window AC unit from the college. They walked around campus and talked about Claire's plans for the summer. Her excitement about her plans was contagious and helped Kelsey spend the day not thinking about the issues she had been experiencing.

The two of them went to the coffee shop on campus that had been recommended and had lunch. They both grabbed an iced coffee before leaving. Kelsey started up the Buick and silently prayed the air conditioner would magically work. However, there was no magical fix for whatever was wrong. They drove home with the windows down, and the radio turned up. Kelsey believed in making the best of whatever was going on.

****

Chris and Helen Hann drove in stony silence toward his office. He had told her when he got home from the hospital this afternoon that he did not want her Buick to sit in the parking lot. They had fallen into their long-standing pattern of silence. Chris had not addressed what had happened yesterday, and Helen had decided to keep her suspicions to herself. She wanted to talk to the attorney Margie recommended before confronting him.

Chris pulled beside Helen's SUV and said, "Please drive straight home."

She opened her door and got out without answering him. Helen waited for him to drive away before going to the back of the SUV. She opened the hatch and lifted the well for the spare tire. She reached inside and grabbed a new bottle of vodka. She was sure Chris had searched for and poured out her stash at home. Helen sat in her SUV and wondered if Chris was going straight home. She decided she was not. She would head out to her farm and finish making her preparations.

Friday April 20, 2018

Minor noted that the farm Helen Hann had inherited was midway between the Moores' farm and Joe Learner's farmhouse. It always amazed her how quickly you could go from being in the city to being out in the country. As they pulled down the driveway of Helen's property, Minor could not help but notice that the driveway seemed to have been freshly lined with gravel. It was no surprise to see the CSI vans and sheriff's cruisers, but a white panel van seemed out of place. A man was sitting in the back of the van, talking on a cell phone.

Sheriff Sumner approached them when Detective Leet and Minor parked and exited their car. He shook both of their hands and indicated to the man sitting in the back cargo area of the van. "That is Mr. Randy Pickens. He was here when my deputy and your CSI technicians arrived. He is a general handyman and reports he has been fixing up this place for Helen Hann for the last six weeks. I asked him to wait until you two got here. I figured you might have a few questions for him."

Leet thanked the sheriff before he and Minor talked to Mr. Pickens. Mr. Pickens stood up as they approached and asked, "Am I in some kind of trouble? Nobody will tell me what is happening, and Ms. Helen isn't answering her phone."

Detective Minor responded, "Mr. Pickens, we have no reason to suspect that you are in any trouble, but would you be willing to answer some questions about the work you have been doing here and Helen Hann?"

Mr. Pickens nodded; Detective Minor continued, "Please tell us about the work you have been doing here."

"Well, I started by redoing the driveway, cleaning up the yard, and repairing the front steps. Ms. Helen liked my work, so she hired me to work on the inside. I have been stripping off all the old wallpaper and painting. When that is done, I will redo the wood floors." Randy Pickens explained.

"How would you describe your interactions with Helen Hann?" asked Detective Minor.

Mr. Pickens responded, "Business-like. She comes out here, meets with me, and checks on the work I have been doing. She is particular about how she wants things to look, but is not rude. She pays me in cash."

Detective Leet asked, "Have you ever seen anyone else with Mrs. Hann?"

Pickens shook his head, "No, she is always alone when she comes out here."

"Would you mind if a CSI Tech looked through your van quickly?" asked Detective Leet.

Pickens agreed to the search, so Leet and Minor went to find a tech. Thirty minutes later, the tech told them the van was full of junk. Some of it was from several decades ago, and he did not think anyone other than the driver could have ridden in the van. Leet went to Mr. Pickens, got his contact information, and told him he could leave.

Detective Leet was headed back toward the house when the lead CSI tech approached him. "There is no sign of Kelsey Learner here. This is not an operational farm. The barn is falling apart, and there is nothing but old hay and cobwebs. The house is undergoing renovations, and thus far, the only shoe prints match those of Mr. Randy Pickens. We have found no obvious ground disturbances, but will continue to use the ground penetrating radar just to be sure."

Leet thanked him for his hard work and the information and went to find Minor. She was in the backyard talking with Sheriff Sumner. They both turned to look at him, and Minor said, "The technicians tell us that they are not finding anything."

"That is what I was just told as well. Let's head back to the station and see if the footage from the DOT has arrived yet," Detective Leet stated.

The two detectives thanked the sheriff, who had offered to have a deputy stay for the time the CSI team was there, and then headed back into town.

Minor wondered, "Why would Helen Hann be fixing up that farmhouse? Did she actually know that Chris was going to leave her?"

Leet had been wondering the same things. "I am still not sure that Helen Hann, especially if she were drunk at the time, would have been able to overpower Kelsey and kidnap her. And if she could do that, where did she take her? The farm seemed like the only place Helen would have gone, but it was not a viable lead."

"I guess we better go back and watch the footage I got from the traffic camera showing Joe Learner turn towards the conference center. Then, we need to expand from there to determine where Helen came from and when Joe Learner left the area."

Sitting together back in the police station media room, Leet and Minor watched the truck they believed was Joe Learners turn towards the parking garage. However, this time, they kept watching to see if Helen Hann drove by this camera. It should be in the wrong direction of the route she would have taken from her house. Detective Minor puts the footage on triple speed, and when the time stamp reached six forty-five pm, she stopped it and rewound. The two detectives watched Helen's Buick come into frame and then turn the corner without stopping at the stop sign.

Minor turned to Leet and said, “Where do you think she was coming from?”

He replied, “No idea, but I better amend my request to the DOT because it won't be the route I asked for.”

They continued to watch the footage at triple speed until it was too dark to make out anything. The detectives had not seen Joe or Helen’s vehicles return through that intersection. It was unclear where either of them went after they turned that corner and equally unclear when either had left the area.

26

Monday April 9, 2018

"I don't think that Monday is anyone's favorite day, Claire, but you have to get a move on", Kelsey commented before heading back downstairs. She hated starting her day with her daughter being cantankerous. Kelsey had learned to walk away in the morning and not argue with Claire. When her daughter was a little girl, she was hard to get going, but once she became a pre-teen, she became a beast in the morning. The less Kelsey said, the better. Kelsey also knew that if she brought up Claire making her late to work, it would start the fight about Claire needing her own car.

It was not as if Claire had a job and would be buying herself a car. No, she expected Kelsey to buy her one. After talking with Joe, Kelsey had decided against giving Clair a car for her high school graduation. She would give her daughter the money she had set aside for the purchase. Then it was up to Claire to decide what to do with the money. She could use it to buy a car or pay tuition. Many students in Missouri took out a student loan for the first year of school and then rolled the reimbursement semester after semester to pay their tuition. When they finished college, the final reimbursement check paid off the student loan. It was not an ideal plan, but Kelsey knew it would work.

Kelsey and Claire pulled out of the driveway, only ten minutes behind schedule. Since going to work for Dr. Hann, Kelsey has had a much more flexible schedule than she had all her years at Memorial Hospital. However, Kelsey had yet to be able to get out of the habit of being right on time. She knew Dr. Hann visited the hospital every morning to check on patients. There would be no appointments until nine in the morning, but Kelsey knew both Becca and Sue would be there right at eight thirty am.

It was already getting hot, reminding Kelsey that she needed to call the dealership about the air conditioning. She would need to ask Sue if there was a day this week when she could pick Kelsey up at the dealership and take her to work.

"Mom?" Claire questioned.

Kelsey replied, "Yes, Claire."

Claire seemed hesitant, "Are you mad at me? I know I was dragging this morning, and you hate to be late. I am sorry."

"I am not mad. I am used to your morning crabbiness." Kelsey responded. She thought about how hard it was to stay mad at her daughter. Claire had such a good heart. "I hope you have a good day today. I should be home right after Mrs. Peterson drops you off."

Claire was already out of the SUV, but turned and said, "Sounds good. Love you, Mom."

"Love you too," Kelsey said as Claire closed the door.

Saturday April 21, 2018

The requests that Minor and Leet had put into the Department of Transportation had come back quickly. With over a hundred traffic cameras in Springfield, they should be able to track both Joe and Helen. The DOT had also provided license plate reader data for locations that had picked up either Joe or Helen's vehicles. This helped both detectives to know where to start watching. Each detective mapped out the routes taken and noted the times. It was clear that Joe had driven straight from his farmhouse to downtown. The route had taken him just over twenty minutes. The last camera that captured his license plate before Kelsey disappeared was the one at the lights he turned at before the convention center.

Detective Minor continued to watch downtown traffic cameras in case Joe drove by one. She concluded that Joe had parked at or near the convention center. Minor looked at the printout from the DOT and saw that the next time a license plate reader had picked up Joe's truck was almost eight thirty pm. She fast-forwarded to that time and watched as Joe came from the same direction, he had gone two hours earlier. He again was caught on traffic cameras heading straight back to his farm. Detective Minor wondered; *Where had Joe Learner been for two and a half hours, and what had he been doing?*

Minor accessed the police department's database of local businesses and individuals with security footage. The police department had started a program allowing private citizens to register that they had a camera system and were willing to share their footage if the police needed it. The program made figuring out where to look for footage much more manageable. Minor was sure many cameras were out there that belonged to people not taking part in the program, but it was an excellent place to start. She had already obtained all the footage from the places closest to the convention center parking garage and watched them days earlier. She now needed to expand her search downtown to figure out where Joe Learner had parked and where he went after he did so.

****

Detective Leet watched as Helen Hann pulled her SUV into a strip mall a few miles from her house. She stayed there for a while. Her vehicle then went in the opposite direction of downtown and was picked up by the cameras heading towards a residential area of Springfield. An hour and a half later, that same plate reader recorded Helen returning through that intersection and turning towards downtown. Leet tracked her driving until she arrived at the intersection and turned toward the convention center. Leet had already noted that the next time Helen's vehicle was picked up was in the morning.

The detectives met back in the conference room and filled each other in. Detective Minor reminded Leet about the private camera database and agreed to search the area where Helen had gone for an hour and a half. Minor returned a half hour later with a dozen names and addresses.

Leet went to get that footage from Helen's route, while Minor went to see about the footage from the downtown locations.

As Detective Leet rang the fifth doorbell today, he thought this felt like good old-fashioned detective work. He acknowledged that technology had helped narrow down whose doors to knock on, but it was still knocking on doors and asking questions. So far, he was striking out. Two people had not been home, and two did not have access to the footage from more than a week ago. The current homeowner had invited him and went to get her laptop. She reversed the footage to the day and time Detective Leet had told her. Together, they watched as Helen Hann's SUV drove by at a quarter to five in the afternoon and then again at quarter after six pm when the SUV returned from the direction, they had watched it go. Leet thanked the homeowner and asked her to email him the footage. At least now he knew which direction to continue to look in.

With a direction to head in, Detective Leet had two more camera locations to check. The first was a large convenience store. After showing him how the system worked, the manager was happy to leave him in the back office to watch what the outside cameras had captured. Sure enough, he saw Helen drive by a few minutes after passing the house. Her SUV turned and drove past the convenience store. As well as drove back past the store an hour and a half later. Detective Leet went and found the manager and asked him to send the footage to his email. Just one more registered camera to check out along what seemed to be Helen Hann's route the night Kelsey disappeared.

He pulled up in front of a brick ranch-style house on a quiet suburban street. The empty lot across the street caught his eye as he exited his car. It seemed out of place in this well-established neighborhood. He realized that a house must've sat on it at some point, as there was still a set of concrete stairs and the remnants of the footings. The owners of the house with the camera were home and happy to help him. They had a system that was motion-activated and one camera that was focused on their front porch and the street. As the footage played, Detective Leet asked the homeowner, "What do you know about the empty lot across the street?"

The homeowner replied, "That was like that when we bought this place seven years ago. A neighbor told my wife that the house burned down and a kid died there."

"Seems strange that a new house was never built."

"I guess so. A service comes by every week and cuts the lawn, and occasionally, an older woman sits on the steps over there,"

Just as he said that, the homeowner and Detective Leet spotted a blue Buick Encore pull up across the street. They watched as an older woman got out and sat on the steps.

The homeowner said, "That is the woman I told you about."

Detective Leet knew just who it was. Helen Hann sat with her back to the camera. He asked the man to speed up the playback. Helen sat on the steps for an hour and a half. She seemed to be drinking and crying. Leet assumed that the house that had burned down and the child had died were connected to Chris and Helen Hann. He suddenly had much more empathy for her and understood how she had become so unhinged.

27

Monday April 9, 2018

Sue and Kelsey sat quietly in the clinic's lunchroom because neither was sure what to say about Dr. Hann's announcement. After a few minutes, Sue stated, "I have been here twenty years, and he has never gone on an impromptu vacation. He and Helen take a week-long vacation to see their kids in the summer and another week at Christmas. That is it. I am still trying to process his announcement. I should go check if Becca needs any help to reschedule his patients."

Kelsey wondered when Dr. Hann said the trip was a surprise for Helen if, in reality, he was planning to get her admitted to rehab. No one in the office talked about the incident from last week, but they all knew that Helen had passed out in Kelsey's office. Kelsey also wondered if Dr. Hann was considering retiring. She did not want to find a new job, but maybe it would work out in the end. If he was retiring, she could look for a better-paying job once Claire left for school without feeling guilty about leaving a job so quickly. Before he left for his vacation at the end of the month, Kelsey would talk with Dr. Hann to find out his plans.

She also needed to call and schedule for her SUV to get fixed. Every day was hotter than the one before, so she needed to fix it. She and Sue had agreed that Kelsey would take any appointment that allowed her to drop the car off at lunchtime. Sue would follow her to the dealership, and Kelsey would buy them lunch on their way back.

Saturday April 21, 2018

Detective Minor was happy to have taken on the task of finding camera footage of Joe Learner downtown. It meant she did not have to drive anywhere. Before leaving the police station, she changed out of her dress shoes and into a pair of tennis shoes. She always tried to look her best even when they were working long hours for many days, but with the walking, practicality won out. She had a list of twenty locations downtown. The downtown business association took security seriously and helped its members install or upgrade to state-of-the-art monitoring systems.

Minor went from business to business, explaining what she was looking for. Her approach differed from her partner. She did not sit and watch the footage at any place she went. Instead, she had them download it and email it to her. She would finish making her requests, note anyone who needed a subpoena to share their video, and then head back to the station. She had not run into trouble at the first dozen locations, but there was no lucky number thirteen today.

The building was a high-end condo that boasted top-of-the-line security monitoring, a doorman, and a locked front entry. The concierge was a pleasant older man who politely told her that allowing her to see the footage would violate their tenants' privacy. She asked why the building had signed up for the camera partnership with the police department if they were unwilling to share the video. He stated, "Well, if a crime happened here or to one of our tenants, that would be different, and we would be happy to help,"

Kass Minor thanked him and went out to talk to the doorman. He, too, could have been more helpful. She thought it was unlikely that Joe Learner would be on this footage since the building was a block west of the convention center, but still, it would have been nice to confirm that. Since she had gotten footage sent to her from the majority of businesses she talked to, she headed back to the police department to watch it. She even found a new coffee shop to get a caramel latte from. Walking back to the station, Detective Minor wondered how Detective Leet was fairing with getting footage of Helen Hann.

Sitting in the media room, Minor watched the clips based on location. She could see Joe pull into a parking lot across the street from the convention center. None of the footage showed Joe getting out of his truck or where he went downtown. The same camera captured Joe's truck entering the parking lot and leaving at eight twenty-five pm. Detective Minor wondered *Whether Joe could have grabbed Kelsey from the convention center parking garage and gotten her across the street to his truck. All while avoiding the security cameras.* It seemed less than plausible, but not impossible.

Minor went to the conference room and started adding to the crime board. She had texted Leet, and he said he was on the way back. She could tell he had learned something when he entered the conference room. Detective Leet shared what he found out about Helen Hann. It was a sad tale of loss that did help to explain how Helen had gotten to this point. The footage that Leet had reviewed showed that Helen Hann had not been at the conference center when Kelsey Learner had disappeared.

Leet went to the crime board and added his information so that it would be there when they reviewed where they were with the case with Commander Davis. Helen Hann had been stalking Kelsey, so she would have to answer to that charge. However, the ADA would need to drop the suspicion of the kidnapping charge. Minor had gone to grab the pizza she had ordered. He knew she would return with a few slices missing from giving them out to other officers on the way back. One thing that was always true about Kass Minor was that she was always looking out for others.

He read all the notes that Minor had added to the crime board before he had gotten back to the station. It was clear that Joe Learner had spent two and a half hours downtown. That was the second lie they needed to confront him with. Leet wondered, *why does Joe Learner keep lying to us? What is he hiding?* He thought back to the start of the investigation. He had thought Detective Minor was wrong at the beginning of this case. She had been sure that Joe Learner had taken his ex-wife, and Leet had not been convinced. Now, the evidence was all pointing in Joe Learner's direction.

After eating dinner, Detective Leet called Commander Davis. The commander agreed they needed to meet with ADA Reinhart to decide what to do next. The meeting was scheduled for eight in the morning the next day. This would give Reinhart time to decide how to proceed before Helen Hann's arraignment on Monday.

28

Tuesday April 10, 2018

Raul had been sick for days. It had come on slowly; first, the headache and exhaustion over the weekend. Today, he also had body aches, and today, he had vomited. He had canceled his appointments and stayed home. Paulina did not seem too concerned about him, but she had gone to the store and returned with his favorite flavor of Gatorade. She had left this morning after telling him he probably had a stomach bug and reminding him to stay hydrated. He had drunk part of one of the Gatorade bottles but threw up almost immediately and could no longer bring himself to drink. He did not want to anger Paulina, so he had been pouring the bottles down the drain, so she would think he was drinking it.

The mailman had brought a package to the door and set their mail on top of it. The rain that had started compelled Raul to grab the package and mail. He carried the items to the table. Paulina always got the mail from their mailbox at the end of the driveway. She managed both their business and personal accounts, so it made sense for her to be in charge of the mail. Raul looked down at the rubber-banded stack of mail. The top envelope was from a bank he did not recognize and was addressed to Paulina. When they married, they agreed not to have separate bank accounts, so Raul was unsure what this envelope could be.

He tried to leave the envelope alone, but it seemed to have a magnetic pull. He kept wandering back into the kitchen in the guise of getting water or hot tea, but in reality, he just stared at the envelope. He went on Google and searched how to open an envelope so someone wouldn't notice. It seemed pretty straightforward. He thought *the worst-case scenario is that I will have to shred it and take the shredding out to the pigs.* As he stood holding the envelope with tongs in the steam from the teakettle, he could not help but wonder how his marriage had gotten to this point.

After carefully opening the envelope, he discovered it contained a bank statement. Paulina had a savings account that he knew nothing about and had almost a quarter of a million dollars in it. She made deposits several times a week for at least a few hundred dollars each. He then saw a monthly recurring charge of nineteen dollars and ninety-five cents for a safe deposit box. He thought back to the key he had found a while back. He had thought about the key on and off, but never dared to ask Paulina about it. There was also a twenty-thousand-dollar cash withdrawal transaction two weeks ago. Raul stood in the kitchen feeling nauseous, but it was not from the stomach bug this time. He had no idea what his wife was up to, but he had an immense feeling of dread about whatever it was.

Sunday April 22, 2018

Before heading into the station, Kass Minor had gone out to the Supreme Bean Coffee Roaster location where Joe and Kelsey met. She had hit the evidence jackpot. The coffee shop stored all its security footage on the cloud and never erased anything. They emailed her the footage from the day on Kelsey's receipt. Detective Minor showed the young barista pictures of Joe and Kelsey and asked if she recognized either. The day they had been in was the barista's first day at the coffee shop, so yes, she remembered them. She remembered commenting to the person training her about people fighting in public. She was sure that the two had argued and that Joe had stormed out. Minor left the coffeehouse, delighted that she had made the trip there.

Balancing four coffees and a bag of donuts, Kass Minor walked into the police station conference room. She had been up for hours trying to figure out what evidence they overlooked. Kelsey Learner had been missing too long. Minor knew there was little chance that Kelsey was still alive. She wondered if the ADA would be willing to make a deal with Joe Learner and his attorney in return for Joe, telling them where to find Kelsey's body. She guessed first that they needed to see if the ADA would agree that they should charge him.

Detective Leet and Commander Davis walked in together. "Thank you for the coffee." Leet and Davis both said.

"Are you two ready to present to the ADA?" Commander Davis inquired.

Detective Minor said, "I have some new information about Joe Learner that I would like to share with the two of you. I went to the Supreme Bean Coffee Roasters this morning."

The other two raised their coffee cups and nodded.

"I went there specifically because I found a charge from there among Kelsey Learner's bank records from two months ago. I have confirmed that is where Joe and Kelsey met, and the barista says they indeed argued. The coffee shop emailed the security camera footage from that day. I have not had time to review it, but I suspect it will confirm what John told Detective Leet and the barista told me."

Commander Davis said, "That is great detective work, Minor."

Leet added, "I agree. I had a thought late last night. Commander Davis, where can we find out if the old tunnels are connected anywhere near the conference center parking garage?"

Minor asked, "What tunnels?"

Leet said, "In the nineteen twenties, Springfield leaders built a series of concrete tunnels under downtown that enclosed the Jordan Creek. The tunnels are not used today, but as far as I know, they are still accessible. Well, at least accessible to some people."

"You have an excellent memory. I will call the city engineer's office after we meet with the ADA and find out about the tunnels' locations, the access points and how someone might get into the tunnels." Commander Davis replied.

"Are you thinking that the tunnels may be how Joe Learner got Kelsey out of the parking garage?" Minor asked.

Detective Leet nodded and said, "Yes, as well as possibly, where he murdered her and left her body. Commander, I think we will need to search the tunnels."

Commander Davis agreed to find out if it was possible to search the tunnels or if they would need special equipment or help.

"I am sorry I am late. I had a meeting with Helen Hann's defense attorney." ADA Reinhart said as she walked in. "What information have you discovered that you wanted to discuss?"

Detectives Leet and Minor told the ADA about Joe Learner lying about the last time he met with Kelsey, where he was, and when his ex-wife disappeared. Next, they explained what they had discovered about Helen Hann.

"What do you think, Ms. Reinhart?" Detective Leet asked.

ADA Reinhart took a deep breath. "I think I need to let my boss know that I am going to offer Helen Hann a plea bargain on the stalking charge. While I am talking to the DA, I would appreciate it if you set up an interview with Joe Learner and his attorney for this afternoon. We will see what Joe Learner has to say for himself and then go from there with what he will be charged with."

Leet set up the appointment, feeling like he and Detective Minor were on the right track this time.

29

Tuesday April 10, 2018

When Robert Matthews applied to the FBI and completed the training program at Quantico, he never imagined being sent to the Springfield, Missouri, field office. His work was drudgery most of the time. Take the latest assignment he was working on. He had been assigned to look into the disappearance of a young man and see if there were any related cases. He had asked the senior field agent, Brad Hollins, if the Assistant Director knew that there were over five hundred thousand missing adults at any time in the United States. Brad had laughed and told him, probably. The senior agent had explained that this guy was the son of a woman who was the Assistant Director's secretary's best friend. Robert had thought, *Ah, nepotism. That beats out logic every time.*

So here he was, compiling a list of missing men from Missouri who had gone missing in the last two years. He started by figuring out what was known about Cory Pratt's disappearance. The sheriff's department that had taken the initial report of Cory being missing had sent him the information they had. They had not investigated his disappearance at all. The conclusion was that Cory lost his job, packed up, and moved away. The problem Matthews found with that theory was that Cory had not been fired until he failed to show up for several days. Agent Matthews also talked with the apartment manager, who had evicted Cory. The man told Matthews he was surprised when Cory stopped paying the rent. In his opinion, Cory took nothing with him when he moved out.

He learned from Cory's mom, Mrs. Lucy Pratt, that Cory loved to run. According to Mrs. Pratt, Cory would leave everything behind and run in just his shorts and athletic shoes. She had often told him it was not safe to leave his car key stuck to the wheel well, but Cory did not listen to her. Mrs. Pratt was sure her son would not have gone almost thirteen months without a call to her and his dad. She was happy the FBI was looking into what had happened to her son.

He used the few facts he had discovered about Cory and his disappearance to narrow the search criteria. He searched for single men who took part in solitary activities and had no ties to criminal activity. His search came up with nine names. He cleared two immediately when he found out the reporting agency had not updated the reports. Both of those men had been found dead after having sports-related accidents. He would have to look more in-depth into the seven remaining cases.

He met with the senior agent, and they decided he should start with the most recent case and work his way backward. The case that met his search criteria and was most recent was that of Aaron Starr. He had been reported missing by his work, Pork Processing of America, when he had failed to show up for several days in a row, and no one could get ahold of him. The Springfield police department had talked to co-workers as well as staff and patrons at a bar called Luke's. They had been able to track Aaron until he left the bar the Sunday evening before the first day he did not show up for work. There was no sign of him since then, and there were no leads for the police to follow.

Matthew's next looked into the disappearance of Pete Taylor, who had been reported missing after not returning from a hike sixteen months ago. The Branson police had done a cursory investigation but had found nothing. Pete's SUV had been abandoned, and no one had heard from him since the morning he left. After reading the case file and talking to Pete's brother Todd, Agent Matthews officially added Pete Taylor's disappearance to his investigation.

That brought him to the case he was looking into today: the disappearance of Sean Anderson. Sean was a twenty-six-year-old competitive bicycle rider who went on long rides alone. It was not uncommon for Sean to take long weekends and bike over a hundred miles. Agent Matthews read the file and then reviewed the list of unidentified bodies for the region. He found a preliminary match for Sean about forty miles from his home. Matthews turned this information over to the Columbia police department so they could get confirmation. Matthews would need to keep digging, but he was not working fast. He still believed that it was implausible that these cases were connected. He called it a day and headed to the gym. He hoped that Kass Minor would be there. He had been trying for months to get the detective to go on a date with him, and he thought he had just the idea to get her to agree.

Sunday April, 22, 2018

Joe had just gotten home from renting a car and was watching a baseball game on TV when he heard his phone ring. He checked the number and saw that it was Mike Davidson calling. As he answered, he wondered why his attorney was calling him on a Sunday.

Mike Davidson wasted no time, "Detective Leet called me, and they want to interview you again. I agreed that you would come in this afternoon at about two."

"What do they want to talk to me about?" Joe asked.

Mike Davidson sighed, "That is not how the police work. They will not disclose their reasons ahead of time. Detective Leet said that some new evidence has come to light, and they have follow-up questions for you. So be at my office by quarter to two this afternoon, and we will walk over together."

Joe agreed to be at Mike's office at the appointed time. He wondered again if he should tell Mike the truth. Joe thought about what was happening as he got ready to leave his house. *Was it possible that the detectives had uncovered his secret? No, it was much more likely that they knew he lied about when he left Columbia.*

****

Mike Davidson waited outside his office for Joe. He was sure that Joe had not been entirely truthful with him. He hated when clients lied to him because it led to surprises. When he knew what was coming, he could plan, and he was a planner. When he got the call from Detective Leet earlier today, he had thought about dropping Joe as a client, but he loved an excellent court fight. Which was where he thought this was headed. He would not be shocked if Joe was arrested today or in the next few days.

Joe parked in the lot across from Mike's office. He saw Mike pacing outside the office building. *Was now the time to come clean with Mike*? Joe thought. He was ready to tell him part of the truth. *The part,* Joe thought, *that he needs to know.*

Joe approached Mike and said, "I need to tell you something. I have not been one hundred percent honest but it has nothing to do with Kelsey."

Mike nodded slightly and said, "Go on. I am listening."

"I was not in Columbia until three thirty in the afternoon when Kelsey disappeared. When a client does not confirm their appointment, I leave it on my calendar and skip it. Then I finish the paperwork without ever visiting that client. It is not an ethical business practice, but I do not believe it is anything illegal." Joe explained.

Mike shook his head and said, "Do you remember the first time we met in my office?"

Joe responded, "Yes."

"I told you then that I needed to know everything. I asked you repeatedly if there was anything you were not telling me. That was when I should have learned about your business misconduct. I doubt that if you had told the detectives the truth about what you did when they first asked, they would have reported it to your employer. However, now they have likely caught you in a lie," Mike told Joe.

Walking to the police station, neither of the men spoke.

30

Wednesday April 11, 2018

Helen drove from her home to the liquor store. She was a frequent customer and appreciated how the people who worked there did not seem to judge her. She bought a case of her favorite vodka and two bottles of wine. The cashier carried the case out to her SUV, and she gave him a tip. She sat in the driver's seat and opened up a wine bottle. She was bewildered at how her life had gotten to this point. She knew she had a drinking problem, but had no idea how to stop. Mainly because stopping would mean she would have to face the things she had done.

After pouring the wine into her waiting thermal tumbler, Helen slowly backed the Buick out of the parking spot. Without thinking, she drove to the lot that had once held her and Chris's first home. She parked in the driveway of the remnants of their former home and got out. She walked from the SUV and sat on the crumbling back concrete steps that now led to nothing. She sat there for a while, drinking and thinking back to the life she, Chris, and their kids had lived in this spot. There were so many happy memories that were all but forgotten because of the trauma they had all suffered here.

****

Kelsey was glad she had attended the conference, but equally glad she was heading home this evening. She had never gotten over the feeling that Helen Hann did not like her, so the thought of sitting with her during the Cardiology dinner was not something Kelsey had even wanted to entertain. She would return in the morning for the second day of the conference having had a nice evening at home. Hopefully, Claire had made no plans because Kelsey looked forward to spending time with her.

Kelsey felt like someone was watching her as she walked to her car. She had called Jana Peterson this morning and left her a message. She had asked if Dan would be around this weekend. She wanted to tell him what had been happening and ask if he thought she should file a police report. She had yet to hear back from Jana, likely because her neighbor needed to check with her husband to verify his work schedule.

She walked around to the passenger side of the SUV. Everything seemed fine, so she opened the door and placed her purse and the bag from the conference on the seat. As she stood up, she sensed someone come up behind her. Before she could turn around, she felt the pierce of a needle in her neck. The world around her quickly faded to black. Kelsey's last thought before passing out was; *I should have talked to the police.*

Sunday April 22, 2018

The desk sergeant notified Detective Leet that Joe Leaner and his attorney had arrived. He and Minor had been busy looking at the plans the City Engineer sent for the downtown underground tunnels. The convention center parking lot was at the end of the tunnel system. Minor had gone to call the City Engineer to find out how the tunnels were accessed and when he would be available to meet them so they could see if this was the lead that would help them close their case. Leet told the desk sergeant to have Joe and Mike escorted back to the main interrogation room.

Leet let Commander Davis know that they were there. He was told that the ADA would be there within five minutes and that they would wait until she gave the go-ahead to start the interview. Minor finished on the phone and returned to Detective Leet's cubicle.

"The engineer says it is possible that someone with some mechanical ability and decent upper body strength would be able to lift the cover

over the tunnel in that parking lot and climb down. He can meet us over there whenever we are ready. I am supposed to call him back when we are ready." Minor filled him in.

Detective Leet responded, "Okay, Joe Learner and his attorney are here. We are waiting for Reinhart, and then we will get started with his interview. Let's plan to call the engineer when we are done with Learner, and then we can go over there. I will ask the commander if he wants us to take a CSI tech."

"Sounds good." Minor agreed, and the two of them went to the observation room to wait for Commander Davis and ADA Reinhart. When they arrived, it was agreed that they would start with the meeting between Joe and Kelsey a few months ago that he had failed to tell them about. Then they would get to his misinformation about where he was on the day Kelsey went missing.

Leet and Minor walked into the interrogation room. Mike Davidson and Joe Learner sat in stony silence while Detective Leet sat down and Minor stood by the door.

"We want to know why you asked Joe to come here again." Mike Davidson stated.

Detective Leet responded, "There are some things we would like to know as well. Before we do so, I need to read Mr. Learner his rights and have him sign off again." Leet took care of the procedure.

"Mr. Learner, when we talked to you last Friday, two days after your ex-wife went missing, you told us that it had been close to two years since you saw Kelsey. Do you remember telling us that?" Detective Leet asked.

This time, Joe knew not to answer without looking at Mike. Mike had been clear that he was likely a suspect and needed to be careful about how he answered everything. Mike shook his head and stated, "My client would not be able to confirm or deny a statement he made the first time you interviewed him. Which I would like to note was without an attorney. He was emotionally distressed regarding the information you had relayed to him."

"Okay. Let me ask this in a different way. When was the last time you saw Kelsey in person?" Detective Leet questioned.

This time, Mike nodded, and Joe responded, "To the best of my recollection, it was about two years ago at a track meet that Claire was in."

"Well, that is very interesting because we have uncovered evidence that you met her at a coffee shop two months ago and had what a witness described as a heated exchange with her. Would you be willing to explain why you did not tell us about that meeting?" Detective Minor asked from her spot by the door.

Leet pulled a few pictures out of the folder he was holding. They were still pictures of the video footage from the coffee shop. He slid them toward Joe and his attorney. There was a picture of Joe sitting alone, one of Kelsey joining him at the table, one of them apparently arguing, and a final one where Joe stood with his finger outstretched towards Kelsey. In the final picture, he appears to be yelling.

Mike Davidson picked up the pictures one at a time and then set them down in a stack. "My client will not be answering that question now," Mike said.

"But..." Joe started

"NO." was all Mike said, and Joe stopped talking.

Detective Minor looked at Leet, who nodded at her.

Minor said, "Well, all right. How about we ask you about another discrepancy that we have found? I understand now that you do not recollect our first meeting. However, you told us that you were in Columbia all day the day Kelsey disappeared. You produced receipts to back up your story, and then your employer sent us those receipts. So, at first, Detective Leet and I were thinking, good Joe told us the truth, but then a funny thing happened. Any idea what that was?"

Joe shook his head, so Minor continued, "Were you aware that Greatlands Insurance has a GPS tracker on your company vehicle and cell phone?"

"Yes, I was aware," Joe said.

Detective Leet picked up the questioning as he laid out the GPS reports on the table. "These reports clearly show that you left Columbia at about twelve thirty and arrived at your farmhouse by three in the afternoon. Why did you lie to us?"

Clearly, Mike Davidson was not shocked by this revelation. Joe answered without looking at Mike. "I made a mistake in not telling you the truth. I apologize. I have not been totally honest in my work practices. Greatlands has a policy that auditors are supposed to visit clients whether or not the client confirms the appointment. This is a giant waste of time. A few years ago, I stopped going to clients who did not confirm. I used to remove those appointments from my calendar and reschedule the audit. Then, I accidentally forgot to do that once before turning in my monthly report. I caught the error a few days later and waited for my manager's reply. He never said a thing, so I stopped going to unconfirmed appointments. When you asked me where I was, I thought about getting into trouble at work. Again, I apologize for being less than honest."

"All right, that explains the lie. So where were you the evening your ex-wife disappeared?" Detective Minor asked.

Joe answered, "I was home all night."

"Now you see, this is why we can't trust you," Detective Leet said as he laid down the pictures from the traffic camera and the license plate reader data. "The Department of Transportation has provided footage and license plate data showing that you drove from your home to downtown that evening."

Before he could finish, Mike Davidson interrupted, "I need to confer with my client."

Detective Minor opened the door, and Detective Leet stood up and said, "That is fine. We need a moment to confer with our commander and the Assistant District Attorney." The two detectives walked out of the interrogation room and closed the door.

31

Thursday April 12, 2018

Kass Minor could not believe she had agreed to go on a date last night. She had a personal rule about not dating others in law enforcement, but over the last few months, Robert Matthews had worn her down. He liked so many of the same things she did, and they did not work for the same agency. She had thought about asking Leet what he thought about her dating an FBI agent, but they were not that close; besides, he was her dad's age.

When Robert had asked her to go ax throwing, she had finally agreed to the date. She had wanted to try her hand at the sport for a while but had no one to go with. They agreed to the ground rule that they would not talk about work at all. Robert had joked that there wasn't much to talk about, as his job was tedious. Kass thought he was joking about that, but had not pursued it.

As cautious as she was, Kass had not let Robert pick her up for the date. Instead, they met at Bullseye Ax Throwing that evening. After a few rounds of ax throwing, Kass agreed she needed a drink. The drink had turned into dinner and a few more drinks. So here she was at six-thirty in the morning, being dropped off at her car by an Uber driver. She would never drink and drive as she had witnessed firsthand as a traffic cop the devastation that could occur.

Both she and Robert had left the bar and grill last night in separate Ubers. They had agreed to call each other and get together again soon. Kass sat in her car drinking coffee before driving to the station. She smiled as she thought back to the previous evening. Robert had made her laugh throughout the evening and was a great sport when she beat him at the game of pool.

Sunday April 22, 2018

Detectives Leet and Minor joined the ADA and their commander in the observation room. ADA Reinhart said, “No matter his answer, arrest him. Before coming here, I went in front of a judge and secured the arrest warrant. He is being charged with obstructing an investigation. At the arraignment, I will ask the judge to hold him until trial, as we suspect he kidnapped and murdered his ex-wife.”

Minor took an audible breath, “Sorry. It is just the first time any of us has said that Kelsey Learner was murdered out loud. I can't imagine what this is going to do to her daughter. Her mom is dead, and her dad is charged with murder.”

“No need to apologize, detective. It is good that you have empathy for crime victims, and believe me, Claire Learner is a victim of this crime, too.” Commander Davis said.

Mike Davidson knocked on the one-way mirror, indicating that he and Joe Learner were ready for the detectives to return to the room. When Leet and Minor reentered, Mike stated, “At this time, my client will not be answering any more questions.”

Detective Leet nodded and said, “We understand. Joe Learner, please stand up and put your hands behind your back. You are under arrest for obstruction of justice in the disappearance of Kelsey Learner. You have been informed of your rights before the start of this interview. However, would you like me to repeat your rights?”

Joe Learner did as Detective Leet instructed and replied, “No, I am aware of my rights.”

Mike Davidson requested to speak to the Assistant District Attorney as Joe was led away by the jail guard.

ADA Reinhart and Mr. Davidson went to a conference room to talk. Mike Davidson quickly told the ADA, “You have nothing but circumstantial evidence against Joe Learner. No jury is going to convict him of kidnapping his ex-wife."

Reinhart chuckled, "First of all, your client, Mr. Learner, is charged with obstruction of justice. I am sure a jury will find him guilty of lying to the police during the active investigation of the disappearance of his ex-wife, Kelsey Learner. Second, when we charge him with the kidnapping and murder of Kelsey Learner, and believe me, we will be charging him, I am not worried because juries are made up of smart people. They know that if they wake up in the morning and there is snow on the ground, they do not need to see the snow falling to know it has snowed. This is not TV; juries convict on circumstantial evidence all the time. If you can convince your client to tell the police where to find Kelsey Learner's body, I will convince my boss, the district attorney, not to seek the death penalty."

"I do not believe that my client had anything to do with the disappearance of his ex-wife, but I will meet with him and let him know about your offer. I assume he will not be arraigned before Wednesday." Mike Davidson replied.

ADA Reinhart agreed that the arraignment would likely be on Wednesday. The courts had seventy-two hours to hold an arraignment, and Reinhart was going to ask for as many of those hours as possible. She needed the detectives to uncover as much evidence as feasible, so she needed to give them time.

32

Wednesday April 11, 2018

Paulina Moore sat next to their daughter's headstone. Paulina was sure Lynn's death was the only one she had ever really mourned. Her daughter had been a ray of sunshine that had helped heal Paulina's broken parts, and the eight years of her life had been the best years of Paulina's.

Losing a child was not something a person got over with time. It was unnatural and had driven Paulina to obsession. Their daughter had gotten influenza that winter and was sick for a few weeks. Lynn had been hospitalized for a few days, getting IV fluids and antibiotics. She seemed to have rallied, but there was a change in their daughter once she came home. The ordinarily bubbly and energetic girl was lethargic. Her doctor assured Paulina and Raul that she was recovering from illness.

When Paulina went to wake her up one morning, she noticed that Lynn's fingernails and lips had a bluish tinge, and her face looked swollen. She knew that the doctor was wrong. They rushed her to the closest hospital, that immediately transferred Lynn to the children's hospital across town. That is where the Moores learned that Lynn had developed myocarditis. She would need a heart transplant to survive.

The weeks Lynn spent in the cardiac center of the children's hospital were a blur. Her Cardiologist, Dr. Chris Hann, had been kind and attentive, but little else could be done without a transplant. Lynn slipped away six years ago to the day in the early morning hours.

Monday April 23, 2018

Helen Hann was led into the courtroom. She felt horrible. Chris had been telling her for a long time that she needed to go to rehab and detox, but she did not think even Chris would have recommended this. She had gone almost twenty hours without alcohol. Helen could not remember the last time she had been sober for this long. This morning, her attorney, Angie Miller, had come by with clean clothes for court. They had talked about what would happen at the arraignment. Helen wished Chris had come to visit. She needed to ask him about Angie's suggestion that she plead guilty and ask for rehab to be part of her sentence. She looked around the courtroom, but Chris was nowhere in sight.

She saw Angie and another woman talking at the front of the courtroom. Helen wondered who the other woman was. The guard from the jail led Helen up to a seat. She sat down, and a few minutes later, Angie approached her.

"That is Assistant District Attorney Reinhart. She just offered you a plea bargain. She will drop the suspicion of kidnapping charge and reduce the stalking charge from first-degree to second-degree if you plead guilty today. Reinhart will also agree to the recommendation that you complete an inpatient alcohol rehabilitation program and then be on probation for five years. As long as you stay out of trouble, you will serve no time in jail." Angie told her.

"How long do I have to decide?" Helen asked.

Angie Miller looked at Helen and replied, "About five minutes. I suggest you take the offer. It will probably be the best outcome for you."

Helen wondered; *what will my kids say? Will Chris ever forgive me? What am I thinking? He is done with me. I have been unwilling to face reality before now but life as I know it is over.*

"All right, I will take the plea agreement," Helen said.

Angie got up and walked over to ADA Reinhart. The two of them spoke briefly and then shook hands. Angie returned to her spot next to Helen just as the judge walked in, and the court was called to order.

ADA Reinhart asked to approach the bench. She spoke briefly to the judge.

Judge Curtis said, "Helen Hann, please rise. ADA Reinhart tells me she and your attorney have reached a plea agreement. Do you understand the terms of the agreement and do you willingly agree to those terms?"

"Yes, your honor, I do," Helen replied.

"What is your plea to the charge of second-degree stalking?" Judge Curtis asked.

Helen looked at Angie Miller, who nodded at her. "I plead guilty."

"Helen Hann, you are convicted of stalking in the second degree and are sentenced to inpatient alcohol treatment. Upon the successful completion of your treatment, you will serve five years of probation, during which you may not consume alcohol or use drugs and must not commit any other crimes. If you do not complete treatment, your sentence will automatically be converted to two years in jail, and a warrant will be issued for your arrest. Do you understand?" Judge Curtis decreed.

Helen replied, "Yes, your honor, I do."

"Mrs. Hann, you will be held in the city jail until arrangements are made for you to enter a treatment center." Judge Curtis said, and then banged his gavel.

Angie turned to Helen and said, "I will work to get you into a treatment facility today or tomorrow at the latest."

Helen thanked her and then asked, "Would you be able to arrange for me to call my kids? I want to tell them what is going on myself."

"I will do everything I can so that you can call them," Angie said as Helen was led back to the jail.

****

Chris Hann could not bring himself to go to his wife's arraignment. He knew their son and daughter would be disappointed in him if they ever found out, but he could not do it. He had been up most of the night thinking about how he had failed Helen. He was a physician and should have done more to help his wife. Chris knew that Helen was clinically depressed after Jackson died, but instead of helping her, he buried himself in his work. He also knew she had been self-medicating with alcohol. Over the years, he had become increasingly aware that Helen was having blackouts and being irrational. Rather than helping his wife, he had made plans to divorce her.

****

Detective Kass Minor pulled up to Kelsey and Claire Learner's house. She was driving Kelsey's Buick Encore to return it to Claire. Forensics had found nothing of value with the SUV, and it was released. Leet and Minor agreed that they would return it to Claire and talk to her about her dad being arrested. Commander Davis and the Mayor will hold a press conference this afternoon regarding the arrest of Joe Learner. Minor suspected that the local media was going to be in a frenzy. The story might even attract national attention. She wanted to be sure that Claire was prepared for the media, but also to hear that her mother might be dead.

Detective Minor had called Claire this morning and told her they were coming by with the SUV. That is when she learned that the girl was living alone in the house she had previously shared with her mother. Minor was concerned with Claire being alone, especially after the news they were sharing. After talking to Claire, she decided she would go by and see the Petersons. She just wanted to give them a heads-up.

Claire walked out of the front door as Detective Minor exited the SUV. "Thank you so much for bringing this back to me. It will make my life so much easier not to find rides." Claire exclaimed.

"You are welcome. Would it be okay if my partner and I came in and talked to you?" Minor responded.

"Umm, sure. Did you find my mom?" Claire asked.

Detective Minor led Claire into the house, with Detective Leet following behind. The three of them walked into the living room and sat down.

"We have not found your mom yet. But we need to tell you that we have arrested your dad," Detective Lett told Claire.

Claire jumped up. "What? No, why?" she said in an alarmed tone.

Detective Minor replied, "Claire, please sit down. We will explain to you what we can."

"Okay, why would you arrest my dad? I know he may not be the best dad in the world, but I cannot see him hurting anybody." Claire told the detectives.

Detective Leet responded, "Your dad was arrested on a charge of obstruction of justice. As we have looked into your mom's disappearance, your dad has lied to us about some key facts. I apologize, but we cannot give you any details."

Claire started to cry. Detective Minor moved over to her and put her arms around the girl. "Do you think my mom is dead?" Claire sobbed.

Minor looked at Leet, who shook his head. They would only say that to Claire once they had definitive proof. "We do not know. We have not figured out what happened to her so far." Detective Minor gently told Claire. "The other thing you need to be prepared for is that there will be a press conference this afternoon regarding your dad's arrest. I suspect the media will be trying to contact you again."

Claire looked at the detectives and asked, "Do I have to talk to them?"

Detective Leet responded, "Absolutely not. It would be best if you did not answer them at all. Do you have any relatives you could stay with for a while?"

"My mom has an aunt in Iowa. I met her a couple of times, but I think I need to stay here, so I am close when you find my mom. She is going to need me." Claire responded.

"That is your choice. Please let us know if you need anything." Detective Leet stated.

Claire looked at him, "Can I see my dad? I need to look him in the eyes and ask him if he did something to my mom."

Minor was unsure that was a good idea, but Detective Leet replied before she could, "Let me see what I can work out. One of us will call you if we can get it arranged."

Claire walked the detectives to the front door. She closed the door and locked it. She suddenly felt like she was an orphan.

33

Monday April 9,2018

Chris Hann was relieved to have told his staff about his plans for his vacation. He knew Sue and Becca had been shocked, as it was beyond his norm. He vowed that when he returned, he would let them know that he and Helen were getting a divorce.

He realized that he actually better tell them before he left. There was no telling how Helen would react. The keys to the clinic and the pass-code for the alarm system would also need to be changed. He decided to call and set that up.

After making his calls, he got back to seeing patients. He had decided that the day before he left on his trip, he would tell his staff the real reason behind it. There was no reason for them to know any sooner than that.

Monday April 23, 2018

Minor turned to Leet as they walked down the street to the Peterson's house. "I don't understand why you would agree to help Claire talk to her dad. He kidnapped and likely murdered her mom."

Detective Leet responded, "I know, but all conversations other than between attorneys and their clients are recorded at the jail. I hope talking with Claire in person will help Joe Learner understand the impact of what he has done. He may slip up and say something to Claire that we can use to help us find Kelsey."

"That makes sense, but at what cost to Claire? Or doesn't that matter?" retorted Minor.

Detective Leet blew out a breath, "Of course, it matters, but at this point, we suspect that her dad kidnapped and murdered her mother. I am not sure that there can be any more damage done. I also believe that Claire will need the closure of burying her mother to move on with her life."

Minor thought about what he had said as they approached the Peterson's front door. She could see his way of thinking; nevertheless, she worried about Claire confronting her dad. Jana Peterson opened the door and welcomed them inside. She led them into the kitchen where her husband, Dan, sat.

"I heard you arrested Joe Learner Sunday," Dan stated.

Detective Leet was not surprised the police officer knew about the arrest. The police station was not a place where a secret was kept; not that Joe Learner's arrest was a secret, but it was not yet public knowledge.

Detective Minor responded, "That is right. We have just come from telling Claire that her father was arrested. There will be a press conference this afternoon, and after that, I expect the media to descend upon your neighborhood and Claire like locusts. We thought we should warn you, so you are prepared to help Claire if needed."

Jana Peterson nodded and responded, "Of course. We welcomed Claire to continue to stay with us, but she wanted to be at home. Do you all have any idea where Kelsey is?"

"Honestly, at this point, we do not." Detective Leet answered.

Jana Peterson took her husband's hand as a tear trickled down her face. "This was Kelsey's worst fear. Kelsey's mom died when Kelsey was in her early twenties, and she never wanted Claire to go through what she did at such a young age. I am afraid that Claire has lost her mom at an even younger age."

Minor and Leet thanked the Petersons for their time and showed themselves out.

Detective Minor turned to her partner as they got in the car, "I noticed that neither of the Petersons told us that they did not believe Joe had anything to do with Kelsey's disappearance."

"Yeah, I noticed that, too. I am sure part of that is Dan Peterson's training as a police officer. He knows that many murderers are not someone people predicted would commit the crime and that most are committed by someone the victim knows." Leet replied to her.

As Detectives Leet and Minor drove back downtown to meet the City Engineer, they were both lost in thought. It had been dusk before they were done with the paperwork to process Joe Learner's arrest last night so they had put off this task for this morning. Usually, when they arrested someone, their part of the process was over, but there were so many loose ends in this case that it was far from true. The most important of which was where Kelsey Learner was.

34

Sunday April 8, 2018

Instead taking the advice he had given his wife, Chris Hann didn't drive straight home, he circled back and went into his office. There was always work to do, and work had always been a way that he could not think about his personal problems. He had considered retiring after his divorce was final, but what would he do with his time? No, he was on the work until-you-die plan.

The amount of paperwork that he had to do had significantly decreased since he hired Kelsey. She had been a real blessing to the practice. He felt terrible that he had misled her about why he could not give her a raise. He needed to set aside as much money as possible so Helen could not access it. Once the dust settled on his divorce and he figured out how much he would have to pay Helen, he would find a way to give Kelsey the raise he owed her.

Monday April 23, 2018

Detectives Leet and Minor met the engineer and the CSI tech in the parking lot behind the convention center parking garage. The engineer explained that most people who enter the tunnels do so through the large openings called portals throughout downtown. These openings are closed with gates and locks, but that did not stop people who wanted to go in. However, if someone wanted to enter the tunnels from this parking lot, they would need to lift the maintenance hole cover and climb down a ladder.

The CSI tech took pictures of the maintenance hole cover and its position in relation to the parking garage. The engineer took out a tire crowbar. He remarked to the detectives, "Now, there is a specialty tool that would make this easier, but I wanted to show how a simple tool that most people have in their trunk could be used."

The engineer pried open the cover and set it aside. He then shined a flashlight down and showed them the ladder. The CSI tech took more pictures, and the four people descended into the darkness. They climbed down about seven feet, all turning on flashlights. They saw mass amounts of graffiti and water flowing along the ground.

The CSI tech commented, "There will probably be no evidence down here. Flowing water is one of the best ways to get rid of the evidence."

Detective Leet agreed and commented, "Let's walk through the whole thing, just in case."

The engineer pointed out that the tunnels went in several directions. It was agreed that they would walk to the first turnoff and continually come back to the tunnel they started in. The walk took them several hours, and there had yet to be a sign of Kelsey Learner. Minor and Leet agreed to note the spots where tunnels came out through the large portals.

After climbing back up to the parking lot, Leet and Minor thanked the city engineer for his time and knowledge. Based on the footage they had viewed, they decided to go to the portal that was in the direction that Joe Learner drove after leaving downtown. Standing with the CSI tech at the portal, it was clear that people came in and went through the gate at will. The chain and lock dangled off the gate. They had walked the underground portion of this tunnel, so they were more interested in what they might find outside.

While Detective Leet and the CSI tech walked the outside perimeter of the portal, Minor went to see if there were any cameras in the neighborhood. None of them found any evidence that showed Kelsey Learner had been there. The CSI tech took pictures of the tire impressions left in the gravel area next to the portal. Maybe they would get lucky, and one of those impressions would match Joe Learner's truck.

35

Sunday April 7, 2018

Dr. Chris Hann hated it when a patient died. Today, his patient was a twenty-year-old man. He had been treating James Mason since he was first diagnosed with a heart defect as a baby. James had undergone multiple surgeries over the years. A few days ago, the most recent one was to fix a growing hole that had emerged from the area that had seen multiple repairs.

James' surgery had gone as expected, and he seemed to be recovering well when Dr. Hann had seen him the evening before. The page Chris had received an hour ago was that James was crashing. The team on the cardiac unit had done all they could, but James had not survived.

Sitting in his office at the hospital, Chris dictated his report. When that was done, he took out the notebook he kept locked in a filing cabinet. He turned to the next empty page and began to write about James Mason. He had started this notebook after his son, Jackson, had died. Every patient he lost after that picked at the scab on his heart.

The hardest ones were the children. He had not lost that many kids in his career. He did not need the notebook to remember their names or cases. He could still see their faces and their parents' faces in his mind. Chris knew some doctors who acted like gods, but he knew better. You just had to be powerless to save one child to know that you are no god.

Monday April 23, 2018

The press conference was scheduled for five that evening. The timing was so it would be shown live on the local news channels. Minor had hoped that she would have time to go home and freshen up when they were done walking through the tunnels and surrounding areas. Time was not on her side, so here she was in the bathroom, washing her face and trying to tame her hair.

Standing behind their commander and the mayor, Detectives Leet and Minor knew they were there just for show.

"Joe Learner has been arrested in connection to his ex-wife Kelsey Learner's disappearance. He is currently charged with obstruction of justice. We urge the public to come forward with any information that might help to locate Kelsey Learner." Commander Davis read the statement.

The mayor then spoke, "The hard work and diligence of the detectives on the Major Crimes Taskforce has led to this development. We will not be taking questions at this time due to this being an ongoing investigation."

He then turned and ushered them off the stage and out a side door. Once the door closed, the mayor turned to the detectives, "I appreciate your hard work, but you need to find Kelsey Learner." He walked away, talking with Commander Davis.

Detective Leet turned to Minor, "I am so glad he cleared that up for us."

Both detectives chuckled as they walked to their desks. They had worked the last nine days straight on this case. They had pursued every lead that they had.

"How about we go to the conference room and start over from the beginning? Maybe we missed something." Detective Leet said to Minor.

Detective Minor agreed. When they got to the conference room, she took out her cell phone and took pictures of everything they had pinned up and written on the whiteboard. She and Leet then began removing everything, and set the items down in chronological order on the conference room table.

36

Friday March 30, 2018

Claire was sitting at the table, finishing her homework. What a lousy way to spend a Friday night, but her mom insisted she finish all her back work, or she would be home all weekend. Her mom had even stated that Claire's track coach had agreed that she would not run in the track meet tomorrow if she was not done with the back classwork.

Claire wondered if she should call her dad and see if she could start going there every other weekend. She knew he would never make her do homework. He probably would not even have a curfew for her. But what good would that do her? He lived clear out in the country, and she had no car to drive. She was sure he would not want to drop her off and pick her up all weekend.

Claire wondered if her mom was still out in the garden. When her mom went back to school, she took it very seriously. She was like that about anything she decided to do, and Claire was proud of her, but she wished her mom would sometimes let her hair down and have some fun. In Claire's opinion, the fact that they were opposites seemed to be the reason for her parent's divorce. Her dad traveled for work, and when he was home, he wanted to have fun. At the same time, her mom worked as a nurse and liked to stay home and putter in the garden. Her mom and dad had argued about housework and about going out all of Claire's life, but she would never have thought they would get a divorce.

Claire thought back to when her mom told her that they were getting divorced. She remembered thinking that she could not believe what she was hearing. Her mom was calm and matter-of-fact, and her dad was already gone. Everyone told her that their parents argued, too. She had even heard Lindsey's parents arguing about whether they should buy a new car. But to get divorced, what reason did they have? Heck, her dad was gone as much as he was here.

She had thought it would suck because she was sure that her parents would think she had to go to her dads on weekends at least, or worse, that she had to live with him half the time. She had wondered where he was even living. Had her parents even thought of her when they decided to get divorced? They had surely never talked to her about it.

Tuesday April 24, 2018

Joe Learner sat in his jail cell, thinking about how he had gotten here. Since childhood, he often only told people what they asked or what he thought they needed to know. He sometimes exaggerated and occasionally outright lied, but didn't everyone? As of yesterday, he had still not told Mike everything.

He could not say why other than he felt he was allowed not to have everyone know his business. Mike had not been to see him since Joe had been arrested. As he spent his first sleepless night in jail, Joe decided that he was going to tell Mike everything. He hoped Mike could get him out of there without his secret being made public.

This morning, one guard commented that he had seen the press conference and that the mayor insinuated that Joe had murdered his ex-wife. Joe was seething about this. Yes, he had lied, but he had murdered no one. He heard his name being called by a guard. The guard stepped to his cell door, saying, "Learner, you have a visitor."

He followed the guard to the visitor's room and was shocked to see Claire sitting there. He sat down across from his daughter and could see the heartbreak on her face. "I did not do anything to your mom. I promise you that I had nothing to do with her disappearance." Joe stated before Claire even spoke.

Claire looked at him and said, "Okay, Dad, I believe you, but why did the police arrest you?"

Joe knew he needed to stop lying, but again, he didn't think he necessarily had to tell the whole truth. “I was not entirely honest with the detectives. It has nothing to do with your mom. I lied about where I was because I should have been working when I was already home. I know it is not right, but it has nothing to do with your mom.”

“I understand why you wouldn't want anyone to know that, but it does not seem like something that could get you arrested,” Claire told him.

Joe responded, “The police are stretching. Basically, they think if you lie about one thing, you are lying about everything.”

“Do you have a good lawyer?” Claire asked.

“Yes, honey, I do. I am sure I can post bail after this goes to court. I will write you a letter so you can go to my bank and get a cashier's check once my bond is set. Are you willing to do that to help me?” Joe asked.

Claire responded, “Of course I am, Dad. Should I come to your court date?”

“That is a great idea. I appreciate it so much. I will have my lawyer, Mike Davidson, call you when the day and time are set.” Joe stated.

Claire and Joe sat and talked about Claire's plans for college and how the track was going the last few weeks. They talked until the guard informed them that their visiting time was over.

Claire stood up and said, “I love you, Dad, and I believe you.”

Joe wished he could hug his daughter, but the signage throughout the room made it clear that physical touching was not allowed. “I love you, too,” Joe said as the guard led him away. He thought about all the times he had missed the opportunity to hug his daughter because he had simply not shown up for her.

37

Friday March 23, 2018

He disagreed with her plan to take Kelsey Learner entirely, but she had him by the short hairs at this point. Two months ago, he was shocked when she first told him what she had planned. The fact that he even entertained taking Kelsey showed how much power she had over him. She knew all of his secrets and had been clear that he either agreed to this or she would demolish his entire life. She had shown him all the information, she had compiled to use against him. He felt powerless to oppose her.

Now, he stood in the pouring rain, hoping not to kill himself with this part of her plan. She learned Kelsey Learner would attend a conference here in a few weeks. The idea she had was that during the next thunderstorm, they would go and tamper with the security camera system. When the storm began an hour ago, he suggested it might be too soon to take out the system. But she was worried that it might be their only opportunity.

The plan was to put a power surge through the camera system to mimic a lightning strike. He had learned that the parking garage still needed to update its security camera system. It was a hard-wired system that was all interconnected. His research showed that just like old fashion Christmas light strands, if he took out one, it would take out the entire system. He started by taking out one camera by hitting it with a paintball. The gun was quiet, but effective in ensuring he was not recorded.

The next step was to stick the cattle prod that delivered a high-voltage strike into the power feed of the disabled camera. He watched as the smoke seeped out, and then came the boom. He had blown the whole thing. He grabbed the cattle prod and then smacked down the camera he had splattered in paint. He picked up the camera and ran towards his vehicle.

To confirm that the system was not operational, a day before Kelsey's conference, she would go into the convention center and ask if they had footage of the parking garage. She would claim someone had scratched her car, and that she wanted to know if there was a way for the police to see them before she spent the time to file a report.

Tuesday April 24, 2018

Detectives Leet and Minor had gone over every piece of evidence they had. They had rearranged them in every conceivable order, but still could not find one more thread to untangle the mystery of where Kelsey was. They still hadn't determined exactly what they were looking for. They just knew they needed something, anything that would lead them to Kelsey.

Leet stood staring at a map where they had placed pins for every place that they had gathered evidence. Minor was very methodical about this task, using blue pins for places they conducted interviews, yellow pins from places they had collected physical evidence, including video footage, and a red pin for the last place Kelsey Learner had been seen. As he looked at the map, he wondered about the James River.

There were no pins there, but many surrounded it, or the James River ran towards them, such as Lake Springfield, where Kelsey Learner's keys and Joe Learner's flip flop had been found. He turned to Minor, "Care to take a ride? I want to look at something."

Minor responded, "I could use a change of scenery. Maybe it will shake something loose. "

The two drove south to the James River, near Helen Hann's farmhouse. They followed the river in their car as closely as possible until it reached Lake Springfield. Then continued to follow the river south until the turnoff for Joe Learner's house was passed. Minor asked, not for the first time, "What are we looking for?"

Leet finally answered, "I wonder if someone tossed Kelsey Learner into the river would her keys could have floated to Lake Springfield. And if this same somebody had lost a flip-flop during the disposal of her body, would that also have made it to the lake as well?"

Detective Minor nodded, "I think you are on to something. We should ask the team to search the James River."

38

Friday March 9, 2018

The man had been watching a documentary about the largest kidnapping in United States history when the idea hit him. If those three guys could bury a semi-trailer and hold people underground, he could do something similar. He had a small patch of wooded land outside of town that he had bought with his girlfriend when they were eighteen. They had dreamed of building a house there one day, but that had never happened.

After watching the documentary, he went to different public library branches to use computers for a couple of weeks. He had decided to buy a used shipping container and have it delivered to his land. He arranged the entire transaction using a prepaid credit card and the library's computers.

The man would not start digging the hole until after the container was delivered. He did not want anyone to see what he was doing. The container was delivered two weeks ago without any issues. He had spent time setting the inside up with the chain attached to the wall and some basic supplies.

Now he stood looking at the hole he had been digging all day. He had borrowed the mini excavator from a farmer he worked with. No money had exchanged hands. The farmer needed a favor, and so did the man.

The container was twelve feet long and eight feet high, so he had dug the hole fourteen feet into the ground. He used his pickup truck to push the container into the hole and then used a torch to cut holes in the top. One for a ladder and two small ones for ventilation. He then inserted tubes into the ventilation holes and covered the large hole with a utility cover. As he carefully back filled the dirt, he thought about how his life had come to this point.

Tuesday April 24, 2018

Savannah Morgan had called her attorney's office when they opened this morning and made an appointment. Her attorney, Gary Taylor, had been in court all day, so it was five in the evening before he could see her. She had poured over all the information she could find on the internet regarding the Kelsey Learner case and the little there was about Joe Learner's arrest.

When she watched the ten o'clock news last night, she was shocked to see Joe's picture and hear that he had been arrested. She had not connected the missing woman and her long-time client until she saw the news. She noted that Joe missed his last few sessions, but he had called to cancel them, so she was not worried.

She was sure that Joe Learner had followed the contract he had signed with her and had not used her as an alibi. When Savannah had the contracts for her clients drawn up, her lawyer had added that clause. She never really thought much about the contract; it was a way to protect her business and clients.

Savannah gathered the materials she had put together between appointments today and headed out to see her attorney. She explained to Gary about seeing the news and knowing that Joe Learner had been with her when his ex-wife disappeared. She handed over a copy of the contract and the swipe records showing that Joe Learner had swiped into the service door at the back of the condo at five fifteen that evening. The service door and the swipe system were under-the-table agreements between Savannah and the building's owner.

By not having her clients come and go through the front door, Savannah avoided others at the building, noticing she was conducting business out of her condo. Before going to the attorneys, she had called the building owner and asked him to print still pictures from the security system. She wanted the time and date-stamped pictures of Joe arriving and leaving.

"I will call the District Attorney's office in the morning. I need to meet with them and get a written guarantee that they will not pursue criminal charges against you. As well as agreeing not to open an investigation into your business. You are risking a lot by coming forward with this. Are you one hundred percent sure this is what you want to do?" Gary Taylor asked.

Savannah had thought about this all day, "Gary, it is the right thing to do. I do not want to live the rest of my life worried that a man went to prison so I could protect myself. I have been thinking of relocating, anyway. So, if you think I need to, I will move out of state. I can always go back to my given name, too."

"All right, I will make the call, and then I will let you know," Gary responded.

39

March 2017

Aaron Starr wondered how his life could have turned out differently. It wasn't that he hated his life, but it seemed to be on a continuous loop of drudgery. He did the same things every day. He worked the first shift Monday through Saturday at the hog rendering plant. He had worked there since he dropped out of high school at seventeen. Every day after work, he would drive back to his rented house, shower, and walk to Luke's bar. The bar was three blocks from his house, so walking made sense. There was no reason to risk a ticket for driving under the influence when he could easily walk. The food and beer at Luke's were cheap, and the bartenders all knew him.

On Sundays, he walked to Luke's by noon to watch sports. He usually stayed until nine each night. Aaron knew he drank more than most, but figured he wasn't harming anyone. After all, he was single and had no kids, and other than some guys at work or the bar, he didn't interact with anyone.

This Sunday was like most; he left the bar after the game and was now walking home. He wondered if it would be too late to call his dad and talk about the game. His parents had relocated to Florida a few years ago, so he did not see them much. He had called them this morning just like he did every Sunday morning, but his dad and he always loved talking sports.

Aaron turned around because he thought he heard footsteps behind him. There was no one there. As he turned back to walk home, he saw a woman sitting on the curb ahead. He could hear her crying. He picked up his pace and walked up to her.

He asked her, "Are you okay?".

****

Aaron never heard an answer as the man had come up behind him and injected him with the tranquilizer. The man and woman quickly moved Aaron into the back of their vehicle and covered him.

After they got him back to their lab and had him strapped in, they began the ritual that had become part of these experiments. The man knew he was improving with the anesthesia and surgery. He hoped that this time the experiment would be more successful.

Two days later, the man wondered if they could call that a success. Aaron lived for two days after the experiment. That was longer than any other subject had so far. The man was not entirely sure what had gone wrong to cause Aaron's death. She said she would analyze the data before they picked another subject. She was sure they were on the cusp of a breakthrough.

Wednesday April 25, 2018

When the ADA calls your commander at nine in the morning and tells him that the four of you need to talk, it generally is not a good thing, Leet thought as he and Minor sat in the conference room waiting for ADA Reinhart and Commander Davis. The two of them were having a closed-door meeting.

Minor asked Leet, "What do you think is going on?"

"No idea, but I feel our case will get more complicated."

Commander Davis and ADA Reinhart walked in at that moment.

"You can say that again," Commander Davis responded.

ADA Reinhart sat down and said, "This morning, an attorney named Gary Taylor called me, and then he came to my office. I met with him and the district attorney. He and his client will come to the station in an hour. She will give a statement and hand over proof of where Joe Learner was the evening that Kelsey Learner disappeared."

Minor was shocked, "What?"

"I do not have the details. I know the district attorney has approved this woman's immunity from prosecution agreement." Reinhart told them.

This time for Detective Leet spoke up, "Wait. She was given immunity when we did not have all the details. Maybe she is part of the disappearance."

Reinhart apologized, "I am sorry I was unclear in what I told you. Her immunity agreement is only for criminal activities unrelated to the Kelsey Learner case."

Detective Leet responded, "Now I am confused. What kind of illegal activity?"

"Let's wait to ask her directly," responded Reinhart.

40

Monday August 21, 2017

Lucy Pratt had been thinking a lot about how life went on even when there was a gaping piece of her heart missing. When a birthday card arrived for her from her best friend from childhood, Carrie Booth. She knew her friend would always be someone she could turn to even though it had been a long time since they last talked. The card had prompted Lucy to call the last number she had for Carrie. Sure enough, it was her friend's voice on the answering machine. She had left a message thanking Carrie for the card and asking her to call when she could.

Carrie called her back this morning and they talked for over an hour, catching up and reminiscing. Lucy told her friend about her frustration with the Miller County, Missouri Sheriff. He did not seem even to care that her son was missing. His theory that Cory had taken off made no sense, but no matter how many times she had told him that, she could not change his mind.

Carrie asked Lucy if it would be okay to ask her boss if the FBI could investigate the case. Carrie worked as a secretary at the FBI since she moved to Virginia in her early twenties. As her boss moved up the ranks, he always took Carrie with him. Now, she was the secretary to the Assistant Director of the FBI's Critical Incident Response Group. Lucy had agreed, but knew it wasn't a case the FBI would generally care about, so it might not happen.

Lucy talked with her husband, Bill, about the small amount of hope she had begun to feel that the FBI would breathe new life into their son's case. He had asked her to please not get her hopes up, but she could not stop praying for a miracle. Their son was out there somewhere, and she needed to know where.

Wednesday April 25, 2018

Detective Leet stood behind the one-way mirror, astonished. While waiting for the witness, his brain tried to figure out what was happening. He had come to conclusions that were far from what he was seeing and hearing. The woman before him, Savannah Morgan, was almost six feet tall, with golden skin and long black hair flowing down her back. She was dressed all in black with leather pants, knee-high boots, and a leather jacket. Her attorney, Gary Taylor, had requested that only one detective take the statement. Commander Davis and ADA Reinhart had agreed that it should be Detective Minor.

The interview started with Savannah reading a written statement. "On the evening of April 11th, Joe Learner arrived at my condo at 5:15 pm. He stayed until eight-fifteen that evening. He is a regular client with standing appointments on Wednesdays and Saturdays. I have brought electronic key fob records showing his arrival and departure. In addition, I have requested that the building supply you with the video surveillance of the door that Joe used."

Gary Taylor slid a folder across the table to Minor. Detective Minor opened the folder and looked over the papers in it. "What is the nature of your business with Mr. Learner?" Minor asked.

"We do not believe that is relevant to this discussion; however, suffice it to say that Ms. Morgan provides adult services to paying customers." Gary Taylor stated.

Minor responded, "Let's say we find that Joe Learner was with Ms. Morgan at the time of his ex-wife's disappearance. Why would Mr. Learner not tell us that when we asked him where he was?"

Gary Taylor slid another folder across the table. "In this file, you will find portions of the contract between Ms. Morgan and Mr. Learner. I flagged the section directly addressing Mr. Learner's agreement not to use Ms. Morgan as an alibi. We assume that Mr. Learner did not want to violate the contract, as that would lead to the automatic end of the business arrangement between himself and Ms. Morgan."

Minor accused, "I wonder if this is not an elaborate cover-up to throw us off Ms. Morgan being a part of the disappearance of Kelsey Learner."

Savannah Morgan stared at Minor, "I had nothing to do with that. The other evidence I have not turned over to you but can, if you feel it is necessary, is video footage of the session that evening. Would you like to see it, Detective Minor?"

Minor was surprised to hear that this woman was recording these quote-on-quote sessions. "I do believe we will need to see this footage. Why did you record this session, and was Mr. Learner aware you recorded this session?"

Ms. Morgan stood up and fished a small flash drive out of a pocket on the inside of her jacket. "Here you go. To answer your questions, I record all my sessions, and all my clients are aware. I do not view the sessions, but I keep them because I have my clients verbally state their desire to participate in the activities of the session and that they are in no way being coerced into the activities. I have a friend and mentor in this line of work. She had an issue many years ago in which a recording like mine would have saved her a lot of expense and headache."

Gary Taylor asked, "Detective Minor, do you have any other questions?"

Minor shook her head and said, "Not at this time. Ms. Morgan, we may have follow-up questions after viewing this and the footage from your condo building. Thank you for coming forward."

Detective Kass Minor watched as Savannah Morgan walked out of the interview room with her attorney. Minor put her head down on the table. She never imagined watching their case against Joe Learner blow up in such a strange way. She knew her partner, ADA Reinhart, and Commander Davis stood behind the mirror watching her. She got up and went to see who was willing to watch the footage on the flash drive with her.

41

Monday April 1, 2013

It had taken them longer than she had wanted to procure their first candidate. He had vetoed many of her choices and wanted them to take their time to be sure they knew as much as possible regarding the specimen. He had wondered if her plan to trap the guy would work, but she was so sure of herself, and it had gone just as she had planned.

She sat and watched him through the live feed of the hidden cameras she had installed. Wishing once again that she could carry this project out on her own, but there was no way. She thought back to the day she had concluded that she would have to involve him. She smiled to herself as she thought about the perfect scene, she had set to soften him up before she told him about the project and his role in making it a success. Luring him into her trap had been the simple part. Men loved how she looked, and she knew how to wrap him around her little finger. She had thought carefully about how to begin to convince him. She decided that the non-direct approach, the one without all the details to start, would most likely be successful.

After they ate dinner and he had a few whiskeys to drink, they talked about what she had been researching and the limitations she kept running into. She knew that if he thought it was his idea that she had just refined; he was much more likely to be agreeable initially, even when it got tough. She had been sure to record him talking once she had led him to the part of the conversation she would need if this project went wrong.

She knew he had been worried about her and that she could leverage that to convince him that the project was the best thing for them. About a month before she told him about the project, their relationship had become so strained that she was sure he would agree to whatever she asked him. She chuckled softly as she enjoyed the memory of how easy he was to convince.

She had done her research and knew how she wished to proceed. She was sure they could be successful by carefully adhering to the protocol she had developed. Then, she could use their knowledge to write her research and convince others to duplicate their results.

It wasn't that she did not value individual human life, but she believed that sometimes sacrifices had to be made for the greater good. Taking a life, whether a human or an animal, never bothered her as long as there was a reason. She knew some would think she was heartless, or maybe even a sociopath, but she disagreed. She remembered vividly every life she had taken. She had never had a partner for this work before, but she would need one with the extent of her project. She knew he was weak enough for her to have him do her bidding, but she wondered if he was strong enough to carry out the project.

His reaction this evening was her worst fear. He may prove incapable of being her partner; then she would be forced to sacrifice him. It's a good thing she had her insurance safely locked away.

Wednesday April 25, 2018

Joe wondered where Mike was. It was almost noon, and there had been no word about his arraignment. He had thought Mike had told him it would happen today for sure. He must have misunderstood him.

He sat in his jail cell, wondering how this had all gone so wrong. Even though he had signed the contract with Savannah, he should have told the truth from the beginning. He wondered how to tell Mike Davidson where he had been the evening when Kelsey disappeared. How pissed was his attorney going to be at him? For what he had already paid him, Joe hoped he was willing to help him get out of this.

Joe stood up when the cell door opened. The deputy told him his attorney was there to see him. Joe walked into the room and saw Mike sitting there.

Mike said, "Why didn't you just tell us about your little hobby? That would have saved us all a lot of headaches."

Joe wondered how Mike had found out. Joe responded, "I signed a contract and knew I had nothing to do with Kelsey's disappearance. So, I never thought the police would scrutinize my whereabouts."

Mike explained that ADA Reinhart had called him and explained that they had potential evidence that might clear Joe. She asked that he sign off on not holding the arraignment first thing this morning. It seemed a woman named Savannah Morgan had come into the police station this morning with her attorney. She had seen the news report about Joe's arrest. She had met with the detectives and provided written and video records that cleared Joe. He had agreed and thought he would hear back from her by mid-morning. It was not until half an hour ago that the ADA called him and told him that the charges against Joe had been dropped and that he would be released in the next few hours.

"You are very lucky because they are not going to charge you with lying to the police or hindering an investigation. In exchange for that, you are never going to sue them or publicly denounce them for wrongful arrest. That is the deal, I made for you. Are you okay with it?"

Joe nodded his head and then thanked Mike for all he had done.

42

April 2012

Paulina and Raul Moore staggered more than walked out of the children's hospital. They had spent virtually all of their time here the last four weeks. Neither of them had worked the entire time Lynn was a patient. Lynn's illness had left both of them feeling overwhelmed. No one prepares a person to have a critically ill child. The illness had come on quickly and escalated from a case of the flu to fatal heart failure.

Raul had returned to work a few days after Lynn's funeral, but Paulina could not bring herself to resume her life. Paulina threw herself into researching heart failure, the issues surrounding the lack of donor organs in the United States, and why there were no alternatives to donated human organs.

She became obsessed with preventing other parents from going through what she had. For several weeks, Paulina read research like it was her job. When Raul told her their largest client, a local corporate pig farm, was considering hiring new vets, she knew she had to start working again. Without the income from their veterinary clinic, she could not begin her burgeoning plan.

Wednesday May 23, 2018

Detective Leet walked over to Minor's desk. "Commander Davis says to shelf the Kelsey Learner case. We have exhausted all leads, and there is little hope that new information will come to light. He is declaring it cold. Now, I can't retire because I have always said I would never retire with a cold case on my record."

For Minor, all she could think of was the question that had started this case, "Where is Kelsey Learner?"

43

October 2003

You know it is going to be a terrible night when you turn down the street your house is on and see a plethora of police cars and fire trucks. Helen pulled over to where the police officer indicated for her to do so and showed him her license. He asked her to stay in her car, and he went back to his. She could not contain herself and got out and ran up to a neighbor. When the neighbor saw her, she grabbed Helen and hugged her. The young police officer found her and said, "Ma'am, I am sorry your house is on fire. The fire department is doing all it can. Do you know if anyone was home this evening?"

She looked at him and replied, "My husband and son were." The officer led her to his cruiser and had her sit in the passenger seat. A few minutes later, her husband, Chris, ran up to her. He was safe, but where was their son Jackson?

Helen asked him, "Where is Jackson?"

She would never forget his reply, "I don't know. I left him home alone. I figured you would be home soon, and he would be okay."

Helen knew Chris was right. She had told him she was running to the store to grab a few things to make cookies for the bake sale at Jackson's school. She had not known about the bake sale until she cleaned out Jackson's backpack after dinner and found the flier. She had known that Chris was on call and might have to leave at any time, but she had run into an old friend at the store, and the two talked for over an hour.

Jackson was a typical pre-teen boy who rarely remembered to pass along school papers. Helen fondly remembered that her oldest son,

Chris Junior, had been the same way when he was twelve. Chris Junior was starting his third year at Mizzou, majoring in the pre-med program. He had grown to be so much like his father. He was organized and driven. The messy little boy had grown into a motivated, successful young man.

Chris and Helen stood together just outside the police barricade, waiting for news. They had decided to wait to call Chris Junior and their daughter Heather until they knew for sure what was going on. Heather had joined her brother at Mizzou just a few weeks ago. Unlike her brother, Heather was a free spirit. She was majoring in Fine Arts with an emphasis on Dance. Helen could not imagine how her older children would react to what was happening.

The fire captain walked up to the Hanns and lifted the police tape. He motioned for them to come under the tape and follow him. He walked away from the crowd and stopped. He turned to them and said, "I am so sorry your house is a total loss. We have not found your son, but we will continue to look."

Helen remembered Chris yelling, "What do you mean, you can't find him? Is he in the house?". She did not remember much more from that night other than praying to God to keep Jackson safe, but he was not all right. Jackson died that night, and his mother was left a shell of the person she had once been.

Wednesday June 6, 2018

Kelsey awoke with a start. It was

still dark all around her. She had figured out that she was in a metal box, possibly a shipping container. A chain around her leg only allowed her to go a few feet. Someone had come and gone every few days, but they were dressed in all black and wearing night vision goggles. When they reached the bottom of the ladder, the person would zap her with a stun gun and inject her with some kind of tranquilizer. They would remove her waste bucket and leave her another jug of water and freeze-dried foods. Kelsey wondered; *Where am I, and Why am I here?*

Dismantling the Farm

Book Two-Secrets in the Heartland Series
Dismantling the Farm
Andrea Crist Heckner

Dedication:

This is book is dedicated to my parents, John and Maryfran Crist. Thank you for going the extra mile to ensure that I am a reader and for supporting my dreams.

Dismantling the Farm-Book Two of the Secrets in the Heartland Series was originally published in 2023. The version contained within this compilation is an edited version with no major changes to the story line or characters.

1

If every person is just six degrees of separation from each other, how many degrees is too close to a serial killer?

Thursday June 11, 2020

Detective Kass Minor entered Jerry's bar. It was a place that many cops in Springfield visited nightly. She was an infrequent patron, but tonight, she needed a drink. She wondered again if her partner, Detective Mitch Leet, had made the right choice by not retiring. It wasn't just the foot chase today that he had not kept up with that had her concerned, but also his apathetic attitude towards everything of late.

Leet often expressed to Minor that the Kelsey Learner case had left him feeling helpless. Kelsey had been missing for twenty-six months at this point. In every other case, he was able to put the pieces together. Leet had built a career on finding the evidence, figuring out the suspect, and then the motives, which equaled arrests and prosecutions. The Kelsey Learner case had not followed that pattern, and he could not shake the feeling that they had failed her and her daughter. Kass was sure they had done all they could to find Kelsey Learner. Now, they just needed someone to slip up or a healthy dose of good luck, but neither had happened, so the case was cold.

As Kass sat down, she looked at the television above the bar. It looked like the FBI, Missouri State Police, and the Christian County Sheriff's Department were raiding a farm outside of Springfield. She wondered what they were saying, but the sound was turned off. Something about the scene on TV of the FBI driving up to the farm niggled at Kass's brain. Where were they? Had she ever been there? The next image on the TV caught her attention even more. It was a picture of two veterinarians, Doctors Raul and Paulina Moore. Now Kass knew how she knew that farm. She and Leet had talked to Raul Moore at that farm while investigating Kelsey Learner's ex-husband.

Minor got up from the bar and headed home. She was sure the twenty-four-hour news channels would be running the story. A call to Robert Matthews might help answer her questions. But she knew he wouldn't answer her call if he was at that farm. As she drove, Kass wondered; *Is this the dose of luck that Leet and I need to solve the Kelsey Learner case?*

April 1994

Paulina Ross stared at the note and plate of cookies. *How dare Tom take these from that girl?* Not only had he accepted the gift, but he had tried to hide it from her. Paulina may never have been the wiser if she had not opened his trunk to look for her missing jacket. Looking around to ensure no one was watching, she grabbed the plate, put it underneath her coat, and walked to her car. When she got to her car, she carefully set down the plate on her passenger seat, took her coat off, and laid the coat over the cookies.

She had caught Tom flirting with other girls before, but he had always sworn that it was harmless. These cookies and this note did not seem harmless to her. He needed to be taught a lesson on how to treat her. Paulina stopped at the grocery store, bought what she needed, and then headed home to bake a fresh batch of cookies. She carefully ground the peanut candies in the blender and poured the mix into the cookies. Tom was always telling everyone that he had an extreme peanut allergy. She was going to put that to the test. She would save his life, and he would be beholden to her for the rest of their lives.

Paulina was sure to wear gloves as she dumped the girl's cookies out and replaced them with the ones she had made. Using the same cling wrap and being careful not to disturb the taped note, she wrapped the new batch of cookies and placed it in the bottom of her backpack. On top of it, Paulina added a picnic for Tom and herself, a blanket, and her camera.

Tom pulled up to the house right on time. Paulina finished eating her peanut butter sandwich and grabbed her packed bag. She tapped on his trunk, and he popped it open. She carefully placed the bag inside. When Paulina got in the car, Tom tried to kiss her. She turned away and said, "Wait, my mom might be watching."

Tom sighed and said, "Yeah, I get it. But we are both eighteen. When is she going to accept that you are grown up?"

"Probably never", Paulina replied with a laugh.

Tom drove to Lake Springfield and parked the car. He jumped out and came around to open the door. When Paulina got out, he put his arms around her and kissed her.

Tom looked at her and said, "You taste weird. What have you been eating?"

Paulina replied, "I ate some cookie dough."

Tom shrugged and went to the trunk to grab the bag that Paulina had put in there. He had completely forgotten about the plate of cookies that Marcie had given him. So, he never noticed that they were not there.

As Paulina and Tom walked down to the spot by the lake they often visited, Tom realized that his mouth and throat were tingling. He turned to Paulina and asked, "Hey, that cookie dough didn't have peanuts, right?"

Paulina replied, "No. I know you are allergic. Why? What is wrong?"

"Nothing, it is probably my hay fever starting up," Tom replied.

Together, they laid out the blanket and unpacked the picnic. Tom grabbed the thermos with lemonade and took a big drink. Paulina handed him a cookie. He took a bite and then kissed her.

Tom said, "These are good. Thanks."

"Better than Marcie's cookies?" Paulina asked.

"What? I have never had any cookies from her." Tom replied. As he spoke, he remembered the plate of cookies Marcie had given him with the note. The note read; *I am waiting whenever you are ready for a real woman again. Love-Marcie.* Tom remembered thinking that Paulina would be irate if she ever saw it. Now he knew that she had.

"I don't know what Marcie's deal is, but I have no interest in her," Tom told Paulina. He was having trouble catching his breath. He wondered if he was having a panic attack over Paulina confronting him.

Paulina was staring at him. She leaned over and kissed him. When she pulled away, she whispered, "I wish I believed you."

Tom realized that he was having an allergic reaction. "Paulina, I need you to go to my car and get my epinephrine kit," Tom said in a strained voice.

Paulina stared down at her boyfriend as he struggled to breathe. She had planned to save Tom and be his hero, but as she watched the life slip out of him, euphoria rushed through her like nothing she had ever experienced. That was when her plans changed. She picked up the picnic meal except for the plate of cookies. Tom was no longer conscious, but still breathing. She rolled him over, picked up her blanket, and walked to his car. Setting her backpack on the ground, she opened the trunk and grabbed Tom's fishing pole and tackle box. Paulina carried his fishing gear back to where he was lying, set it beside him, and then placed the cookie he had bitten in his hand.

As Paulina walked home, she thought about how satisfied she felt. Not only had Tom paid for his infidelity, but Marcie would always believe she was to blame. Paulina knew that she needed to be prepared to act shocked and grief-stricken, but until the time came to do that, she would enjoy this rush of power.

2

Thursday June 11, 2020

Robert Matthews stood looking at the room underneath the Moore's barn. The case he had once thought was a waste of time had turned out to be a major one. He had spent more than two years looking into a series of missing men around Missouri. The list had started with ten missing, but he had narrowed it to seven who were truly unaccounted for. Each had been involved in a solitary activity when they seemingly vanished. When he had found a way to track one of the men, it had quickly led them to the Moore's farm.

Paulina and Raul Moore were not home when the FBI served the warrant. The Fugitive Apprehension Task Force members were out looking for both of them. They were very good at finding people, so Matthews was sure they would be in custody quickly. What he was not sure of was whether he would be the one to interview either of them. Despite his work leading them to the Moores, his short time in the FBI would be why someone else would conduct the interviews. He wondered if his name would even be a footnote in this investigation.

The farm was swarming with agents, state police detectives, deputies from the sheriff's department, and Crime Scene Investigators. Matthews was in the basement of the Moores barn. He was standing in what a fiction writer would describe as an evil lair. It had taken them less than an hour to find and access this room. The room's setup was like an operating room with two operating tables and sets of equipment. An industrial drain was in the middle of the floor, and a power washer was sitting by the large metal sink. Matthews was sure the technicians would pull apart the sink and drain to look for evidence. The FBI crime scene investigators were among the best in the world, so he knew they would do a thorough job. As Matthews walked around, careful not to touch anything, he was sure that something about the room's dimensions were off.

Matthews walked the perimeter of the room again. Now he was sure that something was wrong. Three walls were the standard cinder block type and painted white, but the fourth wall was drywall. He asked the lead CSI tech if he could knock on that wall. The technician looked at Matthews' gloved hands and told him to go for it. Matthews walked along the wall and knocked every few inches. He was listening for a change in sound. Sure enough, the sound differed a few feet into that back wall. Matthews called one of the technicians over, and he agreed that there seemed to be a hollow spot in the wall.

Agent Matthews checked-in with the senior agent at the scene, Agent Hollins, and then took Agent Lee Rivers back to the basement with him. They carefully opened a six-foot wall section and discovered a small room. Once in the smaller room, they found a hidden door. Swinging the door open and walking back through, Matthews closed the hidden door, keeping his hand to mark the spot it connected. He reached towards the spot where the door connected and gently pulled. The door swung open. Rivers shook his head and said, "That was much easier than the first way we got in."

The two agents reentered the hidden room and stared at a large hydraulic scissor lift in the center, then looked at the ceiling and saw a hatch above the lift. Three racks held cassette tapes and three-ring binders against the back wall. Each item had a label with a single letter and a date. Two racks had seven shelves with materials, each containing materials labeled with a different letter and number. The third rack contained medical equipment and supplies.

Agent Matthews picked up the binder marked C 6 on it. He opened it and saw pictures of Cory Pratt. Cory was the young bicyclist whose disappearance had started this investigation. If it wasn't for his mother's connection to the FBI, no one would have searched for Cory or the other six men. He set that binder down and went to the next. Each binder had pictures taken from a distance of a missing man, and after the pictures were pages of typed notes on each man and his routines. In four of the binders, there was a red divider. After the divider, there were details of the man's death. The remaining three binders had an orange divider; these men had also died, but something was different.

The second rack contained seven more sets of materials labeled with the letter P and a number between one and seven. Agent Rivers was looking through these binders. He walked to Matthews with one of the binders and asked, "What do you make of this? Every one of them is basically identical."

Matthews looked at the binder and saw that instead of pictures of men, there were pictures of a pig, from when it was a piglet to a full-grown hog. Matthews replied, "That is weird. Mine are all the missing men I have been looking into. It seems one of the Moores killed all of them."

"One of the Moores? Oh, come on, you know that statistically, serial killers are men. So, Raul Moore killed seven people down here. Where are the bodies, and what is with the binders of pigs?" Rivers asked.

Matthews thought those were both good questions and ones that he did not have the answers to.

July 1994

Raul Moore and Shelby Lansing stood in the wooded lot. It was officially theirs. Legally, it belonged to Shelby because she bought the lot with money she had inherited from her grandma. But they planned to change the deed to both names when they married. Shelby did not consider it to be just hers. She and Raul had found this land while driving around after leaving the wedding reception for Shelby's cousin in Springfield. They had plans. They were both going to Mizzou and would get married when they graduated. This land was where they were going to build their dream house.

Walking around the wooded lot, they talked about the house and the future they would build. Shelby wanted three kids, and Raul thought that would be great. They were both only children, so the idea of a bigger family appealed to them. The land in the woods would be great for raising kids, with plenty of fresh air and outdoor fun. They agreed to have dogs and barn cats.

Raul talked about building a log cabin which was fine with Shelby as long as there was a big front porch and at least two bathrooms. Raul wanted chickens, but Shelby was unsure if she liked that idea. She had heard that they were smelly and required a lot of work. She decided to discuss the chickens when it was time to get them.

Shelby was planning to become an accountant. She had a natural propensity toward math. She loved to solve problems and was very detail-oriented. Raul had wanted to be a veterinarian since he was a child. He loved animals. He was the reason they were vegetarians. He had helped Shelby understand the compassion toward animals that not eating them showed.

3

Friday June 12, 2020

The joint FBI and local law enforcement team had been at the Moores' farm for almost twenty-four hours. The ground-penetrating radar had found no evidence of buried bodies on the property. The house and barn had been thoroughly searched. Except for the basement rooms and their contents, nothing of evidentiary value had been found so far. They had moved on to searching the pig pens. Before this search began, they had to wait for a local farmer to pick up the pigs. Matthews was unsure they would find any evidence in pig pens, but one of the senior agents had grown up on a pig farm, and he explained that pigs would eat everything except for metal.

In the early morning light, Matthews and the other agents watched as the technicians sifted through the two large pigpens. They did this much like archeologists handle a dig site. The technicians had marked off the pens in sections and scooped and sifted materials. They placed items of possible interest on folding tables.

A second group of technicians was carefully washing and cataloging the items found. A rivet from a pair of jeans, several eyelets from shoes, and other unidentified pieces of metal made up the items so far. A CSI tech said, "Agents, you will want to see this."

Matthews and several other agents walked over. The tech pointed out a couple of human teeth with metal caps.

Agent Rivers said, "I think we have discovered how Raul Moore got rid of the bodies."

Matthews asked the tech, "How long do you think the entire search of the pigpens will take?"

The technician said, "We are planning ten days to two weeks."

There was nothing else he could do until the Moores were found and the evidence from the farm had been processed, so Matthews decided to head home and nap. At home, Agent Matthews thought about the call and text he had received from Kass Minor. He and Kass had dated off and on for the last two years. Their work schedules always seemed to be in the way. When Robert was in a lull between cases, Kass was in the midst of a case and vice versa. He knew her call and text were work-related, but it would be nice to connect with her again.

Tuesday May 6, 1997

Shelby and Paulina had shared this dorm room for the last three years. They had become fast friends and discussed getting an off-campus apartment for their senior year of college. Paulina had suggested that Shelby's boyfriend, Raul, also move in with them. Shelby had been very unsure about that idea. She explained to Paulina that she did not want to live with him before marriage. Paulina thought her view was old-fashioned. She also did not think Shelby spent enough time with Raul. Paulina knew from personal experience that keeping an eye on your boyfriend was essential. She had tried to talk with Shelby about it, but Shelby had laughed and said that Raul was not that kind of guy.

Paulina knew the kind of guy that Raul was. She had studied him over the past three years. He certainly did not have a wandering eye. She had paid other girls to try to get him to flirt or more. He had never even responded to any of the attempts. Paulina had decided a few weeks ago that Raul needed a more attentive and caring woman.

Knowing that Shelby needed to be out of the picture for Raul to move on, Paulina devised her plan. She had seen in the forecast that finals week would be unseasonably hot, with temperatures over one hundred. She had gone to the library and studied the schematics of window air conditioners and their installation. This morning, after Shelby headed to class, Paulina cut the wire to the blower fan and then unscrewed the bracket of the window air conditioner unit.

After rigging the air conditioner, Paulina met up with her study group for her advanced biology class. Most people in her study group wanted to be doctors or nurses, but Paulina intended to become a veterinarian. She did not want that much contact with other people. Shelby rarely changed her routine, so Paulina knew she would be gone all day and have dinner at the dining hall where Raul worked. Paulina walked over to the dining hall and had dinner with her roommate.

They watched a movie before returning to their dorm room to study. When they returned to the room, Shelby called Raul, and they talked on the phone for almost an hour. When she hung up the phone, she asked Paulina, "Why is it so hot in here?"

Paulina was standing at the window, looking out at the empty courtyard. She shrugged, "I am not sure. The AC is running, but does not seem to be blowing out cold air."

"Have you tried turning it off and on?" Shelby asked.

"No, I was waiting to ask you what you thought we should do. I am going to find a Resident Assistant." Paulina replied.

Shelby turned to the unit and started fiddling. Paulina pivoted at the door to the room and ran at Shelby. She pushed her roommate with all her might. The air conditioning unit and Shelby fell out the window. As soon as the falling began, Paulina got out of the room. She walked calmly down the hall and into the elevator. She was almost at the Resident Assistant's office when she heard screaming.

Paulina ran from the building along with many others. People were standing around, staring at Shelby's broken, lifeless body. Paulina screamed, "What happened?"

A couple of girls who also lived in the dorm looked at her. One of them asked, "Where were you?"

Paulina was crying and replied, "The air conditioner wasn't working. I went to get one of the RAs."

She felt someone put their arm around her. She turned to see the head RA, Lenny. He led her away from the scene, she sat on the steps to the building and cried. She could hear sirens approaching. She wondered how Raul would hear about Shelby's "accident." She felt someone sit next to her. Looking over, Paulina saw Raul. He seemed to be in shock. He was pale and shaky, with tears streaming down his face.

Paulina whispered to him in what she hoped was a shaky voice, "Is she dead?"

Raul looked at her and nodded. He asked, "What happened?"

Paulina put her head down, "I am not sure. The air conditioner wasn't working. Shelby was fiddling with it, and I went to get help. Then I heard screaming and came outside and saw...."

Paulina did not finish her sentence. She just couldn't. Paulina hoped that Raul interpreted that as her being too upset to talk. In reality, she was working hard to suppress a laugh. It worked. This time, it was an even bigger thrill than when she had handled her problem with Tom. She knew the police would want to talk to her and was prepared. She had been reading about panic attacks and knew she could fake one just as she was pretending to cry right now.

She began to take shallow breaths and put her head on her knees.

Lenny, the RA, walked over to her and asked, "What's wrong?"

Paulina said in between puffs of breath, "I can't breathe. I am going to pass out."

Lenny ran to get one of the paramedics who had responded to the scene. Paulina quickly found herself on a gurney in the back of the ambulance. They gave her oxygen and told her they were taking her to the emergency room. When she was at the hospital, the doctor gave her a sedative and called for the hospital psychiatrist to see her.

The psychiatrist was an overworked man who quickly decided that Paulina's panic attack was unsurprising after seeing her roommate die from a fall. He wrote her a prescription for the sedative and an anti-anxiety medication. He suggested that she might benefit from talking with someone about what she had been through. She agreed that she would do that. All the while knowing she would never go to a counselor.

The next day, Paulina sat in the dean's office with her dad and a police detective. The college had called her father, who had driven up last night. Her dad was a defense attorney and had left his wife and Paulina ten years ago, but had always told Paulina to call him if the cops ever wanted to talk to her. She had listed him as her emergency contact.

The police had never talked to Paulina when Tom died. Everyone believed that his death was a complete accident because of the ingesting of peanuts. Marcie was not back at school that year or at their graduation, but that did nothing to stop the whispering about her. Paulina was not even sure her dad was aware that her high school boyfriend had died. At this moment, she was very glad for his detachment from her life.

The detective asked her, "Please tell me what happened last night."

Paulina looked at her dad, and he asked the detective, "Before my daughter answers you, what is the nature of your questioning?"

"This is a death investigation into your daughter's roommate, Shelby Lansing. Shelby and the window air conditioner fell from their dorm room last night. Shelby died upon impact. What we don't know is what happened right before she fell. I hope your daughter can fill some of those blanks in for us," the detective replied.

Mr. Ross turned to his daughter. "Honey, are you up to answering these questions?" Once again, before Paulina could answer, Shawn Ross turned back to the detective, "I am sure you know that Paulina was taken by ambulance from the scene to the Emergency Room. She had a panic attack. She is currently under the care of a psychiatrist and on medication."

The detective nodded.

Paulina said quietly, "It is okay, Daddy. Our air conditioner wasn't working right. I went to get Lenny the RA, and Shelby tried to get it working. I heard yelling when I got off the elevator and was about to knock on the RA office door. I ran outside and saw..."

Paulina stopped talking and began to cry. She put her head in her lap and did an exaggerated version of the breathing exercise they taught her in the ER.

Her dad asked the detective, “Is that all you need?”

The detective replied, “Yes. We may need to talk with Paulina again, but at this point, this looks like an accident from an improperly installed air conditioning unit.”

4

Friday June 12, 2020

Matthews grabbed a Diet Coke from his refrigerator as he finished getting dressed. He had been asleep for two hours when Agent Hollins called and told him that the fugitive team had Raul Moore. The Moores had been attending a veterinary conference in Kansas City. The apprehension team had arrested Raul in a banquet hall having breakfast. His wife was nowhere to be found. Raul told the team she was at the conference with him, but he did not know where she was.

As Matthews walked into the FBI office, he marveled at how the once quiet office was bursting at the seams with agents, state police detectives, the Christian County Sheriff, and technicians. This case had blown wide open. There had been no real leads in the seven missing persons cases until six weeks ago when he was home flipping through the channels. He stopped on a special about medical advances while he went to grab a beer from his refrigerator. He was only half-paying attention when the show began discussing pacemakers. He heard them say that modern pacemakers transmitted data back to the doctor so they could monitor patients' hearts remotely.

He went to bed that night, not really thinking about the case he was working on or the program he had seen. At two in the morning, he woke with a start. He was sure he had read that one of the missing men, George Jeffers, had a pacemaker. *Was it possible to track his whereabouts from the pacemaker?* He wrote down that thought and went back to sleep.

The next day, Matthews began researching pacemaker technology with much of the information going over his head. He worked with the medical examiner that the FBI used in the area, and she helped him to find out what model pacemaker George Jeffers had. He then contacted the company that manufactured that model of pacemaker. At first, the company denied that tracking the pacemaker's location would be possible based on the data it was sending back.

The computer technicians for the FBI agreed with Agent Matthews that if a device was sending data one way, it was possible to track where that data had come from. One of the computer technicians, Lily Thomas, worked with Matthews to obtain a subpoena for the manufacturer to send all the metadata from George Jeffers' pacemaker.

Lily used the metadata to determine the GPS coordinates of the last data set George's pacemaker ever transmitted. Matthews then pinpointed the Moores' farm as that location, and now that hunch had led to this massive investigation. Robert had talked to his mom the other day and jokingly told her that she was wrong that watching television was a waste of time.

March 2003

The relationship between Raul and Paulina had blossomed from supporting each other after Shelby died to friendship and, in the last two years of veterinary school, into a romance. They graduated from veterinary school a year ago and married in a small civil ceremony two weeks after graduation. Raul was surprised when Paulina took his last name. She was very independent yet, in some ways, very traditional.

They had spent the last year of veterinary school looking at farms to buy and researching the areas around Missouri to decide where to settle. Paulina was pleased they were within half an hour of her mother's home. They had agreed that they did not want to move to an area saturated with large animal veterinarians. Right after graduation, Raul accepted a job as the on-site veterinarian for a corporate pig operation, and Paulina accepted one with a local large animal vet. The veterinarian, Curt Manning, was an older gentleman who had told Paulina that he was considering retiring in a few years and might be willing to sell Raul and her the practice then.

In the past year, the Moores had bought a small farm with two barns and two pig pens. Raul had taken an interest in pigs and recently brought two piglets home. Both piglets were runts and had recently been weaned. Paulina was unsure; she wanted to be a pig farmer but could see the upside. Pigs were living garbage disposals, and you never knew when you would need to make trash disappear. Their shared goals helped them to deepen their relationship. Paulina knew they were meant to be together and was glad everything worked out.

There was only one problem: Curt Manning, the veterinarian that Paulina worked for. Curt treated Paulina more as a veterinarian technician than a fellow veterinarian, and he was no longer talking about retiring and selling the practice. He usually called her "little lady" and sent her on errands. When she had asked him not to, he had laughed and said she was being too sensitive. Paulina had talked to Raul about Manning, and Raul thought they should continue to save up and start their own large animal veterinary service.

However, Paulina had other ideas. Curt Manning stood in the way of what she wanted; even worse, he lied to her. She knew Curt had a heart condition and was on strong medication for it. He had sent her to the pharmacy every month to pick up his prescriptions. She was returning from one of these trips and was fuming when she devised her plan to deal with Curt.

Paulina pulled into the parking lot of the large truck stop. She carefully poured Curt's pills out and studied them, looking at their shape and color. It was essential to find something similar to replace each of these with. She studied the pill book she bought at a second-hand bookstore for the next few weeks. She identified two medications that would be similar enough that Curt should not even notice.

Paulina purchased what she needed and then bided her time until Curt sent her to the pharmacy again. A month later, while driving back to Manning's farm with his pharmacy order, she pulled into the same truck stop parking lot. She carefully poured out the prescriptions and made the swap. She saved all the swapped medications, as she knew she would have to put them back once Curt was gone.

Curt had given Paulina a key to his house when she first started working there. The veterinary practice office was part of the house, and he had put Paulina in charge of all the paperwork. She had gotten very little hands-on work with animals but had learned the business side of running a veterinary practice. Paulina entered Curt's kitchen and saw the two prescription bottles sitting in their usual spot. She switched the old bottles for the new ones. She filled the old bottles with the real prescription and put them into her bag.

As Curt began to feel worse and worse each day, Paulina was thankful for the man's stubbornness. He refused to make a doctor's appointment or to cut back on his work. Two weeks after switching medications, Paulina was walking into the barn on Curt's property. She was carrying the business checkbook so Curt could sign the checks she had written for the practice's expenses.

Paulina immediately saw Curt on the ground inside one of the stables. He was not moving, but the horse in the stable with him was. The horse was agitated and very close to where Curt lay. Paulina turned around and walked out of the barn. She got in her truck, drove to town, visited Curt's favorite diner, and picked up his usual lunch and a salad for herself. She thought as she drove back, smelling Curt's country-fried steak. *That is another thing: How can a veterinarian eat meat?*

Paulina parked her truck in its usual spot, took the lunches inside the house, then walked to the barn. As soon as she opened the door, she could smell the blood. She approached the stable where she had last seen Curt. He was lying in a pool of blood. His favorite horse had trampled him. Paulina carefully opened the stable and watched the horse run from the barn. Returning to the house, she switched back Curt's medications. Paulina wore gloves this time when she handled the bottles and thought about wiping the bottles clean, but there was a reasonable explanation for her fingerprints. It would look suspicious if there were no prints on the bottles.

Walking back to the barn, Paulina practiced what she should say to the nine-one-one dispatcher. She needed to sound shocked and frightened. This state of mind would explain why she did not give very much information. The less she said, the better. Paulina bent down and checked Curt for a pulse. He was dead. This was the first time she had touched a dead body. She found that touching her prey after killing them had a special thrill. Paulina walked to the barn phone and made her call.

"Nine-one-one. What is your emergency?" the dispatcher answered.

Paulina shrieked, "My boss, Curt Manning. He is dead. I need help."

The dispatcher quickly began to try to calm Paulina down, "What is your name, and where are you calling from?"

"Dr. Paulina Moore. I am standing in Doctor Manning's barn. He is lying in a horse stable in a pool of blood," she replied.

"Is the horse still in there with him?" the dispatcher asked.

Paulina broke down crying. She sobbed, "No, I let him out to check on Dr. Manning. He has no pulse."

The dispatcher responded, "Help is on the way. There is a deputy who will be there in two minutes or less. Just stay on the line until he gets there."

Paulina continued to cry into the phone and listen to the dispatcher as he tried to help calm her down.

A sheriff's deputy arrived with his lights and sirens on, and Paulina hung up with the emergency services dispatcher.

The deputy ran to Curt's body and checked his pulse. He then turned to Paulina, "What happened here?"

Paulina breathed and quietly said, "I have no idea. I returned from town with lunch and found Dr. Manning like that."

"Did you touch or move him at all? Where is the animal that trampled him?" the deputy questioned.

"I let the horse out so I could check on Dr. Manning. I checked for a pulse but otherwise did not touch or move him. Would it be all right if I sat outside? I am feeling nauseous and lightheaded." Paulina responded to the deputy.

The deputy knew he could do nothing for Dr. Manning so he led Paulina outside. He then walked to his car and called on the radio. He told the dispatcher they did not need the ambulance but to send the coroner and a detective. He sat by Paulina and waited. She had put her head between her legs and took short, shallow breaths. This trick had worked so well for her in the past that she was sure no one would ask her much this afternoon, and they didn't.

Paulina continued to go to Curt Manning's farm each morning to care for his two horses and the chickens. She called his clients and let them know of Dr. Manning's passing. Many had heard about it before she called and had questions about who would care for their animals. Paulina assured each client she could and asked them to allow her to continue as their veterinarian.

Curt's only living family was a younger brother, Chester, who lived in California. He arrived two days after Curt's death to arrange the funeral and settle his estate. Paulina hoped that Chester would sell Raul and her the veterinary practice.

One week after his death, the coroner called and told Paulina that Curt had a heart attack. He was dead before the horse stomped on him. The coroner had asked her about Curt's medication-taking habits. She told him she never saw him take his medications, but she did pick up the refills monthly and often noticed that he had not finished a bottle before a new one was ready.

5

Saturday June 13, 2020

Raul Moore sat in the jail cell and tried not to melt down completely. The FBI agents who arrested him yesterday spoke to him only for cursory inquiries, such as needing to go to the bathroom. He knew he was being held on seven counts of kidnapping and first-degree murder. What he did not know was how much the FBI knew. He also did not know where Paulina was. What he did know and had always believed was that when the shit hit the fan, she would be nowhere near the back spray.

When a guard came by with his breakfast, Raul asked to call his attorney. He knew Mike Davidson from The Club, and the guy was said to be one of the best criminal defense attorneys in the state. Raul told the guard he didn't know the phone number, and he responded they would look it up before he took Raul to make his call. Twenty minutes later, Raul hung up the phone with Mike Davidson. Mike said he would be there as soon as possible and that Raul was not to talk to anyone.

Walking into the interrogation room in handcuffs and ankle shackles, Raul saw Mike Davidson already sitting down. There were two men in suits across the table from him. Raul thought they looked like cliche FBI agents, in shape with short hair and dark suits. Every mystery book he had ever read described FBI agents this way, and the books had gotten it right.

Mike Davidson looked at the FBI agents and motioned at the shackles. "Is that really necessary?" he asked.

Raul sat down next to Mike. The guard who had led him in unlocked his cuffs and the shackles around his ankles before exiting the room.

The older agent responded, “Your client is charged with seven counts of kidnapping and murder. So, yes, it is.”

The agent then looked at Raul and stated, “I am Agent Hollins, and this is Agent Matthews. You have been read your rights and signed off on your understanding. At this time, are you prepared to answer questions?”

Mike Davidson answered for Raul, “My client and I have not had time to confer, so no, he will not be answering questions until we have had a private discussion.”

Hollins and Matthews stood up, and Hollins said, “We will give you time to talk.” Both men walked out of the room.

“Seven counts of kidnapping and first-degree murder. These are serious charges. What is going on, Raul?” Mike Davidson asks after the agents have left.

Raul was unsure where to start and asked, “What evidence do they have?”

Mike responded, “They have not told me specifically, but said they have physical and forensic evidence from your farm. They served a warrant there two days ago and are still gathering evidence. I also need to tell you that they say that Paulina killed herself.”

Raul gasped and asked, “Is it safe for me to talk to you here? Are they listening?”

Mike replied, “It is safe. We have attorney-client privilege, and they will honor that. Now, you need to explain to me what is going on.”

Raul responded, “It started about eight years ago.”

June 2012

Raul opened the door to the house he shared with his wife of ten years, Paulina. He was not sure how they were going to continue to survive. Their daughter’s death a few months ago had thrown Paulina into a downward spiral. Raul was also grieving, but knew they could not stop living. He believed you had to go through the motions daily until you found a new normal. He was worried about Paulina. She had always been so strong and pulled together that he had not expected this reaction.

Their daughter Lynn's death was not unexpected. She contracted influenza, leading to an infection attacking her heart. The weeks she had spent in the cardiac unit were a blur to Raul. He and Paulina had clung to each other the entire time Lynn was ill, but after she died, Paulina pulled inward. She hardly spoke to Raul or anyone else. She did not go to work and often went days without eating or sleeping.

He knew he needed to tell Paulina that the largest client of their veterinary practice was threatening to hire someone else. Raul could not keep up with all the work. They would need to decide whether to let the client go, find someone to hire to help Raul, or if Paulina would return to work. He was unsure what her reaction would be, but hoped she would talk to him about it.

It only took Paulina a day to let him know she would return to work. She reached out to the client and apologized for her absence. They were very understanding and told her they were happy she was returning to work.

6

Saturday June 13, 2020

Agent Robert Matthews walked to the conference room with his partner, Agent Hollins. The jail guard would come and get them when Raul Moore was ready to talk. There are eight portable bulletin boards set up around the room. Seven of the boards contained copies of the information from each binder on a man who was presumably a victim at the farm. The eighth board was information on seven pigs.

During his initial investigation, Matthews had found ten men in Missouri with suspicious disappearances over seven years. He had narrowed it down to the seven men who were represented on the bulletin boards. The CSI technicians continued to gather forensic materials from the Moore's farm. Matching DNA materials of the victims would strengthen the case against the Moores.

He started at the first board and the materials regarding that man. It was the oldest of the cases, Trevor Dawson. He had disappeared seven years ago and was likely Raul Moore's first victim. He was a twenty-nine-year-old single man from Pittsburg, Missouri, who was an avid rower. It was not a sport many in Missouri took part in or knew much about. Trevor's mom had been a college rower and introduced him to the sport. He lived in a small house right on the Pomme de Terre Lake. He rowed every morning before heading to work.

Trevor's employer reported him missing when he failed to show up for work and had not called in. A co-worker had gone to his house and saw that his car was in the driveway, but Trevor did not answer the door. The local sheriff had done a cursory investigation. The report noted that Trevor's boat, a single scull, was missing from the dock. A few days later, the scull was found washed up on the shore a few miles from Trevor's house. The death was ruled an accidental drowning despite never finding his body.

The information from the binder showed pictures of Trevor coming and going to and from his house, rowing on the lake, and working at a local garage door company. He was alone in every picture. The next items from the binder were detailed notes regarding Trevor's whereabouts for the two weeks before his disappearance. Raul Moore had carefully tracked Trevor's movements before abducting him.

Agent Matthews stared at what seemed like a medical intake form. It listed Trevor's physical statistics, followed by his pulse and heart rate, every fifteen minutes for two hours. Then, a red line was drawn, and the words *unsuccessful experiment* typed just below the line. That was the last page of the binder for Trevor. There was no information on how he died or what Raul Moore did with his body after that. Although there was no proof, Matthews was coming to accept that Moore's pigs had eaten the bodies of all of the victims.

October 2012

When he arrived to a home-cooked meal, Raul knew Paulina was up to something. She had made all his favorite foods and bought him a bottle of expensive whiskey. After they ate dinner, Paulina started telling him what she had been doing while he was working since Lynn died. She told him she had begun researching if more could have been done to save their daughter. She explained that she had come to accept that Dr. Hann and the team had done everything they could have for Lynn. The real issue was the lack of organ donors in the United States.

This shortage led Paulina to delve into research regarding whether there were any alternatives to a human heart for transplant. She explained to Raul that in a bizarre coincidence, Dr. Chris Hann's wife, Dr. Helen Hann, was a human biology researcher thirty-plus years ago who had been researching using pig hearts in humans.

Raul found the whole discussion strange, but sat and listened because Paulina had not been this animated about anything in a very long time. She paused and said, "Here is the important part: Dr. Helen Hann abruptly stopped her research before moving into the experimental stage. That is where we are going to pick up."

"What? How are we going to pick it up?" Raul asked in genuine confusion.

Paulina went on to explain that she believed that to honor their daughter Lynn's memory, they needed to be part of solving the issue of the lack of human organ donors. Raul thought at first that he must be a lot more drunk than he had realized. Surely, his wife was not suggesting that they implant pig hearts in humans.

He decided just to ask her what she was suggesting. "So, you are suggesting that we kidnap people? Bring them to a lab of some kind, sedate them, swap out their heart, and see how it goes?"

Paulina nodded her head. She was sure that once they had perfected the technique, they could find a way to bring it to a doctor to do above-board experiments.

"We will not be recognized for our hard work, but knowing that we were fundamental in preventing deaths like Lynns will make it all worth it," Paulina told him in an animated tone.

Shock and disgust were the most prevalent emotions Raul was feeling while staring at his wife. She was asking him to help her experiment with live people. Instead of an emotional reaction, he decided he would try to help her see that what she was proposing was impossible. He asked, "Where do you think we could conduct these experiments?"

Paulina smiled and said, "The basement of our main barn. I have been down there and have cleaned it up. I think we can get that ready as our operating room." She explained how she was sure they could obtain all the needed equipment with no one growing suspicious. She planned to order everything through the veterinary supply company they used regularly.

He was surprised by how thoroughly she had thought this through. Raul asked her, "Where do you suggest we find these test subjects?"

"Well, my thought is that we can look for men who are single, and then I can lure them in, and you can incapacitate them," Paulina replied without hesitation.

Raul got up from the table and walked over to his wife. He kissed her on the top of the head. He thought they needed to find something fun to do as a couple. While it seemed, his wife had thought they should murder people in the name of science as a couple. He walked out of the dining room and upstairs to their room. He hoped that she would have come to her senses by morning. If not, he was going to have to find help for her because, obviously; she was not coping in a healthy way.

7

Saturday June 13, 2020

Paulina stepped off the bus in Chicago. Riding a bus through the night was a new experience for her. Leaving Raul and Missouri behind was easier than she had ever thought. The closed-circuit hidden camera system she had installed years earlier alerted her as soon as the FBI had arrived at the farm two days ago. While Raul attended the conference, Paulina drove back to Springfield and cleared out her safe deposit box and checking account. The bank had been reluctant to give her a cashier's check for the quarter million dollars she had stashed away with them. Ultimately, the bank had no choice and issued her the check. She left with the cashier's check and fifty thousand in cash from the box.

She drove back to Kansas City and sat in the hotel room reading until Raul walked in.

"I never saw you today," he said as the door closed.

Paulina knew he likely looked for her between sessions and at lunch. "I guess we were in different areas, and I came up here at lunchtime and took a quick nap."

Raul expressed concern, "Are you feeling alright? You don't usually nap."

"I am okay. Just tired today," she assured him.

That evening, Paulina and Raul went to dinner with several colleagues. Paulina knew that she needed to act as if nothing was wrong. She would be gone tomorrow and wanted Raul to be taken by surprise. The next morning, Raul headed to breakfast while Paulina was showering. She had been sure to tell him she was not going to breakfast and that he should go without her. After hearing the door close, Paulina stepped out of the shower and wrapped a towel around her.

Paulina got down on the floor and pulled out the bag she had tucked under the bed. She checked that the bag contained everything she needed and left the hotel. As she got in the van, Paulina thought about how prepared she felt for this day. She parked their van by the side of the bridge over the Missouri River. She set the note she had written on the passenger seat.

I am sorry for not stopping Raul. I can no longer go on knowing what he has done. I am ready to join Lynn.
Paulina

Paulina reached inside her bag and took out the burner cell phone and skull cap. She swept her hair under the cap and put on the blond wig and bright green contacts. She applied makeup and took out her new ID and passport from where she had taped them to the bottom of the driver's seat. She looked just like Michelle Brooks, the woman on those documents. Putting on a face mask a few years ago would have raised suspicions, but post-COVID shutdowns, she and other criminals could conceal most of their faces with no one really taking any notice. Paulina left her purse and cell phone behind and walked to a nearby restaurant, where an Uber driver picked her up and took her to the airport. Paulina took a shuttle from the airport to a hotel one block from the bus station. She paid for her bus ticket to Omaha in cash and was on the bus before the FBI even arrived at the convention center. When she arrived in Omaha, she bought a train ticket to Chicago.

Three and half years ago, when Raul had begun to give her reason to doubt him, she realized that she needed a way out. She had gone to see her dad and hired him as her attorney. She never told him what she and Raul were doing, but just that he needed to receive documents from her and keep them under lock and key. He had agreed without asking many questions. It was as if he already knew she was capable of killing. While planning her getaway, she realized that leaving the country without detection was harder than the movies made it seem. She had traded the pain medication Tramadol for a new birth certificate, driver's license, social security number, and passport.

Becoming Michelle Brooks meant that Paulina had the opportunity to reinvent herself. Michelle walked into the Walgreens across from the train station and purchased a prepaid visa card for five hundred dollars. She would pay as much cash as possible, but knew that a hotel would want a credit card. She would apply for a regular credit card when she got to Lake Geneva. She had purchased a condo in that small Wisconsin town, sight unseen, and handled everything over the internet and through her father. The realtor was holding the keys for her.

Michelle had booked an appointment at a salon downtown to get a haircut and color. She walked into the salon as Paulina Moore and felt and looked like a new woman when she walked out. She took the local train to the end of the line, Kenosha, Wisconsin. There were several small car dealers near the train station. She purchased a used Mini Cooper and paid cash. The registration would arrive in the mail at her new address. As far as she was concerned, Paulina Moore died that day.

Monday April 1, 2013

The construction of the operating area had taken them over six months. Raul devised every excuse he could think of to stop the plan, but did not prevail. When he told Paulina that they would not be able to get a full-grown pig or person down to the basement, she once again surprised him with her cunning. She ordered a hydraulic scissor lift. Together, they created a trapdoor in one of the horse stalls and lowered the lift to the basement. Raul had been sure they would kill themselves getting it down there, but they had somehow succeeded. They then covered the trapdoor with hay. The lift had allowed them to get equipment down to the basement and proceed with Paulina's plan.

Kidnapping Trevor Dawson had gone as smoothly as Paulina planned. She had sat on his boat dock in the early morning and waited. When Trevor walked to the dock, he saw her sitting there with her feet in the water. He walked up and said *good morning* as he unlocked his boat. He had his back to Paulina as he bent and lowered the boat into the water. She injected him in the back of the thigh. He collapsed on the dock as he turned around to figure out what had happened. Paulina pulled out the two-way radios and called Raul, saying, “We are ready for you.”

Raul joined Paulina on the dock, and the two of them carried Trevor into his house. While surveilling him, they learned that he left his back sliding door unlocked every morning when rowing. Once inside, Raul backed their van up to the garage door. They carried Trevor out to the back of the van and strapped him down.

Before they had left to get Trevor, Paulina and Raul had brought one of their pigs down to the room. Raul tranquilized the animal and strapped it to an operating table. Now he was strapping Trevor on an adjacent table. Paulina would operate on the pig and remove its heart while Raul anesthetized Trevor. The plan had been that as soon as Trevor was out, Raul would open him up and prepare to remove his heart. This step would need to be simultaneously completed, so that Paulina handed over the pig's heart just as Raul lifted out Trevor’s.

Paulina had bought some used medical textbooks from an estate sale last year, and Raul had studied the information on anesthesia. Of course, none of those books recommended using animal medications or putting a person under in the basement lair of your barn, but it would have to suffice. He had continually tried to get Paulina to admit they did not have the knowledge, skills, or equipment to make this work. She had not wanted to hear any of his objections. Instead, she always seemed to find a solution.

Opening up Trevor’s chest was terrifying for Raul. As he reached inside, he noticed Trevor's heart barely beat. He turned to Paulina, “I need your help here.”

Paulina replied, “I am busy here. What is it?”

By then, Raul knew this was going terribly wrong: “Trevor’s heart stopped beating.”

“WHAT? No! What did you do?” Paulina screamed as she ran over to Trevor.

Raul could not believe that he had just killed a man. "I think it might have been too much anesthesia."

Paulina ripped off her gloves and threw them on the ground. She stormed up the stairs and left Raul to deal with the mess in their lab. Both Trevor and the pig were dead, and the only thing that they had learned was that Raul did not know how to anesthetize a person.

8

Saturday June 13, 2020

Joe Learner had finished his reports for work and turned on the nightly news. After leaving Greatlands Insurance, he took a job as a Property and Casualty Insurance Complaint Investigator for the state of Missouri. He enjoyed his new job and had grown close to his daughter, Claire. Claire had just finished her second year of college. Recently, she had let him know that she would be transferring to Missouri State University so that she could major in forensic science. He knew that not having answers about her mother's disappearance weighed heavily on Claire. On Tuesday, he would help Claire move back to Springfield and into her childhood home. She had spent last summer with him at his house, and maybe he could convince her to live with him while she finished school. Either way, it would be nice to have her close by.

The local news started with the lead story about a local FBI investigation. Joe was shocked when a picture of Raul and Paulina Moore appeared on the screen. Raul was being questioned for kidnappings and murders, and Paulina was missing and presumed dead. Joe immediately thought about his ex-wife, Kelsey, who had never been found. He had worked hard to put being a suspect in her disappearance behind him.

Joe wondered if Kelsey was among Raul Moore's victims. What a strange coincidence that would be. He knew Raul from The Club and had met his wife a few times. He wondered if the police had looked into Raul back when Kelsey disappeared. There was no way that Joe would reach out to the detectives working his ex-wife's case because he couldn't stand them, and he was sure they had similar feelings.

****

Agent Matthews moved on to the next board in the conference room. Rick Pierce had been a twenty-four-year-old competitive swimmer. He lived in an apartment complex with an indoor and outdoor pool. The Moore's pictures showed him swimming early in the morning and late at night. Matthews knew from his research that Rick worked a series of jobs. Rick would often leave a job to compete in swim meets across the country. When he had failed to show up for a meet, someone from the Missouri Valley Masters Swim team had reported Rick's disappearance. His work history was spotty, but he was highly committed to swimming.

There were pictures of Rick's car, closeups of his license plate, and a handwritten note with a four-digit code. Like with Trevor Dawson, there was a medical intake form with all of Rick's vital statistics, including his heart rate, oxygen level, and blood pressure, in fifteen-minute increments until a bold red line was on the page. Once again, there was no indication of how Rick had died or what Raul had done with his body.

September 2013

The next subject she picked seemed much riskier to Raul. In theory, he met all the specifications that they had agreed to. He was single with no children and was often alone. The issue was that Paulina wanted to drive into his gated apartment complex and snatch him as he left the pool. Raul thought the plan brought too much risk of being caught, but Paulina was sure of herself again. When they had pulled it off, he could tell from her Cheshire cat grin all the way back to the farm that she was proud of herself.

Rick Pierce had been walking back to his apartment with his headphones on. He never even turned around when Raul started walking behind him. Raul watched as Paulina walked out from between the two buildings. Rick paused and said something to her. She reached out her hand as if to show him something. He leaned in to look closer, and Paulina jabbed the hypodermic needle into his neck. He started to shout

out, but never got beyond the first part of the sound. Rick crumbled to the ground, and Raul scooped him up under his armpits. The van was fifty feet away, and they had him in the back and secured within a few minutes of the encounter between Rick and Paulina.

The operation on Rick had been more successful than the previous one, but he did not last long after the operation. After Raul had taken care of the disposal, he and Paulina sat down to discuss what improvements they could make. They both knew their biggest issue was the lack of a heart-lung bypass machine. Knowing that obtaining one of these machines would be difficult, they had to figure out what other improvements to their experiments they could implement. Raul had many questions about the interaction of the blood between what was left in the pig's heart and the blood in the human body that they had transplanted it into. When he first brought it up, Paulina seemed to think he was wrong, but a few days later, she brought home books on hematology and transplants.

Between the two of them, over the next six months, they read over two dozen textbooks and medical journal articles on hematology and transplants. They made a plan for the next subject. During the operation, they would extract the pig's heart first, and Paulina would drain it. At the same time, Raul would extract a liter of the subject's blood, and then they would immerse the pig's heart in it. Paulina would manually pump the heart to move the fresh blood through it until it was time to transplant it into the subject.

9

Saturday June 13, 2020

Agent Matthews wondered if Mike Davidson would let Raul Moore talk to them at all. With the evidence they already had from the farm, it did not matter whether Raul Moore confessed. However, Matthews would like to know the reason behind these murders and knew that these men's families would also want that.

He moved to the third board and looked at the images of Brett Ellis. The pictures and documents followed the same pattern as the first two victims. Brett was an amateur astronomer who worked as a retail merchandiser for an outdoor equipment company. Many pictures were taken at night, with Brett alone in a field using a telescope. Agent Matthews wondered how Raul Moore had been able to go unnoticed to take these pictures.

Matthews remembered reading the missing person's report that Brett's ex-wife had filed. Her making the report seemed a little odd until Matthews saw the note that she became concerned when her child support payment did not arrive for the second month in a row. It seemed that Brett had two children, but besides sending a check, he had little involvement with them or his ex-wife. The file noted that the ex-wife had told the investigators that Brett had major depression and often preferred to be alone. The working theory was that Brett had committed suicide, and his body had not yet been discovered.

Matthews contemplated how the Moores had chosen their victims. Would figuring that out help him find their motive, or were they insane enough that there was no motive? Brad Hollins walked up and stood by him.

"What are you searching for?" he asked.

"A motive! In this case, these crimes just do not make any sense to me. Why would the Moores do all this?" Matthews asked as he swept his hands toward the crime boards.

Agent Hollins thought about all they knew so far before he replied. "I have worked some cases over the years in which the motive was never really clear. Unless Raul Moore explains it, this will probably be one of these cases. Want to go do some interviews with me?"

Agent Matthews was surprised, "I thought we were waiting to question Raul Moore."

Hollins replied, "The boss and I talked, and neither of us thinks that Mike Davidson will let his client answer any questions. So, instead of wasting time waiting to be told that he will not talk, I am headed out to see his parents and Paulina's mom. We need to figure out if Paulina is really dead."

"I agree that Raul Moore won't be answering questions, so yeah, I want to do the interviews with you." Robert Matthews replied.

****

Mike Davidson stared at Raul and said, "So, what you are telling me is that you did murder these men."

Raul slowly nodded his head. "I would have done anything for Paulina when Lynn died. Then, I could not stop once it started because she had tapes and pictures. She was clear that she would turn me in and that I had no evidence to prove she was even a part of it."

Mike was shocked by what he heard, but knew he needed to hear the rest. "Okay, go on. After you killed Rick Pierce, what happened?"

March 2014

Raul had given Paulina an ultimatum that he thought would end this madness. He had told her that she either had to get them a heart-lung bypass machine or he would not do another experiment. He never imagined she could get one of the machines, but she had proved him wrong. Three months ago, when she arrived home and asked for help to unload the van, he had no idea what she needed help with. In the back of their veterinary van was a heart-lung bypass machine. Raul stood staring at the machine in stunned silence.

Paulina smiled in a way that could only be described as evil. "I heard what you said and agreed that this was necessary for our success," she said to Raul.

Raul was able to spit out, "But how?"

Her response was, "The dark web." Nothing more

After they unloaded the machine and set it up, they reviewed the list of possible next subjects. Paulina had never stopped looking for the next man. They agreed on Brett Ellis and followed the man for several weeks. It was clear that they would need to grab him at night when he was stargazing. Luckily for them, he was a creature of habit, so they knew where he would be and when.

Raul watched through the night vision goggles as Brett set up his tent and telescope. He knew that Brett would spend the entire weekend camping and stargazing. The woods belonged to an acquaintance of Brett's who did not mind him camping out there as long as he left nothing behind when he left. Brett parked on the road and hiked in with his gear each weekend. Raul parked right behind him on the unmarked farm road.

The two of them approached the man as quietly as possible. Unlike their previous study participants, Paulina would likely not be able to get close enough to Brett to inject him with a hypodermic needle. She had gotten a taser for this procurement. She had explained to Raul that with a Taser gun, she only needed to get within twenty feet of a person to tase them. Raul thought that was still too close, but Paulina was sure of her ability to sneak up on someone. The plan was to zap Brett and then tranquilize him before he regained control of his faculties, and they had done just that.

After securing the man in the back of their van, they packed all his gear into his trunk. Raul watched as Paulina drove Brett's car away. She had told him that she knew where to take the car and that she had a way back to the farm, so he was not to worry about her. It had gotten to the point where he'd no longer questioned her seedy, criminal ties. Raul got Brett into the lab and secured him to the exam table. He hooked Brett up to the monitors and started an IV while waiting for Paulina to return. Before leaving to get Brett, they had prepared the pig, which lay sedated on the adjacent operating table.

The time waiting for Paulina to return wore on Raul's resolve. He needed to put a stop to this, but he was not sure how. Obviously, Paulina was extremely committed to the plan, and reasoning with her would do him no good. He thought about going to her dad, Shawn Ross, and telling him what was happening. The man was a high-powered defense attorney in St. Louis, but he was unsure that Shawn Ross would be willing to help Raul. Yes, he would help Paulina in any way he could, but that help could be having her turn Raul in and implicate him in the murders. Maybe he needed to hire an attorney of his own.

Paulina walked into the lab as Raul sat with his melancholy. She did not seem to sense, or at least did not comment on, her husband's despondency. "Shall we begin?" was all she said to him.

Raul nodded and got up from his chair. He had been shocked to find as much information as he had on the internet about operating the bypass machine. When Paulina had brought the machine back to the farm, he had asked her if she knew how to operate it. She chuckled and said that a manual wasn't included in the purchase and then suggested that he go to an internet cafe or public library and do some research. He had done just that, sitting at an internet cafe reading the intricacies of the machine.

He was pleased with himself for having successfully hooked Brett up to the machine and getting it running. Paulina walked over and peered down at Brett. She then went back to the pig and extracted its heart. She drained the heart of its blood and manually pumped it in the basin of

Brett’s blood the entire time Raul worked on opening up Brett. When Raul told her he was ready, she walked over with the pig's heart. He had left the back half of both upper chambers in place. She laid the heart on the man's chest, and Raul handed her the man's partial heart. He then took the pig's heart and carefully sewed the front half of the pig’s donor heart to the back half of the old heart. Raul disconnected the heart-lung bypass machine and watched in utter astonishment as the pig's heart began to beat.

Brett lived for almost two days, and Paulina was ecstatic at the results. Of course, once the man had passed, she was not part of the disposal or cleanup, but her happiness was the fuel Raul needed to recommit to her plan

10

Saturday June 13, 2020

Agents Hollins and Matthews went to see Paulina's mother first. No one official had talked to her yet, and they would need to tell of her daughter's apparent suicide. Matthews hated notifying families of deaths, and this would be worse than usual because they were unsure of Paulina's involvement in the seven murders or even if she was dead. The street was quiet, so the press had yet to connect the raid with Heather Ross.

Before they could even ring the doorbell, Paulina's mom, Heather Ross, opened it. She said, "Is my daughter dead?"

Matthews and Hollins were both taken aback; however, Hollins quickly replied, "I am Agent Hollins, and this is Agent Matthews. We are with the FBI and need to talk to you about your daughter and son-in-law."

Ms. Ross opened the door and let the agents step into her home. It was a tidy, nineteen-sixties ranch-style home with pictures of Paulina, Raul, and their daughter Lynn everywhere. "What is going on? Paulina calls me daily, and I have not heard from her in two days. I know something is very wrong." Heather said in a rapid-fire manner to the agents.

Agent Hollins replied, "On Monday, the FBI raided your daughter and son-in-law's farm. Since then, we have arrested your son-in-law Raul, but have been unable to locate your daughter."

Heather looked incredulously at the agents, "What reason would you have for raiding their farm? Is it because they know Donald Trump is the true and real president?"

Matthews almost chuckled out loud; it seemed that Paulina's mom might be just as whacky as her daughter and son-in-law. He replied, "No, ma'am, the raid and subsequent arrest are connected to seven murders."

"Murder? Are you trying to say that Paulina and Raul murdered seven people? Neither of them will even eat meat because they think it is unkind to animals. Who in the world would those two murder?" Heather Ross asked.

Agent Hollins replied, "I don't know anything about their dietary habits. However, we have overwhelming evidence that seven murders happened on their farm. Additionally, there is reason to believe that your daughter has committed suicide."

At that point, Heather Ross began to laugh.

"Care to fill us in on what you find amusing?" Agent Hollins stated.

Heather looked at the agents and said, "It is clear to me that you have never met or talked to my daughter. Paulina was diagnosed with Narcissistic Personality when she was twelve years old. She loves herself. I am pretty sure that she has never loved anyone else besides her daughter, Lynn. Also, her IQ was measured off the charts. She was admitted to Mensa at fourteen. People like her do NOT commit suicide."

Agent Hollins had written down everything that Heather Ross had said. When she finished speaking, he asked, "Do you think your daughter is capable of murder?"

Heather responded, "In the right circumstance, I think all of us are capable of murder. I am done talking to the two of you and would appreciate it if you would leave."

May 2016

Paulina had been so pleased with their small success with the last subject that it had been difficult for Raul to get her to be slow and methodical as they had with each previous selection. Raul had considered Heather Ross falling and breaking her hip six months after Brett Ellis' death to have been a blessing. Not that he wanted his mother-in-law to be hurt but because it had derailed Paulina's murderous rampage for a while. His wife had been so busy taking care of Heather and shuffling her to appointments, that there simply was no time for her to hunt. Once Heather was recovered, it had taken over a year to find and then do enough reconnaissance to be sure they had a viable candidate. He was much older than any of their previous participants which Paulina thought this was positive, as he was much closer to the average age of heart transplant recipients.

Just as they were ready to procure George Jeffers, he left on a trip with his girlfriend. Paulina was livid, but Raul convinced her to wait to see how long he stayed away before looking for an alternative subject. George returned six weeks ago and went right back to his normal routine. They had been able to take him while he was at his favorite fishing spot. Paulina had decided that they would leave his car and personal belongings behind. She had thrown his fishing pole into Perche Creek before returning to the van.

It was not until Raul prepared George Jeffers for surgery that they realized he had a pacemaker. George Jeffers was not the ideal candidate they had planned for. Paulina seemed to think proceeding was fine, since someone like George would likely be a heart transplant candidate. Raul worried about what kind of medication the man might be on and how they might affect the operation. Of course, they did proceed because that is what Paulina wanted.

As Raul connected the pig's heart to the portion of George's heart that was left intact, blood began to seep from everywhere. Raul did not know what to do and called Paulina over for assistance. He watched in horror as more and more of George Jeffers' blood flowed out of the incisions he had made. They could never disconnect George from the bypass machine, so his new heart never took a beat.

11

Saturday June 13, 2020

After leaving the home of Heather Ross, Agents Hollins and Matthews drove towards Raul Moore's parents' home. The drive to Joplin, Missouri, would take them just over an hour.

Matthews asked Hollins, "What do you think we learned from Heather Ross?"

"Well, I think first we learned that Heather Ross is not stable, but more importantly, she divulged Paulina's mental health history. We now know that at least at one point, Paulina saw a psychiatrist and that mental health professional diagnosed her with narcissistic personality disorder. That let us know that we need to try to get a warrant for her medical and psychiatric records. Without her mother's comments, that is not something that I would have pursued." Hollins stated.

Matthews nodded and added, "Also, her mother was convinced that Paulina would never commit suicide. My mom always tells me that a mother knows things about her children that defy explanation. A kind of intuition or sixth sense that is part of the bond that forms between mother and child."

Agent Hollins chuckled and added, "My mom would agree with yours. When I got shot a few years ago, my mom called my cell phone to check on me before the ambulance even got me to the hospital. I think we agree that, at this point, we do not believe that Paulina Moore is dead. After we talk to Raul's parents, I will call the Fugitive Apprehension Task Force lead and let them know what Heather Ross had to say."

Raul had grown up in Joplin, and his parents still lived in the home they raised him in. His parents owned a chain of fast-food franchises, and they both continued to work in them. As far as the agents knew, no one had officially talked to them. However, there had been a news report on the raid on the farm and the arrest of Raul, so members of the press may have contacted them.

When they arrived at the Moore's home, it was clear that the press had found them. The local police had placed barricades on the street, and news vans sat at them, waiting for a chance to see the Moores. Hollins and Matthews showed their badges to the officer and were allowed through. As they approached the Moores' home, they saw someone pull back the curtain and then drop it. Hollins rang the doorbell, and a woman opened the door.

Agent Hollins showed her his badge and said, "Hello, I am FBI Agent Brad Hollins, and this is Agent Robert Matthews. We are here to speak to you and your husband about Raul and Paulina."

The woman gestured for them to enter and stepped aside. The agents followed her into the living room. Troy Moore stood in the room and walked up to the agents. He said, "We have been wondering when you would show up. What we are hearing on the news is utterly ridiculous."

Camilla Moore added, "Please sit and tell us how we can help clear this up. Raul is a good man and has been through so much heartache."

"The news said that Raul was being charged with multiple counts of murder. Is that true?" Troy Moore replied.

"Raul is the prime suspect in seven kidnappings and murders. He is being held in Springfield." Matthews told them.

Troy Moore inquired, "What possible evidence do you have to suspect my son? He is a pacifist and a vegetarian. Does that sound like a murderer to you?"

"We are not at liberty to discuss the case or the evidence. We would like to know more about Raul. Mrs. Moore, you said that he had been through so much heartache. What are you referring to?" Agent Hollins asked.

Camilla Moore's eyes filled with tears, "When Lynn died, it was hard on all of us, but it sent Raul back to a dark place. He loved that little girl so much, and when she was alive, he was back to his laughing, optimistic self. You see, when his girlfriend, Shelby, died in college, his entire personality changed. We had not seen the Raul we knew and loved for many years until Lynn was born. Both he and Paulina were so in love with that little girl."

Troy Moore took over talking when his wife began to cry quietly. "Lynn was everything you could ask for in a child. As a baby, she rarely cried and blossomed into a sweet, intelligent little girl. Her death was so unexpected. I think that is why it was so hard on Raul. He lost two people that he loved in unexpected and uncommon ways."

Agents Matthews and Hollins looked at each other. They knew about Lynn Moore's death eight years earlier, but this was the first they had heard of Shelby or her untimely death. Agent Hollins asked, "Would you please tell us more about Shelby and her death?"

Camilla had stopped crying and replied, "Raul and Shelby had been friends since the second grade when Shelby and her folks moved here. They started dating in high school, and I am sure they planned to marry right after college. They were both attending Mizzou when Shelby somehow fell out of her dorm window and died on impact. For a few months, we were not sure that Raul would stay at Mizzou and continue his education, but he did."

Troy added, "It helped that he had Paulina. They leaned on each other."

"So, Raul and Paulina were already friends when Shelby died?" Agent Matthews asked.

"I would not say they were friends before Shelby's death. Paulina was Shelby's roommate, and the two girls were friends." Troy Moore informed them.

Agent Hollins replied, "Okay, thank you for that background. We have a few other questions as well. How often do you talk to and see your son and daughter-in-law?"

Camilla looked like she might cry again, "Throughout college and while Lynn was alive, we talked to our son several times a week. They would come to visit every few weeks, or we would go to see them. But since Lynn died, we rarely see them. Raul asked us not to visit them. He said they needed time and space to grieve and that he would let us know when they were ready for company. He visits us maybe once a year and calls about once a month."

Hollins asked, "How would you describe Raul and Paulina's relationship?"

Troy replied, "Cold. Paulina was so different from Shelby. Shelby was warm and affectionate and brought out the best in others. The first time Raul brought Paulina home, I remember thinking she was so beautiful, but cold. In all the years that they dated and have been married, I never saw the two of them be affectionate towards each other."

Camilla nodded and added, "I agree that woman is not who I would have imagined Raul with. She was different when Lynn was alive, but returned to her cold, indifferent self after Lynn's death. If anything, she went from being cold to being frigid. I have described her as an ice queen many times over the years. If anyone killed people, it was her!"

Agents Hollins and Matthews had no other questions. The Moores wanted to know when they could see their son. Agent Hollins said, "In a few days from now, there should be a hearing. You would be able to see him in the courtroom. We appreciate your time, and if you can think of anything else, please do not hesitate to contact one of us."

As the two agents drove back towards Springfield, Matthews pulled out his agency-issued tablet and looked up Shelby Lansing. As they drove, he filled his partner in on what he could find on her death, which was not much.

Friday May 6, 2016

Raul stood in the middle of the wooded lot. Today marked nineteen years since Shelby died; this was how he marked the anniversary every year. This place was where he felt closest to her. He missed her every day. Moving on had never been easy, but while Lynn was alive, he had been able to put Shelby in the back of his mind. Since Lynn's death, either Shelby or Lynn or both had been at the forefront of his mind almost all the time. He had been creating stories in his mind about what his life would have been like if either of them had lived.

He knew that if Shelby had lived, Lynn would never have been born, and that had been the salve for his wounds while Lynn was alive. Now that he had lost both of the women he loved and descended into the madness that was Paulina's deadly scheme, he was sure that he had lost all that was good in the world.

Coming here today, he had planned to end his life, but he was not strong enough to do it. Sitting on the fallen tree, he thought about his life since Lynn died. He had stopped talking to and seeing his parents regularly, and his relationship with Paulina had returned to how it was before Lynn was born. His wandering mind screeched to a halt; no, his relationship with Paulina was not how it used to be because now they were killing people, and that was the only time Paulina seemed happy. At least before Lynn was born, their relationship had often felt like a business partnership. The consolation, looking back, was that the business they were partners in before had not been deadly.

Raul thought back to college when he had clung to Paulina after Shelby's death. She had been a rock for him and helped him through the worst of his grief. He remembered the night after finishing their first semester of veterinary school, Paulina kissed him. He was shocked, and she apologized profusely. Up until that point, he had not thought of her as anything more than a friend. Yes, she was attractive, but that part of him seemed to have died with Shelby.

He had not slept much the night that Paulina first kissed him. In the morning, he found Paulina sitting in the quad, drinking a cup of coffee. This time, he kissed her. He told her that he was ready to start really living again. During their first few years together, Paulina was attentive and loving. After they married, it was as if a switch flipped, and the cold, distant Paulina appeared. Back then, he chalked it up to starting their professional careers and then their own practice. Every time Raul got close to ending the relationship, he would get a glimmer of the old Paulina. She would cook dinner or buy him a present, or they would have sex, and Raul would hope that the relationship was back on track.

When Paulina told him she was pregnant, he felt unbridled joy. The first year with Lynn was a blur, as it is for most parents, but Raul clearly remembered that the invisible switch seemed to have flipped again. Paulina was once again loving and attentive not only to Lynn but also to him. Lynn had brought sunshine back into their lives. He had never paused even to consider that she would be gone so quickly. But she was gone, and now he was left with the worst version of Paulina. Not only cold and distant, but murderous as well.

12

Saturday June 13, 2020

Mike Davidson was in shock. For hours, Raul had been confessing what he and Paulina had been doing the last few years. If someone had asked Mike before today who at The Club, he thought was capable of murder, Raul Moore would not have even been a consideration. Mike knew that he needed to know everything, but he did not need to know it tonight.

"Raul, I think we should pause for now, and I will return in the morning. You can finish telling me what has been going on, and we can decide how to proceed. Is that all right with you?" Mike asked.

Raul nodded his head. The man had the most tired and defeated look, but underneath, there seemed to be an air of relief. As Raul was led out of the room, Mike wondered if his client was actually happy to have been caught and stopped. He also wondered if Paulina was really dead.

Mike walked to his car and drove straight home. He often worked at his office until the early morning hours, but tonight, he needed to head home. He needed a shower and a drink. Then he would watch the boxing match he had on his DVR and try not to think of the horrors that Raul Moore had described. His wife, Annie was a teacher on summer break. She was off on a girl's weekend with her best friend, Jo Beth. Tonight, he was glad to not have to tell Annie about his day.

****

When Matthew and Hollins arrived at the FBI field office, they were informed that Raul had been returned to his cell at the Greene County

Jail and that Mike Davidson would return in the morning to continue talking with his client.

"I think we should call it a day. Hopefully, the CSI team will finish their first sweep of the Moore's farm tomorrow. We might even get a crack at talking with the good Doctor Moore," Agent Hollins said to Matthews.

Matthews responded, "Sounds good to me. I want to see Raul Moore's reaction when we tell him about his wife's supposed suicide and her note."

Agent Hollins said, "Yeah, that will be interesting. It will be hard to convince me that the woman killed herself until I see her body."

Matthews and Hollins walked out of the field office together. Matthews thought the other thing they would need to decide tomorrow was who would make the death notifications to the seven families. If he was going to get any sleep tonight, he needed to put that out of his mind. Death notifications were the worst part of the job.

He looked at the last text Kass had sent him. He wondered if the stars would ever align for them to have time off at the same time so that they could spend time together.

He sent a quick text back to her: Are you busy?

Kass replied quickly: No. What's up?

Preferring to talk over texting, Robert hit the button to call her.

"Hi. This is a pleasant surprise. I would have thought you would be knee-deep in the case against the pig farmers." Kass said in a light-hearted manner.

Robert chuckled, "Oh, we are knee deep, but called it quits for the night, and I wanted to hear a friendly voice. Also, I have a question for you."

"I am glad you consider me friendly. What is the question?" Kass inquired.

"My cousin is getting married in three months, and it would be great if I did not show up alone. No pressure, but would you be willing to be my date?" Robert asked before he lost the nerve. He knew that if he brought a date, his mom and aunts would be ecstatic, and they would not try to play matchmaker with all of the single women at the wedding.

Kass responded, “I would love to go. Text me the information, and I will put in for the weekend off. Where is the wedding?”

Robert was pleased she agreed. It would be great to spend the weekend with her and to show up with a beautiful woman by his side. “Lake of the Ozarks. I will send the wedding website to you, too. We can pick which hotel to stay at, and I will reserve a room for each of us. My treat.”

“I will call you next week, and we can work out the details, or maybe we will run into each other at the gym,” Kass replied.

“I look forward to it. Have a great night.” Robert said, as he wondered if the weekend at his cousin's wedding was just what he and Kass needed to solidify their relationship.

Friday May 6, 2016

Paulina stared at the dot on the map on her laptop. Why was Raul out in the countryside? She had installed the GPS tracker on the van months ago to be sure Raul was not betraying her. He had been very distant from her lately. She liked it when the dynamic of their relationship was Raul acting clingy and needy and her being cold and distant. That was the norm for their relationship, and that norm was what she wanted.

She typed the GPS coordinates into a different map and zoomed in. Sure enough, there was nothing there but woods. Paulina logged into the county records site to see if she could figure out if anything was out there, but the records were not listed by GPS coordinates. She would need a physical address, and it did not seem like the woods would have that. Wanting to know what Raul had to say about his whereabouts drove her to text him.

Writing the text was harder than she thought it should be. She had to be careful not to come off like she suspected something, and since she rarely texted him, the text alone may seem that way no matter what she wrote. She settled on: Can you go to the Johnson farm appointment? I am running behind today.

The message was marked delivered; Paulina waited to see it change to read and for Raul to answer her. She tried to distract herself with the bookkeeping, but kept checking her phone and the GPS locator. She would need to head to the Johnson farm, since Raul had not yet answered her. She would indeed be late for this appointment, so she texted the client quickly.

As she pulled into the Johnson farm, her phone buzzed. It had been nearly an hour since she had texted Raul. His text read: Sorry, I left my phone in the van. Do you still need me to go to the Johnsons?

Paulina was fuming. What the hell had he been doing this whole time? Her response was a single word: NO!

Raul would pay for this. He knew that she hated secrets. Well, at least secrets that were not hers.

Saturday May 7, 2016

Paulina drove out to the location and parked her truck. She looked around and then got out. There was a small path that looked like someone had recently walked down it. She followed the path to a clearing. There was a fallen tree on one edge, and Paulina could see a section of grass in front of it that was crushed down. She walked over and sat down. Sitting here gave her no real answers, just more questions. Why would Raul have driven out here and sat for almost two hours? How had he even known about this place?

Paulina walked back to her truck and took out her notepad. She wrote a single word on the center of the page: *PAYBACK!* Walking back to the clearing, she searched for a place to put her note. It needed to be visible enough to be found, but not exposed to the elements enough to be destroyed. Paulina began to pick up rocks. She set the note down in the center of the trampled grass and neatly piled the rocks on top. She was sure that would not go unnoticed.

13

Sunday June 14, 2020

Agent Matthews walked into Hollins' office to discuss what they would do while Raul Moore continued to talk to his lawyer. Matthews thought they should start looking further into Paulina. He was unsure what Hollins was thinking. He knew the Fugitive Apprehension Task Force was still trying to confirm her suicide, but Matthews wanted to follow up on what she had been doing in the days leading up to her disappearance.

Agent Hollins was on the phone when Matthews knocked, but motioned for him to come into the office and close the door. He concluded his phone conversation by saying, "All right, sir, we will see you in about three and a half hours." He turned to Matthews and stated, "We are headed to see Paulina's dad, Shawn Ross, in St. Louis."

"Okay, what do we hope to learn?" Matthews asked.

Hollins said, "I am not sure. Before I called him, I thought we should talk to him like we did to her mom and Raul's parents. But when I called him this morning, Mr. Ross informed me that besides being Paulina's father, he is her attorney and has a file to give us."

Matthews asked, "What kind of file?".

"Mr. Ross said it was a sealed envelope that his daughter gave him with specific instructions never to open it and to give it to the police if they ever came looking for her," Hollins replied.

On the drive to St. Louis, Matthews reviewed the case with Hollins. They began a timeline of the murders and compiled a list of everything they knew for sure. Hollins agreed with Matthews that after talking to

Shawn Ross, they needed to check in with the Fugitive Apprehension Task Force to find out where the search for Paulina Moore stood.

The offices of Shawn Ross Esquire and Associates were in an upscale office building downtown. Agent Hollins griped that the agency would likely not repay him for the parking fee. The offices were surprisingly busy for a Sunday. Shawn Ross's secretary greeted them when they arrived. She told the agents that he was waiting for them and showed them to his office.

Shawn Ross stood and shook both of the agents' hands. "My daughter came to see me about three and half years ago. She hired me to be her attorney, and at that time, she gave me a sealed envelope and asked me to keep it for her. I tried to get her to tell me what was happening, and she repeatedly told me that *every marriage has secrets.* I knew I shouldn't have, but I left it at that."

Agent Hollins, "Okay, so is that the envelope you told me about on the phone?"

Mr. Ross replied, "Well, yes and no. Every six months, Paulina would come to see me, take the envelope I had, and put it into a bigger one. She made me swear that I would never open the envelope, and I never have."

He then picked up a large manila envelope with writing on the front. The label said, *Property of Paulina Moore. To be opened only by the police if I am missing or dead.* "My ex-wife called me last night to say that you had visited her and told her that Paulina may have killed herself. I was expecting your call, but had you not called me this morning, I would have reached out to you to hand over the envelope."

Agent Matthews said, "Thank you for the envelope. Please tell us about your relationship with your daughter."

"One of my only regrets in life is that when I left her mother, I did not stay involved with Paulina. I do not have a father-daughter relationship with her, and so on the occasions when she has reached out for my help, I always tried to be there for her." Shawn Ross sounded genuinely sad as he talked about Paulina.

Matthews looked at Hollins and then asked, “Occasions? Are you talking about when she came to give you the envelopes?”

Shawn Ross nodded and said, “Yes, and one time during college when police questioned her. Although, I think the university called me and not her that time.”

“Why did the police question her in college?” Agen Hollins asked.

Shawn sat quietly, looking like he was searching his memory, and said, “Hold on, let me grab my file on Paulina.”

After he left the room, Matthews asked Hollins, “What kind of father keeps a file on his daughter?”

Hollins chuckled and said, “The kind who is a criminal defense attorney first and a father second.”

Shawn Ross walked back into the office, reading a slim folder. “Yes, it was the college that called me. Paulina’s roommate died in an accident, and Paulina was taken to the hospital. That was the reason they called. When I arrived, I discovered that Paulina was not hurt, just upset over her roommate, and that the police wanted to question my daughter regarding the accident. I stayed and accompanied Paulina to the police interview. The case was ruled an accident, and I did not hear from Paulina again until three and half years ago.”

Matthews asked Shawn, “The roommate's name was Shelby Lansing; is that correct?”

“Yes, that was the girl's name,” Shawn Ross replied.

Hollins thanked Shawn Ross for the envelopes and for talking to them and said, “If you think of anything else, please let us know.”

****

Shawn Ross walked the agents out and returned to his desk. He then took another file about his daughter from his locked desk drawer. This file concerned her recent purchase of a condo in Lake Geneva. A condo she purchased in cash and in the name of Michelle Brooks. He was glad that Paulina had been paying him a retainer. As her attorney, he could not be compelled to testify or be legally required to tell the FBI privileged information about a client as long as they couldn’t prove someone's life was in imminent danger. Never the less, he would burn his file tonight in his backyard firepit.

****

Mike Davidson walked slowly towards the Greene County jail. He knew he needed to finish hearing what his client, Raul Moore, had to say, but the thought of sitting and listening to more horrors filled him with dread. When he decided to be a criminal defense attorney, he knew he would represent some people who were actually guilty, but never had he imagined he would represent a serial killer.

Mike watched as Raul was escorted into the conference room. He wondered if Raul had slept at all last night. Mike took a deep breath and said, "Raul, I need you to finish telling me about what happened at your farm. Then we will need to talk about your case."

Raul nodded and then stared at the wall as he recounted the next killing.

July 2016

One of the reasons their plan had gone so well thus far was that they picked people who were creatures of habit. That was certainly the case when it came to Pete Taylor. He hiked every weekend no matter the weather, and his brother Todd joined him only when the weather was nice. So that Saturday morning, when they woke to drizzle, Paulina declared it was time to pick up Pete.

Whenever Pete hiked alone, he came to the same trail, so they knew that was where they needed to head. Raul let Paulina off at the trailhead and then went and parked a half mile away. They would once again use their walkie-talkies to communicate. Raul watched as Pete Taylor drove by. Ten minutes later, Paulina's voice came over the walkie-talkie, telling him they were ready to be picked up.

Driving back to the parking lot for the trailhead, he wondered what Paulina would do if he never showed up. Instead, he parked the van, unloaded the dolly from the back of it, and carried it up the trail. He was glad that Paulina had intercepted Pete close to the start of the trail.

Together, they rolled Pete onto the dolly and strapped him on. Paulina ran ahead to be sure that no one had arrived. There would be no good explanation for why an unconscious man was strapped to a dolly. The area was deserted, likely because of the rain, so things had gone just as Paulina planned.

As they drove back to the farm, Paulina delighted in telling Raul how she had outwitted Pete. She waited until he pulled into the parking lot and ran up the trail a little way. She ensured she was out of view of the parking lot and then laid down on the ground. As Pete Taylor rounded the bend in the trail, he spotted her on the ground and rushed up. When he bent down to lend aid to her, she injected the hypodermic needle right into his jugular vein. He fell on top of her, and she had to wiggle her way out. Raul was horrified by the delight he heard in Paulina's voice as she retold the event. He could not fathom how his wife enjoyed what they did so much.

The operation on Pete Taylor seemed doomed from the beginning. Raul had difficulty getting his IV started, and the man's pulse and blood pressure were very low from the start. Raul thought he had Pete properly anesthetized, but then, as Raul started the first incision, Pete sat up and screamed. Paulina began yelling at Raul as he struggled to get Pete Taylor strapped back down; she walked over and injected Pete with the tranquilizer again. Raul watched in horror as Pete Taylor's monitor flatlined. Paulina immediately left the operating room, and Raul cleaned up the mess he had made. The whiskey he was drinking had helped to numb him to the reality of what they were doing. Unfortunately, he knew that despite two failures in a row, he would never convince Paulina to abandon this maniacal plan.

14

Sunday June 14, 2020

Michelle sat at the computer station of the Lake Geneva library. She had chatted with the librarian at the service desk, who had helped her to register for the library card. In Michelle's opinion, the librarian had been overly friendly and nosey, but to not be rude, she had answered her questions. Telling her she had moved to the area a few days ago to start fresh after her husband's death. Once again, the ability to wear a face mask was in her favor. Along with the short blond hair and bright green eyes, her resemblance to Paulina Moore was not evident.

Today's goal was to check news stories to discover what was being reported about the FBI raid. She figured by now it was national news. Sure enough, every major news source had a story about the serial murders in Missouri. They all seemed to have the same basic information: the FBI and local law enforcement agencies had raided a farm, one of the farm owners was being held for questioning, and the other had apparently committed suicide. The stories noted that the FBI was not commenting on the investigation at the time, nor were they willing to say how many victims had been identified. Michelle clicked on and read several unrelated news stories, so her search history varied.

Michelle closed the browser and logged off the computer. She had not and would not be getting any internet-capable devices, so she would come to the library whenever she wanted to access the internet. She needed to have as small a digital footprint as possible. Michelle walked to the library's nonfiction section and browsed books on different hobbies. She was already growing restless and knew she needed to find something to occupy her mind. Eventually, she might need to find work, and working as a veterinarian was impossible, but for now, she planned to lie low and watch the events unfold in Missouri. She also needed to find a plastic surgeon and have a little work done. If anyone started looking for her, she needed to have had her face altered enough to throw facial recognition software off.

****

Agents Hollins and Matthews agreed they should go to the St. Louis field office to open the envelope they had received from Shawn Ross. Following FBI procedure, they photographed and documented each step they took. They noted that the envelope seal had Paulina Moore's signature and a date on it, so they used a letter opener to split the envelope open on the top. Once they opened the large envelope, a packet of pictures and documents came out along with a slightly smaller envelope. This envelope also had Paulina Moore's signature and a date over the seal.

Hollins looked at Matthews and said, "Well, do you want to look at this pile first or open the next envelope and see what is in it?"

Matthews was unsure what they were getting into, but thought opening the second envelope before looking at the materials was a logical way to proceed. He replied, "How about we open the second envelope, make a separate pile of whatever is in it, and then look at all we have?"

Hollins nodded and said, "Sounds like a plan," and proceeded to open the second envelope. Like the first, this envelope contained a bundle of pictures and documents and a slightly smaller envelope.

"I say keep going," Matthews said to Agent Hollins

Hollins continued to open envelopes and find the same contents until he had opened seven in total. Each envelope was dated about six months apart, and the smallest envelope was the only one without another envelope inside of it. The last envelope had a handwritten note in it.

Matthews picked up the note and read it aloud.

"I am writing this letter and enclosing pictures and documentation to prove that I am not making up a story. When our daughter Lynn died, it was like a switch flipped in my husband, Raul Moore. He became cold and violent. I was unaware of what he was doing until recently, when I stumbled upon his hidden rooms. I confronted Raul, who told me he was doing everything he could to ensure no child died like Lynn did. I have taken pictures of what I found. I know I should go to the police with this evidence, but I can't imagine losing Raul. I will do everything possible to stop him from hurting anyone else. -Paulina Moore."

Matthews set the note down on the table, and Hollins spread the pictures out on the table next to the note and envelope. The pictures showed Raul Moore dismembering a human body and feeding the Moore's pigs. The agents were shocked at the level of violence and depravity that Paulina Moore had captured in pictures.

Agent Hollins looked up, took a deep breath, and said, “I think the next best step is to pack all this up and take it back to Springfield. We should try to match up the dates of these envelopes with the murder boards, and I want to get forensics started on a few things.”

Matthews slowly gathered each piece of evidence from the first envelope and put it carefully into a clear evidence bag. He then put each of the remaining six envelopes and their contents into individual clear evidence bags.

The two agents were silent on their three-and-a-half-hour journey back. When they had headed to St. Louis this morning, neither could have imagined the Pandora's box that they would be opening.

****

Mike stared at Raul and said, “So, what I think you are trying to tell me is that even though you physically committed the murders, Paulina was just as culpable in the crimes,”

Raul looked up at him, gave the slightest nod, and added, “I am willing to accept the punishment that I have coming to me, but I want to be sure that people know I did not do this alone. Furthermore, unless the police or the FBI can show me Paulina's dead body, I will never believe she killed herself. I am sure this was her contingency plan all along. Be prepared for the pictures and recording she showed me to make their way to the FBI."

Mike Davidson was unsure he could be taken by surprise at this point, but he was glad to have a client laying out all his cards. He tried to sound empathetic as he spoke to Raul, "We will deal with that if and when it happens. You have told me about five men that Paulina and you murdered, but the FBI is saying at least seven. Are there more?"

"Yes, there were two more men that we kidnapped and killed. The next one was a young man named Cory Pratt."

October 2016

Paulina wasted no time in finding their next test subject. She had told Raul that she wanted to get their plan back on track and that failure was not an option. Raul had thought but not commented that, *very obviously, failure was an option, since they had failed with the last two men.*

As Cory Pratt set off on his run, Raul used the walkie-talkie to let Paulina know he was on his way. Their van was parked on the side of the road across from the parking lot for the path. As he stretched and prepared for his run, Cory never glanced at Raul or the van. After Cory took off running, Raul backed up beside his car and waited for Paulina and Cory to return.

Paulina was waiting about an eighth of a mile down the trail. She had strung a fishing line across the trail at ankle height. Cory was running full speed when he hit the line. He catapulted forward and put his hands out to try to stop his fall, breaking both his wrists in the process. As soon as she heard the crash, Paulina came walking from the other direction and feigned shock and concern. She helped Cory first to sit up and then to stand. Together, they walked slowly toward the parking lot.

Paulina chatted with Cory and told him her husband should be waiting for her in the parking lot. She told him that she had been dropped off earlier so she could walk while he went to see his mother. She offered to drive him to the emergency room. He was agreeable to this plan as he knew there was no way he could drive himself and did not want the expense or hassle of having an ambulance come.

As they arrived at the parking lot, they spotted Raul sitting on the van's bumper with both doors open. Paulina led Cory towards the van, and as he approached, she injected him in the neck with the tranquilizer. Once again, Cory Pratt fell forward; however, this time, Raul caught him and pulled him into the van.

There were no surprises with Cory's operation, and they were able to transplant the pig's heart and remove him from the bypass machine. Cory seemed to be doing all right until the third day, when all his organs seemed to fail at once. One minute, the monitor looked like his body was starting to recover from the transplant, and the next, all the alarms were going off. Paulina was not home when Cory died, and Raul was not sure which he dreaded more, the chore of disposing of Cory's body or telling Paulina what had happened.

15

Sunday June 14, 2020

Agent Hollins had called ahead, so the forensics team awaited them when they arrived. Copies of all the documents and Polaroid pictures were made. The originals were sent to be analyzed for fingerprints and DNA. It would be essential when the case went to court to be able to establish that Paulina Moore was indeed the author of the documents, as well as the authenticity of the pictures.

Now that the forensics team was done, it was time for Agents Hollins and Matthews to look through the contents of the envelopes. They started with the small first envelope again. Based on the dates, they matched up the document and pictures that pertained to the murder of Cory Pratt, but something was off. As Matthews studied the pictures of Cory Pratt on the murder board and the pictures sitting on the table from the envelope, he noticed that Cory was a pale redhead who was six foot five inches tall. The pictures from the envelope showed a man with dark hair who appeared to be no more than five foot six inches.

Matthews told Hollins, "I think that the date does not have to do with the victim."

"Why not?" Hollins asked.

"The date is closest to the disappearance of Cory Pratt, but the victim in that photo does not match Cory's physical description," Matthews responded.

Hollins walked over to the murder boards. "All right, so the victim in the photo has dark hair, which limits it to three of the men on this board. He also seems to be under six feet tall and in good shape based on the muscle tone in his legs, so that narrows it down to two of the victims."

Matthews joined Hollins by the boards. "I think that with what we know, Trevor Dawson is most likely the victim in those photos. As far as we know, he is the first victim of Raul Moore."

"But that makes the picture from three and half years before Paulina wrote the letter and went to her father. So that proves her statement that she had just discovered what he was doing false." Hollins commented.

"Do you think there is a way the forensics team can tell when a picture was actually taken?" Matthews asked Hollins.

Hollins responded, "Since they are Polaroids, I have no idea, but we will certainly find out. Let's put the pictures of the victim from the first envelope on the Trevor Dawson murder board, at least for now. Then, let's call it a day. Raul Moore is still talking to his lawyer, so there is no chance we can talk to him today."

****

Mike Davidson stared at Raul Moore. He had decided that his client needed to have a complete psychological exam. The man was so matter-of-fact and emotionless as he described the violent acts he had committed. Mike was unsure that he believed Raul's version that these murders were all Paulina's idea and that she was an active participant. Women serial killers were very rare, and almost all serial killers worked alone.

"Raul, are you up to finishing telling me what happened, or do we need to take another break?" Mike asked his client.

"No, I want to finish. We only killed one more man, so I might as well tell you about him."

Mike silently commented to himself, *only one more.*

March 2017

Aaron Starr was a nondescript man. Average in every way, he was five foot nine and weighed one hundred and ninety-eight pounds. He had light brown hair and brown eyes. Raul was unsure how Paulina had come across him, but he fit the criteria. Aaron went to work at the pork processing plant and sat at a bar or at home when he wasn't working. Every Sunday, he walked to that hole-in-the-wall bar, where he drank and watched sports. For the weeks they had watched, he never had a visitor nor varied his routine.

Raul watched from the parked van as Paulina sat down on the curb. She appeared to be crying, but Raul knew that would never happen. The Ice Queen did not shed genuine tears but was a superior actress who could cry on demand. Raul had come to understand that she constructed their entire relationship and controlled all aspects of their life. He wondered *did she ever love me or was I just another conquest for her.* He had been thinking a lot about Shelby's death. Things had never fully added up, but no one really questioned Paulina's version of events. He contemplated if Paulina had murdered Shelby, too. Was Shelby her first victim?

Aaron came strolling down the sidewalk. It was apparent from his cadence that he was intoxicated. He seemed to speed up a little when he noticed Paulina. He bent down to talk to her, and she plunged the needle into his neck. Raul wondered how the alcohol and the tranquilizer would interact, but he guessed it really did not matter because he was sure Aaron would be dead soon.

Paulina looked up and smiled as Raul pulled the van up to the curb. Raul grabbed Aaron under his arms and dragged him to the back of the van. Paulina had already jumped in the back, and for a brief moment, Raul thought she had a Polaroid camera out and taken a picture. He had hoped that she had stopped taking pictures to use against him, but he wouldn't put anything past her.

Aaron's surgery had been successful, and Paulina was sure that they had taken every step to keep him alive this time. Raul had argued that they needed to stop the transplants until they figured out what anti-rejection medications they needed. Within a day, Paulina had somehow gotten them. She pointed out that they really did not want these men to fully recover, as they would never let them go. But yes, they need to see if the anti-rejection medications kept them alive a little longer.

Raul did his best to keep Aaron alive, including giving him antibiotics, which he had not done for any other subject in the past. The outcome for Aaron didn't differ from Cory's. Aaron died on the third day.

16

Sunday June 14, 2020

Raul let out a loud breath, put his head down on the table, and said, "That's it. Those are the seven men we killed."

"Okay, but I am confused about two things. What did you do with your victims' bodies? And why did you stop abruptly two ago?" Mike asked him.

Raul knew that the first question was the easier one to answer. "I feed the bodies to the pigs. There is very little they won't eat other than metal. Things like keys, I threw into Lake Springfield. Each time we killed someone, I would go out at night, paddle my boat into the middle of the lake, and throw their things in it."

Mike remembered the party he had attended years earlier at the farm. The one where everyone had enjoyed a pig roast. He realized the pig they enjoyed eating that day likely enjoyed eating a person. The thought sickened him, but Raul started answering his other question before he could react.

"The answer to your second question is twofold. First, we had done as much as possible with the experiments, and Paulina needed to think about how she could get our fledgling results to a legitimate researcher. The second and probably the most important reason is that Paulina had a new obsession." Raul answered.

Mike hesitantly asked, "And what was her new obsession?"

****

Calling his ex-wife, much less going to see her in person, was not how Shawn Ross had planned to spend his Sunday evening, but after the FBI agents left, he had lingering questions he hoped Heather would be able to answer. She had not seemed surprised when he called, but refused to talk on the phone because she was sure the FBI was listening. Her paranoia was a major cause of their divorce, and it seemed she had not changed.

Heather opened the door to the home that they had once shared and blew out smoke from her cigarette as a greeting. She then walked into the house without a word. He walked in behind her because, after all, he still owned the place. For a brilliant attorney, he had rolled over when it came to their divorce. He paid off the house, gave it to Heather, and paid a hefty sum in child support until Paulina was twenty-two and was still paying alimony. Heather had never gotten a job, but somehow, she managed on his money.

"I assume you are here because of the bullshit with the FBI," Heather stated as she sat down in the living room.

Shawn looked around; it was like a time capsule. He was sure nothing had changed in the thirty-three years since he had walked out the door for the last time. "Yes, the FBI came to see me today. I want to talk about Paulina," he replied.

Heather looked around as if she was looking for someone or something, and then she said, "Let's go for a walk." She got up and walked out the front door.

Neither said a word as they walked down the sidewalk toward the small neighborhood park. Once at the park, Heather sat down on a swing. Shawn followed suit and asked, "Okay, why can't we talk at the house?"

"I know the FBI is looking for our daughter, and so I am sure they are listening to my calls and have bugged my house," Heather stated matter-of-factly.

During his fifteen-year marriage to Heather, Shawn learned that arguing with her delusions got him nowhere, so he chose not to respond to her statement and steered the conversation to their daughter. "Heather, do you think that Paulina is capable of murder?" he asked.

Heather lit another cigarette and took a long drag off of it, then replied, "Yeah, yeah, I do. I know you know about her college roommate dying, but do you know that her high school boyfriend and former boss also died in accidents?"

"Are you saying that you think our daughter killed those three people and the seven people the FBI is accusing her and Raul of murdering?" Shawn responded.

"Look, when you left, she had not even gotten to puberty yet, but if you really think back, that mean, vindictive side of her was already showing. We both know she killed the neighbor's cat after it scratched her. There were so many small unexplained fires in the neighborhood, which all stopped when she left for college. I have always wanted to believe the best about her, but frankly, she scares me." Heather said.

Shawn had not expected Heather to confirm his suspicions, but it seemed they were on the same page for once. "All right, what about the theory that she killed herself? Do you think that is possible?"

Heather chuckled and said, "Like I told the FBI, she loves herself way too much to have committed suicide. Knowing her, she had an escape plan and is off somewhere living under an assumed name."

Shock radiated through Shawn's body, and he wondered if he should tell his ex-wife what he knew. No, that was a bad idea; as far as he knew, only he and Paulina knew the connection to Michelle Brooks and her brand-new condo in Lake Geneva, Wisconsin. Instead, he said, "If the FBI or any other police agencies come back to question you, just give them my card. You are under no obligation to answer their questions, and don't let them try to intimidate you."

"Thanks, but don't forget I was married to you, so I don't intimidate easily," Heather said in a sarcasm-laden voice.

Shawn got up and walked away. Walking back towards his car, he prayed he would never hear from Paulina or Michelle again.

Saturday May 6, 2017

Paulina had noted this day in your calendar so she would not forget to watch the GPS tracker on the van. She had checked it periodically over the last year and reviewed all the data. Raul had not returned once to that spot in the woods. She had decided that if he did not go out there today; she was wrong to be upset with him, and she would let it go. Maybe he had just stumbled upon it between clients last year and lost track of time. That was the narrative she had made up in her head.

She opened her laptop and logged into the monitoring system. She checked his location and saw he was at a client's farm. All right, she needed to stop this suspicion about her husband. She had lived with her mom's paranoia and knew it could drive others away. There was no way she was going to act like her. Paulina logged into the bookkeeping system and began to work on the monthly credits and debits. She was in the middle of printing bills for clients when the laptop binged. She looked to see what program had made the noise and saw the monitoring system tab blinking. Opening the tab, she thought it was odd that *it had never binged like that before.*

A year ago, when Raul had spent hours at his mystery spot, she had set an alert on the monitoring program to tell her if that location was visited again. That alert was now binging. Raul was back out in the woods. Paulina wanted to get up and drive out there. She wanted to confront Raul and find out what he was hiding, but to do so would give away the fact that she was tracking him. No, she would figure out why Raul was going to this spot on this day and then decide her next step. She watched the dot on the screen blink from the same spot for almost thirty minutes, and then it was on the move again. Had Raul found her note? If he had, would he ask her about it or take his usual scared tail between his legs approach and never say a word?

****

As Raul drove away from Shelby's woods, he knew he had to confront Paulina. He could not kill one more man to prove her theory. He had decided today that if it came down to it; he was okay with Paulina killing him or both of them going to prison, but this would end.

As the workday drew to a close, Raul had to muster his courage to confront Paulina. He would find an attorney and turn himself in if she refused to stop. Raul waited until after dinner to bring up his ultimatum, "I am done," he blurted out.

Paulina looked up from the book she was reading. "Done with what?" she asked.

"All of it. The stalking, the experiments, the disposing of bodies. All of it." Raul said in a shaky voice. He wished he could sound stronger, but Paulina scared him, and it showed in his voice and everything he had done.

A tense silence filled the room, and then Paulina got up and walked away. Raul sat rooted in his seat. He was paralyzed with fear and was sure he was about to die. After an hour, the house was silent, and Paulina had not returned to the living room, so Raul got up and prepared to go to bed. He found Paulina in their room, reading the same book as before but now was lying in bed. Neither spoke as Raul laid down and turned off the light on his side of the bed.

As he lay there, Raul wondered if he should say something. Just as he plucked up the courage to ask Paulina what she was thinking, she spoke, "Okay. We can be done. I need to figure out who I can trust in the medical research community to discuss using non-human hearts for transplant." She then turned off her light and rolled away from Raul.

Raul lay in bed while a terrible uneasiness spread throughout his body. There was no way that Paulina should have been that agreeable. There was something else going on, and Raul feared it was going to be the end of his life.

17

Monday June 15, 2020

Agent Matthews was surprised when the guard came to tell him that Mike Davidson reported that his client was ready to talk. Matthews wondered what Raul Moore would tell them as he walked to get Hollins. The evidence was clear that Raul and Paulina Moore had kidnapped, tortured, and murdered seven men over the last seven years. He had questions for the Moores, but they had more to do with motive than getting a confession. There was no doubt in Matthew's mind that the Moores were serial killers.

Neither Mike Davidson nor Raul Moore acknowledged the agents as they walked in. Once they sat down, Mike Davidson said, "I will read a statement my client and I have prepared, but at this time, Mr. Moore will not be answering questions. Over the last seven years, I have made regrettable choices and participated in incomprehensible actions. I do not believe that my wife, Paulina Moore, killed herself; she is a danger to the general public. Thus, you must find her."

Agent Hollins asked, "Is that all?"

Mike Davidson responded by nodding his head.

Hollins then replied, "That is all well and good. Be assured that we are investigating Paulina Moore and her apparent suicide to ensure she is indeed dead. In the meantime, you don't have to answer any questions, but we have some things to say."

Matthews began to lay out a picture of each victim and pictures of the envelopes left by Paulina. Hollins said, "We know you kidnapped, tortured, and murdered these men. We know this because of physical evidence at your farm and documents that Paulina left with her father. What we do not know is why?"

"Why would two successful veterinarians suddenly begin killing people?" Matthews asked. He was having trouble keeping the disgust for Raul out of his voice.

Neither Mike Davidson nor Raul Moore responded to the agents' questions. Mike Davidson broke the silence. "If that is all, please return my client to his cell. Raul, I will see you tomorrow morning and let you know when your arraignment is scheduled."

****

Michelle parked her car and walked into the office building of Dr. Keith Rodane. When she called this morning to book an appointment to discuss having Botox injections, the receptionist told her that there was a cancelation for today. It was hard not to think the available appointment was more proof that her plan was coming together perfectly. She would have to play the role of an overly vain, insecure woman while discussing ways to improve her appearance. Between that and being a cash payer, she was sure she would leave with a surgical plan and date.

****

Dr. Rodane looked over the file of the woman he had just met with. Michelle Brooks was in her late forties and in terrific shape. She had come in to discuss Botox and left scheduled for Botox, a nose job, and lip filler. Over the years, he had become very good at teasing out people's insecurities about their looks and reeling them in so he could do expensive procedures. He always started small, just like the plan he had laid out for Ms. Brooks, but they would build from there. Her expensive clothes, shoes, handbag, and plan to pay cash told him she would be a lucrative new client.

Wednesday May 10, 2017

Raul knew he should have seen it coming, but he could never have guessed what Paulina wanted to do next. How had the once-loving mother of his daughter turned into a psychopath? Kidnap and murder

Kelsey Learner; that is what she wanted them to do next. Worse yet, it wasn't to help others but to get revenge for Kelsey divorcing Joe Learner. Paulina had gone on and on last night about how Kelsey had a perfect life and that she destroyed that life by kicking Joe out.

As far as Raul knew, Paulina had only met Joe two times, and neither had included a long discussion about his ex-wife. Raul decided to try to get Paulina to tell him more. "What exactly do you know about Kelsey Learner's reason for divorcing Joe?" he asked.

Paulina replied, "I don't know her reason; honestly, it doesn't matter. When you get married, you take vows, and none include words like unless or only if. They are for life. Kelsey and Joe had the perfect family. They have a little girl who was traumatized by her parents' splitting up. Then Kelsey turned Claire against Joe and alienated her from her father. If all that was not enough, do you know who she works for?"

Raul shook his head and said, "No."

"She works for Dr. Hann. You know I do not believe in coincidences. The doctor who could not save our daughter now employs that homewrecker."

It was difficult for Raul to figure out how to approach this with Paulina. She was being unreasonable, but then, when he thought about it, nothing they had been doing for the last seven years was reasonable. Raul decided to take the direct approach, "I won't do it."

"What exactly won't you do?" Paulina said with an angry tone. "You think that you have a say in this? You know I have pictures, videos, and other evidence proving that you stalked, kidnapped, tortured, and murdered seven men? The first time you killed someone, that was the last time you got to make a choice, so you will do what I tell you to." She then walked out of the room.

Raul knew this was her way of saying that the conversation was over.

18

Tuesday June 16, 2020

When Mike Davidson arrived at the Greene County Jail, he wondered how often he would come here to see Raul Moore. His law clerk received a call this morning that the Grand Jury had returned an indictment in Raul's case and that his arraignment would be tomorrow morning. Raul was officially charged with seven counts of first-degree homicide, seven counts of kidnapping, seven counts of stalking with the intent to cause bodily harm, seven counts of concealing a human corpse, and seven counts of cruelty to animals. Mike had not been surprised by the Grand Jury's decision and doubted that Raul would be either.

After signing in and being escorted to the conference room, Mike waited for Raul. He watched as his client shuffled in. Raul never raised his head to look at Mike but just sat down in the chair the guard indicated. Mike laid out the indictment from the grand jury. As he suspected, Raul was not surprised.

"I want to have you examined by a psychiatrist. Are you alright with that?" Mike asked.

Raul shrugged and replied, "Yeah, fine."

Mike was frustrated with Raul's apathetic attitude. "Raul, we are fighting for your life here. If you are found guilty, the prosecutor will no doubt be asking for the death penalty. I will need you to help me mount a defense," he patiently explained.

Raul looked up at Mike for the first time today and said in a dejected tone, "I am guilty, and we both know it, so yeah, maybe I do deserve to die for what I did to those people."

"Do I need to have you put on suicide watch?" Mike asked.

Raul shook his head slowly, then responded, "No, I want to help the police find Paulina more than I want to die."

"Okay, good. Your arraignment is tomorrow morning at nine am. Is there anyone who can bring you clothes to wear for court?" Mike asked.

Raul sat quietly for a moment and then asked Mike, "Do my parents know what is happening?"

Mike had no way of knowing the answer but responded, "Raul, this case has been all over the local and national news. They likely know. I also would not be surprised if the FBI has spoken to them."

"Am I able to call them? They would probably bring me clothes," responded Raul.

"Just tell the guard you want to make a phone call. It shouldn't be a problem. I will set up an account and put money on it before I leave, so you don't have to call collect. If you have to leave a voicemail, give them my number since they cannot call you back. If they call me, I will explain briefly what is happening and ask if they can help get you clothes," Mike explained to Raul.

****

Charles Silver, the Chief Assistant Prosecuting Attorney for the State of Missouri, exited his boss's office. Charles would take the lead in the case against Raul Moore. With each passing hour, the case was gaining more and more notice in the national spotlight. This morning, as he ran on the treadmill, Charles listened to the so-called experts on a national news program discuss the case. According to the experts, it was an open-and-shut case with the only remaining questions: why Raul Moore had killed the seven men and whether Paulina Moore was dead.

The problem for Charles was that he struggled to believe that anything was as straightforward as it seemed. The arraignment was tomorrow, so he just had to familiarize himself with the basics for now. His boss, the Chief Prosecuting Attorney, and Charles agreed they were not interested in a plea deal with Raul Moore and would ask for no bail. This was not the first death penalty case he had prosecuted, but these cases held the highest burden of proof. That is why he and his team would dive deep into the evidence and build an iron-clad case against Dr. Raul Moore.

Hopefully, they would uncover not only the how and why but also any secrets that could take them by surprise during the trial. Charles knew there had to be something more to the case than the talking heads on television knew because Mike Davidson was a fierce criminal defense lawyer. There is no way Mike would have taken a case that was un-winnable.

******

Calling his parents was hard, but seeing them sitting behind plexi-glass waiting to talk to him tore at Raul's heart. He sat down and picked up the phone as his dad picked up the one on their side.

"I am so sorry that I am putting you through this," Raul said in way of a greeting.

His mother Camilla began to cry softly as his father replied, "We love you, son, and want to help in any way we can. We dropped off clothes for you with the guard and deposited money in your jail account so you can buy a notebook and pen like you asked for."

Raul knew he was lucky to have parents willing to help him, no matter the situation. "I appreciate all of your help. I have a lot of regrets, and one of them is you two becoming in any way associated with what Paulina and I did."

"Son, don't talk to us about your case. Everything is recorded here. I talked to your lawyer, Mike Davidson, on the phone while your mom and I drove here. He seemed very capable. Your mother and I will be in court tomorrow, and every other time you have to appear in court." Troy Moore told him.

Camilla put her hand on top of her husband's hand, and he handed her the phone. "You know the love a parent feels towards their child. You had that love for Lynn. We saw that when you were with her. Our love for you is unconditional. We are both disappointed and saddened by this situation, but love you nonetheless."

The sadness in her voice brought tears to Raul's eyes. Before he could respond, the guard indicated that the time for their visit was over, and all three of the Moores rose from their seats. Camilla put her hand on the plexiglass, and Raul pressed his to the same spot on the opposite side and lipped. I *am so very sorry*.

Friday February 2, 2018

Paulina Moore stopped to get a coffee and sandwich after seeing her mom. While waiting for her order number to be called, she looked around the shop and spotted Joe Learner. She was about to walk up to him when she watched his ex-wife sit down. She thought, *"Oh, this is interesting, "* and decided to sit at the table behind Joe's back so he did not see her.

As she sat there, she could hear most of their conversation. They were clearly arguing about money and their daughter, Claire. Kelsey was talking to Joe very condescendingly, and Paulina could hear that he was getting upset. She felt Joe's chair bump into hers as he stood abruptly and heard him say. "Okay then, we won't get her a car. She doesn't need one at school, anyway." Paulina watched Joe storm out of the coffee shop. Kelsey Learner just sat there and did not try to stop Joe or tell him she was sorry.

Paulina did not believe in coincidences. Her being in that particular coffee shop on that day at the same time as Joe and Kelsey was meant to be. She was regaling the tale of what she had witnessed at the coffee shop when she looked up and saw that Raul had a far-off look on his face.

"Raul, did you hear me?" she asked.

Raul once again was unsure how to respond to his wife. He thought it was not a big deal for two married or divorced parents to argue about money and whether to buy a kid a car. But, of course, logic and Paulina were not congruent. "Yes, I heard you. You stopped at a coffee shop and heard an argument between Joe and Kelsey Learner."

"Well, at least I know you don't have a hearing problem." Paulina said condescendingly, then continued, "It was serendipity that led me to that place at that time. It was the universe proving that I was right about taking her. She was horrible to Joe. If she talked to him like that during their marriage, it is no wonder that he pulled away from her."

"People argue. Money is a stressor for families. We really don't know why Joe and Kelsey divorced," Raul responded.

She should have known better than to try to explain to Raul. It always surprised her when he stood up to her even a little. She wondered what had gotten into him. This conversation was not worth her time. "Fine. You don't have to acknowledge that I am right," Paulina said as she turned around and walked out of the living room.

Monday February 5, 2018

Raul chose to sit at Joe Learner's table at The Club instead of his usual table. He wasn't sure what he hoped to learn by making small talk with Joe, but what Paulina said had been on his mind since last night. Was Kelsey Learner really that horrible to him? Had she alienated their daughter Claire from him? Neither of those things was likely to be just brought up while eating dinner at The Club, but he was hoping to steer the conversation somehow that way.

Joe Learner and John Andrews walked in together and sat down. John turned to Raul and said, "What's up, doc?" and then started laughing at his own weak joke.

Raul responded to both men, "Not much. How are both of you?"

Joe and John both indicated that they were well. After the business portion of The Club meeting, dinner was served, and the people at the table began socializing. Both Joe and John were a few drinks in at this point, as was Raul. The liquor gave him the liquid courage to jump into what he wanted to know.

"So, you are both divorced, right?"

Joe chuckled and said, "Yeah, and John has rung that bell twice, so he is the expert on all things divorce."

"Thanks a lot, buddy. Just throw me under the bus. What can I say, doc it was their fault, not mine. Both times." John responded in a joking manner. He then added, "Why are you thinking of going through the big D, doc? I would not recommend it. Definitely a one-star experience."

Raul really wished that John would stop calling him doc, but he did not want to halt the flow of the conversation. "I have thought about it a few times. The time I got most serious and talked to an attorney, he told me that Paulina would rake me over the coals financially. Between child support and alimony, I would be out a lot of money, and the courts would likely give her full custody of our daughter. So, I have made it work since then." All of it was a lie. He had never even dreamed of divorcing Paulina. They meant it when they said to death do us part.

"Wait, Raul. I swore your wife told me you guys have no kids." Joe stated.

John bumped Joe under the table and shot him a look that said, let it go.

"It's okay, John. He doesn't know. Our daughter Lynn died when she was eight. Paulina tells people who didn't know us then that we don't have any kids. It is easier than talking about your child who died," Raul told Joe.

"Sorry, I had no idea. The lawyer was right, though. It took me a long time to get back on solid financial footing after my divorce." Joe told him.

"And now that you are, that bitch asks you for more money. That is called rubbing salt in your wounds, right buddy?" John added in.

Joe sighed and turned to John, "Man, I have told you not to call her that. We are divorced, but she is still the mother of my child, and I work hard to have a decent relationship with her."

John said, "I know what you say, but how has that worked out for you? Your daughter never visits you, and the ex wants you to buy your daughter a car."

Raul was getting the information he had come for and pushed to get a little more. "Do either of you still have feelings for your ex-wife?"

John seemed to find his question hilarious because his only answer was laughter. On the other hand, Joe nodded slightly, "I love Kelsey. I screwed up, but she is the one who ultimately gave up on our marriage and filed for divorce."

Raul left The Club that night, thinking that Paulina was not completely wrong. Her plan was wrong, but she was not.

19

Tuesday June 16, 2020

The forensic team was still at the Moore's farm, and the evidence they had already gathered was being turned over to the prosecutor's office. The Fugitive Apprehension Task Force was looking for Paulina so that left Agents Hollins and Matthews with only reports to type up. As the junior agent, Matthews knew that he would be doing the brunt of the paperwork. He decided to see if Kass had time for lunch before he got started.

A diner was between the FBI field office and the Springfield Police Department, and they agreed to meet there. After ordering their lunch, Kass asked Robert about his current case.

"I would love to tell you all about it, but you know how it is. I can tell you that there is no evidence to tie this case to the cold case you asked about," Robert replied.

Kass nodded and said, "I knew it was a long shot, but it was an odd coincidence that my partner and I went to that farm and talked to your suspect."

"That is a strange coincidence. Was he a suspect in the woman's disappearance?" Robert asked.

"No, he was an acquaintance of her ex-husband. We thought the ex had done it at the time and were trying to gather evidence against him. As I remember, your suspect was of little help to us," Kass replied.

Robert thought back to what Kass had told him about the case and what he had seen in the news. "The ex-husband was ruled out, right?"

"Yes, he was. After that, our case went cold, and the victim was never found. It has been over two years." Kass said with a hit of sadness in her voice.

****

Joe Learner pulled up to the house he used to share with his ex-wife, Kelsey, and daughter, Claire. His daughter was sitting on the front porch, waiting for him. They were moving her back into the house today. He had offered for her to move out to his farmhouse with him, but she did not want to live out of town. They had been collecting rent on the house for the last year while Claire was away at school. The family they rented to had been very understanding when Joe told them they would not renew their lease.

"You beat me here. You must have made good time," Joe said in a way of greeting.

Claire smiled at him and stood up. She responded, "Hi, Dad. There was no traffic, so here I am. Are you going to let me drive your truck?"

Driving the truck was a running joke between the father and daughter. The truck was a mint condition 1993 GMC Sierra that Joe had gotten from his dad. He did not let anyone else drive his truck. He had told Claire that he would let her drive it when he decided to give it to her. That did not stop her from asking whenever the opportunity presented itself.

"No, I will pass on that experience. Are you ready to head to the storage unit, or do we need to go to Starbucks before getting started?" Joe responded.

"I would never turn down a Starbucks drink, especially when you are buying," Claire replied.

As they drove towards the coffee shop, Claire fiddled with the radio. She stopped on a local station, replaying the news story about the arrest of Raul Moore. The Grand Jury had indicted him on multiple counts, and his arraignment was set for this morning. When Claire leaned in to change the station again, she looked sad.

Joe was not good at dealing with emotion, so he jumped in to fill the void. "I know the guy they arrested. What they are saying he did shocks the hell out of me."

"Dad, do you think Mom is one of his victims?" Claire asked in a shaky voice.

Joe could tell she was on the verge of tears and wanted to reassure her. "No, Claire. The news last night clearly said that his victims were seven men." The truth was that Joe had wondered the same thing and had no real answers. He knew they were charging Raul with seven counts of murder, but what if there were more victims? What if Raul Moore was the one who took Kelsey? Joe prayed that his association with Moores had nothing to do with Kelsey's disappearance.

Joe glanced over at Claire and saw tears streaming down her face. "Claire, honey, what can I do to help?"

"Nothing, Dad. I miss Mom. I told you that I had been seeing a counselor on campus. She helped me to accept that Mom is likely never coming home and that I have to grieve. It is just so hard because we never got to say goodbye. There is no closure." Claire's voice was ragged with emotion.

"Do you want to have a memorial service for her?" Joe asked.

A loud sob ripped out of Claire, and she whispered, "No, that is just too final. Until she is found, I will always have a glimmer of hope. Having a memorial service would be like giving up on her; I will never give up trying to find her."

Friday March 2, 2018

Raul sat at the edge of the entrance to the wooded lot. The shipping container should be delivered any minute now. He had laid out four logs for the container to be set on. When he had accepted that there was no way for him to change Paulina's mind about taking Kelsey Learner, he had begun to look for a way to save Kelsey's life. While watching television, he stumbled across a crime show about a kidnapping in the nineteen seventies where a school bus was buried, and the victims were held underground. The victims escaped, and the perpetrators were quickly found, but that seemed to be mostly because of poor planning. Raul thought; *Who would think you could steal a school bus full of kids and not have that end in a manhunt?*

Nevertheless, he used that idea as inspiration for how he would handle his current predicament. Raul was unsure how to get Kelsey out here under Paulina's watchful eye, but he was counting on Paulina, not wanting to get her hands any dirtier than she had with their past crimes. While cleaning the lab, he found the hidden cameras that Paulina must have installed. He would have to cut the feed to those cameras just before they went to get Kelsey.

The truck delivering the shipping container arrived and backed into place. The driver was in a heated discussion on his cell phone, with whom Raul assumed to be his wife or girlfriend. Raul felt bad for the driver as this woman continued screaming at him, but it worked in Raul's favor because the driver paid little to no attention to his customer. After the truck pulled away, Raul opened the shipping container and walked around inside. He decided his plans for the inside would work, so he went to the van and retrieved the items he had brought.

Paulina had made it clear to him that you could learn how to do anything and buy anything online. She was not the only one who could scheme. Years ago, one of the farmers they worked with approached him about helping a migrant worker by stitching the man up. Raul had hesitated but ultimately decided that having someone owe him a favor for once may be useful in the future. He had stitched the worker and did not ask questions despite the story of how the man was injured not adding up to the injury. Since then, he had provided "medical care" to workers at the farm.

A week ago, he asked that farmer if he could have some items delivered there and held for him. The farmer was agreeable, and Raul had been able to get all that he needed for this project. His dad used the phrase "Throwing a Hail Mary" whenever they had no easy ways to get something done, but you had to do something. This was Raul's Hail

Mary to save both Kelsey and himself. After he had Kelsey safely here, he would figure out a way to escape from Paulina and let the authorities know where to find Kelsey.

20

Wednesday June 17, 2020

Mike Davidson watched as Raul Moore was escorted into the courtroom. Mike had gone to see Raul this morning and reviewed what to expect in court again. Raul had not acknowledged him in any way. The guards informed Mike that Raul had been like that since he had been brought back to his cell after his parent's visit yesterday afternoon. His parents had brought him a suit and tie, which were clearly new. The courtroom was packed with spectators and news outlets. Raul's parents, Camila and Troy Moore were sitting right behind the defendant's table. Raul sat down next to Mike at the defense table without even looking back at his parents.

Mike leaned in and whispered, "You will have to enter the plea when the judge asks. Remember to say not guilty. I will ask the judge for an evaluation, and hopefully, we can move your plea to not guilty by reason of mental disease or defect."

Raul nodded but continued to stare downward.

The judge entered the courtroom, and everyone rose. Judge Kent Buckman was known to be a no-nonsense jurist thus he matter of factually read the charges. "Raul Moore, you are charged with seven counts of kidnapping, seven counts of murder in the first degree, seven counts of desecrating a human corpse, and seven counts of animal cruelty. How do you plead?"

"Not Guilty," Raul said in a quiet, flat voice.

Mike Davidson quickly added, "We request a full psychiatric evaluation of my client before trial by a psychiatrist of our choice."

"Are you planning to change the plea to not guilty by reason of mental disease or defect?" Judge Buckman asked.

"We will not make that decision until after a qualified mental health professional has evaluated Dr. Moore," Mike responded.

Judge Buckman then asked the prosecutor, Charles Silver, "Do you have any objection to the request for the psychiatric evaluation?"

"The state does not have any objection to the evaluation," Mr. Silver responded.

"Moving to the matter of bail. I assume the state is asking for remand?" Judge Buckman said.

Mr. Silver nodded and said, "Due to the extensive list of charges and the severity of those charges, the state believes that Raul Moore poses a danger to the public and asks that he be held without bond pending his trial."

Judge Buckman then asked Mike Davidson, "What is your position on bond?"

"We are not asking for bond, but due to Mr. Moore's mental state, we ask that he be held in a secure mental health facility prior to his trial," Mike responded.

The courtroom hummed with anticipation as Judge Buckman mulled over the request. "Raul Moore, you are remanded to custody at the Greene County Jail. If or when a psychiatrist finds that you require inpatient psychiatric care, you will be moved to the secure unit at the Fulton State Hospital. The Circuit Court clerk will set the date for the preliminary hearing no more than thirty days from today." With a bang of his gavel, Judge Buckman rose and exited the courtroom.

Friday March 2, 2018

When she saw the dot representing the van Raul was driving move, Paulina drove out to the wooded lot. Now she stood looking at the shipping container in the middle of the lot. There was an industrial-strength padlock on the door, and she knew she couldn't just cut it off without alerting Raul to the breech. What was he doing having a container delivered here, and what did he have in it that warranted a padlock? She needed a better way to track what Raul was doing out here.

Saturday March 3, 2018

Paulina returned the next day with a pair of trail cameras. She would need to come out and switch out the memory cards every few days, but she had found a way to know what Raul was doing out here. As she scaled up a tree to install the first camera, she chuckled to herself about Raul thinking he could conceal anything from her. Then, she repeated the process to install the second camera in another location. One camera pointed directly at the entrance to the lot, and the other at the shipping container.

The cameras had the capability to be watched live as well as to record on the memory cards. Paulina sat in her truck and checked the feed on both cameras. The cameras could transmit via Bluetooth, but the range was very limited, so she could only watch live when she was here. The lack of real-time data regarding what her husband was doing bothered her, but this setup would have to do for now. If the need arose, she would upgrade to a better system.

Driving away, Paulina was determined to figure out not just what Raul was doing out here, but also why he had picked this lot. She had noticed the fire numbers on some properties as she drove by. So, she drove north on the highway to the first property with a fire number. Pulling next to the number, Paulina wrote down all the information the small sign contained. Then she drove to the next fire number and wrote that information down. After getting the information from four signs on that side of the county highway, she turned around and wrote the numbers for the properties on the other side of the highway. When she had the fire numbers for all the properties before and after the wooded lot going both north and south, she headed back to the farm.

She used the information from the fire numbers to figure out the possible fire number for the wooded lot. She methodically typed each combination into the Greene County property tax search engine. Four numbers in, she got a hit. The wooded lot belonged to the estate of Shelby Lansing. Now, the pieces clicked into place. According to the records, Shelby purchased this lot the summer after she and Raul graduated from high school. Paulina figured that Raul and Shelby had planned to build their dream home on that lot in the woods.

Raul had never really let go of Shelby, at least not in his heart. It was not as if she would claim to have an epic love for him either, but at least her heart did not belong to someone else. She just did not feel romantic feelings towards others. Those feelings had never been something that she had experienced. She had felt great love, unconditional love for their daughter, Lynn. That kind of love was not something that she ever expected to feel. It wasn't until the first time Lynn was handed to her, and they laid their skin to skin, that the love surged through her in a way she had never experienced. So did the maternal need to protect Lynn with all she had. Paulina had already figured out that was why she had reacted so strongly when Lynn died. As her mother, there was nothing she could do to save Lynn, and she felt powerless and experienced self-loathing for the first time in her life.

21

Wednesday June 17, 2020

Agents Hollins and Matthews sat in the conference room, waiting for the rest of the joint operations team to join them. Since the case against Raul was moving to trial, they were turning their collective sights on Paulina Moore. Joining them today was the lead agent for the FBI's Fugitive Apprehension Task Force, a forensic accountant, and the Supervisory Special Agent in Charge of the Moore investigation, Jose Martinez. He was Hollins' and Matthews' boss, but they rarely saw him since he worked in the St. Louis office.

As everyone gathered, pleasantries were exchanged, and Jose got to business. "The CSI team is still at the Moore's farm. I spoke to the lead technician, who said they would gather evidence for at least two more weeks. The prosecutor's office expects Raul Moore's trial to start in forty-five to sixty days, so we should have everything wrapped up for that case in time. This brings us to the subject of Paulina Moore. Hollins, why don't you start us off with what we know for sure?"

"Alright, well, we know that Paulina Moore left her van and belongings, along with a suicide note, by the side of the bridge over the Missouri River. Her mother told Agent Matthews and me that Paulina was diagnosed with narcissistic personality disorder and that she would never commit suicide." Hollins explained to the group. "After that, we went and saw Raul's parents, and they described her as cold and calculating. An interesting but possibly unrelated fact we learned from them is that Raul's college girlfriend died in a freak accident. The strangest part was that Paulina was the girlfriend's roommate and the last person to see her alive."

Agent Landon Kross, the Special Agent in Charge of the Fugitive Apprehension Task Force, asked, "Are you thinking she killed the girlfriend?"

Matthews knew he had no evidence, but he was the kind of investigator who trusted his gut. He replied, "I know this may be an unpopular opinion at this point, but I think that Paulina Moore is the dominant personality of this killing duo. I believe there may be a series of murders she committed alone before she involved Raul in the seven, we are currently investigating."

"What leads you to believe that Paulina is the dominant partner?" Agent Martinez asked.

. "Three days ago, Agent Hollins called Shawn Ross, who is not only Paulina's father but also her attorney. He let Agent Hollins know that he was in possession of an envelope that he needed to turn over to us. We met with Mr. Ross at his office in St. Louis, and he gave us a large manilla envelope."

Matthews paused to catch his breath and take a drink of coffee.

Martinez impatiently asked, "What was in the envelope?"

"Oh, sorry. We went to the St. Louis field office and opened the envelope. We found a note clipped to Polaroid pictures and a slightly smaller envelope inside it. We continued opening envelopes until we had seven in total. Each envelope had a note and Polaroids. The pictures were taken during the actual abductions or murders of the seven victims. In many of the pictures, Raul Moore could clearly be seen." Matthews concluded.

Agent Hollins added, "The smallest envelope in the pile contained a note from three and half years ago and was an attempt to implicate Raul by saying she just found out what he was doing. However, we quickly figured out that the victim in the first set of photos was the Moore's first victim, Trevor Dawson, who went missing seven years ago."

Agent Martinez replied, “Okay, we will work to gather evidence and see if we can prove that. Agent Kross, what has the Fugitive Apprehension Task Force found thus far?”

Landon Kross clicked a button on a remote, and the TV at the farthest end of the conference room came to life. On the screen was a picture of Paulina Moore exiting the hotel in Kansas City, where she had stayed with her husband immediately before his arrest. She was carrying a small black duffle bag and a purse. “This is the last CCTV picture we have found of Paulina Moore. We tracked the van the Moores used for their veterinary business through Kansas City to where it was found next to the bridge. We have used searchers and divers without any sign of Paulina’s body in the Missouri River. This led us to the next part of our investigation, where Ms. White comes in. Ms. White?”

“Thank you. As all of you know, crimes are often solved, and criminals are apprehended by following the money, and that is where the forensic accounting team came in. After speaking with Agent Kross, I deeply explored Paulina and Raul Moores’ finances. Their joint personal and business accounts are very ordinary and of no real help to the case. It got interesting when we found a separate account solely in Paulina’s name. There was a quarter of a million dollars in this account when it was closed the day before you arrested Raul. Mrs. Moore closed the account along with her safe deposit box at the bank and received a cashier's check for the balance.” Trinity White told the team.

Jose Martinez asked, “So, where did that cashier's check trace to?”

Trinity White sighed and replied, “One thing I will say for sure is that Paulina Moore is smart. She deposited the check in a Bitcoin ATM, and from there, the money disappeared into cyberspace.”

“Wait, what?” Agent Kross replied, “Are you saying we can’t trace it?”

“It is not that we can’t trace it, but it will take some time. We got the court order for the records and are now waiting to receive them. I fear she moved the money overseas after converting it, and if she picked the right country, there will be no tracing it,” White replied.

Agent Kross sounded irritated as he replied, “As soon as you know where that money went, my team will start looking for her there. You are right; following the money is a tried-and-true strategy. Additionally, I would like to have Paulina Moore added to the FBI’s ten most wanted list. We have her fingerprints on file from when she got her veterinary license, so I created an alert in CODIS in case she is fingerprinted anywhere else.”

Hollins smiled then said, “I am glad we all agree that Paulina Moore is alive. Matthews and I will continue to work on finding any evidence that ties her to the commission of the kidnappings and murders.”

“Agreed. We will meet again as soon as anyone has an update,” SAC Martinez said as he got up and walked out of the conference room.

Matthews asked Hollins, “Do you think Raul knows where she is? And if he does, would he tell us?”

“No, I don’t think he knows where she is. I think that she was the keeper of the secrets in their relationship. As for your other question, now that he has been formally charged, it is highly doubtful his attorney would let him answer any questions.”

Friday March 9, 2018

Raul picked up the farmer's truck with the small excavator already on the attached trailer early this morning. He had put cattle deworming on his work calendar as an all-day appointment. He used the excavator to dig a hole fourteen feet deep by fourteen feet wide, piling the dirt off to the side.

After digging the hole, he used the truck to push the shipping container into it. The logs underneath it made it possible for the container to roll with a push from the truck. After the container settled into place at the bottom of the hole, he got his plasma cutter out of the truck and cut three holes on the top of the shipping container, one for the ladder and two for ventilation.

He inserted the two pieces of PVC pipe that he had cut ahead of time into the small holes, used sealant to secure them, and then put a cap on each one. Raul returned to the farmer's truck and got the manhole cover and skirt. Again, he was amazed by everything that could be bought online. The template for the manhole cover had allowed him to cut the hole perfectly to size. He eased the manhole skirt into place and then secured the cover. He had constructed a cardboard cut-out to create a form to make a tunnel from the manhole to the ground. With everything in place, Raul completely buried the container by filling the dirt back in, leaving only the vents and access point. He put as much of the dirt as he could in the truck's bed. A construction site was between the lot and the farmer, with a sign asking for clean fill. He would dump this off before he returned the truck.

Raul was exhausted after his day of work, but also very proud of his accomplishments. He drove the truck and trailer back to the farmer, dropping off the dirt on his way, and then picked up his van.

Saturday March 10, 2018

Paulina pulled up to the wooded lot to swap out the memory cards in the trail cameras. So far, there had been nothing besides wildlife and insects on the cameras. She had not figured out what Raul was doing with the shipping container but had been able to order keys for the padlock by using the lock code on the bottom of it. Today was the day she was going to open that container.

Walking onto the lot, Paulina immediately noticed that the container was gone, and there was an area of disturbed ground. She wondered *where has Raul had taken the container.* After retrieving the memory cards, she sat in her truck and inserted the first card into her laptop. She watched a pickup truck hauling a trailer pull into the lot a day before. When Raul stepped out of the truck, Paulina was filled with rage. Where had he gotten this truck and trailer? Watching him back the small excavator off the trailer, she wondered what he was planning to do. It took him hours to dig the massive hole. How had he learned to dig a hole like that? Raul dug three adjoining holes, returned to the first one, and began digging deeper. He dug an ever-deeper hole by digging a ramp for the excavator to drive down as he dug. After he finished the first pass, he repeated the process for the other two.

Raul took a short break, sitting on the back of the truck, and then disconnected the trailer. He then used the truck to push the shipping container slowly towards the hole. She watched as the container plunged into the hole with what she assumed must have been a loud thud. Raul then exited the truck and carried items to the edge of the hole he had made. He jumped into the hole and then grabbed the items on the edge.

After Raul climbed out of the hole, he returned to the truck and carried a large box back to the edge. The box appeared to be heavy. He once again got in the hole and pulled the box in with him. After climbing out of the hole, Raul returned to the excavator and filled the dirt into the hole. He then filled the truck's bed with dirt from the mound. As Paulina watched as Raul reattach the trailer, pull the excavator back on it, drive away she wondered; *What is he planning to do?*

22

Thursday June 18, 2020

Raul stared down at the table as Dr. Vera Triton wrote in her notebook. She was the psychiatrist that Mike Davidson had hired. The psych exam had started with her asking him routine questions to be sure he was oriented to time and place. Then she had moved on to ask Raul about his childhood, and he had told her the basics of a normal, unremarkable upbringing. As she wrote, Raul thought about Shelby and how to describe her to Dr. Triton.

"I had the same girlfriend throughout high school and the first three years of college. Shelby Lansing was the most wonderful woman. She and I had a plan for our lives together. I was devastated when she died at the end of our junior year of college." Raul told her.

Dr. Triton wrote something else and asked, "How did Shelby die?"

It was not easy for Raul to talk about Shelby's death. When people say a death was senseless, that completely described what happened to Shelby. She was happy and healthy at dinner and then dead that evening. Plus, there was the fact that he suspected that it hadn't really been an accident. No, he now knew that Paulina had murdered Shelby but with no way to prove it, he gave the same story he had told for twenty plus years. "It was a freak accident in her dorm room. She fell out of the window because the room's air conditioning unit was not properly installed."

"I am sorry for your loss. It sounds from your voice like you still miss her," Dr. Triton remarked.

"I do. She and my daughter Lynn were the most wonderful and special parts of my life." Raul told her.

Dr. Triton wrote a few more things down and then asked, "So, when did you meet your wife, Paulina?"

Raul knew that the conversation would center around his life with Paulina from this point forward, so he took a moment to think about Shelby before answering. "Paulina was Shelby's roommate since our freshmen year. She and I formed more of a friendship after Shelby's death. During veterinary school, we slowly fell in love," Raul responded.

"Tell me about your early married life." Dr. Triton said in the way of a question.

He thought back to the early years, "We were busy. Busy but happy. We were both working full-time to establish ourselves as veterinarians here in the Springfield area. Then we bought our practice, and things just got busier. We were married for about two years when Paulina got pregnant."

Raul told Dr. Triton about Lynn and their life before she got sick and then about the illness and losing Lynn.

Dr. Triton asked, "How did her death affect both of you?"

"It was hard. I tried to return to our lives, run our veterinary practice, and remember the positives. Paulina could not seem to do that. She went for weeks, barely sleeping or eating. Then she just seemed to snap," Raul answered.

"Snapped?" Dr. Triton used the word as a question

Raul wondered if he used the right word, "Yes, she came up with the idea to kidnap and murder people so we could conduct experiments only after our daughter died. I don't know if that is what you would call snapped, but I do know that a normal person would never have devised her plan."

Dr. Triton looked up from her writing and stared at Raul. He dropped his eyes back down to the table. "Just to be clear, Paulina planned these crimes, but you carried them out?"

"No, not really. Paulina planned all the kidnappings. She stalked the men and decided when and how we would take them. She procured all of the supplies and equipment. We kidnapped them together, and Paulina supervised while I did the so-called surgery," Raul responded.

"Why did you kill for her and continue to kill for her?" Dr. Triton asked him.

Raul had thought about this a lot over the last seven years. Had it been his love for her? No, that was not it. "I cannot understand it for myself, so I doubt I can fully explain it to you, but I will try. When we lost Lynn, I was desperate to restore our lives. When Paulina told me her plan, I never thought we would actually go through with it. But now here I sit in jail seven years later, having committed seven murders."

Dr. Triton wrote in her notebook as Raul sat and sobbed. She had decided that he was being sincere, but there were definitely some unanswered questions.

"The thing is, I told you that Paulina must be psychotic, but the truth is that I have to be just as crazy, too. Because I put my own life in front of saving others. Paulina routinely reminded me of all the evidence she had to show that I alone was a murderer. I did not want to go to prison, but worse than that, I did not want Paulina to abandon me." Raul cried the entire time he tried to explain this to Dr. Triton.

Using a gentle tone hoping to help Raul calm down enough to finish the evaluation, Dr. Triton asked him, "Do you feel like she abandoned you by committing suicide?"

"No, she did not commit suicide, but she did abandon me. I am in jail, and Mike Davidson tells me I may very well get a death sentence. She is out there living a new life." Raul responded with more vigor than he had shown throughout the interview.

It was essential that Dr. Triton not only determine Raul's sanity in terms of his ability to aid his counsel at trial and understand the crimes he had committed, but also whether he was a danger to himself. She had already determined one of those factors and now needed to delve into the other. "Raul, are you planning to hurt or kill yourself?"

Raul barely looked up as he shook his head and replied, "No, I need to take responsibility for what I did and be able to help the FBI find her."

Friday March 23, 2018

Taking Kelsey had to be well-planned, just like the seven men they had kidnapped. The difference between this time and the others was that Kelsey did not live a solitary life. Raul should not have been surprised when Paulina told him that she had found out that Kelsey was registered to attend a conference. Paulina had walked around the convention center and the parking lots and garage. She wanted them to wait for Kelsey after the conference and grab her if she was alone. The only issue Paulina saw was video cameras in the parking areas.

Of course, Paulina had a plan for that, too, and today was when they would deal with the camera system. When the storm began an hour ago, she told him it was time to go. Once they arrived at the convention center, Paulina parked outside the video range. Raul used a paintball gun to obscure the camera outside the parking garage. He walked back to the van and got the ladder and cattle prod. As he climbed the ladder in the pouring rain, he hoped that he would get struck by lightning, and then all of this would be over.

Raul loosened the screws on the camera and then stuck the cattle prod into the housing. He watched as smoke billowed out of the camera. The only reason that this plan worked was because the convention center had never upgraded the camera system. When he fried this camera, it shorted out the entire system. Raul climbed down the ladder and picked up the camera that had fallen off the building. Finding Paulina standing beside the ladder took him by surprise. He put away the supplies and climbed into the passenger seat as she got into the driver's side.

"How will we know for sure that the system has not been replaced before that conference?" Raul asked Paulina.

Paulina replied, "I will go to the conference center the day before the convention Kelsey is registered for. I plan to say someone hit my car in the parking garage, and I want to know if they have video footage. If they do, then this will not be the right spot to take her."

Friday April 10, 2018

Raul was sick with the stomach flu, but Paulina left anyway. She was determined to check the video capabilities at the convention center. He had gotten sick this weekend. First, he had a headache and was exhausted. When he complained to Paulina, she had gone to the store and bought him more of his favorite flavor of Gatorade. She had always nagged him about drinking only Gatorade. Supposedly, the sugar and artificial colors were going to kill him. Raul was sure that Paulina would kill him before the Gatorade ever did.

She left this morning after telling him he probably had a stomach bug and reminding him to stay hydrated. When she had brought the Gatorade home Saturday, he had drunk part of one of the bottles but threw up almost immediately and could no longer bring himself to drink it. He did not want to anger Paulina, so he had been pouring the bottles down the drain the last few days, so she would think he was drinking it. Raul was sure that Paulina had been trying to poison him.

There was no surprise or shock when he realized what she had done. It was likely that she had added antifreeze to his drinks. After getting sick from the first one, he noticed none of the bottles were still sealed. He wondered what her next step would be when he didn't die.

****

Paulina's emotions were all over the place, driving away from the convention center. She was elated that the camera system was fully dysfunctional, so they could hopefully proceed with the plan to take Kelsey tomorrow. At the same time, it enraged her that Raul did not seem to be getting sicker. Paulina no longer had a use for Raul. The ethylene glycol poisoning should have worked.

She had even accepted that she would have to take Kelsey herself because Raul would either be too weak to help or already dead. She had planned to put Raul's body in the basement alongside Kelsey and then light the barn on fire. After the fire department put out the blaze, they would find the bodies, and she would play the shocked widow.

Raul must have figured out that the Gatorade he so loved was tampered with, and he wasn't really drinking it. Fine! She would play this out with him, helping her to get rid of Kelsey Learner and then figure out how to deal with him. He was right two months ago when he told her that he was done.

23

Friday June 19, 2020

Mike Davidson hung up the phone with Troy Moore just as his assistant walked in with Dr. Triton. Troy had agreed to pay Mike's retainer and ongoing expenses to defend his son. The senior Moore would need to get a home equity loan, but Mike was assured that he would get paid. If, in the unlikely event, the courts didn't seize the assets of Raul and Paulina, he would help Troy and Camilla to recoup their expenses.

"I thought we should discuss my findings after meeting with your client, but before I submit my report on Monday to the judge." Dr. Vera Triton stated as she sat down and took a file out of her bag.

Mike thought, from her tone, that he wasn't going to like what she had to say. "Absolutely. What is your professional opinion regarding Raul Moore?" Mike asked.

Dr. Triton opened the folder in her lap and seemed to skim the contents. She then handed the folder to Mike and said, "As you can see, I am going to report that Raul Moore is sane and fully understands the crimes he committed. I also do not believe that Mr. Moore is suicidal."

"Okay, I appreciate you conducting the evaluation," Mike told her.

"Mr. Davidson, there is more. It will not be helpful regarding the competency decision, but may be of assistance during the trial. I have detailed my findings in the report, but I can give you a brief rundown them now if you would like it," Dr. Triton asked.

Mike was disappointed that insanity would not be the defense, but he needed to hear Dr. Triton thought it might be useful for Raul's defense. "Yes, I would appreciate you walking me through your findings."

Vera Triton started by saying, "Let me start with a caveat. These are my preliminary findings. Before being willing to testify, I will want to look at all the evidence and speak with Raul again, probably multiple times."

"That is perfectly understandable, and I appreciate you sharing your initial thoughts," Mike responded.

"I believe that Paulina and Raul Moore were a team of serial killers. Teams of serial killers are very rare and when there is a team, there is always a dominant and a submissive personality type. Paulina Moore was the dominant personality not only in terms of their crimes but in all aspects of their lives.

As they committed more crimes, their bond grew stronger. At first this was because of Raul's feelings of guilt, which made him more submissive to Paulina. Later shame became the major factor for his deepening dependence. In turn, this fueled Paulina to increase the momentum of their crimes.

Raul feared abandonment, which was a fear that was constructed first by the death of his long-term girlfriend, Shelby, and then made worse when his daughter died. The thought that Paulina would leave him drove Raul to be willing to go along with her plans, despite knowing that what they were doing was wrong."

Dr. Triton took a breath, and Mike decided to ask a question.

"Do you think that Paulina is insane?"

Dr. Triton replied, "I would have to evaluate her to arrive at a diagnosis. However, it is pure speculation based on Raul's descriptions during my evaluation of him and the case notes you shared. I would speculate that she is a narcissist with a God complex. She seems to believe she can defy human biology and anatomy based on the experimentation Raul Moore described. I would further speculate that she is also a psychopath. The diagnosis of psychopathic personality disorder and sociopathic personality disorder both fall under the broader diagnosis of antisocial personality disorder. People with antisocial personality disorder are characterized by a long-standing pattern of disregard for the feelings of others.

Both psychopaths and sociopaths are manipulative of others; however, a key reason I lean towards Paulina being a psychopath is that she is described as being very socially adept. Sociopaths cannot hide their lack of regard towards others, are very impulsive, and lack social skills.

Whether Paulina was a psychopath before their crime spree is something that I cannot say with the information that we currently have."

Mike Davidson needed time to think about what Dr. Triton had told him. "I appreciate all of your information, and please stay in touch so that I can provide you with all the access to evidence that the prosecution turns over as well as to Raul," he said as he stood up and walked around his desk. He was about to walk Dr. Triton to the door when his phone started ringing. It was his direct line, which few people had access to.

Dr. Triton stood and said, "Feel free to answer that. I can see myself out."

Mike picked up the phone and asked the person to hold on a second, and put his hand over the receiver. "Dr. Triton, please wait," he said, and then to the person on the phone, "Sorry, please go on. Yes, I understand. Thank you for informing me," hanging up he sat back down.

"What is it, Mr. Davidson?" Dr. Triton asked as she walked towards him.

Mike Davidson seemed stunned into silence for a moment, then he looked at Dr. Triton and said, "Raul Moore hung himself this morning in his cell."

Now, it was Dr. Triton's turn to sit quickly and be stunned.

"How could this have happened? You just told me that Raul was not suicidal," Mike questioned Dr. Triton.

Dr. Triton's voice was laced with remorse, "I think it is clear that I was wrong. What I did not factor in is that many suicidal people are at their most calm when they have resolved to end their lives. I should have probed deeper."

Wednesday April 11, 2018

As Raul slowly drove the van through the parking garage, he was happy that very few cars were left parked here. He had driven through this morning to see if Kelsey had parked in the garage or the street-level parking lot. They had put a magnet on the side of the van for a local construction company that was doing remodeling at the hotel attached to the convention center. Paulina had stolen the magnet two years ago. She had collected things like that in case they found a use for them. Today, that magnet helped their van blend in. He had found Kelsey's SUV on the third level of the garage, which the level that was adjacent to the pedestrian bridge to the convention center.

This time, unlike the morning trip to find Kelsey's SUV, Paulina was harping at him in the passenger seat. She seemed nervous and knew this was riskier than any other person they had taken in the past. As they had planned, Raul backed into a parking spot that was one away from Kelsey's vehicle. He exited the van, opened one of the back doors, and sat down.

Paulina walked to the edge of the pedestrian bridge and appeared to be texting on her phone. Raul knew it was a ruse as neither carried a working cell phone while on a mission. Not leaving a digital footprint was one of the many things Paulina repeatedly lectured him on since they started this seven years ago. It was one of the few things that he thought she was right about.

Raul saw Paulina start walking back to the van, he knew that she had spotted Kelsey and that it was time for him to get into place. He walked to the van's driver's side and stood just before the door. Paulina walked past him slowly and then dropped her purse. She bent down to pick up items, facing the direction that Kelsey would be walking to get to her car. Paulina would stand up when Kelsey was at her car, indicating that he was to grab her.

When Paulina stood up, Raul rounded the van and saw Kelsey leaning into the passenger side of her SUV. He walked up behind her and injected her with the tranquilizer. As Kelsey fell, Raul hauled her to the back of the van and put her in. Paulina was waiting in the back and restrained Kelsey. Driving out of the garage, they turned the opposite way, they had come from. They knew there was a camera this way that had recorded when Raul arrived this morning. The other direction that Raul used to leave the first time and arrive this time had no working cameras for several blocks, so it would appear that the work van arrived this morning and was just now leaving.

When they arrived back at the farm, Paulina said, "Take care of her," and exited the van. Knowing that he had to seem like he was doing what Paulina had told him to, Raul backed the van into the barn. He checked to ensure Kelsey was still unconscious and prepared the pig's usual slop buckets. He used the lift to go into the basement with Kelsey. He had disconnected Paulina's camera down here this morning and now wondered if she had figured that out yet. He hooked Kelsey to the monitor and saw a steady pulse and heart rate. Raul sat down in the basement for thirty minutes. Kelsey's heart rate and pulse increased, so he injected her with more tranquilizer before she could fully regain consciousness. As he waited, he became drenched in sweat due to the fear of not knowing if Paulina would come charging in and confront him about the camera system at any minute or if he would be able to get Kelsey out of there safely.

When a feasible amount of time passed, Raul fed the pigs and got Kelsey back in the van. He always left after one of their victims died to throw their personal belongings into Lake Springfield. Hopefully, sticking to the routine would keep Paulina from suspecting he was not following her plan. He would stash Kelsey in the shipping container and ditch her things in the lake.

****

Did he really think he could outsmart her? Paulina fumed as she watched the lights on the van drive away from the farm. When she got to her home office, she booted up the camera system and saw that the basement camera was no longer working. She had been about to charge over there and confront Raul when she decided to wait and see what he was up to.

Paulina watched the dot that signified the van on the tracking software move across the laptop screen. After a few turns, Paulina figured out where he was headed and what he had been doing out in the woods for the last few weeks. Her laugh rang out, and if anyone had been home to hear it, they would have described it as bone-chillingly evil. Paulina reveled in her thoughts:

Oh my, this is so much better than my plan. He is going to put her in that shipping container that he buried. Does he honestly think being held captive underground is a better fate than dying?

Paulina was glad she had inspected what Raul had done on the lot. He hadn't installed a lock on the top of the manhole cover. She had ordered a lock for the cover the day after Raul buried the container. The lock was in the bed of her truck, so Paulina went to check what tools she needed to install it and then waited until the GPS locator dot left the lot. She knew Raul would be headed to Lake Springfield next, so she needed to get going.

The truck's headlights illuminated the opening to the shipping container, which provided Paulina with enough light to install the lock. She then attached a tag on the lock that said *Ask your wife.* She wondered how long Raul would wait to come see her for the key. A better question was whether she would give him the key.

24

Friday June 19, 2020

Agents Hollins and Matthews stood in SSAC Hernandez's office, reading a copy of Raul Moore's suicide note. The Greene County Jail had called Hernandez at six this morning to tell them that Raul Moore had hung himself in his cell. Hernandez had called Matthews at home and told him to go to the jail and retrieve the suicide note. Matthews had picked up the note that was sealed in an evidence bag and taken it straight to the lab. The technicians would verify that it was Raul Moore's handwriting just so there were no questions in court. The technician had made the copy that Hollins and Matthews were now reading.

To the FBI,

I am guilty of all the crimes I have been charged with, and I cannot live with the things that I have done. When my wife, Paulina, came to me seven years ago with her plan, I should have stopped her then. I felt then and still now feel powerless to stand up to her. I have known from the start of this that she must be psychotic. There is no other explanation for believing we should kidnap seven men and transplant pig hearts into them. When this all started, I thought her psychosis was a grief reaction, but after what we did to Kelsey Learner, I began to really think about Paulina and the tragedies that seem to follow her.

When Shelby died, I, like everyone else, accepted that it was a freak accident. The more I have thought about it in the last few months, the less sense it makes. Maybe touching the AC unit would have caused it to fall out of the window if it wasn't installed right, but how would Shelby have fallen with it? How would she have lost her balance to that degree while standing in her dorm room? Paulina quickly befriended me after and shared with me that she could empathize because her high school boyfriend, Tom, died during their senior year. She only brought it up once, and the few times I ever tried to ask about him, she shut down the conversation, saying it was too hard to talk about.

I am hoping the FBI is reading this note, and if you are, you may be saying come on, accidents happen. But do they happen to three people in your life, all in different freak ways? You see, Paulina's first boss after veterinary school also died in an unusual manner. She hated Dr. Curt Manning and complained about him excessively until about three weeks before his death. I didn't think about it then, but she just stopped telling me all the irritating things he did. Paulina did not tell me about his death, despite being the one to find his body and call for help. No, I found out about it the next day when I went to work, and someone asked me how she was doing. I had no clue what they were talking about, and when I asked her about it that evening, she waved her hand at me and said something like; it seemed like divine intervention to her. We bought his veterinary practice from his brother a few weeks later for far less than Dr. Manning would have ever been willing to sell it for.

Just before we took Kelsey, Paulina attempted to murder me as well. She poisoned my drinks with antifreeze for several weeks. When I got sick, I realized that I was vomiting more after I drank the Gatorade that Paulina had bought me. I poured them out and saw some bluish liquid stuck to the bottles, which I had never seen before. I recovered, and for whatever reason, Paulina didn't try again.

I am telling you all these things for two reasons. First, Paulina is out there. She would never have committed suicide and is dangerous to anyone she decides is in her way or has slighted her. She will kill again. The second reason is that I think the families of the people she murdered, Tom, Shelby, and Curt, deserve to know the truth, and the only way that happens is if you, the FBI, look into their cases.

The final thing that I regret is our kidnapping of Kelsey Learner. Paulina developed a deep hatred for Kelsey and decided she needed to die. I couldn't bring myself to kill Kelsey, but she is likely dead by now. I knew I couldn't stop Paulina, so I helped kidnap Kelsey and hide her. I had planned to let Kelsey escape, but of course, Paulina outsmarted me once again. It has been fourteen days since I have been able to give Kelsey food or water, and I am sure that Paulina would not have, so I am sorry to say she is dead.

I sincerely apologize to my victims, their families, and my parents. I deeply regret that I was not a strong enough person to stop Paulina. I take full responsibility for what I did and hope my death is at least some solace to all I hurt. I committed unforgivable atrocities and am not asking for or expecting forgiveness or absolution for my sins.

Raul Moore

SSAC Hernandez had waited until both Matthews and Hollins had finished reading the letter. "I have already called Silver at the prosecutor's office and let him know. The jail will also call Mike Davidson to inform him, and the Green County Sheriff will inform Raul's parents. Since the sheriff's department is in charge of the jail, they will conduct a death investigation, but there is no reason to suspect that this is anything but a suicide. Our attention now must be on finding Paulina Moore and Kelsey Learner."

Thursday April 12, 2018

Raul stared down at the metal bar and lock now attached to the manhole cover; neither had been there last night when he had brought Kelsey here. Based on the note, he knew who put them there, but he felt he would have known even without the note. Who else would have found this and put a lock on the cover? Paulina! How had she found out? How long had she known about this spot?

Sitting on the ground, Raul was paralyzed with fear. Not only would he not be able to free Kelsey, but it was highly likely that he would die today. It was delusional of him to believe that he would be able to outsmart Paulina. He slowly rose from the ground and went to face the music.

****

Paulina looked at the screen of the laptop that had started beeping. Raul was at the wooded lot. She wondered if he would come straight to see her or if he would be too scared to face her. She had work to finish, so she returned to it while waiting. Three years ago, she formed an LLC using a third identity she created as the owner. Hanna Lewis was the sole owner of a company named Lewis Holdings, LLC. Paulina had found it incredibly easy to use the forms provided online by the State of Missouri to form the LLC and get her tax identification number without assistance.

The mailbox that belonged to Lewis Holdings was at the post office down the road from her mother's house. Paulina kept the items she needed to look like the ID photo of Hanna in a princess' backpack. Hanna was a colorful dresser with bright red hair and even brighter lipstick. Once a month, Paulina went to see her mom and then, after that visit, became Hanna and picked up any items in the P.O. Box, which was almost always just junk mail.

Two months ago, Lewis Holdings had written to the estate of Shelby Lansing at the address listed on the Register of Deeds website and asked to purchase the wooded lot. The letter said that Lewis Holdings was planning to set up a bird sanctuary and thought the lot would be a wonderful location for the birds. It had only taken a week to receive a response from Shelby's father, agreeing to sell the lot. His letter had named a cheap price and had included a simple contract for Hanna Lewis to sign. Hanna had gotten a cashier's check from a check cashing store for the transaction and had the contract notarized by an overworked secretary at a law office that offered the service for a small fee.

Hanna had gone to the P.O. box this morning and found a slip to pick up a certified envelope. She had retrieved the envelope and found the deed for the property. Paulina had scoped out gas stations with antiquated outdoor bathrooms and stopped at one to change her attire and look. She entered the bank where she had her own personal account and went to her safe deposit box. After securing the deed in the box, Paulina headed home to work on the scheduling calendar for their veterinary practice.

She was finishing up the calendar when she heard Raul pull up in the van. He had come straight back after leaving the wooded lot. Paulina stood up, stretched, and walked to the kitchen table to wait for him. She thought, *Let the fun begin.*

****

Raul ended the call with his mom and dad as he pulled into the farm. He had called them to catch up and ensure that the last thing he ever said to them was, "I love you." He was sure that Paulina was lying in wait for him and that the end of his life was only moments away. He parked the van and walked into the house. You could see the kitchen table from the front door, and Raul saw Paulina sitting at the table, staring at him.

He walked into the kitchen and asked, "How did you find out?".

Paulina responded, "Sit down".

After Raul took a seat as far from his wife as he could, Paulina continued, "How did I find out what, Raul? That you have been harboring a thing for Shelby for the past twenty years? Or that you bought a shipping container with God knows what money? Had it delivered, and then you buried it in the ground? Or are you asking, how did I find out that instead of killing Kelsey Leaner, you took her to that container and left her inside for who knows what reason? Which question would you like me to answer first?"

Raul was flabbergasted by all that Paulina knew and was unsure where to start, but he knew he had to answer her. "I just couldn't kill Kelsey, so I took her to the container."

"Now, Raul, please don't treat either of us like we are dumb. You clearly never planned to kill Kelsey. You went through all that effort with the shipping container long before yesterday. What I want you to tell me now is what is your plan for Ms. Learner?" Paulina snapped at him.

There was no way he could tell Paulina the truth that he had planned to let Kelsey go and then turn himself in for the seven murders. She would go ballistic. He decided to try to stall, "I had not thought beyond putting her into the container."

The look Paulina was giving him now said she did not believe him, even for a second. "Raul! That is total bullshit. Were you planning to keep that woman down there forever, or did you have another way you were going to get rid of her?"

Raul had no explanation that would make Paulina happy, so he decided to ask for her help. Maybe if he let her take charge of the situation, she would turn her focus away from him. "I don't know. What do you think we should do next with her?"

"Now that is the right answer. Here is what we are going to do..." Paulina laid out a plan for Raul that made him wonder if he and Kelsey were better off dead.

25

Friday June 19, 2020

Agent Matthews had gotten permission from SSAC Hernandez to update Detectives Minor and Leet about the link to their cold case. He had informed Hernandez of his relationship with Kass Minor, and Hernandez was fine with Matthews taking the lead. His next step was to call Kass and tell her that he and his partner, Agent Hollins, needed to talk to her and her partner. Kass had tried to get him to tell her what was happening over the phone, but he had not relented.

Hollins had driven them to the Springfield Police station, and on the way, Matthews told him that he had told Kass that the cases were unrelated.

"You had no way to know. None of us did. Kelsey Learner doesn't fit their modus operandi. I also don't believe that the Moores didn't kill her. For whatever reason, Raul just wasn't willing to admit to that one murder."

Matthews knew Hollins was right, but felt bad about giving Kass misinformation. As they walked into the police station, Kass was waiting for them; she greeted them as they walked towards a conference room.

"Are you going to tell me what is happening now?" she asked Matthews.

He shook his head and smiled weakly at her.

She shook her head in response and chuckled.

Detective Mitch Leet was already sitting in the conference room as they walked in. He shook both agents' hands and asked, "What is happening?"

"Kass, I have to apologize to you. When we met a few days ago, I assured you that Raul Moore had no connection to the Kelsey Learner abduction case. I was wrong," Matthews explained.

Detective Leet interjected, "WHAT? What do you mean?"

Agent Hollins replied, "Early this morning, Raul Moore committed suicide in his cell at the Greene County Jail. He left a suicide note admitting to kidnapping Kelsey Learner." He slid a copy of the note to each of the detectives.

Once the detectives had read the note, Detective Leet said, "Our case is no longer cold. Do we know where they were holding her?"

Matthews shook his head and said, "For no known reason, Raul Moore did not disclose Kelsey's location in his letter. We have torn the Moore's farm apart and have found no evidence of Kelsey ever having been there."

"The question now is whether the FBI will take over the Kelsey Learner case or the Springfield Police Department will take the lead. I am sure that your gut reaction is to say that it is your case, but talk to your commander and be sure that is what the higher-ups want," Agent Hollins told Minor and Leet.

Mitch Leet nodded, "You are right, Minor, and I want to close this case, but you are also right that both our agencies are ruled by politics. So, we will check with our commander and get back to you as soon as possible."

All four law enforcement officials stood up, and Kass Minor walked Hollins and Matthews back to the front door. Hollins left Matthews and Minor at the door and walked back to their agency-issued car.

Minor turned to Matthews, "Robert, you do not need to apologize. You gave me the best information that you had at the time."

Robert reached out and pulled Kass into a quick hug. "Thanks. I think the one positive thing that may come out of this case is being able to tell eight families what happened to their loved one."

"I want to talk with Joe and Claire Learner before this somehow makes it onto the news. I will see what Commander Davis has to say and get permission to contact the Learners. There are still so many unanswered questions, but at least we have a starting point now." Kass told him then turned and walked away.

Robert Matthews walked to the car and wondered out loud; "Where is Kelsey Learner?"

Thursday April 19, 2018

Raul was freaking out. Yesterday, a detective had left him several messages wanting to talk to him about the disappearance of Kelsey Learner. Raul had not called him back because, quite frankly, he was too scared to do so. How had detectives linked him to Kelsey's disappearance? When he got home last evening, he thought about telling Paulina about the messages, but decided to go to Mike Davidson this morning instead. Hiring an attorney before talking to the police was the smart thing to do.

The doorbell rang just as Raul approached the back door after feeding the chickens and pigs. He heard Paulina answer the door, so he poured himself a cup of coffee. They rarely got visitors at the farm, so he thought it odd to hear Paulina tell them to come in. He looked up when Paulina returned to the kitchen. She told him, "There are two Springfield police detectives here to see you. I showed them to the living room. What the hell is going on?"

"How should I know? What do you want me to say to them?" Raul was shaking as he responded to her.

Paulina wished she could be the one who talked with these detectives, but they had specifically asked to talk to Raul. "Just answer their questions and only their questions. Do not volunteer any information. If they ask you specific questions about her, tell them that you are not comfortable with their questions and that you will get an attorney to contact them. Am I clear?"

Nodding his head in the affirmative, Raul got up and entered the bathroom next to the kitchen. He washed his hands and face, then stood staring at his reflection. He tried to slow his breathing and thought, *Is this the end? When they arrest me, I need to tell them immediately where Kelsey is before Paulina can kill her.*

As he walked into the living room, Raul saw two detectives. He introduced himself, and they did the same in turn.

Detective Leet said, "I left you several messages yesterday, and you did not get back to me. Since time is of the essence, we came out to talk to you this morning."

"Yes, I got those messages. I am sorry I did not have a chance to get back to you yet. We are swamped because it is the birthing season for horses and cattle. I wrote myself a note to call you today. How can I help you?" Raul responded.

The female detective, whose name he could not remember, said, "We would like to know about your relationship with Joe Learner."

"Um, okay. I know him from The Club. He has been out here once for a party, and I think he helped on the playground project that I headed up for The Club. I cannot say that I know him well. Is there something specific that you would like to know?"

Detective Leet asked, "Did you ever talk to him about his ex-wife, Kelsey?"

"Well, I knew he was divorced, and of course, I heard on the news that his ex-wife was missing. He never talked to me about her, so I do not think I can help."

"What is your general impression of Joe?" the female detective asked.

Raul shrugged and said, "He seems like an ordinary guy. Nothing that stands out in my mind."

The detectives stood up and thanked Raul for his time, then Detective Leet handed him a business card and said, "Please contact me if you think of anything else that may help us to find Kelsey Learner."

Raul walked the detectives to the door and watched them leave. As he turned around, he was startled that Paulina was standing less than two feet away.

"What the hell was that?" she asked.

****

Paulina stood right outside the entrance to the living room. She was fuming mad. Her thoughts were already rampant; Detective Leet had just said *he had left Raul messages yesterday. Yet Raul had not told her anything about the messages. She could have coached him through a response if he had told her, and these detectives would not be here now.*

The detective's questions were primarily regarding Joe Learner. Paulina began to think that Raul was not a suspect at all, but that, for some reason, the detectives were focused on Joe. She was sure there was no way they could pin this on Joe because he didn't do it, and she and Raul had not left any evidence behind so there was no reason for them to be suspects.

As they began wrapping up their conversation, Paulina walked back to the kitchen. She heard Raul say goodbye to the detectives, aa she walked up behind him. He was falling apart, and she needed to reel him back in before he ruined everything. However, her anger took over as she asked, "What the hell was that?"

She watched as Raul shrunk away from her. He responded, "They just wanted to know my impression of Joe Learner."

"Oh, I heard that. I want to know why you didn't tell me about the detective leaving you two messages yesterday?" Paulina hissed at him.

Raul knew there was no acceptable answer to her question, so he responded with just one word, "Fear."

Paulina started laughing and asked, "Of the police or me?"

This question he had a definitive answer to, "Both."

His answer made Paulina laugh harder as she walked away from him to get ready for the day.

26

Saturday June 20, 2020

Detective Kass Minor called Joe Learner last evening to set up a time to meet with him and Claire. He had told Kass that Claire had moved home about a week ago. They agreed to meet at Claire's home this morning. Joe would let Claire know he was coming over, but not why. Minor had talked with Detective Leet, and they had agreed that he would start to work on figuring out where Kelsey could be while she was talking to the Learners.

Pulling up to Kelsey and Claire Learner's home, Minor remembered the other times she had been to this home. The last time was when she had brought Claire her mother's SUV back. Since then, Claire called Kass Minor every week to get an update on her mom's case. It had been hard for Kass to tell her that there was no new information, but as hard as that was, she knew that this update would be harder.

As Detective Kass Minor approached the house, Claire opened the door, turned around, and called, "Dad!".

The door was open when she reached it, but no one stood there. She looked in and saw Joe Learner holding a sobbing Claire.

He waved her in and said, "Why don't we sit in the kitchen?". He turned and gently led Claire down the hall, with Detective Minor following them.

"Claire, I have news about your mom," Minor said as they sat down.

In an expectant tone, Claire looked up at her and asked, "Did you find her? Is she alright?".

Detective Minor shook her head and replied, "No, we have not found her, but for the first time, we have a viable lead. Please let me explain, and then you can ask me any questions."

Joe and Claire nodded, and Minor continued, "You have likely heard on the news about the FBI raiding a local farm last week. The owners of that farm, Doctors Raul and Paulina Moore, are part of an ongoing federal investigation into the murders of seven men. I do not have details on that case, so I cannot answer any questions regarding it. Including how the FBI figured out what was happening at the Moores' farm.

Raul Moore was arrested seven days ago, and Paulina Moore was added to the FBI's most-wanted list yesterday. Yesterday, early in the morning, Raul killed himself in his jail cell. He left a suicide note. In that note, he claimed that he and Paulina kidnapped Kelsey. He did not explain why, except to say Paulina hated her.

The letter doesn't tell us where to find your mom, but the FBI has eliminated the Moores' farm. They have thoroughly searched that property, and there is no sign of her there. Detective Leet is working on narrowing down where the Moores may have taken her."

Claire was crying quietly, her head buried in her father Joe's chest. Joe asked, "Are you saying Raul and Paulina Moore murdered Kelsey?"

"The letter left by Raul did not confess to killing Kelsey, only to having taken and held her," Minor answered him.

Claire sat up and asked, "So, my mom may still be alive?".

This was the part that Kass Minor had been dreading. If what he had written in the letter was true, there had been a chance to save Kelsey all these months, but she and Leet had stopped looking. How could she explain that Kelsey had likely died while Raul Moore was in custody? Minor took a deep breath, "It is highly unlikely that your mother is still alive, Claire. I will do everything I can to find her, no matter what."

Joe Learner gently moved his daughter off of him and stood. "Detective, I think it is time for you to leave. I am sure you will contact us if you have any more information." He walked Minor to the front door and added, "Please tell me any news before you tell Claire. She is a very strong young woman, but when it comes to her mother, that is an open wound, and I need to be more prepared to help her than I was today."

Kass Minor stared at Joe Learner for a moment. She realized that she and Leet underestimated his love for Claire. It seemed he had really stepped in to fill a void for Claire in her mother's absence. She responded to Joe, "Of course. I am sorry. I didn't mean to upset Claire, but I promised to tell her if we ever had any leads in the case. I wanted both of you to hear it from me in case it leaks to the media as well."

"I appreciate you telling us yourself. I am hoping that Kelsey's name will not get pulled into the sensationalized story surrounding the Moores and their victims. But I am prepared that will likely happen," Joe said as he opened the front door for Minor.

As she walked back to her car, Detective Kass Minor wondered if it was better for the Learners to know who had taken Kelsey without knowing what they had done to her. With the national news swirling with rumors of what had happened at the farm, she was sure that imagining what may have happened to her mom would haunt Claire. The real question came back to: *Where is Kelsey Learner?*

Sunday June 10, 2018

Raul drove the van into the lot. This was the fourth time he and Paulina had returned to the lot since he had locked Kelsey in the storage container. Each of the last four Sundays, they drove out here together. Paulina would unlock the manhole cover while Raul removed the fire ladder and other supplies from the van. Raul would lower the ladder down the hole, shoot Kelsey with the stun gun, and then inject her with the tranquilizer.

With Kelsey out cold, Paulina would lower the supplies down to him. Raul would clean up any mess Kelsey had made, swap out her latrine bucket, and leave her food and water. This week, Paulina sent a package of shower wipes as well. The last step was to send the old latrine bucket and anything else that needed to be removed up to Paulina. Raul then climbed back up the ladder and pulled it out of the hole. Once the manhole cover and lock were back in place, Paulina would join him in the van.

When Paulina had laid out her plan, she had been clear to tell Raul that if she caught him coming out here without her again, both he and Kelsey would die a horrific death. He did not question that she would be happy to end it that way. Daily, he considered whether to get a lawyer and turn himself in. Somehow, he never found the strength.

****

Claire sat crying in her mom's Buick Encore in their driveway and looked at the house. She had put off leaving for college as long as she could but today, she had to leave and her mom was not there to see her off. It was one of many things her mom had missed out on since she disappeared. Her friend, Lindsey, thought Claire should go to counseling, but she was not ready.

Graduating from high school without her mom was hard, but her friends and her dad surrounded her. Today, she was alone. Lindsey was off with her boyfriend in Florida, visiting her grandparents. Her dad called her at least twice weekly, but she had told him she didn't need his help today. She believed that he would be here if she had, but honestly, the only person she wanted today was her mom, which was impossible.

Her dad had helped her sort out her mom's finances, so she knew that she could go almost a year without renting out the house and be able to pay all the bills. He had told her that when the time came, he would help her with renting out the house. The one positive thing over the last few weeks was how much time she and her dad had spent together. She had never believed that he did anything to hurt her mom and was glad when the police had cleared him. He had never explained what had happened, and she was too worried about her mom to probe him for details.

This morning, she had hung the new note on the inside of the storm door facing out. She had put up a note when her mom disappeared, but decided that there needed to be a new one. The new note read:

Mom-

If you are reading this note, you are home! Nothing is more important than that!

My cellphone number has not changed. My dorm address is:

Missouri University of Science and Technology

1 Constitution Hall

Rollo, MO

I love you! Call me-Claire

The note was on bright orange paper and taped up with box tape. She wanted her mom to know that she was not forgotten. Claire would never stop searching for her mom, and she had told Detective Minor that she would call her every week to check on her mom's case. The detective had assured her that no matter what, she would never let her mom's disappearance be forgotten.

Claire put the SUV in reverse and backed out of the driveway. She started her mom's playlist and cried as she drove towards the next step in her life. Another step without her mom.

27

Saturday June 20, 2020

Michelle Brooks walked from her condo to the library. She picked up a coffee from her new favorite local coffee shop and enjoyed the mild summer day. Her surgery was scheduled for Monday, then she would rest while deciding what to do next. She would have to rely on cable news to keep her up to date with the goings on in Missouri.

Michelle logged on to the computer and thought about how long she could stay here. She didn't believe that the FBI was stupid, just that she had gotten a good head start on them and had put a lot of measures in place to make it hard to track her. After she recovered from her surgery, it would be time to start looking for an off-the-grid cabin to buy. It would likely drain her resources, but she was sure the condo could be rented to make for a decent passive income.

It was tempting to type what she wanted to search into the computer, but she would not do that. If she could set up Google alerts, surely law enforcement could too. She was unsure that they would do that because it would likely lead to hundreds, if not thousands, of hits a day that were perfectly innocent, but she was not willing to take any chances. She clicked on a national news page after reading articles on urban gardening and celebrities. As soon as the page loaded, she saw the headline:

Suspected Serial Killer Raul Moore Kills Himself in Jail

She opened the story as a sense of relief coursed through her. She was in no way surprised that Raul had taken the coward's way out. With him dead, the FBI and police couldn't get any further information out of him. She was unsure what he had already told them, but just the same, she knew the longer he was in custody, the more he would have talked.

The article didn't have a lot of information other than that Raul died yesterday morning and had reportedly left a suicide note. The reporter said that the FBI was actively searching for Paulina Moore and had added her to the Ten Most Wanted list. There were two pictures of her on the wanted poster; one was from the Moore Veterinary Practice website, and the other was captured from the surveillance camera at the bank.

Michelle clicked off the article and then on to other top news on the site. After reading a few unrelated stories, she closed the browser and logged off. Walking back along the trail that looped around Geneva Lake, she wished there was a way to find out how much the FBI knew. She thought about contacting her dad but decided it was in both of their best interest not to call him. When she had planned her identity change, she knew it might be necessary to change her fingerprints at some point. She decided that being added to the FBI's Ten Most Wanted list was that point.

While she recovered from her plastic surgery, she would use dry ice to burn her fingers systematically until all ten fingerprints had been altered. While the process was said to be painful, there was no way she wanted to leave behind identifiable prints.

****

Detective Minor walked towards her cubicle at the Springfield Police Department. She was sure that she would find Leet working at his cubicle which was right across from her. They would be working out of their cubicles this time, unless the commander authorized them to use one of the conference rooms. Sure enough, Mitch Leet was on the phone at his desk. He waved to her as she approached, and she rolled her chair over to his cubicle to wait for him to finish his call.

Leet told the person he was talking to, "Thank you for checking. I appreciate your help." then hung up. Turning to Minor, he said, "That was the Greene County Register of Deeds. I called her and had her check whether Raul Moore, Paulina Moore, or their veterinary practice owned any property other than their farm. She told me there is no record of them owning anything else."

"I assume that Commander Davis approved of us taking the lead on the case," Minor said to Leet.

"You and I are the lead investigators on the case. Commander Davis has asked the FBI Behavioral Analysis Unit to review Raul's suicide note. He is hoping there are clues to where Kelsey may be," Leet told her and continued, "I asked the evidence clerk to bring up the boxes on Kelsey Learner's case."

Detective Minor wondered if any of the old evidence would actually help them. They had gone in the wrong direction twice when first looking for Kelsey. What was worse was that they had gone out to the farm where the Moores committed their crimes. They had talked to Raul Moore, but he was never even been a blip on their radar as a suspect. *Did we miss something when we went there? Would we have been able to save Kelsey if we had realized the Moores were involved?* She thought as she sat there.

"Don't do that!" Detective Leet said, which shook Kass out of her wondering.

She responded, "Do what?"

Detective Leet answered, "The look on your face tells me you were playing the what-if game. Neither of us suspected the Moores. I remember talking about there being something strange about them, but there were no signs they took Kelsey. Instead of thinking about what we could have done differently, we have to put our energy into finding Kelsey."

Minor knew he was right and said, "Alright, let's start a new crime board and look at everything we know."

December 2018

Kelsey woke up with a start. She was cold, and it took her a few seconds to remember that she was still chained in a metal container. The man must have been here because she had the groggy feeling that she got each time he had come by. With no windows, she could not be sure how long she had been being held. She had found a few rocks in the container she was trapped in and had been trying to keep track of the days by making hash marks on the ground.

Kelsey thought back to the first time she woke up in her prison. There was a flashlight in her right hand. She had switched it on and looked around. To her right were seven jugs of water and a bucket containing what she later figured out were twenty-one shelf-stable food packets. To her left was a bucket with a toilet seat on top of it and rolls of toilet paper next to it. She was sitting on an air mattress, with a blanket across her lap and a pillow where her head had laid.

During the first few weeks, at least she thought they were weeks, Kelsey tried to find a way to free herself from the shackle around her left ankle. The chain from the shackle to the wall was welded in both spots and was long enough to allow her to move around about two feet. She walked the full-length multiple times daily, counting her steps as she went. She spent her time remembering Claire's life. She worried about how her daughter was doing. She prayed that Claire knew that she had not left her intentionally.

At some point, the man had brought down more blankets, a sweatshirt, and a coat, which she had been thankful for. Over time, he had replaced her flashlight with a battery-operated lantern and must have routinely replaced the battery in it, as it never stopped working. He occasionally cut her fingernails and toenails and would leave her bathing wipes. There were extra t-shirts that he had left at one of his visits so she could change her shirt. When her pants had begun to fall apart, she woke up and found a slit cut up the left side of her pants and underwear, and a pair of tear-away basketball pants were neatly folded at the base of her bedroll.

One thing Kelsey could not work out in her mind was why this man had taken her. He had never physically harmed her and actually made sure that most of her needs were met. After one of his visits, she had found an old Walkman and some cassette tapes of eighties music in the bottom of the food container. Being trapped had worn down her resolve. Her will to live came from the hope that one day, she would be able to see Claire again, and she was losing hope of that ever happening.

28

Saturday June 20, 2020

After meeting with SSAC Hernandez, Agents Hollins and Matthews had a plan for trying to look for Paulina Moore. It had been ten days since they raided the Moore's farm. They would retrace her steps in the days leading up to her escape. The Fugitive Apprehension Task Force was also looking for her, but Hernandez didn't want to leave any stone unturned. While they looked for Paulina, they hoped they could gather evidence of her involvement in the murders.

The plan was to trace her movements from the day before she left until the last sighting, using surveillance footage and other electronic data. The van that the Moores drove to Kansas City was an older model and did not have GPS. Paulina Moore had left the only cell phone they could link to her behind in the van. She had used no credit cards since the charge for the hotel room at the conference on the veterinary practice's card.

Matthews had obtained a timeline of the sightings of Paulina at the hotel conference center and the bank from the Fugitive Apprehension Task Force. It had taken about forty-five minutes longer for her to make the return trip to the conference center then the trip to the bank had taken her. She had spent about fifteen minutes at the bank, so where had she been for those thirty minutes?

After piecing together what they had, Hollins and Matthews decided to go to the bank to obtain any footage they had from outside. They would also check with nearby businesses in hopes that they could see which direction Paulina Moore drove when she left the bank. Then, they would start getting footage to look for her along the route. It was next to impossible to go undetected in today's high-tech society.

This kind of work was tedious and would take them days and possibly weeks. Matthews wondered if Shawn Ross knew more than he had told them when they met with him. He realized they never asked Shawn Ross if he knew where Paulina was. Agent Matthews had to find out if they could compel Shawn to talk to them or if what he knew was covered by attorney-client privilege. Shawn Ross might be the only person who knew where Paulina was.

****

Charles Silver looked at the two agents sitting across from him. People misunderstood attorney-client privilege and thought it was all-encompassing, but it was not. Missouri law was clear that lawyers could disclose information to prevent death or substantial bodily harm that is reasonably certain to occur. From what they knew about Paulina Moore, it was a safe assumption that she was capable of killing more people. However, since they did not have a known target for this murder, Shawn Ross could easily argue that there was no reasonable certainty of a future crime.

"Agents, you are fine to go and ask Shawn Ross if he knows where Paulina Moore is?" Silver told them and then continued, "If he refuses to answer, let me know, and I will ask the judge to compel him."

Agent Hollins stood and shook Charles Silver's hand, "Thank you. We will let you know what we find out." He looked back and saw that his partner, Agent Matthews, was still sitting.

"Matthews, are you ready to go?" Agent Hollins asked.

Robert Matthews turned and looked at his partner and then back at Charles Silver. "I have a couple more questions."

Silver sat back down and said, "What else can I answer for you?"

Hollins also sat back down, then Matthews asked, "What if Shawn Ross knows something but lies to us?"

"Just like anyone, lying to a federal officer is a crime. I think he is too smart for that. He will either tell you the truth or claim privilege." Silver responded.

"Just one more thing: if he claims privilege and you go to court, how likely is it that a judge will compel him to talk to us?" Matthews asked.

Charles Silver knew it was a fair but tough question to answer. He replied, "Actually, with the evidence we have right now, not likely at all. If you can find more evidence that Paulina was the one who killed those seven men and Kelsey Learner, then it will strengthen my argument."

Robert Matthews wondered if talking to Shawn Ross was a waste of their time. He replied, "Thank you, Mr. Silver. I appreciate your candor."

June 2019

The irony that Claire wasn't taking classes this summer after starting college early last year was not lost on her. She wiped the sweat from her forehead and headed to the truck with another load of boxes. They were moving the furniture in her room and her stuff out to her dad's house and the rest of the things in the house to a storage unit. After they got everything out and the house cleaned, her dad would list the house for rent.

Lindsey and her boyfriend Mack were supposed to be here helping, but they had not shown up so far. Claire sent a quick text telling her they were done at her house and headed to her dad's place. When Claire had told Lindsey she was coming home for the summer, Lindsey had tried to convince her to stay with them at their apartment. Claire had made up a story about how important it was to her dad that she stay with him. The truth was that Claire did not like Mack. He always told Lindsey what to do, and she often canceled plans with Claire because Mack wanted her to stay home with him instead. She never told Lindsey what she thought because she did not want to alienate her friend.

Joe watched as Claire returned to the rental truck with the last box. He had offered to hire a moving company, but she felt it was important to clear her mother's house herself. Several of the guys from The Club had come and helped move all the furniture. Claire's stuff was in the back of his truck, and everything else was in the rental truck. He had found a storage unit a mile from his house, so they would go there first and then to his house. His friend, John, was driving the rental truck and would return it when they finished today.

Claire walked up to her dad, and he enveloped her in a hug. "I know this is hard, honey, but if your mom comes home, we will move you both back in," Joe told her.

Nodding her head, Claire handed him the house keys and walked to the passenger side of his truck.

Thursday July 4, 2019

Spending the Fourth of July with her dad at a cookout for The Club wasn't how Claire had planned to spend the holiday, but she would make the best of it. She and her dad had spent every evening together the past few weeks since she moved in playing board games. They were both fierce Scrabble competitors but sometimes broke up the routine by playing Monopoly or Clue. Claire didn't remember her dad having such a good sense of humor.

She and Lindsey had planned to attend the Fourth celebration downtown, but this morning, Lindsey texted her.

Lindsey: Mack wants us to go to his friend's party tonight. Cool?

Claire: No, I don't want to go to a party. Let's just stick to our plan!

Lindsey: Sorry, I have to go with Mack. Plz come with me!

Claire: Pass. Meet for coffee tomorrow?

Lindsey: SYT

After texting with Lindsey, Claire went to ask her dad if the invite for the barbecue was still open. He had said, of course, it was, so here she was, walking beside him towards a large gathering at a popular local park. She smelled food cooking and saw kids running around playing and many people sitting around talking. She followed her dad as he walked towards a table and introduced her.

"Hi, guys. This is my daughter, Claire. She is home for the summer from college. Claire, this is John, Mike, Jerry, and Raul," Joe said as he pointed around the table.

Claire smiled and said, "Hi everybody," as she sat down along with her dad.

She sat and listened while the men talked about fishing. She laughed along with them when they razzed her dad about his truck. Claire and her dad walked together to get heaping plates of food, and she asked him, "Dad, were we supposed to bring something?"

Joe smiled at her and shrugged, "There is always so much food that I never do."

As they returned to the table, a pretty woman with jet-black hair sat down beside the man her dad had said was Raul. She smiled at Claire and Joe and said, "Joe, is this your daughter?"

"Yes, this is my daughter, Claire," Joe responded.

The woman reached across the table, extended her hand to Claire, and said, "It is so nice to meet you. I'm Dr. Paulina Moore."

While the men continued their conversation, Paulina Moore got up, moved to sit next to Claire, and asked, "Your dad says you are going to college. Where are you going?"

"I'm attending Missouri University of Science and Technology in Rollo. I'm home for the summer. What kind of doctor are you?" Claire responded.

Paulina smiled at her and said, "I'm a large animal veterinarian. What are you studying?"

Claire had taken general education classes this past year and was unsure what she would major in. Before her mom disappeared, Claire had wanted to major in physical therapy and athletic training. Since starting school, she had been very unsure, and her advisor had told her to concentrate on her two years of required general education classes.

"I haven't declared a major yet. I am trying to figure out what I want to do as a career," Claire responded.

Paulina smiled, "You have your whole life to figure it out. I am glad you get to spend your summer with your dad." She then stood up and walked away.

****

Paulina was feeling practically giddy driving away from The Club's summer get-together. "Raul, did you see it? I was right."

"See what?" Raul responded while keeping his eyes on the road. He knew that if he made even the smallest driving error, she would unleash on him about his inadequacies.

"Raul, how is it you are so obtuse? You sat with them almost the whole time we were there. I am talking about Joe Learner and his daughter Claire. He has stepped up for her, and they have developed a loving relationship," Paulina explained to him.

Raul did not really understand why she cared so much, "That's nice."

"You really don't get it, do you?" Paulina asked, with the edge of impatience creeping into her voice.

"No, I don't," Raul responded. He was tired. Physically tired and mentally exhausted from dealing with Paulina and her constant mind games. He had no energy to try to figure out what she was going on about.

"Our latest project, you idiot! I told you that with Kelsey Learner gone, Joe and his daughter could develop a strong relationship. What we saw today tells me that I was right." Paulina responded.

"Does that mean we can let Kelsey go?" Raul asked and regretted it as soon as the words left his mouth. He knew the answer before she started screaming at him.

29

Sunday June 21, 2020

Hollins had called SSAC Hernandez after the meeting with Charles Silver. It was decided that Agents Hollins and Matthews should go to St. Louis to talk with Shawn Ross today. After that, they would work on gathering video to track Paulina when she had come back to Springfield. Hernandez had been clear that they were to keep working on the Paulina Moore case until they found her or a more pressing matter presented itself.

While they drove, Matthews told Hollins, “Based on Raul Moore’s suicide letter, he and Paulina were transplanting pig hearts into their victims. I guess that was the motive that we could not figure out.”

Hollins nodded and replied, “It is probably the strangest motive I have ever heard of, but that does seem to be theirs. Do you think she had planned to try to go public with the experiments?”

“Go public? Why would she go public? If she went public, how would she explain the dead people without admitting to murder?” Matthews asked in response.

Agent Hollins replied, “Exactly what I don’t understand. For there to be a medical benefit, other researchers and, eventually, heart surgeons would have to know about the experiments. As you pointed out, this would lead to knowing that Paulina and Raul murdered people.”

“Maybe Paulina is delusional, as well as a psychopath. If that is the case, we will never understand her thought process. It only needed to make sense to her. One woman’s logic is another woman's crazy,” Matthews commented.

Hollins nodded and then added, "I forgot to ask Charles Silver if we can get Mike Davidson's notes on Raul Moore. There may be information in what Raul said to him that will help us find Paulina."

"I will call Silver when you are driving back after we talk to Shawn Ross. That way, we can tell him what Ross said and get an answer to your question." Matthews replied.

****

Although they hadn't call ahead; Shawn Ross wasn't surprised to see Agents Hollins and Matthews back welcomed them into his office. "How can I help you? I assume it is about Paulina again?"

Agent Hollins asked, "Do you know where Paulina is?"

Shawn had been amazed that the agents had not asked him that when they were here the first time. The question's phrasing made it so he could answer them without lying or claiming privilege. "No, I do not know where Paulina Moore is. Do you have any other questions?"

"Not at this time. Thank you for your time," Agent Hollins said and shook Mr. Ross's hand.

Walking out of the office, Matthews asked Hollins, "Did you find it weird how he said his daughter's full name when he answered you?".

"I think he is very precise with his answers because he is a defense attorney. Remember, Silver told us that if Shawn Ross told us he did not know where she was, he was probably telling the truth. My opinion is there is no more information to gain from Shawn Ross." Hollins answered.

Matthews knew what Silver had said, and that Hollins was likely right, but something about how Shawn Ross answered bothered him.

When they returned to the office, there was a note from SSAC Hernandez; he had Agent Lee Rivers gather footage from business and traffic cameras around the bank. The footage was waiting for them on flash drives in the conference room that housed all the information on the case.

"Do you want to start tonight or wait until tomorrow?" Matthews asked Hollins.

Hollins responded, "Let's divide the footage up by the two directions she could have driven off. Then, watch the two from the closest locations in each direction. I hope we can at least figure out the direction she went in, and then tomorrow, we just have to watch the videos from that way."

"Sounds like a good plan. I will pull up the map of the area and read off the businesses north of the bank," Matthews told Hollins.

An hour later, they had compiled two piles of flash drives. Hollins first put the drive for the pizza place next to the bank to the north into the computer. He cued up the footage to the time when Paulina was in the bank, and they started watching. When the time that Paulina left the bank had come and gone without them seeing her van go by the pizza place, Hollins stopped the footage and removed the flash drive.

"Okay, so hopefully, we will see her on the hair salon camera going south. Here goes nothing," Hollins said as he put the second flash drive in.

He cued up the footage following the same process as with the first flash drive. Sure enough, the veterinary van drove by three minutes after Paulina walked out of the bank and towards the parking lot.

Matthews commented, "Well, at least we know which way she went and that she left right after she got done in the bank."

"Yep, let's call it a night, and then we can start watching everything to the south until we have to get more footage," Hollins said.

December 2019

Claire had started therapy in her third week of college. Her advisor had strongly suggested this after Claire began sobbing during her psychology class. The professor was talking about the importance of mother and child bonding on healthy development. The professor and her advisor were very kind about the incident, but thought that Claire would benefit from having someone to talk to. Since then, she saw her counselor once a week, and yes, it was helping.

Her therapist, Ellie Shephard, was a doctoral student in psychology whose mother had died in a car accident when she was a baby. Her ability to empathize with Claire's loss was the primary reason that Claire clicked with her. Every week between sessions, Claire had homework: writing a letter to her mom. It could be to share a memory or tell her about something that had happened that week, like the kind of things that she would have normally called her to tell her.

At first, writing the letters seemed impossible, and she would show up with hardly anything on the page. Ellie had been gentle with Claire and helped her to understand that the letters gave her a concrete way to detail what was going on in her life so that she could share them with her mother if she ever came back. While simultaneously allowing Claire to start processing that her mother may be gone forever and begin to grieve. The letter was clutched in her hands as she waited for today's appointment was about the week her mom disappeared. Writing it had been gut-wrenching, and she knew she would be reading to Ellie soon.

Ellie walked out to the waiting room and waved Claire back. They started with small talk, and then Ellie said, "I see you are holding tight to that letter. You know you don't have to read it to me if you don't want to."

Claire nodded and said, "I know, but it does help to read them to you then for us to talk about what I wrote and the meaning of it."

She then unfolded the letter and began to read:

Mom,

I came home from track practice on Wednesday, and you were not there. I remembered you went to that conference. It sounded so boring to me, but you were looking forward to it. When you weren't home by six, I had the leftovers in the fridge and then watched a movie. I tried to call you at about nine, but you didn't answer. I figured you decided to stay at the conference after all and had forgotten your phone charger again. I know I should have been worried because you had never not been where I expected you to be, but I was thinking about prom, graduation, and going to college.

I went to school on Thursday and just figured you would be home when I came back. After school, Lindsey and I went shopping for prom dresses and out for dinner, and then I went to her house to sleep. There was no school on Friday, so we had the plans for weeks, and you had it on the calendar in the kitchen, so I knew that you wouldn't worry about me. I told Lindsey about you not texting me or coming home Wednesday night, and we joked that maybe you finally met someone. Lindsey told me not to bug you because you might actually be having fun. I feel so bad because we laughed about it, and now, I know that something bad happened to you.

Friday morning, I went to track practice because there was no school then I headed home. When I walked in, it was clear you weren't there. The first clue was that mail from Thursday was on the floor just under the slot. I checked your room, and you were not there, so I looked in the garage, and the Buick was gone. That is when I panicked and called nine-one-one. I can't believe I waited to call. Would they have found you if I called right away? All those TV shows about crime say that the first forty-eight hours are the most important to find a missing person. The cops did not even know about you being missing until like thirty-six hours after, so most of those critical hours had already passed. I don't know how I will ever forgive myself if, when they finally solve your case, it turns out that if the police knew sooner, you would be alive.

Love-Claire

Claire had cried most of the time as she read her letter aloud, and when she finished, she sobbed uncontrollably. Ellie handed her the tissue box and said, "That was a very powerful letter you wrote. How did you feel when you wrote it and when you read it?"

"It is the first time I ever admitted to anyone, including myself, that I might be somehow to blame for the police not finding my mom," Claire answered quietly as she worked to bring her crying under control.

Ellie replied, "Oh, Claire. I am so sorry you have been carrying around that guilt. I know that you intellectually know that you have nothing to feel guilty for, but your heart doesn't know that. It is a very common reaction for crime victims' family members.

I think that your questions are the kind that will never be answered. You may need to just let the questions and the guilt go. You have to feel these wounds so that you are able to start healing. People say that time heals all wounds, but I will be honest with you. It is not healing like a scraped knee. When you scrap your knee, and it heals, there is no scar; after a while, you forget about it. Healing from losing a parent, especially when you do not know what happened or even if they are actually dead, is more like a broken bone. With time and therapy, you get to a place where your bone heals, but if a doctor orders an x-ray, there is always evidence of the break. Claire, do not build healing up to be miraculous. We are working towards acceptance, and you are building a happy life, not towards the loss of your mom, not hurting."

This was another one of the reasons that Claire liked Ellie so much; she was honest. Claire would never forget or give up on her mom, but she would try to build the kind of life her mom would want her to have.

30

Monday June 22,2020

The assistant at Dr. Rodane's office had helped Michelle set up medical transport to and from the outpatient surgery center. This morning, promptly at six a.m., the van had arrived. The older gentleman driver talked the entire ten-minute drive. Even though she couldn't care less, she now knew he was a retired city employee who had worked his entire life in the water department. He had become bored with retirement within three months and had been driving people to their medical appointments since. He took her silence for nervousness; she knew this for sure because he had told her just that.

When they arrived at the surgery center, he wished her luck and told her that someone else would pick her up that afternoon as he was off by the time she would be ready to go home. Taking the card with instructions for getting her ride home, Michelle got out of the van and walked into the surgery center. Hopefully, once she was healed, she would be able to stop wearing her mask.

The check-in and prep process went quickly, and Michelle lay in the hospital bed waiting for the anesthesiologist to leave. The doctor was going on and on about her medical history and the procedures she was having. Michelle told him that besides having her tonsils out as a child, which was a procedure she did not remember, she had never been under anesthesia. He stopped talking mid-sentence and said, "Oh, you are wearing contacts, aren't you? Those will have to come out."

Michelle tried to avoid this for as long as possible and responded, "I know. It is just that I forgot my glasses at home and can hardly see without correction."

The anesthesiologist responded, "I understand, but now is the time to remove them. You will be going back for your procedures in less than ten minutes, so you don't have to worry about being unable to see. Would you like me to send in a nurse with supplies?"

"Yes, please," Michelle responded. The next thing she remembered was waking up with a nurse standing by her, taking her vitals. The nurse smiled down at her and said, "Your procedures went well. Dr. Rodane should be in to check on you soon," then she walked out of the room.

Michelle slipped back into sleeping and awoke as she felt someone bend down near her ear. A male voice whispered, "Paulina, you will look amazing after you recover."

Michelle's eyes popped open, and she watched Dr. Rodane leave the room. She wondered; *was I dreaming? Or is the anesthesia was making me hear odd things? Or did he really just call me Paulina? If I heard him correctly, how had he figured out who I am, and more importantly, what did he plan to do with the information?*

****

Claire woke up and thought about the nightmare she was having. Her mom was trapped somewhere and was cold and scared. Claire had started crying in her sleep and was still crying as she sat on her bed thinking about her mom. When her mom had first disappeared, there had been so many questions: *Who had taken her? What had they done to her? Where was she?* Now they knew one answer for sure: Raul Moore had taken her.

Claire thought back to having met the Moores at the Fourth of July Barbecue last summer. They had both seemed nice at the time. She remembered that Paulina Moore had sat with her and chatted about college. How had they both been so nice to her dad and her, all the while knowing what they did to her mom? It made her feel physically sick to think back on having spent time with the two of them. What was wrong with them?

Making her way downstairs, she went to the kitchen and poured a cup of coffee. Gone were the days when she would only drink fancy, blended coffee drinks. There was free coffee at several places around campus, so Claire had learned to drink her coffee with cream and sugar. Her dad called it cotton candy coffee the one time he had grabbed her mug instead of his and taken a big swallow. Wandering towards her dad's home office, she hoped he wasn't busy with an online meeting. She needed to talk to him.

****

Joe Learner looked up as Claire walked in. Sometimes, when he saw her, he was momentarily transported back to when he met her mom in college. Claire could be Kelsey's twin at that age. This morning, Claire looked rough. Her hair was messy, her face pale and splotchy, and her eyes puffy and red-rimmed. His daughter had clearly spent most of the night crying. He got up from his chair, walked up to her and pulled her into a hug.

He was not a hugger by nature but had found the last two years that Claire was comforted by his touch. "Honey, how can I help?" he asked her.

She clung to him and cried, "Daddy, why would they do that to my mom?"

Joe had no answer to that and knew that, other than Paulina Moore, no living soul did. "Claire, they were both crazy. There is no way to figure out what motivates an insane person, much less two of them."

Claire straightened her body and pulled away from her dad. "Do you have time to talk?" she asked.

"I always have time for you. I was just working on reports for work. Come sit down." Joe walked back to his office chair and watched as Claire sat on the loveseat in his office.

"How well did you know the Moores? I remember them from that barbecue you took me to last summer."

"I have been thinking about that since Detective Minor left yesterday after letting us know about Raul's suicide note. I met him about three and half years ago when I joined The Club. Since then, I have seen him once or twice a week, and he seemed average to me. He and I never talked about your mom when she disappeared. I only met his wife, Paulina, a handful of times. She was a little too aggressive for my taste. She asked lots of personal questions and sat too close to me, but I never would have guessed she was a psychopath." Joe told Claire. He wondered if the FBI or the Springfield police would be coming around, wanting him to tell them about his relationship with the Moores.

The look on Claire's face told Joe there was something else on her mind. "Dad, why did you and mom get divorced?"

He had always wondered what Kelsey had told their daughter about the divorce, and Claire had never asked him directly about it before. He needed to know how much she knew before he answered her, "What did your mom tell you the reason was?"

"She never told me anything about why. The few times I asked her, she just said something like the two of you wanted different things in life."

Joe decided that Claire deserved the truth, "Your mom and I were very young when we got married. Neither of us had matured enough to know what we really wanted in a relationship or life. In the end, though, the divorce was totally my fault. I cheated on your mom, and she forgave me, but then I did it again."

Claire stared at her dad and asked, "How could you have done that?"

"The details and my reasons are not something I want to discuss with you. After all, you are my daughter, but know that I regret it. Your mom was a loving, caring person, and I hurt her. I was selfish and immature." Joe confessed to Claire.

She wondered if her mom would have ever told her the truth. Maybe as an adult, Kelsey would have told her to try to prevent Claire from making the same mistake. "Okay, Dad. You are right; I don't want to know the details. Thank you for being honest with me. I guess I have always wondered if Mom would have never disappeared if the two of you were still married."

Joe was startled by Claire's thought process, but before he could respond, she continued.

"My counselor at school told me it is what if thinking. I do it a lot about Mom and her kidnapping. I know it is impossible to change the past, but I just wonder if things would have been different if you two were still together. Maybe she would be here today." Claire seemed to have run out of steam after she explained her thoughts and started to doze off.

Joe thought it best to let his daughter rest rather than respond to her attempts to change the past.

March 2019

Claire had finally decided to major in Forensic Science. She wanted to help solve crimes, but couldn't see herself as an actual police officer. Forensics would allow her to apply her love of science and her desire to help crime victims. She knew that her mom never having been found was the driving force behind her decision, but she thought it would be a great way to honor her mom. She could stay at Missouri University of Science and Technology, where she was finishing her sophomore year, but she was lonely. A quick internet search told her she could transfer to Missouri State and be back in Springfield without causing a delay in earning her degree.

Her advisor had been very understanding about her desire to transfer and helped her to complete all the paperwork. She had a month left here in Rollo and then would return home. She and Ellie had talked about her change in the last few sessions. Ellie had wanted her to be prepared that moving back home may not be the cure for the loneliness that she was seeking. It was true the thing that she was loneliest for was her mom, and being back in Springfield would not solve that.

When she had called her dad to let him know her decision, he had offered to have her live with him. She had stayed with him last summer, but really wanted to be back in her own home. He let the renters know that their lease would not be renewed and told her he would have some friends move her things back to the house the week before she returned. All that would be left to do would be to go to the storage unit and get furniture for the rest of the house. They had agreed to do that together when she got back.

Lindsey had been complaining about her boyfriend Mack every time she and Claire talked for the last few weeks. Claire was hoping that Lindsey would move into the house with her, but so far, Lindsey wasn't ready to. Maybe one day, Lindsey would realize that her relationship was not healthy, and when she did, Claire would be there to support her.

31

Thursday June 25, 2020

Kelsey thought back to the second time she had woken up after being kidnapped, there were twenty-one packets of food. At first, she had been very conservative and ate only when she could no longer stand the hunger pains. Over time, she concluded that the twenty-one packets were meant to be three meals a day for seven days and that the man brought more every seven days, along with the seven jugs of water. The man never took away the food packets or water that she had not finished, so she has a small stockpile.

To keep track of days, each time she woke with a dizzy feeling and taser marks, she would start new piles of food wrappers and make a mark on the ground representing the wrappers the man had taken away. She would put the wrappers in a pile based on what she thought a day was three wrappers per day until she had seven piles. Kelsey had become skilled at counting the days correctly, which made her worry. By her count, it had been eighteen days since he had been here. He had never been late before. Something was wrong.

On the eighth day, when he had not come by, she returned to her original pattern of eating only one packet of food and drinking less than half a gallon of water daily. As each day passed, Kelsey became more and more concerned. She had come to accept that she would die down here, but dying due to starvation would be a slow, painful way to go. Kelsey used the rocks she had piled up to scratch out a message to Claire on the floor. She had not done that until now because it felt like giving up.

One of the other habits that she had gotten into early in her captivity was to turn off the lantern and flashlight when she was going to sleep. She feared being awake in total darkness, so it helped her to know that she was conserving the batteries on her two light sources. The lantern seemed like a high-end model and had lasted until now. As she went to switch on the flashlight before switching off the lantern, the flashlight only came on dimly and then went out. Kelsey began to sob and thought *one light source gone, and no idea how long the other will last.*

Thursday May 28, 2020

When Paulina found two different people to make her new identification documents, she also found a whole other way of living. One that was all about how to get one over on people and the government. The forger who made Hanna Lewis' documents was named Two-Bit. Paulina was sure that was not his given name, but it was what he had told her to call him. His sister ran a non-profit daycare that watched no children. The concept made absolutely no sense to Paulina when he first mentioned it to her as a way to move money from Paulina's accounts to Hanna.

He went on to explain that mothers that his sister knew who were on welfare enrolled their kids at the daycare, and his sister Charlene collected the state daycare assistance payment. These same mothers worked for Charlene's daycare or one of her two other nonprofits. Except those mothers never actually worked, and the kids never actually came to the daycare other than on days when the state inspector would be there. Charlene would pay the mothers twenty percent of what she collected from the state. This meant the moms could collect welfare from the state's welfare-to-work program without working, and Charlene collected state daycare funds without watching kids or having employees.

Hanna met with Charlene after an introduction from Two-Bit, and the two women came to a mutually agreeable deal. Hanna would be listed as an employee of the non-profit, and Paulina would make donations to each of the three non-profits from herself and her business.

Charlene would deposit fifty percent of the donations into Hanna's online savings account as paychecks. Three years of this arrangement had been lucrative for the two women.

Today, she was meeting with Charlene at her request. Paulina listened as Charlene outlined the legal troubles she was starting to experience. It seemed that someone at the state level had begun to question the interconnectedness of the mom's employment and their daycare provider. This led to several unannounced visits by the state daycare inspector. She found no one at the business each time she came by and had carefully documented those dates. When Charlene and the daycare moms submitted the reimbursement request last month, the inspector and an auditor for the state had checked against the dates that no one had been there. Of course, since Charlene had not known the inspector stopped by, those dates were on all reimbursement requests.

Paulina was unsure how this affected her until Charlene said her attorney had called this morning to say that the state had a subpoena for all her employment and donation records. Paulina and Hanna were all over those records.

"Are my business and I your only donors?" Paulina asked.

Charlene shook her head, "No, I have a bunch of other people who donated in the same way."

"Okay, so the donations should look legitimate. If asked, I will tell the police I heard about your non-profits through an acquaintance. As for Hanna, when did you last pay her?" Paulina asked.

"It will have been two weeks on Friday. I pay her every two weeks, as that makes it look like a regular paycheck."

"Well, Hanna quit a month ago, so that was her last paycheck. I will write her resignation letter right now, and you will add it to her employment file. If this all blows over, Hanna can return to work for you. How does that sound?" Paulina knew that she needed to distance herself from this mess.

"That works for me," Charlene replied.

So, Paulina wrote a quick note:

Charlene,

Thank you so much for hiring me three years ago. I have learned so much from you while working here. I have decided that I am going to move to Las Vegas. My last day will be next Friday.

Hanna Lewis

Paulina handed the note to Charlene and then shook her hand. She was sure that Charlene would be going to prison for fraud and that she had done what she could to put distance between them.

32

Friday June 26, 2020

Michelle checked the notes she had taken while using the library computer against the atlas she bought at the second-hand bookstore. Healing from her surgery was going well, and with the mask on, no one could see the small amount of bruising she had. Her fingers hurt more than anything else, but knowing that her fingerprints were permanently changed made it worth it.

She planned to start her drive to St. Louis tonight, sticking to state highways and back roads. She wanted to have minimal contact with people and cameras on her way. It was risky to return to Missouri, but a loose end needed to be taken care of. Her dad's house was in the suburbs, and she had seen on the computer at the library that there was a cheap rent-by-the-week hotel only a mile away. It was the kind of place where you didn't need a reservation, took cash payments, and did not ask for an ID. Michelle had packed some cleaning supplies, clean sheets, blankets, and towels for her stay there.

She would be spending several days watching her dad so she could successfully carry out her plan. She hoped he had not changed his habits too much in the thirty-three years since she lived with him. The pictures, ribbons, and medals she had seen in his office when she went there over the last few years indicated that he was still an avid bike rider. When she was little, he would leave every morning between five and five-thirty and ride his bike. During the week, he would be gone for about an hour, but on the weekends, he was often gone most of the day.

As she drove, she thought back on one of the fights her parents had routinely had when they were married. It was about the amount of time and money he spent on biking. Her mom thought it was a waste of both resources and often accused him of having an affair and meeting up with someone instead of really biking that much. Her dad stayed so calm during these arguments and continually reminded her how important exercise was for managing his diabetes.

That was another thing she counted on; her dad still injecting himself with insulin. She had four preloaded insulin jet injectors that she had bought for cash off an internet sales site. The cost of insulin had created a large and prosperous black market with patients filling prescriptions using insurance and then selling the medication for cash. The man Michelle had bought the four injector pens from was extremely obese and likely needed to be actually using the medication, but that was his problem, not hers.

If everything went as planned, she would run on the route that he biked and come from the opposite direction. Just before he arrived, she would string a fishing line across the route to trip her dad like they had with Cory Pratt. Shawn would flip off his bike, and if he was not unconscious from the fall, she would hit him in the head with a rock to get him there. She planned to pull up his shirt, find the freshest injection spots from his insulin shots, and inject him with all four insulin jet pens. As long as the trail wasn't busy, she foresaw no issues with her plan.

Once her dad was dead, there was only one other loose end, and she had not yet come up with a way to deal with her. Right now, she needed to hope there really was honor among thieves and concentrate on one problem at a time.

Tuesday June 9, 2020

Paulina finished packing the van to head to the veterinary conference in Kansas City. It was the first time she would be away from the farm since they had started their mission, which worried her. She had packed all the usual things, like clothes and toiletries, but she had also added a large plastic storage container to the back of the van. In that container, she put the hard drive for the computer she used for their practice, the laptop she used for herself, and the old laptop she kept notes on. She placed Hanna's princess backpack with her ID, debit card, and Michelle Brooks' papers under the van's driver's side seat. One could never be too prepared.

Raul seemed shocked when she told him to take her truck to the clients he was at now. She had explained that she wanted to get the van packed so they could leave as soon as he was done working. The truth was, she wanted to remove the GPS tracker before they left. The tracker was a loose end that caused her some degree of anxiety. If Raul was ever caught and the tracker was still in place, the police would know that there was data telling where that van had been somewhere. That was fine with Paulina when they had been working on phase one of the plan. She figured it was just more evidence to stack against Raul. But now that they were in phase two, she did not want the GPS data to lead to Kelsey Learner.

****

Agent Matthews looked in the mirror one more time before heading into the conference room. He had compiled all the information on the kidnapping and probable murders of seven men by Dr. Raul Moore. He first presented everything to his senior agent, Hollins, who agreed it was a good case. From there, it was decided to call a meeting with SSAC Hernandez. It would take a lot of manpower to raid the farm and arrest the Moores.

As Matthews entered the room, he saw Agent Hollins, SSAC Hernandez, Lily Thomas, the Christian County Sheriff, a couple of commanders from the Missouri State Police, and several other FBI agents he didn't know were sitting around the table.

"Thank you, everyone, for being here today. As you may or may not be aware, twenty-six months ago, I was assigned by the FBI's Assistant Director to look into Cory Pratt's disappearance. When I started looking into his disappearance, I discovered that the Miller County Sheriff did not investigate because he figured Cory had just moved on. I found evidence that Cory likely did not leave on his own accord. All the information on Cory's case is in the folder each of you have.

As I looked into Cory's disappearance, I began to find other missing men from around Missouri. I found a total of ten missing men whose disappearances were questionable. From there, I was able to eliminate three of the men, one who was found dead and the other two who did leave on their own accord. The folders contain information about all seven of the men who are still unaccounted for." Matthews told the group.

Each team member opened their folder, and while they looked over the information, Matthews got a cup of coffee. He hoped that he had answers to any questions that came up.

No one raised any questions, so Matthews continued, "The men were tied together because they all lead primarily solitary lives and participate in solo activities. I had no definitive answers where the seven men had gone until about two months ago. By chance, I watched a program on pacemakers and technology that said that modern pacemakers transmit data to doctors so they can check on their patients. I remembered one of the missing men, George Jeffers, had a pacemaker. I contacted our technology department, and Ms. Thomas was able to help obtain the data. Since that is her area of expertise, I have asked her to take over this part of the briefing."

Lily Thomas stood up and pointed a remote at the television at the front of the room. "When Agent Matthews contacted me about the pacemaker data, I contacted the medical equipment company that manufactured George Jeffers' pacemaker. The company denied that tracking the pacemaker's location would be possible based on the data it sent back. Agent Matthews and I secured a subpoena for the data, and the company complied by inundating me with massive amounts of metadata to sort through. As shown on the screen, I used the metadata to determine the GPS coordinates of the last data set George's pacemaker ever transmitted. Then Agent Matthews used the GPS coordinates to find the location." Lily sat back down as she concluded her portion.

"That brings us to today. I am asking for a team to raid the Moore farm and arrest Raul and Paulina Moore." Matthews told the group.

SSAC Hernandez raised the first question, "Is it your belief that Raul Moore not only killed George Jeffers, but the other six men in these folders?"

"Sir, I am not sure how many of the men Raul killed, but I think it was more than George Jeffers," Matthews answered.

"You said you believe that Dr. Raul Moore is the killer, but you also said we should arrest both Raul and his wife, Paulina. What is your reasoning for that?" Hernandez asked.

He had expected this question: "I do not believe it would be possible for Raul Moore to have killed multiple people at their farm without his wife knowing anything."

"Alright, we will assemble a team and get the needed warrants. It should take about forty-eight hours for us to be ready. If the state police and you, Sheriff Tripp, are okay with it, the FBI will take the lead on this case." SSAC Hernandez stated.

All the other law enforcement agencies were fine with that suggestion. Everyone's budgets were stretched thin, and if Agent Matthews was correct, this investigation would be extensive and expensive.

Hernandez continued, "Agents Hollins and Matthews, I expect the two of you to be there and keep me in the loop. Good Job Agent Matthews." SSAC Hernandez said as he stood and walked out of the room.

33

Tuesday June 30, 2020

Robert Matthews was running on the treadmill and reading news articles on his tablet. So far this morning, he had read about changing tide patterns, raising interest rates, and the best way to bake cookies. He was flipping through headlines, looking for the next article to read. He stopped not just scrolling, but running.

The headline read Local Attorney Found Dead on Popular Bike Trail. There was a picture of Shawn Ross under the headline.

Sitting down on his weight bench, Robert read the brief article.

Shawn Moore, age 72, a local criminal defense attorney, was found dead on Grant's trail yesterday morning. The police are saying that the preliminary reports point to a diabetic incident that led to him suffering a cardiac arrest. There are no details on funeral arrangements at this time.

Matthews headed for the shower and finished getting ready to head into the office. On the way there, he called the Detective Bureau of the St. Louis Police Department. A frazzled-sounding Detective Caleb Brown answered the phone. Matthews told him who he was and the case he was working on and then asked about Shawn Ross' death.

Detective Brown told him, "There isn't an open investigation into his death. The medical examiner was all but sure that Exercise-Induced Hypoglycemia had caused his death, so unless she calls me to tell me something different, it is an accidental death. Nothing at the scene, his home or workplace, suggested anything different. I have too many active cases to go looking for trouble."

Matthews thanked the detective for the information and tried to call Agent Brad Hollins. His call went right to voicemail, so he hung up. When he got to the Springfield FBI field office, the first thing he noticed was that there were only five cars in the parking lot. The crush of people that had descended on the small office had all scattered. Likely on to other cases, but for him and Hollins, the Moore case was their continued focus. Charles Silver, the state prosecutor, had been clear that at this point, even if they did find Paulina, the most that she would be charged with was as an accessory after the fact and fleeing to avoid prosecution. While the Fugitive Apprehension Task Force looked for, Paulina, Matthews and Hollins looked for evidence.

Agent Hollins was sitting in his office, staring at the paperwork in front of him, when Matthews walked in.

"Are you hoping that paperwork will do itself if you stare at it long enough?" Matthews joked as he sat down.

Hollins chuckled and replied, "Nope. I am just waiting for the agent with less seniority to arrive so I can delegate all this to him. Think of it as a learning experience."

"Great, thanks! I want to show you something before I start on all that learning." Matthews replied and handed his iPad across the desk. The screen was open to the news story on Shawn Ross.

Hollins quickly read the blurb and replied, "Wow. He is dead, too."

Matthews continued, "Yeah. It is like Raul Moore said in his suicide letter: accidents happen to people all around Paulina."

"You think that Paulina killed her dad?" Hollins questioned.

Matthews knew there was nothing to suggest he was right, but his gut told him that it was no accident that Shawn Ross was dead. "Yes, I do, but when I called the St. Louis Police Department this morning."

"Wait, What? You called the St. Louis PD?" Hollins interrupted.

"Yep, and I was told they are not investigating Shawn Ross' death. It has been ruled to be accidental due to his diabetes." Matthews told him.

Hollins thought about what Agent Matthews had said and replied, "Let's add Shawn Ross to the file on accidents occurring close to

Paulina Moore. His is the freshest case, so it is the easiest to find evidence for. How about you call the medical examiner in St. Louis and explain the concern? Hopefully, they will look closely at the evidence to ensure this was a medical issue, not a murder."

Thursday June 11, 2020

Raul sensed something was very wrong when he couldn't find Paulina at the conference. He had gone back up to their hotel room during the lunch break, and she was not there either. He sat down on the bed to think about what could be going on. His phone slipped out of his pocket and onto the floor. He knelt down to get it and somehow inadvertently kicked it under the bed. That is when he saw the duffle bag.

Thinking that the guest before them had put it there and that the housekeeping staff did not notice it when they had cleaned the room, he pulled it out. It was a nondescript black duffel, so Raul decided to unzip it. He was surprised to see a blond wig, makeup kit, contact container, a cell phone, and a bundle of cash.

She is planning to run; raced through his mind repeatedly as he held the bag. Then he added to the thought: *She is planning to run, and she isn't taking me. What does she know that I don't?* Raul sat on the floor for what felt like an eternity before putting everything back in the bag, pushing it back under the bed, and then standing up. He looked at the clock on the nightstand. He had been up in the room for nearly thirty minutes. He needed to get back to the conference.

When he returned to the room at the end of the conference day, he was surprised to see Paulina sitting there. "Hi, honey. I didn't see you at all today," he said to her while silently praying she had not noticed that he had touched her duffel bag.

Paulina smiled at him and replied, "I guess we weren't in the same place at the same time. At lunchtime, I came up here and closed my eyes."

Raul knew that wasn't true because he was in the room at lunchtime. "Oh, are you feeling, okay?"

Paulina assured him that she was fine, and they went to have dinner with their colleagues.

34

Friday July 3, 2020

Shasta Peters was so happy to be home. Her time in jail was not something she ever wanted to repeat. She was glad that she had her brother Two-Bit create an alias for her years ago. Charlene Peterson, on paper, seemed to be an employee of Shasta's non-profit. In actuality, that name was a way for people not to know Shasta's real name and for Shasta to hide away money. It was the money in Charlene's bank account that Two-Bit had used to post Shasta's bail.

After taking a shower, ordering delivery from her favorite Chinese restaurant, and mixing up a lemonade and vodka, Shasta plopped herself on the couch and turned on the television. The local news was on, and she was about to start channel surfing when a familiar face appeared on the screen. It seemed that while Shasta sat in jail on fraud charges, Paulina Moore had gotten herself on the FBI's Ten Most Wanted list. The news anchor briefly mentioned that Paulina's father, a prominent St. Louis attorney, was laid to rest that morning, with the FBI surveilling the funeral for any signs of Paulina.

The doorbell rang, and Shasta got up and lumbered over to it. She knew she needed to lose weight, but had been big her whole life. All the women in her family were big. She vowed that if she found a way to stay out of prison, she would start to take better care of herself. After collecting her food, Shasta sat at the kitchen counter, eating and catching up on all the stories about the Moores. *Wow, I guess I am lucky she did not kill me. I wonder if Two-Bit knows about this;* she thought as she read the most recent article.

After making another drink, Shasta called her brother, who, of course, did not answer. He never answered his phone. The best she could hope for was that he would call her back in the next day or so. Sitting on the couch with a movie playing in the background, Shasta started to drift to sleep. She woke up an hour later with a crook in her neck and a plan. One thing none of those news articles mentioned was Paulina's other name, Hanna Lewis.

Now she had something to trade with the prosecutor. She would tell him everything she knew about Paulina/Hanna, and he would drop all the charges against her. At least, she hoped it would work that way. On Monday, she would call an attorney who was not court-appointed and make an appointment.

****

Kelsey shivered. She knew that it was because she was cold, but also due to fear. The lantern had stopped working. She had run out of food and had only half a jug of water left. Weeping, she laid down on the mattress and prayed for sleep.

Remembering the Farm

Secrets in the Heartland Series-Book 3
Remembering the Farm
By Andrea Crist Heckner

Dedication:

To my sons, Anthony, Matthew and Robert, who have always been and will always be my greatest achievements. I love you all and am proud of the men you have become.

Remembering the Farm-Book Three of the Secrets in the Heartland Series was originally published in 2024. The version contained within this compilation is an edited version with no major changes to the story line or characters.

1

They say that there is nothing worse than not knowing the truth. But sometimes, knowing too much is actually worse.

Chapter 1

Thursday May 26, 2022

James Adams watched as his brother, Jessie, approached the pickup truck. Asking a stranger for a ride was a bad idea, but getting home late might be worse. When their mom, Trixie, got mad at them, she went on for days. James knew that if they biked all the way to Lake Springfield, it would take a long time. There was no way they could get there, fish, and be home on time, so Jessie had decided they should try to hitch a ride. He assured James that as long as they stuck together, they would be okay.

Jessie ran back and said, "Grab your bike and throw it in the back. He is going to give us a ride."

James watched as his brother grabbed his bike and the fishing gear, putting them in the truck bed. Jessie turned around and yelled, "Come on!"

He could not let his brother get in that truck alone. Besides, what if this worked out? Then Jessie would get to fish all day, and James would be stuck at the trailer park. Throwing his bike next to his brothers, James walked around to the truck cab and got in with his brother.

******

Claire Learner walked out of the Springfield Police Department on cloud nine. Her first day as a Crime Scene Technician had gone really well. Everyone on the team was very welcoming, and no one brought up her mom. She figured Kelsey would be a topic of conversation in time, but either people had not made the connection yet, or they were too nice to talk about it. When she applied for the position six weeks ago, she had reached out to Detective Minor for a reference. The detective had been happy to help her. Claire was ecstatic; first to get an interview and then a job offer. She wondered if she and Detective Minor would end up on the same case soon. It was a small enough police department that it was bound to happen.

Pulling up to her house, she saw that Lindsey's car was parked on the street in its usual spot. Lindsey had moved in eight months ago when she and her boyfriend Mack broke up. Claire loved living with her best friend, but she had been worried about Lindsey. Her once outgoing, bubbly personality was much more subdued. Claire was sure that could be squarely placed on the treatment Lindsey had endured from Mack, although Lindsey never talked about what had gone on. All Claire knew for sure was that Lindsey had called her to ask her to move in, and when Claire went to see her, she saw that Lindsey's wrist was broken. Claire knew that Officer Peterson, Lindsey's dad, and his partner had gone to see Mack but again did not know the details of what occurred at that visit, just that Claire had not seen Mack around since then.

Claire parked and walked through the garage entrance, going through the process of disarming and rearming the house alarm from rote memory. One time when they had both been drinking, she and Lindsey joked about who was more cautious. It was part of the reason why living together worked out so well. Neither thought the other was over-sensitive about security. Claire called out Lindsey's name on the way to her own bedroom. There was no answer. *Hmm, I wonder if she walked over to her parent's house,* Claire thought as she changed into her gym clothes.

******

James Adams worried about how much trouble they would be in because he was sure they would be late getting home. Sitting on the dock fishing all day with his brother had been great. They had thrown back all the fish they caught because their mom did not like the smell of fish, so it wasn't like she would cook them. When they had run out of snacks and water, James suggested they should start heading home, and for once, Jessie did not argue with him.

It was a long ride home, which they had never done before because usually, they fished at the creek by their mobile home park. Jessie had lied to the guy who gave them a ride and told him their mom was picking them up when she finished work. It wasn't like they had never been to Lake Springfield to fish, but it had always been with their mom's friend, Eddie Learner. When they got to the highway's edge, James asked Jessie, "Do we turn left or right?"

Jessie's face had a flash of panic before he said, "I thought you knew."

"Wait, what? I don't know how to get home. You said you did."

"When? When did I say that?"

James thought about it and could not recall his brother actually saying he knew how to get home. He had just said something like; *don't worry about it. I got this.* "Okay, let me think about how the man drove us here this morning, and we will go back the same way."

Jessie smiled, "I knew you would have a plan."

"Let's turn left, and if we see a familiar road, we will turn again. How does that sound?"

"Great. We got this."

Tuesday July 7, 2020

Shasta Peters sat with her attorney in the interview room of the Springfield FBI field office. To say she was scared was an understatement because, in her world, people did not willingly talk to the authorities, plus the whole turning against a serial killer on the loose thing was enough to scare anyone. But this was her only way to avoid prison, which she did not want to face because jail was a bad enough experience.

The deal her attorney had worked out would allow her to stay out of prison but be on probation for ten years. Worse yet, the state of Missouri would seize all of her assets. Her part of this agreement was to tell the FBI all that she knew about Paulina Moore and her alternate identity, Hanna Lewis.

A young, handsome FBI agent walked into the room and introduced himself while shaking both their hands. "Hello, I am Special Agent Robert Matthews. The State of Missouri Prosecutor's office says you have some information that may be very helpful in our search for Paulina Moore."

Howard Blaston, Shasta's lawyer, responded, "That is correct. Charles Silver, the Chief Assistant Prosecuting Attorney for the State of Missouri, has signed an agreement with my client regarding her cooperation in the case for consideration of a fraud case against her. Per the agreement, some of what she will tell you pertains to the fraud and is not admissible in court."

Agent Matthews nodded his head and replied, "Understood."

Howard turned to Shasta and said, "Go ahead and tell him what you know about Paulina Moore."

"Okay, so it is like this: sometimes people with a lot of money want a way for that money to be less traceable. That was a service that I offered through my non-profit. I met Paulina Moore when she came in to become a client of this service. She had a fake ID and other documents for a person named Hanna Lewis. On paper, I hired Hanna, and when Paulina donated to my business, I paid Hanna fifty percent of that donation. I brought a copy of the employment file for Hanna so you can have all the paperwork I had on her."

Shasta slid the file over to Agent Matthews, who opened it and took out a copy of the driver's license and social security card. The picture of the woman on the license bore a resemblance to Paulina Moore. The license said Hanna Lewis was five years younger than Paulina and had red hair and green eyes. The height on the license said that Hanna was five-foot one inch tall, whereas Paulina Moore was only four foot eleven.

"Do you know where Paulina got these documents?" Matthews asked Shasta.

"No, that was none of my business. My business worked because I didn't ask many questions, and neither did my donors."

"When was the last time you saw or heard from Paulina?"

"I called her number and left her a message when I discovered I had to turn over all my employment and donation records. That was like five weeks ago. She came to see me the next day and wrote that note in the file about Hanna quitting. I have not heard from or seen her since, and with all this stuff about her and her old man being serial killers, I hope I never see her again. Do you think I am in danger?"

Agent Matthews thought about what to say. He was the only person who believed that Paulina Moore had been in St. Louis and killed her father. Knowing that any answer other than an assurance would likely get him reprimanded, he gave the obligatory answer. "No, ma'am, it is highly unlikely that Paulina Moore would come out of hiding to travel back to Springfield. However, at the same time, it is always a good idea to be vigilant and report anything suspicious."

"Ok, thanks, I guess." Shasta was not sure that she felt reassured.

Mr. Blaston said, "If you do not have any further questions, we will be leaving. You have my contact information if you would like to follow up with Ms. Peterson."

"Thank you for this information. It may be just what this investigation needed. I will let Mr. Silver know that you were very helpful and forthcoming."

Agent Matthews showed them to the door and then went to find Agent Hollis. He hoped this was the break they needed to find Paulina Moore, aka Hanna Lewis. She had been on the run for almost a month, and they had no leads until now. Robert Matthews knew he was the only person fully convinced that Paulina Moore was a serial killer. Most other agents and police officers who had worked on this case thought that she was complicit in the killings, but that Raul was the actual murderer.

2

Thursday May 26, 2022

Trixie swatted at the cardboard box she used as a nightstand and turned off the alarm on her cell phone. Working nights sucked, but the pay was so much better that she could not even begin to think about getting a day job. Plus, it meant being home when her kids were, which was especially helpful in the summer when they had no school. They were old enough that she didn't have to pay anyone to watch them anymore. Heck, her mom would take off for days by the time she was eleven, and Trixie had four younger brothers and sisters that she had to watch. Her oldest, Jessie, who was eleven, only had to look after his younger brother, James. Plus, it was more like James, looked after Jessie because Jessie was reckless, like his daddy.

After a long hot shower, Trixie made her way to the trailer kitchen to figure out something to make for dinner. It looked like it was macaroni and cheese again. Before the boys returned, she needed to mix the powdered milk and get it in the empty milk jug. She didn't think the powdered milk was as bad as her entitled kids made it out to be. After getting the milk made and put away, Trixie sat on the couch to watch TV until her kids made it home. No one liked reheated macaroni, so it was best not to make it yet.

When she woke back up at eight p.m., she realized two things: the couch was lumpy as hell, and her kids weren't home. They knew they were supposed to be home by six. Trixie walked two trailers down to her on-again, off-again boyfriend, Eddie Learner's place. The boys loved to hang out there because Eddie had an enormous flat-screen TV, the newest video game system, and massive amounts of junk food. He had told her plenty of times that she didn't have to knock because she was always welcome, but that did not stop her. If she started coming and going to his place as she wanted, he might think he could do the same with her trailer, and that wasn't anything she wanted to start. As Trixie waited for an answer, she wondered if she should punish her kids. Her conclusion was *Nah, who cares as long as they aren't causing trouble?* She had grown up hating how many rules her ma'ama had but only enforced on a whim.

After a few minutes, no one answered, so Trixie tried the handle on the trailer. Locked, she walked back to her trailer, wondering *where have my damn kids gone off to.* Worry set in as the sky turned from dusk to dark, and the time for Trixie to head to work at the factory drew closer. She was pretty sure you could not report someone missing for like two days, so she figured the police were not going to help her. Plus, calling the police was like inviting trouble into your home. Trixie wrote a note and put it on the boys' bedroom door.

Jessie and James,

You are in so much trouble. I had to go to work, but your asses are going to get it when I get home in the morning.

Mom

That would have to do because she could not miss her shift. The factory operated off a strict point system, and calling in at the last minute would be enough points that she would be dangerously close to being fired. She still had two points on her record because she and her best friend, Porsche, had been caught propping a side door open while they smoked a cigarette. The floor supervisor had gone on and on, not just about the safety violation of propping the door open, but also that they were not on their scheduled break. As she drove to work, she thought about calling her ex, the boy's dad, Chase, but why bother? He had been clear that he wanted nothing to do with any of them.

******

Porsche clocked into work with just one minute to spare. She was a night owl, but coming to work wasn't something she looked forward to. Payday now, that was something to look forward to. As she headed to her machine, she thought about when to tell her friend Trixie that she had enrolled in cosmetology school. Porsche didn't want to work nights in a box-making factory for the rest of her life. She didn't know how Trixie did it. Trixie had been at the plant since they graduated from high school. How had she stood in this place for twelve years? Working nights and taking care of her kids must be hell. Porsche wanted more from her life, but didn't want Trixie to think she looked down on her. It wasn't like she was lighting the world on fire. She had jumped from job to job and man to man over the last twelve years, but turning thirty last week made her realize that if she was going to do something else, now was the time.

Where is Trixie? Porsche wondered. Neither of them could afford to be late. Then, as if thinking about her made Trixie appear, she watched her friend walk out of the bathroom and to the machine next to hers.

"Girl, I thought you were late."

"Naw, I actually clocked in five minutes early, but then I went to the bathroom because of all the coffee I drank. I am running on fumes tonight."

"Is something wrong?"

"Yeah, my boys are out running around like hoodlums. They were not even home when I left tonight."

"That's pretty late to be out at their age. Do you think they are okay?"

"Yeah, I think so. Plus, what am I supposed to do, call into work and call the cops?"

"I don't know, maybe. I mean, nowadays, there are a lot of bad things that happen to kids."

"No, let me tell you what would have happened if I had called into this place and called the cops. My boys would have come home on their own or been found at a friend's house, and then I would have two problems instead of one. Problem number one would be that I am out of a job, and problem number two, social services would be all up in my business, saying I shouldn't be sleeping while my kids are awake and my kids shouldn't be sleeping with no adults at home when I am at work."

"Okay, I get it, but call me if they aren't home in the morning. I will come over, and we can call the cops together."

"Fine, I will, but I am telling you, if those two are not waiting for me when I get home, there will be hell to pay."

******

Jessie was scared, but would never admit that to his little brother. It was dark, and they were out in the middle of nowhere. "James, I got to use it. Let's stop and rest, too."

He stopped his bike and pointed to what looked like an old gravel drive, "James, let's go there. I don't think it belongs to anyone."

"Don't you think maybe we should go to one of the farmhouses we have been riding by? They can call Mom so she can come and get us."

"Or they will be psycho killers, and no one will ever find our bodies. You know they never found that lady serial killer; what if she is still around here?"

James pulled the flashlight Eddie had given them out of his backpack, and the boys walked their bikes down the overgrown drive and into the woods. A large fallen tree was off to one side, and James plopped down on it. He handed Jessie the flashlight and watched his brother walk toward the trees. They probably should just stay the night here and ride home in the light. James closed his eyes and started to drift off to sleep when he heard Jessie scream and then a loud thump.

Friday July 10, 2020

Michelle Brooks parked her car and looked around. The parking lot was strangely deserted for a Friday evening, which was likely why he chose this as a meeting spot. It had taken her forty-five minutes to drive to Janesville, Wisconsin, and find the address that Keith had given to her. She had arrived fifteen minutes early, mostly to study her surroundings. One could never be too prepared when facing an adversary. Opening the trunk, she unzipped her bag to be sure she had not forgotten anything, although she already knew she hadn't. One of her life mantras was *preparation is the key to success*. Watching his SUV pull into the lot, Michelle wondered who the victor of this clandestine weekend away would be. Because she knew there would be only one winner.

After parking his SUV, Dr. Keith Rodane approached Michelle and reached out to take her bag. She handed it to him and closed her trunk. They walked silently back to the SUV. Once they were both in and Keith had started driving, he turned to Michelle and said, "You packed a lot for a week away. You do know we will be staying in the entire week," then chuckled, as if he had said something especially witty.

"You can never be too prepared," Michelle responded and returned to looking out the window. What did two people talk about when one was blackmailing the other for sex? Nothing.

At some point during the two-hour drive, she dozed off. The slowing of the SUV as they pulled into town woke her up. The sign at the edge of town read Welcome to Sheboygan, The Malibu of the Midwest. Looking around, she could not see the appeal of owning a second home in this town. Everything seemed to be chain stores and restaurants or factories, with a few run-down, abandoned buildings sprinkled in between. "How did you ever decide to buy here?" she asked Keith.

Again, with that annoying chuckle, he replied, "Once you see the lakefront, you will understand. We were looking for a place on Lake Michigan and toured places all up and down the shore. We even went to the Michigan side of the lake to look at a few properties. We have owned this place for about eight years, and my wife thinks we should sell it because we rarely come here. It's true that as a family, we might come here once a year, but I come to this place far more often."

Michelle did not really need any more evidence that Keith Rodane was a louse, but he kept piling on to her case against him. "Alright, I will reserve my judgment."

Within ten minutes, they drove along the road next to Lake Michigan, and Michelle could see some of the appeal. Keith turned into a driveway and pressed the button to open the garage door. They had arrived. He exited the SUV, shut the garage door, and went to the alarm panel to disarm it. Michelle slowly opened her door. The alarm was a complication she had not prepared for, and she would need to think about how to handle it. Lost in her thoughts, she was unaware that Keith had walked to her side of the vehicle until he slid his arms around her from behind. He whispered in her ear, "Let's go in and start to enjoying our time together."

Michelle disengaged herself from Keith and went to the back of the SUV to get her bag, with Keith following her. As they stood there, Keith's phone rang. He pulled it from his pocket, looked at the screen, and told Michelle, "I have to get this, then I will grab the bags. Why don't you go in and make us a drink?"

This was the perfect setup for her plan. She wondered *is he even a little fearful of me.* It seemed that he wasn't. She must have really sold the idea that Raul had manipulated and threatened her during his killing spree and that she was innocent of what the media had reported she had taken part in. For a smart man, he was easily fooled.

The house was laid out in a typical fashion, so Michelle could easily locate the wet bar right off the kitchen. The bar was well stocked. She put on the vinyl gloves that she had in her pocket, grabbed the one whiskey glass that was not a match to the others, and a stemless wine glass. She reached back into her pocket and slowly removed a slim, brown bottle. She listened for Keith to come into the kitchen, but he was still talking on the phone in the garage. She twisted the top off the bottle and pulled out the stopper. The man who sold this to her said that Liquid Ecstasy was very potent, so only use a drop or two. She added ten drops to Keith's glass, just to be sure.

The Pappy Van Winkle Bourbon bottle looked expensive, which seemed like a great choice for Keith's last drink. She poured a generous amount into the glass, stirred it, and then used the tongs to add the clear ice ball to the drink. She then poured herself a glass of merlot. She picked up Keith's glass and her wine and wandered into the living room. She set both drinks down on coasters on the coffee table, slid open the door to the deck overlooking the lake then she stripped off her gloves and shoved them back into her pocket. Opening that door was the perfect solution to the alarm. As long as Keith did not shut it, this would allow her to leave without the alarm recording the time it was opened as being after he died.

Michelle sunk into the soft, buttery leather chair and heard Keith still on the phone. She looked out over the lake and thought about how she had gotten to this point. Six weeks ago, when she had walked into Dr. Rodane's medical office and found everyone but the dear doctor gone for the day, she knew that she hadn't imagined him calling her Paulina. He was sitting in the waiting room, just lingering until she arrived. It seemed he had given everyone in the office the afternoon off and canceled her appointment in the office calendar.

He led her back to his office, telling her what he knew about her real identity and being on the FBI's Ten Most Wanted list, then asked her for her side of the story. She explained that Raul was abusive and a killer, and she had been trapped in a marriage she was afraid to escape. When he asked her why she had not gone to the police, she explained that Raul was well-connected in Springfield and that he had made it clear that no one would believe her. If Dr. Keith Rodane had really thought about her story, he could have poked some real holes in it. Such as how she had created a new identity or where the money, she was living off of came from. After all, if she could do all that, why had she not been able to get away from her husband?

Instead, he chose to believe that she was an innocent but wanted woman and had laid out what he wanted—an ongoing sexual relationship with him in exchange for his silence. Michelle had been lucky that until now, he had not been able to get away to cash in on her end of the bargain. When he called her last week to tell her that his wife and daughter were headed to Nantucket for two weeks to see his wife's family, she knew it was time to put her plan into motion. She had been toying with the idea of going along with Keith's demands because, after all, a woman had needs, too. That was until she researched his personal life and discovered he had a wife and an eight-year-old daughter—another person who planned to destroy a perfect family. There was no way she would let him get away with both blackmailing her and ruining his family. The blackmail was something that she could understand, not that she had ever blackmailed anyone. Well, other than Raul, but that was different. But to not appreciate having a perfect family and putting that family at risk was unforgivable.

3

Friday May 27, 2022

Detective Kass Minor walked towards the Springfield Police Department, hoping to have a quiet day so that she would be able to catch up on paperwork. She had thought when her former partner, Detective Mitch Leet, retired and she was assigned a new partner that she would be the one doing less paperwork. Her new partner, Detective Devin Wilcox, was young and cocky, but worse, he was very well-connected in the department. All the men in his family had been part of the Springfield PD, with his father being the current Commander of the Uniform Operations Bureau. These connections made Wilcox feel he was above menial tasks such as paperwork and that he had little to nothing to learn from Minor.

Contemplating putting in for a transfer to the cold case division was occupying much of Kass's mental space. Two things were driving her decision: her new partner and never having found Kelsey Learner. She and Robert had discussed all her options, and she knew she needed to decide soon. A half-hour into the paperwork, she heard her commander call out.

"Minor, Wilcox, you are next up for a case. Come into my office, and I will tell you what we have so far."

Detective Minor walked toward the commander's office, scanning the unit for her partner.

The first thing their commander said to her was, "Where is Detective Wilcox?"

"I do not know, sir. I have not seen him yet today."

"Okay, when we get done talking, your first order of business will be to find your partner."

"Understood. What is the case?"

"The dispatch center got a call about forty minutes ago from a woman reporting that her two sons were not at home. An officer went out there to get the story and now requested our assistance. He thinks the boys may be in danger and says he doesn't believe the mother is telling him everything."

"Do we know the ages of the boys?"

Commander Davis looked down at the legal pad he had taken notes on and replied, "They are eleven and ten years old. Their names are Jessie and James Adams."

He then handed the paper to Minor. The notes contained the mother's name, address, and information Davis had relayed.

Detective Minor stopped at each desk as she made her way back to her cubicle. It seemed no one had seen Detective Wilcox this morning. She called him using her desk phone and left a message to meet her at the trailer park. Having no idea how else to get ahold of her partner, she headed out on her own.

******

As Detective Minor exited her car, she watched the late-model silver Corvette stop behind her department-issued sedan. The driver didn't have to get out for Minor to know it was Wilcox; he was the flashiest person in the department. She thought, *well, at least he was here, so I will not have to explain where my partner is to Commander Davis.*

"Hey, I got your message. What have we got so far?" Wilcox said as he walked towards her.

"I just got here, so nothing other than what I told you in the voicemail. I thought we would start by talking to the mother."

"You do that; I will look around and talk to Officer Grant."

Minor walked towards the trailer, mentally shaking her head. Why was she even stalling about putting in for a transfer? There was no way this would be a long-time, productive partnership. It was probably better that Wilcox didn't talk to the boy's mom because she figured that he would be less than reassuring and not open to listening to the woman's version of events. Knocking on the door, Kass observed a slew of abandoned toys and junk outside the trailer. There was a shed on the back side of the trailer, but it was unlikely it held anything of importance since one of the doors hung sideways off of its hinges.

"Just come in." Minor heard a voice from inside the trailer call out.

Walking in, she silently prayed that the brothers would be found quickly and in good health. Two women were sitting on the couch in the living area.

"Hello, I am Detective Kass Minor; I am here to help you find your kids."

"Thank you. I am Trixie Corman, and this is my friend Porsche Rowen. My boys, Jessie and James, weren't here when I got home from work today. I checked with their friends, but no one knows where they are."

"Alright, do you have a picture of your sons?"

"A bunch on my phone." Trixie pulled up a picture and handed her phone to Detective Minor.

Minor texted the photo to her own phone and then said, "Please tell me about your sons."

"Jessie is eleven, and he is reckless. He has broken a couple of bones and more than a few skateboards and bikes doing jumps and stunts. James is ten. He is my responsible kid and would never stay out all night."

"Has Jessie ever stayed out all night before?"

"A couple of times, but James was here and knew where his brother was, so I didn't worry. Basically, he spent the night at a friend's house without permission. He knows that he isn't supposed to leave this trailer while I am at work, but like I said, he is reckless." Trixie thought to herself *raising boys is not for the weak.*

"Who supervises your boys while you are at work?"

"Nobody. They are old enough to be alone at home to sleep." The edge of defiance had found its way into Trixie's voice.

Detective Minor picked up on the change in Trixie's attitude and decided to adapt her tactic. "Is it alright if I look at the boy's room?"

"Sure, it is the first door down the hall. It is a mess because, well, they're boys."

"No problem." Detective Minor said, walking into the boy's bedroom. It was a complete mess, and she wasn't sure that even the best CSI technician would be able to find anything of evidentiary value in there. She turned and walked back past the living room and into the kitchen without Trixie or Porsche even looking up at her as she passed them. Looking around, she saw dirty dishes in the sink and the garbage can almost overflowing. As she turned to head back to talk with Trixie again, a crumpled piece of paper on the top of the trash caught her eye.

Reaching into her pocket, she pulled out and put on a pair of gloves, then grabbed the paper and smoothed it out on the countertop. On the side facing up was a receipt from the local convenience store dated about a month ago, but it was what was on the other side that interested Kass. The handwritten note read:

Jessie and James,

You are in so much trouble. I had to go to work, but your asses are going to get it when I get home in the morning.

Mom

She grabbed an evidence bag out of her pocket and slid it. Kass thought about how her former partner often joked that she kept more in her pockets than a ma'ama kangaroo. Kass thought of it more as always being prepared. The responding officer had been right; Trixie Corman was not being forthright with them.

Friday July 10, 2020

Michelle heard Keith walk into the condo and then approach the living room. He reached down, picked up the tumbler, and finished the drink in one large swig.

"I am going to get a refill. Do you want another?"

"I would like what you are having."

"Alright, two whiskeys coming right up."

As Keith walked back into the kitchen, Michelle wondered how long it would take for him to feel the effects of the drug. It took him only a few minutes to return with two glasses of whiskey. She noticed that his gait was already a bit unsteady, but that did not stop him from taking a long drink of the whiskey and setting the glass on the coffee table.

"Wow. Maybe I should have eaten something before drinking."

Michelle smiled at him and said, "Maybe we should head to the bedroom."

He slowly nodded and used the side table to help him stand. Michelle helped him walk to the bedroom and said, "I am going into the bathroom to get ready. How about you get undressed and wait in bed for me?"

In a very eager tone, Keith said, "Sounds perfect, baby!"

As soon as she entered the bathroom, Michelle put back on the gloves she had in her pocket. Looking around the bathroom, she realized that the main closet was part of this room and couldn't help herself from snooping around. There were only a few items in the closet, so the large stack of sweaters was clearly out of place. Michelle picked them up and saw that they were there in an attempt to hide a safe. The door to the safe wasn't fully closed, so naturally, she had to peek inside. There was a stack of cash and a gun sitting in the safe. *I don't mind if I do;* she thought to herself as she removed the items, then closed the safe door, twisting the lock mechanism and replacing the stack of sweaters.

Walking back into the bedroom, it was clear that Keith had passed out. He lay in the center of the bed naked as the day he was born. He had neatly folded his clothes and put them on the dresser, along with his wallet. She placed both of Keith's hands on what she was sure was his favorite body part, then grabbed his necktie and secured it around his bedpost, then his neck. She applied enough pressure to cut off his breathing. Taking the bottle out of her pocket, she wrapped his fingers around it and set it on the nightstand. Next, she returned to the living room and grabbed the glass of whiskey he had prepared for her. She poured the whiskey down the drain and put the glass on his nightstand. She set the flip-flops that had been in the closet by the back door and went to finish cleaning up.

After washing, drying, and putting away the other two glasses, Michelle looked around the condo. Seeing two sets of footprints in the thick, lush carpet, she thought, *Good thing I have all night* as she pulled the vacuum cleaner out of the hall closet. She started vacuuming in the bedroom, working toward the living room and then backing down to the closet where she had found the vacuum. She removed the dust bin from the vacuum and emptied it into a plastic store bag. Luckily, the hallway had hardwood floors, so she could walk back to the door to the garage where their shoes and bags sat. She put the bag of garbage and her shoes in her bag, then slipped her feet into Keith's flip-flops. She walked to the open French doors in the living room, slid the screen away, and stepped out into the chilly night air. Walking on the sand beside the lake, she stared at the moon and thought about her daughter Lynn. Once she had the perfect family, then tragedy ripped that away from her. Now, her daughter and husband were both dead, and she was left feeling untethered to anything good in this world.

4

Tuesday May 26, 2022

Sitting back down in the living room, Detective Minor looked at Trixie and asked, "When was the last time you saw Jessie and James?"

Trixie didn't look up when she replied, "Yesterday, before I went to work."

Minor took the note from her bag and put it on her lap. "Really? Because I found this note crumbled in the kitchen trash, so I will ask you again, when did you last see your sons?"

Trixie looked up at Minor and responded, "Well, it was yesterday, and it was before I went to work last night. I just didn't say how long before. When I got home yesterday morning, both boys were already awake, sitting in front of the television, eating cereal out of the box. We talked for a little bit, and then, at about nine, the boys headed out to ride their bikes, and I went to sleep. That is what we have done all summer; until now, there haven't been any problems."

"So, your kids have been potentially missing since about nine a.m. yesterday. I am going to ask you and your friend to leave the trailer, and we will have the CSI team sweep for clues. I am going to walk you out, talk to my partner, and call my commander. We have a rapid missing child response team that will be brought in. Trixie, it is essential that from this point forward, you are one hundred percent forthcoming with us. Is that understood?"

"Yeah, I get it. I just want my kids home."

"When the team is done here, I suggest that you and Porsche clean this place up while you wait. I can almost guarantee that social services will pay you a visit regarding your son's disappearance. You are not to leave the trailer park unless myself, my partner, Detective Wilcox, or the police Commander Davis tell you to. Are we on the same page?"

"Yes, Detective Minor, just bring my son's home."

******

Detective Wilcox and Office Grant stood at the Corvette with the hood open. Kass was sure that whatever they were discussing had nothing to do with this case and would do nothing to bring Jessie and James Adams' home.

"Wilcox, I want to update you before I call Commander Davis." She called over to the two of them and watched as Wilcox walked towards her.

"What's up?"

"The two boys have been missing since nine a.m. yesterday, and their bikes were not here. Their mom, Trixie, has called all their friends' homes, and no one has seen them. Our next step will be letting Commander Davis know what is happening and having the CSI and RMCR teams get out here."

"Okay, what do you want me to do?"

"Will you take Officer Grant and go through the trailer park door to door? We need to know if anyone saw the boys and where they were headed."

"Ten-four," he replied and then walked back to Officer Grant.

Minor placed her call to Commander Davis and then walked to the stairs of the trailer where Trixie and Porsche sat. "Tell me about the boy's father."

"His name is Chase Adams. He is a loser. I met him when I was in high school, and I thought he was so cool. I got pregnant when I was nineteen, and by the time I was six months along, Chase was headed to jail. He got out when Jessie was two months old, and I was exhausted, so when he said he wanted to live with us and be a family, I was okay with it.

Chase didn't make it long on the outside; he was back in jail by the time Jessie was four months old, and the next month, I found out I was pregnant with James. When Chase got out of jail two years later, I didn't take him back again. At first, he would come by to see me and the kids, but that quickly tapered off. The last time he came by, I told him I was suing him for child support. He got really angry and started screaming and throwing stuff. One of the neighbors called the cops, and Chase went back to jail for violating his probation."

Detective Minor knew that they would need to look into Chase Adams. "Do either of the boys have a cell phone?"

"No, they both really want one, but I can't afford it. My phone is one of those prepaid kinds. It is Porsche's old phone, and I just put minutes on it when I have a little money for it. Now, I wish I would have gotten one for them. I know you can track phones, so if they had one, then we would know where my boys are."

Just as Minor was about to ask her next question, all three women's cell phones began screeching an alarm. It was the Amber Alert for Jessie and James; Trixie broke down and started sobbing. Porsche just stared at her phone, and Detective Minor silenced hers.

Commander Davis, the CSI and RMCR teams, and several patrol cars pulled into the trailer park just as Officer Grant came jogging toward Minor.

"Detective Minor, there is a little girl three trailers down who may have witnessed something."

Minor jumped up, and they both ran back towards the potential witness. A sense of dread had settled in since she had learned that the boys had been gone almost twenty-four hours before Trixie called it in. A possible witness sighting was a glimmer of hope.

Thursday July 16, 2020

Sheboygan Detective Chris Dyer hated calls for dead bodies that had been found days after death. The sights and smells of these scenes were not something anyone ever needed to experience once, much less multiple times in a lifetime. He was sure that the woman for the cleaning service who stumbled on the scene when she had gone to do a regular cleaning job would be scarred by her experience. The condo on the lake was beautiful on the outside. Chris walked around outside and noted that the only condo without security cameras was of course the one where the dead body had been found.

The Crime Scene Team was already inside the condo, processing the scene and waiting for the medical examiner to arrive. Detective Dyer needed to head inside to look at the scene and, more importantly, the body. He walked the scene whenever possible before the body was removed, which helped him to better visualize what had happened. The responding officer had already made a preliminary identification based on the wallet found near the body. Dr. Keith Rodane and his wife, Beatrice from Lake Geneva, owned this condo, and there had never been any police calls to the address. The body of Dr. Keith Rodane was lying alone on his bed.

The woman from the cleaning service sat on a bench outside that looked out over the lake. She was clearly crying, but Detective Dyer needed to get her statement before he could let her head home.

"Hello, ma'am, I am Detective Chris Dyer. I know what you saw today was very jarring, but I need to ask you a few questions. Are you up to talking?"

"Okay, sure."

"Are you the person who regularly cleans this condo?"

"Yes, I clean every Thursday. Most of the time, no one has even been here between my cleanings, but the Rodane's contract is for weekly cleaning, so I clean it weekly. Until today, it was absolutely my easiest job."

"Do you have a key to the house?"

"No, I have a code for the garage door and one for the alarm."

"When you entered the garage today, what was the first thing you noticed?"

"That Dr. Rodane's SUV was parked in there."

"Walk me through the rest of what happened until you called 911."

"I sent Dr. Rodane a text asking if he wanted me to clean today, but got no answer. I waited ten minutes and then went to disarm the alarm and found that it was off, so I knocked on the door to the house. No one responded, so I went in, and that is when I smelled that awful odor. I thought the Rodane's had left some meat out that was rotting. I walked towards the kitchen, but there was nothing out of place.

I kept walking towards the bedrooms. Thinking back, I should have turned around. There was like a silent, internal alarm going off in my head saying get out, get out, but I rarely listen to that alarm, so I kept walking. The smell was ungodly when I opened the primary bedroom door. Then I saw Dr. Rodane on the bed. I mean all of Dr. Rodane. I screamed and ran out of the house. That is when I called 911."

Detective Dyer was now sure that this woman would never forget this day. "I appreciate you talking me through that. I know it wasn't easy. I have just one more question; besides Dr. Rodane, did you notice anything else unusual or out of place?"

"The only other thing was that I could feel a cool breeze as I walked past the living room. I looked into the room and saw that the French doors were open."

"Thank you for your help. Here is my card; if you think of anything else, I might need to know or you just need to talk, please do not hesitate to call."

Dyer returned to the condo and into the garage, where the CSI team had left the required gear. Putting on the crime scene body suit, booties, and mask, he walked into the condo and looked around. The condo was pristinely clean and well-appointed. He walked from room to room, looking around, seeing nothing that stood out. That was until he entered the main bedroom; Dr. Keith Rodane was lying naked on the bed with a tie around his neck then wound around the headboard.

Next to the bed on the nightstand was an empty whiskey glass, with what were presumably the doctor's folded clothes in a pile on the dresser and wallet set on top of the pile. There was no sign that anyone else had been there. Detective Dyer's initial reaction was that this was an accidental death due to suffocation during a solo sex act. He was standing looking at the body when the medical examiner walked up next to him.

"Well, we don't see that every day here in good ol Sheboygan, now do we?"

Dyer had gotten used to the medical examiner's odd sense of humor. It seemed to Dyer that any doctor who chose to work with the dead instead of the living must be a little off. "I know I have never seen a case of it before, but I know about it from training."

"I will do my part here and then transport him back to the morgue. I will let you know in a day or two what my ruling is, but it is looking like an accident."

As Detective Dyer was walking back to his car, one of the CSI techs called him back into the condo.

"Detective Dyer, we have found something you will want to take a look at."

Dryer looked at the evidence bag that held a small brown bottle.

"What do you think it is?"

"No idea, but it is a liquid and appears to have rolled off the nightstand. We will send it to the lab to be fingerprinted and figure out what it contains. The other thing is in the closet."

Detective Dryer walked with the technician into the closet, where a safe was clearly visible.

"I didn't notice that before."

"Yeah, it was behind a stack of sweaters. We took pictures before moving them. The safe is locked."

"I will ask the wife for the combination when I speak to her after the local police in Lake Geneva notify her of the death."

5

Friday May 27, 2022

The witness turned out to be an eight-year-old girl named Bailey, who lived three doors down from where Jessie and James did. She told Detective Minor that she had walked to the trailer park office to buy a soda from the vending machine yesterday morning. Her mom added that it was a little before eleven in the morning, and she had been sitting on the porch playing on her phone while Bailey walked there and back. Detective Minor could see the office from the trailer's porch as well as the road that ran in front of the turn-in for the trailer park.

"Bailey, please tell me what you saw yesterday?" Detective Minor asked the little girl.

"Sure. I saw those boys. You know Jessie and James; they were riding their bikes. They ride their bikes all the time. Then I saw Jessie get off his bike and walk towards the road. Once I got my grape pop, I saw Jessie talking to a man in a green truck. Then he went and talked to James, then they put their bikes in the back of the green truck and got in."

"Do you know who drives that green truck?" Minor asked the child.

"No, I have never seen it in my life, but it is probably their daddy because you ain't supposed to get rides from strangers."

"You are right; you should not get rides from strangers. Did you see the man who was driving?"

"Nope."

"How do you know it was a man?"

Bailey shrugged her little shoulders and replied, "Cuz, men drive trucks."

"Got it. Did you see which way the truck was going?"

"Yep, it drove that way." Bailey was pointing north.

"Thank you so much for helping us."

"You're welcome."

Detective Kass Minor handed Bailey's mom her card and then went to fill her partner and the rest of the team in on the lead.

When she had finished relaying the information that Bailey and her mom had reported, Commander Davis asked, "Do we think she is a reliable witness?"

"As reliable as an eight-year-old could be. Her mom corroborated that she was at the park office when Bailey said she was; besides, I do not know what she would gain from lying. Plus, we have nothing else to go off of."

Detective Wilcox spoke up, "I agree with Minor on this one. Finding the green truck as well as its driver makes the most sense to me, too."

Minor was surprised that Wilcox actually agreed with her, but she would not turn down the backup.

Commander Davis, "Alright, let's start looking for camera footage around here for that green truck."

Minor walked to her department-issued car and was startled when her partner opened the door and got in. "Where to first?" he asked.

"I will drive north and stop at the first business I see. Hopefully, they will have a security camera, and we might get lucky and see this mystery truck."

She did just what she had planned and pulled into an older gas station about a half mile from the trailer park.

"Let's go see if we can get lucky," Wilcox said, and then quickly began to try to retract his statement. "I didn't mean that how it sounded. I just meant that maybe we would be lucky enough, at the first place, to score... Oh, God."

"I know what you were trying to say; maybe just stop talking," Minor said, chuckling as they walked into the station.

After introductions to the store owner who was working behind the counter and an explanation of what they were looking for, Minor and Wilcox found themselves in a cramped back room watching footage from the outside camera. The camera was pointed at the four pumps, but you could also see the road. Minor had teed up the footage to ten thirty a.m. the day before and started watching at double speed. Until they saw it. A green truck drove past the station at four minutes after eleven in the morning. You could see a driver and two children but could not clearly make out faces or anything descriptive. Worse yet, the license plate was not visible from the angle of the video.

"At least we know that little girl wasn't lying, or if she was, it is a hell of a coincidence."

"No, Wilcox, I think we can safely say she didn't lie to us. It is time for us to go find some more footage."

******

James woke Jessie up as soon as he saw the light coming down from the hole. "Jessie, we got to find a way out."

Last night, after hearing his brother scream, James had run in the direction he had last seen him. It was dark, and the only flashlight was with Jessie, who wasn't answering him as he screamed his name repeatedly. James fell into the hole in what he figured was the same way his brother had. James had read that you should try to land on your butt if you are falling, so he rolled into a ball and did just that. The landing hurt, but he was pretty sure nothing was broken. He felt around and found Jessie's leg.

"Jessie, are you okay?"

His brother moaned and then said, "I can't stand up. I think I broke my leg. Where are we?"

"I don't know, but it is some kind of hole. Where is the flashlight?"

"I dropped it when I fell. I tried to feel around for it, but it hurts to move, so I stopped."

James also tried to feel around for the flashlight, but he also didn't go far from Jessie. He didn't want to remind Jessie about the fact that he was afraid of the dark. It was better to just sit by his brother and wait for the morning, and now here it was. He looked up at the light streaming down at them. The hole they had fallen through was really far up, and there was no ladder.

"Jessie, are you awake?" This time, he nudged his brother as he asked.

"Yeah, but man, I am hurt bad."

James could see around them, although the light was dim down here, and he could tell that his brother's leg was bent weirdly. The next thing he noticed was the flashlight. It had been just out of the area he searched last night. He walked over and grabbed it and was surprised when it turned right on.

Turning, he beamed the light towards his brother. Now he could see that Jessie had dried blood on one of his hands. "Jessie, where did that blood come from?"

"I think it's from my leg. When I landed down here, I rubbed my leg because it hurt so bad, and my hand felt wet."

James grabbed the fishing knife out of his old backpack that they used as a tackle box. Everything in it had been given to them by Eddie about a year ago when the boys showed an interest in fishing. Sitting beside Jessie, James told him, "I am going to cut open your pants."

"Why? It ain't like you can do anything for my leg."

"If it is still bleeding, we have to put pressure on it. We learned that in the after-school boys' club. Don't you remember?"

"I guess so. I didn't really pay attention. Mom just made us stay at that so she could get extra sleep. I only liked the days we played basketball."

James looked at his brother's leg. There was a bunch of dry blood just above where his leg turned the wrong way. "It isn't bleeding right now. I am going to walk around down here and see if there is a way out."

Monday July 20, 2020

Agent Matthews was frustrated, and running was the best way he had found to calm down when he was frustrated. But this morning, running wasn't helping. He had been so hopeful a month ago when they had gotten the information on Paulina Moore's alias. Hanna Lewis's trail had seemed like it was going to get them somewhere at first, but nothing was as straightforward as it seemed when it came to Dr. Paulina Moore. It had been three months, and they had not found any trace of her.

Looking ahead, he could see Kass Minor running towards him; hopefully, seeing her would be a calming force. This had become their new routine for the last two weeks; each morning, they would text each other and then run towards the park in the middle of the route between their condos. Once they met at the park, they ran the trail together and then returned to their respective homes. When he shared this routine with his mom, she said that it was not dating, but for him and Kass, it was.

When he told Kass what his mom had said, she laughed and told him that her mom felt just the opposite way. Her mom had told her that the cornerstone of a long-lasting relationship was finding things to enjoy together, and if running was their thing, that was great. Robert agreed with Kass's mom's sentiment because, with both of their busy schedules, running was a great way for them to spend time together.

"Good morning, Kass."

"You made good time getting here, or I am slow this morning."

"I was in the zone running today. I can't figure out what to do next in the search for Paulina Moore, so I took my frustration out on the running path."

"That is a feeling I can relate to. I was hopeful we would find Kelsey Learner once Raul Moore confessed to kidnapping and holding her in his suicide letter. But we are no closer than before to finding out where she is. I take it the lead you got about the alias was a dead end."

"The informant was being truthful about Paulina's alias, but all we have uncovered is a closed P.O. Box on the north side of Springfield and a closed bank account with money transferred into Bitcoin, just like her other account. The forensic accountant says that the bitcoin was converted to currency overseas. She has been trying to trace both transfers, but many countries do not cooperate with the US government."

"When did she close her PO Box?"

"The day she came back to Springfield to clear out her accounts. Agent Hollins and I could not account for 30 minutes of her time, but now we know she went to the post office and closed her box."

"I read an article a couple of days ago about some notorious serial killers who were not caught for decades. Do you think Paulina Moore will join their ranks?"

"Honestly, that is what scares me the most. If she is out there, I don't believe her killings will stop."

"So, you believe what Raul accused her of in his suicide note?"

"Yes, I do. I also think she had something to do with her dad's recent death."

"Wow."

"Any news on a new partner?"

"No, Leet will be around for a couple more weeks, and then I will probably be partnered with whoever gets promoted or hired into his job."

"I am still surprised that Leet is retiring, especially since Kelsey hasn't been found, so her case is still open."

"He told me that he trusts me to close the case. I just hope he hasn't put too much faith in me."

Running beside each other, they both fell silent and concentrated on keeping up with the pace. Matthews broke the silence as they returned to the start of the path, where they would part ways to run home. "Are you ready for this weekend?"

"I am packed and ready to go. My commander knows I am leaving for a long weekend, so I'm not up for a new case until I return. So, this will be my big chance to catch up on paperwork. How about you?"

"I am more of the throw a few items in a bag at the last-minute kind of guy."

"If that works for you, more power to you, but I cannot function that way. Plus, I will meet your family for the first time and want to make a good impression."

"When you packed your bag is likely not something that will come up in conversation."

"Probably true, but being prepared will help me to feel like I can handle anything."

"Are you not looking forward to going?"

"No, that isn't it. I am definitely looking forward to going to the wedding, meeting your family, and spending time away with you. I just worry about what people think of me."

"Please don't worry. My mom is so overjoyed that I am bringing someone you could show up in a clown suit, and she would think you were wonderful."

Minor started laughing, "I can definitely do better than that."

Matthews reached over and pulled her in for a hug, and they kissed briefly before they ran their separate ways.

6

Friday May 27, 2022

The forensic team combed through the trailer while uniform police officers and volunteers searched the woods and fields surrounding the trailer park. Minor and Wilcox had been driving from business to business, watching footage for hours. So far, there had been no sign of the boys and no more than quick glances of the truck as it drove north. Wilcox had been complaining about being hungry and sick of being in the car, and Minor was ready to take him back to get his car and continue on her own.

"Alright, after we meet with the park rangers here at Lake Springfield, I will take you back to your car." She said as she parked at the ranger station. When she called the ranger, she told Minor that the state had not installed any cameras at the lake. Still, there were several cameras that environmental scientists from the university had installed to monitor wildlife. The ranger had told Minor that she would call one of the scientists and have him meet them as well.

"I just hope this isn't a giant waste of time. We don't even know if the truck came here."

"I get it, Wilcox, but Commander Davis made a list, and we need to check the lake off our list of footage we have looked at."

"Fine!" he said as he got out and slammed the car door.

Detective Minor followed her partner into the ranger station and made introductions.

"Nice to meet both of you. I am Park Ranger Abby Cranshaw, and this is Dr. Marco Flores from the University of Missouri. Dr. Flores and I were just discussing what his cameras might have captured. We thought you would want to start with the footage from the one with the boat launch and shore. The rest of the cameras are throughout the woods."

"I have cued up the footage to yesterday morning, as that is when Abby told me you were looking for a green truck."

"Have you watched it yet?" Detective Wilcox addressed his question to Dr. Flores.

"No, I got here about five minutes before you."

The four watched as Dr. Flores started the footage at five minutes after eleven yesterday morning. Fifteen minutes later, they saw a man launch a small boat, and a couple of birds fly by, then the front of a green truck pull into the parking lot. They could only see the front end, but could clearly make out a license plate. The slight movement indicated that someone had gotten out of the truck, but no one came into view of the camera. Five minutes later, the truck went into reverse and left the camera's view.

"Oh my, I think we might have a really good lead. I am going to call in the license plate. Dr. Flores, please email me the footage and what your other cameras caught that morning. I will have forensics examine it for any clue as to who got out and where they went for those five minutes." Kass Minor slid her business card over to him so he would have her email address.

"No problem. I hope you find the missing kids."

"Thank you. We certainly hope so, too."

As they walked out, Minor called the plate into the dispatch and listened as they relayed the information that was found.

"Thank you. Please put a Be on the Lookout for that license plate."

"What do we know?" Detective Wilcox asked when Minor hung up the phone.

"The truck is registered to Dan Becker of Hot Springs, Arkansas. His truck is registered under his company name, Becker Construction. He is the sole proprietor of that business."

Detective Kass Minor grabbed her department-issued laptop and did a Google search of Dan Becker.

"He is a divorced, fifty-one-year-old who specializes in restoration carpentry. He has a twelve-year-old daughter, and she and his ex-wife live in Springfield."

"Well, that explains why he was here. Does he have a record?"

"That isn't something I can find out on Google. Let's head back to your car and then meet back at the station. We can do an extensive search on the criminal records database."

"I guess you plan to pull an all-nighter."

"I will work as long as I physically can until we find these children."

"Fine."

Minor once again wondered about her partner's commitment to this job. Most of the detectives she had worked with over the years put in super long hours during a major case.

Monday August 3, 2020

When Michelle had returned from her trip to Sheboygan a month ago, she hoped she would never have to spend hours on a bus again. The first thing she did was call Dr. Rodane's office and make an appointment for later this month. The receptionist was her normal cheery self, so Michelle knew that his body had yet to be discovered. Now, as she read the letter she had just received from his office, it was clear that whatever investigation the Sheboygan police had done it did not involve murder.

To the Patients of Dr. Keith Rodane,

We regret to inform you that Dr. Rodane died last month in a tragic accident. We have

included a list of board-certified plastic surgeons currently accepting new patients in the

area. Dr. Rodane's office will stay open for another six weeks to fulfill records requests

and close out the billing for the office.

Sincerely,
The office staff of Dr. Keith Rodane

She hadn't been to the library since her trip to Sheboygan, so she didn't know whether there had been an obituary or a news story surrounding his death. Since she had another errand to run, she would go to the library just to fulfill her curiosity. Soon, she would need to leave Lake Geneva and reinvent herself again. It was time to start preparing for her move.

Standing in the post office lobby, Michelle was fuming mad, and she knew who was going to pay for the cause of her anger: Charlene Peterson! When Michelle had headed to the little town of Twin Lakes just outside of Lake Geneva to rent a post office box, she hadn't been planning to stop and look at the wanted posters. The problem was that the post office closed for an hour for lunch each day, and she had arrived ten minutes before they reopened. Standing in the lobby, she found herself staring at the display of wanted posters. They were hung on a two-ring clipboard that was mounted to the wall. She flipped through the first few papers and then stopped at the wanted poster for Paulina Moore. She had seen the poster on the library computer, but touching it made it so much more real. Being famous was not her goal, much less being infamous, but there she was in black and white on a wanted poster. She skimmed the information and stopped short when she saw the section on known aliases. The name Hanna Lewis was listed with a picture of her counterfeit driver's license. That information was not on the original poster she had seen on the internet six weeks ago.

There was no honor amongst criminals, after all. Michelle wondered what kind of deal Charlene had gotten for ratting her out. The library was in the same strip mall complex as the post office, and the systems were interconnected throughout the county, so using their computer system to look up Charlene's case presented no issues for Michelle. The first thing she learned was that Charlene was an alias for Shasta Peters, but that didn't surprise Michelle. She thought, *of course, she told me an alias. After all, her brother was Two-bit.* The information in the Springfield newspaper said that Shasta Peters and the State of Missouri had entered into a plea deal in exchange for information that Shasta had provided the FBI. Shasta had all her assets seized and was on probation for ten years.

Michelle searched for Shasta's current address but kept coming up with the house that the state had seized and would be auctioned off next month. Finding Shasta wouldn't be as easy as a Google search, but determination and persistence were things that Michelle prided herself on. Now, instead of moving away from Lake Geneva, it was time for Michelle to take another trip to Missouri.

7

Friday May 27, 2022

By the time Detective Kass Minor got back to the Springfield police department, the sun was setting, and the search parties were being called in for the night. She could only imagine the terror that Jessie and James must be feeling by now. Holding out hope that both boys remained alive, she vowed to track down every lead she could until they were found. Their dad, Chase Adams, had been cleared as a suspect by a quick database search that showed he was sitting in jail in St. Louis awaiting trial for robbery.

Commander Davis called her into his office and repeated a question he had asked her this morning: "Where's your partner?"

Just like this morning, Minor did not know Wilcox's location, so she just shrugged.

Davis shook his head and said, "Fine, you can fill him in when you find him. The Arkansas State Patrol stopped Dan Becker on I-530, just outside Little Rock. He denies having anything to do with the Adams boys' disappearance, but they are bringing him here for questioning."

"That is fabulous. What is the ETA?"

"They will be here in about two hours."

"I am going to go get some dinner. Do you want anything?"

"No, I am going to make some calls and eat the food the wife packed me."

"Okay, I will be back long before the state patrol gets Dan Becker."

"While you are out, find your partner and tell him to make sure his ass is here before Dan Becker is too!"

Minor nodded in acknowledgment of what Davis had said and walked away.

******

Kass called Robert as she walked to the diner, and he answered on the first ring, saying, "Hi, Hun. How are you?"

"Not so good. I hate cases like this. Then add that Wilcox is a crappy partner, and the commander keeps ordering me to find him."

Robert laughed and replied, "I think these are signs from the universe that you need to put in for that transfer."

"I hear you. As soon as these boys are found, I will sit down with Commander Davis."

"Good. I am glad you are finally doing what is best for you."

"I am going to be working late tonight. The state police are bringing in our only suspect, so don't wait up."

******

James sat next to Jessie, too terrified to move. He had stopped shaking a while ago, but now that it was getting dark again, he started to feel the fear, starting the tremors again. How were they supposed to make it down here in the dark another night?

Jessie asked him again for the first time in hours, "Are you sure it was a real human skeleton? Not just like a Halloween one?"

James nodded, but he wasn't sure if his brother could see him as the darkness had begun to surround them. "No, it was a person. There was hair and everything."

Jessie wished he could get up and go over to see it, but he knew he couldn't stand up, much less walk. He also knew that James was afraid of the dark, so he was worried about how long the flashlight would last. They had sat below the hole they had fallen through since James had run back over here. "James, let's try to keep the flashlight off as much as possible. I don't want it to stop working."

"Don't you think people are looking for us?"

"Yeah, I am sure they are, but we are lost, so they may not know where to look."

"I don't want to die down here."

"Come on, bro, we aren't going to die."

"We don't have any food or water. How long can we last?"

"About three days from the last time we had water."

"How do you know that for sure?"

"The boys' club."

James sat next to his brother in the dark and cried silently. What he didn't know was that Jessie was crying, too.

Thursday September 24, 2020

Michelle got off the bus in Columbia, Missouri. She had never imagined that life on the run would mean sitting on a bus so often. The guy from the rental car company was in the parking lot, ready to pick her up. She had made a reservation at a hotel here in Columbia for a couple of days and secured a few job interviews. All of this would explain why Michelle had traveled from Lake Geneva to Columbia if anyone ever even bothered to look into it.

After finishing her paperwork at the rental car agency, Michelle checked into the hotel and walked across the street to the big box store parking lot. The car she had come to buy was sitting in the back of the parking lot with a young man sitting on the hood.

"Hi, you must be Tony. I am Jenny." Michelle put her hand out to shake his.

The man shook her hand and said, "So, do you want to test drive the car?"

"Of course."

She got in the driver's seat, and Tony got in the passenger one, then she drove around the parking lot first. Tony gave her directions to the interstate, and she drove for two miles and then exited. She drove through town, carefully following the directions to get back to the big box store.

"This car will work great for me."

Tony gave her a perplexed look, then replied, “I gotta say you are not the kind of person I was expecting to buy my car.”

“Really, why is that?”

“It is a 1985 Oldsmobile Cutlass Brougham sedan with a custom paint job and lift package. I am selling it because my wife and I are expecting our first kid and need to have a more suitable ride.”

“I’ll be honest with you. My brother had a car just like this in high school, and I am buying this one to surprise him.”

“Wow. I wish my sister would buy me something like this.”

When they got back to the big box store parking lot, Tony had her pull up next to the Toyota Camry. They both got out, and Michelle pulled an envelope out of her purse.

“Wait, before you pay me, I have to tell you that I don’t have the title for the car. Well, I have it, but we can’t find it. You can get one by writing to the Motor Vehicle Department.”

Michelle was sure that she would not be able to get a duplicate title, but that did not matter to her. She never planned to title it anyway, but now Michelle knew for sure that this sale was not on the up and up. That made this car even more perfect for her needs.

Her hesitation made Tony try to reassure her, “I will knock five grand off the listed price if you buy it now in cash.”

“Okay, I think we can make that work.”

Michelle counted out the money and handed it to Tony. He walked to the Brougham, removed the license plates, shook Michelle’s hand again, and got into the Camry.

Michelle locked the Cutlass and walked back to the hotel. She went up to her room to get a good night's sleep. As she lay in the bed drifting off to sleep, she thought about the positives of riding the bus, such as they didn’t check your luggage or bags. She had brought the Smith and Wesson 22 caliber gun that she had stolen from Dr. Keith Rodane’s condo with her on this trip.

Friday September 25, 2020

Michelle attended her three job interviews and then walked around downtown. She had a nice dinner at a small restaurant, then parked the rental car at the hotel, walked back to the big box store parking lot, and got into the Cutlass. The drive to Springfield would take her almost three hours, which was perfect. She would arrive after dark, which was necessary for her plan to work. The car had a full gas tank, and she could get to Springfield and take care of her business without needing to stop for gas.

At first, finding Shasta's address had been difficult, but of course, all it really took was perseverance. Michelle had pulled up every listing for rentals in the Springfield area and then whittled it down to ones with low rent in questionable neighborhoods. She started with the ones closest to where she had met Two-bit and interacted with Shasta. She called the numbers listed in the ads and asked about the properties. The ones that were still available, she crossed off her list. There were two that had been rented since the week before she called. Tonight, she would drive to each and try to figure out which one, if either, was the new home of Shasta Peters, then she could make a plan for taking care of this particular issue.

******

Shasta Peters was exhausted. Moving was not as hard as it would be for most people, because the state of Missouri now owned most of her former belongings. The little that the marshals overseeing the seizure had let her take from her former home fit into a dozen boxes. She bought used furniture from a social media site. Her brother Two-bit thought she should have just tapped the money in Charlene's accounts, but Shasta didn't want to draw attention to herself. Renting this row house in her old neighborhood was a good place to restart her life.

Mixing up her favorite beverage of vodka and lemonade, she grabbed her cigarettes and went to sit on the stoop. Her brother lived a block over in the row house they grew up in. When their mom died a few years ago, Shasta had no desire to live in that house and didn't need the money they would get for selling it. So, when Two-bit told her he wanted it, she signed over her share of it. It was likely that Two-Bit was sitting on his own stoop, hanging out with the same few guys he had hung out with all his life.

A supped-up Oldsmobile Cutlass Brougham drove slowly by; Shasta had never understood the money guys put into these old cars. Give her a brand-new high-end car any day over an old car without technology any day. But cars like the one she just saw were very popular in this neighborhood, so she knew there was a strong appeal for some. Shasta needed to buy a new car, since that was yet another thing that had been seized. That was something that she would use Charlene's money for. Nothing flashy, but without a job, financing wasn't an option. Two-bit had agreed to buy the car and register it in his name so that the state did not know about her new ride.

Shasta pulled out her phone and began searching for cars for sale. A noise made her look up. That same Cutlass Brougham she had seen drive by a few minutes ago was now sitting right in front of her row house. The passenger window was rolled down, and a rap song from a couple of years back about snitches and rats was blaring. Shasta reached for her drink just as the first shot rang out. The glass shattered as she dropped it while jumping up to run inside, but she never even reached the door.

******

Michelle couldn't believe her luck. Shasta had been just sitting on the steps at the first place that Michelle drove by. Driving around the corner, she rolled down both windows and put in the mixtape she had brought. There would be one chance to get this right, so Michelle took a few moments to prepare herself. Pulling up to the curb in front of Shasta's new place, she watched as Shasta stared at her phone, paying no attention to the car or its driver. Michelle picked up the gun and leaned over towards the passenger side window. Pulling the trigger was like a release of anger that she loved. Her mom had taught to shoot and she had forgotten how much she loved it.

Watching Shasta scramble to her feet, Michelle emptied the rest of the shots. Then she sat back up in the driver's seat and put the car in drive. There was a park at the end of the street with a bus stop that she had found on a map. The city bus was a great way for her to get out of the area. Leaving the Cutlass running, she popped out her mixtape, put the gun in her book bag, got out, and walked to the bus stop. Buses were the bane of her existence, but they provided her with transportation, so she was developing a love-hate relationship with them.

8

Friday May 27, 2022

Detective Kass Minor had left a voicemail for her partner, letting him know that Dan Becker had been apprehended and that Commander Davis had said that Detective Wilcox had better beat the suspect back to the precinct. Short of that, she didn't know anything else to do to ensure her partner was there. She had gotten her dinner to go and treated herself to a strawberry milkshake, which she had recently developed a great fondness for. Now she was sitting at her desk, eating her meal while preparing to interview Dan Becker. She had learned that he had no criminal history, but nothing else of significance since her initial Google search.

Wilcox walked up and sat down in Minor's cubicle.

Trying to keep her annoyance out of her voice, she turned to him and asked, "Where have you been?"

"Home. I knew you would call me if anything came up."

"You do know that we are actively investigating two missing and presumably kidnapped children, right?"

"Yeah, I know, but like I said, I also knew you would call me if anything big came up, and you did."

Minor didn't want to lecture him, and no witty retort came to mind, so moving on was the only thing to do. "We are expecting the state police to bring Dan Becker in about an hour. The search has been called off for the night unless Becker tells where to find the boys."

"Or their bodies," Wilcox added unnecessarily.

They passed their hour of waiting in very different ways, Minor watching footage from business cameras showing the most likely route from Lake Springfield to the interstate. Meanwhile, Wilcox wandered around socializing with anyone and everyone who would engage with him.

"Minor, Wilcox, we are ready for you in interview room one." Commander Davis called out.

Minor got up and grabbed her notebook and favorite pen.

"What are those for?" Wilcox asked.

"Taking notes."

"You know they record all interviews, right?"

"Yes, I know, but I note things I want to look into right away. There is always a delay before the interview footage is available."

"Old school. Got it."

Minor and Wilcox walked to the observation area adjacent to the interview room, where Commander Davis and Assistant District Attorney Liza Reinhart waited.

"We talked about it and will have Detective Minor interview Dan Becker alone. He seems to be very skittish, and we don't want him to invoke his right to a lawyer. Are you ready, Minor?" Commander Davis told the two detectives with his tone, leaving no room for debate.

"Yes, sir."

Liza Reinhart reminded Minor before she walked out of the room, "If he asks for a lawyer, stop the questioning. I want to find these kids as much as anyone, but I also want our case against this guy to hold up in court."

Davis added, "When he denies knowing where the boys are because we all know he will tell him they are missing to see his reaction."

"I completely understand what both of you are saying," Minor replied.

Detective Kass Minor walked into the interview room and sat down.

"Hello, Mr. Becker, I am Detective Kass Minor. Do you need anything to drink?"

"No, I am fine. I just want to understand why I was arrested and brought here."

"Where were you this morning at about eleven a.m.?"

"Here, I mean in Springfield, obviously, not at the police department. I visited my daughter. I spent three days and two nights in Springfield. My ex-wife and I agreed it would be easier for our daughter, JJ, if I spent time with her here. They moved to Springfield six months ago to be closer to my ex's parents. It has been a big adjustment for JJ, so taking her back and forth to Little Rock for visits would be a strain."

"So, at eleven this morning, you were with your daughter?"

"No, I left her at her moms about eight a.m. and went to consult on a restoration job for a guy I used to work with. That's what I do, restoration carpentry."

"Alright, so where were you at eleven?"

"Oh, I know what this is about. Those two boys that I gave a ride to the lake. Did something happen to them?"

"We don't know. How about you tell me what happened to them?"

"Listen, I know that giving kids a ride as a single man is probably not the smartest thing I could have done, but I did not hurt those kids. I dropped them off at the lake by the boat launch so they could fish. They told me their mom was going to pick them up."

"Why would you do that? Why would you give two kids you don't know a ride?"

"I remember being young like that and riding my bike everywhere. I was trying to do something nice for them."

"The boys are missing."

"Missing? What do you mean, missing?"

"What I mean is that the last time the boys were seen was when a witness watched them get into your pickup truck. Now, here we sit thirty-five hours later, and no one knows where those kids are. Well, actually, we think no one other than you knows where those boys are."

"Wait, just a minute. The only thing I did was give them a ride. I did not hurt those kids. You know what, I want a lawyer."

There was a distinct rap on the glass behind Detective Minor's head.

"That would be my boss. I will have a deputy bring you a phone so you can call a lawyer."

Saturday September 26, 2020

Since Robert Matthews had started running with Kass, he no longer read news stories while he ran on the treadmill. That was until today when Kass was out of town for the weekend with her best friend. It was raining, and he had no motivation to run in the rain if he wasn't even going to see her. Last night, he called his mom and dad to tell them he planned to ask Kass to marry him. They were both ecstatic and encouraged him to send them a video of the proposal.

Two months ago, at his cousin's wedding, while dancing with Kass, he realized he loved her and could not imagine his life without her. Their dating continued with running together almost every day, in addition to lunches and dinners. He had met her family a few weekends ago, which had gone great. Her parents, Steve and Lacy, had welcomed him into their home with a family dinner that included her older brother, Ray, and younger sister, Franny. With Kass away and him not working on an active case, he planned to drive to Marionville this afternoon and ask Kass's parents for her hand in marriage. He knew that was an old-fashioned custom, but he wanted everything to be just right when it came to this momentous event.

He shook his head to clear the daydreaming and focused on his tablet. He flipped to the local Springfield online edition; the headlines were about rising interest rates and the Mississippi River water level decreasing, but those stories held no interest for him. He continued to flip until he got to a small story about a local woman being murdered in an apparent drive-by shooting. It was Shasta Peters, the woman who had turned over information on Paulina Moore's alias in exchange for a plea deal.

Robert jabbed at the button to turn off the treadmill and grabbed his cell phone. He dialed his supervisor, SSA Brad Hollins, who picked up on the first ring.

"What's going on, Matthews? You do know it is Saturday, right?"

"Yeah, sorry, are you busy?"

"No, I am the only human awake in the house right now, so go ahead."

"Did you happen to read the newspaper this morning?"

"Can't say I have had that privilege as of yet. Why, what did you read in it that you are calling me at the butt crack of dawn on a Saturday?"

"Shasta Peters was killed in what the paper is calling a probable drive-by shooting."

"When and where did this happen?"

"The article says last night on Battlefield Road."

"Well, Battlefield Road is a dangerous area, so it may actually be a drive-by. Before you say it, I know you are thinking about Shasta's link to Paulina Moore. Why don't you call Detective Minor and find out what they know about the shooting?"

"Because she is out of town this weekend, but I will call the department and see what I can find out and let you know."

******

Detective Ronnie Brewer was not overjoyed to be assigned to yet another drive-by shooting. People in the neighborhood never wanted to talk to the police in order to solve these crimes. He had one decent lead: a grainy video from the corner store's outside camera footage. A 1985 Oldsmobile Cutlass Brougham had driven by the store two times within ten minutes. There was no way to identify the driver, see how many people were in the car, or the license plate number. The Cutlass appeared to have a custom multi-tone paint job, spinner rims, and a lift package. Ronnie Brewer loved cars and worked on his 1964 1/2 Mustang every chance he got. When he was off work, he was likely at a car show if he wasn't working on his Mustang. So, identify the year, make and model of the car in the video had been easy for him.

He had put out a radio call for patrol officers to watch for cars meeting that description and had to hope that they found their shooter that way. Ronnie wished he had grabbed a good cup of coffee before returning to the station because now he was stuck with the sludge that passed for coffee here for his caffeine fix. Looking into the victim in this case, Shasta Peters, was his next step. The internet seemed to be running incredibly slow this morning, but that wasn't all that unusual at the police department. While he waited for the police databases to load, Ronnie did a Google search on his smartphone.

He skimmed several news articles about Shasta Peters' fraud of state daycare funds and one about her accepting a plea deal after providing information to the FBI. The database was finally ready, so he typed in the victim's name and read the information. He learned nothing that wasn't on Google, so he knew talking with the FBI was the only way he might find out what information Shasta had given them. Instinct told him that if the FBI thought she was in danger, they would have put her in witness protection, but still, he needed to check.

Detective Brewer was about to pick up his desk phone when it started ringing. When he answered the phone and found it was none other than FBI Special Agent Robert Matthews on the other end. He thought, *Hmmm, that was right on cue, as if in some cheesy detective novel or television show.*

"How can I help you today, Agent Matthews?"

"I understand from your commander that you are the lead detective on the Shasta Peters murder. What can you tell me about the case?"

"We are just getting started on it, but it looks like a drive-by to me. There has been increasing gang tensions in that neighborhood."

"Okay, but Shasta Peters wasn't a gang member, right?"

"Doesn't look like it. By the way, I was getting ready to call your office when you called me. Are you able to tell me what information Ms. Peters supplied the FBI in exchange for her reduced sentence?"

"Probably not all the specifics, but in general terms, she told us some previously unknown information about Paulina Moore. You do know who Paulina Moore is, right?"

"Yep, the wife of the serial killer who committed suicide while awaiting trial."

"Right, she is a wanted fugitive in that investigation, which is why I called you. There is a possibility that she is the one who killed Ms. Peters."

"Oh, so the FBI thinks Moore is still in the area. Why wasn't Shasta Peters in protective custody then?"

"Well, no, the FBI doesn't think that Paulina Moore is in the Springfield area. We have no leads on her whereabouts, but the thing is that a lot of people with connections to Dr. Paulina Moore die. Please let me know the case updates, and if you find any links to Moore, call me ASAP."

"No problem, but my gut says this is a drive-by, and Ms. Peters was just in the wrong place at the wrong time."

9

Friday May 27, 2022

Detective Kass Minor was exhausted, but the lawyer for their only suspect in the disappearance of Jessie and James Adams had only arrived fifteen minutes ago. She and Detective Wilcox were still waiting to see if they would be able to speak with Dan Becker again tonight. It wouldn't surprise Minor at all if the lawyer advised the no-comment answer to all questions. Her phone rang as she considered whether she should have a cup of coffee.

"Detective Minor, here."

"I am glad you answered, Detective Minor; this is Abe from the Computer Forensics division. Are you and your partner able to come up here?"

"Yes, we will be there in five minutes."

After waking up Detective Wilcox, who had fallen asleep at his desk, the two of them went to the Computer Forensics department two floors up. Minor wondered if the technician had found the evidence that they needed to locate the Adams boys.

"Okay, so I was analyzing Dan Becker's phone and found that he has an app for tracking his mileage for tax reasons. The program also tracks his locations and routes, so a lot of data is saved. On my screen, you will see Dan Becker's route after he finished the job, as well as where he went all the way until he got arrested in Arkansas."

Minor peered at the monitor. According to what she was seeing, Dan Becker had only stopped twice, and both times were only for about five minutes. His first stop was right outside the trailer park; at the time, they knew the boys got a ride from him, and the second was at the boat launch.

"In addition to that information about yesterday, I can also tell you that in the last thirty days, Dan Becker has never stopped at either of those locations before."

"Thank you for letting us know. Will you please print a copy of this information and email it to both of us, as well as Commander Davis and ADA Reinhart?"

As Minor and Wilcox waited while the technician printed the report, Minor texted their commander. He had left the precinct after Dan Becker had asked for a lawyer, but now he needed to know that they had evidence that showed it was impossible for Dan Becker to be responsible for the Adams boys' disappearance.

Her phone rang twenty minutes later, and Commander Davis, in his regular style, skipped pleasantries and got right to business.

"I talked to Reinhart, and based on what the Computer Forensics Technician found, we are letting Dan Becker go. Please tell Mr. Becker and his lawyer that he is free to go. I have already called the patrol division, and one of the officers will drive Mr. Becker back to his truck. Be sure to apologize for any inconvenience."

"Okay, will do."

"Then head home to get some sleep, so you are ready to join one of the search

parties in the morning."

Again, Detective Kass Minor gave an affirmative answer to Commander Davis's order, and he unceremoniously hung up the phone. She found Wilcox just sitting in his cubicle, staring into space.

"Commander Davis told me to cut Becker loose and then head home. You are

welcome to leave now."

"Great. See you tomorrow."

"First thing in the morning, we are to report to the command center set up for the search."

"Gotcha."

Minor knocked on the door to the interview room and then walked in.

Dan Becker's attorney, Cliff Marshall, quickly said, "We are not ready to speak to

you."

"Please, just listen. Mr. Becker, we have reviewed your cell phone, which you

willingly provided for us to examine, and found an app you use to track mileage for business. That app also tracks your routes and location when you have activated it, which you did yesterday morning. I am saying all this to tell you that you are no longer a suspect in the disappearance of Jessie and James Adams. You are free to go."

Dan looked from Detective Minor to his attorney, then back again, "I am happy to

hear that and sincerely hope you find those kids."

"I personally apologize to you for any inconvenience. Here is your wallet, keys,

and cell phone. An officer is waiting out front to drive you back to your truck."

Detective Minor watched Dan Becker and his attorney walk out of the conference room door with them, taking the only lead they had to find the Adams brothers with them.

Monday January 25, 2021

The proposal this weekend had been perfect. He had taken Kass to her favorite Italian restaurant for dinner with her parents. Her mom had set up the dinner, saying she and Kass's dad would be passing through on their way to their vacation. Robert had met with the manager that morning, and the restaurant had prepared a special dessert plate. It was a piece of cherry cheesecake with "Will You Marry Me?" written on the plate in chocolate syrup.

The only hitch was when Kass said she didn't want dessert, so he had to order the cheesecake. The waiter caught on without any prompting, and when he brought out the plate, he set it in front of Kass. She had started to explain that the dessert was Robert's and not hers, but stopped mid-sentence when she saw the question. As she turned to Robert, he dropped to one knee and opened the box. It was his grandmother's engagement ring, and he thought it was perfect for Kass when his dad offered it to him. The round diamond surrounded by rubies was not a typical engagement ring, and Kass was not a typical fiancee.

She had accepted with tears in her eyes and loved the ring. Her mom immediately started talking about wedding plans. Neither he nor Kass cared all that much about the details. The only thing Kass told her for sure was that they would not have a long engagement. He would never forget her saying, "I have waited a very long time to find the right man, so now that I have and we are getting married, I don't want to draw out the engagement time." Her mother laughed and said planning a perfect wedding took at least a year.

Kass responded, "I will give you about six months, and we don't need a perfect wedding."

******

Agent Matthews had just shut down his computer for the day and was packing up to leave when his desk phone rang. He was going to ignore it until he saw that it was Detective Ronnie Brewer.

"This is Agent Matthews."

"Hi, Matthews; it is Detective Ronnie Brewer over here at Springfield PD. When we talked a few months ago about the drive-by shooting of Shasta Peters, I promised to update you when we found something. So that is what I am doing. We arrested two juveniles, and as of this morning, they were both charged with first-degree murder."

"Okay, that is not what I was expecting. Why were they both charged?"

"Oh, the same old song and dance. Neither will admit to being the shooter or pin it in on the other kid. They have some BS story that they found the car running with keys in it about ten minutes after Ms. Peters was killed."

"I take it there is no chance that is true."

"It would be wild if it was. The car was stolen out of St. Louis a week before the murder, and the St. Louis police told me it belonged to a known gang member. It just so happens the car's rightful owner is a rival gang member of the gang the two young men we arrested are affiliated with. Plus, the night the car was stolen, both young men had been gone from home for several days. One of their older gang members got a speeding ticket on the way to St. Louis the day before the car was stolen."

"Got it. What about the gun?"

"We haven't found it, but these gangs swap around guns constantly, so our only real chance of recovering it is if they use it in another crime."

"Why would they have shot Shasta, though?"

"Yeah, that is another tie between them and this crime. It seems Ms. Peters had only moved into that row house the day of the shooting. Before that, it had been occupied by a rival gang member. So, it really was the wrong place at the wrong time for her."

"Thanks for the update. It sounds like her death is not connected to Paulina Moore."

Hanging up the phone, Robert Matthews was not one hundred percent sure that the Springfield police department had gotten this one right. He had learned that Paulina Moore was extremely smart and manipulative; thus, she might have somehow set those boys up to take the fall for Shasta Peters' murder.

10

Saturday May 28, 2022

Kass had a fitful night of sleep and was sure she had disrupted Robert's sleep. At least it was a Saturday, and he didn't have to work today, but he got up with her, anyway.

"I am going to volunteer to search for the kids today, and I called a bunch of the guys from the office. All of them are planning to come." Robert told her as they got ready for the day.

"Thank you. We can use all the help we can get. Do you want to drive over together?"

"Sure. Do we have time for a run?"

"No, I want to be there as soon as there is enough light to start searching."

When they arrived at the trailer park, it was clear that the command center had been set up at the office. There were already several dozen volunteers and officers waiting to start searching. Minor walked into the office and joined Commanders Davis and Wilcox at a table that had maps on it. They had marked the areas that were searched yesterday with a yellow highlighter and were currently discussing where to send the groups of searchers.

As Minor listened, she realized they were only covering the areas that were the direct route back from Lake Springfield to the trailer park. "Sir's not to interrupt, but what if the boys went in the wrong direction?"

Davis turned and looked at her, "We discussed it and decided to cover all of these areas first," pointing back to the route they had been discussing.

Kass walked back out to the waiting searchers and joined Robert, who was standing with a group of off-duty firefighters, FBI agents, and cops.

"Hey, Minor. What's the plan?" one of the Springfield officers asked her.

Minor wished she knew because even though she was the lead detective on this case, she was not in charge. "Just waiting on the commanders to let us know."

As she said that, the door to the office opened, and Commanders Davis and Wilcox exited. Wilcox grabbed a bullhorn and began barking orders in a manner that fit his personality to a tee.

"There will be six groups of searchers. Each group will be led by one of the detectives from the Springfield police department. Wilcox, Brewer, Lancaster, Smith, Diaz, and Minor, come up here and grab the map of the area you will be searching. The rest of you count off by six and then join the group leader."

It was not lost on Detective Kass Minor that Commander Wilcox had called his own son's name first and her name last. She caught Robert's eyes as she walked up to the front. He winked and smiled at her. Unremarkably, Robert ended up in her group, along with many other off-duty FBI agents and police officers. They were searching the farthest area from the trailer park, so the searchers in her team drove to the nearby park to start the search.

Working in a grid pattern, they covered a six-by-two-mile area in just over two hours, finding nothing. The plan was to switch spots and walk back in the other direction of the area covered, but first, they were taking a break. Kass was sitting in the grass beside Robert when her phone started ringing.

"Hello, this is Detective Minor."

"Detective Minor, this is the dispatch center. We got a call regarding a possible sighting of Jessie and James Adams. The caller identified himself as Richard Hathaway and said that he saw the boys riding their bikes on Thursday evening. He was headed home from work, and it wasn't until the news described one of the boys having two fishing poles strapped on like antennae that he realized that the kids he saw were the missing kids."

After getting the address and phone information from the dispatcher for Richard Hathaway, Minor hung up and called Commander Davis. He agreed that Agent Matthews could take over the search team while she went to talk to Mr. Hathaway. She filled Robert in on the plan, walked back to her car, and programmed the address into her GPS. It was in the opposite direction of where they had been searching. Sometimes, she did not like to be right.

Thursday February 4, 2021

"Remind me again, why are we walking around an empty wooded lot after the only accumulated snow in Springfield, Mo, in over a decade?" Agent Brent Hollins sarcastically asked.

Agent Robert Matthews suppressed a sigh and replied, "Ha-ha, very funny. You know as well as I do that Paulina Moore bought this lot using the shell corporation that she formed. We are here to find out why?"

"By walking around in the snow?"

"Do you want to leave and wait a few days for the snow to melt?"

"No, we are here now; we might as well walk around."

The two agents proceeded to walk in different directions and then back towards each other when they reached the end of the lot. As they approached each other, Agent Matthews pointed up in a tree at a camera that had been mounted there.

"I see it; how are your tree climbing skills?"

"I used to be the fastest tree climber in my neighborhood, but that was many years ago. Let's hope it is like they say about riding a bike, and the skill is still part of my muscle memory."

"I am sure the bureau's human resources department would say climbing a tree without proper equipment is a safety violation, but I won't tell if you don't."

Matthews laughed, thinking about the yearly mandatory videos that showed an agent using a chair to get something off a high shelf and falling. Those videos were a joke around the office, as he was sure they were in settings all over that used them. Climbing a tree did come back to him as soon as he began shimming up; when he reached the camera, he put his hand in his pocket and retrieved his pocket knife. He cut the camera free from the zip ties then put it and his knife in his back pocket.

After he was safely back on the ground, he handed the camera to Hollins, who looked it over.

"Looks to have been up there awhile. There is a spot for an SD card, but it is empty. We should send it to the technicians in the Computer Forensics department to see if they can tell us anything else about it. Did you see anything else of interest?"

"No, how about you?"

"Nope, I go back to thinking that Paulina bought this lot just to mess with Raul's mind since his dead girlfriend owned it before Paulina."

"Seems that way. I will add the information to the file we have on her. I was really hoping that this place would help us figure out where she might be and where the two of them might have put Kelsey Learner."

"I know that you are deeply invested in this case, but there are no leads for us to chase. You and I both know that fugitives that are not caught within the first few days or weeks will probably go years, decades, and sometimes forever without being found."

"I get it. I really do, but she is dangerous. I may be the only one who believes it, but she is behind her dad's and Shasta Peterson's deaths."

Hollins shook his head, "Look, Matthews, I admire your tenacity in wanting to track her down and possibly stop her from killing more people. But here is the thing, until there is a solid lead, you need to back off.

I am telling you this as your friend before I get told to tell it to you as your supervisor."

"Understood," Matthews replied in an irritated tone. It had taken years for the connection between the seven missing men and the horror at the Moore's farm to be discovered. He feared that with no one really searching for her that Paulina Moore would be out there for years to come. Because of that, he was sure that when she was finally apprehended, the same kind of connections would be made to new unsolved cases.

11

Saturday May 28, 2022

While she drove to talk to the witness, Kass called her best friend, Amy.

"Hi, are you busy?"

"Never too busy for you. What's up?"

"I am driving and wondering if you would look something up and read it to me."

"Sure, what am I looking up?"

"I am going to see a possible witness, and he told the dispatcher that he saw a news story this morning about the missing boys whose case I am working on. The witness mentioned something about one of the boys' bikes that he heard on the news. I am wondering who they got that information from."

"Okay, here goes, I will read it to you:

The Springfield Police have no leads regarding the whereabouts of Jessie or James Adams, who have been missing since Thursday morning. The two brothers are ages eleven and ten and were last seen at Lake Springfield fishing. According to Eddie Learner, a long-time neighbor and family friend, the boys love to go fishing and are both very resourceful. Mr. Learner told Channel 9 News, 'They came up with a way to attach both their fishing poles to one bike using bungee cords. It looked like the bike had two antennae sticking up.' Anyone with any information regarding the brothers is urged to call the Springfield Police Department.

There are a couple of other articles. Do you want me to read them too and call you back if they have any more information in them?"

"That would be great. Thanks."

Detective Minor was almost to the address dispatch had given her for Mr. Hathaway, but she needed to call her partner first.

"Wilcox, here."

"Hi, it is Minor. I have a quick question."

"Okay, what's up?"

"I am heading to talk to someone who called into dispatch saying that he saw the Adams boys on Thursday evening. My question for you is, did you or Officer Grant speak to Eddie Learner when you canvased the trailer park yesterday?"

"Let me check my notes. Okay, yeah, I talked to Mr. Learner, and my note said he had been at work at the time the boys went missing and had not seen them before work or after he got home that day. Why? Is he the witness you are going to talk to?"

"No, he isn't, but a local television station interviewed him, and he seemed to

know a lot about the boys and their habits."

"Do you need me to go talk to him again?"

"Let's wait on that until I see what the witness has to say. I will call you back."

"Ten-four," Wilcox commented and ended the call.

******

Richard Hathaway was a sixty-seven-year-old semi-retired truck driver living with his wife in the farmhouse she had inherited from her parents. Mr. and Mrs. Hathaway had welcomed Detective Minor into their home, and now she was sipping a glass of cold water at their dining room table.

"Mr. Hathaway..."

"Call me Rich; everybody does.", he interrupted as Minor was gearing up to figure out what, if anything, he knew.

"Alright, Rich. You told the dispatcher when you called in that you saw Jessie and James Adams riding their bikes on Thursday evening. Please describe where and what time that was."

"Sure thing. First, if I had known it was the two missing kids I saw, I would have called immediately. It wasn't until we were watching the news this morning and they interviewed that man who described the boys' fishing poles like antennae that it hit me that I had seen them."

"I understand. Thank you for calling when you realized that you had information."

"You're welcome. These days, I only drive local routes, mostly just when Stateline Trucking, who I work for, is in a pinch. I drove for them for forty years, and they were always good to me, so I try to help out when I can."

These were the kind of superlative details that Detective Minor couldn't stand. Knowing all the details of this man's work history did nothing to help her solve the case, but she had learned over the years not to rush a storyteller.

"So, Thursday, George over at Stateline called me and asked me to run a route down to the Ozarks and back. We weren't doing anything, and as I told you already, I try to help out when I can, so I took the job. I got back to town about seven thirty and was driving home on South Farm Road One-Seventy-Five when I saw the two kids biking. I didn't recognize them, but figured they must be headed home because it was starting to get dark. That was a bit before eight o'clock Thursday night."

"Do you know where you saw them on One-Seventy-Five?"

"Not exactly, sorry. The road is only a couple miles long, and I drove from one end to the other."

"Are you sure the kids you saw were the Adams brothers?"

"Well, see, that is why I didn't call at first, but yeah, after hearing what they were wearing and the fishing poles sticking up from a bike. I am sure. I saw two boys, both in jeans and white t-shirts, riding together, and one of them had the poles sticking up just like the man on the news said."

"Great. Thank you so much for your call and the information."

Tuesday March 16, 2020

"I can't believe you are making me do this," Robert told Kass, as they ran along the path.

"Come on, I am not making you do anything. Claire is just trying to find closure on her mom's disappearance. If talking with you helps her to do that, isn't that worth your time?"

"Honestly, sweetheart, if you weren't the one asking me to talk to her, I wouldn't be. There is very little I can tell her about the case against the Moore's because it is still an open investigation."

"I know that, and I warned Claire about that when she asked me to set this up. Are you sure you don't want me to be there?"

"No, I can handle it alone. I just hope that she gets what she needs."

"Me, too!"

******

Later that morning, when Agent Robert Matthews walked into the FBI field office, Claire Learner was waiting for him in the small reception area.

Matthews looked down at his smartwatch, and Claire quickly said, "I am early."

"Okay, give me a few minutes to check on some things, and then I will come back and get you."

"Sounds good. Thanks."

Walking away, Matthews wondered if he should have had Kass join them. He had no idea what Claire wanted to ask him about the Moores, but he was concerned about her emotional well-being. As he walked past Agent Lee Rivers' cubicle, he paused and asked, "Rivers, are you busy this morning?"

"No, what's up?"

"Would you mind sitting in on a meeting with me? Claire Learner, the daughter of Kelsey Learner, has asked to meet with me."

"Sure, no problem."

"Thanks. Meet us in the conference room in ten minutes."

After checking his voicemail and emails, Matthews went to the conference room and turned on the lights. He thought about starting a pot of coffee but decided against it because making Claire Learner too comfortable might prolong this meeting. Walking back to get Claire, he thought about what they knew about Kelsey's kidnapping. The FBI had not been involved in her case until Raul Moore admitted to having taken her in his suicide note. He didn't know any other information and was still unsure how talking to him would help Claire. but he had agreed, so he might as well get this over with.

Once all three of them were seated in the conference room and introductions were made, Matthews asked Claire, "How can I help you today?"

"I am not sure if Detective Minor told you, but I am studying Forensic Science and planning to become a Crime Scene Analyst. One of my current classes is Criminal Psychology, and we just finished studying serial killers. Studying those people and their traits left me with a lot of questions about how my mom fit into the Moore's crimes. I guess my question is, why did it take the FBI so long to figure out that the Moores were serial killers?"

Claire knew even as she asked the question that the agents might be hostile about it, but she had to know. It seemed that her mom was Moore's last victim, so if the FBI had figured it out sooner, her mom would be with her now.

Agent Lee Rivers looked at Agent Matthews and raised an eyebrow, but he said nothing. Matthews cleared his throat and thought back to his training; he decided to stick to the FBI's official stance.

"In order to analyze the possibility of a serial killer, we look for a signature. A signature is a rare combination of modus operandi, otherwise referred to as a method of operation and ritual. This allows agents to link cases over time and geographical distance and then put together a behavioral profile of who the suspect might be. One of the major factors is multiple murders that are known about and unsolved, which we didn't have with the Moores. I began looking into men's disappearances in our area about two years ago, but never fathomed that I was tracking serial killers. The Moore's didn't fit the typical pattern, so it was hard for law enforcement to connect the men's disappearances to them."

Claire knew all the facts that Agent Matthews had just shared, but still, it seemed like the Moores had slipped through the cracks. When she talked to her dad about this meeting, he told her not to point that out to the agents unless she wanted to get no information. So, she suppressed telling them how she felt and asked her next question, "Is it your belief that both Raul and Paulina Moore were killers, or was it just Raul Moore?"

"We have evidence that proves beyond a shadow of a doubt that Raul Moore killed seven men at his farm outside of town. Paulina Moore is on the most wanted list because of her involvement in those kidnappings and murders as well as your mom's kidnapping." Agent Matthews explained, hoping he had provided her with enough, but not too much, information.

"I don't think you actually answered my question, so I will ask it more directly. Did Paulina Moore kill those men? Yes, or no?"

This time, Agent Rivers jumped in to answer her question, "We are not at liberty to answer that because the case against Paulina Moore is still an open investigation. Is there anything else we can answer unrelated to our open investigation?"

"No, there isn't. Thank you both for your time." Claire stood up, and Agent Matthews walked her to the door. She had wanted to ask them why the Moores had taken her mom, but she knew that no one other than Raul and Paulina could answer that. He was dead, and she was on the run. Claire needed to work on accepting that they may never know the reason.

******

Matthews could smell coffee brewing when he walked back into the conference room. Lee Rivers was sitting in the same spot he had been when Matthews had left the room, but now he was on his tablet.

Matthews poured them both a cup of coffee and sat down next to his colleague and friend. “You know, I have often wondered myself if the Moores could have been stopped. Did we miss something?”

“I have read the files, including the Springfield police file on the kidnapping of Kelsey Learner, and I really don’t think anyone could have deduced that Raul and Paulina Moore were behind all of those cases.”

“I agree, but what bothers me the most is that I think wherever Paulina Moore is, she is still killing people.”

“The entire office knows that you think she killed her dad and your witness, Shasta Peters, but you know the brass doesn’t agree. You might want to start keeping your theories about Paulina Moore to yourself until you have some solid evidence. You don’t want to be labeled obsessive.”

“Thanks, Agent Hollins already gave me that speech. Don’t forget I was right about the disappearance of the seven men being linked, and when I am right about Paulina Moore, I would like an apology.”

“How about this? IF and that is big, if you are right and prove it, I will buy you a beer and publicly apologize.”

The two agents shook on the deal and then walked back to their cubicles to return to the mundane tasks that filled their days.

12

Saturday May 28, 2022

Calling Commander Davis should have been the next thing that she did, but she decided that time was of the essence, so she called Robert instead.

"Hi Kass, we are re-walking our area. How did it go with the witness?"

"I have a lead on the boys and need your help. Please gather up the search party and meet me on the north end of South Farm Road One-Seventy-Five."

"Okay, I will round everyone up. Will other search parties be joining us?"

"I don't know; I have to call Davis and find out how he wants to handle this."

Robert snickered before replying, "You do that, honey. We will see you in a bit."

After ending her first call, Minor dialed Commander Davis and filled him in on the information that Rick Hathaway had provided.

"I would like to have the search party I am leading relocate to South Farm Road One-Seventy-Five, and we will look for the boys."

"Yeah, Minor, take them out there, but I don't think your witness is right about the kids he saw being the Adams brothers. South Farm Road One-Seventy-Five is the wrong direction for the kids to have gone. Keep me updated if you find anything."

"Thanks, Commander Davis, I will."

******

While waiting for the other search party members to arrive, Detective Minor pulled up the map of the area and zoomed in using the street view feature. Noting each possible driveway and turn-in, she devised a plan to split up the search party into threes. She was thankful that her team included several off-duty police officers and FBI agents. She assigned at least one of them in each triad to lead the searches. They would need to get permission from landowners wherever and whenever possible, and it would help that a member of law enforcement would be asking. She needed help to make a digital map and knew just the person to ask. She opened her contacts and selected the one she needed and was thankful when the call was picked up on the first ring.

"Abe, it is Detective Minor. Are you able to help me with a quick project?"

"Sure, detective, what do you need?"

"I just emailed a link to a map. It is for South Farm Road One-Seventy-Five, which is about two miles long. Will you divide the land up into twelve areas so we can search it?

"Okay, no problem; how many miles in for each one?"

"Let's start with two miles. We can always cover more if we need to."

"Alright, I just emailed it back to you."

"Wow, you are fast."

"The software is fast as long as you know what you are doing, and I do."

"Thanks, Abe."

"Good Luck, Detective Minor. I hope you find those boys."

"Me, too, Abe. Me, too!"

******

As she watched the searchers arrive, Kass sent up a silent prayer that this was not a misdirection. The Adams boys had been missing for almost three days, and she had no idea when they had last eaten or drank anything. Time may be running out even if nothing nefarious happened to them. Once the searchers got out of their vehicles, Kass broke them out in triads and electronically shared the map Abe had made with each of them. The plan was for two groups to work on a half-mile by two-mile grid, walking towards each other so they would know when they had searched the entire area. Then, those same two teams would repeat the process in another two areas. In the end, each search team would cover two areas, and the entire road would be covered for two miles in. The searchers had the phone numbers of all the other searchers and knew to call Kass if they found anything.

She and Robert were on the two teams that were in the areas that had no homes or other structures on them. Minor and her team were methodically walking in the first area when her cell phone started ringing.

"Minor, here."

"This is Agent Lee Rivers. I am with my team in Area 11, and we have found the boys. They fell down a well or something."

"Are they okay?"

"The boys report that Jessie broke his leg, but otherwise, they are okay. We threw some bottles of water down to them. I think we will need help from the fire department to get them out."

"Okay, I will call them now."

"Wait, Minor, before you hang up, James told me that there is a skeleton down there with them. He is terrified."

"We will get them out of there as quickly as possible and then figure out what they saw down there."

Detective Minor called Commander Davis, "We have found them!" she shouted into the phone.

"That is great news. What is the address so we can send a cruiser and an ambulance?"

Before answering, Minor thought to herself; *Yeah, and be sure you and Commander Wilcox are here before the news crews arrive.*

"Sir, the boys are stuck in what FBI Agent Lee Rivers believes may be an abandoned well. We need the fire department to respond and bring every piece of equipment they think they might need to get them out."

"Alright, I will call the fire chief. What is the address?"

Detective Minor relayed the fire number of the wooded lot to Commander Davis. She then sent a mass text to the searchers she was working with that the boys had been found and they should meet there.

Saturday July 17, 2021

Kass sat with her shoes off and her feet up, looking around the reception hall. Like all weddings she had ever attended, there were things about this one she loved and things she could have done without. The major difference was this was Robert and her wedding, and the things she didn't love about it were really all her own fault. When you let two other people plan your wedding for you and show little to no interest in those plans, you can't really complain about the outcome.

Their moms had been more than happy to plan the celebration. The only thing they had made Kass decide on was her wedding dress; even though they had pre-chosen gowns for her to try on to make it as quick as possible, she was happy with the arrangement. The ceremony had been simple but elegant at the church Kass and her family had attended her whole life, which she had loved. Her best friend, Amy, was her Matron of Honor, and her sister, Franny, was the only other bridesmaid. Robert's brother, Kyle, was his best man, and Kass's brother, Ray, was his other groomsman. Her mother had helped out-of-town guests figure out places to stay, as there was only one hotel and one bed and breakfast in Marionville.

Her lack of involvement in planning explained why she was sitting there hungry long after the dinner and cake had been served. Dinner had been a fancy chicken dish full of cilantro, an herb that she could not stand the taste of. She would never tell either Mom this complaint or her yearning for chocolate cake versus the white cake with a raspberry filling that had been served.

Mitch Leet sat beside her and smiled, "I am really happy for you and Robert. This was quite a shindig, thanks for inviting me. I can't help but notice that I am your only work friend here."

Kass chuckled, "That is because you are the only person from work, I would want here, and you are retired from work."

Leet smiled and asked, "Where are you all going on your honeymoon?"

"Well, that is the one thing we did not let our mom's plan. We are camping and hiking at Yosemite National Park."

"That seems about right for the two of you. I hope you have a great time. I am headed home; staying out late is a young people's game."

"Thanks again for coming, Mitch."

Kass surveyed the room, looking for Robert, finding him leaning against the bar and talking to her dad and brother. She and Robert were the first of their parents' kids to get married so far, but from the looks of it, her brother seemed to be in love with the date he had brought. Her mom might get lucky and be able to plan another wedding. Kass wondered how long the mothers would take to ask about a grandchild. She and Robert had a friendly bet about whose mom would be the first to bring it up. Each of them was betting against their own mom.

The crowd was thinning out, and she wondered if it would be rude for them to leave. They had a flight to California in the morning, so a few hours of sleep sounded ideal to her. Robert seemed to sense her eyes on her as he looked up, nodded, then patted both men on the back and made his way across the hall to her.

"Well, Mrs. Kassandra Lacy Matthews, are you ready to head out?"

"Absolutely, Mr. Robert Anthony Matthews."

He leaned down and put Kass's shoes back on, and then they walked around saying goodbye to people. The happiness for them that shone in so many people's eyes made all the hoopla worthwhile to Kass.

******

July had always been Michelle's favorite month. She loved the heat, the sunshine and all of the outdoor activities. However, she had lived nowhere except for Missouri, and July in Wisconsin was colder than she preferred. The librarian had mentioned that they were expecting another rainy week with the temperatures in the high sixties.

As she walked back home, Michelle was also contemplating her need to get a job. More to keep her mind engaged than for economic gain, but there was the minor issue of references. She had seen the multiple papers looking for volunteers on the community board at the front of the library. Volunteering would be a great way for her to build references and fill her time. She was going to start with the local humane society. Household pets were not her favorite animals, but she missed working with animals, so it was a place to start.

13

Saturday May 28, 2022

It shouldn't have surprised Detective Minor when her partner, Detective Wilcox, did not answer her call, but it did piss her off. She had wanted him to go tell Trixie in person that they had found her kids, but since he didn't pick up, she would have to notify Trixie over the phone.

"Hi Trixie, it is Detective Minor. We have found Jessie and James. They are both alive."

"Oh my God, thank you so much. Where are they? I need to see them."

"Here is the thing: they fell down what we think is an abandoned well. The fire department is on the way to get them out, but we don't know how long that will take. We do know that the boys are reporting that Jessie broke his leg."

"I need to be where they are. I have to talk to them."

"Understood, there is a patrol car sitting at the trailer park office. The officer there will bring you to the site, and you can talk to them, but then you have to wait in a patrol car while the fire department does its job."

"Yeah, yeah, that is fine."

Minor called the officer at the trailer park and then went and talked to the patrol officer, blocking the turn into the lot. After telling him that he could let Trixie come back there when she arrived, she walked back to where Robert and some other FBI agents were standing. They seemed to be having an intense conversation.

"What's going on?" Kass asked Robert.

She saw Lee Rivers and another agent she didn't remember the name of shake their heads and walk over to another group of searchers.

"The guys think I am connecting things that aren't related, but I am sure this is the lot that Paulina Moore bought under the holding company she created using the Hanna Lewis alias."

"What? I'm not following you."

"Okay, so do you remember that almost two years ago, a woman named Shasta Peters provided the FBI with an alias that Paulina Moore had used? That alias was Hanna Lewis, and I chased that clue as far as I could. I found that Paulina had a P.O. box in Hanna's name, not far from her mother's house. She closed that box the day that she came back to Springfield when we were raiding her farm.

It took eight months for us to track down that Paulina had started an LLC using the name of Hanna Lewis and bought this lot of land. Agent Hollis and I drove out here and walked around, but that was the winter with the freak snowstorm, and there was snow on the ground. The only thing we found was a camera mounted in trees with no memory card in it. We concluded that since the lot had belonged to the estate of Shelby Lansing, who was Raul's deceased former girlfriend, Paulina bought it just to mess with Raul."

"Are you sure it was this lot?" Kass asked as she looked around the lot. It seemed like, until the searchers arrived, it had been abandoned for a long time.

"That is what the guys were asking me, too but, I am sure. I texted Hollins and asked him to check the file because all the information was in it."

"Not to be rude, but why did it take you so long to figure out that this belonged to her?"

"She incorporated overseas using the name Lewis Holdings, LLC, and the only address was the closed P.O. box, so it wasn't a Google search kind of find. I really don't think the agents working in technical analysis saw finding it as a priority either."

"Got it. Just one more thing: why does it matter that this land belongs to Paulina Moore? Or is it just a strange coincidence?"

"That is the other thing that Rivers said to me. He told me I am obsessed, and at this point, I have synchronicity syndrome when it comes to all things: Paulina Moore. I, of course, disagree; I do think that, however improbable, when something or someone has a tie to Dr. Moore, there is a reason for that. I get that I cannot make the causal connection between her dad's death, Shasta's murder, or even the Adams boys being stuck on this lot. But I just think that woman is evil, and there are no coincidences when it comes to her."

"Okay, let's get these boys out of here safely, and then we will work together to figure out what is happening."

******

The fire department, Commanders Davis and Wilcox, along with Trixie arrived simultaneously, creating a bit of chaos that was magnified by the media being close on their heels. As Minor predicted, Davis and Wilcox quickly took over with the media while the fire department assessed the situation, and Trixie waited for a chance to talk to her kids. Standing next to Trixie, Minor could practically feel her anxiety as she bounced from foot to foot while smoking. Fifteen minutes later, the fire chief approached. He turned to Trixie, "Ma'am, you may walk over to the hole with Firefighter Fritz, and he will assure your safety while you talk to your boys."

"Thank you so much'" Trixie said as she walked off with the firefighter.

The chief now spoke to Detective Minor, "You're the lead detective on this case, right?"

"Yes, sir, I am."

"I am going to brief you before I go talk to the police commanders. The good news is that we have a plan for getting Jessie and James out of there with minimal risk of further injury."

"Great, is there bad news?"

"I don't know if it is necessarily bad, but we have determined they did not fall into a well, but rather a metal shipping container that is buried underground. None of us has ever seen anything like that before. When their mom has had a chance to talk to them, we are going to start by removing the earth from the top of the container. After that is done, we plan to use a reciprocating saw, well, actually several reciprocating saws to cut the top off the container. After we have cut the area that is nowhere near the kids, we will peel the top back, which will create a large opening through which we will lower several ladders. We will climb down to the boys and bring them up the way we came down."

"Sounds like a good plan. I don't understand why there would be a shipping container buried out here, but right now, our first priority is to get those kids out safely. Were you told that the boys are reporting a dead body down there as well?"

"I am, and in fact, James told one of my men it was a skeleton with hair. After we have the kids out, we will turn the whole area over to you as a crime scene."

"Thank you for all your help and for letting me know what is going on."

"You betcha; now I am going to try to get the PD brass away from the cameras so I can update them. Wish me luck; it may be the most difficult part of this mission."

"Good luck," Detective Minor said, smiling, and then watched the Fire Chief walk away.

Saturday August 7, 2021

As Claire watched her dad and Lindsey's dad, Officer Peterson, carry in the last load of Lindsey's stuff, she hoped that she could be the friend that Lindsey needed right now. When Lindsey called her two nights ago, she had just gotten home from the Emergency Room and had a broken wrist; she didn't tell her much that night, just asked to move in. Claire agreed without hesitation, but was worried about her friend. Yesterday, she had sat in the Peterson's kitchen staring at her friend, whom she once knew so well but was now almost a stranger.

Thinking back over the time since she had moved back to Springfield, Claire realized how little she had seen Lindsey. The two had once been inseparable, but in the last year or so, Lindsey simply never agreed to or canceled all the plans they had. Her once vibrant friend sat across from her, looking emaciated and exhausted while drinking black coffee. Mrs. Peterson glanced back and forth between the young women and then said, "Lindsey, are you sure you don't need anything else?"

In an exasperated tone, Lindsey replied, "No, mom. I am fine."

"Alright, I am going to do some laundry and other chores. Holler if you need me."

Claire watched as Mrs. Peterson walked out of the room, thinking about the last time her own mom had offered to take care of her. She knew that Lindsey was not in a place to hear how lucky she was to have her mom there to care for her, but one day, Claire was going to tell her friend how she felt.

"Want to tell me what happened?"

"No."

"Okay, want to tell me why you are drinking coffee black, because that is gross."

"It only has five calories when you don't add junk to it."

"Looks to me like you don't need to watch your calories."

"I worked really hard to get to this weight, and I do not want to be fat again."

"Fat? When were you ever fat? When we shopped for senior prom, you wore a size eight, and I cannot think of a time when I visited that you looked any bigger than that."

"Can we please not talk about this? My weight is a topic my mom harps on, so I do not need you to jump on that track, too. Okay?"

"Sure. Is talking about you moving in with me an okay topic?"

Claire heard Lindsey sigh and put her head down on her arms, which were folded on the table.

"Lindsey, I love you. You have been my friend since we were little girls, and you saw me through my mom's disappearance. I am not trying to push you. I just don't know what to say or do because, clearly, you went through something traumatic. Let's start over, okay? Would you like my mom's old room, my room, or the spare bedroom?"

"The spare bedroom is fine."

"Actually, that is the hardest one for you to have because I have been just piling things in there since I moved back in. If you are okay with it, I think you should have my mom's room. I cannot imagine sleeping in there, but I think it would be great for you. I know my mom would want you to have a comfortable spot."

"If you're sure, then that is fine. I don't want to be an imposition or a burden or anything."

"Lindsey, listen to me; you are my best friend, and you could never be an imposition or a burden to me. I am looking forward to us being roommates. It will be like an extended sleepover."

"Thank you, Claire. I love you, too, but I am not ready to talk about what happened with Mack."

"When you are, know that I am here for you. Want to walk over, and we can talk about what you need to move?"

"Yes, let's do that."

14

Saturday May 28, 2022

Watching the fire department working to open the container, Detective Minor stood with Agent Matthews, trying to figure out what they were going to find. The noise of the saws was deafening, but everyone who had been allowed to stay at the site had been given noise-canceling headphones, including James and Jessie. Despite the headphones, the whirring of the saws could still be heard and felt reverberating through the ground.

Thirty minutes later, when the saws turned off, Minor was sure that she would be hearing that noise in her head for a long time to come. She was about to pull her headphones off when Robert put his hand on them to stop her. She was going to ask why she couldn't take her headphones off when a new noise ripped through the air. The fire department had attached a hook to one end of the metal and was peeling the container open using a wench. It was like watching a gigantic can of oysters be opened.

Not even ten minutes later, James Adams climbed out of the container, followed closely by a member of the fire department. He was dirty but seemed to be unharmed; nonetheless, the plan was for him to be transported to the emergency room to be checked. It took another twenty minutes before they watched a group of firefighters emerge, pulling a gurney with Jessie Adams strapped to it. The boy was conscious and chatting animatedly with the firefighter closest to his head.

Trixie ran up to Minor and embraced her, "Thank you so much for finding my kids. I promise I will watch them better from now on."

"Just doing my job, ma'am. Now go be with your kids."

As both kids were loaded into the ambulance along with their mom, Trixie, the fire chief walked up to Minor. "My people report that there is indeed a human skeleton down there, and it appears that he or she was chained inside. We are officially turning this back over to you as a crime scene. When the police department is done processing it, let me know, and I will have it back filled with dirt so no one else can fall in."

"Thank you."

As the fire chief went to give the commanders a status update, Minor called the coroner, Dr. Reeves, and the lead technician, Gabby Simms, for the CSI team. After talking to them, she let Matthews know what was going on, and then she and Detective Brewer climbed down the ladder the fire department had left secured for their use. Brewer had asked her where her partner was, and she shrugged, to which he responded with a laugh.

Like all crime scenes that they looked at, the two detectives took precautions to disturb as little as possible while trying to figure out what they were looking at. Two feet from where they had climbed off the ladder lay a skeleton in the fetal position with some tattered clothes hanging off of it. One ankle had a maniacal attached to it that had a two-foot chain to the wall behind. There was a bucket with a toilet seat on it and several piles of other things. There were empty gallon water jugs, a large plastic container with a faded picture of survivalist-type food on the label, and an old Walkman-type tape player.

After walking the entire container, Minor was bent down looking at the skeleton when she thought she saw something on the floor, but the dust had obscured whatever it was. Minor took out her cell phone, snapped a couple of pictures, and then, with Brewer looking over her shoulder, she gently brushed the dust off. A gasp escaped her as the words scratched into the floor came into view.

Claire, I love you! Mom

"What is it?" Brewer asked.

"I think that is the skeleton of Kelsey Learner. We have to be sure that her daughter Claire is not on the CSI team that is responding."

"Wait, her daughter is a CSI Tech with our department?"

"Yes, she started a few days ago."

"Alright, let's go back up and wait for the techs."

"Okay, they need to process this scene before we know anything else."

Waiting for the medical examiner and the CSI team to arrive, Kass filled Robert in on what they had seen in the container.

"So that explains why Paulina Moore bought this lot; the Moores brought her here and held her captive underground. What was their end game?" Robert asked himself as much as Kass.

"I have no idea, but I think keeping Kelsey captive in the dark with no outside contact was worse than killing her immediately."

"No doubt being trapped like that would be psychological torture, but why did they want to do that to her? The seven men that they killed were medical experiments, and the people that Raul accused Paulina of killing on her own had personal connections."

"I don't understand the mind of psychopaths, but a smart FBI agent told me that Paulina Moore is off the charts smart and unimaginably evil. Her motives are something that we normal people may never understand. She is the only one who had to make sense for her to commit the crime."

"Tell me more about this FBI agent. Is he handsome, too?"

Tuesday October 12, 2021

Michelle looked over the reports on the Humane Society Director's desk; it amazed her that these people were so trusting. She had only been volunteering for a few months, but when the closing employee left work sick, no one thought twice about leaving Michelle alone to lock up. So here she was, poking around in the director's office, trying to figure out what had prompted the notice on the front desk regarding dog adoptions. The report detailed a slew of dead or gravely injured dogs found around the county. The animals had suffered injuries, including puncture wounds, lacerations, blood loss, crushing injuries, and broken bones. The police were sure that someone was running a dog fighting club in the area, but had no leads. They had informed the Humane Society in more as a precaution so that they would look out for a person adopting multiple dogs in a short period. Michelle didn't think that someone who was fighting dogs would come to get them from a legitimate source. It was more likely that the person was picking up strays, answering ads in the paper, and breeding their own dogs as their source for fighters.

That was what law-abiding citizens failed to comprehend: that criminals didn't think like them and, therefore, didn't act like them. In order to find this person, it would be necessary for her to get on the dark web to find these fights. That would entail her firing up the used laptop she had bought from an estate sale to find the liquid Ecstasy. Up until now she had avoided using the laptop again, but animals' lives were in danger. Someone needed to be held accountable for that. It was a good thing that her neighbor used a password that a child could have figured out.

******

When Kass and Robert had gotten engaged, they agreed to put both of their condos up for sale and see which one sold first. The problem with that plan was the boom in the housing market, which had brought both of them multiple offers on the first day that the condos went up for sale. Now, they were living in a one-bedroom rental with a lot of their collective belongings in storage. A booming housing market is great when you are selling, but it is enough to drive buyers to feel discouraged. Kass's dad had suggested that they continue to rent and save the money they made until the market cooled, and after several lost bids, they had settled on his plan.

Both of their hectic schedules meant that they often only spent time together at night, so the small apartment was not that big of a burden.

Plus, they were newlyweds, so their new home being cozy was a welcome feeling. Other than when Robert was running on his treadmill early on a Saturday morning when Kass wanted to sleep. She got up and started the coffee; while it brewed, she opened her laptop and moved a dedicated workout room from a want to a must-have on the house-hunting checklist. Adding the preference that it not be on the same floor as the bedrooms.

Robert walked up to her and said, “I thought you were going to sleep in. What are you working on?”

“Nothing, really. I thought we were going to train later today, but you were already on the treadmill.”

“Oh, we are still going to train. Don’t think I am letting you out of training for the triathlon. You threw down the gauntlet about who would place higher in their class.”

“Extra running is not what you need. Your swim skills are weak, and mine are top-notch.”

“You talk a lot of smack for a woman who rides a bike like a toddler.”

“Let me get ready, and then we will head to the gym.”

15

Saturday May 28, 2022

When the medical examiner, Dr. Reeves, arrived he first examined the skeletal remains, and then came back up to discuss what he saw with Detective Minor.

"My preliminary analysis is that the skeletal remains are that of a woman in her late thirties of Caucasian descent. She has been down there a while. I will have to run some tests, but I estimate that she has been dead close to two years."

"Please expedite a DNA comparison test from the victim and Kelsey Learner. Her DNA profile is on record since her missing person's case was opened four years ago."

"Absolutely. As soon as the CSI team arrives, we will remove the remains, and the DNA extraction will be my first priority when I get back to the morgue."

Dr. Reeves and Detective Minor watched as two vans pulled in carrying the CSI team and their equipment. They had gotten lucky, and Claire was on a different team of forensic technicians. Detective Minor was sure to talk with each member of the responding team, telling them that it was imperative they not discuss this case even with other members of the department. They were now constructing a large tent around the site where the container sat peeled open.

Minor tried again to call her partner, Detective Wilcox, but the call went straight to voicemail.

She placed another call, but this time to someone who answered on a much more regular basis, Robert.

He picked up on the first ring and asked, "How's it going?"

"About as you expect, it is really just a wait-and-see operation for me right now. Would you be willing to do me a favor?"

"Of course; how can I help?"

"Actually, two things. Will you bring me some lunch and, on the way, see if Wilcox is at his place and if he is there tell him that the commander expects him to be out here?"

"I take it that he is once again not answering your calls."

"Yes, and I am sorry to make you his babysitter, but you know that I have no official channels to go through to deal with this."

"I know, and I will go by his place, but I want to remind you this is one of the major reasons we have talked about you transferring. Having an unreliable partner puts a law enforcement agent in danger."

"We can talk about it tonight, but I have decided that I am going to tell Davis on Monday."

January 5, 2022

Becoming a cop was never a choice for Devin Wilcox; it was in his blood; it was an expectation, a nonnegotiable. He had not enjoyed the police academy, and being a beat cop had just straight out sucked. Putting little to no effort into his job had not been a detriment to his career thus far. He was a guy's guy who bought the rounds at the bar and always picked up the tab for the shift meal. He didn't ask for time off for holidays or weekends because, other than his dad, he had no one to be with during those times. His mom had died when he was twelve, and two hard-headed Wilcox men living together had not been pretty.

So, when his dad had told him that he was sitting for the detective exam, he just did it. All the other detectives had bachelor's degrees or decades on the force, but none of that mattered to Commander Wilcox. Devin also knew there was no way he got the almost-perfect score that was reported. Supposedly, Detective Mitch Leet was preparing to retire, and his dad had told him the paperwork for his promotion was just waiting on that day.

******

Michelle had forgotten how much she loved the dark web. It not only validated her darkness but also made her feel less alone in the world. On the dark web, any and all levels of depravity and perversity lived, or, to put it another way, as she had once heard in a movie, it was a place where people flew their freak flags proudly. Sure, there were still codes, innuendos, and lots of half-truths, but they were not done for social graces or preserving friendships; no, they were done, so only people who could see the darkness knew what they were looking at.

That was why the police had so far not been able to figure out where, when, or even who was running the dog fighting ring. It was all there to be seen if you just knew where and what to look for. There were ads looking to sell American Pit Bull Terrier pups and others about the availability of breeding stock. Each of these ads didn't have a phone number or even an email address, just a website to respond to. It wasn't the same website in each ad, but the addresses were close facsimiles of each other, and low and behold, when you went to them, they looked almost identical.

She had gone through all the necessary steps to bc admitted into the website's portal by claiming that she had a female dog to breed. After many back-and-forth exchanges, a price had been arranged, as well as a time and place to meet. Now, she had to figure out where to get a female pit bull before then.

16

Saturday May 28, 2022

The process of bringing the evidence up from the container was done systematically. The CSI team had laid out a tarp and taped out the exact dimensions of the container so that each time something was brought up, it was put in the spot it was found down there. Minor looked over the items that had been brought up as far: the empty gallon water jugs, a large plastic container with a faded picture of survivalist-type food on the label, an old Walkman-type cassette tape player, a blanket, a mattress, a comb, and the chain with the manacle on the end of it.

The lead technician, Gabby Simms, walked up to her, "That is all that was down there that we can remove. We are taking photos of the walls and floor where there are some markings. Then we will dust for fingerprints and be done down there for now."

As they watched, a forensic technician opened the lid of the food container and pulled out several empty packages. Minor presumed they had once contained freeze-dried food. Next, he pulled out six cassette tapes and set them on the tarp in the order he took them out.

"What are those?" Gabby Simms asked.

"Cassette tapes," Minor replied.

"No, I knew that. I guess I was actually asking what is on the tapes."

"That is a very good question, but I think we will have to let the forensic computer technicians be sure that we can listen to the contents without destroying them. Hopefully, they are not just mix tapes."

"What is a mixtape?"

"Something people used to make in the eighties and nineties. My parents had them."

******

After everyone else packed up and headed off the wooded lot to continue processing the evidence they had gathered, Detective Minor descended the ladder one more time. She sat down where they had found Kelsey Learner's skeleton and let the tears run down her face. Yes, she logically knew that she needed to wait for the DNA analysis before closing the case, but in her heart, she knew it was Kelsey. Standing up, she walked two feet in the three directions that she could and sat back down. *This had been Kelsey's reality for two years.* Kass thought; No, *actually, Kelsey's reality had been a lot darker. Considering that now with the lid of the container three-quarters removed and sunlight streamed in and she was down here with the top sealed shut.*

Why had the Moores trapped Kelsey down here? What had she endured under their evil hands? Minor knew that she would need to bring Mitch Leet and Claire Learner here because there was no way she could answer their questions in a way that sitting here would. After they come out here, they could probably have the container backfilled, but that would likely take a court order. Nothing moved fast when multiple government agencies were involved. Chances were, the FBI would want to say it was their crime scene due to the connection to the Moores. Since no crime had been committed in relation to the Adams boys, Minor didn't see how the Springfield PD could claim jurisdiction for that case. However, this was the site of Kelsey Learner's murder so perhaps what happened to the lot would be the decision of the Springfield PD.

As the sun began to set, Kass felt the temperature dropping and knew she needed to get up and head home, but the thoughts of Kelsey's suffering seemed to have rooted her in this spot. The need to use the bathroom finally drove her to head home, feeling more grateful for the life that she had than she had had before solving these two cases.

February 11, 2022

Joe Learner watched as Claire drove up the driveway to his farmhouse. He hoped he was handling this situation the right way. Introducing the first woman he had seriously dated since divorcing her mom to his daughter would have been difficult enough. But with Kelsey still being missing the complicated situation was even worse. Dawn, his new girlfriend, thought he should have been casually mentioning her for months so that it was not a bombshell when they met. Joe had never figured out how to work it into conversation, so here they were.

As Claire entered the house, he heard her call out, "Wow, Dad, something smells great. I thought you lived on the bachelor diet of takeout and frozen meals."

He met her halfway to the kitchen and hugged her. "That is a funny sweetheart. Actually, we are having your favorite meal, chicken carbonara, for dinner. My friend Dawn is making it."

Claire raised one eyebrow and said, "Friend?"

"Yes, Claire, I have been seeing Dawn for about eight months, and I want the two of you to meet."

"Dad, you could have told me sooner."

"Probably should have, but I wanted to be sure."

"Okay, let's go into the kitchen so you can make introductions."

February 12, 2022

Meeting her dad's new friend, Dawn, last night had gone well, and Claire was happy for them. It had been decades since she saw her dad this happy; actually, this might be the first time she had ever seen him happy like this. She wasn't sure she would ever find that kind of happiness. The therapist she had been seeing since returning to Springfield had described her as acting like a skittish rabbit. It had become her norm to be shy and stay away from people until she got to know them.

The problem was compounded by the fact that she didn't engage with anyone. Sure, there were other students in her classes and people at her job, but she never let them in. She had never had more than a surface conversation with any of them. At this point, other than talking to Lindsey and her dad, she had concluded that she was no longer capable of having an actual conversation with another human being.

Lindsey had vowed never to date again, so they had agreed to live together until they were little old ladies. That was why Claire had headed to the Humane Society today to adopt a kitten: if you are going to have a couple of single women living together, you might as well have a cat. Here she was, walking out with a cardboard box with two small kittens because the ladies inside had her convinced that adopting two at the same was better for the cats.

When she got home, she found Lindsey sitting in her room, scrolling on her phone.

"Will you please come downstairs? I have something I need to show you.?"

"Okay, I need more coffee anyway."

Lindsey followed her friend to the living room and wondered what Claire could possibly have to show her. Sitting on the coffee table was a cardboard box. Before Lindsey could figure out what was in the box, two little kitten heads poked up.

"You got us each a kitten!" Lindsey said as she lifted both of them out of the box. "Which one is mine?"

"You can pick, but I think we should name them something cute that goes together."

"Are they girls or boys?"

"They are girls and sisters."

Lindsey handed Claire the kitten with the black spot on her nose, and they spent an hour discussing names and drinking coffee.

17

Monday May 30, 2022

Detective Kass Minor set down her bag and walked toward her commander's office. "Sir, do you have a few minutes?"

"Sure. By the way, good job closing the Adams case so quickly and with both the kids basically okay. I will never be able to publicly say this to you, but you were right that we needed to be searching in both directions. In the end, the boys did go the wrong way, and your team found them."

"Thank you, sir. If it weren't for the witness, Mr. Hathaway, I wouldn't have known where to look. I am pleased this case had a happy ending."

"It also looks like you will be closing a cold case as well. Dr. Reeves, the medical examiner, is inclined to agree with your assessment that the skeleton in the container is the remains of Kelsey Learner."

"With your permission, I would like to update Mitch Leet about the finding, and once the DNA confirms her identity, I would like to be the one to tell Claire Learner."

"Both those requests are approved. Was there anything else you needed to discuss?"

Before Minor could respond, Detective Brewer barged in; "Sorry to interrupt, but there is a situation downstairs in the holding cells, and they are asking for you to respond."

Commander Davis stood up, then turned to Minor, "If there was anything else, come back and see me later."

Minor nodded as she watched the commander walk away. Explaining why she hadn't requested a transfer was going to be a bit tricky with Robert, but what else could she do? Paperwork, that was what.

******

Detective Minor called Mitch Leet, and they agreed to meet for lunch at their favorite diner. Walking over to the diner, Minor thought about all the times they had eaten here when they were partners and all that she had learned from Leet. She had always known he was a great partner, but having an unreliable one now was shining a spotlight on just how much she appreciated Leet.

Since she had arrived first, Minor sat in the booth facing the front door and ordered a strawberry milkshake. Watching Leet walk in, she immediately noticed his relaxed posture, the contentment that shone on his face, and heard him laugh at something that whoever he was on the phone with had said. He ended his phone call and joined her in the booth.

"How have you been, Minor?"

"Good, Leet. I have been good. How about you?"

"I am really good. I should have retired a long time ago because I feel better than I have in years."

"That's great."

The waitress walked up, and they both placed their orders since they had been here enough to know what they liked. After she walked away, Leet looked at Minor and said, "I am assuming this is not just a social call."

"No, it isn't." She replied and opened the Kelsey Learner file to the new section she had added this morning. Sliding it across the table to her former partner, Minor said, "We found her."

Mitch took time to look through the information and pictures, then shut the file and slid it back across the table. "I am happy that her daughter can have closure, but what they did to her. That is just messed up."

"I couldn't agree more. Obviously, we have to wait for the DNA analysis before officially closing the case, but I highly doubt there will be any surprises found."

"What is on those cassette tapes that were found?"

"That is the million-dollar question. Abe is working on it in computer forensics."

"Does he even know what a cassette tape is?" Leet asked with laughter in his voice.

"Seems he does, and he has some fancy equipment to digitize whatever is on the tapes. He explained to me that with the age of the tapes, each time they are played increases the chances of them breaking."

"If it is possible, I would like an update on what was on the tapes."

"Absolutely, Mitch. Do you want me to request permission to have you go out to the site with me?"

"No, the pictures are enough. I don't need any more gruesome images running around in my head. I already have plenty up there."

Detective Minor's phone buzzed, and she looked down and saw a text from Abe.

"Abe has the first side of the first tape ready to be listened to. I am going to head back." She reached into her bag to get her wallet, but Leet held up his hand.

"I've got lunch. It was good to see you, and I am proud that you will deliver closure for the Learners."

March 14, 2022

Claire sat in front of the dealership, waiting for her dad. The SUV had major problems, and the service writer had said it might not be worth it to put that much money into it. The thing that he didn't understand was that the SUV was her mom's. Her dad had told her many times that it was hers and that if her mom ever made it home, the least of her concerns would be that SUV. Claire would never consider the Buick to be hers.

Watching her dad pull up in his Sierra truck, she figured he would understand sentimental value. After all, wasn't that a big part of what the truck was to him? Once he came to a stop, she climbed into the cab. "Hi, Daddy."

"Hmm, it must be bad if you are calling me daddy," he laughed as he drove towards her house.

Claire began to tell him what they had told her about the SUV. The aluminum cylinder head was warped, which was why it was overheating. There was a small amount of antifreeze in the oil, and the dealership suggested she not drive it again.

"Why didn't you just call me when it started having issues?"

"Mom always took it back to the dealership, so I have just done that, too. I have gotten the oil changed, new tires, and all the stuff that needed to be done, so when the overheating started, I just brought it in here."

"Okay, so I agree at the prices the dealership will charge, it isn't worth it. However, since it is worth it to you, I can get some help and fix it up for you. But remember, I work full time, so this is going to be a slow project. You will need to find a car to buy in the meantime. Do you want me to ask Dawn?"

"Thanks, Dad, for fixing it, but I don't understand how Dawn can help me."

"She owns Emmitt auto with her brother, and that is where I am going to get some of the more extensive work done on your SUV. They sell cars that they fixed up."

"I guess I didn't ask her much about herself when we met."

"That's okay, honey. I know I stunned you."

******

Infiltrating a criminal enterprise, no matter the nature of the crime, took time and patience, both of which Michelle had plenty of. Getting a female Pit bull was not difficult; an ad on a social media site for Pit bull puppies had led her to a breeder an hour away. At first, the woman was reluctant to sell the mama dog, but as the saying goes, for the right price, everything is for sale. Having a dog in her condo was not ideal, but the dog herself was very well-trained and spent the majority of her time in her crate, even when the door was open to it.

Michelle had taken the dog to the initial breeding meeting a few weeks ago, and the owner of the male pit bull, who called himself Octavius, had been pleased. She had taken the dog back several times before the dog became impregnated with the puppies that were due any day now. Michelle had been using a vet that the animal shelter recommended to people, and the vet and she had agreed that the puppies would be fine to be born at home. Turning the puppies over to Octavius when they were weaned would not be easy for her, as she knew that the dogs would be abused and taught to fight. However, building trust and rapport was necessary to be invited further into the ring.

18

Monday May 30, 2022

Kass Minor walked through the detective division on the off chance her partner was actually at his desk. He wasn't, so she wrote him a sticky note and headed up to the computer forensics division to see Abe.

"Hi, Minor. I have digitized side one of the first one of those tapes. It is indeed Kelsey Learner, and she addresses the police in it. I will cue it up for you to listen to and then get started on the flip side."

"Thanks, Abe. I appreciate all of your hard work. How much of it did you listen to?"

"All of it, several times. It is rough."

"Thank you for the warning," Minor said as she put on the headphones and waited for Abe to start the recording.

My name is Kelsey Learner, and I am making this recording for the police. If you are not the police and are listening to this, please take this and the other tapes to the police. If you are the Son of a Bitch, who kidnapped and kept me down here, you have no right to listen to these tapes. I hope you burn in hell.

For the police: My name again is Kelsey Learner; I am going to record this one side of a tape to tell you what I know so you can find the man who took me. If by some chance, however unlikely it is, I am found alive, then none of these tapes will be necessary. However, since it is highly unlikely, I am getting out of here alive, here goes. The rest of the tapes are for my daughter, Claire; please be sure they get to her.

The last thing I remember before waking up down here is leaving a conference I attended with my employer, Dr. Chris Hann. The conference was held in downtown Springfield, Missouri, on Wednesday, April 11th 2018. That is also the last date that I know for sure. I have been trying to have a system of counting the days and weeks using the trash from my food rations and scratching a mark on the wall every time it has been a week. From my count, I have been down here for almost two years.

The man and I call him that because I have never clearly seen him but cannot imagine that a woman would have done this, comes down here every seven days. He wears a mask with a headlamp when he first descends down and then shoots me with a stun gun. While I am out cold, he injects me with some kind of tranquilizer and cleans up down here. He leaves me food and water every time and often other things such as these tapes and the Walkman. He routinely cuts my fingernails and toenails and leaves me new clothes to wear, and the two flashlights he left for me have never run out of battery life. Other than taking me and the tasering, tranquilizer ritual, he has never hurt me.

I have no idea why he took me, but I was being stalked before my kidnapping. Someone followed me often; a message using cut-up letters was left on my doorstep, and lipstick was used to write Homewrecker on my windshield. I know I should have reported the incidents to the police, but I didn't. I am sorry I cannot be of more help in finding my kidnapper. I simply do not know anything.

Kass took off the headphones and looked over at Abe, who was hard at work. He noticed her looking over without her headphones off. "Do you want me to cue it up again?"

"No, but I do think we need to get it transcribed."

"The software already did that, and the reason I listened to it several times was to edit that transcription. Would you like me to print you a copy?"

"Yes, please. Can you send me a digital copy of the recording?"

"No problem."

"Thanks, Abe. I appreciate you prioritizing this."

"Glad to help. "

Taking the printout Abe had given her, she detoured once again, but this time on the same floor but over to where the Crime Scene techs worked. She looked around for Claire but did not see her. Another tech walked up to her, “Can I help you, detective?”

“I am looking for Claire Learner.”

“She was done at three today.”

Detective Minor looked at the clock on the wall. She had no idea where the time had gone, but it was almost five o'clock.

“Thanks. I will catch up with her another time.”

******

Kass walked into the apartment, tired from her day, and smelled something cooking. This was one of the things that worked so well about her and Robert’s relationship; they did what they needed to do. No squabbling over whose job or turn it was.

“What are you making for dinner?”

“Beef and Broccoli; It was one of those meal kits from the freezer. How did your talk with Davis go?”

“It didn’t. I went to talk to him, but he got called away, and every time I checked back, he wasn’t in his office.”

“I guess another day won’t make a difference.”

Kass walked over and kissed him.

Saturday April 2, 2022

Kass was so upset that she had food poisoning this morning. She and Robert had been training for the last year for this triathlon. Robert had headed to the twenty-four-hour pharmacy to get her some electrolyte sports drink because there was no way she was missing the race. He was smart enough not to mention that he said he thought sushi from the gas station was a bad idea last night. In her own defense, she had worked late, was starving when she stopped for gas and loved sushi. Well, she had loved sushi before this morning. She wasn’t sure that she would ever eat sushi again.

After consuming large amounts of electrolyte drinks, she felt ready to go, and although Robert had suggested they could skip the race, there was no way she was going to let that happen. In hindsight, Robert had been right, not that she would be telling him that anytime soon; at least she should have skipped the race. A lot of people would have been happy to have come in at the middle of their class, but to Kass, it felt like a loss. Robert had, of course, won their bet by placing third in his class, so she knew that she would have to pay up. The rest of the weekend would be nonstop spaghetti westerns, chicken wings, and salt and vinegar chips.

******

Robert watched as Kass slept curled up on the couch while his favorite movie played in the background. He had gotten up to answer the door with their food delivery and came back to find her sound asleep. As he watched her sleep, he thought about how lucky he was to have met her and for her to have ever agreed to go on that first date with him. He knew that he did not need to wake her up. Just sitting here with her was a great way to spend the evening.

Sunday April 3, 2022

Kass woke up to blissful silence as she rolled over and picked up her phone. She was startled to see it was almost ten in the morning. Kass was not sure when the last time she had slept in this late was, but it had to have been during college. After going to the bathroom and brushing her teeth, she walked into the living room/kitchen combo area to find Robert. She found a note on the counter:

Hi Honey,

You must have been really wiped out, so I let you sleep in. I am going to meet Rivers for breakfast. See you around noon

Love-Robert

Kass started a pot of coffee, but as the steam rose and the smell wafted towards her, she ran to the bathroom and got sick. *Wow, this food poisoning has really got a grip on me,* she thought as she brushed her teeth for the second time this morning. She sat on the couch and wondered if there was any more of that electrolyte drink left. Sipping on the grape-flavored drink, she called Amy, thinking a quiet apartment would be a great opportunity to catch up. Almost an hour later, Amy asked about the triathlon, and Kass told her about the food poisoning and her horrible race finish.

When she told Amy about how she was still feeling the effects, such as being tired and getting sick again this morning, Amy started laughing.

"How is this funny to you?"

"I am so sorry, Hun, but I think you are pregnant, and you think it was sushi."

Kass was too stunned to respond. *Was that possible? Well, yes, it was biologically possible, but we take precautions.*

"Amy, I will call you back later."

"Yep, after you pee on a stick, right?"

"Yes, Amy. Goodbye!"

19

Tuesday May 31, 2022

Detective Minor walked towards her commander's office again this morning, hoping that this was not going to be her new routine.

"Commander, do you have a moment to talk?"

"Yep, come in."

This time, Detective Minor closed the door behind her in hopes they could finish this conversation. She was sure Robert would want her to start with the transfer request, but instead, she started with the tape.

"Abe, up in computer forensics, was able to digitize the first side of one of the tapes we found in the container. I listened to it and have an electronic copy to send you, as well as the transcript. The tape is of Kelsey Learner, and she explains what she knows about her kidnapping and captivity. She also says all the other tapes are for Claire."

"Oh my. Have you told Claire yet?"

"No, I am going to ask her supervisor to send her down to me if she isn't too busy and explain she may need the rest of the day off. I think I need to tell her sooner rather than later because the more people who know, the more it will be all over this place."

"I agree. Go and tell her unless there is something else."

"Yes, there was. I would like to transfer to the cold case division when Xavier Moss retires."

"Okay, I didn't see that coming. Why? You worked so hard to get into the detective bureau, and cold cases are where people go to coast out their careers."

"With all due respect, I think cold cases deserve the same degree of professionalism and dedication as the new ones. Hell, maybe they deserve more."

"I will sign your transfer paperwork when it comes across my desk, but you need to know that Moss talked to some pencil pusher with the retirement association. Now he says that he is going to stay for another nine months or so to optimize his benefits, so you will have to wait a while."

"The timing will work well for me, sir, because the thing is, I am having a baby in six months. I plan to take the full twelve weeks of leave that I am allowed."

"Wow, now that I didn't see that coming at all. Congratulations."

"Commander Davis, I would prefer that my pregnancy not be discussed with others until or unless it is necessary."

"Of course."

******

While she waited for Claire, Detective Minor placed a phone call that went straight to voicemail.

"Mr. Learner, this is Detective Kass Minor. I am calling you to discuss a development in Kelsey's case. I have asked Claire to come and see me; if you get this message in the next few minutes, please call me back, and I will put you on speaker while we talk."

It only took fifteen minutes for Claire to come down to the detective division and find Minor, who walked her to the conference room. Joe Learner hadn't called Minor back, so she moved on with what she needed to tell Claire.

"Thanks for coming down to see me. This is about your mom, so if you prefer, we can leave the station and talk somewhere else, and your dad can be there."

"No, please tell me what you have found out."

"I am sure you heard about the missing Adams boys and their rescue."

"Yes, it is all the talk of the station and the town. How is that related to my mom?"

"The boys fell through a hole that had rusted through a shipping container that was buried in a wooded lot. To make a long story short, that wooded lot belonged to Paulina Moore."

Claire gasped as her imagination about what Detective Minor was going to say next took flight.

"When the fire department opened up the container to save the boys, skeletal remains were found in the container. I would like to show you a few things if you are up to it."

Claire nodded, but didn't verbally respond.

Detective Minor had put this file for Claire together before she left last night because there was no way she wanted her to look at the official police file. Pulling out the picture of the words that had been scratched into the floor of the container, Minor slid it over to Claire.

She picked it up, tears streaming down her face. "You found her."

"We are waiting on definitive proof, but yes, we did. There is something else I want you to listen to if you are up for it."

"Listen to?"

"Yes, your mom left some tapes behind. We are working on digitizing them so that they can be listened to, but the first side of the first one is done. Now, I don't want you to listen to the whole thing just a little from the beginning. If you could verify that it is your mom's voice, that would be helpful."

"Okay."

Minor pulled her phone out of her pocket and cued up the recording to the part she wanted Claire to listen to.

My name again is Kelsey Learner; I am going to record this one side of a tape to tell you what I know so you can find the man who took me. If by some chance, however unlikely it is, I am found alive, then this won't make a difference, but here goes. The rest of the tapes are for my daughter, Claire; please be sure they get to her.

Claire began to sob and choked out a yes.

Saturday April 16, 2022

Each time that Michelle met up with Octavious, the location was different, and this was no exception. As she drove further into the country along narrow, winding roads with four puppies in the back of her car, Michelle wondered if this was a fool's errand. Why was she so invested in stopping the dog fighters? It wasn't as if she was a big dog lover, nor was it that she had never killed an innocent. For her, it was that the killing of these dogs was purely for profit and enjoyment; there was no great good coming from their sacrifices.

She made a right when the GPS told her to and arrived at a locked gate with a speaker box. After pressing the button and giving her name, the gate swung open, and she proceeded up the gravel drive. At the end of the drive was a large square building in the middle, with a rectangular building on either side, and a large gravel parking lot with several cars parked in it. As Michelle got out of her car, the crescendo of barking dogs was deafening and like nothing she had ever experienced before. Walking around the car, she opened the passenger side door and picked up the box of puppies. As she turned around, Octavious approached her from the middle building.

"I see you found the place. I can carry them for you."

"Thanks," Michelle said as she handed over the box and then followed Octavious towards the building on the right where he was headed.

"Before you come in here, I need to make sure you are prepared for what we are doing. But first, I need to pat you down for a wire and be sure you aren't carrying a cell phone."

"Go ahead; my cell is in the car, and I'm not wearing a wire."

After Octavius took care of assuring himself and whoever else she was sure was watching them from the cameras mounted all around, he asked, "What do you think we are doing out here with the dogs?"

Michelle wondered if the move was to play dumb or, to be honest, but decided just to tell him what she thought.

"I believe that this is a dog fighting breed operation and maybe even where the fights happen."

"I told them you were a smart one. Why do you want to be involved?"

"Money!" It was a simple answer, but one that she thought was the only one that would be accepted.

"Well, there is money to be made. Let's go check out the pups you brought."

Michelle followed Octavious into one of the buildings and was surprised to see two men sitting at a table. There was nothing else in the building. Michelle turned to Octavius and asked, "What is going on?"

"We have to be careful, so anyone who will be doing business with us has to have a complete background check."

"You didn't think to mention this to me ahead of time."

"Is it a problem?"

"Yes, it is. I will just leave."

The two other men walked towards Michelle and Octavious, and one of them said, "Octavious, what is the problem here?"

"I'm not sure, but Michelle isn't comfortable with our arrangement."

"I want to leave. You can just pay me for the puppies, or I will take them with me, and I will leave and never contact any of you."

The man who had spoken to Octavious grabbed Michelle by the wrist and said, "Oh no, now you are being fingerprinted because if you are a fed or a cop, this will not end well for you."

The other man walked over to the table, grabbed something, and returned to where Michelle was struggling to get free.

“This is a portable fingerprint scanner, so in a few moments, we will know who you really are, lady.” He then pressed the scanner against Michelle’s fingertips. The machine beeped, then the man walked back to the table and opened a laptop.

“Okay, let’s try again because it errored out.”

Octavius questioned, “Why would it do that?”

“I don’t know. It has never done that before, but I will just scan her other hand. Lady, if you know what is good for you, no squirming around.”

The man repeated the scanning procedure, then walked back to Michelle and inspected her hands. “What happened to your fingers?”

“My ex-husband was abusive and would burn my fingers along with the countless other horrible things that he did. I will level with all of you; if you run my name, there is no record. I am on the run from my husband, and I was only trying to sell the puppies to raise some money.”

The first man who had talked reached into his pocket and pulled out a roll of hundred-dollar bills. He counted five of them off and handed them to Michelle. “Here you go; now get out of here.”

Michelle did not have to be told twice. She turned around and walked out the same door that she had entered with Octavious a few minutes before. Her days of chasing these dog fighters were over.

******

“Why did you just let her leave? What if she is an undercover cop, and that was just some bullshit story?” The man who had attempted to scan Michelle’s fingerprints asked.

“Listen, no cop, no matter how dedicated, is going to mutilate their hands like that. To burn off your fingerprints would be agony. Plus, my mom had a super abusive boyfriend for a long time, and I know it is really hard for these women to leave their abusers. If I can help that woman in some way to not go back to the man who did that to her, I am good with that.”

Octavius had not said anything during this entire interaction, but he knew these guys well enough not to leave until they told him he could.

"Oc, take the puppies over to the kennel, and then you can head out."

Octavius picked up the box of puppies and headed to the other rectangular building. He was relieved that neither of the men seemed to be blaming him for bringing Michelle here. She had seemed harmless to him, but he knew that the men he worked for expected him to show a high level of discretion in regard to who he brought into their world.

20

Tuesday May 31, 2022

Claire drove straight to her dad's farm after talking to Detective Minor. She knew he wouldn't be home from work yet, but she needed to go there. She pulled up the driveway, parked behind the garage, and walked up to the stall door. After putting in the code, the door opened, and she got into the SUV, which was sitting in the garage with the hood open and the engine out. That was how Claire felt right now, a hollowed-out core of herself. The SUV was the place she felt closest to her mom. Claire could smell her mom for a long time when she got in the Buick. Not in a bad way, but in terms of her shampoo, perfume, and natural scent, it was a comfort. So much so that when Kelsey first disappeared, Claire had slept in her mom's bed until that smell went away. Until they cleared the house for the renters on the really bad days, she would sit in her mom's closet and try to capture that essence.

Today was a bad day, so she reached under the driver's seat and took out her mom's favorite sweatshirt, which she and Lindsey had vacuum-sealed when they found it while packing up the house. Lindsey had called it an emergency plan, and Claire had carried that bag in the SUV since. Pulling open the bag, the smell wafted towards her, and Claire began to sob. Her mom was and had been dead for a long time. That small shred of hope that she had, that her mom was still alive, was now gone, and Claire was not sure how to go on. All she wanted was her mom. Hearing her voice again after so many years was a gift, and Claire couldn't wait to listen to the other tapes.

When her dad opened the passenger door and sat down, Claire wasn't sure what time it was, so she had no idea how long she had been there.

"What is going on, honey?" Joe asked in a voice tinged with worry.

"They found her, daddy! They found my mommy!" Claire answered before breaking into sobs again.

She wasn't aware that her dad had gotten out of the SUV until he opened the driver's side door and pulled her into a hug.

"Come inside with me, honey, and tell me everything," he softly pleaded.

All Claire could do was nod and let her dad lead him into his house.

******

Joe was kicking his own butt for not calling Detective Minor back. He had let your call go straight to voicemail and had yet to listen to her message. Letting his hatred for the detective cost him being there when his daughter got the worst news of her life. After settling Claire in the living room with some hot tea and tissues, Joe sat down next to her.

"Claire, are you ready to tell me what you learned today?"

"I'll try. Detective Minor had me come down to see her at work. She offered to talk somewhere else, but I just wanted her to tell me, so she did. When working on another case, they found a skeleton that has been tentatively identified as Mom."

"Tentatively?" Joe could feel his blood pressure rise. He thought, Why *would that detective have told her this when they are not sure yet?*

"Dad, it is her. She left me a message scratched in the ground, and there are tapes."

Now Joe was even more concerned because his mind instantly wondered *what kind of tapes we were talking about.* "Tapes?"

"Cassette tapes; I don't know details or how she did it, but mom recorded tapes while she was in captivity. Detective Minor played a very small part of what she called the first one. It was Mom, for sure. Mom said the rest of the tapes are for me."

"In captivity? Your mom was held in captivity before she died?"

"Yes, Dad; they found her remains in a shipping container that was buried under the ground on a wooded lot that Paulina Moore owned. Detective Minor didn't tell me any of the details because I never gave her a chance. I started sobbing after listening to Mom's voice and came straight here."

"Okay, Hun. I don't need the details. What can I do to help you?"

"Daddy, tell me a story about mom. A happy one that you have never told me before."

Joe thought for a few minutes and started to chuckle.

"Okay, so when I met your mom, we were both freshmen in college, and I was a know-it-all. Somehow, I convinced your mom to go on a second date, and there was a new restaurant in town, so I decided to take her there.

The restaurant had a salad bar that came with every meal, so we both went up to get a salad. I was not much of a salad eater at nineteen, so I was happy when I saw cottage cheese, potato salad, and pudding. I loaded up my plate and headed back to the table with your mom. She looked over at my plate and said something like, 'What are you going to do with that?' She was pointing at the big pile of pudding, so I said, 'Eat it.'

Kelsey had the strangest look on her face and said, 'It's butter,' to which I replied, 'No, it is vanilla pudding,' and then I took a big bite of whipped butter. I would have spit it out, but your mom was staring at me, so I took another bite and then another and another until I ate all that butter.

Your mom was laughing so hard by the time our meal came that tears were rolling down her face, and she was having trouble catching her breath. The server asked if she was okay, and she somehow was able to get coherent words out and told him, "No, my date would like some rolls, please." That is when I started laughing, too. Many times, over the years, your mom would ask me if I needed more butter, or I would ask her for more butter, and we would both laugh."

By the time he finished the story, Claire was laughing along with her father.

Tuesday April 26, 2022

Robert and Kass decided to spend a long weekend telling their parents they were going to be grandparents. Both of them took Friday and Monday off and first headed to the Ozarks to see Robert's parents. The entire four days were a blur of celebration, happy tears, and driving. Both of their moms seemed shocked that it had happened already, and the dads were worried about them finding a house to live in. The latter was a concern for Kass and Robert as well, so looking at houses would be put back on the front burner.

******

The decision not to change her last name professionally was not a difficult one for Kass. She was known as Detective Minor and did not want to have people lose that connection to her stellar reputation. Robert had completely understood, as the majority of female FBI agents didn't change their last names either. However, this morning, when her mother called her at work, she answered the phone: *Detective Minor, how can I help you?* It had started a conversation that she now had to finish.

"Hi, mom. I am calling you back after work just like I promised."

"Thank you. I was so startled when I called you, and you didn't answer as Detective Matthews. Why didn't you change your name? What will happen when you and Robert have this baby? Whose last name will your baby have?"

"Mom, legally, my name is Kassandra Minor Matthews, so Robert and my baby will have Matthews as a last name. However, as a police detective, I will be Detective Minor as long as I am with the Springfield police department."

"Are you trying to tell me who may not be staying at the police department?"

Suppressing a sigh was a skill that children of opinionated mothers learned early, so that is what Kass did. “No, Mom, I am planning to be with the Springfield PD for the foreseeable future.”

******

Lindsey watched as Claire pulled away from the house. Lying to her best friend was something that Lindsey hated to do, but she knew that Claire would never understand why she was having coffee with Mack. Worse yet, Claire might tell Lindsey's parents, who would be upset with her. No one ever had the nerve to bring up what had happened between Lindsey and Mack, and she had shared very little, so she was sure that their imaginations had run wild. There was no way her parents or Claire would believe that Mack had not meant to break her wrist that night.

They had been arguing, which was something that Lindsey knew was a bad idea, but a worse idea was that she tried to walk away from Mack. He hated when she walked away from him, and she knew that too. When he grabbed her wrist and twisted it, she knew she had gone too far and tried to apologize. Mack stormed out of the apartment, but they must have been loud because a neighbor had called the police. The officers who responded knew Lindsey’s dad and insisted she get checked out by the EMTs.

Having her parents pick her up at the emergency room was a very embarrassing low for Lindsey. Feeling that low was why she had agreed to press charges, get a restraining order, and move out on Mack. No one wanted to hear that he was sorry or that they loved each other, but both of those things were true. The last few weeks, Lindsey had been meeting Mack out of town on their days off. He had been so sweet and attentive, just like at the beginning of their relationship.

******

As Claire drove to class, she wondered if her imagination was getting away from her again. She could swear Lindsey was hiding something from her, but what would her best friend have to hide? The uptick in Lindsey's mood and her smiles when she read a text were likely not secrets, just her friend getting back to her happy-go-lucky self. More than once over the last few months, Claire had started to ask Lindsey what had gone on with Mack, but she had always stopped herself.

After her first class, Claire followed her usual routine and headed to the on-campus coffee shop for a latte while she worked on her last paper for her criminal psychology class. After ordering her drink, she turned to head to a comfy chair when a guy carrying a drink carrier with four beverages ran right into her. That was the reason she was arriving home now covered in coffee, because changing before her next class was a must.

Their cats, Monica and Rachel, met her at the door, meowing like crazy. Claire had thought Lindsey would be at home today because it was her day off, but her car was gone, and the cats only greeted people when no one else was home. After changing, she brewed a cup of coffee into her to-go cup; while she waited for the coffee, she straightened up the kitchen. The grocery list she and Lindsey wrote last night was under the napkins, along with the hundred dollars Claire had left to help cover the items. She took a picture of the list and fired off a text to Lindsey.

Claire: I stopped home and saw the list and money. Here is a picture of the list, so you can go straight to the store if you want to.

Claire grabbed her stuff and headed out, thinking how odd it was for Lindsey not to text her back, even just a thumbs up or the letter K. In a few months, Claire would be graduating, but she didn't think anything would really need to change. The only difference would be that she would have a little more money. Living together had worked well for both of them, and neither was dating, so they were heading towards being crazy cat ladies.

21

Tuesday June 13, 2022

Abe called Detective Minor and let her know that he was done digitizing the tapes. He asked her if she would like to come up to his office to review them. Before going up to see Abe, she let Commander Davis know what was going on and looked for Wilcox, who was not in the detective bureau.

"Hi, Detective. I know I could have just emailed you the transcripts and recordings, but I wanted to go over how I chose to label them. If you think there is a better way, I will redo the labels."

"Okay, sounds good."

"Like the first tape indicated, each of the rest of them is exclusively for Claire. There is nothing that I think is evidence, but I will let you be the judge of that. I labeled each recording with when Claire is supposed to listen to them."

"When she is supposed to listen to them?"

"Yes, like, for example, the first one I labeled 'When you first get these tapes,' and there is one labeled, 'When you become a mom.' because that is how they start."

"Oh my. Let me see the list."

1. When you first get these tapes
2. When you graduate from college
3. When you fall in love
4. When someone breaks your heart
5. When you get married

6. When you find out you are going to have a baby
7. When you become a mom
8. When you are missing me
9. When you are angry about what happened to me
10. When you face a hard choice
11. When you are celebrating a great success

"Tell me again how you decided on the labels?" Minor asked Abe.

"Like I said, each tape starts out with something similar. They all start the same with Kelsey saying 'Claire, this tape is for...' then it continues with the when statement that I used for the labels."

"I think the labels are perfect. Thank you for doing this."

"I took the time to take out bled-through sounds, like snippets of music that were likely what Kelsey recorded over. The original unaltered records are also available, but those I labeled Tape A, Side 1, etcetera."

"That works for me. I am going to go ask Commander Davis about releasing the recordings to Claire. Would you be able to put them on a portable hard drive?"

"Sure, if you or Claire bring me one, I will put them on it."

"Great. Thank you again."

"You're welcome. I am happy to have helped you close this case."

Monday May 2, 2022

Porsche hung up when her sister Mercedes didn't answer yet again. It had been weeks since her sister had answered her calls, and her voicemail had said it was full when she tried to call her the last few times. Porsche wondered what was going on with her sister, who usually called just to talk a couple of times a week and at least a month to ask for money. The sisters were each other's only living relatives and were barely a year apart in age. Their mom died of a drug overdose when they were both still in elementary school, and their granny had raised them. Mercedes was still living with Gran rent-free when their granny passed in her sleep.

With no job and the beginning of a drug problem, Mercedes floated from place to place, including Porsche's efficiency apartment, until she took off one day. Porsche had been worried sick about her sister, who called her a few days after to say she was making her way to Florida. From that day on, every payday, Porsche put minutes on her sister's cell so she could call, and until a few weeks ago, that had worked fine. The last place she knew her sister to be was in Mobile, Alabama, because, like most things Mercedes did, she did not make it all the way to Florida before she ran out of steam.

Filing a missing person report took knowing information that Porsche simply didn't have. She didn't know where her sister had been staying. Heck, she couldn't even say for sure that her sister was missing. Mobile was too big an area for Porsche just to drive down there and look for her sister, but there had to be something she could do.

22

Monday June 13, 2022

As she walked by the Commander's office, Detective Minor saw that the door was shut, and Detective Wilcox and his dad, Commander Wilcox, were sitting inside. Her inquiry into the next steps with the Kelsey Learner tapes would have to wait. The voicemail light was flashing on her phone, so listening to her voicemail was the first thing she took care of. There were two messages, one from a local reporter wanting to do a follow-up story on finding the Adams boys and the other from the desk sergeant.

The desk sergeant's message was, "There is a Porsche Rowen here to see you. Call down if you want me to have someone bring her up."

Minor wondered, *what does Porsche Rowen need to see me about?* The message was only five minutes old, so she called down and asked the Desk Sergeant if Porsche was still there. When he told her that she was, Minor had him send her up and met Porsche and the officer who escorted her at the elevator.

"Thank you, Officer; I will escort Ms. Rowen the rest of the way."

"You're welcome, Detective," the officer said as he turned and got back on the elevator.

Turning to Porsche Rowen, Minor put out her hand to direct the woman to follow her down the hall and then opened the door to the conference room. After both of the women were seated, Detective Minor asked, "How can I help you, Ms. Rowen?"

"Please call me Porsche when you say Ms. Rowen, I think you're talking about my granny."

"Okay, no problem. How can I help you, Porsche?"

"I think my sister is missing, and I'm not sure what to do."

"You think she is missing?"

"Here is the thing: she doesn't stay around here anymore, so I am not here to report her missing to you. I am here because you are the only cop I know, and I need some cop-type advice."

Detective Minor smiled slightly, thinking of all the people she had arrested over the years who could have used some cop-type advice. "All right, tell me about your sister."

"First, I want to say that I watch enough TV to know that a lot of people, including the police, write off people like my sister, but no matter how she is living her life, she is my sister, and I love her. Mercedes, that is my sister's name, started taking painkillers when she was sixteen. My granny and I didn't know it then, but it escalated, and we quickly realized she was using. She lived with Gran until about three years ago when our granny passed.

Mercedes got worse after that and became homeless, which is when I think she began prostituting, but it is nothing she ever told me, nor did I ever ask her directly. After about six months of that here, she got it in her head to float down to Florida, but she only ever made it as far as Mobile, Alabama. We talk every couple of days, and I make sure she always has minutes on her phone. But it has been almost a month, and I haven't been able to get ahold of my little sister."

Porsche took a breath, and Detective Minor decided to ask some questions while she had the chance. "Are you sure she is in Mobile?"

"No, I'm not sure. She was there when we talked last, but with it being a month, she could have moved on."

Detective Minor could see how if Porsche reported her sister as missing to the Mobile police, honestly, to almost any police department, there would be little to no investigation.

"Do you have her last known address?"

"No. She told me she was renting a room at a place with a couple of other girls she met down there. I learned over the years that if I want

Mercedes to stay in contact, I don't push her for details or ask a lot of questions."

"Alright, I am going to be honest with you. The Mobile police department may not be willing to take your missing person's report, but you should still try. I would also suggest that you call the hospitals in the area and give them a description of your sister so they can check if she was admitted. The final thing I am going to suggest is hard to do, but when you call the Mobile Police Department, even if they don't open a missing person's case on Mercedes, you need to ask them to check the morgue for anyone matching your sister's description."

Minor heard Porsche gasp and knew the woman had not thought of her sister as possibly being dead.

"Please let me know if Mobile opens a case. Besides the things I have told you to do, I will put your sister's name and description in the system as someone I want to speak to. If she is picked up for a crime and she uses her real name, I will get a call."

"Thank you so much, Detective Minor. I will go home and make those calls and then call you to let you know what I find out."

As the two women stood, Detective Minor pulled her business card out of her pocket and handed it to Porsche, then opened the door to the conference room. Commander Davis was standing in the hall across from the door.

He said, "Minor, after you see her out, come to my office," then turned and walked away, not even waiting for the detective's response.

Porsche turned to Detective Minor, "I hope I didn't get you in trouble or something."

"No, he is just like that, and I am sure you aren't the reason he wants to talk to me."

Thursday May 12, 2022

Meeting Mack had become how Lindsey spent her days off, and she wondered how long she could continue to keep it a secret from Claire.

It wasn't that she was ashamed of her choice to see Mack. No, it was Mack who was adamant that they had to keep their relationship secret. He wouldn't tell her exactly what happened between her dad and himself, but she was sure that her dad had threatened Mack. There was also the issue of the restraining order that her parents had convinced her to get. She would need to file paperwork to have the order dismissed, but Lindsey was afraid that her dad would find out.

Mack had been very attentive and sweet since they had been seeing each other again. He told her that if they moved back in together; he was willing to go to couples' counseling. She wasn't ready to move back in with him, but spending time together and rebuilding their relationship was making her happy. Today, she was going to talk to Mack about starting counseling now so they could get their relationship back on track.

23

Monday June 13, 2022

Detective Minor could have sworn that all the other detectives were staring at her as she walked to Commander Davis's office.

The commander motioned for Minor to take a seat as he closed the door. She heard him sigh as he sat down, but he didn't immediately start talking. As the tension built, Minor ran through the last few days and then cases in her mind, but nothing stood out as being out of the ordinary.

"Alright, I feel like a Middle School Principal because Wilcox, the father and the son, came to see me to complain that you are not being nice to Detective Wilcox."

"What? Really, are you joking? How am I mean to him?"

"Detective Wilcox stated that you often don't keep him in the loop during active cases and that you ask him to complete menial tasks while you go off on your own. Now, I will be honest with you: I think the real issue is that the news reported you as the detective who saved the Adams boys. Now, several reporters have called, specifically asking to interview you. Commander Wilcox wants to be the next police chief, and so the limelight is especially important to him. Do you want to tell me your side of the story?"

"What would you like me to say? On a regular basis, I don't know where Detective Wilcox is, and he often doesn't answer my calls or texts. I would love to have a partner who works with me."

"Alright, well, I told Commander Wilcox that you were being transferred to the cold case unit when Detective Moss retires. That seemed to appease Commander Wilcox to some degree, but I will also be assigning Detective Wilcox to work with Ronnie Brewer."

"What about Detective Diaz? He and Brewer have been partners since before I started here."

"Diaz has put in his retirement papers for six weeks from now. He will finish his career working with you, then you and I will figure out if you want to stay in the field until your leave starts. Is that alright with you, or do I need to get the police union involved?"

Minor knew that not having to work with Wilcox for the next few months would reduce her stress level tremendously, but she felt bad that he was being pushed off onto Brewer.

"Commander Davis, I am agreeable to your plan as long as my file doesn't have any mention of the Wilcox's bullshit."

"There will be absolutely no mention of it, and I figure that Brewer isn't going to be as kind as you have been."

Davis got up and walked to the door, and motioned for Minor to head out. She followed him out of his office, watched as he walked over to Brewer and Diaz, and then the three of them walked back to Davis's office.

Entering Mercedes Rowen's information into the computer system was easier than Detective Minor had thought it would be. There was an open bench warrant from the Springfield court for Mercedes not showing up for court on a prostitution charge, so Minor added her name to the case as the contact instead of just the general police department number. The other positive was that Mercedes's fingerprints were in the system, so Minor could run the prints through the database for missing and unidentified persons. There were no hits, so she could let Porsche know that her sister was not a known dead person.

Tuesday May 17, 2022

Detective Elijah Greene had been undercover in a dog fighting ring for almost eighteen months now. He found the people that he had interacted with and the things they were doing reprehensible, but that was the job. Today, he was meeting with his handler to update him on the case and discuss how much more evidence they needed to gather before busting the ring. In order to protect Greene's identity, the two of them were meeting on a walking trail in a county park.

As they wrapped up their conversation about the dog fighting ring, Greene turned over the footage that he had captured with his cell phone.

"Do we, or any other agency, have someone else trying to infiltrate this ring?"

"Absolutely not. This investigation is a joint county, state, and federal case; there is no one else. Why?"

"A month or so ago, there was a strange interaction with a woman. She came to sell some puppies, and when I went to scan her fingerprints, we found that her hands had severe healed burns; thus, she had no fingerprints. She said it was because she was a victim of abuse who was on the run, but something felt very off to me."

"It takes a lot to obliterate fingerprints, so I understand why it would raise red flags. So, is this lady part of the dog fighting ring?"

"No, she isn't. Roger doesn't allow anyone into the ring without a full background check, which is why my cover has worked so well. While I am running the background checks for Roger, we get all that information on the people who are part of this criminal enterprise."

"What do you want to do about this mystery woman?"

"Nothing for now. When we wrap this case up, I will try to track her down and figure out what is really going on with her."

"Works for me."

24

Monday June 13, 2022

Minor waited until the dust seemed to have settled down a little in the detective bureau before heading back to see Commander Davis. She knocked and, when he looked up, said, "Sir, I need to speak to you about something."

He looked up and acknowledged her request with a nod of his head, which she took to mean come in and have a seat.

"Is this about the Wilcox situation?" he asked once she sat down.

"No, sir, it is about the Kelsey Learner case."

He didn't reply verbally, but Detective Minor could see some of the tension leave his face and body.

"Abe in Computer Forensics is done converting the cassette tapes to digital files and making the transcripts of the files. He told me that they were all personal messages for Claire and that there was no information about her abduction and captivity. Is there a procedure I need to follow prior to handing a copy of the digital files over to Claire Learner?"

"Have you listened to them?"

"No sir, I have not."

"Start with listening to all of them, and while you determine if there is anything of evidentiary value, I will contact Liza Reinhart in the DA's office. We will let her make the final decision as to how to handle handing over the files."

"Alright, I will start listening to them tonight."

"I think it can wait for tomorrow. Head home."

"Will do, sir. Have a nice night."

"Thanks, you too."

Kass Minor had no intention of waiting until tomorrow to start listening to the files. After talking to the commander earlier today, she went to the local technology store and purchased an external hard drive. Abe had already transferred the files, and the drive was sitting on her desk. She would take the drive home with her and start listening. Hopefully, within a day or two, she could turn the hard drive and all its files over to Claire and close the Kelsey Learner case.

******

Robert agreed to listen to the recordings with Kass, so that is how they spent their evening. Each recording was thirty minutes in length and, as Abe had told her, started with Kelsey telling Claire when to listen to them. After listening to each recording, they would take a break and discuss if either of them thought there was anything of evidentiary value. Many of the recordings made Kass cry, which she told Robert was the pregnancy hormones, but it was also the pain she could hear in Kelsey's voice and imagine Claire would feel when she listened to them.

It took them all evening to listen to all the recordings, and they both agreed that there was no information that a lawyer, whether defense or prosecution, would find to be something that should have been kept only for court.

"Do you think Claire will wait to listen to them when they are labeled for?" Robert asked Kass.

"I don't know. I think it would be really tempting to listen to them all at once and then go back and listen to them again when they are labeled for. On the other hand, it may be really hard for Claire to listen to her mom, so she may need to break it up."

"I have to say that I admire Kelsey Learner for thinking of making these for her daughter. She must have been terrified down in that container, but knew that she wanted her daughter to have a way to always stay connected to her."

"You're right. It is a wonderful gift under horrible circumstances."

Monday May 23, 2022

Eddie Learner sat on the small deck of his trailer, enjoying the early summer heat and sun. It was the only day he had off this week, and he planned to spend it outside. He watched as Jessie and James Adams raced by on their bikes and wondered if their mom, Trixie, was awake. She was the one reason he could be persuaded to spend time inside today, so he went into his trailer and grabbed a six-pack out of the fridge. Most people would frown on a beer at ten in the morning, but he worked second shift, and Trixie worked third, so their time clocks differed from most people.

Just before Eddie could knock on the door of Trixie's place, Jessie said, "I wouldn't do that if I were you."

"Okay, buddy, why not?"

"She's asleep and was really crabby before she headed to bed."

"Thanks for the heads up. I guess I will pack up my truck and go fishing."

"Umm, can James and I go too?"

"I am pretty sure your mom has told the both of you many times that you aren't allowed to leave the trailer park when she is sleeping. So, I am going to have to say no."

"But she means just us leaving, not with an adult. Plus, she knows you, and I would leave her a note."

"Sorry, it's not going to happen, but here's what I will do. Next time I talk to your mom, I will ask her if, in the future, when she is sleeping, if it is okay for me to take you and James fishing."

"Whatever," Jessie replied and rode off on his bike to find his brother.

Eddie thought about the kids as he packed up his truck and wondered how much longer it would be before they stopped following their mom's rules altogether. He thought about talking to Trixie about her sleeping while her kids were out and about with no checking in on them. But he decided it wasn't his place, plus what did he know about raising kids? It wasn't like he had any of his own.

25

Tuesday June 14, 2022

Staying up late was not something that was working for Detective Kass Minor anymore. After listening to all the recordings and talking them over with Robert, Kass had trouble falling asleep last night. Now, she faced a long day at the precinct and no caffeine. As she walked towards her desk, she could see that her voicemail indicator light was already flashing. Being busy was what she needed today.

The message was from the medical examiner, Dr. Reeves, asking her to come and see him at the morgue today. For a brief moment, Minor contemplated just calling Dr. Reeves because the smell of the morgue was not something her sensitive stomach would handle well. She decided that if she was going to learn to balance her career and motherhood; she needed to go to the morgue. The Green County Medical Examiner's office and the morgue were less than a half mile from the police department, so Minor decided to walk over.

Not being sure who her partner officially was, she taped a note on her computer screen regarding where she was headed in case anyone looked for her. The brisk walk helped to clear the fatigue, so she was feeling ready to face the malodor that she knew would hit her when she entered. She spoke briefly with the administrative assistant, who sat by the door and then was admitted to go talk with Dr. Reeves. The administrative assistant had told her that he was in his office, so Minor lifted a silent thank you to the heavens that she might be spared actually entering the morgue.

Knocking on the open door, Minor looked around Dr. Reeves' office and saw books and files stacked all around the room. The doctor looked up and said, "Oh good, you're here, Detective Minor. Come on in."

As she walked in, she was careful not to bump into anything as she hoped the doctor had some kind of system of organization that she simply did not see.

"Sorry, the place is such a mess. We are understaffed like everyone else, so things like filing and straightening up haven't been happening."

"No problem," Minor said as she took a seat across from Dr. Reeves.

"I have made a positive identification of the skeletal remains that were found in the container that the Adams boys fell into. It is Kelsey Learner per both dental records and DNA."

"Thank you for letting me know. What did you rule her cause of death to be?"

"Homicide by unknown cause. There is no obvious trauma to her remains. Still, there are signs of malnutrition as well as a lack of Vitamin D. Although I cannot be entirely certain, with the evidence that was collected along with Ms. Learner's remains, my educated guess is she died due to a lack of water."

"That makes sense and sounds like a horrible way to die."

"It is a long and arduous process but largely pain-free from what is reported in research. Do you want to inform her daughter of the identification, or would you prefer that I did?"

"She is aware that we preliminarily identified the remains as her mother based on the evidence at the scene. If you have time, I think you letting her know about the definitive identification would be best, so if she has questions, you might be able to answer them. Is that alright with you?"

"That is fine. Although I don't have very many answers to give, I will try to be forthright with her."

"Thank you. When do you think you will notify her? Because I am sure my commander will want to hold a press conference, and I absolutely don't want it to be until after Claire has been told."

"I have a family coming in to make an identification in the next half hour, and once that is concluded, I will call Claire Learner. Would you like me to call you when the notification has happened?"

"That would be helpful."

As Detective Minor walked back to the station, sadness for Claire occupied her mind. Each step of this case had left unanswered questions, but Minor hoped that being able to bury her mom would provide some solace to Claire. Walking back to her desk, she saw that the note she had written was right where she had left it. Crumbling it up, she threw it in the trash can before walking to Commander Davis's office. She had spent too much time in his office the last few days.

Commander Davis saw her coming and said, "Come on in, Minor," as she got to his office door.

"I spoke with Liza Reinhart, and as soon as you confirm that the tapes are personal in nature, you may release a digital copy to Claire Learner."

"Great, sir. I listened to the recordings last night, and I confirm that they are personal in nature. I also needed to let you know that Dr. Reeves has positively identified the remains as Kelsey Learner. He is informing Claire Learner this morning, and I am closing the case."

"Great job, Minor. I will coordinate with the Media Department to do a press announcement. You will need to be there, and we likely need to have Detective Wilcox there, too."

"Alright, sir, just let me know when and where."

Tuesday May 24, 2022

Mack Tiswell sat in the parking lot of the big box store and watched Lindsey flirting with the guy who was taking in carts. He knew if he asked her about it, she would deny flirting and say they were just talking.

When she had left him, he tried just to move on, but he knew they were destined to be together, so now he was having to try to woo her back. Mack knew that Lindsey's parents and her friend Claire had tried to poison her against him, but they were soul mates, and he just had to help her see that again.

The night that Lindsey had gotten hurt and her parents coerced her to leave him, Mack knew that he had gone too far, and he was sorry. The thing was, Lindsey knew that he hated when people walked away from him when they were talking. She had started the argument by not having dinner ready and then suggesting that they just order pizza. She knew that his work hours had been cut back, and that they were on a budget. When they started to argue, she told him that she would pay for the pizza even though she knew he didn't want a woman paying his way. When he told her that he expected dinner made, she had turned her back on him. He saw red and reached out for her. He just wanted to stop her from walking away.

Mack watched as she sauntered into the store like she didn't have a care in the world. He thought back to that night when he had come home to find her dad, Officer Dan Peterson, and his partner sitting in his apartment. Officer Peterson told him that Lindsey was returning her key, would no longer be living there, and there was a pending restraining order. Mack laughed when he mentioned the restraining order and then found himself face-first against the wall with his arm bent behind his back. Dan Peterson got close to his face and said, "Stay away from my daughter, or a restraining order will be the least of your problems."

His friends told him there were plenty of other girls out there and that he didn't need the headaches that Lindsey had brought to his life. Mack had tried to date others, but so many women were too arrogant and modern for his taste. Online dating and apps had a lot of liars on them, everything from their age, size, and having kids; it didn't seem honesty was something that most women on those sites believed in. He had been on one of those dates a few months ago when he saw Lindsey and her friend Claire walk by the restaurant window. They each were licking an ice cream cone and laughing their heads off. Seeing her made him realize that she was the only one for him, and that is when he devised his plan to get her back.

It had been easier than he thought to convince her to meet at the diner out of town to talk. All he did was send her a text and ask her to meet so that he could apologize, and she agreed. He had been trying to ease her back into their relationship, but he knew she wasn't sure yet; that is why he said he would go to counseling once they lived together again. He never intended to go to counseling, but she didn't need to know that. Lindsey just needed to be back with him where she belonged.

26

Tuesday June 14, 2022

The police department media department set up the press conference for that afternoon. When Detective Minor arrived at the staging area, she saw that Claire and Joe Learner, Detective Wilcox, Commander Davis, and the media relations person, Jennifer Hurtz, were standing around. She asked, "Are we ready?"

"No, we are waiting for Commander Wilcox and Chief Anderson to arrive. Chief Anderson will be making the statement, and we will not be taking questions." Commander Davis responded.

"We will enter the following way: Chief Anderson, Commander Davis, Commander Wilcox, myself, Detective Minor, Claire and Joe Learner, and Detective Wilcox. I will speak first to introduce Chief Anderson, with the two commanders standing next to him and the rest of us creating a row behind them." Ms. Hurtz told all of them.

The chief walked in, talking with Commander Wilcox, "Hurtz, have you briefed everyone on the plan?"

"Yes, sir, we are all set."

"Good, let's go." The chief turned and walked through the door to the press room.

Detective Minor watched Joe Learner take Claire's hand as they began to walk towards the door. Claire had already started to cry silently, and Kass felt tears welling up in her eyes. She was glad that she wouldn't be answering questions today because she was not sure she could trust herself not to break down.

As they all got on stage, Ms. Hurtz introduced the chief, and he stepped forward, saying, "Thank you all for coming. During an unrelated investigation, the remains of Kelsey Learner were found and have been positively identified. Paulina Moore is wanted for questioning in this case as well as by the Federal Bureau of Investigation regarding the kidnapping and murders of seven men. If any member of the public has information on the whereabouts of Paulina Moore, we urge you to call the FBI tip line. Our condolences go out to the family of Kelsey Learner during this difficult time. We will not be taking questions."

The chief turned and walked out, followed by everyone else on the stage. Once they were back in the staging area, he turned to Detective Minor and said, "Good job, never giving up on this case." He then shook hands with everyone and walked out.

As the others left, Minor stopped Claire and Joe Leaner, saying, "Claire, I am so sorry for your loss. This is a portable hard drive that contains all eleven of the recordings that your mom made for you. They are labeled based on the start of each recording."

"Thank you, but I don't understand the labels."

"Please, just listen to the first one with your dad when you get home, and then, if you still have questions, call me."

Joe Learner reached out and took the drive from Detective Minor, "Thank you, detective. Claire will call you if there are any lingering questions."

Tuesday May 24, 2022

Michelle was packing her suitcases when she heard a knock at the door. It was a sound that she so rarely heard that it took her brain a minute to register what she was hearing. Looking out the peephole, she could see a young man in an ill-fitting suit standing on the front step. She opened the door, leaving the chain in place.

"May I help you?"

"Yes, ma'am. I am sorry to disturb you; I am Detective Leon Harris from the Lake Geneva police department." He held up his identification and badge for Michelle to see.

Her heart had begun to beat rapidly, and she wondered, *Is this how it ends? I imagined a bunch of FBI agents kicking down my door, not some rookie detective knocking and introducing himself.*

"Would it be possible for me to come inside and ask you a couple of questions about your neighbor?"

Relief flooded her body as she realized this visit had nothing to do with her. "Of course, let me just unchain the door." She softly closed the door, removed the chain, and reopened the door to let the detective in. When she did, she noted there were several police cars in front of her neighbor's condo, and the front door was wide open. She had been so wrapped up in figuring out where she was going and what to do about her condo that she had not even realized there was a commotion next door.

Detective Harris followed her into the living room and sat down. "Ma'am. What is your name?"

"Michelle Brooks. What is going on over at Rose's place?" She only knew her neighbor's name because mail for her had been misplaced in Michelle's mailbox on more than one occasion. The woman had stopped by once looking for her missing cat but admitting to not knowing the woman would stop the detective from asking his questions and from Michelle figuring out what was going on.

"Ms. Brooks, how well do you know Rose Callahan?"

"We have had coffee a few times and chatted. I wouldn't say we are friends, but

we are friendly. Is Rose, okay?"

"Rose Callahan is missing. She did not report to work yesterday or today, and when an officer went to do a welfare check, he noted that her front door was not closed all the way. When was the last time you saw Ms. Callahan?"

Michelle thought back in order to try to figure out when she had seen her neighbor because, in reality, other than the incorrectly placed mail and occasional waving, she did not know the woman.

"I saw her Saturday as she was leaving home, and I was getting back from buying groceries."

"What time was that?"

"I would say about six o'clock in the evening, maybe a little after."

"Have you been in her condo in the last few weeks?"

"Yes, we had coffee about a week ago."

"Did you notice anything unusual in the past few days? A person you didn't recognize in the area, or maybe a car you had never seen before at Ms. Callahan's place."

"No, sorry, I didn't."

"Are you aware if Rose was seeing anyone?"

"As far as I know, she wasn't dating anyone."

"Is there anything else you can think of that might help our investigation?"

"No, I am sorry. I can't really help. I hope Rose is okay."

Detective Harris stood up, reached into his pocket, and handed Michelle a business card. "Please call me if you think of anything else?"

Michelle nodded, walked the detective to her front door, then locked the door again and went to sit down.

A missing neighbor who was around her same age and height was like a gift from the universe. All Michelle had to do was figure out a way to get into Rose's place, find her birth certificate, and a new identity for Michelle would be born.

27

Tuesday June 14, 2022

Claire sat in her dad's car, clutching the hard drive that Detective Minor had given her. Her mom's last words were on here. She was so torn because she couldn't wait to hear her mom's voice and what she had wanted Claire to know, but on the other hand, she knew her mom well enough to know these recordings were her way of saying goodbye. Even though she knew it was over, Claire could still not bring herself to say goodbye.

Her dad pulled up to the house that Claire had lived in with her mom and now shared with Lindsey. He started a pot of coffee while Claire went to get her laptop and wireless speaker. After everything was set up, Claire opened the hard drive on the screen of her laptop, and the two of them started at the list of rccordings.

"I guess we just start with the first one," Claire said as she opened that file, and her mom's voice filled the kitchen.

Hi Claire, it's mom. I know that if you are listening to this tape; the police have found my body, and you know that I am gone. When I figured out that I was probably never getting out of here alive, I decided to make these tapes for you. I love you, Claire, with all my heart and soul. Being your mom is the thing I am proudest of in my life. I know that right before I was taken; we weren't always getting along, but I hope you know that is just a normal part of a mother-daughter relationship. I never doubted for a moment that you loved me, and I hope you never doubted my love, either.

I told the police on the first side of this tape that I had no idea who took me or why, and that is true. I will probably never know what craziness led this to be the way my life ended, and I don't know if you will ever have those answers either. What I want you to learn from this is to trust your gut. I say this because I felt like someone was stalking me in the weeks before I was taken, and I didn't report it to the police. Maybe this all could have turned out differently if I had.

I cannot imagine how sad and upset you must feel. I have some degree of empathy because I lost my mom when I was young, too, but the difference was that I had the opportunity to say goodbye to her. Her battle with cancer was difficult, but it gave us the opportunity to talk about so many things. I am sad that you and I will never have that opportunity. These tapes are my way of memorializing the things I want to be sure to tell you. Most of all, they are a way for you to always know how much I love you.

The day I became your mom, my whole world shifted. I will never forget staring into your little face as we lay together in that hospital bed the night you were born. You were a perfect baby, from your little tuft of hair to your cupid's bow of a mouth and teeny perfect little fingers and toes. Staring at you, I suddenly understood the sentiment of parents who said they would die for their children. My only solace as I sit here and wait to die is that it isn't you locked down here.

Watching you grow from a newborn to a toddler, the delight on your face each time you conjured a new skill, brought me so much joy. The day you walked on your own for the first time, your face beamed with pride, and then you sat down and clapped for several minutes. That is how you approached life: working hard to get what mattered to you and appreciating it when you achieved your goals. I was always so proud of how hard you worked and your ability to be confidently humble.

No matter what you put your mind to, you have accomplished it, and I am so very proud of you. Claire bear, yes, I know you asked me to stop calling you that but indulge me just a little because, in my heart, you will always be my Claire bear. Please don't let what happened to me stop you from living your life, and that includes finding someone to love.

I am going to record tapes for you for certain occasions in your life that I imagine we would have talked about. Whether you choose to listen to all of the recordings when you first get them or on the occasions, I have made them for, it is up to you. Please do whatever your heart tells you is best, and know that if I could be there for you, I would be.

Love always-Mom

P.S. If you are wondering how I recorded this without sobbing, know that it took me four tries to do so.

Joe reached over, hit the end button, and handed his daughter another tissue. They both sat in silence, contemplating what they had just listened to, until Joe finally said, "Do you want to listen to another one?"

"No, Daddy, I want to go lay down."

"Are you going to be, okay? Do you want me to stay?"

"I will be fine. Hearing her voice and the fact that she spent her time making these recordings for me is just a lot to process. You don't need to stay. I will text you later."

"Okay, honey. Let me know if you need me to come back. Love you."

"I love you too, daddy. Thank you for all your support today."

Joe watched as his daughter walked slowly up the staircase towards her bedroom. He sat remembering when they had baby gates on those stairs to stop Claire from getting hurt. He wished there was a simple solution like that to stop his daughter's pain now.

Wednesday May 25, 2022

Michelle had to get into Rose's condo, but the police were still all over the place.

What she needed was a convincing lie to have a reason to go over there. She had thought back over the last few days to come up with something that would be a reason to talk to the detective again. Then it hit her, Rose's cat. That stupid cat had been at her backdoor meowing up a storm the other morning. She knew it was Rose's cat because it had escaped one other time, and Rose had stopped by looking for it. In fact, that was the only conversation she had ever had with her neighbor. Rose had described the cat in detail as an orange and white tabby with a part of its right ear missing, wearing a collar with red roses on it and a bell attached. Rose had called the cat Chrysanthemum, which had struck Michelle as an odd name for a cat.

Walking next door, Michelle was hoping to be able to swipe a key to the place so that she could later let herself back in. Luckily, it was cold enough that no one would question why she was wearing gloves because there was no way she was getting near an active police investigation without them on. Counting on all of these condos being set up the same way, with the garage door leading into the kitchen, she planned to walk in through the garage. The Lake Geneva police were making it easy on her since the garage door was wide open; she just walked right in and softly knocked on the door to the house. When no one answered, Michelle slowly turned the knob and eased open the door. The vast majority of people would keep their keys right by their garage door, and sure enough, she was in Rose's kitchen, and there was a shelf with hooks right above the countertop, with a set of keys on it. Michelle quickly reached out, grabbed the keys, and put them in her pocket; then she loudly said, "Hello, is anyone here?" She knew it was a strange thing to say since there were four police cars at the condo, but she thought acting a little spacey might help her get away with entering the condo.

A uniformed police officer came practically sprinting into the kitchen; he took one look at her and said, "Ma'am, you cannot be in here. It is a crime scene."

"Oh, I am so sorry. I was looking for Detective Harris. He came to see me yesterday and said if I thought of anything else, that might help find Rose to let him know."

"Ma'am, I am sure Detective Harris meant for you to call him not to enter her residence looking for him. He isn't here. I assume you have his card."

"Yes, I do have his business card."

"What did you say your name is?"

"I didn't say, but since you're asking, it is Michelle Brooks. I am Rose's neighbor, and I am worried about her."

"That is understandable, but I need you to leave now. Please be sure to call Detective Harris to talk to him about what it is you remember."

"Sorry for any rules I broke; I was only trying to help. I will go home and call the detective."

******

Michelle chose to call the detective's work number instead of his cell, betting that she would get his voicemail, and she did. She left her message and hoped to never hear from Detective Harris again.

"Hi, Detective Harris, this is Michelle Brooks, Rose Callahan's neighbor. You stopped by yesterday and told me to let you know if I thought of anything else to let you know. Early this morning, I remembered that Rose's cat Chrysanthemum was by my back sliding door Sunday morning. She didn't let that cat out of the house and was really worried the last time he got out. I am sure if she was home, she would have come by looking for the cat."

Now it was time to gather her materials for tonight when she planned to let herself into Rose's condo. She had bought some Night Vision goggles when she thought they might be helpful with her investigation into the dog fighters. She set them on the charger and got out her headlamp, gloves, mittens, hat, and coat. To pass the time, she went back to packing since she was meeting with the real estate agent tomorrow about renting out her condo.

At dusk, Michelle headed out to walk the loop that went behind the entire condo complex. She walked the loop often so no one would think it was out of the ordinary. With each pass, she saw fewer police vehicles at Roses. When the last one pulled away, Michelle walked back to her condo, being sure to take off one mitten and drop it just behind Rose's condo. She let herself back into her condo, turned on lights and the radio, then grabbed the night vision goggles and put the headlamp in her fanny pack along with the penlight. When she arrived at Rose's back door to the garage, she inserted the key and turned the knob. She would be turning on no lights just in case someone noticed, but really, she didn't need to because the goggles made her able to see what she needed to.

There was a piece of crime scene tape across the door to the house from the garage, but it was easy enough to detach it on one side and let it hang down. Once inside, Michelle headed straight down the hall to where the two bedrooms and two bathrooms sat. The first room she looked in was clearly Rose's bedroom, but the room across the hall was a home office. Michelle closed the door behind her and made sure the blinds and curtains were closed. Looking around, she saw a desk with a two-drawer filing cabinet at one end. That was the logical place to start, so she pulled open the top drawer and turned on her headlamp. The very first file was labeled *Important Documents,* so Michelle took it out and set it on the floor.

Flipping through the documents, Michelle felt like she had hit the jackpot as she took out Rose's birth certificate and social security card. She was almost ready to put the file back when she saw a large white envelope labeled Adoption Documents. This piqued her interest as she wondered, *Whose adoption? Because,* as far as she knew, Rose had no kids. She slid the documents out of the envelope, noting that everything was clipped together. The first item was a birth certificate for Chrysanthemum Rose Farmington, which Michelle compared to Rose's birth certificate. There were two glaring differences: the name on the first one she had taken out was Rose Lynn Callahan, and the names of the parents were different on each one.

Michelle instantly knew that she could never have imagined such a great turn of events: Rose was adopted. Unclipping the birth certificate, she came to the adoption papers, which were of no interest to Michelle, so she set them aside. There was a social security card for Chrysanthemum Rose Farmington, so Michelle compared the numbers, and they weren't the same. Having all that she needed, Michelle slid the papers she did not want back into the envelope, put it back in the file folder, and then returned Rose's birth certificate and social security card.

It would take her a while to wrap her head around being named Chrysanthemum, but it was a small price to pay for a new, clean identity. Michelle turned off the headlamp, put her night vision goggles back on, and headed to the kitchen. She hung Rose's keys back up on the hook where she had found them this afternoon and then let herself out, putting the crime scene tape back right where she had found it. When she got back to her garage, Michelle swapped the night vision goggles for her headlamp and walked back to get her mitten. It was just one more precaution in case anyone had seen her near Rose's place; she had simply been looking for her mitten.

28

Thursday June 16, 2022

A positive of working for the police department that had investigated your mother's disappearance and recovered her remains was that no one questioned her need for days off. It had been two days since the press conference and listening to the first of her mom's recordings. Claire hadn't been able to listen to any of the other recordings, but had played the first one many times over. She knew that she needed to get up, shower, and leave the house today. Lindsey had checked on her before she left to go to the gym, and Claire had promised to get out of the house today.

Going to her mom's favorite diner in Stafford and eating the meal that her mom always ordered seemed like a good outing. It had always been a joke between them that if her mom got to choose where they were going out to eat, it would be the Stafford diner. Never mind that it was twenty minutes away in a little town that you would miss if you blinked while you drove through it. Claire pulled into the parking lot and was surprised to see Lindsey's car. She knew for sure that it was her friends car because Lindsey had a thing for stuffed kittens and kept them in her back window. Claire wondered *what Lindsey was doing here. She told me she had to work.*

Claire got out of her car, but before she started walking towards the restaurant, her eyes were drawn towards the front window. She saw Lindsey sitting with Mack; they were holding hands and laughing. Claire wondered *what is going on? Why would Lindsey be with him?* There was no way Claire was walking in there. She needed to talk to

Lindsey privately about this, but before she did that, she snapped a few pictures. One was of Lindsey's car and one of her and Mack sitting together. When she confronted Lindsey, there was no way she was going to let her friend gaslight her by saying that it wasn't her at the diner.

As she drove back home, Claire kept hearing her mom's voice in her head saying, "Trust your gut." Her gut told her that Lindsey was in danger, but that her friend wouldn't see it that way.

******

Lindsey parked her car in front of the house and sat there, staring forward. Lunch with Mack was going great today, and she had been feeling optimistic about their relationship. Until Mack brought up moving away together, it seemed not only did he want them to live together, but he wanted to do so far away from Lindsey's family and friends. He had a cousin in Colorado who had told Mack he could get him a job there. She had told Mack that she didn't want to move away, and he had gotten upset. He told her that she was going to have to choose him or her family and Claire because she couldn't have all of them. Then he stormed out of the diner.

Deciding that sitting in her car wasn't solving anything, Lindsey headed inside and was surprised to see Claire in the kitchen.

"Hi, are you feeling better?"

"A little. I know my mom didn't make those tapes for me so I would sit around and marinade in my sadness, so I got up and went to do something that made her happy."

"Oh, yeah, what did you do?"

"I drove out to the Stafford Diner to have an open-faced turkey sandwich. That was her favorite place and what she always ordered?"

Lindsey felt the dread building in her body as soon as her friend had said the Stafford Diner. What were the chances that they had missed each other and Claire didn't know what Lindsey had been up to?

"How was it?"

"I don't know because I never went in, and do you want to know why?"

"I am pretty sure I already do, so say what it is you have to?"

"Really, Lindsey? You are back with Mack after all that went down between the two of you."

"You know what, Claire, first of all, you don't know what went down between us, and second, I didn't ask for nor do I want or need your advice. You have never been in a relationship. You are too afraid to get hurt to even try. I am an adult, and I am free to date whoever I want to."

Claire was stunned into silence. It wasn't like she had expected Lindsey to be happy about being confronted, but the attack had been personal.

"What about the restraining order? and What will your parents say?"

"I am going to take care of the restraining order, and if you were ever my friend, you wouldn't even think about letting my parents know."

Lindsey stormed up to her bedroom, wondering *if Mack was right. Do we need to move away in order to be happy together?*

******

Admonishing himself for losing his cool, Mack Tiswell finished another beer and read the text he hadn't yet sent to Lindsey. He hated apologizing, especially when it wasn't his fault because, once again, Lindsey was being unreasonable. She was becoming even more unmanageable, and he knew that was because she lived with Claire. He should have approached the moving to Colorado discussion differently by just asking Lindsey to go on a trip there with him. She had not needed to know that he had no intention of either of them returning to Missouri.

Staring at his phone was not a solution to this issue, so he wrote the text.

Mack: Lindsey, I am sorry I lost my cool. I love you and just want us to build a happy life together.

The text was immediately marked as read, and Mack watched as the three dots indicating that Lindsey was texting him back appeared.

Lindsey: I love you, too, and want us to be happy. Let's talk about Colorado.

It was more than Mack had hoped for. He jumped up and did a fist bump with the air. He was going to get her back, and this time, there would be no breaking up.

******

Claire quietly retreated to her bedroom and took out her laptop and headphones. Hopefully, listening to her mom's voice would help her calm down. As she pulled up the files of the recordings her mom had made for her, she intended to listen to the first one again. Then her eyes slid down the list and settled on tape number ten: When you are facing a hard choice. That was what was happening right now, because she knew that she either had to risk her friendship with Lindsey or the very real possibility that Mack would hurt Lindsey again. Her gut was telling her that she needed to go tell Mr. and Mrs. Peterson what was going on so they could help her intervene in the situation, but she knew if she did, Lindsey would never speak to her again.

Cueing up recording number ten, Claire settled on her headphones and prepared to listen to her mom's wisdom.

Thursday May 26, 2022

Michelle walked out of the realtor's office with a smile on her face. The realtor was sure he would have her condo sell quickly. He had bought her story that she was headed to Los Angeles to care for her dying mother and had no idea when she would be back. She would be able to receive offers and sign all the necessary paperwork from anywhere that had internet. The money from the sale would be wired to the account she provided. She also told him a story about how her ex-husband was an abusive cop, and the relator had agreed to call her if anyone came looking for her and not to give her number to anyone.

Walking back to the condo, Michelle hoped that she would never find herself back in this small town in Wisconsin or, for that matter, anywhere in Wisconsin. She had taken care of all the loose ends in her life that she knew of but had also long ago accepted to never say never. Since she was leaving all the furniture in the condo, just like she had bought it two years ago, she had to put her suitcase and her bin of documents into her car, and she would be off.

There was only one police car by Rose's condo today. It seemed like the police reaction was already cooling down. Michelle wondered if this was how the investigations into the seven men that she and Raul had procured had gone. A swift and intense initial investigation that quickly burned out when there was no trail to follow. Maybe missing people weren't all that important to anyone but their family and friends.

******

She stood up, stretching as far as the chain would allow her; she wondered how someone would end up chained in a shipping container with a bucket for a toilet. Mercedes Rowen knew there were five other women in here with her because she had talked to all of them, so at least she was not alone. All five were like her drug addicts, who had turned to prostitution to feed their habits. *That's the thing,* Mercedes thought, *I know how I ended up here. I remember the first time I got high by taking Granny's pain pills. I remember the first time I traded sex for more drugs, and when I decided to leave Springfield so that at least when I slept outside, it was never cold.*

The other thing that Mercedes knew was that she had agreed to a too-good-to-be-true deal a month ago. A man in a nice car had pulled up next to her and asked if she did weekend-long bachelor parties. She had never done something like that and was going to tell him no when he took out a roll of money and told her she would be paid three thousand for the weekend as well as possible tips. It was too much money to pass up, and she had agreed. She went to the hotel room she shared with two other sex workers and packed her meager belongings in the backpack her Granny had bought her for her junior year in high school. The backpack was ratting with one broken strap, but Mercedes would never want to get rid of it.

She had walked back to the black town car, gotten in the back, and taken the glass of wine the man offered her. Her next memory was waking up in this container and realizing she was in deep trouble. Every few days, the back of the container would open, and the same man from the car would walk in, usually with another girl. He would hand each girl a bag of food and jug of water and then clean up around the container. The one-time Mercedes had tried to kick him when he got close, she had gotten the worst beating of her life. Two weeks ago, the women all woke up to being jostled towards the front of the container as it tipped up. Then the container leveled off, and they could feel the motion of moving, followed by an almost soothing rhythm of driving down the interstate.

Mercedes felt the container tipping again and wondered; *Where am I? and Why am I here?*

School Days

Secrets in the Heartland Series Book 4
School Days
Andrea Heckner

Dedication:

We all need a ride or die friend who gets us and our need to at least write about killing people. I will not name names to protect the innocent or the guilty but to my ride or dies this one is for you!

School Days-Book Four of the Secrets in the Heartland Series was originally published in 2024. The version contained within this compilation is an edited version with no major changes to the story line or characters.

1

Prologue

Revenge is a dish best served cold. Suppose the English Proverb from the eighteen-hundreds is to be believed. In that case, revenge is most satisfying when the avenger has had time to devise a plan of vengeance that has been thoroughly planned and is either long-feared or unexpected.

Chapter 1

Saturday, February 3, 2024

Frank Waters parked his truck in the same spot he did every day for work. The difference was that today was not a workday; it was a Saturday, and the school district administrative building was deserted. He sat and looked at the building for a moment, allowing himself to enjoy the beauty of the brick and glass structure. It was such a stark difference to the former administrative building downtown that was run down. When the city approached the school district a few years ago with the deal to buy the land and partially constructed building for a dollar, the community was supportive of the idea. The several million dollars that it took to finish the building had brought a less than enthusiastic community response. The city officials' hope that by having the district office built on the outskirts of town, would bring other businesses to build out there too had yet to come to fruition. So, the building sat alone in the area except for the large cemetery that was kitty corner.

He knew that his wife Marcia's office building parking lot would be a totally different story this morning. As a tax accountant, she had left early this morning for work, and he knew that she would likely work late as well. Marcia had been grumbling about being too old to keep working the hours that tax season brought with it, but Frank was always happiest during this time of year because she did not come up with things for them to do as a couple. Of course, he was smart enough not to have ever told Marcia that.

Walking to the back door, he thought about the perks of his current position, including having unfettered access to this and all the buildings in the district. If anyone ever reviewed the alarm data and video, they would assume that he was working, and if they asked him, he would be honest that he had misplaced his wallet. After an extensive search of his house and truck, he had decided he needed to check at work. He had worked for this school district since his college graduation, first as a Physical Education teacher, then as a dean of students, and later as a principal. He had moved to being a district administrator ten years before and had held a myriad of different jobs. His favorite position so far has been as the Director of Student Relations and Activities for the past six months. Mostly because no one was really sure what he was supposed to be doing, so he did as little as possible and got paid very well for it.

Taking the elevator to the second floor, he strolled past the Superintendent and Assistant Superintendent's offices on the way to his own. He thought about the brief time he spent in both those positions and how he felt that he had done a better job than the people who currently held the positions. Each time one of them came up with a new directive or plan, he reminded himself that they would move on like so many before them had. He flipped on the light in his office and began searching for his wallet on his desk. Not immediately finding it, he sat in his chair and reached into the crevices to see if it had fallen into one of them. Grabbing his cell phone, he turned on the flashlight and shone it under his desk. Sure enough, in the far back corner sat his wallet. He could see the lines the vacuum cleaner had made as it pushed the wallet as far as it could go before hitting the desk's back facade.

Getting down on the floor, Frank crawled under the desk and grabbed his wallet. As he clamored back out, he never realized that he was not, after all, alone in the office. The first blow with the tire iron struck Frank at the base of the neck and skull, incapacitating him immediately. He was dazed and did not register the feeling of being tugged by his ankles the rest of the way out from under the desk. The five blows to his skull that came next finished the job that the killer had come there to do. Frank Waters was dead. Justice had been served.

******

Marcia Waters walked into her dark house, wondering where her husband Frank was. It was after ten at night, and she thought he would be home, but his truck was not in the garage. After mixing herself a drink, Marcia sat down in the recliner in the living room and turned on the television while she waited for Frank. She would not stay up very long because she had to go back into the office in the morning. She called and then texted Frank, but the call went to voicemail, and the text remained unread. If she cared more, she would be angry about this, but as it was, she felt apathetic as she drifted off to sleep.

May 1992

Walking across campus, Frank Waters thought about how much he was going to miss this place. College had been the best four years of his life. When he was recruited to play football here, his parents and high school coach, and it seemed the entire community had been so proud; the four years here had gone by in a flash of parties, girls, and football. He was graduating in a week with a degree in Physical Education and had a job lined up teaching in Springfield.

Going back to Missouri would bring major changes to his lifestyle, but he had sown his wild oats and was ready to settle down. His high school girlfriend, Marcia, had gone to college right there in Springfield and lived at home. The six-hour one-way trip between their campuses had made their relationship over the last four years very hands-off. A long-distance relationship had worked well for Frank; He could party and live the frat life without his girlfriend seeing what was going on.

The college had been cracking down on fraternity and sorority parties, so Frank's fraternity Psi Sigma Epsilon had been moving their parties around. The party tonight was off campus at Charlie, the frat treasurer's parents' lake house. Picking up the kegs of beer was Frank's contribution, so now he was driving the four kegs toward Charlie's house. The younger guys on the team would lug them inside and get them set up in the buckets of ice. The frat had arranged a party bus to pick people up on campus and bring them out here. Each person had to have a numbered ticket to get on the bus, with each ticket being good for two admissions onto the bus. The guys in the frat each had ten tickets to give out, except for the senior leaders, who had unlimited tickets to give out.

By the time the party had officially started, Frank and his buddies were several drinks in and were already having a great time in the pool. They watched as girls walked out of the pool house in their bikinis, which left little to the imagination. At each of these parties, Frank picked out a new girl to party with, and tonight would be no exception. A young blond walked towards the pool with a friend, perking his interest, so he jumped out of the pool and went over to her. Introductions were made, and Frank went to get Jenny and her friend Heather a drink. He had learned early on at these parties the key was to shower these girls with two things: attention and drinks.

Hours later, Frank led Jenny towards the bedroom that Charlie had given him the key to. He woke up to find Jenny getting dressed and crying, so he got out of bed and went to walk her out. When he touched her arm, she screamed, "You raped me! Let me go!" and then she ran from the room. There was no way that Frank was going to let her leave saying that shit about him, so he went after her. He saw her running out the back door and into the pouring rain. She must have been turned around because instead of heading towards the driveway, she headed into the woods with Frank right behind her.

Chasing her into the woods, Frank wondered how he would calm her down and help her remember that she had been fine with having sex with him when they headed upstairs. He would have moved on to another girl if she had been a prude. He could barely see her as the rain poured down, but saw her stumble and fall, giving him the opportunity to catch up. He reached down to help her up, and she began screaming again, saying, "Stay away from me. I am calling the cops." Frank saw red; there was no way he was going to let this girl ruin his life. He grabbed Jenny and slammed her down on the ground. She went limp, and he put his hands around her throat, squeezing. It seemed to take forever, but it was more like six or seven minutes until she completely stopped breathing. Walking back to the house, Frank felt numb and wasn't sure if it was from what he had just done, the rain that had soaked him to the bone, the alcohol, or a combination of all of them.

He looked down and noticed that his swim trunks and feet were covered in mud, so he decided to jump into the pool. After dunking himself several times, Frank got out and walked to the pool house. He found several passed-out people sleeping there, but no one stirred as he made his way to the shower. After washing up, Frank put on one of the extra pairs of swim trunks that Charlie's family kept in the pool house. He picked up his wet swim trunks and headed into the house to get a couple of hours of sleep. The rain was continuing to come down in sheets, and Frank saw that his muddy footprints leading up to the pool had completely washed away.

Later that morning, all the guys from the frat house cleaned up, packing all the trash and remnants from the party into their cars and trucks. Charlie did not want there to be any sign of the party. He said the housekeeper would be back on Monday morning and she would finish cleaning, but that they needed to make it seem like only a few people had been there. Driving back to campus with a car full of garbage, Frank felt sick and the smell of old beer and pizza was making it worse. He was more than ready to put this entire weekend behind him.

******

Finals week on the campus of a large university is chaotic with no one having their usual schedule, students moving out of their dorms after they took their last exam, and graduating seniors welcoming guests who poured into town for the festivities. It was Wednesday before Jenny Clark was reported missing; her roommate had been sleeping at her boyfriend's apartment and had come back that morning to pack up her half of the dorm room. When Jenny did not return to the room on Wednesday night, her roommate went to their Resident Assistant who called campus security. After campus security had established that Jenny had not taken her finals scheduled for the last three days, they called the local police department.

The detectives talked with Jenny's friend Heather, who had told them about going to the party together. She told them Jenny had gone off with Frank Waters, and Heather headed back to campus on the party bus. She and Jenny had no classes together this semester, so she had not noticed that Jenny wasn't around. They were supposed to have lunch together that Thursday after both of them took their last exam. Then they were both heading home for the summer, but instead, Heather was talking to detectives, and Jenny was missing.

Frank Waters was supervising the move-out happening at the Psi Sigma Epsilon fraternity house when the police arrived. He did not hesitate to talk to them, saying that he and Jenny had hooked up, and then she had left. He stated that he thought she took the party bus back to campus but had not actually seen her leave. No one else that the detectives interviewed had seen Jenny leave the house, and the party bus driver was unsure if he saw Jenny or not. Armed with a warrant, the police department searched the house the party was held at and the pool area where the party had taken place and found nothing. The search of the woods behind the house began after they finished inside the house, and Jenny's body was found after only a few minutes.

The medical examiner had determined her cause of death to be strangulation, with a time of death somewhere between midnight and six on Sunday morning. But there was little evidence that could be collected because of the twelve-plus hours of rain the morning she disappeared and the time that it had taken to find Jenny. Although the lead detective suspected that Frank Waters may have played a role in Jenny Clark's death, but with no evidence, the case went cold.

2

Sunday, February 4, 2024

The cell phone alarm woke Marcia Waters up at six in the morning in the recliner, where she had dozed off the previous night. Making her way to the primary bedroom, she wondered again where Frank was, but it was not the first time he had stayed out all night without telling her where he was. She had put up with his antics for thirty years, but she was too old to continue to live a charade. Now was not the time to worry about him; she had to get to work. They were so far behind, and as a partner in the firm, she needed to concentrate on work, which was pretty much what she had done their whole marriage.

Before leaving for work, Marcia packed a bag and sent her sister, Corine, a text about staying with her for a few days. Corine was no fan of Frank's and had been urging Marcia to leave him almost from the beginning of their marriage. Marcia had stayed for their kids, along with the foolish hope that Frank might one day change, but his wandering eyes and other body parts never ceased. In their thirty-two years of marriage, they had talked to counselors and priests, and Frank would stop straying for a while, but whatever it was that drove him to be unfaithful was never dealt with, so inevitably, it never lasted.

Their respective careers had flourished; they had a beautiful home and had raised two productive and seemingly happy kids. Marcia wondered if the reason neither their son nor daughter had married yet was because they had witnessed their parents' cold marriage. Until a few years ago, she had been unsure that either of them knew about their dad's infidelity and the impact of it on their mom. It was not a subject that she was ever going to bring up to either of them. Closing the door to the house, she wondered how long it would take Frank to notice she had not returned home from work. Unlike him, she would answer her cell phone when he called.

******

Kass Matthews walked into the bedroom that she and her husband Robert used as a supposed shared office.

"Emma is finally down for her nap. I could use another cup of coffee. Do you want one?"

Robert looked up from his computer and said, "Yeah, but how about you take a seat and I will go make them?"

Kass looked around the office while Robert was in the kitchen. All the walls had been turned into a case board for one single case, Dr. Paulina Moore. She knew that her husband's fellow agents thought Robert was obsessed with finding the fugitive, and they had not even seen this room. He spent a lot of his free time trying to put together leads and looking at unsolved murders from around the country to see if he could connect them to Dr. Moore.

When they first bought this house, Kass had been eight months pregnant and much more concerned with setting up the nursery than the office. During the first six months of their daughter's life, she barely noticed how much space Robert was taking up in the home office with his investigation. It really wasn't until he told her he had taken a week of vacation time and was heading to Wyoming to talk with a detective who might have a lead that she, too, accused him of being obsessed.

It had been their first real fight as a couple, and in the end, Kass and baby Emma joined him on the road trip. The trip had turned out to be enjoyable for the family, even though the lead did not pan out. While driving back, she and Robert had discussed his pursuit of Paulina Moore, and Kass acquiesced that she did understand as an investigator, not wanting to have a cold case. The fact that she had been working in the cold case unit for three months at the time made her acutely aware of how much an enemy time was on solving an investigation.

******

Chrysanthemum Farmington walked along the beach, enjoying the early morning quiet. Having been here almost two years, she hoped that Gulf Shores, Alabama, could be her home for a while longer. The people were friendly but not nosey, and with the tourist trade bringing unfamiliar faces through town all the time, it was easy to blend in. She had found a small apartment to rent over the garage of an older man. He had poor vision and worse hearing, so it was very unlikely he would be an issue for her. The apartment had come fully furnished along with all the utilities, including cable and internet, which was ideal for her situation.

The few people in town she talked to called her Chris, which was how she introduced herself. She had been Chris long enough now that if someone said that name, she would respond. Of course, if someone called for Michelle, she also always turned and looked, and because Paulina was such a rare name, if someone had said that, she would run.

As she left the beach, she walked to the sidewalk to get in her car and head back to her apartment; Chris observed a young girl walking with her backpack on. The girl was likely walking to school, and it bothered Chris that there was no adult with her. Didn't her parents realize how precious their daughter was? A van pulled behind the girl and parked. As she watched from across the street, a man jumped out of the passenger side, sliding through the back door, and grabbed the girl. Before Chris could react, the van sped away.

Stunned, Chris watched in horror as the van made a U-turn and headed toward where she was standing on the sidewalk. Not knowing what else to do, she took out her cell phone and took pictures of the van. First, the front and license plate, then the side and back as it passed her. The van never slowed down, and the driver did not seem to even notice her. For a fleeting moment, Chris thought about calling the police to report the crime, but self-preservation stopped her. She thought, No, I have to handle this on my own.

Getting in her car, Chris headed the same way as the van and saw that it was stuck by a train passing through just a mile away. As she closed the gap on the van, the train gates opened, and the van sped through. Chris stayed on their tail until they pulled into the garage of an old, dilapidated house on the edge of town. Driving by, Chris began to formulate a plan for freeing that little girl and dealing with the scumbags that took her.

Leaving the girl there was not ideal, but entering the house with no plan and no weapon would put both the girl and Chris at risk. Driving back to her apartment, Chris thought about her daughter Lynn and how much different life would have been if Lynn had lived. The girl those scumbags had taken was about the same age as Lynn had been when she died. Saving this girl would allow Chris to do what she couldn't for her own daughter. It was like a second chance.

March 2004

Lance Clark had been ten years old when his big sister, Jenny, had been murdered at the end of her sophomore year of college. Jenny's death had ruined their family, with their mom becoming deeply depressed, their dad turning to alcohol, and then their eventual divorce. Lance had not understood as a child why his sister's murder had gone unsolved, but now he was going to find out. At twenty-two, Lance had finished college, was in his first year of law school, and was determined to have his sister's case reopened. He had spoken to the cold case detective at the Champaign County Sheriff's office and been informed that unless there was additional evidence, his sister's case would not be reopened. That was when he requested her file and decided to see if there was anything he thought had been overlooked.

The copy of her cold case file had arrived this morning, and he was going to read every bit of it, no matter how hard it would be to know the details. Opening the envelope, he was surprised that the file was not thicker. A total of fourteen pages made up his sister's murder investigation, with another ten pages of pictures. The end of his sister's life had been reduced to so little, and it made Lance wonder how hard the initial investigators had worked to solve her case.

As he read through the case file, it made Lance sad that his sister had been missing for over four days before anyone noticed. On the form that had moved her case from active to cold, there was a note written that the delay in reporting her disappearance and finding her body had created a major problem for the investigators. Lance learned that his sister had been found in the woods dressed in her bikini with a sundress over it and one jelly shoe still on. The other jelly shoe was found stuck in the mud a few feet from her body. Because there had been several days of heavy rain, there was no DNA or other trace evidence to be found. The medical examiner had put her time of death as sometime early Sunday morning, with her cause of death being manual strangulation, but she had her head bashed in first. There was evidence that she had been sexually active in the hours prior to her death, but no way to determine whether or not it was consensual. Once again, because of the delay in finding Jenny, there was no way to determine if she had been drinking or using drugs.

Lance took a walk around the block after reading about the initial investigation and his sister's autopsy. Several interviews had been conducted that he needed to read through next, but it was harder than he thought it would be to delve into the details of Jenny's death. Before she left for college, his sister had been like a second mother to him, often taking care of him after school when their folks were at work. She was a happy, high-spirited teenager who often blasted pop music and danced around the house. Jenny never acted like taking care of Lance or having him tag along on her adventures was a burden.

Stopping to pick up a coffee and sandwich before heading back home, Lance wondered how different all of their lives would have been had Jenny lived. The house had been quieter once she went to college and fell silent after her death. Someone had taken Jenny's life and was still out there, living their own. He wondered if the person had killed other women, too, or if Jenny had been his only victim. Did this man, because, let's face it, a man had killed his sister, have any remorse for what he had done? Most of the interviews were brief, with people having little to no helpful information, but one name kept coming up over and over: Frank Waters.

It would seem that Frank Waters was the last person Jenny had been seen alive with, and he did not deny being with her. There was only one interview with Frank Waters, and Lance had to wonder why the detectives had not looked more closely at him. Lance started up his home computer and connected to the internet; listening to the dial-up noises, he thought about how his sister had never even used the internet. Opening the Webcrawler search page, Lance typed in Frank Waters' name. The top of the interview page contained information that had been redacted prior to sending Lance the file, so he had little to go on other than the man's name. It was likely that Frank Waters was Jenny's age or a couple of years older, so he used that to narrow his search.

Finding that the search netted him mostly information about a writer who had been an elderly man living in the southwest when Jenny died, Lance decided that a trip to the campus in Champaign-Urbana to look at old yearbooks would be the next step to figuring out who the Frank Waters in his sister's murder case file was.

3

Sunday, February 4, 2024

Chris parked her car and ran up the stairs to her apartment; she knew just the look she was going for. Having kept her body in great shape, she knew that men hardly noticed her age because they were too busy looking at her assets. A sports bra, spandex short shorts, a bouncy ponytail, and a full face of makeup were the perfect get-up for this occasion. After Chris checked her appearance one more time, she grabbed the finishing touch, the gun she had stolen from the late Dr. Keith Rodane.

It was a risk to use this gun again, but she had never replaced it, and she had to have a gun to save this girl. She parked down the block from the house, walked up to the door, and started crying at the same moment she started knocking on the door. Chris had perfected crying on demand when she was a young girl because she had discovered the power of tears with her dad. Her dad couldn't deny her anything when she cried, and that had continued to be true with every man she had ever turned the waterworks on for.

The door slowly opened, and a rough, dirty-looking man peered through the crack formed as the chain lock held the door secure.

"Do I know you?" he barked out as he peered at Chris.

"Please, you have to help me. My boyfriend kicked me out of the car, and he said I better run and hide, or he will find me and kill me."

The door closed and then reopened fully, with the man motioning for Chris to come in. "Come on in, honey; my brother and I will be happy to help you."

As Chris walked through the door, following the man who had opened it, she pulled the gun out of her fanny pack. As they entered the living room, she saw the man who had kidnapped the little girl sitting on a dirty recliner surrounded by junk food wrappers and beer bottles.

He turned around and said, "Ty, who the hell is this broad?"

The man who had let Chris in, who was evidently named Ty, stepped aside so his brother could fully see who he had let in. As he did, he turned around and saw that Chris had raised her gun and was pointing at him.

"What the hell are you doing?"

"You two scumbags took a little girl this morning, and now karma has come back for you."

"Just put that gun down, and we will straighten this out."

"My mom used to listen to old country music, and one song sticks in my mind for this occasion. It went something like this: you go to know when to hold them, when to fold them, when to walk away, and when to run. Boys, you should have run."

Chris fired two shots, which hit each man dead center in the forehead. She had been going to the shooting range since she was twelve years old, first with her mother and then on her own. Thirty-plus years of practice had paid off. Both men lay dead on the living room floor. Now she had to find that girl, and the screaming that she heard coming from the basement was the best place to start looking. There was a padlock on the basement door, so Chris shot the lock and opened the door.

As she made her way down the dark, rickety stairs, the screams grew louder, and Chris braced herself for what she might find at the bottom. When she got to the bottom of the stairs, she saw a string hanging down and pulled it. It turned on a single bulb swinging from the ceiling. It provided a small amount of light, but was enough to lead her to the next bulb on a string. After pulling the next light on, Chris saw the girl sitting on a mattress in the corner. She was wearing only a pair of panties and was crying and screaming. When the girl looked up and saw Chris; she said, "Please don't hurt me."

Chris untied the girl as she replied, “I am not here to hurt you. I am here to get you out of here. Do you know where your clothes are?”

“No. One of those men took them.”

“Did they hurt you?”

“Not really. They grabbed me, brought me to this house, then down to this basement, made me take off my clothes, and took pictures of me. Then they tied me up and left me down here. I fell asleep but woke up when I heard shooting.”

“Yeah, that was me. Now, let’s get you out of here and back home.” Chris replied, then grabbed a small blanket that was lying on the bed and wrapped it around her.

The girl grabbed a backpack that was near the bottom of the steps, and by the time they got to the front door, the girl had shed the blanket and was wearing a t-shirt and shorts.

As they walked out of the house, Chris said, “By the way, what is your name?”

“Delilah, my name is Delilah Young. Thank you for getting me out of there.”

“You’re welcome. So, Delilah, what is your address? I am going to drop you off at home, but you can’t tell anyone anything about me.”

“You can just drop me off at the beach.”

“No, no, I can’t. How old are you?”

“I’m eight and a half years old, and I am begging you not to take me back to where I live.”

“I think we need to talk. Are you hungry?”

“I am so hungry. Can we get McDonalds?”

Driving through the line to pick up the food she had just ordered, Chris could not stop herself from thinking about her daughter Lynn. Before Lynn had gotten sick, she had been becoming a fiercely independent child and had been wanting her parents to let her ride the bus to school instead of being dropped off. Chris wondered if that was what happened to Delilah. Did she beg her parents to let her walk to school? Why would she not want to be taken back home? Was she afraid that they would never let her be independent again? Chris needed answers, and she needed them fast because driving around town with a child she did not know in her back seat was a recipe for disaster.

April 2005

Watching Frank Waters had become an obsession for Lance Clark, which led him to transfer to the University of Missouri to finish law school. Law school was brutal, and he should have spent all of his non-class time studying and writing papers, but instead, he often found himself making the drive to Springfield to watch Frank. Lance had been surprised when he found Frank living a seemingly normal life. Frank was married, had two middle school-age children, and worked as a high school Physical Education teacher.

Lance had driven to Springfield a dozen times since figuring out that this Frank Waters was the one connected to Jenny's murder. The first time he had come here, he expected to find that Frank Waters was a low-life criminal who had been hurting and killing women his entire adult life. Instead, he found this high school gym teacher who shuttled his kids around in a mini-van. After a few trips that netted him the same information, Lance began to question if Frank Waters was actually his sister's killer. After all, it didn't seem possible to have murdered someone and just put it behind you. He decided to make one more trip just to confirm that there was nothing to connect Frank to Jenny's murder.

Arriving in Springfield just in time to follow Frank out of the high school parking lot, Lance followed and watched as Frank went through what he had come to know was his normal routine. Pick up the kids, run a couple of errands, and then head home. As Lance sat across the street watching Frank's house, he decided it was time to move on and was preparing to head back to Columbia when Frank's garage door opened. Leaving was not the usual pattern, so Lance followed Frank's mini-van as he dropped each kid off at a different house and then headed to a local bar.

In all the times he had followed Frank, the man had never gone out without his wife or kids, so the bar was not expected. Lance parked across the parking lot from Frank's van and walked into the bar. Frank was with a large group of people, several of whom Lance recognized from the high school parking lot. This appeared to be a co-worker get-together, which Lance knew was common in many workplaces. Sitting at a booth close to the door, Lance ordered a burger and a beer and watched Frank and the group he was with for a couple of hours. As the group began to shrink, he saw Frank casually put his arm around a woman who was not his wife. Frank leaned over and whispered something in the woman's ear, and she laughed. To Lance, her laugh sounded both nervous and intoxicated, but he saw Frank smile at her like he had just told the best joke.

After a couple more rounds of drinks, the woman excused herself and headed to the front door, with Frank close behind her. Lance was closer to the door, so he got up, held it open for both of the departing patrons, and then walked out behind them. He watched as Frank steered the woman towards his van by her elbow and then as he swooped in to kiss her. The woman ducked her head and stepped away from him. Lance heard Frank shout, "What's your problem, Courtney? I thought we had a good thing going?"

Lance stepped closer so he could hear Courtney's response.

"Frank, I told you when I got engaged that I was done fooling around with you."

"And I told you that I was not okay with that. This arrangement is mutually beneficial, and I am not just talking about the great sex. Do you honestly think you would have been made the head girl's basketball coach your second year of teaching if it wasn't for me?"

"What are you saying? That I am only a coach because I slept with you?"

"I am saying you scratched my back, and I scratched yours. I would hate to see you throw away all your future career opportunities over a little thing like marriage."

"A little thing? I take my commitment seriously, even though I know you don't. I am done discussing this with you. Goodbye!"

Lance watched as Courtney ducked under Frank's arms and started striding across the parking lot, with Frank close behind her.

"Don't you walk away from me! This is over when I say it is over!" Frank yelled as he reached out and grabbed Courtney by both arms.

Lance was horrified by what he was watching and wondered, Is he going to kill her like he did my sister? Is this what happened to Jenny? Did she try to walk away from Frank Waters? Not knowing what else to do but knowing that he could not stand by and watch Courtney get hurt, Lance called out, "Hey, is everything alright?"

Watching as Frank and Courtney both stopped moving, he waited for one of them to reply, and was not surprised when he heard Frank's voice.

"We are fine. She has had a little too much and is refusing to not drive."

"I think you should let go of her and let her speak for herself."

"Buddy, this is not your business, and I think you need to go back inside or get in your car and leave."

Lance noted that Frank had indeed let go of Courtney and turned towards Lance. At this opportunity, Courtney ran to her car and got in. The slamming of her car door made Frank whip back around and run towards her car. She had the car in reverse before he got there and was backing up quickly. Frank had to jump out of the way to not get hit, and he banged his fists on her car as it passed.

Lance took this opportunity to get into his car and followed Courtney out of the parking lot to see which way she turned. He pulled up to the curb just beyond the entrance and waited to see which way Frank would go. When Frank's van came flying out of the parking lot and turned in the opposite direction Courtney had headed, Lance followed him. Frank drove straight home, and Lance sat across the street, watching several more hours before deciding it was time to head home. However, he knew he would be back. After what he had just witnessed, he was sure that Frank Waters was capable of murder.

4

Sunday, February 4, 2024

Chris and Delilah sat on a bench looking at the ocean while Delilah polished off her large meal, and Chris drank her diet soda.

"Alright, tell me why you don't want me to take you home?" Chris said when she saw Delilah's eating begin to slow.

"It isn't really my home. It is a foster placement, and it is awful."

"Two questions: first, where are your parents? And second, how is the foster placement awful?"

"My parents were killed in a car accident right before my birthday, and the foster people don't care about anyone but themselves. They lock us in our room and leave for long periods of time, and we have to do all kinds of chores."

"Who is we? Are there other kids there, too?"

"There were two other girls living there when I was placed there, but they are gone, and now it is just me. Last night, the Simmons, my foster parents, went out to party and must have forgotten to put the padlock on my door. I realized early this morning that it wasn't locked, so I packed my stuff in my backpack and left. I doubt they have even noticed yet."

"I am sure they have called the police by now."

"No, they haven't."

"Why do you say that?"

"These are not the call the police kind of people. They don't even let me go to school, and they keep their foster kids locked up unless they are making us work. My social worker dropped me off at this place and came back one time. I haven't seen her since that visit, so it isn't like they have to worry about her knowing I am gone. Plus, those two guys who took me have been to the house before, so they know my foster people."

Chris was stunned, which was not a thing that happened often to her, but she could not believe that no one wanted this little girl. Children were meant to be loved and protected, not locked in rooms, and made to feel like they were not important.

"Where were you headed when those men took you?"

"I have twenty-three dollars, so I was going to take a bus wherever that much money took me."

"Do you know where the bus station is?"

"Not exactly."

"Hmm, that would have been an issue. I also don't think the people at the bus company would have let a child buy a ticket and ride the bus out of town."

"Really, why do people treat kids like we can't do stuff?"

"Adults are supposed to protect children, and that includes not letting them ride the bus out of town alone. We need a plan, since you don't want to go back to your foster placement."

"I can just live with you."

"What? No, that is not a good idea."

"Why not? Are you some kind of serial killing psychopath?"

"It's complicated."

******

Sophie Waters tried to call her dad again. It wasn't like him not to call her back, but she left him two messages yesterday and another one this morning. They had talked every Saturday since Sophie's divorce. Like every other difficult time in her life, her dad was there for her, even if this time it was over the phone more than in person. Living in Florida was a dream come true for Sophie, with the only drawback being that she was so far away from her dad.

Calling her mom was not in Sophie's plans, but now she was worried. Her mom was testy during tax season and would likely not appreciate being called, but Sophie had to be sure her dad was okay. Growing up, her dad was the one who took Sophie and her younger brother Kyle to and from school and all their activities. He was in the stands at every sporting event, concert, and play either of them had taken part in. When Sophie had struggled academically in high school, it was her dad who sat with her every night, going over the material and helping her to keep on top of her work.

Now, here she was at thirty years old, calling her mom because her dad wasn't answering his phone. As the phone rang, Sophie prayed that her dad was okay. She wasn't ready to deal with losing a parent. The conversation with her mom was short, with her mom saying that she hadn't seen Frank since Saturday morning, but that she wasn't worried about him. Sophie was worried, so she decided to fly home. As a nurse, she worked a four-days-on-four-days-off schedule and finished her last shift this morning.

After booking a flight for the next morning, Sophie tried her dad's phone again and left him a voicemail. She let him know that she was coming home tomorrow and asked him to pick her up at the airport in St. Louis. She prayed that he would be there.

May 2010

After graduating from law school and passing the Bar Exam, Lance accepted a job at the District Attorney's office in Springfield. It was not the job he had imagined when he dreamed of becoming a lawyer as a teenager and during undergrad, but since most of his law school years were spent driving back and forth to Springfield watching Frank Waters, a job in town, was ideal. Plus, working at the District Attorney's office gave him the ability to keep tabs on Frank Waters in ways that he had not had access to before.

Frank continued to have no criminal history and was moving up the ranks in the school district, but Lance knew he was not a good person. There had never been any new evidence for the detectives in Champagne to reopen Jenny's case, but Lance knew that Frank had killed his sister. He may never be able to prove that in court, but he could keep a close enough eye on Frank to catch him in another criminal act and make sure that he at least paid for that.

The condo that Lance had bought in town gave him the perfect excuse to drive by Frank's house, both on his way to work and on the way home. So Lance had timed his schedule around Frank's so that he often followed him as both men went to work in the morning and then drove by as Marcia Waters arrived home most evenings. Since moving here and starting daily surveillance, it had become clear to Lance that Frank was a serial philanderer and a heavy drinker. Today, when he logged on to his computer at work, there was an alert waiting for him. Frank Waters had been arrested and cited for disorderly conduct last night.

Lance opened the police report and read the minimal information that was contained in it. There had been a fight at the same bar that Lance had followed Frank to four years ago between Frank and a man named Tom Clayton. Both men had denied wanting to press charges, and so the officers issued the tickets and sent them both home. There was no mention as to what had led to the fight, but Lance intended to find out.

On his lunch hour, Lance drove to the home of Tom and Courtney Clayton to follow up on the fight and provide Tom the opportunity to press charges against Frank. As soon as Lance saw the name of Tom's wife, he deduced that it was the same Courtney who Frank had followed out of the bar four years ago. After introducing himself, Tom Clayton led Lance into the kitchen and sat down with him.

"I appreciate you following up, but like I told the cop last night, I don't want to press charges. Frank and I have known each other awhile, we were both drinking, exchanged words, and then I punched him."

"You punched him first?"

"Yeah, I'm not proud of it, but I am going through a rough time. My wife Courtney moved out last week and is talking about filing for divorce. I'm heartbroken, and drinking made that worse."

Even though Lance felt like he already knew the answer, he wanted to see if Tom would tell him how the two things were connected. "Okay, so how does that tie in with the fight you were in?"

"Before Courtney and I were an item, she was involved with Frank, and last night, he made a derogatory remark about her not being that good in bed. It pissed me off, so I punched him."

Lance knew that he would not be able to bring a case against Frank Waters and just had to be satisfied for the time being with the man getting the snot beat out of him. He thanked Tom for his time and wished him luck with his marital situation before heading back to the office.

5

Monday, February 5, 2024

Porsche Rowen pulled up to the Springfield School District administrative office with one minute to spare before her shift began. Working as a custodian at the school district had not been her dream, but beauty school had not gone well, and this was a better job than the box factory. She was surprised to see a truck in the parking lot already, as she usually was the first person to arrive at the building. Even more surprising was finding the back door not fully closed and the alarm system off. Deciding that it was not a good idea to walk into the building, Porsche called her supervisor, who told her to wait in her car.

Fifteen minutes later, the head of security for the district, the superintendent, and a police car pulled into the parking lot one after another. Porsche got out of her car and spoke with them about what she had found when she arrived. The head of security assured her she had done the right thing and that it was likely an inadvertent slip-up that had left the building unsecured. Sitting back in her car, Porsche wondered if her supervisor was going to let her adjust her timecard when she finally got to go inside and punch in.

She looked up from playing on her phone when three more police cars arrived. Looking over at the back door, she realized that the three men who had initially responded were still standing there. They had not entered the building. As she watched the newly arrived police officers draw their weapons and enter the building from all different doors, she thought, *Wow, they are really taking this seriously*. It took less than five minutes for one of the police officers to come out and begin having what looked like an intense conversation with the district personnel, who were still standing at the back door.

The officer then walked up to Porsche's car, and she once again got out of it. He took her official statement about what she found this morning and asked her what she had touched, which amounted to the door handle on both sides. She explained that she had been ready to use her electronic key fob to unlock the door when she saw that it was not fully closed. She pulled the door open and walked to the alarm box. That was when she saw that the alarm was off, and she called her supervisor, who had told her to wait in her car. The officer was not willing to answer any of her questions about what was going on, and as he walked away, her phone began ringing. Her supervisor was on the phone and told her she would work at the high school that day and that she could head over there now.

******

Today was Detective Kass Minor's first day back in the Major Crimes Division of the Springfield Police Department. She had spent the last year working in the Cold Case Division, which she had requested to be moved to after her maternity leave. Kass had planned to stay there at least until her daughter, Emma, started school. However, the recent shakeup in the police department had resulted in, among other things, her involuntary transfer back to the Major Crimes Division.

Like most shake-ups, it began with one person complaining to the right person, who, in this case, was the Attorney General. An investigation into allegations of falsified detective exams, preferential treatment, and discrimination had resulted in Commander Wilcox taking early retirement and his son, Detective Wilcox, resigning from the department altogether, as well as her former commander, Davis, taking early retirement for his role in the scandal. Detective Ronnie Brewer was promoted to the position of commander of the Major Crimes Division. Minor liked Ronnie Brewer and felt that he was going to be a good boss.

After dropping her daughter off at daycare, Kass was driving towards the station when her phone rang. Surprised that Commander Brewer was calling her already, she checked the time before answering the call. She wasn't late, so this must be about a case.

"Minor, here. How can I help you, Commander Brewer?"

"Morning Minor. I'm not sure I am used to the whole commander thing, so just call me Brewer, as always. I need you to meet your new partner, Detective Nichols, at the Springfield School District building. We have a dead body, and it looks like it is a homicide."

"Well, that is one way for me to start back."

"Yeah, welcome back. Either you or Nichols should call me as soon as you know anything. I already have the CSI team and the medical examiner headed over there as well."

"Will do."

Ending the call, Kass turned towards the school district administrative offices. This case would be a true test of whether she could juggle being a detective in Major Crimes and a mom. After parking her car, she fired off a text to her husband, Robert, to let him know that she had a case. Luckily, he was not involved with an active investigation, so he would be able to pick up the slack while she put in long hours.

******

Chris stared down at Delilah sleeping on her couch and couldn't believe that she had let the little girl stay with her, but neither of them could come up with a better plan yesterday. So, they agreed that Delilah could stay with Chris unless there was a news report or an Amber Alert or they came up with a plan. One thing Chris knew for sure was that if Delilah was going to stay with her, they could not stay in Gulf Shores for long. She had decided that they would wait three more days to be sure that the police were not looking for Delilah and then head out to a new location.

Last night, while they ate pizza and watched television, Chris tried to get more details about what Delilah had been through. The girl had been vague, and Chris could not decide if she was deliberately trying not to tell her things or if she just did not understand everything because she was eight years old. Chris had learned enough to know the couple that Delilah had been placed with did not provide any care and had no business being in charge of children. She wondered if they had sold Delilah to those men. It seemed awfully convenient that the men grabbed her off the street on the morning after the foster parents stayed out all night and left Delilah's room unlocked. When she combined those two facts with Delilah's assurance that the men had partied at the Simmons' house in the past, in Chris's mind, it led straight to a set-up.

Chris turned on the TV to watch the morning news as she drank her coffee. The top story was about two known local drug dealers being found shot to death in their home. The pictures of Delilah's kidnappers that the news displayed were obviously mug shots and did the men no favors. The reporter said that both men had long criminal histories and that a source close to the investigation had told the news channel that the working theory of the Gulf Shores police department was that they were shot in a drug deal gone wrong. The police department issued a statement in which they said: "The investigation is ongoing, and there is currently no danger to the public."

There was no mention of Delilah, and the police seemed to be heading in a direction that had no chance of leading to Chris. As the news program moved on to other stories, Chris allowed her mind to wander. What would life be like if she raised Delilah as her own? Would it be too hard on Delilah to live on the run? Was it unfair of her to even consider taking the girl with her?

******

When Cherry Lane decided to get her Master's in Social Work and then accepted a job with the Alabama Department of Child Protective Services three years ago, she never imagined the crushing caseload. In theory, each case worker was supposed to manage twenty-five to thirty families, but they were chronically understaffed. The lowest caseload Cherry had managed was forty-eight, and she currently had fifty-two families to case manage. To make matters worse, she had cases in Baldwin and Mobile counties, and there were over three hundred and fifty miles between her two farthest families.

Driving to Gulf Shores to check on Delilah Young had been on her to-do list for months, and today, she was going to do just that. She had four cases in Gulf Shores, so she would check in on all of those families while she was here. The Simmons', whom she placed Delilah with six months ago, were long-time foster parents with the agency, and there had never been an issue with them. That was a large part of the reason Cherry had made do with phone check-ins for Delilah. There had been something about the Simmons' that just seemed off to Cherry, and when she described them to her mentor, the other social worker was surprised by the description. Her mentor had placed kids with them throughout the years and said the way Cherry was describing the Simmons differed greatly from how she remembered them.

The drive to Gulf Shores had been problem-free, and she was able to finish listening to her current audiobook. As she pulled her car up to the foster home where Delilah lived, she checked her emails on her tablet just to be sure nothing was pressing that she needed to respond to. In the hour the drive had taken her, she had received seventy-six emails, but almost all were either spam or messages she was simply carbon copied on. She sent a quick text to her supervisor letting her know she was heading into the Simmons' as it was procedure, then grabbed her stuff and walked to the front door.

After knocking and ringing the bell several times, she heard someone yell, "Coming" from inside the door. Jordy Simmons yanked open the door wearing boxer shorts and a white t-shirt. He nor the clothes appeared to have been washed in days.

"Yeah, what do you want?" Jordy asked as he looked Cherry up and down.

"Mr. Simmons, I am Cherry Lane from the Department of Child Protective Services. I am here to see Delilah and do a welfare check."

"Sorry. I just woke up. Come on in and have a seat in the living room while I go get dressed and send Debbie down to the living room."

As Cherry walked into the home and looked around the living room, she was surprised by the odor of cigarette smoke and the general disarray she was seeing. This was not how the home had been when she brought Delilah here, nor when she had come for her announced visit a month later. Cherry wondered what was going on here? She used her tablet to take some pictures of the kitchen and living room and noted how long she was made to wait. Sixteen minutes after Jordy Simmons headed upstairs, he and his wife, Debbie, walked into the living room.

Although Jordy had cleaned himself up a bit, both of the Simmons looked rough, and Debbie immediately began talking.

"I'm so sorry. We have both been sick with the stomach flu, so it might be better if you come back another day."

"Mrs. Simmons, you have been a foster parent for over ten years, so surely you know that I can not do that. Once I start an unannounced visit, I have to finish it. Please, just have Delilah come down here, and I will talk with her and the both of you."

"Oh, Delilah isn't here. She is at school."

"What? When she was placed here, we agreed that she would be enrolled in the Alabama Virtual Academy and that you would oversee her learning. You are being paid an additional monthly stipend for that. When did she start going to school?"

This time, it was Mr. Simmons who answered, "Delilah hated that virtual school business, so we sent her to Lincoln Elementary down the street. She wanted to be around other kids her own age. I know it was wrong to keep taking the extra money, but things have been tight here since I lost my job eight months ago. I apologize."

Something was very wrong. It should have been impossible for the Simmons to enroll Delilah in school without Cherry signing the paperwork and providing records. CPS had custody of Delilah as they did all kids in the Alabama foster care system.

"Alright, we will work out the details of her schooling later; for now, I will walk around the house and check on the living conditions. Then I will head over to Delilah's new school to check on her."

Both of the Simmons simply nodded and sat down on the sagging couch in the living room. As Cherry walked through the house, she took more pictures of the less-than-stellar living conditions. She was startled to see that the room that Delilah shared with two other foster girls was devoid of any signs that three kids lived in it. All three beds were stripped bare, and a single dresser sat empty beside the closet, which was also empty except for two wire hangers. Even more startling to Cherry were the holes on the outer door frame that clearly had once held a clasp lock in place. *Why would the Simmons have installed a lock on the outside of the children's door?* Cherry wondered as she headed back towards the living room.

She was torn between confronting the Simmons and finding Delilah to verify she was okay. When she saw no signs of the girls living there in any other part of the house, her decision was made. She walked out of the house without saying a word to the Simmons and drove the three blocks to Lincoln Elementary School. After talking with the school office staff and learning they had never heard of or seen Delilah, Cherry stumbled back to her car. She could hear her blood coursing through her veins, and her head felt like it was going to explode in panic.

Delilah Young was missing!

May 2014

Marcia Waters walked from her attorney's office back to her own after meeting with him to discuss the probable outcomes that divorcing Frank would bring. She had waited to even consider this until both of their kids graduated from high school and moved out. Now that their daughter was a junior in college and their son was in the Army, Marcia did not see a reason to keep up the pretense of being married. That was until she talked with her attorney and realized just what it was going to cost her. Her attorney had told her that Missouri judges divide marital assets based on an equitable split and that among the factors that a judge may consider for this was the conduct of the parties during the marriage.

She could not prove his multiple affairs over the years, so she would have to seek a no-fault divorce and thus split everything with Frank. So, her attorney told her it was highly likely that Marcia may end up getting less than fifty percent since she would be the one filing and was a higher income earner.

While walking, she searched her memories for the first time that she realized that Frank was not the wonderful guy she and others thought he was. They had started dating their junior year of high school and dated throughout college. Frank had been a great boyfriend throughout all that time. He was always doing sweet, romantic gestures like leaving her notes, sending her mom flowers, or always not wanting to be the first one to hang up when they talked on the phone. It was like a switch flipped when he moved home to Springfield after college graduation, and they got married. That summer before their wedding in August, Marcia remembered thinking that it was just the stresses of moving, getting married, and starting a new job that had Frank so on edge. She realized now that he had never gone back to the sweet, loveable young man she had fallen in love with.

Twenty-two years had passed, and she had done her best to make their home a happy, safe place for their kids to grow up, but she had also stopped trying to have a loving relationship with Frank. Since that part of her life was a bust, she had poured her energy into her career as a tax accountant. She had been mortified when Frank showed up drunk to the dinner celebrating her making partner five years ago. It had been the water cooler talk around the office for weeks and the last time she had invited him to anything dealing with her work.

There was no way she wanted Frank to benefit from her financially any more than he already did, so she had told her attorney that she was not ready to file for divorce. Her sister, Corine, would be disappointed in her decision, but that was something that Marcia was willing to live with. When she got home that evening, she moved all of Frank's belongings to the guest room and informed him he would not be sleeping in their bed ever again. He hadn't even seemed fazed by her words or actions and had simply gone back to watching a baseball game on television in the den.

6

Monday, February 5, 2024

As Claire Learner pulled up to the Springfield School District Administrative building in the CSI van, she realized despite having lived almost her entire life in Springfield; she had never been here. The building looked to be only a few years old and was larger than she had expected. *How many people does it take to run a school district*, she wondered as she parked?

This would be the first case that Claire would be the lead technician on, so she wanted to make sure she did everything by the book. She took out her police department-issued tablet and opened the application for logging case information. After signing into the app, she pulled up this current case and navigated to the evidence collection tab, where she signed herself and her team in with the date and time. The rest of the team met her at the back of the van, and they unloaded the supplies and equipment they needed.

There was a vestibule area by the front door, where she had been directed to set up the supply station. From this point forward, anyone who entered the crime scene would wear full gear that included gloves, goggles or a face mask, booties, and a jumpsuit. The less contamination of the crime scene, the better. They would already need to gather forensic information from the officers who had responded to the scene, as well as any civilians who had entered the building prior to the discovery of the body.

The two detectives, Kass Minor and Ethan Nichols, walked into the vestibule as Claire was finishing setting up the supplies. They had both received an alert from the app that the CSI team was there and knew that they needed to come down and suit up.

Claire greeted both of them and was super happy to see Detective Minor. They had not had a chance to work together before Minor had moved to the Cold Case division. Detective Minor had worked on her mother's case and was the one who had finally found her mom's body and closed the case. Claire shared a bond with her that neither could fully explain.

"Everything is ready to go, and my team is collecting evidence from the likely victim's truck, the parking lot, and the backdoor area. Then we will head up to where the victim is."

"Sounds good. Both Nichols and I were up there to see the scene but did not step into the office, as one of the responding officers had already confirmed the victim was deceased. He is logged in as the only one who breached the crime scene, and all of his forensic details should be in the system."

"Alright, I'm going to head up and take pictures before the medical examiner arrives. I know he is delayed because of the major accident on the interstate, but we can get a lot of work done prior to his arrival."

Minor and Nichols followed Claire up to the office where the victim was. Once the responding officer had confirmed that the man was deceased, he left the room without touching anything else. The truck in the parking lot had been identified as belonging to Frank Waters, and the office the victim was found in was assigned to him as well. Now, they needed to see if they could confirm who the victim was. Claire took pictures as they made their way upstairs; the stair rails and elevator buttons would be dusted for fingerprints as well as the floors vacuumed, and the material collected would be examined for hairs and fibers.

So far, there was no sign outside of the office that a crime had been committed there, which told Claire that whoever the killer was, they had either been well prepared or very lucky. Arriving at the office of Frank Waters, they observed the feet of a man sticking out from the edge of the desk as well as cast-off blood spray on the walls and ceiling surrounding the desk. The smell of decomposition hit them with its nauseating waves of odor. There was a clean spot on the carpet in the pattern of dried blood that likely indicated where the killer had stood. This was a brutal and messy scene, and Claire knew that the killer would have had blood on them from the commission of the crime.

The victim lay face down in a pool of blood, which had dried, so the responding officer had not tracked any of the blood as he checked the man for signs of life. Claire wondered why Officer Peterson had even bothered, since the odor alone told them that the victim had been dead for at least a couple of days. They would not turn the body over until the medical examiner arrived, so for now, Claire got to work photographing the scene.

Detectives Minor and Nichols walked around to the other side of the desk and crouched down to get a better look at the body. In one of his hands was a wallet, which was presumably his, so Minor motioned for Claire to join them on that side of the desk.

"Please take a picture of his hands and the wallet so that I can retrieve it and make an initial identification."

After taking the requested photos, Claire went back to the photo procedure she had been using. She took photos from left to right and up and down at each crime scene and used several points of reference within the room, such as the door, window, and desk, to help orient where the photos were shot from. Her team had checked in and was now collecting evidence from the stairs and elevator. They would methodically work their way from both the elevator and the stairs until they reached the office that Claire and the detectives were working in.

******

Cherry Lane ended the call with her supervisor, Pam Drummond, as she pulled into the parking lot of the Gulf Shores Police Department. After reading her the riot act about just how bad this was going to look for Cherry and the entire department, Pam had told her to file a police report and ask the police to go back to the Simmons' home with her. Pam was also going to make a few calls in order to be sure that Cherry's report was taken seriously right away and to find out where the other two girls who were supposed to be living with the Simmons were.

After Cherry had asked at the front desk of the Gulf Shores Police Department to make a report regarding a missing eight-year-old child, it seemed that everything went into hyper speed. She spoke with two detectives, who made a couple of calls and then informed Cherry that they, as well as two uniformed police officers, would accompany her back to the Simmons' house. Nothing in her training had prepared Cherry for dealing with this. The kids on her caseload were her responsibility, and she had failed Delilah. She was in no condition to drive, so she rode over with the Detectives Fisher and Jackson.

When they arrived at the Simmons' house, Cherry pointed out to the detectives that the Simmons' minivan was no longer in the driveway.

"Ms. Lane, we need you to stay in the car while we make sure that the house is secure." Detective Fisher said as he parked.

Cherry watched as the detectives and police officers walked around the house and then to the front door. It seemed that the front door was not all the way closed because as soon as Detective Jackson knocked; the door swung open. Ten minutes later, Detective Fisher walked back to the car.

"There is no one in the house. It looks like they left in a hurry. The forensics team is on the way. In the meantime, please come inside with me so you can tell us if you notice anything missing from your visit earlier."

"Was there any sign of the three girls living there?"

"The bedroom was as sparse as you told us, and the only sign that kids ever lived here were some boxes in the basement. We haven't gone through the boxes, but they each are labeled with a name, and there is one on the floor at the bottom of the stairs labeled Delilah. That box is open, and from what I saw, it has clothes and possibly a blanket."

Cherry began to cry silently as she followed Detective Fisher into the house. She could not imagine being a social worker anymore if she even still had a job after this. Walking around the house, Cherry noticed that it was even more disheveled than before, with drawers and doors open and papers all over the dining room table.

"When I was here this morning, the house was a mess, but the drawers and doors were closed, and those papers were not all over the table. I took some pictures on my tablet when I was here. Do you want to see them?"

"Absolutely, the pictures may be of assistance. When we get back to the station, I will have you share them with us. Alright, let's go and let the Forensic team gather any evidence they can find. In the meantime, Detective Jackson has put an APB for the Simmons' minivan, and an Amber Alert is going to be issued for Delilah. We need to go back to the station so we can delve deeper into the timeline of when Delilah went missing."

February 2016

Lance studied his notes one more time before he went to meet with Colin Bruno, the former football coach at North Springfield High School, and his attorney. Colin was being charged with over twenty counts of embezzlement and misuse of public funds. Yesterday, his attorney, Gary Taylor, called Lance and asked for this meeting to discuss an exchange of information for a plea agreement. Plea agreements were a preferred outcome for Lance's boss because they saved the taxpayers the expense of a trial while still punishing an offender.

Walking out to the conference room where he knew Colin and Gary were waiting, Lance wondered what type of information a football coach really had to trade. Both men stood as he entered the room; when they were all seated, Gary Taylor started right in.

"Thank you for meeting with us, Mr. Clark. As I stated on the phone, my client, Mr. Bruno, has information that he would like to share in exchange for a plea bargain. Before he shares what he knows, we would like to know if you are open to a plea that does not involve prison time."

Lance should have seen this coming; no one wants to go to prison. He carefully chose his words as he responded, "Nothing is off the table at this point. It will really depend on the value of the information that Mr. Bruno shares, as well as the ability to prove what he says."

Gary Taylor nodded at his client, and Colin Bruno began, "I will admit that I embezzled money from the school district, but I didn't do it alone. Frank Waters, who is the district Athletic Director, came up with the idea and got half the money."

"Alright, let's say I believe you. How did this arrangement work?"

"I made up invoices for items that had been purchased in the past and put fake company names on them. Then I submitted the invoices for payment, and Frank Waters signed off on them. Before we started, I incorporated a business with a bunch of DBAs, you know, doing business as names under it. That way, I could make invoices with all different companies but cash them without issue. When the checks arrived from the district, I cashed them and gave half the money in cash to Frank."

Lance was practically jumping out of his chair at the opportunity to put Frank Waters in prison, but he knew that he had to act discreetly.

"Do you have proof of Frank Waters' involvement?"

"Well, not really, other than to ask you to look at the financial transactions and note that I only ever deposited half the money."

"Mr. Bruno, this is what I intend to prove in court against you, that you put into place an elaborate plan to defraud the school district. This plan included the multiple business names and addresses, the purchase by you of substandard equipment and supplies, as well as the purchases you have made over the last five years that far out exceed your means. I have witnesses that will testify to your large purchases made entirely in cash, so that you always took half the checks in cash does not provide evidence that anyone else was involved."

Gary Taylor cleared his throat, "Will you at least have your investigator look into it?"

Lance nodded his head and responded, "I will, and if we are able to prove what Mr. Bruno is claiming and he is willing to testify against

Frank Waters, then I will recommend a suspended sentence for any prison time imposed."

Colin Bruno looked discouraged, but Gary Taylor responded, "That is really all we can ask for. Thank you for your time."

After Colin and his attorney left, Lance walked back to his office. When Colin had first told him that Frank Waters was involved, Lance had a surge of hope. But with no evidence, it was highly unlikely that he would prove Frank had committed this crime any more than he had proved he had murdered Jenny.

He assigned an investigator to look into Frank Waters and see if they could prove what Colin Bruno was accusing him of. In the end, the investigator came up with the fact that Frank was messing around with another woman again, but there was no trail of money to prove the accusations of embezzlement. No lavish spending, no cash deposits, no overseas accounts or trips. A whole lot of nothing. It was as if Frank Waters was coated in Teflon, and the dirt never stuck to him.

7

Monday, February 5, 2024

"Do you want to interview the superintendent or the head of security?" Detective Nichols asked as he and Detective Minor walked back down the stairs.

"I will meet with the head of security, and then we can meet back up and make a list of everyone else we need to talk with," Minor responded.

Nichols nodded his head, then replied, "Don't forget that we need to notify the next of kin."

"Okay, so let's talk to the superintendent and head of security since they are here now and were here when the victim was found. Hopefully, one of them will provide us with the name and contact information for the next of kin; then we will go do the notification."

Detective Kass Minor went to find Trey LaMan, the head of security for the school district. He was seated at the front desk of the administrative building, answering a continuously ringing phone. Between calls, Detective Minor requested, "Is there someone who can fill in for you here so we can talk?"

Trey nodded his head, stood up, and walked to the room directly behind the front desk. A few minutes later, he and two women walked out of the room, and the women sat down in the two empty chairs.

"Detective, we can talk in the administrative room right here if that is alright with you."

"That would be fine," she said and followed Mr. LaMan into the room that he had just walked out of.

Before Minor could ask any question, Trey LaMan tried to take over the conversation by asking, "Who is the victim that was found? Is it Frank Waters because that is his truck in the parking lot?"

Minor was used to men who thought they could run all over her, and so it did not even phase her. "We are not able to comment on the victim or the investigation at this time. Please explain the circumstances that led you to be here this morning and to call for police assistance."

"I am the head of security for the Springfield School District, and per policy fourteen point two, when Ms. Rowen from the janitorial service arrived this morning and found the building to not be secured, she contacted her supervisor. The supervisor then called me, and I called the superintendent, Dr. Sydney Trappen, and the non-emergency number for the police department. That is also part of policy fourteen, which states that if a building is found to be unlocked and not alarmed, the police are to come and secure the building."

"What did you find when you got here?"

"Ms. Rowen was sitting in her car, and so we talked to her, then went to see what was going on for ourselves."

"And by we, you are referring to yourself, Dr. Trappen, and Officer Peterson, correct?"

"Yes, that is who I meant. We saw that the backdoor was indeed not securely closed. Officer Peterson put on gloves, opened the door wide enough for me to step inside, and confirmed that the alarm was disarmed, as Ms. Rowen had stated. The alarm was off, so he then told us we all needed to leave the building immediately. Dr. Trappen and I waited in our vehicles until we were allowed into the front area of the building in order to secure the building in terms of letting people know not to report to work here and coordinate with the IT department to get the camera system back online."

"Officer Peterson let my partner and I know that the camera system was not functional all weekend. Why did that happen?"

"It was a planned update. The only way to completely update the system was to take it offline for up to forty-eight hours. The IT guys were supposed to be putting it back online this morning, but it seems to be something they can only do on-site, and at this point, they are not allowed in the building."

"Who knew about the camera system being offline?"

"Well, um, everyone with a school district email address. That is an unfortunate coincidence with what happened, but I assure you it was a simple mistake."

"Alright. Please explain, and I will reserve my judgment regarding what happened."

"The secretary who was told to email the employees who work in this building accidentally emailed all employees regarding the system upgrade and camera outage."

Detective Minor said nothing about the email, but she was not one to believe in coincidences. She tried very hard as a detective not to jump ahead in investigations, but she would be shocked if an employee of the district was not the killer.

"Have you been in touch with the alarm company, and if so, were they able to tell you what time the alarm was disarmed?"

"I called them, and they have the alarm being disengaged at nine forty-five Saturday morning and not being rearmed since."

"Do you find it odd that they did not contact you to let you know that this building was not alarmed most of the weekend?"

"No, because we don't have them do that. The reason being that all the district buildings get used at odd hours, and having them call would cause a lot of unnecessary calls."

"What would be an example of why a building would need to be disarmed for almost two days?"

"I have no example of an alarm needing to be off for that long, but I am just saying that the alarm company doesn't monitor our systems for being disarmed."

"Got it. Have there been any threats made to the school district or any specific employees that you are aware of?"

"Absolutely not. We would take something like that very seriously. There are complaints, threats to sue us or report us to the state education department, but threats of violence, no, that has not happened as long as I have been here."

"Who would handle these complaints, threats to sue you or report you to the state education department?"

"The Director of Human Resources, Star Crespo, would handle complaints from employees about other employees, and the superintendent's office would handle all the rest of those issues."

"Is Ms. Crespo here?"

"No, we, meaning Dr. Trappen and I, called all the employees and had them work from home today except the two front desk secretaries. As you saw and heard, the phones were ringing off the hook, and we wanted to be sure calls were answered."

"What are they telling callers who ask what is going on?"

"We wrote them a script that reads; There is an ongoing police investigation regarding a potential crime at the administrative building. This building is the only one affected, and there is no danger or threat at this time. The administrative building is closed until further notice. We told them to say no comment to any other questions."

"Is there anything else that you can think of that we need to know?"

"No, but would it be alright for the IT department to come into work so we can get the camera system back up?"

"When the CSI techs are done with their evidence collection, we will let you know, and then IT people could be let back in. I would appreciate it if you would get Ms. Crespo's contact information."

"No problem. Please let me know if there is anything else we can do to help."

Holding a copy of the Head of Human Resources emergency contact card, Detective Kass Minor sent her partner a text: I am ready to go make the notification. Let me know where to meet you.

Less than a minute later, Detective Nichols wrote back: Just finishing up. Let's meet by our cars.

January 2019

Jo Beth Kalan sighed as she settled into her car after another after-work meeting. She had worked for the Springfield School District for the last fifteen years as a Literacy Specialist after staying home with her kids until they were all in school full-time. Teaching students to read was a job she loved, but the bureaucracy of the school district made her think about quitting regularly. In the time she had worked for the district, there had been ten superintendents and just as many administrative structures. Frank Waters had been her supervisor off and on for the entire fifteen years, and she could not stand the guy.

It was things like this evening's meeting that drove her up the wall. The meeting had been a waste of time, as all the meetings he had were. All the information shared would have been just as effectively shared via email. Frank Waters loved the sound of his own voice. On the occasions that Jo Beth complained to her husband Noah about Frank, he laughed and told her that many people didn't like their bosses. But it wasn't just the evening meetings that Jo Beth hated. Her issues with Frank included the unanswered emails, the condescending tone of his voice, his lack of follow-up on things that he agreed to do, his spineless way of never standing up to his superiors who challenged his decisions, and, of course, his way of continually rising to the top and staying there.

There had been rumors of Frank sexually harassing a female employee, but Jo Beth had never had that issue with him. That being said, she believed that he was capable of that and more. When she complained to Noah yesterday about this meeting, he told her to quit at the end of the school year. Their youngest daughter was a sophomore in college, so he suggested that they downsize their house and that she could either get a job in another district or be done working. Jo Beth just couldn't do it. She liked her financial freedom and wanted to put in another five years toward her state retirement plan. Starting over in another school district was not something that a woman in her mid-fifties wanted to do under the best of circumstances, much less to get away from a terrible boss. No, Jo Beth was going to put her head down, do her job, and stay as far away from Frank Waters as she could.

At home, Jo Beth settled into her favorite chair with the bag of fast food she had picked up on her way home, a glass of wine, and the remote. Noah was bowling this evening, so she was on her own and was ready to settle in to watch forensic television. It was her guilty pleasure, well, that and fast food—oh, and wine and chocolate. Okay, so she had a lot of guilty pleasures. She looked at the coffee table and saw a gift bag with her name on it in Noah's distinctive handwriting. She read the note first:

Jo Beth,

I know work has sucked lately, so I got you this gift to make you smile. Remember, we work to live, not live to work. Wear these to your next meeting and smile in a way that makes others wish they knew the joke.

Love always-Noah

Opening the gift bag, she pulled out a pair of socks, wondering why Noah thought they would make her smile. Then she saw the bottom of the socks that said, **This Meeting is Bullshit!** She burst out laughing and vowed to wear these socks to every meeting Frank Waters ever held.

As the episode started, Jo Beth wondered why all these criminals did not think things through better. In almost every episode, there was a video of them at a big box store buying either the murder weapons or stuff to clean up after. The one time she had shared with Noah how she would buy everything from garage sales, he had asked her if he should be in fear for his life. They had both laughed because while Jo Beth was a careful planner; she deplored violence and loved Noah.

8

Monday, February 5, 2024

As Detective Minor waited by her car for her partner, she watched as the medical examiner, Dr. Reeves, pulled into the parking lot. She approached the ME's van as he and his technician were unloading supplies from the back.

"Morning, Dr. Reeves. Sounds like you have already had a busy day. Nichols and I were wrapping up here and headed to notify the wife."

"You already have an id?"

"Preliminary based on the victim's truck being the only vehicle here prior to discovery, the body being in that same man's office, the wallet the victim had in his outstretched hand, and the basic match to the demographics. We want to be sure that his wife hears from us before there is a leak of information."

"Sounds good. Please let her know that she will need to come down to the morgue in a couple of hours to make a positive identification. I assume his body was not moved."

"Not in the least. The responding officer checked for a pulse, then Nichols, the CSI techs, and I looked over the scene. Pictures were taken before we retrieved his wallet."

"Great. After all the shake-ups and scandals this department has been through, the brass is on all of us to do everything by the book, but I am sure you know that. By the way, I am glad you're back with Major Crimes."

"Thanks, I think," Minor replied with a chuckle as she spotted her new partner, Detective Nichols, walking towards them.

After leaving the school district administrative building, Detectives Minor and Nichols drove to the station to leave their cars in the parking lot. Nichols had told Minor that Dr. Trappen had given him a copy of Frank Water's emergency contact form and told him that Marcia Waters was likely at work. The office building where Marcia worked was four blocks from the police station, and it was a nice day for February, so the detectives had agreed to walk over.

The accounting firm that Marcia Waters was a partner in was located on the sixth, seventh, and eighth floors of the office building. They checked in with the security guard in the lobby, rode the elevator up to the sixth floor, and were greeted by a receptionist.

"Hello. We need to speak with Marcia Waters." Detective Nichols told the young woman behind the reception desk as he flashed his badge.

"Do you have an appointment with Mrs. Waters?"

"No, we do not, but this is urgent police business," Nichols replied.

The woman nodded, then made a phone call as well as seemingly sending an instant message or email on her computer. Minor watched as the girl's fingers flew across the keyboard and wondered if this messaging was related to their visit or something else.

"If you would like to take a seat, Mrs. Waters' secretary will be down in a few minutes to escort you to her office. In the meantime, would you like anything to drink? We have coffee, water, and an assortment of sodas."

Both detectives declined the offer and turned towards the elevators in anticipation. Five minutes later, the elevator doors opened, and a smartly dressed middle-aged woman walked towards the detectives.

"Hello, I am Marcia Waters. How can I be of help to the Springfield police?"

"Mrs. Waters, is there somewhere private that we could speak to you?"

"Oh, of course, please follow me."

Following Marcia Waters a short way down the hall, she opened the door to what appeared to be a conference room and gestured for the detectives to enter. After all three of them sat down, Marcia Waters turned to the detectives, "I don't mean to be rude, but this is a very busy time of year here, so how is it I can be of assistance?"

"Ma'am, we are so sorry to have to inform you that this morning, your husband, Frank Waters, was found deceased in his office." Detective Nichols had long ago found that when making a death notification, it was best to just be straightforward. This approach helped there to be no misinterpretation of what was said, but also allowed him to gauge the initial reactions of the victims' families. He watched as the blood drained out of Marcia Waters' face, her hands began to shake, and her breathing became rapid—a genuine reaction to shocking news.

"What? How? When?" The questions seemed to tumble out of Marcia Waters as tears rolled down her cheeks.

"We are investigating your husband's death, as it does not appear to be from natural causes. When was the last time that you saw and heard from Frank?"

Marcia Waters stood, walked to the built-in refrigerator at the back of the room, and grabbed a small bottle of water. After gulping down the water, she placed the bottle in the recycling bin by the refrigerator and grabbed another bottle.

"Saturday morning. That is when I last saw or talked to Frank. I was getting ready to leave for work, and he was just waking up. As I mentioned, this is the busiest time of year for me; tax season for a tax accountant is like a marathon. We start running in early January and don't stop until mid-April. I work seven days a week, usually fourteen or fifteen hours a day, so it is not uncommon for Frank and I to pass like ships in the night this time of year. What am I supposed to tell our kids?"

"At this point, it would be best to just let them know that their father has passed. Where do your kids live?"

"Sophie...oh my God, Sophie." Marcia Waters began to sob.

"Mrs. Waters, what is it?" Detective Minor inquired.

"Sophie called me yesterday. She was upset that she had not been able to get ahold of her dad for their regular Saturday call. I blew off her concerns. She is going to be devastated."

"Where does Sophie live?"

"Clearwater Florida. She is a nurse there. I need to go call my kids."

"Before you do that, we would like to ask you a few more questions. Is that alright?"

"Yes, of course. I apologize. My mind is going a mile a minute, and I am feeling very scattered." Marcia Waters said as she sat back down.

Detective Kass Minor looked at her partner, who gave the slightest of nods.

"You said, kids. How many kids do you and Frank have, and where do the others live?"

"Two, including Sophie. Kyle is a contractor with the Department of Defense, so I don't know how to answer where he lives. His home address is with Frank and me, but he hasn't stayed more than a night or two in five-plus years."

"Mrs. Waters, what time on Saturday morning was it when you last saw your husband?"

"I got to the office at eight, and it takes about twenty minutes to get here, so it was around seven thirty that morning. When I got home Saturday night at about ten, I remember being surprised that Frank wasn't home yet. But not worried because Frank is an extreme extravert. He can't stand to be alone with his thoughts. He is always out and about doing something. I figured he was out with friends, then I fell asleep."

"Did you try to get a hold of him at all Saturday night or Sunday?"

"I called and texted him both Saturday and Sunday but got no replies. Looking back now that I know he is dead, I should have been concerned by this, but to be honest with you, it is not the first time Frank has been gone for a few days without me knowing where he is."

"Where was your husband those other times?"

"Usually with his girlfriend du jour at his fishing cabin up north and maybe occasionally actually fishing. I figured that was where he was when he wasn't home and didn't answer my calls and messages."

"Do you know the name of his current girlfriend, and are you alright with this arrangement?"

"I am not sure he is currently involved with someone else, to be honest. We have been to counseling more times than I can count regarding his infidelity, so no, I'm not alright with his proclivity to be unfaithful. I have become numb to our situation because first, I stayed for our kids to have a stable home. After they both were out of the house, it would have been a financial calamity for me to divorce him."

"Interesting, so will you benefit from your husband's death financially?"

"Not really. The school district provides a very minimal life insurance policy, and the state retirement program will give me a one time payout. I am actually better off from a monetary sense for Frank to live and us to stay married."

"From what you have told us, you were here all day Saturday and Sunday; is that correct?"

"Yes, Saturday from eight in the morning until about nine-thirty that evening and then Sunday from about seven until two. Most people take Sundays off here, even during the busy season, but I find it is the best day to finish things up and get organized for the week to come. Yesterday, I finished up all my pending reviews and planned out this week."

"Is there any way for us to verify the times you were here?"

"Absolutely. We have a double badge in and out system for the seventh and eighth floors. By that, I mean you have to have your employee badge to make the elevator go to those floors, and then once you are on the floor, you have to use your badge again to get through the doors to the offices. Security is at those doors and requires everyone to swipe their own badge to get in. So there are electronic records and the security guards themselves."

"Is there a security guard here twenty-four hours a day?"

"Yes, well, not on the seventh and eighth floors, but downstairs there is. They cover security from ten at night until six in the morning."

"We may need those records, but for now, we will leave you to make your calls. Here is my card with the number for the medical examiner's office on the back. Please call them and make arrangements to positively identify your late husband. Again, you and your family have our condolences. Please call us if you think of anything else that may help us with our investigation. We will be back in touch to update you as well."

Marcia Waters walked the detectives to the elevators and shook both their hands before heading to the stairwell and back up to her office. Her head was throbbing, and she kept silently repeating, *Frank is dead!* as she climbed the stairs. She was sad for her kids, but the overwhelming emotion that she felt was relief.

April 2020

Lance sat on the ground next to his sister Jenny's grave, holding his mother's hand as she wept. Today would have been Jenny's forty-eighth birthday, and each year on her birthday, Lance and their mom, Aleesa, came to Jenny's grave together. Lance and Jenny's dad, Ted, had died three months earlier and been buried next to Jenny. Despite having been divorced for over twenty years, his mom had been devastated by her ex-husband's death. On his deathbed, Lance had told his dad that he believed that Frank Waters was the person who had murdered Jenny, but had no way to prove it. His dad had made him promise not to stop trying. Now, it was as if both Jenny and his dad's ghosts were chasing him to find a way to get justice for Jenny.

Lance had used the life insurance money that he had received from his dad to hire a private investigator to look into the case. The investigator, Cliff Alrich, was a retired homicide detective from Denver who exclusively took on cold-case murders. Cliff sent Lance updates every week or so and thus far had not found anything that Lance did not previously know. The passage of twenty-eight years made it difficult to find anyone who remembered the night Jenny was killed. No one who did recall details provided nothing that was not already known. Cliff's email yesterday was that he was going to come to Springfield next week and talk with Frank Waters. Cliff had commented on the odd coincidence of Lance and Frank, both living in Springfield. Since he had not wanted to say that he had moved to Springfield just to be near Frank, Lance ignored the comment.

He must have been lost in his thoughts, because he was startled when his mom placed her hand on his shoulder. She was standing next to him, and he had not even realized that she had gotten up.

"Lance, let's go and get some lunch."

He stood and walked with his mom to the car. There was no question where they would go for lunch because they went to the same place each year for Jenny's birthday. He also knew that his mom would ask for a table for three and order Jenny's favorite meal for her. When they finished eating, she would have the server put the food she ordered Jenny into a box and take it home.

A few years ago, at Thanksgiving, he had been surprised to find all of those previous birthday lunch boxes in his mom's deep freezer. Each was labeled with the date and how old Jenny would have been. Not knowing what to say or do about the frozen relics of meals, he never mentioned them. He supposed one day when his mom passed away, he would need to throw all those chicken salad croissants with a side of fruit away. He just hoped by then justice had been served for Jenny.

9

Monday, February 5, 2024

The Amber Alert went off as Chris and Delilah were making a list of things that they needed to get from the store before they left town. The piercing tone of the alert startled both of them, and Chris knew before she even looked at the television that it was for Delilah.

"Kiddo, the jig is up. They are looking for you."

Delilah sat at the table crying, "Please, I don't want to go."

"I am sorry, but I told you from the beginning that you could not stay with me if the cops started looking for you."

"Why not?"

"I would be charged with kidnapping, and even though I don't want you to be upset, I am not going to prison."

Delilah nodded her head, "I don't want you to go to prison. What are we going to do?"

Chris knew she needed to get Delilah out of her apartment and then pack up and leave town. *No good deed goes unpunished*, she thought as she planned where to drop her young visitor off.

"Alright, I am going to drive you back near where I saw you get taken. There is a hotel that is closed and has a parking garage. On our way there, I will have you lie down in the back seat; then, when we get there, you can get out and walk to the playground on the beach. How does that sound?"

"Fine."

"Delilah, honey, I know you are upset, but someone cared enough to contact the police. When you are found, you need to tell the police about what living at the Simmons' has been like for you. Oh, and about the other girls who disappeared. I can almost guarantee that they will not make you go back there."

"Okay, I will tell the cops about the Simmons and the parties, and the drugs, and the locking me in a room. What about the guys who took me?"

Chris had been thinking about how to handle this part of where Delilah had been. One thing she knew was that it was best to stick as close to the truth as possible. "Tell the cops about being kidnapped and what those scumbags did to you. Then tell them you heard gunshots and someone started coming down the basement stairs, but then they left, so you ran out of there. Tell them you walked around and slept in the parking garage, where I will drop you off."

"Got it!"

"Whatever you do, please do not tell them about me."

"I won't. I promise."

Chris knew that extracting that promise from an eight-year-old probably was not something to rely on. She just hoped that it would buy her a little extra time.

Dropping Delilah off in the parking garage and watching her walk slowly away tore at Chris's heart. The idea of the chance for a fresh start had begun to take seed in her heart, but she should have known that happiness was not something she would ever find again. After she packed her meager belongings into her car, Chris wrote a note to her landlord.

Mr. Hummbold,

I apologize for the lack of notice, but I am moving out because of a family emergency. Here is my rent payment for next month and please keep my security deposit because of my lack of notice. I appreciate your understanding.

Chris Farmington.

Chris put the note in an envelope and slipped it into the slot on Mr. Hummbold's back door, where she left her rent each month. There was no time to dawdle because her identity and, hence, her freedom were now in the hands of an eight-year-old, so she needed to put as much distance between herself and the child whose life she had saved.

******

Marcia Water's cell phone sat on her desk next to the landline. She had four missed calls with voicemails from Sophie, two on her cell and two on her desk phone, as well as a text message. Marcia decided to start with the text message: Mom, I am at the airport in St. Louis. I left Dad messages asking him to pick me up, but he isn't here, and you aren't answering. So, I am taking the bus to Springfield. Hopefully, one of you will be at the bus station to pick me up.

The voicemail messages were basically the same as the text messages, except that Marcia could hear the anxiety in her daughter's voice. Marcia wondered if she should call her daughter back or wait to tell her about Frank when she picked her up. Deciding on the latter, Marcia texted Sophie back: Sophie, I will be there to pick you up. What time does your bus get to town?

Marcia saw that Sophie was writing her back, so she waited before setting her cell phone back down.

Mom, WHAT IS GOING ON? WHERE IS DAD? I am on the bus so don't call but you better be prepared to answer me when I get there!!

Texting back, Marcia replied: Please be calm. We will talk when you get here. I love you.

Sophie's return text came seconds later: Fine. My bus will be there at 1:20. Please tell me Dad is okay.

Marcia did not want to lie to her daughter, but she was also not going to tell her that her father was dead via text message. Deciding that ignoring the message was the best course of action, Marcia made a call to the number her son Kyle had given her in case of emergencies.

Kyle worked for the Department of Defense and he often went long periods of time with little to no communication. The number went right to a voicemail with a computer-generated message that simply repeated the phone number.

"Hello, this is Marcia Waters, and I am trying to get a hold of my son Kyle Waters. Please have him call me as soon as possible due to a family emergency."

Marcia looked at the piles of work on her desk and knew that her next step needed to be telling the other partners what was going on. Well, at least what she knew about what was going on. Marcia called her secretary, Luisa, into her office and had her close the door when she arrived.

"As you know, two detectives from the Springfield police department were just here to speak to me. My husband, Frank, was found dead this morning. They did not give me any details other than that his death was not an accident."

"Oh my, Mrs. Waters, I am so sorry. What can I do to help you?"

"Please call the secretaries of the other partners and tell them I need to have an emergency meeting in the next thirty minutes."

"Will do. I will be back as soon as I confirm with the others that they will be there. I am assuming you would like me not to tell the others what is going on?"

"I would appreciate it. After I tell the partners, I will send an email to the staff so everyone is aware of the reason behind my lack of presence during this critical time."

Marcia watched Luisa leave her office before she picked up her cell phone again. There were six messages, all from Sophie.

Mom! Answer my question!

Mom, please, I am freaking out! Is Dad OK?

I am stuck on this bus freaking out, and you are ignoring me.

WTF, Mom!

Do you even give a shit about Dad or me?

Forget it. I will get my own ride, and I am going to see the cops when I get there!

Marcia thought *this is one of the times that I hate technology*. Ignoring her daughter's request not to call, Marcia dialed Sophie's phone number. The call went straight to voicemail, so Marcia left a message. "Sophie, honey, calm down. I know where Dad is, and we will talk when I get to the bus station to pick you up."

February 2021

The funeral was over, but Jo Beth Kalan could not bring herself to leave the church. Noah's death had been a total shock to her, as well as to everyone else in their lives. He was the healthy one in their relationship, well, that was until he had a massive heart attack and died. She was not prepared to go on without him, and she knew who to blame for Noah's death. Frank Waters!

Frank had scheduled one of his nonsense meetings for the evening that Noah had died. While her husband took his last breaths alone at home, Jo Beth listened to Frank's ridiculous ideas and participated in team-building exercises no one wanted to do. After the meeting, Jo Beth was surprised when she opened the garage door, and Noah's car was in its usual spot. It was his league bowling night, and he should have left fifteen minutes before she arrived.

Dread filled her as she walked into the house, called out for Noah, and got no response. She found him on the floor in the living room in front of his favorite chair. A partially eaten sandwich sat on a table next to the chair, along with an open can of diet soda. She had been trained in first aid and CPR, so she knew how to check him for a pulse and breathing. He was warm to the touch, so she called 911 and started CPR. The paramedics arrived within minutes and took over the life-saving efforts. At the emergency room, the doctor told her that Noah had suffered a suspected massive heart attack and had been declared dead. Jo Beth knew that if she had been at home when Noah started showing symptoms, she would have called for help and Noah would have gotten the medical care that would have saved his life.

The day after Noah's death, Jo Beth told her best friend, Annie, about her anger at Frank. Annie was sympathetic to Jo Beth's pain but thought that blaming Frank Waters was a stretch. She tried to tell Jo Beth that even if she had been home, Noah might still have died. Annie pointed out that Noah had not gone to the doctor in years and that he had been complaining about feeling tired the last few months. Jo Beth knew that Annie was wrong. She knew the statistics that CPR, administered immediately after a cardiac arrest, can double or triple a person's chance of survival. That was what Frank Waters had taken away from her beloved Noah: that increased chance of living. She would never be able to forgive him for keeping her at that stupid, unnecessary meeting.

10

Monday, February 5, 2024

Driving to pick up her daughter from the bus station, Marcia thought back to the meeting she had with her partners. They had all been shocked to hear of Frank's passing, and when Marcia had shared that it was two homicide detectives who had notified her, the partners stared at her in horror. They had so many questions; How?, Where?, Who?, When?, and to all of those questions, Marcia had no answers. When she said that the police would likely want the logs of her coming and going from work this past weekend as well as to talk to the guards, the head partner Heather Johanson had been appalled that the police would even imply that Marcia had somehow been involved. Marcia assured all of the partners that the police were just doing their jobs and that she was not really a suspect.

Marcia's clients had been divided up, with it being agreed that Louisa would call each of them and tell them that Marcia's husband had died unexpectedly. That was also what Marcia stated in her email to the staff regarding her sudden and likely prolonged absence. She was sure that it would not be long before Frank's murder was in the news, and then people would fill in the blanks, but she believed that the best way to handle things was with discretion.

Pulling into the bus station, Marcia noted that she was fifteen minutes early, just as she had planned. She thought about calling the number for Kyle again, but decided that leaving a second voicemail would likely not make him call her back any sooner. Instead, she called the Medical Examiner's Office and set up to identify Frank's body immediately after picking up Sophie. She had decided that if her daughter wanted to know what was going on so badly, she could help with this distasteful task.

Marcia called her sister Corine, who picked up on the first ring.

"Hi, Marcia. What are you doing calling me in the middle of the day during tax season? What's wrong?"

"Frank's dead."

"Whoa, wait, what? Marcia, no lead-in, just Frank's dead. What the hell happened?"

"Corine, I don't know. Two homicide detectives came to see me at the office and told me he was found dead at work this morning. They seemed perturbed by the fact that I had not seen or heard from him since Saturday morning and that I wasn't worried."

"Where are you? Do you need a lawyer?"

Marcia could hear the anxiety creeping into her sister's voice and quickly reassured her, "I am fine. I did not kill Frank, and I was at work all weekend, so no, I do not need a lawyer. Right now I am at the bus station waiting to pick up Sophie."

"How did Sophie get there so quickly?"

"Oh, she was already on her way because she was worried about Frank not returning her calls and texts. I am sure this will be further proof to her that I am a cold-hearted bitch."

"Oh, come on, Sophie is a sweetheart and a daddy's girl; she doesn't hate you."

"Who said anything about hating me?" Marcia needed to be done with this call. "Don't answer that, Corine. I need to go. Will you do me two favors? The first is to bring my stuff that is at your house back to mine. And second, will you please call Mom and Dad and tell them about Frank?"

"Of course I will. Let me know if there is anything else I can do to help. I am in shock."

"You and me both, Corine. You and me both."

******

As the bus drove into Springfield, Sophie Waters powered her phone back on. She had turned it off halfway here in a fit of rage with her mom for not answering her messages, as well as being frantic about where her dad was. It was likely not the most rational thing to do, but it had served a purpose of making her feel more in control. As the phone came to life, the notifications began to buzz. A missed call from her mom with a voicemail that was so like Marcia to not respect what Sophie had told her and to call, anyway.

The text from Kyle was a surprise: What is the emergency mom said I need to call about?

Sophie stared at her brother's message with thoughts rapidly firing in her head, so there *was an emergency. Why hadn't their mom told her? Maybe she told me? I need to listen to her voicemail. Oh my God, what had happened to Dad?* Dialing her voicemail number, Sophie sent up another silent prayer that her dad was okay.

Her mom's message sounded like she was upset: "Sophie, honey, calm down. I know where Dad is, and we will talk when I get to the bus station to pick you up."

Sophie thought, *Well, that doesn't tell me shit.* Realizing that the bus was pulling into the station, Sophie put away her phone and steeled herself to deal with her mother and whatever the hell was going on with her dad. As the bus doors opened, she thought, *God, I have not missed Springfield. Please don't make me have to be here long.*

January 2022

Anger is the second stage in the stages of grief, and Jo Beth had been stuck in this stage for almost a year. There had been moments when depression had almost crippled her. Still, those were predictable events like Noah's birthday, their wedding anniversary, Christmas, and the anniversary of his death, and she always swung back to anger quickly. Her daughters had convinced her to start seeing a counselor, and the therapist had suggested that Jo Beth find something constructive to focus her anger on. The counselor's suggestions were things like kickboxing or chopping wood, but none of those appealed to Jo Beth.

The idea hit her as she lay in bed, unable to fall asleep. Jo Beth was going to turn her over the top organizational skills, and years of knowledge from watching crime shows and listening to true crime podcasts into a constructive hobby, planning ways to kill Frank Waters and get away with it. It was not a project she could discuss with anyone, and the truth of the matter was that it was more an exercise in fictitious murder than something she would ever carry out. The first step was to stop talking to everyone about her anger at Frank and act like she was starting to move on to sadness. It wasn't like she had not been sad about losing Noah; she had been devastated, but her anger just kept overwhelming everything else.

Jo Beth grabbed a half-used spiral notebook from her basement and began her list:

Buy all items below from garage sales
Duffle bag
Gloves (multiple pairs)
Paint suit
Knives
Ski mask
Sunglasses
Wig
Trash bags
Tarp
Duct tape
Goggles
Follow FW and figure out his patterns/schedule
Carry bag with you at all times

When she woke up the next morning and realized she had slept through the night for the first time since Noah's death, it was as if a weight had been lifted. The therapist was right; she needed an outlet for her anger, and she had found it by coming up with fictional ways to kill Frank Waters. Tonight after work, she decided she would write about a way to kill him and how to get away with it. Writing might just be the outlet she needed for her anger.

11

Monday, February 5, 2024

Sophie Waters stumbled out of the Medical Examiner's office sobbing. When her mom had picked her up twenty minutes ago and driven straight here, Sophie could not process what was being said. Dead, her dad was dead, murdered... She was not sure she would have believed it if she had not seen her dad's body for herself. There were so many questions, and her mom was inside, calmly filling out paperwork. This was a prime example of what she meant when she told people that her mom was cold. How does one fill out paperwork after seeing your dead husband's body?

Pulling her phone out of her purse, Sophie started to answer her brother's text. She knew that neither of her parents had this number and that it was a burner phone and would change as soon as this message stream stopped. Her brother was all cloak and dagger about his work and seemed more than a little paranoid to Sophie, but what did she know about national security stuff? She erased another message and suddenly realized why her mom had not texted her back. How do you text someone something so awful and life-changing? She settled on: It is an emergency! Call her! and then put her phone away, closed her eyes, let her head fall back, and resumed sobbing.

******

Marcia stood outside the door of the Medical Examiner's office, holding the copies that the secretary had just handed her. She could see Sophie sitting in the car sobbing and did not know how to comfort her daughter. Both of Marcia's parents were alive and well, enjoying their retirement in Arizona, so she had never had to deal with the loss of a parent. Add into the mix the strained relationship she and Sophie had, and Marcia was left clueless. Her phone began to ring in her bag, and Marcia grabbed it. The screen read unavailable number, and she prayed it was Kyle and not some pesky telemarketer.

"Hi, Mom, it's Kyle. I got your message. What is wrong?"

"Oh, Kyle, I am so glad you called. I wish there was some way for me not to tell you this over the phone." Marcia paused, gathering her thoughts and choosing her words carefully.

"Mom, just tell me."

"Your dad is dead. Someone murdered him."

"What? Who murdered him?"

"I don't know because the police are not telling me much."

"Alright, Mom, I will make arrangements to be home ASAP. I will text you this phone number and let you know my ETA. Please call me back if you find out anything."

"I will. I love you, Kyle."

"I love you too, Mom."

Marcia looked at her phone, waiting for Kyle's text. An actual number that he would answer. Marcia felt a small amount of joy at that little piece of connection to her son.

Sophie looked over at her as she sat down in the driver's seat.

"Your brother just called me. He is on the way home."

"Okay. Do you have a number and name for the detectives on Dad's case?"

"Yes, I have their card. Why?"

"I want to talk to them, that's why?"

"Okay, well, they wanted to talk to you too." Marcia shuffled around in her bag and pulled out the card that detectives had given her. The front was printed with the information for the Major Crimes unit of the Springfield Police Department, and on the back, one of them had written both their names, as well as the phone number for the Medical

Examiner's office. She handed the card to her daughter, then put the car in drive and headed home to plan a funeral for her husband.

******

Detectives Minor and Nichols sat across the desk from Ms. Star Crespo, the head of Human Resources for the Springfield School District. When Detective Minor had called Ms. Crespo, the woman had asked if it would be possible for her to gain access to the administrative building and her office and for them to meet there. She had explained that while she had electronic files she could access from home; she kept sensitive information on paper only and so would need Frank Water's physical personal file.

They had decided on the way over that Nichols would start the interview, and Minor would take notes, then she would ask any follow-up questions she had. So, after settling into the office and exchanging basic information, Nichols began,

"Ms. Crespo, what can you tell us about any issues Frank Waters had while working here?"

"Frank worked for the district for the last thirty-two years, so there have been some bumps in the road. I read through his file while I was waiting for the two of you, and there is one major incident to tell you about and two notes that seem inconsequential, but I will definitely tell you about those as well."

"How about we start with the major incident and go from there?"

"In April 2018, Tessa Lee made a complaint to my office that Frank Waters had propositioned her sexually and tried to grab her. We investigated and found that the incident occurred, and Frank was disciplined. Here is what my office's investigation found: several employees from the district attended a conference that was held in the Ozarks. On the second day of the conference, the majority of the people from the district went to dinner together after the conference concluded for the day. They walked from the hotel to a local restaurant, and after dinner, some of them stayed and had drinks.

The last two people from the district to leave were Ms. Lee and Mr. Waters, so they walked together back to the hotel. As Ms. Lee got off the elevator at the hotel to go to her room, Mr. Waters followed her and stated quote "How about I join you in your room for the night?" Ms. Lee told him no and to leave her alone and turned to walk away from him. At that time, he reached out to grab her, and in her words, she "pivoted and he face planted onto the hotel hallway carpet." She left him there, locked her room, and returned home in the morning.

During the course of our investigation, Frank Waters admitted to the incident, although he was foggy on the details. He stated that he had an issue with drinking too much and agreed to enter a substance abuse program. He was out on administrative leave while he completed the program. Ms. Lee left the district at the end of the school year and was paid two hundred thousand dollars by the district in a settlement agreement." Ms. Crespo looked up from the documents she had been reading.

"I agree that was a major incident, and from what you said, the police were never involved?"

"Well, no, because most importantly, Ms. Lee requested that they not be and second, because workplace sexual harassment rarely rises to the level of a crime unless there is a repetitive pattern. At least, that is what the district lawyers told me at the time."

"Are the other two issues you mentioned also complaints of sexual harassment?"

"No, they aren't. There have been no further complaints of Mr. Waters sexually harassing anyone. Would you like me to tell you about the other incidents?"

"Yes, please do, but first, we will need Ms. Lee's contact information before we leave."

"No problem, I pulled her file too and made a copy of the contact information that we used to mail her last W-2." Ms. Crespo handed the photocopy to Detective Nichols and then continued telling the detectives about Frank Waters' misbehavior.

"The next incident actually happened two years before the one with Ms. Lee, and it was a police matter. I do not know if either of you remembers when Colin Bruno, the football coach at Springfield North, was convicted of embezzlement. Mr. Bruno, while out on bail, came to my office and filed a complaint. He alleged that Frank Waters was his co-conspirator in the embezzlement, but he had no evidence to prove it. We looked into it, and I know the district attorney's office did, too, because I met with an investigator from that office. No one could prove that Frank had anything to do with the misappropriated funds. We changed our policy after that, and invoices require more signatures to get paid as well as adding a system to verify that vendors actually exist and provide the district with something of value."

"We will definitely look into Mr. Bruno's whereabouts?"

"Oh, he is in prison. He took a plea bargain and has to serve a minimum of ten of his thirty years."

"Well, after we verify that being in prison would rule him out as the actual murderer. So, tell us about the third complaint against Mr. Waters."

"This one is much less straightforward. There is an employee named Jo Beth Kalan who has made numerous complaints about Mr. Waters over the years. None of these have risen to the point that we could do anything about them, but after the last one, I have tried my best to make sure that he didn't supervise her."

"What kind of complaints?"

"What we here in HR call nuisance complaints, but we looked into each of them. I will read them in order the order that they occurred:

January 2010-Frank Waters holds extraneous after-hours meetings with no regard to anyone else's needs.

May 2014- Frank Waters completed my evaluation without spending time to truly observe me working and having discussions after those observations. He marked me down in areas that he never expressed were an issue.

August 2020-Request to be assigned to a different supervisor. Frank Waters and I have long-standing issues, which I have expressed to HR on multiple occasions. He treats me with disrespect and is a misogynist. For example, at a district meeting last week, Mr. Waters was spreading misinformation, so I raised my hand and stated the correct information. Mr. Waters then pointed his finger at me and said, and I quote, "Jo Beth, suck those words right back into your mouth. The rest of you can just disregard what you just heard." Several people in the room snickered, and so after the meeting, I tried to talk to Mr. Waters, but he told me he was too busy to deal with me.

Those are the written complaints, but I will tell you that Jo Beth has been in this office no less than six other times over her fifteen years of employment to gripe about Mr. Waters."

Detective Nichols looked at Kass Minor, and she knew that it was her turn to ask follow-up questions.

"We will also need the contact information for Jo Beth Kalan."

"No problem. I expected that and made a copy of her emergency card as well." Ms. Crespo handed this photocopy to Detective Minor.

"Thank you. Who is Frank Waters' direct supervisor?"

"That would be the Assistant Superintendent, Sandy Frances, and you will find her with Dr. Trappen and the school board members in the conference room of South High School. That is where they have set up the incident command center to deal with Mr. Waters' murder."

"Did Mr. Waters have a secretary?"

"Not a personal one, but the department secretary is Roland LaRue. He should be working at South High School along with most of the administrative building staff"

"Is there anything else that you can think of that might help us with the investigation into Frank Waters' murder?"

"As an HR Director, I try not to repeat rumors, but in this case, I will tell you that Frank Waters is known to be a serial cheater. He has had multiple girlfriends who have worked for the school districts, all while being married. When the incident with Ms. Lee happened, I told him to be sure that he kept his wandering eye away from women he supervised and even better if it would stay out of the district. He laughed and then winked at me."

"We appreciate your candor and your time. Please let us know if you think of anything else."

March 2023

Frank Waters walked out of the closing company's office with the check folded neatly in his wallet. Settling his mom's estate had taken almost eighteen months and was a thankless job up until this point. The check for just over two hundred thousand dollars was a nice thank you from his mom. When his mom had been diagnosed with breast cancer, she had told him where to find her will and that she had named him the executor of her estate. What she hadn't told Frank was that it was the will that had been written twenty years ago, right after his dad died.

At the time Esther Waters wrote the will, Frank's brother George was in and out of drug rehabilitation, which was the only thing that explained why she had left George out of the will altogether. She left everything to Frank. George had tried to sue him in court, saying that the estate should be split fifty-fifty, but the court upheld Esther's will. George had shown up at his house the weekend after the court ruling, and the two of them had gotten into a verbal argument. It ended when Marcia told George he needed to leave or she would call the cops.

During the estate sale three months ago, at their mom's house, George had shown up there, and once again, the two brothers argued. The company running the estate sale had asked both brothers to leave, and they did, but not before George screamed, "One day, Frank, you are going to get what is coming to you, and no one is going to mourn your passing." The woman who ran the estate sale had called Frank and let him know that she had names and numbers of people who had witnessed the confrontation and George's threat. In case Frank wanted to press charges against his brother, which he didn't, but it was nice to know that he had proof, if needed, of George's threats.

Marcia had tried to convince him to give half the money from the house sale to George as a sign of good faith and to mend the relationship, but Frank refused. If his mother had wanted to change her will and include George, she would have. His wife's reasoning that they didn't need the money, or that George had turned his life around, wasn't really what mattered to Frank. In his opinion, that money was all his, and he wasn't about to share it with George or, for that matter, Marcia. When she said they didn't need the money, it was another way for her to hold her higher income over his head. He wondered what she would say if he asked her about having separate accounts. It had been her idea a few years ago when they were in counseling, but he had resisted it and said that it was another way for her to show her lack of trust in him. The marriage counselor had agreed with him, and Marcia had dropped the idea. She would likely see right through his suggestion and refuse.

It wasn't as if Marcia spent any money. She was the biggest tightwad that he had ever known, so the money was his to spend. Despite being a partner in her accounting firm, she bought her clothes, purses, and shoes from consignment stores and drove a twenty-year-old Acura.

12

Monday, February 5, 2024

When you are a fugitive from the FBI, it is essential to always have an escape route and plan, so Chris developed several over the past two years while living in Gulf Shores. She knew every back road, out-of-the-way gas station, and low-end car dealer for a hundred miles around. Being prepared had helped her stay at least one step in front of the law for the past four years. This preparation is what led Chris to turn into this less-than-reputable small car lot an hour after she left her apartment.

As she watched the salesman walking towards her, she almost burst out laughing. He was the most cliche person she had ever encountered in her life. Long stringy hair that did nothing to cover his bald spot pulled into a haphazard ponytail, along with wrinkled khaki pants that were slightly too tight and too short. The polo-type shirt he wore with his name and the name of the car lot stitched on had seen better days as well.

"Welcome, welcome to Best Cars Ever. I am the owner, Gus. What can I do for you, little miss?"

"I saw your sign that you buy cars and would like to sell you my car."

"Well, let's go out for a little drive, and I can give you an offer."

"Would it be okay if I wait here and look at the cars on your lot while you drive my car?"

"Oh, a trade is what you are after. Great, you go ahead and look around. I won't be long."

Chris didn't doubt that he would be back quickly; her car was a three-year-old Volkswagon Jetta with less than fifty thousand miles on it, and the cars on his lot were fifteen to twenty years old with hundreds of thousands of miles on each. While Gus was gone, Chris walked around to the back of his lot where cars not for sale sat. Sure enough, three of them still had valid license plates on. She grabbed her multi-tool out of her tote and removed a set of plates from a black Dodge Neon.

Five minutes later, Chris was standing next to a 2005 dark blue Dodge Neon; she watched as Gus pulled her car back into the lot.

"This is a great little runner. Why do you want to sell?"

"The usual, I need the money. So how much can you give me if I trade for this Neon?"

"Don't you want to drive it?"

"Gus, are you saying that I can't trust you?"

"Of course, you can trust me, but I have never sold a car without a test drive."

"I was joking. I absolutely want to test drive this car."

"Let me go grab you the keys, and while you are gone, I will write up the sale so we can review the numbers when you get back."

Chris returned fifteen minutes later, signed the papers, and took her five thousand in cash. Gus had transferred her license plate onto the Neon and given her the paperwork to send to the state to transfer the ownership. He didn't need to know that she would never mail those papers in. She was sure that he thought he had made the deal of the century, and she hoped that he was able to sell her car before anyone from law enforcement came looking for it.

******

Kass Minor ended her call with her husband Robert as she pulled up to the Waters home. She and Detective Nichols had decided to divide and conquer the list of interviews they needed to complete after meeting with Ms. Crespo. After they each conducted the interviews, they would meet back at the station and see where they were at. Minor had volunteered to be the one to go to the Waters home and talk with both Marcia and Sophie Waters, while Detective Nichols talked with the department secretary and Frank's boss.

Sophie Waters had left both Minor and Nichols messages while they were talking with Ms. Crespo. Detective Minor had briefly considered calling ahead but, in the end, decided to just show up. This was not a social call; it was a murder investigation. Ringing the doorbell, Minor wondered how many people would be at the residence. It was common for families to gather as news of death spread. It might be necessary for her to have Sophie and Marcia join her at the station to talk. Marcia Waters opened the door with the chain lock still attached, "Oh, it is you, detective. Hold on a second."

The door closed, and Minor could hear the chain lock being disengaged. This time, when the door opened, it was fully. Marcia Waters was dressed just as she had been at her office this morning, expect for the slippers on her feet.

"Come on in, Detective. Sophie is in the den."

"Thank you so much. Are you and Sophie the only ones here?"

Marcia looked at her inquisitively. "Who else would be here?"

"I have no idea. I was just checking that we can speak freely."

"No, there is no one but Sophie and I here. I know she is anxious to talk to you."

The room that Marcia Waters had referred to as a den had a wall of windows that looked over the woods behind it. A young woman, who was presumably Sophie Waters, sat staring out those windows and turned as they walked into the room.

"Hello, Sophie. I am Detective Minor from the Springfield Police Department. I got your messages, and I am here to answer questions that I am able to but also to ask you some questions."

"Absolutely. I want to help in any way that I can to catch my dad's killer."

"Your mom told my partner and me this morning that you were already on your way home because you were worried about your dad. Tell me about that."

"Dad and I talk every Saturday afternoon. We are both college sports fans and discuss the games that day, as well as how our favorite teams are doing. I called at twelve-thirty as usual, and he didn't answer. It has happened before, but he always calls me right back. He didn't, so I texted and kept calling. I was worried when he still hadn't reached out by Sunday morning, so I called Mom. She wasn't worried."

Marcia Waters let out a loud sigh.

"Well, you weren't mom. It was like you didn't even care where he was."

"Sophie, your dad is an adult and can do as he likes."

"NO MOM, HE WAS AN ADULT. He is dead." Sophie began to sob.

"Oh, honey, I know," Marcia said as she attempted to gather her daughter into her arms but was rebuffed by the young woman.

Detective Minor watched the interaction between the two women, noting not only what was being said but also what wasn't. It seemed that Marcia Waters had no intention of dragging out Frank's supposed girlfriends or weekends at this fishing cabin to explain to her daughter why she had responded as she had. As Sophie's crying subsided, Detective Minor asked, "Are you up to finishing this evening?"

Both women nodded and so Minor continued, "Do either of you know of anyone who would want to hurt Frank?"

"Not that I can think of," Marcia replied a little too quickly for Minor's liking.

"Mom, what about Uncle George?"

Marcia Waters didn't respond, so Minor asked, "Uncle George?"

"She is referring to Frank's brother George, who I just realized I need to call and tell him his brother is dead."

"Sophie, why do you think your Uncle George may have wanted to hurt your dad?"

"My mom could probably tell you more than I know. It is just that, Dad and he had a bunch of arguments after my grandma died."

"George and Frank were never close, and Frank made sure to sever any chance of them having a relationship. Frank's dad died twenty-plus years ago, and his mom always favored Frank. Her will named Frank as her only heir, and it turned ugly. I wasn't there, but Frank told me that George showed up at the estate sale and threatened him."

"Mrs. Waters, I am going to ask you not to call your brother-in-law before I have had a chance to talk to him. Is there anyone else that the two of you can think of that we should look into regarding Frank's murder?"

Sophie's phone began to ring, and she pulled it from her pocket. "I am sorry I have to take this; it is my boss." She said as she walked out of the room.

"Detective, I was going to call you when Sophie was not around, but now the opportunity to speak candidly has presented itself. There is one other person, Tessa Lee. She used to work for the school district and accused Frank of attempting to sexually assault her. He ended up admitting to what he did and blaming drinking, which was total bullshit, but because of that, they told him to go to rehab, and the whole thing blew over. Well, that was only after the school district paid the woman a nice settlement."

"Are you implying that Tessa Lee may have killed your husband?"

"No, not her. Her brother. He showed up here a couple of weeks after Frank came home from the rehab center. The two of them screamed at each other and then exchanged punches. Our neighbor across the street came out and told them that she had called the police. By the time the officer got here, Ms. Lee's brother was gone, and Frank told the officer that it was a private matter, which I suppose was true."

"Did you ever see or hear from this man again?"

"No, and before you ask, I don't know his name. It was Frank who told me who he was."

Sophie walked back into the room, "Mom, my boss told me to take all the time I need here, so I will be here until we know who killed Daddy. Detective Minor, do you mind if I ask you a few questions?"

"Okay, but this is an active investigation and so there is little I can tell you."

"I understand. My first three questions are: where, when, and how?"

"Your dad was killed at his office sometime on Saturday. The medical examiner hasn't yet informed us of the cause of death or the exact time. I will tell you that there is no chance this is anything other than a homicide."

Sophie was crying again, but this time, it was just a flow of tears, not the sobbing from before. "Thank you for telling us that. I guess I have only one more question, do you have any suspects? But I think I know the answer, since you asked us for possibilities."

"We are at the very preliminary stage of the investigation into your dad's murder. I promise you we will do all that we can to solve this case." Detective Kass Minor knew better than to promise to solve the case. Her time in the Cold Case Unit had solidified her understanding that no matter how hard detectives tried, some cases were never solved.

Marcia Waters responded this time, "That is all we really can ask of you. Please keep us informed and know that we will do anything we can to help you solve Frank's murder."

"Please don't hesitate to reach out to me or my partner, Detective Nichols, if you think of anything else? Also, when Kyle gets home, I would appreciate it if you would have him call me."

"We will do that, but I do not see how he will have anything to share with you that will help the investigation. As I mentioned, it has been almost two years since he has come home."

"I understand, but sometimes it is a small thing that a person doesn't even realize is important that helps us solve a case. Family members generally have the most insight into someone's life."

May 2023

Sitting in the hot afternoon sun, Frank allowed his mind to wander back thirty-one years. He only allowed himself to think about Jenny on this day. Every year, he took the day off and found a quiet place to sit and reflect on his life. He had never discussed what happened with anyone nor talked about what he did this day. As far as he knew, his wife Marcia wasn't even aware that he had been taking the same day off for thirty years.

When the parks department offered the opportunity to buy a bench at the new botanical gardens, he hadn't hesitated. When Marcia saw the check, she told him how lovely it was that he had bought the bench in memory of his dad, who had just passed away. That was the story he went with from that point forward. He had donated the bench anonymously, and the quote by Mitch Albom, "There is no fair in life and death. If it were, no good men would die young" was engraved on the donation plate. The quote worked for his dad since he had been in his mid-fifties when the massive heart attack took his life, but it was chosen for Jenny.

After her death, Frank vowed never to express anger through violence again and to lead a life that he could be proud of. Every year when he sat here, he reflected on whether he could hold himself to those two promises. He had slipped up on the no-violence promise a few times, but he had never started the fights, and he hadn't physically hurt a woman since Jenny. It was the second promise that always made him melancholy when he embarked on this journey of self-reflection. He had been unfaithful to Marcia more times than he cared to admit, even to himself. In the beginning, he hadn't wanted to grow too emotionally attached to her and wanted her to be relieved if he went away because he was sure any day the cops would knock on the door and arrest him for Jenny's murder. As the years went by and that knock never came, he began to feel invincible. Who wouldn't? He often thought, *I got away with murder.*

******

Lance Clark sat at his sister's grave. He came here every year alone on the day that she died. His mom could never get out of bed on this day, and when his dad was alive, he drank the day away. So he came alone, sat with his sister, talked to his sister, and cried for his sister. It had been thirty-one years since his sister was murdered and twenty-one years since Lance had zeroed in on Frank Waters as her killer. In those twenty-one years, he had come no closer to proving what he knew in his heart. The private investigator he had hired, Cliff Alrich, had found nothing that investigators did not already know, and his investigation had gotten them no closer to making a case.

The last time that Cliff and Lance had spoken, the private investigator had said,

"I think you have tunnel vision about your sister's murder and it is not helping to solve her case. I am going to keep working on finding Jenny's killer, but I am no longer focusing on Frank Waters. I suggest that you allow myself and the Champagne Cold Case Unit to investigate while you move on with your life."

From an outsider's view, he could see how someone would think that he was stuck and had foregone having a full life because of his obsession with Frank Waters. Maybe he could have had a more well-rounded life if his parents had handled Jenny's death in a healthier way. But that was not how it had been, and no amount of reflection or what-if thinking could change the past.

13

Monday, February 5, 2024

Detective Kass Minor ended her phone call with Tessa Lee and headed into the police station. Nichols had texted her he was back and had ordered them a pizza. She hoped that he had found something out to move this investigation along because, so far, she had nothing. On her way back to the station, she had stopped at home to see Robert and Emma. Robert had assured that he could handle things at home while she worked the case so she didn't linger at home long.

Approaching the conference room, she could see that Detective Nichols was eating pizza while adding to the murder board he had created.

"Thanks for starting, Nichols."

"No problem; I feel like we have to be missing something, so I figured we better organize what we have and see where we are at."

"I take it that your interviews didn't reveal Frank Waters' killer."

"Nah, no TV show instant solves here. How about you eat and I will tell you about my two interviews?"

"Sounds like a plan."

"I started with the department secretary, Roland LaRue, who was working at South High School just as Ms. Crespo said he would be. Mr. LaRue did not have a lot to add to what we already knew because he has only been with the school district for five months. He said that Frank was a friendly guy who loved to talk sports and often brought treats for the entire office. In the short time that Mr. LaRue has worked at the school district, he hasn't heard anyone complain about Frank and did not know who, and I quote, 'would do something to such a standup guy.' end quote."

"I agree that the interview was of no evidentiary value. What about Frank's supervisor? What was her take on the guy?"

"Sandy Frances was also at South High School, so at least I did not spend my time tracking these people down. She's been with the district for a year and a half and was not so flattering towards Mr. Waters, but also did not know who would kill him. She reported that he often was late to meetings, did not have his work done on time, and had a laissez-faire attitude towards his job. Mrs. Frances had never met Marcia Waters and said that Frank rarely spoke of his family. She added that most women who interacted with him were not a fan of his."

"But no specific suspects, and I assume that both of them have alibis."

"Both said they were home most of Saturday other than a few errands. Oh, and Mrs. Frances went out to dinner that evening with her husband and some friends. I asked neither of them for corroboration because I just don't think they are suspects. Anything from your interviews with Sophie and Marica Waters?"

"Mother and daughter seem to have a very strained relationship, which may always be the case or may be because of the circumstance. They provided me with two names to look into. The first was Tessa Lee, who Ms. Crespo also provided, but it seems that Ms. Crespo was unaware that there had been a fight between who Frank Waters said was Tessa's brother and himself."

"I am confused. What do you mean Frank said it was Tessa's brother that he fought with?"

"So, here's the thing on the way back here: I called Tessa Lee on the number that Ms. Crespo provided. Ms. Lee, who is now Mrs. Winchester, lives in San Diego, California, with her husband Graham and two-week-old baby Yvette. When I asked about the fight between Frank and her brother, she hesitated and then told me that she doesn't have a brother. The person who Frank Waters fought with was her then-boyfriend, now husband, Graham. She said that Graham lost his cool when she told him what Frank did and confronted him. Tessa did not know why Frank told his wife that Graham was her brother. I think we can rule Tessa and Graham Winchester out as suspects, since they live in California and have a newborn."

"I agree with that conclusion, so who was the second name?"

"George Waters, Frank's brother. Both Sophie and Marcia indicated that Frank and George had a falling out after their mother died. It seems that their mother left George out of her will, and he did not take it well. Marcia told me that George publicly threatened Frank at the estate sale."

"So we need to find George Waters and interview him. Anything else?"

"No, that is all I have so far, but what do you think about talking to the other two people who Ms. Crespo told us about?"

"Oh, I forgot; I confirmed that Colin Bruno is still doing time in the Algoa Correctional Center. We should probably look into his communications in and out of the prison to be sure this was not a hit, but I think that is a long shot for an embezzlement case."

"Let's put him in the unlikely column along with Tessa Winchester and her husband Graham."

"Are you okay with putting Marcia Waters in that same column?"

"Yes, although I suppose that we should look into whether she arranged his murder. Although, like Mr. Bruno, I don't think that is what we are looking at. So that leaves us with George Waters."

"Yeah, and that other woman Ms. Crespo told us about, Jo Beth Kalan."

"Do you honestly think a woman who hates her boss's meetings would resort to murder?"

"We have both worked cases that had less of an obvious motive, haven't we?"

"Yeah, we have; so do we start with George or Jo Beth?"

"Let's start with George because it sounds like he has more of a motive."

******

Detective Nichols drove to the address that they had found for George Waters while Detective Minor looked for information on him.

"George Waters has some drug-related offenses dating back to the early two thousands but nothing more recent. The address on George's driver's license that we are headed to now is for Fresh Start Sober Living House."

"That is interesting. Do you think he actually lives there, or are we chasing a dead end?"

"I guess we are about to find out." Detective Minor replied as they pulled up to the building.

Minor pressed the intercom button on the front door, and a voice answered, "Welcome to Fresh Start. How can I help you?"

"This is Detectives Minor and Nichols from the Springfield Police Department. Is there a George Waters here?"

"Yes, this is he. I will buzz you in."

George Waters met the detectives at the door and showed them to the office.

"How can I help the Springfield Police Department today?"

"Mr. Waters, do you live here?"

"Yes, I do. I am the resident manager here at Fresh Start Sober Living for the last ten years. I have been clean and sober for the last sixteen years. I moved in here after the last time I got out of rehab and stayed for six months. After that, I started volunteering and then got a job working every other weekend. When the resident manager position opened, I knew that it was a great fit for me. The position is a live-in one, and that works well for me. May I ask again what this is about?"

"We are sorry to inform you that your brother Frank was murdered on Saturday."

"Wait, what? Wow, why didn't Marcia let me know? Murdered? What happened?"

"We can not answer most questions, as this is an ongoing investigation. Just so you are aware, I asked Marcia not to call you. Where were you on Saturday morning?"

"Where was I? Are you saying I am a suspect? I was here. I have every other weekend off, but this past one wasn't one of them. We have a video monitoring system, so I can get you a video of the time frame if you would like it."

"That would be extremely helpful. We were told that you and your brother were not on speaking terms and that you threatened him."

"That is true. We were never close, and when our mom died, it got ugly. I was expecting to get half of her estate, but Frank got it all. We exchanged words on several occasions, and I admit I told him something about nobody caring when he dies. But I never threatened to harm him physically. "

"We appreciate your candor, and I know you said you were not close to Frank, but can you think of anything that might help us catch your brother's killer?"

"I am really sorry, but I can not think of anyone specific, but when I told Frank that no one would care when he died, it wasn't completely true. I am sure that Sophie and Kyle will be devastated, but other than them, I doubt there is anyone else because Frank was only ever out for what was best for Frank. Yes, he screwed me over, but I was just another in a long string of people who Frank treated with disdain."

Detective Minor fished her card out and handed it to George Waters. "Please email me that footage from Saturday to me and call if you think of anything. We are sorry for your loss."

******

As they got back into the car, Nichols turned to Minor, "So, another person to cross off the list. Do you want to go talk to the Kalan woman this evening or leave it until the morning?"

"Let's go ahead and talk with her yet tonight. I figure this will be a quick one, and then tomorrow, we can go over any forensic evidence that is ready and start finding a video from around the area. We are going to need a break in order to solve this case."

"Sounds good to me. Mind if we stop for a coffee on the way over? I am wiped out."

"Works for me."

July 2023

Jo Beth had been looking forward to this girl's weekend since Annie had suggested it. With Annie's husband out of town at a law conference, the two friends were planning a weekend of doing nothing but drinking, talking and watching romcom movies. Jo Beth had stocked up on ice cream and wine, as well as taking Girl Scout cookies out of her freezer.

Saturday evening, they both got really drunk and were talking when Annie brought up Noah.

"You seem to be doing better dealing with losing Noah. I am glad the therapy is helping."

"Thanks. The therapist gave me the idea of finding something constructive to focus my anger on, and that is what I did. It really helps."

"Great. What constructive thing did you start doing?"

When Jo Beth started laughing, Annie lost it too. When the friends stopped giggling and caught their breath, Annie asked, "Pole Dancing? Only Fans? Video Poker? What is it you started doing to refocus your energy? Because from the way you were laughing, it has to be something outrageous."

"I started plotting how to murder Frank Waters."

"What are you talking about?"

"Well, you know how I love true crime and forensics shows?"

"Yeah, but that is a long way from plotting a real person's murder. What exactly did you do?"

"I made a list of things I would need for my murder bag and then went to garage and estate sales and the flea market and gathered everything. When I found myself getting upset, I would write out detailed plans for killing him."

"WHAT? Jo Beth, that is in no way healthy and not at all what the therapist meant!"

"Come on, you know I would never actually hurt anyone, right?"

"I don't know because you are telling me that you actually bought things to make a murder bag. Show me this bag?"

Jo Beth got up off the couch and walked out to her van in the garage. Annie was shocked when she returned with a large black duffle bag. Jo Beth set the bag down in front of her and unzipped it. Annie watched as she pulled items out: garbage bags, a couple of knives, a wig, gloves and more.

"Wow, you really thought of everything. I have to be honest and tell you that this worries me." Annie had found Jo Beth's confession to be sobering, and she was wondering if her friend had suffered a psychotic break.

Jo Beth did not respond as she packed the items back into the bag and carried it back to her van. When she returned, she sat next to Annie and hugged her friend.

"You have to know that I would never actually murder anyone. I get that you do not understand what I am doing, but it has become a release valve for when my anger feels like it is going to boil over. I promise that is all it is. Fantasy. A way to feel like I am regaining my power over my life. I know that you never agreed with me about Frank, but I will always know that I wasn't here when Noah died. It is easier for me to blame Frank than myself."

"Oh sweetie. I can't imagine what you have been through. If I lost Mike as suddenly as you did Noah, I would be devastated. You have no reason to blame yourself. Noah had a massive heart attack. Please promise me that you will find a different way to handle things. Planning to murder someone even if you don't intend to do it is no way to relieve the hate you have for him."

14

Monday, February 5, 2024

Sitting on the floor of her living room, Jo Beth looked at the sea of boxes. Packing up the home you have lived in for almost thirty years was a massive undertaking, but it would all be worth it once she moved to Columbia. The offer she had put in on the condo yesterday had been accepted, and she was not sure who was more excited, her daughter Angie or herself. Angie's first baby was due in July and Jo Beth couldn't wait to be a part of her grandbaby's life. A month ago, when Angie and her husband Jose had asked Jo Beth to consider moving to Columbia and provide childcare for their new baby, she had hesitated at first. The more she thought about the idea, the happier it made her. She had loved being a stay-at-home mom before her girls started full-time school and imagined this would be even better because she did not have to be awake at night with the baby.

The ringing of the doorbell startled her because it was seven at night, and no one ever stopped by her house. She peered at the app her son-in-law had added to her phone when he installed the doorbell camera. A woman and a man stood on the porch, each holding up their badges. Jo Beth took a deep breath and got up to answer the door.

"Hello, how can I help you?"

"Mrs. Kalan, I am Detective Kass Minor from the Springfield Police Department, and this is Detective Nichols. May we please come in?"

"Of course. Please excuse the disorder. I am in the middle of sorting and packing the house to move."

"Where and when are you moving?"

"I am moving to Columbia at the end of the school year to live near my daughter and her family."

"Are you aware that Frank Waters was murdered this weekend?"

"Yes, it was all anyone talked about today at school."

"We have been told that you and Mr. Waters had ongoing issues. Please tell us about that."

Sighing, Jo Beth shook her head, "Look, I never liked the guy. When he was my supervisor, I complained. We were like oil and water, but it was just work. He stopped being my supervisor at the end of last school year when he got his new job, so I rarely interact with him."

"When was the last time you saw Mr. Waters and or were in his office?"

"Last week Thursday, actually. I was at the administrative building for a meeting, and he had ordered some items from the school fundraiser. My principal asked me to drop them off to him, so I did. We exchanged pleasantries, and I left."

"Mrs. Kalan, where were you this Saturday?"

"Me? I went to Columbia for the entire weekend. My daughter and I looked at condos and I put an offer in on one. I got back late last night. Why am I a suspect?"

"We are talking to people who had connections to Mr. Waters. Would you be able to provide corroboration of your trip?"

"Sure, I have the receipt for the hotel in the kitchen and can give you the realtor's contact information. Is there anything else that you need?"

"That should do it for now. We appreciate your time. If you think of or hear anything that may help our investigation, please be sure to call."

"Sure, of course, but I have no idea who would bludgeon Frank Waters in the head to death."

Minor turned to look at Detective Nichols, who was staring wide-eyed at Jo Beth.

"Jo Beth Kalan, put your hands behind your back. You are under arrest for the murder of Frank Waters."

******

Standing next to Detectives Minor and Nichols, Lance Clark thought this had to be fate or maybe karma. A half hour ago, when his phone rang, he was home, mindlessly watching a movie he had seen at least a dozen times and wishing he was not the Assistant District Attorney on call this week so he could have a few beers. When Detective Minor had said that she and her partner Nichols had just arrested someone for the murder of Frank Waters, he felt his stomach drop, and his head began to buzz. He told the detectives that he would meet them at the station ASAP and did just that while repeating over and over in his head, *Frank Waters is dead!*

"Please explain to me how it is you came to arrest Jo Beth Kalan and what you need from me?"

"We went to interview her this evening because the HR director for the school district had given us her name as a person who did not like Mr. Waters. Quite frankly, neither Nichols nor I thought it was going to be anything other than an elimination interview. We talked to her for about ten minutes, and she had a decent alibi for the time that the medical examiner said Waters was murdered, so we were getting ready to leave. As we did, she said, 'I have no idea who would bludgeon Frank Waters in the head to death.' which is a detail that, aside from the responding officer, Nichols, myself, the medical examiner, and the CSI team, no one knows. Well, other than the killer, that is."

"What has she said since you arrested her?"

"Nothing other than I want a lawyer. She made her one phone call, and we have been waiting for the lawyer since."

"While we wait, why don't the two of you tell me everything we have so far?"

Nichols looked at Minor, who nodded her head, so he started. "We got called to the Springfield School District Administrative Office this morning at about 7:30 am. Officer Peterson had responded to an unlocked door with the alarm system off and had found a deceased body that appeared to have been murdered. Minor and I, along with the CSI team, inspected the scene and found a dead male, who we preliminarily identified as Frank Waters based on the driver's license in the wallet he was holding, the fact that the body was in his office, and that his truck was outside in the parking lot.

The medical examiner has made a positive identification at this point based on his wife and daughter's agreement. Dr. Reeves puts Mr. Waters' time of death at about ten in the morning on Saturday and the manner of death as homicide by blunt force trauma."

"Nichols and I notified Mrs. Marica Waters at her office this morning, and I subsequently interviewed her and their daughter Sophie late this afternoon," Minor added as Nichols took a drink of the sludge that passed for coffee here at the station.

"Before that, I spoke with the school superintendent, Dr. Sydney Trappen, and Minor spoke to the head of security, Trey Laman. Both confirmed that the camera system was down for maintenance all weekend and that all the district employees had been accidentally told about the update and outage. Neither gave us any real leads, so we did the notification and then spoke with the head of Human Resources, Star Crespo. She was more helpful as far as possible suspects."

"How so?" Lance asked in a way that he hoped sounded interested, but not too interested. Since the detectives had informed him of Frank Waters' murder, he had been practicing every breathing and calming technique that he had ever learned and employed in court. It would be a major red flag if an Assistant District Attorney showed giddiness over the murder of an outwardly appearing decent citizen.

"She gave us three names: Tessa Lee, Colin Bruno, and Jo Beth Kalan. Each had filed complaints against Frank Waters over the years."

"I know the Colin Bruno case because I prosecuted him and he implicated Mr. Waters in the embezzlement scheme. The investigator for my office could find no evidence to back up this claim, so we never charged Mr. Waters. I assume Mr. Bruno's complaint was regarding the case. What about the two women? What were their complaints?"

"Yes, Colin Bruno's complaint was that Frank Waters was the mastermind of the embezzlement scheme. The first woman that Ms. Crespo told us about was Tessa Lee, and hers was the most serious of the two complaints because it involved an unwanted sexual advance and attempted groping. However, Minor spoke with her, and she lives in California and has a newborn baby, so we eliminated her. The second is Jo Beth Kalan, who filed a series of seemingly petty complaints against Mr. Waters over the past fifteen years. Ms. Crespo also told us that Mrs. Kalan had been in the HR office multiple times to make verbal complaints about Mr. Waters."

"What kind of petty complaints?"

Detective Minor opened her notebook and scanned the notes she had taken during their interview with Star Crespo. "Complaints about the number of and timing of meetings, her evaluation and Mr. Waters speaking to her condescendingly in front of a group of people."

"Yeah, those seem to be trivial, commonplace work complaints, but yet you arrested her for Mr. Waters' murder."

"Minor and I really went there just to dot the i's and cross the t's. We even talked on the way over that neither of us considered her a real suspect. It was her statement about Mr. Waters being bludgeoned to death that led to her arrest."

"What kind of forensic evidence is there?"

"At this point, none. The CSI Techs found no fingerprints other than Mr. Waters, and we do not have the murder weapon. Whoever killed Frank Waters really covered their tracks, which leads me to believe that it was a well-planned event. The medical examiner, Dr. Reeves, reported that the manner is homicide by the use of blunt force trauma."

"And you think that Mrs. Kalan is the killer?"

"Well, honestly, if she isn't the actual killer, she knows who is and leaked that detail about his death inadvertently. That is why we need a warrant to search Mrs. Kalan's car and her house, as well as to get her GPS and cell phone records."

Before Lance could respond, a uniformed officer walked up to the three of them, saying, "Sorry to interrupt, but the attorney for your suspect in the interview room said they are ready to talk."

"Thank you, Officer Jones." Detective Kass Minor responded, then turned to her partner and the Assistant District Attorney. "Let's go see if we have solved this murder, shall we?"

December 2023

Jo Beth looked around her house as she tried to motivate herself to decorate for Christmas. Her daughters and their husbands would be here in a couple of days and would be concerned if they found the house undecorated, like they had the last two years. Decorating without Noah was joyless for Jo Beth. The first year she had tried, she really had but broke down sobbing with each Christmas song that played and box she tried to look through. She and Noah had built Christmas decorating traditions, and like all of their traditions, his untimely death had robbed her of them. The first Christmas after his death, she put on the Christmas playlist that she and Noah had created and was flooded with memories. In the end that year, her daughters and their then-boyfriends had gone out, got a tree, decorated it, and helped her to make the best of a very rough holiday.

The next year, she had hoped it would be easier, but it actually seemed harder. Every day that drew closer to the holiday, Jo Beth slipped farther into a dark place until she found herself driving by Frank Waters's house to see what his holiday preparations looked like. The outside lights that shone brightly, the immense decorated Christmas tree in the front picture window, and the cheery blowup characters on the lawn made her despise him even more. His life was so picture-perfect, and hers was ruined. When her daughters arrived last year, not only did they find the house not decorated, but they found their mom in bed as she had been for several days. Unlike the year before, even her daughters did not attempt to decorate.

Jo Beth went and grabbed her notebook from its hiding place under her bed, thinking *maybe planning another way to kill Frank will get me out of this funk*. So far, she had written plans that involved tampering with his brake lines, stabbing him in his bed while he slept, and burning down his house with his wife, not in it, of course. Jo Beth began to write:

Poisoning is an up close and personal death, so in order to make this work, I will need to volunteer to be on the committee that he chairs. That alone might raise a few eyebrows because I have complained about the fuck wad for so long, but I will have to really sell that the committee is more important to me than my issues with him. Each time the committee meets, I will have to bring his favorite energy drink from the coffee shop downtown and offer it to him. I will do this under the guise of trying to bury the hatchet. HA HA!! I was able to get the arsenic rat poisoning at the flea market this summer and will need to mix it up so I can stir it into these drinks.

Jo Beth paused in her writing, thinking *poisoning will never work*. No one will believe that I am that willing to look past that deplorable man's issues and go out of my way to bring him drinks. Then there is how I would continue to get him the drinks after he gets too sick to work. Ripping the page out of her notebook, she got up and started a fire in her fireplace and burned that plan as she had all the others she had written before it. She turned her wireless speaker system and started blasting eighties hair bands as she decorated. Noah hated this music, so it was perfect for completing this task without him.

******

Marcia Waters sat alone in her house, staring at the Christmas tree. Neither of her kids had come home for Christmas this year. Sophie had decided to work the holidays when the hospital system offered nurses triple time and Kyle was God knows where doing God knows what. Both of them had called this morning, and both seemed surprised to find that their dad was not home. After finding out the kids were not coming home, Frank had spent the week at his fishing cottage, which was probably for the best. Spending an entire week with her husband would have been torture for both of them. Her sister had asked her to join her at their parents' house in Arizona, but Marcia had passed on that too. Tax season was starting soon and Marcia needed a week of nothing to do and no one harping at her. Yes, she would have loved for children to be home for the holidays, but being alone was the next best thing.

By the time Frank got home from his trip, she would have all the indoor decorations put away and the house back in its usual orderly state. Deciding to start with laundry, Marcia grabbed the hamper from her room and then went to the guest room, which was now Frank's room. She shook her head at the mess that she saw. He was as bad a teenage boy, there were clothes, dishes and wrappers all over the room. She should shut the door and walk away, but her fastidious nature would not allow for that. She grabbed an empty hamper and a garbage bag and got to work in the room. She reached under the bed to grab an errant sock that was sticking out, and her hand bumped into a box.

Using both hands, Marcia pulled the box out from under the bed and opened the lid. The box contained cash and a lot of it. *What the hell, where did all this come from?* Marcia wondered as she stared at the money. They had joint accounts and there had been no large cash withdrawals in all their years of marriage, so where had Frank gotten all this and why was it under the guest room bed in a box? The money was bundled and wrapped in stacks of ten thousand dollars apiece. She methodically removed them, counting as she went. Under the stacks of money were more paper bands. Some of them had been torn off, and some appeared to have yet to be used. He had two hundred and fifty thousand dollars in cash in a recycled delivery box under a bed in their house. Actually, Marcia thought *he used to have two-hundred and fifty thousand dollars in cash in a box under the bed that he slept in when he felt like it. Now I have two hundred and fifty thousand dollars in cash and no reason not to divorce his sorry ass.*

15

Monday, February 5, 2024

Jo Beth had used her one phone call to reach out to her best friend, Annie, who was married to an attorney. When Mike Davidson had arrived a few minutes ago, he immediately asked Jo Beth why she had been arrested and she had told him she did not know. She went on to explain that two detectives had stopped by her house this evening asking questions about her former boss, Frank Waters. Since Annie worked for the district too, she had already told Mike about Frank being found dead this morning in his office.

Mike listened to Jo Beth and then posed the question that every attorney hopes their client will answer truthfully. "Did you have anything to do with the murder?"

"No, of course not." While waiting for Mike to arrive, Jo Beth had sat and thought about what had made the detectives arrest her and she knew it was the comment about bludgeoning, but she did not tell Mike this.

After they talked for a while longer, Mike went to let the detectives know that she was ready to answer their questions. He had told her several times that she should wait for him to nod before she said anything and that she was to answer precisely the question she was asked. He had told her he thought the detectives were on a quote unquote fishing expedition and that she needed to not get caught in their net.

With Mike sitting next to her, Jo Beth watched the detectives enter the room and sat down. Mike waited a moment and when no one spoke, he asked, "Why is my client here?"

Detective Nichols smiled and responded, “Well, because we suspect that she murdered Frank Waters.”

“Why? What possible evidence do you have?”

“Mrs. Kalan, how about you explain to us how you knew Mr. Waters' manner of death?”

“Oh, um, I heard it at work. A bunch of us were talking about Frank and someone said that they had heard that.”

“Who? Who said it?”

“I am sorry, I don’t remember.”

“Interesting. Moving on...let’s review where you were on Saturday morning.”

“As I told you, I went to Columbia to visit my daughter and look at condos.”

“Right, what time did you leave for Columbia?”

“It was about nine-thirty that morning. I remember texting my daughter Angie just before I left to tell her I was on the way.”

“So, what time did you arrive in Columbia?”

“Around one in the afternoon.”

“It is a two hour and forty-five minute drive and it took you three and a half hours. Did you stop somewhere?”

“Yes, I did. I stopped at Hilltop cemetery to talk to my husband, Noah.”

“Does he work there?”

“No, he is buried there. I visit him almost every Saturday and talk to him about how things are going. Not being close to him is the one thing that will be tough for me when I move to Columbia.”

“We will be getting a warrant for your cell phone data, house and car. What are we going to find?”

Mike Davidson put his hand up to stop Jo Beth from responding. “Detectives, I highly doubt a judge will give you any warrants based on my client repeating a rumor.”

A knock on the observation window interrupted the conversation before either of the detectives could respond.

Detective Minor rose from her seat and said, “I will be right back.” Standing on the other side of the interview room were Lance Clark and Commander Brewer, both looking grim.

“Mr. Davidson is right. We have no cause to hold her or to be able to get warrants. Cut her loose and try to find more evidence to either prove Jo Beth Kalan did or did not have something to do with this murder,” Commander Brewer said.

Minor knew better than to argue with her commander, so she nodded her head and headed back to the interview room.

“Mrs. Kalan, you are free to go at this time.”

Mike Davidson smiled at his client, stood and held out his hand for Jo Beth to do the same. The two of them walked out of the police station without another word.

Commander Brewer walked into the interview room, “Detectives, head home and tomorrow get to work on triangulating cell phone data and hopefully forensics will have something more for us.”

January 1, 2024

Frank Waters stared at the box that he had just pulled from under the bed. All that was in it now were some paper money bands. All his cash was gone. *Where had it gone? Who had taken it?* Frank’s thoughts whirled in his head. *Should I confront Marcia?* That could backfire in a major way if she hadn’t taken it. How would he explain where the money had come from and why he was keeping it in cash under the guest room bed? But who else could have taken it? Kyle? He knew that Marcia believed he never came home, but Frank was sure he did. Several times, Frank had come home and found the dryer warm, the shower slightly wet and food eaten with the dishes washed and put away. He had concluded that these instances were times that Kyle stopped at home but did not let his parents know.

He had used most of the money he had gotten through Colin, but he knew there was still two hundred and fifty thousand in the box with the majority of that coming from his mom's estate. He had been careful all these years to spend the cash in ways that did not raise questions. He had financed his new truck despite the cash in the box and did not buy flashy items. No, he spent the cash on women and they were an expensive habit. Knowing it was a long shot, Frank went into the primary bedroom to look for his money.

The bedroom looked just as he suspected with its perfect vacuum lines, precisely made bed and not one speck of dust. He opened the door to the walk-in closet and saw that the only change from when he had shared it was that his side sat completely empty. Marcia had moved none of her stuff over when she took his belongings out, but that was true to her nature. Her clothes were hung on color coded hangers and consisting of blue and white silk blouses, both short and long sleeves and black and blue pencil skirts. There were a few dresses, all black on the back of the rack, as well as four pairs of black trousers. Her shoes were lined up precisely with two pairs of blue heels, one pair of black heels, which meant she was wearing the other pair of black ones today, and a pair of athletic shoes. Closing the closet door after finding no sign of the money, Frank walked into the en suite bathroom and checked the cupboards and drawers, to no avail. If Marcia had taken his money, she had not hid it in the bathroom or the closet. On a whim, he got down to check under her bed and that is when he saw the cardboard box.

The box appeared to be almost the same size and shape as the one he had under the guest room bed, and that was not likely to be a coincidence. Frank reached under the bed and pulled the box out. He opened the lid and saw an upside-down stack of pictures and a letter sitting in the box. He decided to start with the note, which read:

Mom,
Here is all the proof you should ever need to divorce him!
K

There were six pictures in all, with first being his fishing cabin with two vehicles parked in front of it, his and Gwen's. The next photo was of him and Gwen sitting on the porch of the cabin, sharing a blanket and a cup of coffee. The third was of him and Gwen kissing as she left the cabin and the fourth was a picture of Frank entering Gwen's condo building carrying flowers. The fifth was a picture of a framed picture that was in Frank and Marcia's den. It was Kyle's senior prom picture and, on their son's, arm was Gwen and the last picture was of Gwen's bank statement showing the cash deposits.

Stunned, Frank put all the items back in the box, closed it and slid it under the bed. He wondered how long has Marcia had these? Why hasn't she done anything about it? He had admitted to cheating in the past during their failed counseling attempts, but never to how much cash he had given some of his lady friends. Which brought him to the crux of his problem with the missing money, Gwen!

An hour later, he sat in Gwen's condo, watching her pace. She was angrier than he had expected and he did not know how to calm her down.

"What the hell do you mean, all your money is gone? Gone, where?"

"I do not know. I told you that. I can take out enough to cover this month's expenses, but after that, we are going to have to come up with something different."

"Something different, something different. If I have to get a job, then I am done with this arrangement with you. Being with you for the last two years has been my job, and I have earned every penny. Now get out of my condo until you come up with money."

Frank rose from the couch and tried to reach for Gwen, but she shoved him away.

"Frank, what part of get out has you confused? We have had a mutually beneficial relationship up until this point, but if you can't keep up your end of the bargain, it is over!"

"Okay, I get it and I will do everything I can to sort this out."

16

Tuesday, February 6, 2024

Kyle Waters slipped into the backdoor of the only place he had ever called home, hoping not to wake his mom or sister. He was exhausted from his last assignment and traveling to come home under the circumstances. As he walked into the kitchen, he saw that luck was not with him, his sister Sophie was sitting at the breakfast bar drinking what he suspected was room temperature coffee.

"Hi sis. Is the coffee hot and fresh?"

"Hello to you too. No, it is old and cold. You know, like our mom. I am so glad you are home. I was sitting here thinking about the fact that neither you nor I came home for Christmas the last few years. It took our dad being murdered to get us both back under this roof at the same time. Why do you think that is?"

"I am going to start some fresh coffee before we dive into the deep end of analyzing all that was wrong with our upbringing. Is that okay with you?"

"Sure, that is fine. Want to sit in the sun room so we don't wake mom up?"

"Sounds like a plan." The siblings sat in silence listening to the coffee brew, both lost in thought. When the machine beeped, Kyle jumped up and poured a large mug and held the pot out for his sister.

Sophie got up from the stool and poured her old cold coffee down the sink drain, and made a fresh cup. She then followed her little brother out into the sun room.

"Sophie, I know you always worshiped the ground that dad walked on but did you ever wonder why mom or their marriage was the way it was?"

"Of course I wondered. I mean, Aunt Corine is so lighthearted and fun and then there is mom. I guess I always wondered why dad married her in the first place and why he stayed with her."

"You really are clueless when it comes to dad aren't you? He was not a great husband. He cheated on mom countless times. I tried to get her to leave him once both of us were out of the house, but she just wouldn't. That is why I rarely come home. I can't stand him and I have been angry with her for staying with him. She deserves better."

"What? Did SHE tell you those lies about dad? He would never have done that."

"No, I witnessed it and I do mean witnessed it for myself."

"What do you mean, you witnessed it?"

"Do you remember when Grandpa Don had his heart attack, I was seventeen, and you were a freshman in college?"

"Yes?"

"Well, mom and Aunt Corine flew to Tucson and that Friday morning when dad and I were both getting ready to head out for a regular day, he told me that a colleague could not attend a conference in Columbia so he was going in their place and would be back on Sunday night. I was like cool and did what most seventeen-year-old guys would. I planned a party with my boys. Thinking we were less likely to get busted if we went to dad's fishing cabin instead of here."

"Okay?"

"After school, my friends and I gathered all the stuff we could and drove to the cabin. I was surprised when we pulled up and dad's van was there. Jimmy got out of the car and ran in the house yelling 'Coach, we are here.' and I was right behind him because I didn't want to get in trouble with dad. Dad had a woman bent over the back of the couch as we ran in, and I am not sure who was more mortified. Me, dad or that chick who, by the way, was like your age. Jimmy and I ran out of the house and dad came out after us, all the while pulling up and zipping his pants."

"Oh, my God. What did you do?"

"Drove home and the kicker was dad did not come home until Sunday evening as he had originally planned to and when he did, he was like 'You're almost a man, so you know that sometimes you gotta scratch the itch.' I told him that he was gross and he shrugged and walked away."

"Did you tell mom?"

"Yes, I did when she got back home. She said she was sorry that I saw that and found out what he was doing. I told her to leave him and she said that she had long ago accepted that he was not faithful to her. I was shocked."

"No way! Why didn't you tell me?"

"I didn't think you would believe me and, oh, it gets better. Well, actually worse because two years ago I came home between assignments. I told neither mom nor dad, I was coming because I wasn't sure if I would make it. Do you remember Gwendoline, who I dated in high school and took to senior prom?"

"She was the blond, perky cheerleader, right?"

"Well, yes, but that kind of describes all my high school girlfriends, but you remembering her isn't that essential. Just know I dated her and really liked her. The last time I visited, I arrived in the middle of the day on a Wednesday. I was dead tired like I am now and headed right to my old room, which, as you know, has been dad's bedroom for a while now. Dad and Gwendoline were in bed together. She hollered when I walked in and dad ordered me out of the room. I didn't just leave the room, I left the house and went right to mom's office. She and I got into an argument about why she didn't leave him. I was mad, and she was hurt, so I have stayed away from visits that involve both of them, but actually I come to see mom several times a year. What is your excuse?"

Sophie was staring at her brother, almost gaping at him. It was hard for her to integrate what Kyle had told her with the dad she knew and loved, but she knew that Kyle gained nothing by lying to her about this.

"Kyle, I am shocked. Why didn't you tell me any of this before now?"

"Sis, mostly because I know you worshiped the ground that dad walked on and I did not see how enlightening you would result in anything positive. Plus, I did not think you would believe me. Are you going to answer my question?"

"You mean why don't I come home?" Sophie asked and Kyle nodded, so she continued, "Now it seems like a horrible reason, but basically I hated seeing the way mom and dad interacted. I always blamed her for being so cold to him, but after what you just told me, I am questioning so much of what I believed about them."

"Yeah, mom isn't really the cold, heartless witch you make her out to be. She is career driven, which if she was a man would be seen only positively and she was cold towards dad because he had hurt her so much."

"Where does that leave us now?"

"I think we both need to rebuild a relationship with mom and bury dad both physically and metaphorically."

"All of that will be easier said than done. I have spent most of my life judging mom in a harsh negative light and as you said worshiping the ground daddy walked on."

******

Marcia Waters stood on the edge of the kitchen, listening to her children talk about Frank and herself. She had woken up when she smelled the coffee brewing and had been walking to get a cup when she heard Sophie ask Kyle what his reason for not coming home was. Marcia believed she already knew the answer but decided to stop where she was because you could not see the hall from the sun room and listen to them talk. The venom she heard in her son's voice when he was talking about what he had seen and experienced made Marcia question if her choice to stay with Frank all these years had been worth the price she and her kids paid.

Sensing a lull in the conversation, Marcia walked to the coffeemaker in full view of her kids. She poured her coffee and turned towards the sun room, "Morning. Kyle, I am so glad you are home."

Kyle stood and opened his arms to hug his mom. The hug was a bigger dopamine hit for Marcia than even the coffee. Kyle's hug was reassurance that all her decisions and actions as a mom had not been wrong. Unbeknownst to Frank, Kyle came home between each of his assignments, usually just for a few hours, but he always came to see her. She knew he wanted nothing to do with his dad and so they kept the visits between them, but the effort that he made to see her was a bright spot in her life. As they parted, Sophie stood up with tears trickling down her cheeks.

"I love you, mom. I am sorry for judging you without all the facts. Why didn't you ever tell me what was going on?"

"I love you too, Sophie. I did not see a purpose in telling you about your dad's infidelity. Your dad's inability to be faithful was between him and I. It really had nothing to do with his relationship with you."

"But mom, it changed the relationship between you and me!"

"I know and I regret that, but as an adult, bashing your father to your children would have been very immature. I love you and Kyle too much to put you in the middle of the issues your dad and I had."

Kyle looked between his mom and sister and thought not for the first time of the positive outcomes that his father's murder would have on his family.

"Alright ladies, I am exhausted, so I am going to take a quick shower and get a few hours of sleep. Mom, when I get up, we should start planning dad's funeral."

"I suppose you are right. I have not wrapped my head around the arrangements that need to be made. Oh, and by the way, the police detectives working your dad's case want to talk to you."

"Why? It is not as if I live here."

"Honey, they are just doing their jobs, so when you wake up, please call one of them. I will leave their cards on the kitchen counter for you."

"I assume you and Sophie have already talked to them."

"Yes, I have talked to them twice, and they talked with Sophie yesterday evening."

"Did you tell them about dad's affairs and his fights with Uncle George?"

"Yes, to both. Sophie told them about Uncle George, and I let them know about your dad's infidelity."

"I will call one of them later today."

****

As Kass and Robert ran, she marveled at how easily Emma slept while being bounced along in the jogging stroller. Of course, their daughter was used to it because unless the weather was nasty, this ride while her parents ran was part of her everyday routine since she was a few weeks old. Kass had just finished filling Robert in on where her case was at.

"I am frustrated by Lance Clark's attitude. I have always liked him mostly because he was so amicable to help us cops, but last night he kept putting up stumbling blocks. I don't understand what his issue is in this case."

"I have to be honest with you; I am not sure that I believe that an overweight, middle-aged widow bludgeoned her former boss to death with a tire iron. Then this same woman drives almost three hours, spends the weekend with her pregnant daughter, looks at and makes an offer on a condo. Furthermore, this woman leaves no evidence behind and calmly goes to work two days later. So either she had nothing to do with the murder or she is a psychopath. Maybe that is what Clark was thinking as well. When will you get forensics back?"

"Today we should at least get some preliminary reports, and I emailed Abe in the cyber tech department to ask him to get the triangulation data for the cell towers in the area. Without warrants for Jo Beth's home and car, I am not sure what else we will find but Nichols and I are going to head to Hilltop cemetery to find out if there is any way to corroborate her story that she was there before she headed to Columbia.

The strange thing is that the cemetery is the only other thing out there by the school district administrative office. You know how I feel about coincidences."

"It is odd that a good portion of your prime suspect's alibi puts her in the same area as your murder scene. Hopefully, the cemetery has surveillance cameras since the school districts were so conveniently not working."

"This case is already so frustrating. Either this killer is very sophisticated or very lucky, but either way, getting justice for Frank Waters is proving to be difficult."

******

Detective Nichols dropped Detective Minor off at the station after they had been to the cemetery. Nichols had to testify in a different case, so he would be at court the rest of the day. The groundskeeper had been cooperative but not provided them with any real information. The cemetery had no cameras, and he had been working on the far side of the lot at the time Jo Beth Kalan reported that she had been there. There were fresh flowers on Noah Kalan's grave, but there was no way to know if they were placed there on Saturday or another recent day. Another dead end.

Minor planned to go over all the information and evidence they had so far to see if they missed something. The light on her desk phone was flashing to let her know she had voicemail messages. The first was from Abe to let her know he had gotten her request and, in turn, had he had put in for the records with the cell phone providers. The second was from Kyle Waters, letting her know that he had arrived in Springfield and would prefer to speak with her away from his mother and sister. She quickly called him back.

"Kyle Waters here."

"Hello Mr. Waters, this Detective Kass Minor. I am returning your call. Would you be willing to come to the station to talk?"

"Sure. When?"

"How about in thirty minutes?"

"No problem. I will see you then."

Minor began reading her notes from her interviews thus far, searching for an elusive clue. The interview with Kyle Waters was likely to be routine and not lead to anything new, but she could always hope that despite not having lived in Springfield for the last eleven years that he knew something.

Kyle Waters arrived right on time and Minor walked him to the interview room.

"Thank you for coming in to talk to me. First, let me express my condolences for the loss of your dad. I am sure you are anxious to get back to your mom and sister, so this will not take a long time. Do you have any idea who may have wanted to harm your dad?"

"I am sure my mom told you I have not lived with them since I joined the Army eleven years ago, so I do not have knowledge of his day-to-day life. My mom told me that she had already informed you of his infidelity. Have you spoken with Gwendoline?"

"Gwendoline? Who would she be?"

"Gwendoline Marks is my dad's mistress, the last I knew. I take it my mother didn't tell you, her name."

"No, she did not and how is it you know who she is?"

"Two years ago, I caught the two of them together in a compromising position. I guess it is possible he has moved on, but I have a feeling it was an ongoing relationship."

"I will definitely add her name to my list of people to speak with. As a matter of procedure, I need to ask you where you were on Saturday morning."

"I apologize, but that is not a question that I am able to answer."

"Why not?"

"Because I am sure you do not have the necessary level of clearance for me to share those details with you."

"Clearance Level? What type of clearance level would I need for you to answer a straightforward question?"

"A pretty high one, actually." Kyle took out his wallet and handed a business card to Detective Minor. "You are welcome to call or have your commanding officer call this number and my superiors will contact me if I am authorized to share the details of my location with you."

Detective Minor looked down at the card, it had no information on it other than a phone number that started with a Virginia area code.

"Who should we ask for when we call?"

"You will have to leave a message with your request. Be sure to tell them my name and date of birth and someone will get back to you. Do you need my date of birth, or are you able to find that out on your own?"

"I have all of your demographic information from the Department of Motor Vehicles. Is there anything else that you can share with me that might help me to eliminate you as a suspect or solve your father's murder?"

Kyle Waters chuckled and stood up. "Detective, I am sorry if I offended you, but it isn't that I am trying to be difficult, but the work I do for our government is classified and not in any way related to my dad's untimely demise. I will be staying with my mom for a while, so you know where to find me if there is anything else."

Detective Minor walked over to Commander Brewer's office to tell him about her interview with Kyle Waters and ask him to call the mystery number, but found that he was in a meeting. Back at her desk, she called Robert.

"Hi Hon. This is a pleasant surprise. How is your day going?"

"Frustrating. How about yours?"

"I am just working on paperwork again. Why has your day been frustrating?"

"You know how they say bad things come in threes, here are my three. The cemetery had no cameras, and no one could verify if my prime suspect was or wasn't there on Saturday. The second is Abe having to wait for the cell companies to give him the tower data. Then my victim's son came in voluntarily but then when I asked him where he was when his father was killed, he pulled the 'it's above your clearance level card' so I am left wondering what the hell is he hiding."

"Above your clearance level? What is that supposed to mean?"

"My understanding is that he works for the Department of Defense, so I guess his whereabouts are confidential. Any chance you could try to find out who this guy actually works for?"

"Sure, just give me his information and I will run it. It will only take a few minutes."

After providing the information, Detective Minor went to grab a snack and diet soda while waiting for her husband to call her back. She found Gwendoline Marks' contact information and decided to head over to her condo after Robert called to tell her what he had found out about Kyle Waters. She thought about calling Gwen first, but decided that the element of surprise would be helpful in this situation. On the first ring, Kass answered her phone without looking at the caller id.

"Hi Kass, sorry it took me longer than planned. So, I ran your victim's son through the FBI database and hit a brick wall. I was about to call you back when Hollins called me into his office. Unit Chief Sanchez called Hollins and asked him why I was looking into Kyle Waters. Hollins, of course, knows nothing about it and tells Sanchez that, to which Sanchez replies that he did not really care, but the FBI is not looking into Kyle Waters.

Hollins asked what I was investigating, and I told him about your case and Kyle Waters' answer to your question regarding his whereabouts when his father was murdered. He wasn't upset that I ran the name and said that Kyle must be pretty high up the food chain at some alphabet soup agency. His advice to you is that unless you and Nichols have solid evidence to prove that Kyle Waters was involved in his father's murder to let this one go.

Sorry that I'm likely adding to your frustration today. If there is anything else I can do that doesn't involve Kyle Waters, let me know."

"Thanks for trying. I apologize for getting you into trouble at work. I don't suspect Kyle Waters killed his dad. His answer to his whereabouts threw me for a loop, but maybe he really is just not authorized to disclose his location to me."

Saturday, February 3, 2024

Being on call on the weekend was a rotating duty in the district attorney's office, but Lance Clark often volunteered for the duty, so his colleagues were able to spend time with their families. This was his third weekend in a row on call, which usually amounted to him staying in town, not drinking, and getting warrants for active cases. He honestly didn't mind the duty, and he knew that his supervisors appreciated his willingness to take it on.

Getting coffee and a pastry was part of his Saturday routine, which he followed up by either sitting in the bakery reading the online newspapers he subscribed to or driving around town. The bakery owner, Monica, knew him by name as well as his usual order and lately had been giving him a discount when he came in. He had noticed that she didn't wear a wedding ring and always took time to come by his table to chat. This morning he had handed her his card and let her know that if she would like to have dinner to please text him. Yes, he had decided that Jenny wouldn't be happy with the way he and their parents had led their lives since her murder and that he needed to try to find happiness. Monica had smiled when he gave her the card, then texted him while she was still standing at his table. They were meeting for dinner on Tuesday.

Before leaving the bakery, Lance got a to-go cup of coffee and now was driving around Springfield with the radio turned up, enjoying the sunshine and feeling of positive anticipation about his upcoming date. As he crested the hill on the outskirts of town, he watched the sun glint off the windows of the school district administrative building. Frank Waters briefly popped into his head, but Lance made a conscious effort to dismiss the thoughts of him. Driving down the hill, he glanced at the parking lot of the building and was surprised to see Frank Waters' truck and another vehicle in the parking lot. Pulling over, Lance wondered who was with Frank Waters alone in that building and concluded that it must be his latest conquest.

17

Tuesday, February 6, 2024

Gwen Marks looked at the display screen from the building's doorbell system, the woman who rang her doorbell was not someone she knew.

"How can I help you?"

"Hello, this is Detective Kass Minor with the Springfield Police Department. I am looking for Gwen Marks. Is that who I am speaking to?" The detective was now holding her badge and identification up in front of the camera.

"Yes, this is Gwen Marks. How can I help you?"

"It would be best if I came in to talk if that is alright with you."

Ever since Gwen had heard that Frank Waters had been murdered, she had been expecting the police to show up, but thinking about it and dealing with it in reality were two very different things. Gwen took a deep breath, smoothed her hair despite the fact that the camera system was one way and the detective could not see her and replied, "Of course, I will buzz the door. Take the elevator to the top floor. My condo is number thirteen."

After hitting the button to start the fancy coffee maker brewing, Gwen unlocked her front door and stood leaning against the doorjamb. When the detective stepped off the elevator, Gwen waved her into the condo.

"Hello, I am Gwen Marks. Please come in and have a seat. Would you like a cup of coffee? I just started a fresh pot."

Although some police officers turned down all offers for drinks, Detective Minor saw nothing wrong with accepting a glass of water or cup of coffee when offered. "I would love a cup of coffee with a touch of cream if you have it."

"Absolutely. I will be right back."

Watching Gwen walk out of the living room, Detective Minor took the opportunity to look around. The layout of the condo was much like the one she had owned before she got married and bought a house with Robert. The living room and dining room were a combined space with a sliding door to a small balcony. There were four condos on each floor, so based on the size of the building, the condo was larger than her former one and would likely have two bedrooms. There was artwork on the walls and a few pictures on the fireplace mantle. Detective Minor walked over to look at the photographs which appeared to be of Gwen with an older couple who were likely her parents and a family photo that was taken at the same time based on the same clothes in both pictures. The third picture was of Gwen and two young women about her age on a beach.

"In case you are wondering, the two pictures are from Christmas this year with my parents. They love to take family photos and the third one is of me and my girlfriends in the Dominican Republic three years ago."

Detective Minor had not heard Gwen walk back into the room, but the plush carpet likely deadened any noise her stocking feet made.

"I think the pictures that people display in their homes tell a lot about what is important to them." Taking her cup of coffee, Detective Minor sat in the chair that Gwen had motioned to her.

"I assume that you are here to talk about my relationship with Frank Waters. What is it you would like to know?"

"That is correct. I am here to ask about your relationship with Frank Waters. What was your relationship with him?"

"Mutually beneficial. He wanted sex and I hate working, so he got what he wanted and I got financially taken care of. It is a tale as old as time; an older man pays the bills for his young mistress. It didn't start out that way. Frank and I bumped into each other in a bar two and half years ago and hooked up that night. We were pretty casual until a couple months later when I lost my job and took one in retail. He didn't like that I had to work nights and weekends, so he suggested our arrangement. He rented this condo, and we saw each other regularly for the next two years. That is until right after this last Christmas when Frank and I ended our arrangement."

"He ended it, or you ended it?"

"Technically, I ended it, but really Frank did with his declaration that he no longer had the money to pay my bills. He had some lame story about the money he had been using being in a box under his bed and just disappearing. According to him, it was likely his wife or son who took the money, but he was not willing to confront either of them."

"How much money are we talking about?"

Gwen shrugged before replying, "I am not sure, but enough to keep me in this condo for the foreseeable future."

"You said he suspected his wife or son. Are you referring to Kyle Waters?"

"Yeah, as far as I know, that is the only son Frank has...had."

"It is my understanding that Kyle has not been home in over two years. Why would Frank suspect him?"

"No idea. It is not like Frank, and I talked about his wife and kids when we were together. Plus, I dated Kyle a little bit in high school, so talking about him would have been extra weird."

The information that Kyle and Gwen had dated in high school surprised Detective Minor and she wondered if Kyle had left it out purposefully. Like a lot of cases that she had worked on over the years, the victim was not the most likable person, but that did not change her commitment to solving this crime.

"Were you upset about the breakup?"

"The relationship had run its course. I had been looking for ways to move on from Frank for a while before he dropped the no money bombshell. I have a job at an art gallery now and have come to realize that I had lost respect for myself during my years with Frank, so now I am working on building that back up."

"How do you think that your name came up in this investigation?"

"I assume that Kyle Waters told you about his dad and I having an affair. A couple of weeks before Frank rented this condo, he walked in on us being intimate in the family home."

"Alright just one more thing. Where were you on Saturday morning?"

"I worked at the gallery from nine am to four pm. The gallery has a lot of surveillance cameras, so you can confirm it with them."

"We will do that. I appreciate you taking the time to answer my questions. I am going to leave my card with you. If you think of anything that may assist our investigation, please do not hesitate to contact me."

"I will, detective, but the more you look into Frank, the less you are going to like him."

"What do you mean by that?"

"I wasn't Frank's first mistress and I am sure had he lived, I would not have been his last. There was something broken in Frank. I don't know how to describe it to you, but it was like he was unable to completely trust other people to truly know him. I have no idea what they were, but I know Frank had secrets and I truly believe that they were sinister in nature."

"It is a good thing that it is not part of my job to like a victim in order to fully investigate the crime committed against them. Again, please reach out if you have any other information."

******

Her next stop was at the elementary school that Jo Beth Kalan worked at. Detective Minor hoped that there was someone there who liked to gossip. She just wanted to see if there was any validity to Jo Beth's claim that she had simply heard the manner of Frank's death through gossip. As she was buzzed into the main office, the secretary greeted her, "Hello. Welcome to King Elementary. How can we help you today?"

"Hi. I am Detective Kass Minor with the Springfield Police Department. I am one of the detectives who is investigating Frank Water's murder. Did you know Mr. Waters?"

"Sure, he came in from time to time. He was a friendly enough guy. I heard about him getting killed in his office on Saturday. Would you like me to get the principal? She probably knew him better than I did."

"That would be great, but first, how did you hear about his murder?"

"Umm, everyone in the district is talking about it, but I first heard about it from my friend Lizzie. She is one of the secretaries at the main desk of the administrative building."

"Okay, do you remember exactly what Lizzie told you?"

"Exactly, probably not, but pretty much, she said that the janitor came in to work on Monday morning and found Frank dead. He was in his office and someone beat him to death. I remember thinking that it was a horrible way to die, made worse by being at work on Saturday when it happened. Why? Lizzie isn't in trouble for telling me, right?"

"She is not in trouble with me. I am trying to piece together what information is out there and what isn't. It helps when we interrogate a suspect to know what only the killer would know."

"Oh, that makes sense. Let me call Mrs. Dover for you."

After speaking briefly with the principal, Mrs. Mary Dover, Detective Minor left King Elementary and drove to the administrative building of the school district. It would seem that Jo Beth Kalan may well have heard through the grapevine how Frank was murdered, but Kass wondered out loud: *How did Lizzie, a secretary at the school district office, know Frank's manner of death?* That was the next question that she needed to answer.

******

They had released use of the school district admin building except for Frank Waters' office late yesterday afternoon, and today the parking lot was full when Kass arrived. She found Lizzie Bach sitting at the reception desk answering phone calls, just as she had yesterday. As Lizzie hung up the call she was on, she looked up and spotted Minor, "How can I help you today, detective?" she asked cheerfully.

"Actually, I need to speak with you? Is there someone who can cover your desk and place where we can talk?"

"Okay, hold on." Lizzie made a phone call and then the two of them waited a few minutes until another secretary walked out from the door behind Lizzie.

"Please follow me, detective." Lizzie indicated towards a room marked Small Conference room and used her badge to unlock the door. "Sharise, over at King Elementary, already called me. I apologize if my gossiping has messed up your investigation."

Detective Minor suppressed her sigh because, of course, the secretaries called each other; it was not as if she had told Sharise she shouldn't call Lizzie. "Alright, so what I want to know is how you found out the information that you shared?"

"I listen when people talk. By that, I mean that secretaries are the kind of professions that fade into the woodwork for some people. They continue their conversations, often private ones, without any regard for the fact that I am sitting right there. Yesterday, I heard conversations between Dr. Trappen and Trey LaMan, the guys from the medical examiner's office, and the school board members who gathered to talk about what was going on. Is there a specific thing that I said that you want to know how I heard it?"

"Do you remember who you overheard talking about how Mr. Waters died?"

"I am pretty sure that was guys from the medical examiner's office. They stopped right by the door and talked about what they needed to do to preserve the evidence when transporting Mr. Waters. Honestly, it was kind of gross because one of them said that they needed to bag his head because the wounds were so deep. Then the other one replied that they would do it the same way they did with the last victim they had who had been beaten to death."

"Wow. Okay, I apologize to you because that is not a conversation that you should have ever overheard. That is really all I needed to know."

******

Detective Nichols texted Minor as she was driving back to the police station to let her know he was done in court and would meet her back at the department. She had a lot to fill him in on, but none of it seemed to have gotten them any closer to solving the murder of Frank Waters. In fact, some of what she had learned today actually moved them farther away from their prime suspect.

Having beaten Nichols back to work, Kass went to see Abe in the Cyber Crimes Tech department to get an update. As she had suspected, his answer was, these things take time. Her next stop was the forensics department and Claire Learner's cubicle.

"Hi Claire. How's it going on analyzing the evidence from the Frank Waters' crime scene?"

"Frustrating. I am afraid that this time forensics won't be what cracks the case. Frank Waters' fingerprints are on his door, desk and chair and there is one other set, but that comes back to the head janitor and there were just a few of those."

"Her prints are in the system?"

"Yep. Like everyone else who works for the school district, her fingerprints were taken as part of the background check they do before hiring someone."

"Nichols talked with Ms. Rowan and told me she said she was the last to leave on Friday because she covered another person's shift that evening. It is likely that she touched some surfaces when she cleaned his office."

"I agree, but what it also tells me is that the killer didn't wipe things down, so they were probably wearing gloves. We didn't find any blood outside of Mr. Waters' office, but there was that patch of carpet that was strangely devoid of blood in his office. I measured it and the width is that of a standard contractor garbage bag, but the length is off, which makes me think that it was more than one bag."

"Like someone rolled out a walkway of bags?"

"Exactly, and then stood on them to commit the murder. Whoever the killer is, this was a well planned and carried out murder."

"Thanks for your hard work on this."

"Even though it gives you nothing to go on?"

"Yep, this entire case is shaping up to be like that."

Saturday, February 3, 2024

Jo Beth took another load of boxes to her van. She was taking Angie her things that were still at the house and her younger daughter Allie was coming home next week to get her boxes. She needed to grab the things she was donating to the charity thrift store, and then she would be ready to hit the road. She sent Angie a text letting her know that she was leaving, then turned off her phone and put it in her bag. She had been in a fender bender six months ago. The accident was her fault because she was texting, so since then, she had developed the habit of keeping her phone turned off and put away.

Her first stop was at Angie's favorite bakery to pick up the danishes that her daughter loved and a latte for herself. The thrift store was a few blocks over and although not open yet, they had a drop box. The items to be donated were on the first row of seats in the back of her minivan. As she grabbed the last bag of donations, she spotted the bag under the seat. Pulling the duffel bag that she meticulously prepared out, she set it on the passenger side front seat. When she returned from Columbia, she would take it into the house, unpack it and then put the items in boxes for her upcoming move. After all, the items in the bag were really just ordinary household things that she could use for non-lethal purposes.

As she drove to Hilltop Cemetery to talk to Noah before leaving town, she put on her favorite mixtape. Her daughters gave her a hard time for still driving her nineteen ninety-eight minivan, but she saw nothing wrong with it. So, what that it had no modern bells and whistles, the Honda ran like a champ and all those gadgets were just more things to go wrong. When Noah had been alive, he had joked that she would get three hundred thousand miles out of that van, which would make it the best thing he ever invested in, and she planned to do just that.

18

Tuesday, February 6, 2024

"How was court?" Detective Minor asked Nichols as she sat down in her office chair next to his cubicle.

"Boring. I sat in that room waiting to be called to testify and then the ADA came in and said that the defendant had agreed to a plea bargain and the trial was over. Did you solve Frank Water's murder while I twiddled my thumbs?"

"No, but I had some interesting interviews. I think we should start a murder board."

"Sounds good, but just so you know, we have gone digital since you were last in this department. Our days of printouts and thumb tacks are over, so grab your laptop and we will head to the conference room."

"So, how does this work?" Detective Minor asked once they were seated in the conference room.

"While I turn on these smart TVs, open that evidence management software icon and then we will start putting what we know into it. It is the same application that the CSI Techs are using to log everyone who enters a crime scene now, as well as all the evidence they collect and analyze."

They entered the information and pictures that they had previously taken into the software and started creating the timeline and tree of people connected to Frank Waters.

"This is great. Why don't all the departments have this software?"

"The Major Crimes Department is the first to get it, but if we find it helpful, it will be rolled out to all detectives."

"Oh, so we are the guinea pigs. Got it."

"Pretty much. Let's start with listing the people we completely ruled out as suspects, then the people who are highly unlikely, but we need to confirm their alibis and finally anyone who is still a person of interest."

"Sounds like a good plan. I would say we have not completely ruled out anyone because we need to confirm a lot of alibis. So, the alibis to confirm that will rule them out include Sophie, Marcia and George Waters."

"I agree with those three being in the unlikely but need to confirm their alibis, but I disagree that there is no one for the completely ruled out. Colin Bruno is serving time, and we confirmed that he is securely incarcerated at the Algoa Correctional Center."

"Oh, that's right, I had forgotten about Colin. We can also add Tessa Lee, now Winchester and her husband Graham, to the list of unlikely suspects whose alibis we need to verify. I also need to tell you about the interviews I conducted after you headed to court so we can decide where to put Kyle Waters and Jo Beth Kalan."

"I am all ears but unless you found something earth shattering, I am ready to put Jo Beth Kalan down as our only person of interest."

"Kyle Waters called to say he was in town and willing to come in to talk. He told me the name of his dad's current girlfriend but left off that he dated the young women when they were in high school together. He also refused to tell me where he was Saturday morning and stated that his location was above my level of clearance. Which led me to asking Robert to check the guy out, which led to Robert's supervisor's supervisor calling and saying not to look into Kyle Waters."

"Okay, so Frank's son is some kind of super spy. I did not see that one coming."

"Well, I don't know if he is a super spy, but he is something, that is for sure."

"Yeah, like the kind of guy who blows up things using a drone that our government later denies our country blew up. That kind of guy."

"Possibly."

"Do you think he killed his dad?"

"He certainly didn't seem upset that Frank is dead and there is the matter of his dad being intimately involved with a woman that Kyle once dated. I would certainly put him on the person of interest list."

"Okay, so Kyle definitely goes on to the possible suspect list. What makes that problematic is that we cannot really investigate the younger Mr. Waters, so if he killed his father, I think we are going to run into a lot of barriers. Tell me about this woman."

"Her name is Gwendoline Marks, and I interviewed her, too. She is every cliche about mistresses; pretty, young, and did not work while involved with Frank. According to Gwen, Frank set her up in her current condo and paid all her bills until a month ago when he told her he was out of money."

"He suddenly ran out of money. That seems odd."

"According to Gwen, Frank told her that either Marcia or Kyle took the money. So, I deduced that Frank kept this money in cash somewhere in the house. What is odd to me, well other than the fact that he seemingly kept large sums of cash in his house, is that both Marcia and Kyle stated that Kyle had not been home in over two years but Gwen said that Frank indicated Kyle may have taken the money."

"I think that what we have been told about and by Kyle Waters needs to be taken with a grain of salt. Let's go on the belief that Kyle has been back to Springfield far more often than we were led to believe. That fits with him being a possible suspect in the murder of his father. So, what makes you question whether Jo Beth Kalan does not also belong on the list of possible suspects?"

"After I finished at Gwen's, I did some good old detective work and went to the elementary school that Jo Beth works at. The secretary was a chatty young lady who told me that she had heard about Frank Waters' cause of death from her friend Lizzie Bach who is the front desk receptionist at the school district administrative building."

"I am going to assume that you headed to the administrative building next to interview Lizzie Bach."

"You are correct. Ms. Bach told me she overheard two of the technicians from the medical examiner's office discussing the best way to transport Mr. Waters because of his head wound. She then admitted to me she gossiped about his murder to other secretaries, which leads me to Jo Beth Kalan's statement. It is quite possible that Jo Beth did hear about the cause of death from gossip and that statement really was our only evidence that she was involved."

"Great, so now we are down to the victim's son, whose whereabouts are unknown and likely will never be known."

"That about sums it up."

"Why don't we call it a night and tomorrow we will work on confirming all of our unlikely suspects' alibis and meet with the commander to give him an update."

"Okay, I feel like we have hit a brick wall, so hopefully a good night's sleep helps us process all this and come up with something."

Sunday February 4, 2024

Carrying around bloody coveralls, plastic bags and a murder weapon in your vehicle is a cause for anxiety, but how do you get rid of these things and not get caught? One at a time? Throw the whole thing in the lake? Find a dumpster? These thoughts had plagued the killer throughout the night, making sleep next to impossible. The only hope was that a solution would present itself just like the opportunity to murder Frank had.

19

Saturday, February 17, 2024

In the detective movies that Robert and Kass enjoyed watching together, attending a murder victim's funeral always brought a resolution to an investigation. Sitting in the back of the large Catholic church watching the mourners come in and speak to Frank's family before finding a seat, Kass Minor was not hopeful that would happen in real life. The past ten days had brought detectives, Minor and Nichols, no closer to solving the murder of Frank Waters. They had spent the last week and half verifying the alibis of all the people that they had interviewed and they had all checked out as well as interviewing twenty plus people who hung out with or worked with Frank or both. There turned out to be nothing of evidentiary value from the materials that the CSI team had collected and processed.

They were looking for anyone who did not seem to belong at the service, as well as anyone who really should be in attendance who was not. No one seemed out of place or was acting strangely, but Kass noticed that Gwen was not in attendance. She wondered if Frank's former mistress had stayed away because she did not mourn him or out of respect for his family. Either way, it seemed to Kass to be the right decision. As the service wrapped up, Minor turned to her partner, Detective Nichols, "Are we headed to the cemetery and then the lunch, or are we done here?"

"I say we are done here. When did you schedule to meet with the Waters family to discuss the attendees today?"

"Tomorrow afternoon at one, since it seems both Kyle and Sophie are leaving on Monday morning. Marcia requested that we meet at the family's home. You are welcome to join me, but don't feel obligated. I don't think I am going to learn anything that breaks the case wide open, nor do I feel that there is any danger from the Waters family."

"Since you don't mind, I am going to let you handle the interview on your own. I promised my kids we would go to the park tomorrow. Are you planning to ask them about the money that Gwen told you Frank said was stolen?"

"Yes, I plan to. I know that we thoroughly reviewed all of Frank and Marcia's accounts and there are no large sums of money that were withdrawn or deposited. Do you think the money Gwen referred to was cash?"

"Yep, that is what I think. I just wonder where Frank was keeping it. Neither he nor Marcia have a safe deposit box and we found nothing when we searched his fishing cabin, so I guess somewhere in the house."

"How much money do you think we are talking about?"

"Well, we know he got a check for approximately two hundred thousand after he settled his mom's estate and the bank manager confirmed that he took that money in cash."

"That would be a lot of money to take in cash and keep in your house. I think you need to ask if the Waters have a safe or lock box at the house."

"I will ask, but I somehow doubt that I am going to get any straighter answers than I did about Kyle's whereabouts."

As they drove back to the station, Minor asked, "Do you think that attending his funeral was a waste of time?"

"Pretty much, although I noticed that Jo Beth was not there."

"I would have found it stranger if she was. After all, Frank was her former boss and she admittedly could not stand the guy. To me, there would be no reason for her to be at his funeral."

"I see your point. It was just the only thing that I really noticed."

"I noticed that there were far more men there than women, but that also made sense to me. Our twenty plus interviews of friends and colleagues had a theme that most of the men liked Frank and most of the women had visceral negative responses to him."

"Well, other than the men whose girlfriends or wives he had cheated with or tried to cheat with. They certainly had nothing positive to say about him."

"Agreed. Those men were more in line with the women and I think that it was close to eighty-five percent of women who could not stand the guy."

"How do you explain his being able to woo so many women over the years, since women seemed to get a creep vibe from him?"

"It has been my experience that most women don't learn to listen to their inner voice until they are a little older. One thing we know for sure is that no matter how old Frank Waters was, his mistresses were all in their twenties. I think he preyed on women who had lower self-esteems or were less sure of themselves. His former mistresses all had not developed the ability to listen to their inner voice when it comes to people who don't have your best interest at heart."

"That makes sense to me and not just in this case, but in so many cases we work when young women have been hurt or killed. As far as solving the murder of Frank Waters, I don't think any of those interviews got us any closer. Do you?"

"No. I still hope that when we get the cell phone tower data, there will be some actionable information for pinning down a suspect."

"Does Abe have any idea when the company will provide that information?"

"When I talked to him yesterday, he hoped that we will have it by early next week. He also told me that since it is a primarily rural area and the warrant only allowed the information for an hour before until an hour after when the medical examiner put Frank Waters time of death, we won't likely be having to wade through tons of data."

"With the way this case has been going so far, I feel like the killer probably either did not have a cell phone with them or had it off."

"I hate to agree with you, but I will be shocked since they covered their crime so thoroughly thus far that data from a cell phone cracks the case."

****

Annie Davidson sat with the other people from the school district that paid their respects to Frank Waters. She had been struggling with a crisis of consciousness ever since hearing that Frank had been murdered. Eight months ago, her best friend Jo Beth and she had a girl's weekend, which consisted of hanging out at Jo Beth's house eating pizza, ice cream, girl scout cookies and drinking wine. As well as a healthy dose of reminiscing and laughter, late into both Friday and Saturday nights. On Saturday night, they were both feeling the effects of the three bottles of wine they had consumed and Annie decided to broach the topic of Noah. That was when Jo Beth had told her about her murder bag and writing out detailed plans to murder Frank.

The question of whether her friend had actually followed through on one of her plans had been swirling in Annie's head since hearing about Frank's death. Since the night that Mike had gone to the police station to represent Jo Beth, Annie had wondered if she should tell her husband about the things Jo Beth had told her during the girls' weekend. But when days went by and Jo Beth was never questioned by the police again, Annie decided that her friend's fantasy about killing Frank had been just that a fantasy. The fact that someone murdered Frank had nothing to do with Jo Beth. At least Annie prayed it didn't.

Wednesday, February 7, 2024

Chris had planned her next destination months in advance. The small cabin in the Appalachian Mountains of Kentucky was a perfect hideaway. The closest small town was Whitley City, but it was a stretch to call it a town as it was unincorporated, but there was a gas station, a grocery store and a library there and that is all Chris needed. People here in McCreary County were naturally reticent of strangers, law enforcement and especially the FBI so it was essential that Chris be sure to align herself with the right people.

When she had found the advertisement for the cabin online six months ago, she was elated at the low price and willingness of the seller to leave all the furnishings. The cash sale had been registered to Jane Smith and the cheap copy of a forged driver's license had not raised any questions. Chris had driven up for the sale and it was the first time she saw the cabin in person; it had also been her opportunity to let slip that she was running from her ex who was an FBI agent.

As Chris pulled into the Whitley Gas and Go, she wondered how many people the real estate agent had gossiped to by now. After filling her car, she wandered inside for some groceries and essentials. As she walked around the store, it was clear that she was being watched and knew she needed to be sure everyone in the store knew who she supposedly was.

Approaching the cash register, Chris put down her basket, "Hi I am Jane. I bought the McBride cabin up the road."

"Well, hello nice to meet you. My husband, Gordie and I were wondering when you would be in. I am Linda Sue. Gordie and I own this here, Gas and Go. If there is anything you need that we don't have, you just let me know."

"Thank you. I will be sure to do that."

"Just so you know we watch out for our own around here. Does the cabin still have the same phone number?"

"Yes, the realtor said it was easier that way because getting the phone company out here is a pain and there is spotty cell service."

"Well, that is good to know in case we ever need to get a hold of you. You take care now."

"Thank you. I will."

Chris put her bags in the back seat and drove towards her cabin, sure that the whole little town knew her back story. Hopefully, she could settle here and stay for a long time. For that, she would need to be sure to stay out of other people's business, especially little girls in distress.

20

Sunday, February 18, 2024

Marcia Waters was relieved that Frank's funeral was over and, if she was being honest, the fact that her kids were headed home tomorrow was also a relief. Well, she did not really know where Kyle was headed, but he was leaving when Sophie headed back to Florida. Kyle had offered to stay longer, but there really was no reason, so she had told him that it was fine for him to leave when Sophie did. Some people at her office would be surprised to see her back at work tomorrow, but she needed to get back to her routine. Plus, it was tax season, so the very worst time for her to be off work. It was just like Frank to get himself murdered during her busiest time of the year. He never had any regard for her needs. When Detective Minor had called her on Thursday to explain about attending Frank's funeral with her partner, Marcia had concluded that they were no closer to finding Frank's killer than they had been the day he was found.

The detective was due to come by in a few minutes, but Marcia was not sure what she thought they could tell her. Marcia had talked with Kyle and Sophie last night, and none of them had seen or heard anything out of place at the funeral. Although Marcia could not really blame the person who killed her husband, she had no idea who the murderer was. Opening the refrigerator, Marcia looked at the abundance of food that had been dropped off by people paying their respects. She would bring most of it to the office break room, hoping that someone there would eat it.

When the doorbell rang, Kyle called out that he would answer it, so Marcia headed straight for the living room. Kyle walked in with Detective Minor just as Sophie entered from her bedroom. Once everyone was seated and holding a fresh cup of coffee, Detective Minor launched right in with her questions.

"I appreciate you all meeting with me again. Unfortunately, the apprehension of Frank's killer has not been straightforward. Was there anyone at the funeral yesterday that you thought seemed out of place or who was acting strangely?"

All three of the Waters shook their heads and Marcia responded, "We discussed it last night and there is nothing from the funeral that we thought was off in any way."

"That is the same conclusion my partner, Detective Nichols, and I came to. I have some sensitive questions and wondered, Mrs. Waters, if you might want me to ask them without your children in the room?"

"No, they can stay. One thing that all this has brought to light is that keeping secrets has not been healthy."

"What kind of secrets?"

"I am talking about Frank's cheating. I thought I was protecting my children by staying with him and not explaining to them what was going on. Kyle found out years ago by accident and that put a major strain on his relationship with his father and eventually on our relationship as well. Sophie only found out after her dad died and she and I have had some heart-to-heart discussions about our strained relationship and the fact that her being in the dark led to some false conclusions. All three of us are determined to work on building stronger relationships, so go ahead and ask your sensitive questions."

"During the course of this investigation, it came to light that Frank was having an ongoing relationship with Gwen Marks."

Kyle interrupted and sarcastically added, "What she means is I told her."

"Yes, Kyle is who provided me with Ms. Marks' name which I followed up on by interviewing her. During this interview Ms. Marks indicated that she and Frank broke up after Christmas and that the reason for the breakup was that Frank told her that he no longer could afford to support her."

"Wait, my dad was supporting his mistress? In what way?" Sophie could not keep the sense of outrage out of her voice.

"Frank was paying the bills for her condo and daily living expenses."

"Wow, just wow, and where was he getting the money to do that? Mom, did you know about this?"

Marcia Waters shook her head, "No, I didn't and I assure you all that money was not coming out of our joint accounts. I watch those accounts very close and have alerts set to tell me whenever over two hundred dollars is spent."

"Actually, that is what I wanted to ask you about? Gwen stated that Frank had told her that his money was missing and that either you Marcia or you Kyle took it. Which leads us to have a lot of questions. First, do either of you know anything about this money?"

Marcia looked at Kyle, and he nodded his head for her to answer first. "Absolutely not. How much money are we talking about and where would Frank have supposedly gotten this money?"

"We do not know how much money there was when Frank told Gwen it was gone, but what we do know is that once your husband settled his mother's estate, he cashed a check for two hundred thousand dollars."

"No, that isn't right. Frank told me that after he settled all of his mom's debts that he got twenty-five hundred dollars, not two hundred thousand. Where did you get the idea that he inherited that much money?"

"We got a subpoena for your bank records and while the accounts that you and Frank held jointly showed no irregularity, but the account he held with his mother was another story."

"You mean his mom's account that she gave him access to in order to help her stay on top of her finances?"

"Yes, she actually made it a joint account and after he settled her estate, he cashed a check for just over two hundred thousand dollars and then closed the account. The bank manager remembers it explicitly because he cautioned Frank against taking that much cash and he told him that there was a couple of days' waiting period while the bank gathered the funds."

"That is a lot of money and I take it. Those are the funds that you believe he supported his mistress with."

"Yes, but back to my question. Kyle, did you take cash from your dad? I ask because the part of that story that my partner and I can't reconcile is that you and your mom have said repeatedly that you have not been home in over two years."

Before answering, Kyle sighed loudly, "I have been home several times in the last two years, but only for a few hours each time. It was always between work assignments and not really authorized for me to do, so that is why mom and I said I had not been home. I never saw my dad on those visits and certainly did not take money from him. Plus, I have to tell you that I think that the money suddenly going missing was a convenient excuse for my dad to get Gwen to end things."

"Why would you say that?"

"Two reasons, first my dad hated being the bad guy. He had this way of turning things, situations, and people into the ones who were in the wrong. Second, and probably more important, if he wasn't ready for something to be done and you tried to end it, he became a bully. For example, when I wanted to quit baseball after my sophomore year of high school, he had a told meltdown about how I needed to show commitment and that I wasn't done until he said I was done. So if he was ready to move on from Gwen, he would have wanted her to end it and telling her the money was gone worked really well, didn't it?"

"Why do you think your dad wanted to end things with Gwen?"

"I guess it always surprised me he stayed with her for so long. I thought his mistresses were short-term flings."

"Marcia, do you have any thoughts about what Kyle is saying?"

"Just that I tried not to think about Frank and his mistresses, but Kyle is right that Frank was highly manipulative when he wanted you to do his dirty work. He never told the kids no to anything they wanted, but always got me to. I always had to be the heavy when it came to parenting."

"Thank you for sharing that theory. By the way, is there a safe in this house?"

"No, there is not. If Frank, as you say, took all that cash, I highly doubt he would have kept it here. Have you searched his cabin?"

"Yes, we did, and there was nothing of evidentiary value. Mrs. Waters, when was the last time you were at the cabin?"

"I went there one time right after Frank bought it. Twenty years ago. I do not enjoy roughing it or fishing, so it was not a place I ever felt compelled to go. When the kids were little, Frank would take them with him to the cabin, which gave me a few weekends a year alone. I felt like that was a good exchange." Marcia smiled at both her kids and continued, "Please don't get me wrong. I love both of my kids, but as a working mom, sometimes the thing you need most is a quiet house."

"Well, that explains why we did not find your fingerprints anywhere in the cabin. Have any of you thought of anything else that might be important to this investigation?"

All three of the Waters shook their heads and Marcia stood up. "If there is nothing else, I would like to spend some time with my kids before they head out."

"No, there isn't anything else at this time. I promise you all that we will update you as we continue the investigation."

"I am sure I speak for all of us when I say thank you for the work you and your partner are doing to attempt to solve Frank's murder."

21

Monday, February 19, 2024

The text from Abe came in while Detective Minor was parking her car at the station and read simply: I have the records. Stopping briefly at her desk, she let Nichols know that she was headed to the fourth floor to see Abe and would return with the cell phone tower records. He reminded her not to get her hopes too high.

Entering Abe's work space, Kass thought once again about all the equipment that this man had mastered and that she had no idea what it even did, much less how to operate it.

"Good morning, Detective. I assume you got my text."

"Yep, I sure did. What do you have for me?"

"The cell phone tower provider complied with the warrant and sent the data. The good news is that there is very little cell traffic off that tower for the time of the warrant."

"Okay, so what is the bad news?"

"The warrant is for what is called a geofence. Are you familiar with it?"

"I think so, but please remind me."

"So basically, a geofence warrant allows us to get records for an area serviced by a cell tower for a specific period of time. In this case, the warrant covered from an hour before the earliest time Frank Waters may have been murdered to an hour after the latest time of the estimated time of death. The geofence tells us which phones pinged off that tower, when and how often. These records include six separate phone numbers."

"So how accurate to the place are these records?"

"See, that is the biggest drawback to the geofence; it is almost six hundred square feet or about thirteen acres."

"How is this supposed to help?"

"It is the best we can do since the supreme court ruled that we need probable cause to search a cell phone's location history. If one of the numbers that we got from the geofence matches one of your suspects, get me a warrant for their cell phone location data and I can pinpoint their location with precision."

"Thank you. I appreciate your help and will get back to you if we can get a specific warrant."

"Detective Minor, just one more thing and it is not work related. Do you have a second?"

"Sure, what's up Abe?"

"Do you think it would be wrong for me to ask Claire Learner out on a date?"

"No, it isn't against department policy."

"That wasn't what I was thinking about. You know that I listened to all those tapes that her mom made, so I feel like I have knowledge of Claire that she may not be comfortable with me having."

"Ah, I see. I can definitely see where you are coming from. Those recordings were deeply personal, and we can not even be sure that Claire has even listened to all of them at this point. I think it is essential that you are honest about having heard them so my suggestion is to ask her out and if the two of you hit it off then after a few dates, you tell her about being the one who listened to the tapes her mom made her."

"Thanks, I will do that."

"Abe, I would suggest that you never bring up something that you heard in one of those recordings."

"Why would I do that?"

"I am thinking down the road if you and Claire develop a relationship, there may be a time when you get into an argument and are tempted to remind her of something her mom said. I am just warning you now that it would be a major mistake."

"I will try to remember that. Thanks for your advice, detective."

After returning to the Major Crimes division, Minor filled Nichols in on what Abe had told her.

"Great, so if Jo Beth's phone number is on this list, it proves nothing since she admitted to being at the cemetery, which is in that same zone."

"Right. I think that you were one hundred percent correct when you told me not to pin any hope on the cell phone tower data, but let's at least look through it. How about I read a phone number and you look up who it belongs to?"

"Sounds good. Fire away."

The first number, which was the one that appeared most often, belonged to Frank Waters, so was of no surprise to the detectives.

"I wonder what application he had running that was tracking his location."

"It is probably something as innocuous as a weather app because I think if someone had a tracking application on his phone that Abe would have told us that when he examined it."

"You are probably right. What is the next number?"

Detective Minor read a few more numbers that appeared one time and Nichols wrote the names of the people. As she started to read the next number, Minor stopped, "I think I know this number but I am not sure whose it is."

"Well, finish reading it to me and I will tell you," Nichols replied in a joking manner.

After Minor told him the number and Nichols entered it into the database, he looked at her and said, "You will never believe this. That number belongs to the Assistant District Attorney, Lance Clark. Is it just the one time, like maybe, he drove by?"

"No, it is listed several times in about a half hour window. What the hell is that about?"

"Before we find out, I think we need to loop the boss in on this, because I have a feeling that questioning an ADA's whereabouts in relation to an open homicide investigation may ruffle some feathers. Are there any other numbers on that list?"

"Just one." Minor read him the final cell phone number. "You know what is odd is that none of these numbers belong to Jo Beth Kalan. You would think she would have her phone on her if she was heading out of town."

"Could be that she just doesn't allow any applications to track her location, and she did not use the phone while at the cemetery. Sometimes the simplest explanation is the right one."

****

Commander Brewer told them to tread lightly when asking Clark about his phone pinging off the cell tower by the school district administrative office during the time period that Frank was murdered. Detective Minor had called Clark at his office and asked if he could come to the station to go over where they were at in the investigation. She and Nichols were now waiting in the conference room with their digital crime board ready to go.

"Hello detectives. Hopefully, you have made some headway in this investigation because I am sure your boss is breathing down your back like mine is."

"Let's review what we have found out so far, and then we can discuss what we think the next steps should be." Nichols replied and pointed at the smart television.

The screen displayed Frank Water's picture with lines running to each person they had investigated thus far.

Detective Minor started by asking Clark, "Have you used this technology yet?"

"No, I heard that it was being used here in Major Crimes, but I have yet to try a case that it was used for. Please walk me through it."

"No problem. The pictures that are bordered by red lines are people we have eliminated as playing a role in Frank Waters' murder. If we were to click on a picture, it would take us to the file for each individual which contains all the pertinent information that we have on them. Most of the people were never actually suspects or persons of interest, but they are somehow connected to Frank and so we confirmed their alibis."

"Alright, so that leaves two people who are bordered in yellow. Let's talk about them."

"I will start with Jo Beth Kalan, as my partner doesn't think she should still be a suspect."

Nichols laughed and responded, "That is true, I think her picture could be bordered in red, but I am trusting your intuition about leaving her as a possibility."

"As you know, we brought Jo Beth in for questioning the Monday following the murder and after speaking to her with her lawyer, it was decided that we did not have enough to charge her. We have subsequently learned that a rumor regarding Frank Waters' cause of death was being spread in the district, so her assurance that she had heard it casually can't be proven or disproven. We have found no other evidence that she is the murderer, but my gut tells me she is not being honest with us."

"Did her alibi check out?"

"No, there is no way to corroborate her alibi that she stopped at the cemetery, so that is another thing that we can't say for sure."

"This is where Minor loses me on keeping Jo Beth as a suspect. I believe that it is possible to be alone and not be able to corroborate what you were doing. Last night I spent the evening at home alone, reading a book and then sleeping. If I needed to have some way to corroborate my alibi, I would be out of luck."

"I get that, but as I have said, it is my instinct that tells me that Jo Beth is the killer, not evidence."

"Sorry detective, my office would never bring charges against someone based on a detective's gut."

"I know, but I am not willing to eliminate her until we have proven someone else did it or that she could not have been the one. I will have

Nichols tell you about our other suspect, as he likes Kyle Waters for the murder."

"The victim's son?"

"Yep,"

"Kyle Water is the only son of Marcia and Frank Waters and, by all reports, despises his dad and loves his mom. He is the person who told us about Gwen Marks."

"Who is she again?" Lance Clark asked.

"Gwen was Frank Waters' long-time mistress and get this Kyle Waters prom date."

"That has a real ick factor that a jury would get. So, what is his alibi?"

"Oh, he won't give us one. He told Minor that it is above our clearance level and that seems to be true since our commander and Minor's FBI agent husband were told to back off of Kyle."

"Told to back off by who?"

Minor decided that she would be the one to try to explain this one. "When I interviewed Kyle and asked his whereabouts, I had no reason to suspect him of being involved, but when he pulled that clearance level BS, I called my husband. I figured Robert would run his name and tell me where Kyle had been and that would be that. Instead, Robert called into his supervisor's office and told the Unit Chief had called and said they were not to look into Kyle Waters."

"When Minor told me about Kyle and the warning that her husband got when he ran his name, I went to Commander Brewer and he ran it up the flagpole here. The response that the Chief of Police gave to Brewer was almost verbatim to what Agent Matthews got. Kyle Waters' whereabouts and actions are not to be looked into. Which is why he stays on the possible suspect list as far as I'm concerned."

"So, let me see if I have this straight, the only suspects you have are a middle-aged woman with an extremely shaky motive and no corroborated alibi and the son of the victim with a strong motive but who refuses to give an alibi?"

"That pretty much sums it up."

"No forensics at all? No DNA? No fingerprints? No videos?"

"Nope, we have drawn a big fat goose egg in the forensic evidence column, which is another reason I lean towards Kyle and not Jo Beth as the killer. I mean, come on, who is more likely to pull off a murder with no evidence, a middle-aged, heavyset teacher or a young, buff probable government agent?"

"I concede your point on who is more likely to be the killer, but I am just not ready to eliminate Jo Beth, which brings us to the cell phone tower data. The geofence warrant you got for us Lance finally resulted in the cell phone provider sending the data." Detective Nichols clicked to that screen as Minor talked.

"Neither Jo Beth nor Kyle Waters' cell numbers appear on that data."

"Further eliminating them as suspects, right?"

"Actually, it is an anomaly with both of them."

"How so?"

"Jo Beth has a cell phone and admitted to being in the geographical zone during the time that the warrant covered but did not ping one time. Detective Nichols believes this may be because she is not allowing her phone's location to be tracked by any apps, but I find it suspect. If she had gone to the school district admin office to kill Frank, turning her phone off would be a great forensic countermeasure."

"And Kyle Waters has no cell phone in his name, nor does he have a phone on his parents' or sister's plan. As far as we could find, there is no phone connected to him, nor does he have any social media presence. Doesn't that seem suspect for a man in his late twenties?"

"I would say that all those points would be something that I could bring up to the jury if I was to take either of them to trial for this murder, but there is not strong enough evidence to charge them. It seems that the cell tower data yielded little useful information."

"Actually, the only phone number of interest on the list is yours. Why were you in that area during the time frame that Frank Waters died?"

"Is that actually why you wanted to talk to me? You could have just come right and asked me. I have nothing to hide. There is a parking spot to enter the trail that leads to Lost Hill Park out there. I like to hike and on the weekends that I am on call, it is one of my favorite spots because it feels out of the city but is close enough for me to be back here quickly if needed."

"See, you have a perfectly plausible but unconfirmable alibi," Detective Nichols said in a joking manner, "and when we add that to you not knowing the victim and had no reason to murder him, you are eliminated."

"So, for a blip in time, you actually suspected me?"

Both detectives shook their heads, "No, actually I hoped that you might have seen something since you were out that way."

"Since you filled me in on the Frank Waters murder when you brought Jo Beth in for questioning, I thought back to that Saturday and can honestly say that I saw nothing that would be of help in solving this crime."

"It might have been helpful, counselor, if you had told us that you were out that way when Frank was murdered."

"Hmm, I think it would have been odd for me to insert my whereabouts into the murder investigation when I had nothing to share. We will have to agree to disagree on this. If there is nothing else, I am going to head back to my office, but let me know if you need anything else or come up with a viable suspect."

******

As Lance Clark walked back to his office in the courthouse, he thought maybe he should have gone into acting because he had just given the performance of a lifetime inside the police station. All of what the detective had shared about Frank Waters and his family was old news to Lance, but he had not let on in any way that he was an expert in all things Frank Waters. Then add on the detectives asking him about why he was near the crime scene when the murder took place and his convenient story about hiking. There was no way the detectives could ever get a warrant for his cell phone and see that he was actually much closer to the office where Frank had met his demise than the trail parking lot. No, nothing about his life connected Frank to him other than the fact that Frank had murdered his sister all those years ago and gotten away with it.

Sunday, February 11, 2024

Driving around the back roads of McCreary County for the last few days, had given Chris the start of a plan for how to escape if she ever needed to run. Other than driving around, she had been hiking and jogging a lot to get her body used to the change in altitude. The scenery in her new home was phenomenal, so that helped engage her mind a lot of the time, but she could not help but wonder about Delilah.

The risk of going to the library and looking up the story seemed low, so that was where Chris was headed today. She was armed with the utility bill and bill of sale in Jane Smith's name so that she could get a library card. Hopefully, the librarian would be willing to see past the lack of an id because while the bad forgery had worked as a scanned photo copy, it was clearly not real in person.

The library was housed in a brick building on Main St that had likely once been a store of some kind. Chris parked her car and looked at the building. She thought about the library in Lake Geneva with its wall of windows looking out over the lake and the multiple library locations in Springfield. Libraries and books had always been essential in Chris's life and she wondered how well used this one was.

The librarian greeted her as she entered, "Welcome to the McCreary County Library. How can we be of help today?"

"Hi, I am new to the area and would like to get a library card." Chris said as she handed over the paperwork she had brought with.

"That is wonderful, Jane. Do you have a photo id with you?"

"No, I apologize but I lost it and haven't been able to get a new one yet on account of not having my birth certificate. Do I have to wait to use the library until I get that all straightened out?"

The librarian looked at Chris, "The usual procedure is for me to verify with an id but there is no harm in getting you a library card without it. Now is there?"

"No ma'am, I promise I just want to read books and look on the internet for recipes."

"Then let's get you all set."

Twenty minutes later, Chris sat alone in a small computer room browsing the internet. In order to cover her tracks, she searched for hotel rooms and vacation rentals all along the gulf coast and for each possible vacation spot she read the local town's recent news stories. There was only a short snippet of a story in the Gulf Shores News about an eight-year-old girl who had been found safe after she ran away from her foster home. There was no follow up to the story and Chris could think of no other way to check up on Delilah. After looking at several other possible beach vacation towns, Chris closed the internet browser and logged off the computer.

She took her books about gardening in Kentucky and preserving food to the counter to check out.

"You really must come back on Tuesday mornings. That is when the gardening and homesteading group meets. They have all kinds of tips and tricks, I think you would appreciate it."

"I will have to try to do that. Thank you for all your help today."

"No problem. You take care, Jane."

22

Monday, February 19, 2024

The alert from the National Integrated Ballistic Information Network of a possible hit on the case Robert was monitoring was like a beacon to the agent. He only had one alert set, and it was for the bullet that had killed Shasta Peters. It was not even his case and as far as the Springfield Police Department was concerned; it was a closed case. Two young African American men were in prison for the drive-by shooting of Shasta, but Agent Robert Matthews had never believed that they had killed her.

Shasta had been a key witness in his case against the fugitive Paulina Moore, and people who crossed Paulina ended up dead. The FBI's interest in Paulina was her connection to her serial killer husband Raul Moore, who had committed suicide after his arrest. In his suicide note, Raul had indicated that Paulina was the mastermind behind the seven murders he was accused of and furthermore that his wife had killed before and would likely kill again. The fugitive apprehension unit was working on finding Paulina, but Robert could not let it go. He had chased leads all over the country but had to do so on his off time. Most people in the FBI did not believe that Paulina was a murderer, much less a serial killer, but believed that Agent Robert Matthews was obsessed with her case.

Opening the email, he saw that the bullet he had entered was linked to a double murder in Gulf Shores, Alabama that happened two weeks ago. Robert clicked to open the case information and saw that two known drug dealers, brothers Ty and Wes Abernathy, had been shot at point blank range in their house. The police had ruled that it was drug and gang related and while the case remained unsolved, there were no notes newer than a few days after the shooting, which told Robert that the police were likely not actively investigating the case. It also told him he needed to head to Gulf Shores, Alabama, which presented issues of its own for him. His wife was knee deep in an active murder investigation so he would need to have someone come help with their daughter, Emma. He wondered if he should talk to Kass first about his plans or call his mom and secure her ability to come up and help them.

******

"What do you think of Clark's explanation?" Detective Nichols asked Minor when the ADA had left.

"I think it is like you said because of the area that cell tower data covers and the fact that Lance Clark's alibi is the type that cannot be corroborated, we are left with no choice but to believe him. Plus, there is no connection between Clark and Frank Waters, so it is not like he is a suspect in the murder. It is a coincidence, but you know how I hate coincidences, especially during a homicide investigation."

"Agreed, but sometimes a coincidence is just that. You never told me about your interview at the Waters' home yesterday."

"Oh yeah, sorry, we got so caught up with the cell phone tower data. There isn't much to tell, both Marcia and Kyle deny any knowledge of the money, much less having stolen it from Frank. In fact, Kyle theorized that no one took the money, and that Frank used the money, or more accurately, the lack of it, to get Gwen to end the relationship."

"That is an interesting theory. Did he say why he thought his father would do that?"

"No, not really, just that he was shocked that his dad had stayed with Gwen so long because he thought his dad kind of moved from mistress to mistress rather quickly."

"Did you ask if there was a safe or lock box in the house?"

"I did and Marcia Waters denied that there was. I left the conversation really questioning what Frank Waters did with all that money."

"You know, maybe that is what we are missing. How many murders over the years have we investigated that were about money?"

"A lot of them, but who, other than Frank, knew about that money?"

"Well, Gwen for sure, and what about his brother George? Wasn't their falling out over Frank not splitting the estate with him?"

"Right, but we have eliminated both of them."

"What we haven't done is look if either of them could have hired someone to kill Frank?"

"True, but I doubt Clark would be willing or able to get us warrants for their financial records. Even if he did, I think that we would be talking about a cash transaction, wouldn't you?"

"Yep, for sure, probably the cash that Frank said was stolen. No, the only way we will ever catch someone at this point is if the murderer starts talking about it."

"That is one thing I have never understood about criminals, why they feel the need to brag about the crimes they have gotten away with."

"Street credit, that is what I think it is. Every time I have busted someone for a crime and they have been telling others about what they did, it has come down to trying to gain street credit."

"Well then, let's hope that Frank's murderer feels the need to get some of that street credit because, at this point, we have nothing."

******

Kass Minor had spent the afternoon calling the other numbers on the cell phone tower data list. No one had anything to report because none of them had driven towards the school district office. She had called Mike Davidson and left a message asking him to ask his client why her cell phone had not pinged off the tower since she had already admitted to being in the area.

As she pulled onto her street, her mother-in-law's unmistakable orange Kia sat in their driveway. Kass was sure that she wasn't aware that Lenora Matthews was coming today. Not that she minded her mother-in-law Lenora visiting, or that she didn't like her, but Kass was exhausted from this investigation and was sure that her house was a mess. As she walked in through the door from the garage, Lenora was in the dining area just off the kitchen feeding Emma, who was in her high chair. Kass walked up to the two of them and kissed Emma on the head.

"Hi Lenora. I am sorry I forgot you were coming today."

"No, you didn't, dear, Robert called me a couple of hours to ask if I could stay because he needed to leave town and you are in the middle of a murder case."

"Well, that at least explains that I am not losing my mind. Is Robert still here?"

"Yes, he is in your bedroom packing."

Robert looked up from his packing to find his wife standing in the doorway. "Hi honey, I am glad you made it home before I left."

"Were you going to tell me that you were leaving and that your mom was coming?"

"I texted you and asked you to call me and you asked if it was an emergency. When I told you no, you responded, let's talk tonight at home. So, I figured you were busy. Sorry."

"You're right, but in the future, I think you need to just tell me in a text that you need to leave town for work and that we need to talk."

"I can do that, but there is one thing."

"Oh yeah, what's that?"

"I am not exactly leaving for work. While my trip is related to my work at the FBI, it is not a work sponsored trip."

"I take it you have another lead on Doctor Moore?"

"Yes! Do you remember Shasta Peters, the witness who told us about Paulina's money laundering and her alias?"

"I remember her and the fact that she was killed in a drive by shooting. Two kids are serving time for her murder."

"Bullets from the same gun that was used to kill Shasta were used in a double homicide in Gulf Shores, Alabama. The detectives are saying it was drug and gang related, but you know that I have always believed that Paulina killed Shasta and that those two kids should not be in prison.

I am headed to Gulf Shores to find out more about the two men who were shot and try to see if I can track down Paulina."

"Did you tell the fugitive task force about this lead? Or how about Hollins?"

"I told Hollins, and he approved my using personal time. But you know that no one else supports my belief that Shasta's murder is tied to Paulina, so the Fugitive Apprehension Task Force would not be interested in my lead. Are you okay with my mom being here to help?"

"Of course I am okay with it. You are following the plan that we made if one of us has to leave town. My case is at a standstill, but you and I both know that my schedule is unpredictable. Please be careful because while I may not be sure that the murders in Gulf Shores are tied to your fugitive, I have always agreed with you that Paulina is extremely dangerous."

23

Tuesday, February 20, 2024

Robert Matthews drove through the night to Gulf Shores fueled by energy drinks and candy, listening to an audio book on the invasions of World War Two and wondering if he was chasing another dead end. Arriving at six in the morning, he parked along the beach boulevard, put the backseat of his sedan down, and stretched out to take a nap. First, he sent a text to his wife to let her know he had arrived safely, then he set an alarm on his phone for nine. He had an appointment with the detective in charge of the homicide of Ty and Wes Abernathy. Detective Fisher was clear that little investigating had gone into the double homicide because of being swamped with other cases and the brothers' known gang and drug affiliations.

As Matthews walked into the lobby of the Gulf Shores Police Department, Detective Fisher met him.

"Hi, I am Detective Reggie Fisher and I assume that you are Agent Robert Matthews."

"What gave me a way?"

"Oh, you know, the dark suit and sunglasses that scream FBI might have been my first clue. Do you mind if we sit outside and I smoke?"

"That is fine."

Sitting in the sun, Detective Fisher lit his cigarette, exhaling he said, "Tell me again what the FBI's interest is in the Abernathy brothers' murder."

"The gun that was used in that murder was used to murder a key witness in an ongoing FBI investigation. I am trying to figure out how the gun made it here and if the person who murdered our witness is here. Tell me about your investigation into the Abernathy brother's killing."

"Both Wes and Ty have long rap sheets that include drug manufacturing and sales, robbery, and lots of petty offenses. They are known members of a local gang which have ties to not only to drugs but also human trafficking. My confidential informant told me that the Abernathy brothers recently ripped off a member of a rival gang during a drug sale. The theory is that the other gang took the brothers out as retaliation. Is your case gang or drug related?"

"No, I am tracking a fugitive who is a serial killer. She is wanted in at least seven murders, but it is highly likely that there are at least a dozen victims."

"She? Well, that is unusual. Aren't most serial killers men?"

"Absolutely right. Over ninety percent of all known serial killers are or were men, and what makes Dr. Paulina Moore even more of an anomaly is that she killed alongside her husband. Serial Killer couples are an extreme anomaly."

"So, she killed this witness in Springfield, Missouri. Then the gun is used in the murder of two low life drug dealers here and you are trying to figure out how the gun or she or both got here?"

"That about sums it up."

"As I said on the phone when we talked, we find that guns are often traded amongst the gangs, so it would not shock me if your serial killer somehow traded her gun for another. The dark web has opened up a lot of opportunities for criminals. That being said, how can I help you with your investigation?"

"Would you mind if I look through police reports for the day of and a few days after the Abernathy brothers' murder?"

"No problem. Are you looking for something in particular?"

"Not really, but hopefully if she was here, there is a bread crumb that Paulina Moore did not realize she left behind."

Hours of reading police reports on very little sleep led to Robert having a headache. He needed to take a break from staring at the computer screen. As it was, he had three reports that he planned to follow up on; A woman who reported that someone had broken in and stolen her driver's license and cash from her wallet, a small car dealer who had reported that a woman stole a set of license plates and a farmer who reported that he found a pair of women's jeans and a few other items of clothing while cleaning out his pig pens.

Matthews approached Detective Fisher, "Hey, I am going to head out and follow up on a few reports. Thank you for your help today. I will let you know if I turn anything up."

"You're welcome. I hope you catch your fugitive."

******

Marjorie Tubbs, the woman who had reported her license and cash stolen, lived in a middle-class neighborhood in the heart of Gulf Shores. Matthews rang the doorbell and waited. It was five thirty in the evening, so most people were likely home.

A woman in her early sixty opened the door, holding a small, loud, yapping dog. "Hello, how can I help you?"

Matthews held up his FBI credentials as he replied, "Are you Marjorie Tubbs?"

"Yes, that is me, but what does the FBI want with me?"

"Ma'am, I am following up on a police report that you filed about your license and money being stolen."

"The FBI now cares about petty crimes. I would think you would have much bigger things to spend your time on and anyway, it turns out my grand-niece was the culprit. She took my id thinking she would be able to buy booze with it and the money to pay for that booze. However, she was dumb enough to go to the same liquor store that I have been for the last thirty years. The owner got my id back and held onto my grand-niece until I got down there. So, you see, it is really a family matter, not a police matter, and certainly not an FBI matter."

"I thank you for your time in explaining the circumstances and I will let you get back to your evening."

Walking back to his car, Matthews thought *this is why the fugitive task force and even my own partner don't follow up on my hunches.*

According to their website, Best Cars Ever was open until seven this evening, so it would be Robert's next stop. In the police report, Gus Diesen, the owner of the dealership, had stated that he was reasonably sure that a woman who had traded a car with him was the one who stole the license plates. He identified the woman as Chris Farmington and said that she had been alone on his car lot while he test drove her trade in. That evening, as Gus was headed to his car to go home, he noticed that the license plates were missing from his nephew's car, which was sitting in the back lot while they waited on a part.

Best Cars Ever was on the edge of town and was like most small car lots that Robert had ever been to. He was barely out of his car when a man approached him.

"Welcome to Best Cars Ever, I am Gus. What brings you in today?"

"Hello Gus, I am Agent Robert Matthews with the FBI and I would like to ask you a few questions about a police report you filed regarding stolen license plates."

"The FBI? Hmm, I knew something was fishy about that lady. Who trades in a newer, lower mileage car for a few thousand in cash and a crappy car? I checked and she never even bothered to get a title for the car she traded me for."

Robert pulled out his phone and opened the picture app to the head shot of Dr. Paulina Moore. "Is this the woman that you referred to as Chris Farmington?"

Gus stared at the picture and shook his head, "Nah, although it could be her sister or cousin, I suppose. Chris was little like that, you know less than five foot and not a hundred pounds sopping wet, but she had long blond hair, bright blue eyes and a cute little upturned nose."

Writing down all the details that Gus had shared, Matthews then asked, "Is there anything else you noticed about her?"

"Well, one real odd thing, when we were doing the paperwork for the sale, I saw that her hands, well really just her fingertips, looked all burned and shriveled up. I have never seen anything like that before, but being a gentleman, I did not mention it to her."

"Thank you, that is a very helpful detail. Here is my card, if you think of anything else."

Robert needed to go check into his hotel and then he had a hunch he was going to follow up on. Paulina Moore may well have messed up this time.

******

Face timing with his wife and daughter had been an enjoyable break from work, but Robert could feel himself growing weary. The cat nap in his car after twelve hours of driving was long worn off, so he knew he needed to do his work before he crashed for the night. Pulling up the FBI database of license plate reader information, he marveled at all the information that was collected by law enforcement and other authorities, with much of the public being unaware. This database contained license plate information from Automatic License Plate Readers or ALPRs in patrol cars from around the country along with tollbooth readers and mounted on objects like road signs and bridges. The database contained the license plate number, and the date, time, and location of every scan, so all Robert had to do was put in the stolen license plate number and wait.

The locations began popping up within seconds and the list was for the past sixty days, so the first step was to narrow it down between the date the plates were stolen and today. This was a far more manageable list and showed a clear pattern. After leaving the dealership, the license plates were recorded at regular intervals, traveling through Alabama into Tennessee and then to Kentucky. After entering Kentucky, there was only one more record of the car from a Kentucky State Troopers ALPR just outside of Whitley City two days ago.

The last thing that Robert needed to do before turning in for the night was email his boss, Supervisory Special Agent Brad Hollins, with an update. Although Hollins thought Robert was off on a wild goose chase, he would have his back if it was ever needed. If the tales of the Appalachians were true, Robert may need some backup when he got there tomorrow.

****

Kass sighed as she got up from the couch after talking with Robert on Facetime. He was so sure that he was on the trail of Paulina Moore and she hoped he wasn't disappointed once again. Her current case had become cold and Commander Brewer had told her and Nichols that he needed them to move on, as there were other major crimes to be investigated. The murder of Frank Waters was seemingly destined to make its way to the Cold Case Unit and Kass felt like it would get little attention. From her time in the unit, she knew that they prioritized cases in which family members stayed in touch for updates. The time she had spent with the Waters family told her it was highly unlikely that any of them would hound the department to not forget Frank's case.

No, it would be up to her to never let it be forgotten. She had added Frank's picture to the small mural of pictures on her cubicle wall. Each was a victim of an unsolved crime that she had investigated, but Frank's was the only one that had not been cold when she started investigating. She and Nichols were still in disagreement about who the prime suspect was, but she had come to agree with her partner that if it was Jo Beth Kalan, there must be more to the motive than they had uncovered.

24

Wednesday, February 21, 2024

Stepping out of his car and stretching, Robert Matthews wondered how over the road truck drivers and sales people did it. All this windshield time he had amassed the past forty-eight hours had left him feeling twitchy. Main Street Whitley City had several small shops, a diner, the library and gas station. He walked from place to place, showing Dr. Paulina Moore's picture, asking shopkeepers and patrons if they had seen her. Everyone he approached barely looked at the picture and denied any knowledge of Paulina. The Whitley City Gas and Go was the last place he walked in and he struck out once again before heading back to his car.

It was four in the afternoon, so with a few hours of daylight left, Robert decided to do old fashion police work. He drove through Whitley City looking for the black Dodge Neon in parking lots, driveways on the street. As he turned onto Highway 478 heading east, he quickly realized that he would need to turn into driveways in order to see the homes and carports to check for the Neon. Each time he pulled in only far enough to see if the Neon was on the property, then backed out and got back on the highway.

As the sun began to set, Robert knew he needed to turn around and head to the travel lodge on the other side of Whitley City. He would continue his driveway explorations in the morning. The next driveway off the highway was on his left-hand side, which was perfect because he could use it to turn around and head back. He would pull in and drop a pin on the map on his phone so he knew where to start tomorrow, but he might as well check for the Neon while he was here.

****

The phone in the cabin had not rung since Chris had moved in, so it startled her when the noise pierced the silence. Knowing that it was likely either a telemarketer or someone looking for the former owner of the cabin, she picked up the receiver, anyway.

"Hello."

"Is this Jane? It is Linda Sue at the Gas and Go."

"Oh, hello. Yes, it is Jane."

"Hun, this may be nothing but a G man was in here a little bit ago, showing a picture of a woman who could be your sister. I know it isn't my business, but I also know you have had issues with your ex who is with the FBI, so I figured it was better to tell you than not."

"Thank you. You were right to call. What did you tell the agent?"

"Nothing, no one in town talked to him. This is not the kinda place that appreciates the kind of fishing that lawmen like to do."

"I appreciate it and will be vigilant."

Hanging up the phone, Chris wondered if her time on the run was coming to an end. As with everything else in her life, she was prepared for this eventuality. Walking into the bedroom, she unlocked the gun box and withdrew the gun she had stolen from Dr. Keith Rodane. The gun had served her well so far, and she was glad she had never gotten rid of it. First, she cleaned and then reloaded the gun, then she took the mix tape out of the container with the boombox. Making mix tapes had been a part of Chris's life since high school and although she knew that most people now kept their music in a digital format, she loved her tapes.

This was the only mix tape that she still had, and she had made it when she first got to Lake Geneva. The tape was made specifically for when her past caught up to her. Plugging the boombox in, she set it on the small table next to the front door and put the tape in. Chris carried a chair from the kitchen, set it next to the table by the open front door, sat down, and pressed play.

The song Blaze of Glory by John Bon Jovi was first up and she vowed she would not be taken alive. An hour later, a car slowly pulled into the driveway and Chris slowly eased open the screen door and whispered, "Lynn, I am coming to you. I love you, honey." As the car came to a stop twenty feet behind her Dodge Neon, she watched as a man with a flattop haircut appeared to be talking on the phone. While he was distracted, she slipped out onto the porch and fired a shot at his head.

******

Robert Matthews was shocked to see the car he was looking for parked off to the side of the small cabin. He unbuckled his seat belt and opened the driver's side door, but before he got out, he decided to call Hollins.

"Hollins, it is Matthews. I found the car with the stolen plates. I sent you a text with a pin of my location."

"You need to get out of there and wait for backup. If this really is Paulina, she is deadly. I will call the state police and the closest FBI field office."

Matthews leaned out to grab the door handle and close the door to do what Hollins had told him when the shot rang out. A bullet came through the windshield, grazed the right side of his head, and embedded itself in the dead center of the headrest. Blood slid down his head as he dropped his body onto the ground behind the open car door, Robert pulled his gun out of its holster. As he began to crouch into a position to return fire, a bullet ripped through the car door and hit him in the chest. Falling backwards, Robert fought to catch his breath. He had promised Kass this morning on the phone that he would wear his vest, and now he knew he owed his life to that promise.

Getting back up, he positioned his gun in the gap between the car door and body of the car, poking his head up to see the shooter, he aimed then unloaded his clip and crouched back down to reload. As he reloaded, he noted the only sounds were Hollins screaming his name over and over through the bluetooth speaker in his car, the ringing in his ears, and sirens in the distance. He peeked through the gap towards the cabin's porch and could see a person laying on the steps. Now he would wait for backup.

25

Monday, February 26, 2024

Although they were still waiting on DNA verification, the hunt for Paulina Moore was all but considered closed. Hollins was the one who drove to Kentucky to collect Robert from the hospital. They had driven together to Frankfort, Kentucky, to talk to the state police and collect his car from their impound lot. Robert had not wanted to worry Kass when she was working on an open murder investigation, and so he chose to downplay what had gone on in Kentucky. He texted her from the ambulance and told her he had shot Paulina dead and that Hollins was on the way to help him with the officer involved shooting protocols. It wasn't until he arrived home and walked in with the bandage still wrapped around his head that he told her the entire story. He led off by thanking her for reminding him to wear his vest because it saved his life.

Last night Hollins had made good on his promise and taken Robert out for that steak dinner last night and this morning, Supervisory Special Agent Martinez had called him to say good job. Martinez had told him that the five days he had taken of vacation time would be returned to him as he was actually working and said he could put in for expenses as well. Matthews did not have the nerve to ask him if that included a new windshield and body work for his car.

He and Kass had decided the night he had gotten home that he would wait to tell Claire Learner until the DNA confirmed the identity of the body he shot at the cabin. Claire had been through so much and neither he nor Kass wanted to give her false information that both of the people responsible for her mother's murder were dead.

******

Like most people nowadays, almost all the mail that Claire got was junk, which had led to her piling it up and going through it on her days off. Sitting at the kitchen table drinking coffee, she began sorting the almost two weeks of mail. The recycling bin sat right next to her on the floor and she was just chucking things into it without even bothering to open them. As she threw the nondescript white envelope in the bin on the top of the pile, she paused and looked at it again. Something about the handwriting of her name and address was eerily familiar. The envelope had no return address and had been machine stamped, which had initially led Claire to believe that it was junk.

She picked the envelope up out of the trash can and slit it open. A small torn off a piece of paper fluttered to the table. Claire picked it up and saw that written on one side was Large Pineapple Anchovy Pizza, she turned it over and there was an address in Denver, Colorado. The paper slipped from Claire's fingers back onto the table. Large Pineapple Anchovy Pizza was the code phrase that she and Lindsey had used since they were young girls. Claire's mom, Kelsey, had come up with it so that the girls would know if someone was safe for them to go with if there was ever an emergency. Later, when they were teenagers, they had agreed to keep using the phrase, if either of them needed help or felt unsafe. One time at a party in high school, Claire had said to Lindsey, "I'm hungry, let's go get a large pineapple anchovy pizza" and Lindsey had left with her immediately. Claire told her as they drove home that she had seen some guys pouring something into the punch and felt like they needed to get out of there.

It had been almost two years since any of them had heard from Lindsey, and Claire knew now for sure that her friend was in trouble. The question was should she tell the Peterson's or head to Denver on her own.

******

Lance Clark walked into the small Russian restaurant on the edge of downtown and asked for a table for two. It was lunchtime, and the restaurant was busy as usual. As he sat at the table waiting, he thought back over the past four weeks since Frank Waters had been murdered. This morning, he had met with the detectives and their commander again to go over the evidence that they had. Nothing had really changed since they had confronted him about his cell phone pinging near the murder scene. He had declined to take the case of Jo Beth Kalan or Kyle Waters in front of the grand jury, and the investigation was now considered cold.

The waiter interrupted Lance's thoughts, "Sir, would you like to keep waiting for your lunch companion or place an order?"

"I will order for both of us. We will each have the Borscht soup and a cup of Kvass. Thank you."

When the food arrived and the waiter departed, Lance raised his teacup and whispered, "Well, sis, it is over. He is dead and your death has been avenged. I know it took a long time, but like this Borscht, revenge is a dish best served cold."

Lance then stood up, placed money on the table for the bill, and walked out of the restaurant, feeling lighter than he had in thirty years.

Saturday, February 3, 2024

Jo Beth could not leave town without going to Noah's grave first. As she drove out to the cemetery, she thought about how different her life would be if her husband were still alive. She highly doubted that she would be moving to Columbia to care for her new grand baby full time. Cresting the hill, Jo Beth looked at the Springfield School Administrative building in all of its shining reflective glory and wondered again how big a raise the educational staff of the district could have gotten if this monstrosity was never built. She took a glance at the parking lot as she drove past, fully expecting it to be empty, and was shocked to see Frank Water's truck coming to a stop. Slowing down, she watched Frank get out of his truck and saunter towards the building without a care in the world.

Without conscious thought, Jo Beth pulled into the parking lot and parked beside Frank's truck. She remembered the email that had been mistakenly sent to the entire district that the video monitoring system was off line at the admin building all weekend. Was this a sign from Noah that she finally had an opportunity to avenge his death? The bag she had assembled of supplies was sitting in plain view on the passenger side front seat. Grabbing the bag, she headed to the side door nearest where she and Frank had parked. If the door was unlocked, she would go in and if not, she would head to the cemetery and forget all this nonsense about murdering Frank.

The door was slightly ajar as she got to it, so Jo Beth put her duffle bag down, pulled out and put on a pair of gloves. Entering the building, she could hear Frank whistling as he plodded up the stairs otherwise, the building was completely silent. Jo Beth ducked into the women's bathroom that was in the hall by the stairwell and pulled the painter's suit and skull cap out of the bag. Then she followed Frank up the stairs, but unlike him, she was silent and took soft, deliberate steps. Once again, she sat the bag down, this time in the hallway just outside his office. Peering into the window by his office door, Jo Beth could see Frank rifling through his messy desk, and then he got on the floor and crawled under it.

This was her opportunity; she grabbed the roll of contractor bags and the crowbar. Quickly unrolling the bags to create a pathway just like she had seen on a forensic crime show, she walked into Frank's office and saw his feet sticking out from under his desk. He was still whistling and as he began to back out from under the desk, Jo Beth raised the crow bar above her head and summoned all of her anger. She brought that crow bar down against the back of his neck and Frank collapsed fully to the ground. Using the adrenaline coursing through her body, she pulled Frank's unconscious but still breathing body out from under his desk and beat him several more times. With each blow, Jo Beth let out a primal scream.

Out of breath, Jo Beth stood over Frank's body crying, she was shocked at what she had done but needed to get out of there. She walked backwards on the garbage bags, rolling them up as she went. When she got to the midway point of her path, she stripped out of her shoes, gloves, the painter's suit and skull cap. Placing the crowbar on top of the discarded protective gear, she continued to roll up the bags. As she entered the hallway, she stopped, tore off the roll of bags and opened two bags to stuff the roll of bags and items into. Double layering the garbage bag then stuffing all of it back in the duffle took a little effort, but Jo Beth used the last of the adrenaline she felt to finish up.

******

Lance had sat sipping his coffee staring at the administrative building, wondering if Marcia Waters was aware of her husband's string of indiscretions. A movement by the backdoor caught his eye. He was shocked to see who walked out of the building and got into the unknown vehicle. Before driving away, Lance thought, *What the hell was that about?* The past twenty years had taught him that Frank Waters unequivocally had a type, twenties, athletic and energetic. The woman he was watching walk to her old Honda minivan fit none of these demographics.

She was in her mid-fifties, heavy set and disheveled. Lance was close enough to see that she seemed to be breathing hard and sweating profusely. Maybe she was messing around with Frank but something just wasn't right.

****

Setting the bag back on the passenger seat of her van, she drove across the way to talk to Noah. As she sat at her husband's grave sobbing, she confessed what she had done and decided right there and then never to tell another soul. After all, who would ever suspect her? Other than Annie, she had told no one that she wanted to kill Frank because she blamed him for Noah's death. As she collected herself to get on the road to see her daughter, Jo Beth realized that for the first time in her life she truly understood the expression that revenge was a dish best served cold.